*This one is for all the Edward fans, who by their letters, questions,
and sheer interest let me know that they were as interested in
knowing more about him as I was.*

ACKNOWLEDGMENTS

Michael Miller who told me more about guns, and weapons in general, than I'd ever hoped to know. To Masaad Ayoob, who caught last-minute gun mistakes. He did not have the opportunity to read the entire book before final edit, so any missed gun mistakes are mine and mine alone. Steve (S. M.) and Jan Stirling, who read the book over to make sure I'd captured the flavor of the Santa Fe area. To all the people who made me feel so welcome in Santa Fe and Albuquerque while I wandered around asking questions and absorbing the atmosphere. And for my daughter, Trinity, who shared my office chair while I finished the last third of this book. Chuck Holmes of the Bernallio County Sheriff's Department, who answered my last-minute questions. To Deborah Millitello, who deserves special thanks for braving the wilds of New Mexico with me, sprained ankle and all. As always to my writing group, the Alternate Historians, who have been with me from the beginning: Deborah Millitello, Mark Sumner, Sharon Shinn, Marella Sands, Tom Drennan. Due to time constraints not everyone got to read this book, so it will be new to you guys as well. What a switch.

AUTHOR'S NOTE

For those of you who have never read an Anita Blake novel before, let me tell you a bit about her world.

It's just like the world we all live in – except that the creatures of the night – vampires, werewolves, zombies and such – are not the stuff of fiction. They are here-and-now. We co-exist with them – not always happily, not always peacefully.

And sometimes we get to know them all too well . . .

I

I was covered in blood, but it wasn't mine, so it was okay. Not only was it not my blood, but it was all animal blood. If the worst casualties of the night were six chickens and a goat, I could live with it, and so could everyone else. I'd raised seven corpses in one night. It was a record even for me.

I pulled into my driveway at a quarter 'til dawn with the sky still dark and star-filled. I left the Jeep in the driveway, too tired to mess with the garage. It was May, but it felt like April. Spring in St Louis was usually a two-day event between the end of winter and the beginning of summer. One day you were freezing your ass off and the next day it'd be eighty plus. But this year it had been spring, a wet gentle spring.

Except for the high number of zombies I'd raised, it had been a typical night. Everything from raising a civil war soldier for a local historical society to question, to a will that needed a final signature, to a son's last confrontation with his abusive mother. I'd been neck deep in lawyers and therapists most of the night. If I heard, 'How does that make you feel, Jonathan (or Cathy, or whoever)?' one more time tonight, I'd scream. I did not want to watch one more person 'go with his or her feelings' ever. At least with most of the lawyers the bereaved didn't come to the graveside. The court-appointed lawyer would ascertain that the zombies raised had enough cognitive ability to know what they were signing, then he would sign off on the contract as a witness. If the zombie couldn't answer the questions, then no legal signature. The corpse had to be of 'sound' mind to sign a legally binding signature. I'd

never raised a zombie that couldn't pass the legal definition of
soundness, but it happened sometimes. Jamison, a fellow animator
at Animator's Inc., had a pair of lawyers come to blows on top of
the grave. What fun.

The air was cool enough to make me shiver as I walked down
the sidewalk to my door. I could hear the phone ringing as I fumbled
the key into the lock. I hit the door with my shoulder because no
one ever calls just before dawn unless it's important. For me that
usually meant the police, which meant a murder scene. I kicked the
door closed and ran for the phone in the kitchen. My answering
machine had clicked on. My voice died on the machine and Edward's
voice came on.

'Anita, it's Edward. If you're there, pick up.' Silence.

I was running full out and skidded on my high heels, grabbing
the receiver as I slid into the wall and nearly dropped the phone.
I yelled into the receiver as I juggled the phone, 'Edward, Edward,
it's me! I'm here!'

Edward was laughing softly when I could finally hear him.

'Glad I could be amusing. What's up?' I asked.

'I'm calling in my favor,' he said quietly.

It was my turn for silence. Once upon a time Edward had come
to my aid, been my backup. He'd brought a friend, Harley, with
him as more backup. I'd ended up killing Harley. Now, Harley had
tried to kill me first, and I'd just been quicker, but Edward had
taken the killing personally. Picky, picky. Edward had given me a
choice: either he and I could draw down on each other and find
out once and for all which of us was better, or I could owe him a
favor. Some day he would call me up and ask for me to be his
backup like Harley. I'd agreed to the favor. I never wanted to come
up against Edward for real. Because if I did, I was pretty sure I'd
end up dead.

Edward was a hit man. He specialized in monsters. Vampires,
shapeshifters, anything and everything. There were people like me

that did it legal, but Edward didn't sweat the legalities, or hell, the ethics. He even occasionally did a human, but only if they had some sort of dangerous reputation. Other assassins, criminals, bad men, or women. Edward was an equal opportunity killer. He never discriminated, not for sex, religion, race, or even species. If it was dangerous, Edward would hunt it and kill it. It's what he lived for, what he was — a predator's predator.

He'd been offered a contract on my life once. He'd turned it down and had come to town as my bodyguard, bringing Harley with him. I'd asked him why he hadn't taken the contract. His answer had been simple. If he took the contract, he only got to kill me. If he protected me, he thought he'd get to kill more people. Perfect Edward reasoning.

He's either a sociopath or so close it makes little difference. I may be one of the few friends that Edward has, but it's like being friends with a tame leopard. It may curl on the foot of your bed and let you pet its head, but it can still eat your throat out. It just won't do it tonight.

'Anita, you still there?'

'I'm here, Edward.'

'You don't sound happy to hear from me.'

'Let's just say I'm cautious,' I said.

He laughed again. 'Cautious. No, you're not cautious. You're suspicious.'

'Yeah,' I said. 'So what's the favor?'

'I need backup,' he said.

'What could be so terrible that Death needs backup?'

'Ted Forrester needs backup from Anita Blake, vampire executioner.'

Ted Forrester was Edward's alter ego, his only legal identity that I was aware of. Ted was a bounty hunter who specialized in preternatural creatures that weren't vampires. As a general rule vamps were a specialty item, which was one of the reasons that there were licensed vamp executioners but not licensed anything else executioners. Maybe vampires just have a better political lobby, but whatever, they get the most press. Bounty hunters like Ted filled in the blanks between the police and the licensed executioners. They worked mostly in rancher-run states where it was still legal to hunt down varmints and kill them for money. Varmints still included lycanthropes. You could shoot them on sight in about six states as long as later a blood test proves they were lycanthropes. Some of the killings had been taken to court and were being contested, but nothing had changed yet on a local level.

'So, what does Ted need me for?' Though truthfully I was relieved that it was Ted asking and not Edward. Edward on his own probably meant illegal, maybe even murder. I wasn't quite into cold-blooded murder. Not yet.

'Come to Santa Fe and find out,' he said.

'New Mexico? Santa Fe, New Mexico?'

'Yes.'

'When?' I asked.

'Now.'

'Since I'm coming as Anita Blake, vamp executioner, I can flash my executioner's license and bring my arsenal.'

'Bring what you want,' Edward said. 'I'll share my toys with you when you arrive.'

'I haven't been to bed yet. Do I have time to get some sleep before I get on a plane?'

'Get a few hours' sleep, but be here by afternoon. We've moved the bodies, but we're saving the rest of the crime scene for you.'

'What sort of crime scene?'

'I'd say murder, but that's not quite the right word. Slaughter, butcher, torture. Yes,' he said, as if trying the word over in his mind, 'a torture scene.'

'Are you trying to scare me?' I asked.

'No,' he said.

'Then stop the theatrics and just tell me what the hell happened.'

He sighed, and for the first time I heard a dragging tiredness in his voice. 'We've got ten missing. Twelve confirmed dead.'

'Shit,' I said. 'Why haven't I heard anything on the news?'

'The disappearances made the tabloids. I think the headline was, "Bermuda Triangle in the Desert." The twelve dead were three families. Neighbors just found them today.'

'How long had they been dead?' I asked.

'Days, nearly two weeks for one family.'

'Jesus, why didn't someone miss them sooner?'

'In the last ten years almost the entire population of Santa Fe has changed. We've got a huge influx of new people. Plus a lot of people have what amounts to vacation homes up here. The locals call the newcomers Californicators.'

'Cute,' I said, 'but is Ted Forrester a local?'

'Ted lives near the city, yeah.'

A thrill went through me from the soles of my feet to the top of my head. Edward was the ultimate mystery man. I knew almost nothing about him, really. 'Does this mean I get to see where you live?'

'You'll be staying with Ted Forrester,' he said.

'But you're Ted Forrester, Edward. I'll be staying at your house, right?'

He was quiet for a heartbeat, then, 'Yes.'

Suddenly, the whole trip seemed much more attractive. I was going to see Edward's house. I was going to be able to pry into his personal life, if he had one. What could be better?

Though one thing was bothering me. 'When you said families were the victims, does that include kids?'

'Strangely, no,' he said.

'Well, thank goodness for small blessings,' I said.

'You always were a soft touch for the kiddies,' he said.

'Does it really not bother you to see dead children?'

'No,' he said.

I just listened to him breathe for a second or two. I knew that nothing bothered Edward. Nothing moved him. But children . . . every cop I knew hated to go to a scene where the vic was a child. There was something personal about it. Even those of us without children took it hard. That Edward didn't, bothered me. Funny, but it did.

'It bothers me,' I said.

'I know,' he said, 'one of your more serious faults.' There was an edge of humor to his voice.

'The fact that you're a sociopath, and that I'm not, is one of the things I take great pride in.'

'You don't have to be a sociopath to back me up, just a shooter, and you are that, Anita. You kill as easily as I do, if the circumstances are right.'

I didn't try and argue, because I couldn't. I decided to concentrate on the crime instead of my moral decay. 'So Santa Fe has a large transient population.'

'Not transient,' Edward said, 'but mobile, very mobile. We have a lot of tourism, and a lot of people moving in and out on a semi-permanent basis.'

'So no one knows their neighbors,' I said, 'or what their schedules should be.'

'Exactly.' His voice was bland, empty, with that thread of tiredness underneath, and under that was something else. A tone – something.

'You think there's more bodies that you haven't found yet,' I said. I made it a statement.

He was quiet for a second, then said, 'You heard it in my voice, didn't you?'

'Yeah,' I said.

'I'm not sure I like that. You being able to read me that well.'

'Sorry. I'll try to be less intuitive.'

'Don't bother. Your intuition is one of the things that's kept you alive this long.'

'Are you making a joke about women's intuition?' I asked.

'No, I'm saying that you're someone who works from your gut, your emotions, not your head. It's a strength for you, and a weakness.'

'Too tenderhearted, am I?'

'Sometimes, and sometimes you're just as dead inside as I am.'

Hearing him state it like that was almost scary. Not that he was including me in the same breath as himself, but that Edward knew something had died inside of him.

'You ever miss the parts that are gone?' I asked. It was the closest thing to a personal question I'd ever asked him.

'No,' he said. 'Do you?'

I thought about that for a moment. I started to say yes, automatically, then stopped myself. Truth, always truth between us. 'No, I guess I don't.'

He made a small sound, almost a laugh. 'That's my girl.'

I was both flattered and vaguely irritated that I was 'his girl.' When in doubt, concentrate on the job. 'What kind of monster is it, Edward?' I asked.

'I've no idea.'

That stopped me. Edward had been hunting preternatural bad guys years longer than I had. He knew monsters almost as well as I did, and he'd traveled the world killing monsters, so he had firsthand knowledge of things I'd only read about.

'What do you mean, you have no idea?'

'I've never seen anything kill like this, Anita.' I heard an undercurrent in his voice that I'd almost never heard – fear. Edward, whose nickname among the vamps and shapeshifters was Death, was afraid. It was a very bad sign.

'You're shook, Edward. That's not like you.'

'Wait until you see the victims. I've saved you photos of the other scenes, but the last one I kept intact, just for you.'

'How did the local law enforcement like putting a ribbon around a crime scene and wrapping it up just for little ol' me?'

'The local cops all like Ted. He's a good ol' boy. If Ted tells them you can help, they believe him.'

'But you're Ted Forrester,' I said, 'and you're not a good ol' boy.'

'But Ted is,' he said, voice empty.

'Your secret identity,' I said.

'Yeah,' he said.

'Fine, I'll fly into Santa Fe this afternoon, or early evening.'

'Fly into Albuquerque instead. I'll meet you at the airport. Just call me and give me the time.'

'I can rent a car,' I said

'I'll be in Albuquerque on other business. It's not a problem.'

'What aren't you telling me?' I asked.

'Me, keeping secrets?' There was a thread of amusement in his voice again.

'You're the original mystery man, Edward. You love keeping secrets. It gives you a sense of power.'

'Does it?' he made it a question.

'Yeah, it does.'

He laughed softly. 'Maybe it does. Make the ticket reservations and call me with the flight times. I've got to go.' His voice went low as if someone else had come into the room.

I hadn't asked what the urgency was. Ten missing, twelve confirmed dead. It was urgent. I hadn't asked if he'd be waiting for my call. Edward, who never spooked, was scared. He'd be waiting for my call.

2

It turned out that the only flight I could get that wasn't full was a noon flight, which meant I got about five hours of sleep before I had to get up and run for the airport. I also missed Kenpo class, a type of karate that I'd just started a few weeks ago. I'd have much rather been in class than on a plane. I hate to fly. I'd driven to as many of the out of town appointments as possible, but I'd been doing a lot of flying lately. It had lessened the actual terror, but I was still phobic. I hated to be in a plane being flown by someone I didn't know, who I had not personally drug tested. I just wasn't the trusting sort.

Neither are the airlines. Carrying a concealed weapon on a plane was a pain in the ass. I'd had to take the two-hour FAA course on carrying concealed on a plane. I had a certificate to prove I'd taken the course. I could not get on the plane without the certificate. I also had a letter stating that I was on official business that required me to carry a gun. Sergeant Rudolf (Dolf) Storr, head of the Regional Preternatural Investigation Team, had faxed me the letter on taskforce letterhead, always impressive. Someone who was a real policeperson had to give me something to legitimize my status. If it were real police business, even if Dolf weren't directly involved, he'd usually give me what I needed. If Edward had called me in to help in an unofficial case, i.e., illegal, I would have avoided Dolf. Mr Law and Order wasn't real fond of Edward, a.k.a. Ted Forrester. 'Ted' was around a lot when there were bodies on the ground. It made Dolf not trust him.

I did not look out the window. I read and tried to pretend I was on a very cramped bus. I'd finally figured out that one of the reasons I didn't like to fly was that I also have claustrophobia. A 727 full of people was close enough to make it hard to breathe. I turned the little fan above my seat on high and read. I was reading Sharon Shinn. She was an author that I trusted to hold my attention even hundreds of feet above the ground with a thin metal sheet between me and eternity.

So I can't tell you what Albuquerque looks like from the air, and the little walkway that led into the airport was like every other one I'd ever walked through. Even in the tunnel you could feel the heat pressing like a giant hand hovering over the thin plastic. It may have been spring in St Louis, but it was summer in Albuquerque. I scanned the crowd for Edward and actually looked past him once before realizing it was him. Part of it was the fact that he was wearing a hat, a cowboy hat. There was a fan of feathers tucked into the front of the hat band, but it had the look of a hat that had been worn well. The brim was curved back on both sides as if he'd worked at the stiff material until the brim had formed a new shape under the constant run of his hands. His shirt was white and short-sleeved like something you'd get at any department store. It was matched with dark blue jeans that looked new and a pair of hiking boots that weren't.

Hiking boots? Edward? He'd never impressed me as a country boy. No, definitely a city fellow, but there he stood, looking sort of down-homey and comfortable. It didn't look like Edward at all until I met his eyes. Wrap him up in whatever disguise you want, you could dress him like Prince Charming on a Disney float, but as long as you could glimpse his eyes, you would still run screaming.

His eyes are blue and cold as winter skies. He is the epitome of WASP breeding with his blond hair and slender paleness. He can look harmless if he wants to. He is the consummate actor, but unless he works at it, his eyes give him away. If the eyes are the mirror to the soul, then Edward's in trouble because no one is home.

He smiled at me, and it thawed his eyes to something close to warmth. He was glad to see me, genuinely glad. Or as glad as he ever was to see anyone. It wasn't comforting. In a way it was unnerving because one of the main reasons Edward liked me was that together we always got to kill more than we did apart. Or at least I did. For all I knew, Edward might have been mowing down entire armies when he wasn't with me.

'Anita,' he said.

'Edward,' I said.

The smile turned into a grin. 'You don't seem happy to see me.'

'You being this happy to see me makes me nervous, Edward. You're relieved I'm here, and that scares me.'

The grin faded, and I watched all the humor, all the welcome, drain out of his face like water leaving a glass through a crack — empty. 'I'm not relieved,' he said, but his voice was too bland.

'Liar,' I said. I would have liked to say it softly, but the noise of the airport was like the crash of the ocean, a continuous roar.

He looked at me with those pitiless eyes and gave one small nod. An acknowledgment that he was relieved I arrived. Maybe he would have verbalized it, but suddenly a woman appeared at his side. She was smiling, her arms sliding around him until she cuddled against him. She looked thirtyish, older than Edward appeared, though I wasn't sure of his actual age. Her hair was short, brown, a no-nonsense style, but flattering. She wore almost no makeup, but was still lovely. There were lines at her eyes and mouth that made me jump her from thirty to forty something. She was smaller than Edward, taller than me, but still petite, though she didn't look soft. She was tanned darker than was healthy, which probably explained the lines on her face. There was a quiet strength to her as she stood there smiling at me, holding Edward's arm.

She wore jeans that looked so neat they must have been pressed, a white short-sleeved shirt that was sheer enough that she'd put a spaghetti strap tank top under it, and a brown leather purse almost as large as my carry-on bag. I wondered for a second if Edward had picked her up from a plane, too, but there was something too fresh and unhurried about her. She hadn't come off a plane.

'I'm Donna. You have to be Anita.' She held out her hand, and we shook. She had a firm handshake, and her hand wasn't soft. She'd worked, this one had. She also knew how to shake hands. Most women never really got the knack of it. I liked her instantly, instinctively, and mistrusted the feeling just as quickly.

'Ted's told me so much about you,' Donna said.

I glanced up at Edward. He was smiling, and even his eyes were full of humor. The entire set of his face and body had changed. He slouched slightly, and the smile was lazy. He vibrated with good ol' boy charm. It was an Oscar-winning performance, as if he'd traded skins with someone else.

I looked at Edward/Ted and said, 'He's told you a lot about me, has he?'

'Oh, yes,' Donna said, touching my arm while still holding onto Edward. Of course, she would be a casual toucher. My shapeshifter friends were getting me accustomed to touchie-feelie stuff, but it still wasn't my best thing. What the hell was Edward – Ted – doing with this woman?

Edward spoke, but there was a slight Texas-like drawl to his voice like an old accent almost forgotten. Edward had no accent whatsoever. His voice was one of the cleanest and hardest to place I'd ever heard, as if even his voice was never touched by the places and people he saw.

'Anita Blake, I'd like you to meet Donna Parnell, my fiancée.'

My jaw dropped to the carpet, and I just gaped at him. I usually try and be a little more sophisticated than that, or hell, more polite. I knew that astonishment, nay shock, showed, but I couldn't help it.

Donna laughed, and it was a good laugh, warm and chuckly, a good mom laugh. She squeezed Edward's arm. 'Oh, you were right, Ted. Her reaction was worth the trip.'

'Told ya, honey-pot,' Edward said, hugging her and planting a kiss on the top of her head.

I closed my mouth and tried to recover. I managed to mumble, 'That's . . . great. I mean really . . . I . . .' I finally extended my hand and said, 'Congratulations.' But I couldn't manage a smile.

Donna used the handshake to draw me into a hug. 'Ted said you'd never believe he'd finally agreed to tie the knot.' She hugged me again, laughing. 'But, my God, girl, I've never seen such pure shock.' She retreated back to Edward's arms and his smiling Ted face.

I am not nearly as good an actor as Edward. It's taken me years to perfect a blank face let alone outright lying by facial expression and body language. So I kept my face blank and tried to tell Edward with my eyes that he had some explaining to do.

With his face slightly turned from Donna, he gave me his close, secretive smile. Which pissed me off. Edward was enjoying his surprise. Damn him.

'Ted, where are your manners? Take her bag,' Donna said.

Edward and I both stared at the small carry-on bag I had in my left hand. He gave me Ted's smile, but he said Edward's line. 'Anita likes to carry her own weight.'

Donna looked at me for confirmation as if this couldn't possibly be true. Maybe she wasn't as strong and independent as she appeared, or maybe she was a decade older than she appeared. A different generation, you know.

'Ted's right,' I said, putting a little too much emphasis on his name. 'I like to carry my own bags.'

Donna looked like she'd have liked to correct my obviously wrong thinking but was too polite to say it out loud. The expression, not the silence, reminded me of my stepmother Judith. Which made me push Donna's age over fifty. She was either a mightily well preserved fifty-something, forty-something, or a sun-aged thirty-something. I just couldn't tell.

They walked ahead of me through the airport, arm in arm. I followed behind them, not because my suitcase was too heavy but because I needed a few minutes to recover. I watched Donna bump her head against Edward's shoulder, her face turning to him, smiling, glowing. Edward/Ted bent over her, face tender, whispering something that made her laugh.

I was going to be sick. What the hell was Edward doing with this woman? Was she another assassin, as good an actor as he was? Somehow I didn't think so. And if she was exactly what she appeared – a woman in love with Ted Forrester, who didn't exist – I was going to kick Edward's metaphorical ass. How dare he involve some innocent woman in his cover story! Or – and this was a very strange thought – was Edward/Ted really in love? If you'd asked me ten minutes ago, I'd have said he wasn't capable of such depth of emotion, but now . . . now I was just plain confused.

The Albuquerque airport broke my rule that all airports look nearly identical and you can't really tell what part of the country, or even the world, that you're in just from the airport. If there are decorations, they're usually from a different culture entirely, like inland bars having seaside motifs. But not here. Here there were hints of a southwestern flavor everywhere. Multi-colored tile or paint leaning to turquoise and cobalt blue lined most of the shops and store fronts. A small covered stand sold silver jewelry in the middle of the large hallway leading from the gates to the rest of the airport. We'd left the crowd behind and with it the noise. We moved in a world of nearly ringing silence, heightened by the white-white walls and the large windows on either side. Albuquerque stretched outside those windows like some great flat plain with a ring of black mountains at the edge, like the backdrop to a play, somehow unreal. The heat pressed down even through the air conditioning, not really hot, but letting you know it was going to be. The landscape was totally alien, adding to my sense of having been cut adrift. One of the things I liked about Edward is that he never changed. He was what he was, and now Edward, dependable in his own psychotic way, had thrown me a curve ball so wild I didn't even know how to swing at it.

Donna stopped and turned, drawing Edward with her. 'Anita, that bag is just too heavy for you. Please let Ted carry it.' She gave him a little good-natured push in my direction.

Edward walked towards me. Even his walk was a rolling sort of gait like someone who spent a lot of time on horseback or on a boat. He kept Ted's smile on his face. Only his eyes slipped and showed through the mask. Dead, those eyes, empty. No love shone in them. Damn him. He actually leaned over, his hand started to close over mine and the handle.

I hissed, 'Don't.' I let that one word hold all the anger I was feeling.

His eyes widened just a bit, and he knew I wasn't talking about just the carry-on bag. He straightened up and called back to Donna, 'She doesn't want my help.' He put emphasis on the 'my.'

She tsked under her breath and walked back to us. 'You're just being stubborn, Anita. Let Ted help you.'

I looked up at her and knew my face wasn't neutral, but I couldn't drain all the anger out of my face.

Donna's eyes widened just a bit. 'Have I offended you in some way?' she asked.

I shook my head. 'I'm not upset with you.'

She looked at Edward. 'Ted, dear, I think she's angry with you.'

'I think you're right,' Edward said. His eyes had gone back to sparkling with love and good humor.

I tried to salvage the situation. 'It's just that Ted should have told me about the engagement. I don't like surprises.'

Donna put her head to one side, giving me a long considering look. She started to say something, then seemed to think better of it. 'Well, I'll try and make sure you don't get any more surprises from me.' She settled herself a little more securely on Edward's arm, and the look in her brown eyes was just a tad less friendly than it had been before.

I realized with a sigh that Donna now thought I was jealous. My reaction wasn't normal for a mere friend and business acquaintance. Since I couldn't tell her the real reason I was upset, I let it go. Better she think Ted and I had been an item once, than know the truth. Though Heaven knew she'd probably prefer we'd been lovers to the real truth about her 'Ted.' She was in love with a man who did not exist, no matter how real the arm she was holding happened to be.

I tightened my grip on my bag and moved up so I was walking on the other side of Donna as we moved up through the airport. She wasn't comfortable with me trailing behind so I'd keep up. I'm not good at small talk at the best of times, but now, I couldn't think of a damn thing to say, so we moved in a silence that grew progressively uncomfortable for me, and for Donna. Her, because she was a woman and naturally friendly. Me, because I knew silence would make her uncomfortable. I didn't want to make her more uncomfortable.

She broke first. 'Ted tells me you're an animator and vampire hunter.'

'I prefer vampire executioner, but yeah.' In a desperate attempt to be polite I asked, 'What do you do?'

She flashed me a brilliant smile that showed the smile lines on either side of her mouth like a frame for her thin, oh-so-slightly lipsticked mouth. I was glad I'd worn no makeup. Maybe that would help her realize I wasn't after Edward/Ted. 'I own a shop in Santa Fe.'

Edward added, 'She sells psychic paraphernalia.' He gave me a smile over her head.

My face hardened, and I fought to keep it blank. 'What sort of paraphernalia?'

'Crystals, tarot decks, books, everything and anything that catches my fancy.'

I wanted to say, 'But you're not psychic,' but I didn't. I'd met people before that were convinced they had psychic gifts when they didn't. If Donna was one of the successfully deluded, who was I to burst her bubble? Instead, I said, 'Is there much of a market for that sort of thing in Santa Fe?'

'Oh, there used to be a lot of shops like mine. The new age was really big in Santa Fe, but the property taxes have skyrocketed and most of the new psychics have moved farther into the mountains to Taos. Santa Fe's energy has changed in the last five years, or so. It's still a very positive place, but Taos has better energy now. I'm not sure why.'

She talked about 'energy' like it was an accepted fact, and didn't try to explain it, as if I would understand her. She was assuming, like so many people did, that if you raised the dead for a living you were psychic in other areas, too. Which was often true, but not always. What she called 'energy,' I called the 'feel' of a place. Some places did have a 'feel' to them, good or bad, energizing or draining. The old idea of *genius loci* was alive and well in the new age movement under a different name.

'Do you read cards?' I asked. It was a polite way of finding out if she believed she had powers.

'Oh, no,' Donna said. 'My gifts are very small. I'd love to be able to read cards or crystals, but I'm only a proprietor. My talent in this life is helping others discover their strengths.'

It sounded like something a therapist who believed in past lives would have said. I'd been meeting enough of them at graveside to know the lingo. 'So you're not a psychic,' I said. I just wanted to be sure she knew it.

'Oh, heavens no.' She shook her head for emphasis, and I noticed her small gold earrings were ankhs.

'Most people who go into the business usually are,' I said.

She sighed. 'The psychic I'm going to now says that I'm blocked in this life because of misuse of my gifts last time around. She says I'll be able to work magic next time.'

Again, she assumed I believed in reincarnation and past life therapy, probably because of what I did for a living. Either that or Edward/Ted had been lying to her about me just to amuse himself. But I didn't point out that I was a Christian and didn't believe in reincarnation. There are, after all, more religions on the planet that believe in reincarnation than ones that don't. Who am I to quibble?

I just couldn't help the next question. 'And have you met Ted before in a past life?'

'No, actually he's brand new to me, though Brenda says he is a very old soul.'

'Brenda, your psychic?' I asked.

She nodded.

'I'll agree with the old soul part,' I said.

Edward gave me a look over her head where she couldn't see him. It was a suspicious look.

'You've felt it, too, then, the way he resonates. That's what Brenda calls it, like a great heavy bell in her head whenever he's around.'

Alarm bells more likely, I thought. Aloud I said, 'Sometimes you can make your soul heavy in one lifetime.'

She gave me a puzzled look. She wasn't stupid. There was intelligence in those brown eyes, but she was naive. Donna wanted to believe. It made her an easy mark for a certain kind of liar, like would-be psychics and men like Edward. Men who lied about who and what they were.

'I'd like to meet Brenda before I go home,' I said.

Edward's eyes widened where she couldn't see them.

Donna smiled delightedly. 'I'd love to introduce the two of you. She's never met an animator before. I know she'd get a kick out of meeting you.'

'I'll bet,' I said. I did want to meet Brenda, because I wanted to see if she was truly a psychic or just a charlatan. If she was professing to abilities she didn't possess, it was a crime, and I'd turn her in. I hated seeing supposed psychics take advantage of people. It was always amazing to me with the number of genuine talents around, how many fakes still managed to prosper.

We were passing a restaurant decorated in more blue and fuschia tiles with small daisy-like flowers painted in the edges. There was a mural on one wall showing Spanish conquistadors and breechcloth-clad Native Americans as we came down the escalators. I was still managing to balance my carry-on without any trouble. All that weightlifting I guess.

There was a bank of pay phones set to one side. 'Let me try to get hold of the kids one more time,' Donna said. She kissed Edward's cheek and moved off towards the phones before I could react.

'Kids?' I said.

'Yes,' he said, voice careful.

'How many?' I asked.

'Two.'

'Ages?'

'Boy, fourteen; girl, six,' he said.

'Where's their father?'

'Donna is a widow.'

I looked at him, and the look was enough.

'No, I didn't do it. He died years before I met Donna.'

I stepped close to him, turning my back so that Donna wouldn't see my face from the phones. 'What are you playing at, Edward? She has children and is so in love with you, it makes me gag. What on God's green earth could you be thinking?'

'Donna and Ted have been dating for about two years. They're lovers. She expected him to propose so he did.' His face was still smiling Ted, but the voice was matter of fact and totally unemotional.

'You're talking like Ted's a third person, Edward.'

'You're going to have to start calling me Ted, Anita. I know you. If you don't make it a habit, you'll forget.'

I stepped into him in the relative silence, lowering my voice to a furious whisper.

'Fuck that. He is you, and you're fucking engaged. Are you going to marry her?'

He gave a small shrug.

'Shit,' I said. 'You can't. You cannot marry this woman.'

His smile widened, and he stepped around me holding his hands out to Donna. He kissed her and asked, 'How are the munchkins?' He turned her in his arms so he was half-hugging her, and had her turned away from me. His face was Ted, relaxed, but his eyes were warning me, 'Don't screw this up.' It was important to him for some reason.

Donna turned so she could see my face, and I fought to give blank face. 'What were you two whispering about so urgently?'

'The case,' Edward said.

'Oh, pooh,' she said.

I raised eyebrows at Edward. Oh, pooh. The most dangerous man I'd ever met was engaged to a mother of two that said things like, 'Oh, pooh.' It was just too weird.

Donna's eyes widened. 'Where is your purse? Did you leave it on the plane?'

'I didn't bring one,' I said. 'I knew I'd have the bag and pockets.'

She looked at me as if I'd spoken in tongues. 'My god, I wouldn't know what to do without my monstrosity in tow.' She pulled the huge purse around in front of her. 'I'm such a pack rat.'

'Where are your kids?' I asked.

'With my neighbors. They're a retired couple and are just great with my little girl, Becca.' She frowned. 'Of course, nothing seems to make Peter happy right now.' She glanced at me. 'Peter's my son. He's fourteen going on forty, and seems to have hit his teenage years with a vengeance. Everyone told me a teenager was hard, but I never dreamed how hard.'

'Has he been getting into trouble?' I asked.

'Not really. I mean he's not into anything criminal.' She added the last a little too quickly. 'But he's just stopped listening to me. Two weeks ago he was supposed to come home from school and watch Becca. Instead, he went to a friend's house. When I came home after the shop closed, the house was empty, and I didn't know where either of them were. The Hendersons had been out so Becca wasn't there. God, I was frantic. Another neighbor had taken her in, but if they hadn't been home, she'd have just had to wander the neighborhood for hours. Peter came home and just wasn't sorry. By the time he came home, I'd convinced myself he'd been abducted by someone and was lying dead in a ditch somewhere. Then he just comes strolling in as if nothing's wrong.'

'Is he still grounded?' I asked.

She nodded, face very firm. 'You bet he is. Grounded for a month, and I've taken every privilege I can think of away from him.'

'What does he think of you and Ted getting married?' It was a sadistic question, and I knew it, but I just couldn't help myself.

Donna looked stricken, truly stricken. 'He's not too keen on the idea.'

Keen? 'Well, he's fourteen, and a boy,' I said. 'He's bound to resent another male coming into his turf.'

Donna nodded. 'Yes, I'm afraid so.'

Ted hugged her. 'It'll be all right, honeypot. Pete and I will come to an understanding. Don't you worry.'

I didn't like Edward's phrasing on that. I watched his face but couldn't see anything behind his Ted mask. It was as if for minutes at a time he just vanished into his alter ego. I hadn't been on the ground an hour and his Jekyll/Hyde act was already beginning to get on my nerves.

'Do you have any other bags?' Edward asked.

'Of course, she does,' Donna said. 'She's a woman.'

Edward gave a small laugh that was more his own than Ted's.

It was a small cynical sound that made Donna glance at him and made me feel better.

'Anita isn't like any other woman I've ever met.'

Donna gave him another look. Edward had phrased it that way on purpose. He'd caught her jealous reasoning just as I had, and now he was playing to it. It was one way to explain my strange reaction to the engagement news without risk of blowing his cover. I guess I couldn't blame him, but in a way I knew it was payback for my lack of social skills. His cover was important enough to him to let Donna think we'd been a couple, which meant it was pretty important to him. Edward and I had never had a single romantic thought about each other in our lives.

'I've got luggage,' I said.

'See,' Donna said, tugging on his arm.

'The carry-on bag wouldn't hold all the guns.'

Donna stopped in the middle of saying something to Edward, then turned slowly to stare at me. Edward and I stopped walking because she had stopped. Her eyes were a little wide. She seemed to have caught her breath. She was staring at me, but not at my face. If it had been a guy, I might have accused him of staring at my chest, but that wasn't exactly what she was looking at. I followed her gaze and found that my jacket had slipped back over my left side exposing my gun. It must have happened when I readjusted the bag coming off the escalator. Careless of me. I'm usually pretty careful about exposing my arsenal in public. It tends to make people nervous, just like now. I shifted the bag so that my jacket slid back over the shoulder holster like a curtain dropping back in place.

Donna drew a quick breath, blinked, and looked at my face. 'You really do carry a gun.' Her voice held a sort of wonderment.

'I told you she did,' Edward said in his Ted voice.

'I know, I know,' Donna said. She shook her head. 'I've just never been around a woman that . . . Do you kill as easily as Ted does?'

It was a very intelligent question, and meant that she'd been paying more attention to the real Edward than I'd given her credit for. So I answered the question truthfully. 'No.'

Edward hugged her to him, eyes warning me over her head. 'Anita doesn't believe shifters are animals. She still thinks the monsters can be saved. It makes her squeamish sometimes.'

Donna stared at me. 'My husband was killed by a werewolf. He was killed in front of me and Peter. Peter was only eight.'

I didn't know what reaction she expected so I didn't give her one. My face was neutral, interested, far from shocked. 'What saved you?'

She nodded slowly, understanding the question. A werewolf tore her husband apart in front of her and her son, yet they were still alive and the husband wasn't. Something had interceded, something had saved them.

'John, my husband, had loaded a rifle with silver shot. He'd dropped the gun in the attack. He'd wounded it but not enough.' Her eyes had gone distant with remembering. We stood in the bright airport, three people huddled in a small circle of silence and hushed voices and Donna's wide eyes. I didn't have to look at Edward to know that his face was as neutral as mine. She'd fallen silent, the horror still too fresh in her eyes. The look was enough. There was worse to come, or worse to her. Something she felt guilty about at the very least.

'John had just showed Peter how to shoot the week before. He was so little, but I let him take that gun. I let him shoot that monster. I let him stand his ground in the face of that thing, while I just huddled on the floor, frozen.'

That was it. That was the true horror for Donna. She'd allowed her child to protect her. Allowed her child to take the adult role of protector in the face of a nightmare. She'd failed the big test, and little Peter had passed into adulthood at a very tender age. No wonder he hated Edward. Peter had earned his right to be man of the house. He'd earned it in blood, and now his mother was going to remarry. Yeah, right.

Donna turned those haunted eyes to me. She blinked and seemed to be drawing herself back from the past as if it were a physical effort. She hadn't made peace with the scene, or it wouldn't have remained so vivid. If you can begin to make peace, you can tell the most horrible stories as if they happened to someone else, unemotional. Or, maybe you haven't made peace, but you still tell it like it was an interesting story that happened a long time ago, nothing important. I've seen cops that had to get drunk before the pain spilled out into their stories.

Donna was hurting. Peter was hurting. Edward wasn't hurting. I looked up at him, past Donna's softly horrified face. His eyes were empty as he looked at me, as waiting and patient as any predator. How dare he step into their lives like this! How dare he cause them more pain! Because whatever happened, whether he married her or didn't, it was going to be painful. Painful for everyone but Edward. Though maybe I could fix that. If he fucked up Donna's life, maybe I could fuck up his. Yeah, I liked that. I'd spread the rain around all over his parade.

It must have shone in my eyes for a second or two, because Edward's eyes narrowed, and for a moment I felt that shiver he could send down my spine with just a glance. He was a very dangerous man, but to protect this family I'd test his limits, and mine. Edward had finally found something that pissed me off enough to maybe press a button that I'd never wanted to touch. He had to leave Donna and her family alone. He had to get out of their lives. I'd see him out of their lives, or else. And there is only one 'or else' when you're dealing with Edward. Death.

We stared at each other over Donna's head while he hugged her to his chest, stroking her hair, mouthing soothing words to her. But his eyes, his face were all for me, and I knew as we stared at each other that he knew exactly what I was thinking. He knew the conclusion I'd come to, though he might never understand why his involvement with Donna and her kids was the straw that broke the camel's back. But the look in his eyes was enough. He might not understand why, but he knew the camel was broken in fucking two and there was no way to fix it except to do what I wanted him to do, or die. Just like that, I knew I'd do it. I knew I could look down the barrel of a gun and shoot Edward, and I wouldn't aim to wound. It was like a cold weight inside my body, a surety that made me feel stronger and a little lonelier. Edward had saved my life more than once. I'd saved his more than once. Yet . . . yet . . . I'd miss Edward, but I'd kill him if I had to. Edward wonders why I'm so sympathetic to the monsters. The answer is simple. Because I am one.

3

We walked out into the heat, and it blasted against our skin on the edge of a hot wind. It had the feel of a serious heat, and considering that it was only May, it probably would be a real barnburner when true summer finally hit. But it is true that eighty plus without humidity isn't nearly as miserable as eighty plus with humidity, so it wasn't horrible. In fact, once you blinked into the sunlight and just got adjusted to the heat, you sort of forgot about it. It was only attention-getting for the first, oh, fifteen minutes or so. St Louis would probably be ninety plus by the time I got home, and with eighty to a hundred percent humidity. Of course, that meant I'd be going home. If I really drew down on Edward, that was a debatable option. There was a very real possibility that he'd kill me. I hoped, seriously hoped, that I could talk him out of Donna and her family without resorting to violence.

Maybe the heat didn't seem bad because of the landscape. Albuquerque was a flat empty plain running out and out to a circle of black mountains, as if everything of worth had been strip-mined away and the waste had been lumped into those forbidden black mountains like giant mounds of coal. Yeah, it looked like the world's largest strip-mining operation, and it had that feel to it of waste and desolation. Of things spoiled, and an alien hostility, as if you weren't quite welcome. I guess Donna would say, bad energy. I'd never felt anyplace that had such an instant alienness to it. Edward was carrying both my suitcases that had come off the carousel. Normally, I'd have carried one, but not now. Now I wanted Edward's hands full of something besides guns. I wanted him at a disadvantage. I wasn't going to start shooting on the way to the car, but Edward is more practical than I am. If he decided I was more danger than help, he might be able to arrange an accident on the way to the car. It'd be tough with Donna in tow, but not impossible. Not for Edward.

It was also why I was letting him lead the way and putting me at his back instead of him at mine. It wasn't paranoia, not with Edward. With Edward it was simply good survival thinking.

Edward got Donna to go ahead of us and unlock the car. He dropped back to walk beside me, and I put some distance between us so that we were standing in the middle of the sidewalk staring at each other like two old-fashioned movie gunfighters.

He kept the suitcases in his hands. I think he knew that I was too keyed up. I think he knew if he dropped the suitcases, I was going to have a gun in my hand. 'You want to know why I wasn't bothered with you following behind me?'

'You knew I wouldn't shoot you in the back,' I said.

He smiled. 'And you knew I might.'

I cocked my head to one side, almost squinting into the sun. Edward was wearing sunglasses, of course. But since his eyes rarely gave anything away, it didn't matter. His eyes weren't what I had to worry about.

'You like the personal danger, Edward. That's why you only hunt monsters. You have to be taking the big risk every time you come up to bat, or it's no fun.'

A couple came walking by with a cart full of suitcases. We waited in silence until they passed us. The woman glanced at us as they hurried past, picking up on the tension. The man jerked her back to face front and they pushed past us.

'You have a point?' Edward asked.

'You want to know which of us is better, Edward. You've wanted to know for a long time. If you take me from ambush, the question will never be answered and that would bug you.'

His smile both widened and faded, as if it wasn't a humorous smile anymore. 'So, I won't shoot you in the back.'

'That's right,' I said.

'So why go to so much trouble to fill my hands and make me walk in front.'

'This would be a hell of a time to be wrong.'

He laughed then, soft and vaguely sinister. That one sound said it all. He was excited about the idea of going up against me. 'I would love to hunt you, Anita. I've dreamed about it.' He sighed, and it was almost sad. 'But I need you. I need you to help solve this case. And as much as I'd like the big question answered, I'd miss you. You may be one of the only people in the world that I would miss.'

'What about Donna?' I asked.

'What about her?' he asked.

'Don't be cute, Edward.' I looked past him to find Donna waving to us from the parking lot. 'We're being paged.'

He glanced back towards her, lifting one of the suitcases to make a vague wave. It would have been easier to do if he'd dropped one of the cases but in his own way, Edward was being cautious, too.

He turned back to me. 'You won't be able to do your job if you're looking over your shoulder for me. So a truce until the case is solved.'

'Your word?' I asked.

He nodded. 'My word.'

'Good enough,' I said.

He smiled, and it was genuine. 'The only reason you can take my word at face value is that if you give your word, you'll keep it.'

I shook my head and started closing the distance between us. 'I keep my word, but I don't take most people's oaths very seriously.' I was even with him and could feel the weight of his gaze even through the black lenses of the sunglasses. He was intense, was Edward.

'But you take mine.'

'You've never lied to me, Edward, not once you've given your word. You do what you say you'll do, even if it's a bad thing. You don't hide what you are, at least not from me.'

We both glanced back at Donna, and started walking side by side toward her as if we'd discussed it. 'How the hell did you let it get so far? How could you have let Ted propose?'

He was quiet for so long, I didn't think he'd answer. We walked in silence in the sun-warmed heat. But finally, he did answer, 'I don't know. I think one night I just got too caught up in my role. The mood was right and Ted proposed, and I think for just a second I forgot that I'd be the one getting married.'

I glanced at him. 'You've told me more personal shit in the last half hour than in the entire five years I've known you. Are you always such a jabberbox when you're on Ted's home turf?'

He shook his head. 'I knew you wouldn't like Donna being involved. I didn't know how strongly you'd react, but I knew you wouldn't like it. Which meant to keep the peace I had to be willing to talk about it. I knew that when I called you.'

We stepped off the curb, both of us smiling and me waving to Donna. I said through the smile like a ventriloquist, 'How can we know each other this well, and would miss each other if we died, yet still be willing to pull the trigger? I know it's the truth, but I don't understand it.'

'Isn't it enough to know it's true? Do you have to explain it?' he asked as we wove through the cars toward Donna.

'Yes, I need to explain it.'

'Why?' he asked.

'Because I'm a girl,' I said.

That made him laugh, a surprise burst of sound, and it made my heart ache because I could count on one hand the number of times I'd heard Edward surprised into laughter. I valued the sound of that particular laugh because it was like an old sound from a younger, more innocent Edward. I wondered if I was the only one that could force that laugh from him. How could we be talking calmly about killing each other? No, it wasn't enough to know we could do it. There had to be a why to it, and saying we were both monsters or sociopaths wasn't enough explanation. At least not for me.

Donna looked at me rather narrowly as we walked up. She made a big show of kissing him and when he sat the suitcases down and had his hands free, she put on an even better show. They kissed, hugged, and body-pressed like a couple of teenagers. If Edward was in any way reluctant, it didn't show. In fact, he slipped off his hat and melded into her like he was happy to be there.

I stood, leaning against the side of the car close enough to touch them. If they wanted privacy, they could get a room. It went on long enough that I wondered if checking my watch would be hint enough, but resisted the urge. I decided that leaning against the car, arms crossed over my stomach, looking bored might be hint enough.

Edward drew back with a sigh. 'After last night, I wouldn't think you'd be missing me this much.'

'I always miss you,' she said in a voice halfway between sultry and a giggle. Donna gazed at me, hands still encircling him, very possessive. She looked right at me and said, 'Sorry, didn't mean to embarrass you.'

I pushed away from the car. 'I don't embarrass that easy.'

The happy light in her eyes turned to something fierce and protective. The look and her next words were not friendly. 'And just what would it take to embarrass you?'

I shook my head. 'Is this my cue to say, a lot more than you've got?'

She stiffened.

'Don't worry, Donna. I am not now, nor have I ever been interested in . . . Ted in a romantic way.'

'I never thought . . .' she started to say.

'Save it,' I said. 'Let's try something really unique. Let's be honest. You were worried about me with Edward,' I changed it very quickly to, 'Ted, which was why you did the teeny-bopper makeout session. You don't need to mark your territory for my sake, Donna.' The last was said in something of a rush because I hoped she hadn't noticed my slip on the names, but of course she had, and I knew Edward had. 'Ted's too much like me to ever consider dating. It'd be like incest.'

She blushed even through the tan. 'My, you are direct.'

'She's direct even for a man,' Edward said. 'For a woman she's like a battering ram.'

'It saves time,' I said.

'That it does,' Edward said. He drew Donna into a quick but thorough kiss. 'I'll see you tomorrow, honeypot.'

I raised eyebrows at that.

Edward looked at me with Ted's warm eyes. 'Donna drove her own car in so we could spend part of the day together. Now she's going to drive home to the kiddies, so we can do business.' Donna turned from him, giving me a long searching look. 'I'm taking you at your word, Anita. I believe you, but I'm also picking up some strange vibes from you like you're hiding something.'

I was hiding something, I thought. If she only knew.

Donna continued, face very serious. 'I'm trusting you with the third most important person in my life. Ted is right behind my kids for me. Don't screw up the best thing I've had since my husband died.'

'See,' Edward said, 'Donna knows how to be blunt, too.'

'That she does,' I said.

Donna gave me one last searching look, then turned to Edward. She drew him away towards a car three down from us. They talked quietly together while I waited in the still, dry, heat. Since Donna had tried for privacy, I gave it to them, turning away and gazing off at the distant mountains. They looked very close, but it's always been my experience that mountains are seldom as close as they appear. They're like dreams, distant things to set your sights on, but not truly to be trusted to be there when you need them.

I heard Edward's boots crunch on the pavement before he spoke. I was facing him, arms crossed lightly over my stomach, which put my right hand nicely close to the gun under my arm. I believed Edward when he said we had a truce on, but . . . better cautious than sorry.

He stopped by the car one slot over, leaning his butt against it, arms crossing to mirror me. But he didn't have a gun under his arm. I wasn't sure that a bounty hunter's license was enough to get him through an airport metal detector, so he shouldn't have been able to have a gun or large blade on him. Unless of course he'd picked it up from one of the cars, where he'd hidden it. It would be something that Edward would do. Better to assume the worst and be wrong than assume the best and be wrong. Pessimism will keep you alive, optimism won't, not in our line of business anyway.

Our line of business. Strange phrase. Edward was an assassin. I wasn't. But somehow we were in the same business. I couldn't quite explain it, but it was true.

Edward gave me a pure Edward smile, a smile meant to make me uneasy and suspicious. It also usually meant that he meant me no harm and was just yanking my chain. Of course, he knew I knew what the smile usually meant, so he might use it to lull me into a false sense of security. Or it could mean just what it seemed to. I was overthinking things and that was bad all on its own. Edward was right, I was at my best when I let my gut work and kept my higher functions in the background. Not a recipe for going through life, but a good one for a gunfight.

'We have a truce,' I said.

He nodded. 'I said we did.'

'You make me nervous,' I said.

The smile widened. 'Glad to hear you're still scared of me. I was beginning to wonder.'

'The day you stop being afraid of the monsters is the day they kill you.'

'And I'm a monster?' He made it a question.

'You know exactly what you are, Edward.'

His eyes narrowed. 'You called me Edward in front of Donna. She didn't say anything, but you are going to have to be more careful.'

I nodded. 'I'm sorry, I caught it, too. I will try but I'm not half as good a liar as you are. Besides, Ted is a nickname for Edward.'

'Not if the full name on my driver's license is Theodore.'

'Now, if I can call you Teddy, maybe I'd remember.'

'Teddy is fine,' he said, voice totally unchanged.

'You are a very hard man to tease, Ed . . . Ted.'

'Names don't mean anything, Anita. They're too easy to change.'

'Is Edward really your first name?'

'It is now.'

I shook my head. 'I'd really like to know.'

'Why?' He gazed at me from the black sunglasses, and the weight of his interest burned through the glass. The question wasn't idle. Of course, Edward seldom asked any question he didn't want an answer to.

'Because I've known you for five years, and I don't even know if your first name is real.'

'It's real enough,' he said.

'It bugs me not to know,' I said.

'Why?' he asked again.

I shrugged and eased my hand away from my gun because it wasn't necessary, not right this minute, not today. But even as I did it, I knew there would be other days, and for the first time I really wasn't sure that both of us would see the end of my little visit. It made me sad and grumpy.

'Maybe I just want to know what name to put on the tombstone,' I said.

He laughed. 'Confidence is a fine trait. Overconfidence isn't.' The laughter faded and left his face around the glasses cool and unreadable. I didn't have to see his eyes to know they were cold and distant as winter skies.

I pushed away from the car, hands empty at my sides. 'Look, Edward, Ted, whatever the hell you call yourself, I don't like being invited here to play monster bait, and find you dating the new age mom of the year. It's thrown me, and I don't like that either. We have a truce until the case is solved, then what?'

'Then we'll see,' he said.

'You couldn't just agree to stop being engaged to Donna?'

'No.' His voice was small, careful.

'Why not?' I asked.

'I'd need to give her a good enough reason to break her heart and the kids'. Remember, I've been spending a lot of time with the kids. How would it look to just vanish on them?'

'I think her son wouldn't mind. Peter, wasn't it? I think he'd love it if Ted would vanish.'

Edward turned his head to one side. 'Yeah, Peter would love it, but what about Becca? I've been in her life for over two years and she's only six. Donna trusts me to pick her up after school. I drive her once a week to dance lessons so Donna doesn't have to close the shop early.' His voice and face never changed as he spoke, as if it was just facts and meant nothing.

Anger tightened my shoulders and traveled down my arms. I put my hands in fists just to have something to do with my body. 'You bastard.'

'Maybe,' he said, 'but be careful what you ask me to do, Anita. Just walking out could do more damage than the truth.'

I stared at him, trying to see behind that blank face. 'Have you thought about telling Donna the truth?'

'No.'

'Damn you.'

'Do you really think she could handle the truth, the entire truth about me?' he asked.

I thought about that for nearly a full minute while we stood in the heat-soaked parking lot. Finally, I said, 'No.' I didn't like saying it, but truth was truth.

'You're sure she couldn't play wife to an assassin? I mean you've only met her for half an hour. How can you be so sure?'

'Now you're teasing me,' I said.

His lips twitched almost a smile. 'I think you are exactly right. I don't think Donna could handle the truth.'

I shook my head, hard enough that my hair lashed my face. I literally threw my hands in the air. 'Fuck it, for now. I didn't get on a plane at a moment's notice to stand in the heat and discuss your love life. Don't we have a crime to solve or something?'

'We could discuss your love life,' he said. 'Werewolf or vampire, which are you fucking now?' There was something close to bitterness in his voice. It wasn't jealousy, but utter disapproval. You killed the monsters. You did not date them. It was one of Edward's rules, and used to be one of mine. Just another example of my moral downfall.

'Neither, actually, and that is all I'm going to say on the subject.'

He lowered his sunglasses enough so I could see his pale blue eyes. 'You dumped them both?' He actually sounded interested.

I shook my head. 'If I feel like sharing, I'll let you know. Now tell me what the hell you've dragged me into besides your sordid love life. Tell me about the murders, Edward. Tell me why I'm really here.'

He slipped the glasses back over his eyes and gave a small nod. 'Okay.' He opened the driver's side door and left me to let myself into the passenger side. He'd held Donna's door for her, but that wasn't the kind of relationship Edward and I had. If we might have to start shooting each other, I'd get my own doors.

4

The car belonged to Ted, even though Edward was driving it. It was a square and big something between a Jeep, a truck, and an ugly car. It was covered in red clay mud as if he'd been driving through ditches. The windshield was so dirty only two fans of clear space remained where the windshield wipers had washed away the mud, everything else had dried to a reddish-brown patina of dirt.

'Gee, Edward,' I said, as he opened the back hatch, 'what have you been doing to this poor whatever it is. I've never seen a car so dirty.'

'This is a Hummer, and cost more than most people's houses.' He raised the hatch and started putting my bags inside. I offered him my carry-on, and when I was close could smell that new car smell, which explained why the carpeting in back was still nearly pristine.

'If it costs that much, then why doesn't it rate better care?' I asked.

He took the carry-on and put it on the new carpet. 'I bought it because it could go over almost any terrain in almost any weather. If I didn't want it to get dirty, I'd have bought something else.' He slammed the hatch shut.

'How can Ted afford something like this?'

'Actually, Ted makes a fine living off varmint hunting.'

'Not this good,' I said, 'not off of bounty hunting.'

'How do you know what a bounty hunter makes?' he asked, peering around the filthy car at me.

He had a point. 'I guess I don't.'

'Most people don't know what a bounty hunter makes so I can get away with some purchases that might be out of Ted's price range.' He walked around the car toward the driver's side, only the top of his white hat showing above the mud-caked roof.

I tried the passenger side door, and it opened. It took a little bit of work to climb into the seat, and I was glad I wasn't wearing a skirt. One nice thing about working with Edward was that he wouldn't expect me to wear business attire. It was jeans and Nikes for this trip.

The only business thing I was wearing was the black jacket slung over my cotton shirt and jeans. The jacket was to hide the gun, nothing more. 'What are the gun laws like in New Mexico?'

Edward started the car and glanced at me. 'Why?'

I put on my seatbelt. Evidently, we were in a hurry. 'I want to know if I can ditch the jacket and wear my gun naked, or whether I'm going to have to hide the gun for the entire trip.'

His lips twitched. 'New Mexico lets you carry as long as it's not concealed. Concealed carry without a permit is illegal.'

'Let me test my understanding. I can wear the gun in full view of everyone with or without a carry permit, but if I put a jacket over it, concealing it, and don't have a carry permit, it's illegal?'

The twitch turned into a smile. 'That's right.'

'Western state gun laws are always so interesting,' I said, but I started sliding out of the jacket. You can wiggle out of almost anything while remaining seatbelted in a car. Since I always wear a seatbelt, I'd had a lot of practice.

'But the police may still stop you if they see you walking around armed. Just make sure you're not here to kill anybody.' He half smiled when he said the last.

'So I can carry as long as it's not concealed, but not really, not without getting questioned by the police.'

'And you can't carry a gun of any kind, even unloaded, into a bar.'

'I don't drink. I think I can avoid the bars.'

A wire fence edged the road he pulled onto, but did nothing to take away the flat, flat distances and the strange black mountains. 'What are the mountains called?'

'Sangre del Cristo – the blood of Christ,' he said. I looked at him to see if he was kidding. Of course, he wasn't. 'Why?'

'Why what?'

'Why call them the blood of Christ?'

'I don't know.'

'How long has Ted lived out here?'

'Almost four years,' he said.

'And you don't know why the mountains are named Sangre del Cristo? Do you have no curiosity?'

'Not about things that don't affect the job.'

He didn't say, a job, but the job. I thought it was odd phrasing. 'What if this monster that we're hunting is some kind of local bugaboo? Knowing why the mountains are named what they're named may mean nothing, or it may have to do with a legend, a story, a hint about some great blood bath in the past. There are very localized monsters, Edward, things that only come above ground every century or so like really long-lived cicadas.'

'Cicadas?' he asked.

'Yeah, cicadas. The immature form stays in the ground until every thirteen or seven or whatever their cycle is years, they climb out, molt, and become adults. They're the insects that make all that noise in the summertime.'

'Whatever did those people wasn't a giant cicada, Anita.'

'That's not the point, Edward. My point is that there are types of living creatures that stay hidden, almost totally hidden, for years, then resurface. Monsters are still a part of the natural world. Preternatural biology is still biology. So maybe old myths and legends would give us a clue.'

'I didn't bring you down here to play Nancy Drew,' he said.

'Yes, you did,' I said.

He looked at me long enough to make me want to tell him to watch the road. 'What are you talking about?'

'If you just wanted someone to point and shoot, you'd have brought in someone else. You want my expertise, not just my gun. Right?'

He'd turned back to the road, much to my relief. There were small houses on either side, most of them made of adobe, or faux-adobe. I didn't know enough about it to judge. The yards were small but well tended, running high to cacti and huge lilac bushes with surprisingly small bundles of pale lavender flowers on them. It looked like a different variety from the lilacs in the Midwest. Maybe it took less water.

Silence had filled the car and I let it, watching the scenery. I'd never been to Albuquerque, and I'd play tourist while I could. Edward finally answered me when he turned onto Lomos Street. 'You're right. I didn't ask you down here just to shoot things. I already have backup for that.'

'Who?' I asked.

'You don't know them, but you'll meet them in Santa Fe.'

'We're driving straight to Santa Fe now? I haven't eaten yet today. I was sort of hoping to catch some lunch.'

'The latest crime scene is in Albuquerque. We'll catch it, then lunch.'

'Will I feel like eating afterwards?'

'Maybe.'

'I don't suppose I could talk you into lunch first then.'

'We've got a stop before we hit the house,' he said.

'What other stop?' I asked.

He just gave that small smile, which meant it was going to be a surprise. Edward loved to try my patience.

Maybe he'd answer a different question. 'Who's your other backup?'

'I told you, you don't know them.'

'You keep saying them. Are you saying that you already have two people for backup, and you still needed to call me in, too?'

He didn't say anything to that.

'Three people backing you on this. Geez, Edward, you must be desperate.' I'd meant for it to be a joke, sort of. He didn't take it that way.

'I want this case solved, Anita, whatever it takes.' He looked grim when he said it. So much for my sense of humor.

'Do these two backups owe you a favor?'

'One does.'

'Are they assassins?'

'Sometimes.'

'Bounty hunters like Ted?'

'Bernardo is.'

At least I had a name. 'Bernardo is a sometimes assassin and a bounty hunter like Ted. You mean he uses his bounty hunting identity like you use yours as a legal identity?'

'Sometimes he's a bodyguard, too.'

'A man of many talents,' I said.

'Not really,' he said. Which was a strange thing to say.

'What about the other guy?'

'Olaf.'

'Olaf, okay. He's sometimes an assassin, not a bounty hunter, not a bodyguard, and what else?'

Edward shook his head.

His noncommittal answers were beginning to get on my nerves. 'Do either of them have any other special abilities besides being willing to kill?'

'Yes.'

He'd reached my limit on 'yes, no' answers. 'I didn't come down here to play twenty questions, Edward. Just tell me about the other backups.'

'You'll meet them soon enough.'

'Fine, then tell me where the other stop is.'

He gave a small shake of his head.

'Look, Edward, you're getting on my nerves, and you've already pissed me off, so cut the mysterious crap, and talk to me.'

He glanced sideways at me, a glimpse of eyes from the edges of the dark glasses. 'My, my, aren't we touchy today.'

'This isn't even close to touchy for me, Edward, and you know it. But keep up the noncommittal crap and you are going to truly piss me off.'

'I thought you were already pissed off about Donna.'

'I am,' I said. 'But I'm willing to get interested in the case and forget to be continuously pissed. But I can't get interested in the case if you don't answer questions about it. As far as I'm concerned your backup is part of the case, so either start sharing info or drive me back to the damn airport.'

'I didn't tell Olaf and Bernardo you're shacking up with a vampire and a werewolf.'

'Actually, I'm not dating either of them anymore, but that's not the point. I don't want to know about their sex life, Edward. I just want to know why you called them in. What are their areas of expertise?'

'You broke up with Jean-Claude and Richard both?' For one of the few times since I'd met him I heard real curiosity in his voice. I wasn't sure if it was nice to know or disturbing that my personal life interested Edward.

'I don't know if we broke up, it's more like we aren't seeing each other. I need some time away from them before I decide what to do.'

'What are you thinking about doing to them?' And there was a note of eagerness now.

Edward was only eager about one thing. 'I am not planning to kill either of them, if that's what you're hinting at.'

'I can't say I'm not disappointed,' Edward said. 'I think you should have killed Jean-Claude yourself before it all got too deep.'

'You're talking about killing someone who has been my lover off and on for over a year, Edward. Maybe you could strangle Donna in her bed, but I'd lose sleep over something like that.'

'Do you love him?'

The question stopped me, not because of the question but because of who was asking it. It seemed a truly odd question coming from Edward. 'Yeah, I think I do.'

'Do you love Richard?'

Again, it seemed odd talking about my emotional life with Edward. I have a few male friends, and most of them would rather have a root canal than talk about 'feelings.' Of all my male friends I was talking to the one I thought would never discuss love with me. It just wasn't my year for understanding men.

'Yes, I love Richard.'

'You say, you think you love the vampire, but you simply answer yes about Richard. Kill the vampire, Anita. I'll help you do it.'

'Not to put too fine a point on it, Edward, but I'm Jean-Claude's human servant. Richard is his animal to call. The three of us are bound by vampire marks into a nice little ménage à trois. If one of us dies, we may all die.'

'Maybe, or maybe that's what the vampire tells you. It wouldn't be the first time he's lied to you.'

It was impossible to argue without looking like a fool, so I didn't try. 'When I want your advice on my personal life, I'll ask for it. Until people start ice skating in hell, save your breath. Now, tell me about the case.'

'You get to tell me who to date and who not to, but I can't return the favor?' he asked.

I looked at him. 'Are you angry with me about my stand on Donna?'

'Not exactly, but if you get to give me advice on dating, why can't I return the favor?'

'It's not the same thing, Edward. Richard doesn't have kids.'

'Children make that big a difference to you?' he asked.

I nodded. 'Yeah, they do.'

'I never figured you as the maternal type.'

'I'm not, but kids are people, Edward, little people trapped by the choices the adults around them make. Donna's old enough to make her own mistakes, but when you screw her, you're screwing her kids, too. I know that doesn't bother you, but it bothers me.'

'I knew it would. I even knew how you'd react, but I don't know why.'

'Well, you're one ahead of me. I never dreamed you were boffing new age widows with munchkins. I figured you more for the pay as you go plan.'

'Ted doesn't pay for it,' he said.

'How about Edward?'

He shrugged. 'It's like eating, just another need.'

The cold bluntness of it was actually reassuring. 'See, that's the Edward I've grown to know and be afraid of.'

'You're afraid of me, but yet you'd come against me for a woman you just met and two kids you don't even know. I'm not even planning to kill any of them and yet you'd push the ultimate question between us.' He shook his head. 'I don't understand that.'

'Don't understand it, Edward. Just know it's true.'

'I believe you, Anita. You're the only person I know, except for me, that never bluffs.'

'Bernardo and Olaf bluff?' I gave it that extra little lilt, making it a question.

He shook his head and laughed. The tension that had been building eased with that laugh. 'No, I'm not giving you anything on them.'

'Why?' I asked.

'Because,' he said, and he almost smiled.

I looked at his careful profile. 'You're enjoying this. You're enjoying Olaf and Bernardo meeting me.' I didn't try and keep the surprise out of my voice.

'Just like I enjoyed you meeting Donna.'

'Even though you knew I'd be pissed,' I said.

He nodded. 'The look on your face was almost worth a death threat.'

I shook my head. 'You're beginning to worry me, Edward.'

'Just beginning to worry you? I must be losing my touch.'

'Fine, don't tell me about them. Tell me about the case.'

He pulled into a parking lot. I looked up to find a hospital looming over us. 'Is this the crime scene?'

'No.' He pulled into a parking spot, and shut the engine off.

'What gives, Edward? Why are we at a hospital?'

'The survivors are here.'

My eyes widened. 'What survivors?'

He looked at me. 'The survivors from the attacks.' He opened his door, and I grabbed his arm, holding him in the car.

Edward turned slowly and looked at my hand on the bare skin of his arm. He looked at my hand a long time with his disapproval at the touch radiating from him, but it was a trick I'd pulled myself more than once. If the person makes it known that they don't want to be touched, most people that don't mean you violence will back off. I didn't back off. I dug my fingers into his skin, not to hurt, just to let him know he wasn't getting rid of me that easily.

'Talk to me, Edward. What survivors?'

He shifted his gaze from my hand to my face. I had an urge to snatch the sunglasses from his face but fought it. His eyes wouldn't show me anything anyway.

'I told you there were injured people.' His voice was mild.

'No, you didn't. You made it sound like there were no survivors.'

'My oversight,' he said.

'My ass,' I said. 'I know you enjoy being mysterious, Edward, but it's getting tedious.'

'Let go of my arm.' He said it the way you'd say, hello, or nice day, no inflection at all.

'Will you answer my questions if I do?'

'No,' he said, still with that same pleasant empty voice. 'But if you make this a pissing contest, Anita, I'll feel compelled to make you let go. You wouldn't like that.'

The voice never changed. There was even a slight smile to his mouth. But I let go, slowly, drawing back into my seat. If Edward said I wouldn't like it, I believed him.

'Talk to me, Edward.'

He gave me a big ol' smile. 'Call me Ted.' Then the son of a bitch got out of the car. I sat in the car, watching him walk across the parking lot. He stopped at the edge with the hospital just across a small road from him. He took off the sunglasses, slipped one of the ear pieces into his shirt front, and stared back at the car, waiting.

It would serve him right if I didn't get out. It would serve him right if I went back to St Louis and let him clean up his own mess. But I opened the door and got out. Why, you might ask. One, he'd asked me for a favor, and being Edward he'd reveal all in his own sadistic time. Two, I wanted to know. I wanted to know what had finally cut through all that coldness and scared him. I wanted to know. Curiosity is both a strength and a weakness. Which one this particular curiosity was wouldn't be answered for a while. I was betting on weakness.

5

Saint Lucia Hospital was big and one of the few buildings of any size in Albuquerque that I'd seen that didn't have a southwest theme to it. It was just big and blocky, a generic hospital. Maybe they didn't expect the tourists to see the hospital. Lucky tourists.

As hospitals go, it was nice, but it was still a hospital. A place I only go when things have gone wrong. The only up side this time was that it wasn't me or anyone I knew in the rooms.

We were in a long pale corridor with lots of closed doors, but there was a uniformed police officer in front of one of them. Call it a hunch, but I figured that was our room.

Edward walked up to the policeman and introduced himself. He was at his good ol' boy best, harmless and jovial, in a subdued hospital sort of way. They knew each other on sight which should have sped things up considerably.

The uniform looked past Edward to me. He looked young, but his eyes were cool and gray, cop eyes. You have to be on the job a while before your eyes go empty. But he looked at me too long and too intently. You could almost feel the testosterone rising to the surface. The challenging look said that either he was insecure in his own masculinity, his own copness, or that he hadn't been on the job all that long. Not a rookie, but not much beyond it either.

If he expected me to squirm under the scrutiny, he was going to be disappointed. I faced him, smiling, calm, eyes blank and close to bored. Passing inspection had never been my favorite thing.

He blinked first. 'The lieutenant is inside. He wants to see her before she goes inside.'

'Why?' Edward asked, voice still likable.

The officer shrugged. 'I'm just following orders, Mr Forrester. I don't question my lieutenant. Wait here.' He opened the door and slipped inside without giving much of a glimpse inside. He shut the door behind him, not waiting for the weight and hinges to do it for him.

Edward was frowning. 'I don't know what's going on.'

'I do,' I said.

He looked at me, raising an eyebrow, as if to say, go ahead.

'I'm a girl and technically a civilian. A lot of cops don't trust me to do the job.'

'I vouched for you.'

'Gee, Ed . . . Ted, I guess your opinion doesn't carry as much weight as you thought it did.'

He was still frowning at me with Edward's eyes when the door swung open. I was watching his face as he transformed into Ted. The eyes sparkled, the lips curved, the entire set of his face remade itself, as if it were a mask. His own personality vanished like magic. Watching the show this up close and personal made me shiver just a bit. The ease with which he switched back and forth was just plain creepy.

The man in the doorway was short, not many inches above me, maybe five foot six at best. I wondered if their police force didn't have a height requirement. His hair was a golden sun-streaked blond cut very short and close to his square-jawed face. He was tanned a nice soft gold, as if it were as dark a tan as his pale skin were capable of. First Donna, now the lieutenant. Didn't anyone sweat skin cancer here? He looked at me with green-gold eyes, the color of new spring leaves. They were beautiful eyes with long golden lashes and softened his face to an almost feminine appearance. Only the masculine jut of the jaw saved him from being one of those men who is beautiful instead of handsome. The jaw both ruined his face and saved it from perfection.

The eyes may have been lovely, but they weren't friendly. It wasn't even the coolness of cop eyes. It was hostile. Since I'd never met him before, it had to be the fact that I was a woman, a civilian, and/or an animator. He was either a chauvinist or superstitious. I wasn't sure which I preferred.

He let me have a nice long dose of glaring. I just gave a blank face, waiting for him to get tired of it. I could stand there all day and be peacefully blank. Standing in a nice safe hospital corridor wasn't even close to the worst thing I'd had to do lately. It was always sort of peaceful when no one was trying to kill me.

Edward tried to break the stalemate. 'Lieutenant Marks, this is Anita Blake. Chief Appleton called you about her.' He was still using Ted's happy voice, but there was a set to his shoulders that was stiff and not so happy.

'You're Anita Blake.' Lieutenant Marks managed to sound doubtful.

I nodded. 'Yep.'

His eyes narrowed. 'I don't like civilians messing in my case.' He jerked a thumb at Edward. 'Forrester here has proven himself valuable.' He pointed a finger at me. 'You haven't.'

Edward started to say something, but Marks cut him off with a sharp movement of his hand. 'No, let her answer for herself.'

'I'll answer a question if you'll ask one,' I said.

'What's that supposed to mean?'

'It means you haven't asked a question yet, Lieutenant. You've just made statements.'

'I don't need shit from some fucking zombie queen.'

Ah, he was prejudiced. One mystery solved. 'I was invited down here, Lieutenant Marks. I was invited to help you solve this case. Now if you don't want my help, fine, but I'll need someone from the city government to explain to my boss why the hell I got on a plane to New Mexico when I wasn't sure of my welcome.'

'I don't treat you right and you run to the powers that be, is that it?'

I shook my head. 'Who got your panties in a twist, Marks?'

He frowned. 'What?'

'Do I remind you of your ex-wife?'

'I'm married to my only wife.' He sounded indignant.

'Congratulations. Is it the voodoo that I use to raise the dead? Are you nervous around the mystical arts?'

'I don't like black magic.' He fingered the cross-shaped tie tack that was standard police issue almost everywhere, but somehow I thought Marks was serious about it.

'I don't do black magic, Marks.' I drew on the silver chain around my neck until the crucifix spilled into the light. 'I'm Christian, Episcopalian actually. I don't know what you've heard about what I do, but it's not evil.'

'You would say that,' he said.

'The state of my immortal soul is between God and myself, Lieutenant Marks. Judge not lest ye be judged yourself. Or do you skip that part and just keep the parts you like?'

His face darkened, and a vein in his forehead started to pulse. This level of anger, even if he was a right-winger Christian extremist, was over the top. 'What in hell is behind that door to have you both so spooked?' I asked.

Marks blinked at me. 'I am not spooked.'

I shrugged. 'Yeah, you are. You're all bent out of shape about the survivors and you're taking it out on me.'

'You don't know me,' he said.

'No, but I know a lot of policemen, and I know when someone's scared.'

He stepped close enough to me that if it had been a fight, I'd have stepped back, put space between us. Instead, I stood my ground. I wasn't really expecting the lieutenant to take a swing at me.

'You think you're so fucking tough?'

I blinked at him, close enough that if I'd risen on tiptoe, I could have kissed him. 'I don't think, Lieutenant. I know.'

He smiled at that, but not like he was happy. 'You think you can take it, be my guest.' He stepped to one side, making a sweeping motion towards the door.

I wanted to ask what was behind the door. What could possibly be so horrible that it had Edward and a police lieutenant this shaken? I stared at the closed door, smooth, hiding all its secrets.

'What are you waiting for, Ms Blake? Go ahead. Open the door.'

I glanced back at Edward. 'I don't suppose you'd give me a hint.'

'Open the door, Anita.'

I muttered, 'Bastard,' under my breath and opened the door.

6

The door didn't lead directly into the room. It led into a small antechamber with another sealed, mostly glass door beyond. There was a hush of air circulating through the room as if the room had its own separate air supply. A man stood to one side wearing green surgical scrubs complete with little plastic booties over his feet, a mask hanging loose from his neck. He was tall and slender without looking weak. He was also one of the first New Mexicans that I'd met without a tan. He handed me a pile of scrubs. 'Put this on.'

I took the clothes. 'Are you the doctor on this case?'

'No, I'm a nurse.'

'You got a name?'

He gave a small smile. 'Ben, I'm Ben.'

'Thanks, Ben. I'm Anita. Why do I need the scrubs?'

'To guard against infection.'

I didn't argue with him. My expertise was more in the line of taking lives, not preserving them. I'd bow to the experts. I put the scrubs over my jeans, tying the string tie as tight as it would go. The legs of the pants still bagged around my feet.

Ben the nurse was smiling. 'We weren't expecting them to send us a policeman so . . . petite.'

I frowned at him. 'Smile when you say that.'

His smile brightened in a flash of white teeth. The smile softened the face and made him seem less like Nurse Ratched and more like a human being.

'And I'm not a cop.'

His eyes flicked to the gun in its shoulder holster. The gun was very black and very noticeable against the red shirt. 'You're carrying a gun.'

I slipped a short-sleeved shirt over my head, and the offending gun. 'New Mexico law says I can carry as long as it's not concealed.'

'If you're not a policeman, then why do you need the gun?'

'I'm a vampire executioner.'

He held a long-sleeved gown out towards me. I slipped my arms through the sleeves. It tied in the back like most hospital gowns. Ben tied it for me. 'I thought you couldn't kill a vampire with bullets.'

'Silver bullets can slow them down, and if they're not too old or too powerful, blowing a hole in their brain or heart works. Sometimes,' I added. Wouldn't want Ben to get the wrong idea and try to take out an intruding vamp with silver ammo and get munched because he trusted my opinion.

We had some trouble getting my hair up under the little plastic hair thing but finally managed it, though the thin ridge of elastic that held it in place scraped the back of my neck every time I moved my head. Ben tried to help me with the surgical gloves, but I put them on myself, no problem.

He raised eyebrows at me. 'You've put on gloves before.' It wasn't a question.

'I wear them at crime scenes and when I don't want blood under my fingernails.'

He helped me tie the mask around my neck. 'You must see a lot of blood in your line of work.'

'Not as much blood as you see, I bet.' I turned with the mask over my mouth and nose. Only my eyes were left uncovered and real. Ben looked down at me, and his face looked thoughtful. 'I'm not a surgical nurse.'

'What is your specialty?' I asked.

'Burn unit.'

My eyes widened. 'Are the survivors burned?'

He shook his head. 'No, but their bodies are still like open wounds, just like a burn. The protocol is similar.'

'What do you mean their bodies are an open wound?'

Someone tapped on the glass behind me, and I jumped, turning to see another man in an outfit just like mine glaring at me with pale eyes. He hit an intercom button, and his voice came clear enough to hear the irritation in it. 'If you're coming inside, then do it. I want to sedate them again, and I can't do that until you've had a chance to question them, or so I'm told.' He let go of the button and walked farther away behind a white curtain that hid the rest of the room from view.

'Gee, I'm just on everybody's happy list today.'

Ben put on his mask and said, 'Don't take it personally. Doctor Evans is good at what he does, one of the best.'

If you want to find a good doctor in a hospital, don't ask other doctors or referral services. Ask a nurse. Nurses always know who's good and who's not. They may not say the bad stuff aloud, but if they say something good about a doctor, you can take it to the bank.

Ben touched something on the wall that was a little too big to be called a button, and the doors whooshed open with a sound like an air lock opening. I stepped inside, and the doors hushed closed behind me. Nothing but the white curtain now.

I didn't want to pull that curtain aside. Everyone was too damned upset. It was going to be bad. Their bodies were like open wounds, Ben had said, but not a burn. What had happened to them? As the old saying goes, only one way to find out. I took a deep breath and pushed the curtain aside.

The room beyond was white and antiseptic looking, a very hospital of a hospital room. Outside this room there had been some attempt at pastels and a pretense that it was just a building, just hallways, just ordinary rooms. All pretense ended at the curtain, and reality was harsh.

There were six beds, each with a whitish plastic hood/tent over the head of the beds and the upper bodies of the patients. Doctor Evans was standing beside the nearest bed. A woman in matching scrubs was farther into the room, checking one of the many blinking, beeping pieces of equipment that huddled around each bed. She glanced up, and the small area of her face that showed was a startling darkness. African American, female, and not fat, but beyond that and height I couldn't tell anything underneath the protective clothing. I wouldn't recognize her again without the scrubs. It was strangely anonymous and disturbing. Or maybe that was just me. She dropped her gaze and moved to another bed, doing the same checks, writing something down on a clip board.

I walked towards the closest bed. Doctor Evans never turned around or acknowledged me in any way. White sheets formed tents over each patient, held up by some sort of framework to keep the sheet from touching them.

Doctor Evans finally turned to one side so I could see the face of the patient. I blinked and my eyes refused to see it, or maybe my brain just rejected what I was seeing. The face was red and raw as if it should be bleeding, but it didn't bleed. It was like looking at raw meat in the shape of a human face, no meaty skull. The nose had been cut off, leaving bloody holes for the plastic tubes to be shoved inside. The man rolled brown eyes in his sockets, staring up at me. There was something wrong with his eyes beyond the lack of skin around them. It took me a few seconds to realize his eyelids had been cut off.

The room was suddenly warm, so warm, and the mask was suffocating me. I wanted to pull it off so I could breathe. I must have made some movement because the doctor grabbed my wrist.

'Don't take anything off. I'm risking their lives with every new person that comes in here.' He let go of my wrist. 'Make the risk worth it. Tell me what did this.'

I shook my head, concentrating on breathing slowly in and out.

When I could talk, I asked, 'What's the rest of the body look like?'

He stared at me, his eyes demanding. I met his gaze. Anything was better than looking at what lay in the bed. 'You're pale already. Are you sure you want to see the rest?'

'No,' I said, truthfully.

Even with just his eyes visible I could see the surprise on his face.

'I would like nothing better than to turn and walk out of this room and keep walking,' I said. 'I don't need any new nightmares, Doctor Evans, but I was called in here to give my expert opinion. I can't form an opinion without seeing the whole show. If I thought I didn't need to see it all, trust me, I wouldn't ask.'

'What do you hope to gain by it?' he asked.

'I'm not here to gape at them, Doctor. But I'm looking for clues to what did this. Most of the time the clues are on the bodies of the victims.'

The man in the bed made small jerks, head tossing from side to side as if he were in a great deal of pain. Small helpless noises came from his lipless mouth. I closed my eyes and tried to breathe normally. 'Please, Doctor, I need to see.' I opened my eyes in time to see him rolling back the sheet. I watched him roll it back, folding it carefully, revealing the man's body an inch at a time. By the time I saw him to the waist, I knew that he'd been skinned alive. I'd hoped it was just the face. That was awful enough on its own, but it takes a hell of a long time to skin a grown man's entire body, a long screaming eternity to do it this well and this thoroughly.

When the sheet rolled back over the groin, I swayed, just a little. It wasn't a man. The groin area was smooth and raw. I glanced back up at the chest. The bone structure looked male. I shook my head. 'Is this a man or a woman?'

'Man,' he said.

I stared down and couldn't keep from staring at the groin and what was missing. 'Shit,' I said softly. I closed my eyes again. It was so hot, so very hot. With my eyes closed, I could hear the hiss of the oxygen, the whisper of the nurse's booties as she came towards us, and small sounds from the bed as he twitched and strained against padded restraints at his wrists and ankles.

Restraints? I'd seen them but hadn't really registered them. All I could see was the body. Yes, body. I couldn't keep thinking of the man as a 'he.' I had to distance myself or I was going to lose it.

Concentrate on business. I opened my eyes. 'Why the restraints?' My voice was breathy but clear. I glanced down at the body, then back up, giving Doctor Evans the most complete eye contact I'd ever given. I'd stare at him until I memorized the light crows-feet around his eyes, if I just didn't have to keep looking at what lay on the bed.

'They keep trying to get up and leave,' he said.

I frowned, not that he could see it under the mask. 'Surely, they're too hurt to get far.'

'We've got them on some very strong painkillers. When the pain dies down, they try to leave.'

'All of them?' I asked.

He nodded.

I made myself look back to the bed. 'Why isn't this just a case of a serial . . . not killer. What would you call it? A serial . . .' I shook my head. I couldn't think of a word for it. 'Why was I called in? I'm a preternatural expert, and this could have been done by a person.'

'There are no blade marks on the tissue,' Doctor Evans said.

I stared up at him. 'What do you mean?'

'I mean that no blade did this because no matter how good they are at torture, there are always telltale signs of the instrument used. You're right when you say the bodies of the victims have the best clues, but not these bodies. It's almost as if their skin just dissolved away.'

'Any corrosive agent that could take someone's skin and soft tissue like nose and groin wouldn't just stop at the skin. It would keep eating through the body.'

He nodded. 'Unless it was washed off immediately, but there's no residue of any known corrosive agent. More than that, the body isn't patterned on an acid burn. The nose and groin were torn away. There are signs of tearing and damage that aren't present elsewhere. It's almost as if whoever did the skinning, skinned them then tore off the extra pieces.' He shook his head. 'I've traveled all over the world to help catch torturers. I thought I'd seen it all, but I was wrong.'

'Are you a forensic pathologist?' I asked.

'Yes.'

'But they're not dead,' I said.

He looked at me. 'No, they're not dead, but the same skills that let me judge a dead body work here, too.'

'Ted Forrester said there were deaths. Did they die from the skinning?' Now that I was 'working,' the room didn't seem so hot. If I concentrated very carefully on the business stuff, maybe I wouldn't throw up on the patients.

'No, they were cut into pieces and left where they fell.'

'Blade marks on the cut-up bodies, I assume, or you wouldn't have used the word cut.'

'There were marks of a cutting tool, but it was like no knife or sword, or hell, bayonet that I'd ever seen. The cuts were deep but not clean, something less refined than a steel blade was used.'

'What?' I asked.

He shook his head. 'I don't know. The blade didn't cut through the bones, though. Whoever cut the bodies up pulled the bodies apart at the joints. No human would have the strength to do that, not multiple times.'

'Probably not,' I said.

'You really think a human being could have done this?' he asked, motioning at the bed.

'Are you asking me if a person could do this to another person? If you travel the world testifying in cases of death by torture, then you know exactly what people are capable of doing to each other.'

'I'm not saying a person wouldn't do this,' he said. 'I'm saying I don't think it would be physically possible to do it.'

I nodded. 'The cutting and tearing, I think might have been human, but I agree with the skinning. If it were done by a human, then there would be tool marks of some kind.'

'You say tool marks, not blade marks. Most people assume it takes a blade to skin someone.'

'Anything that holds an edge can do it,' I said, 'though it's slower and usually messier. This is strangely clean.'

'Yes,' he said, nodding. 'Yes, that's a good phrase for it. As horrible as it is, it's still very neatly done, except for the extra tissue that was removed. That was not neatly done, but brutally done.'

'Almost like we have two different . . .' I kept wanting to say killers, but these people were still alive. 'Perpetrators,' I said finally.

'What do you mean?'

'Cutting up a body with a dull tool that isn't strong enough to tear through bone, then pulling a person apart with bare hands is something more in the line of a disorganized serial killer. The careful skinning is something an organized serial killer might do. Why go to the trouble of carefully skinning the face and groin, then pulling off the pieces? It's either two different mutilators, or it's two different personalities.'

'A multiple personality?' He made it a question.

'Not exactly, but not all serial killers are so easy to put in one category or another. Some organized criminals have moments of savagery that resemble the disorganized killer, and some organized minds become more disorganized as they escalate their killing. The same isn't true of a disorganized killer. There aren't enough brownies in the pan for them to ape organized methods.'

'So either an organized killer with savage moments of

disorganization, or . . . or what?' The good doctor was talking very reasonably to me, not angry anymore. I'd either impressed him or at least hadn't disappointed him. Not yet, anyway.

'It could be a pair of killers, an organized killer being the brains of the operation and the disorganized being the follower. It's not that unusual to find killers working in tandem.'

'Like the Hillside Strangler or rather Stranglers,' he said.

I smiled behind the mask. 'There have been a lot more cases than just that one where we had two killers. Sometimes it's two men. Sometimes it's a man and a woman. In that case the man is the dominant personality. Or at least in every case I've ever heard of, except one. Either way one is dominant and the other is to a lesser or greater degree in the control of the other. It can be a near complete domination so that the other person is unable to say no, or it can be more of a partnership. But even in more equal relationships one person is primarily dominant while the other is the follower.'

'And you're sure it's a serial mutilator?' he asked.

'No,' I said.

'What do you mean?'

'The serial mutilator idea is the most normal solution I can come up with, but I'm a preternatural expert, Doctor Evans. I'm rarely called in when the answer wears a human face, no matter how monstrous. Someone thinks this wasn't done by human hands, or I wouldn't be here.'

'The FBI agent seemed very sure,' Doctor Evans said.

I looked at him. 'Have I just wasted both our times here? Did the Feds come in and say pretty much what I just said?'

'Pretty much,' he said.

'Then you don't need me.'

'The FBI is convinced that it's a serial mutilator, a person.'

'Sometimes the Feds can be very sure of themselves, and once they've committed themselves, they don't like to be wrong.

Policemen in general can be like that. It is usually the easy answer when it comes to crime. If a husband dies, the wife probably did do it. Cops aren't encouraged to complicate a case. They're encouraged to simplify it.'

'Why aren't you taking the simple solution?' he asked.

'Several reasons. One, if it was a serial anything, a human, I'd think the police, Feds, whatever would have some clues by now. The level of fear and uncertainty among the men is too high. If they had a clue to what was happening, they'd be less panicked. Two, I don't have a superior to report to. No one's going to slap my hand or demote me in rank if I guess and I'm wrong. My job and income don't depend on pleasing anyone but myself.'

'You do have a boss to answer to?' he said.

'Yeah, but I don't have to give regular written reports. He's more a business manager than anything. He doesn't give a rat's ass how I do the job, as long as I do it and don't insult too many people along the way. I raise the dead for a living, Doctor Evans. It's a specialized skill. If my boss gives me too much grief, there are two other animating firms in this country that would take me in a hot minute. I could even go freelance.'

'You're that good?' he said.

I nodded. 'I seem to be, and that frees me from a lot of the red tape and politics that the police have to mess with. My goal is to keep this from happening to anyone else. If I look a little foolish or indecisive along the way, that's just fine. Though I'll probably get some pressure to make up my mind and pick a bogeyman. Not from my boss, but from the police and the Feds. Solving something like this could make a cop's career. Being wrong and failing to solve it could be the end of a career.'

'But if you're wrong, you aren't hurt,' Evans said.

I looked at him. 'If I'm wrong, then no harm, no foul. If everybody's looking in the wrong direction, me, the cops, the Feds, everybody, then this is going to keep on happening.' I looked down at the man on the bed. 'That will hurt.'

'Why? Why will it hurt you?'

'Because we're the good guys, and whoever or whatever is doing this, is the bad guy. Good is supposed to triumph over evil, Doctor Evans, or what's a Heaven for?'

'You're Christian?'

I nodded.

'I didn't think you could be Christian and raise zombies.'

'Surprise,' I said.

He nodded, though I wasn't sure what he was agreeing with. 'Do you need to see the others, or is this enough?'

'You can cover him back up, but yeah, I should at least look at the others. If I don't, then I'll wonder if I missed something by not looking.'

'No one else has made it all the way around the room without having to leave, and that includes me the first time I walked in here.' He was walking to the next bed as he spoke. I followed behind, not happy to be there, but feeling better. I could do this if I just concentrated on solving the crime and shoved my empathy in a tight dark box. At that moment sympathy was a luxury I couldn't afford.

The second man was almost identical to the first except for height and eye color. Blue eyes this time, and I had to look away. If I locked gazes with any of them, they'd become people, and I'd run screaming.

The third bed was different. The wounds on the chest seemed different somehow, and when Doctor Evans rolled the sheet over the groin, I realized it was a woman. My gaze went back to her chest where something had ripped away her breasts. Her eyes rolled wildly, mouth opening and closing, making small sounds, and I saw for the first time why no one was talking. The tongue was just a ruined stump, rolling like a butchered worm in that lipless, skinless opening.

Heat washed over me in a rush. The room swam. I couldn't breathe. The mask molded itself to my open, gaping mouth. I turned and went for the doors. I walked slowly. I didn't run, but if I didn't get out of there I was going to lose what little I had in my stomach or maybe faint. Of the two, I think I preferred throwing up. Doctor Evans pressed the pad that opened the door without a word. The doors opened, and I went through.

Ben the nurse turned to me, mask hastily held in place with a gloved hand. When the doors shut behind me, he let the mask drop. 'You all right?'

I shook my head, not trusting my voice. I jerked the mask off my face and still couldn't seem to get enough air. It was too quiet in the little room. The only sound the soft hush of the air whooshing in, recycling. The small movement of cloth as Ben moved towards me. I needed noise, human voices. I needed out of there.

I jerked the plastic thingie off my head. My hair fell around my shoulders, brushed my face. I still couldn't get enough air. 'I'm sorry,' I said, and my voice sounded distant. 'I'll be back.' I opened the outer door and escaped.

7

The hall felt cooler, though I knew it wasn't. I leaned beside the closed door, eyes closed, breathing in great draughts of air. The corridor was full of noise after that silent hissing room. People walking, moving, and Lieutenant Marks' voice, 'Not so fucking tough after all, eh, Ms Blake.'

I opened my eyes and looked at him. He was sitting in the chair that had probably been brought up for the uniform guarding the door. The uniformed officer was nowhere to be seen. Only Edward leaned against the far wall, hands behind his back. He was watching my face, watching me, as if he'd memorize my fear. 'I made it through three patients before I had to leave the room. How many did you see before you had to go outside, Marks?'

'I didn't have to leave the fucking room.'

'Doctor Evans said that no one has made it through the room, all the way through the room without having to run out. That means you didn't make it either, Marks. So piss off.'

He was on his feet now. 'You . . . you witch.' He spat the last word at me as if it were the worst insult he could come up with.

'Don't you mean bitch?' I said. I was feeling better out here in the hallway. Trading insults with Marks was a cakewalk compared to my other choices.

'I said what I meant.'

'If you don't know the difference between a real witch and an animator, no wonder you haven't caught the thing that's doing this.'

'What do you mean "thing"?' he asked.

'Thing, thing, monster.'

'The Feds think it's a serial mutilator,' he said.

I glanced at Edward. 'Nice of someone to tell me what the Feds said.'

Edward didn't look guilty in the least. He was pleasant, unreadable, and I turned my attention back to Marks. 'Then why aren't there any tool marks from the skinning?'

Marks glanced down the corridor where a nurse was pushing a small cart. 'We don't discuss an ongoing investigation in the open, where anyone can hear us.'

'Fine, then after I've gone back in there and looked at the last three . . . bodies, we'll go someplace more private and talk about the case.'

I think he paled just a bit. 'You're going back in there?'

'The victims are the clues, Lieutenant. You know that.'

'We can take you to the crime scenes,' he said. It was the nicest thing he'd ever said to me.

'Great, and I need to see them, but right this moment we're here and the only possible clues are inside that room.' My breathing had returned to normal and the sick sweat had dried on my forehead. Maybe I was a touch pale myself, but I was mobile and felt almost normal.

I walked into the middle of the hall and motioned Edward over to me, as if I had something for his ears alone. He pushed away from the wall and came toward me. When he was close enough, I faked a low kick. He looked down for just an instant, reacting to it, and the second, higher kick caught him in the jaw. He went backwards hard. He had his arms up to defend his face. He knew enough to defend the vital areas, and worry about standing later.

My heart was thudding in my chest, not from exertion, but from adrenaline. I'd never used my new-found Kenpo skills in a fight. Trying it out for real for the very first time on Edward was probably not my best idea, but hey, it had worked. Though truthfully, I was a little surprised it had worked that easily. In the back of my head a voice wondered if Edward had let me take him down. The front of my head said that he had too much ego for that. I believed the second voice. I stayed where I was in a modified horse stance. It was pretty much the only stance I knew well enough to go back to once a kick was launched. I had my fists up, waiting, but didn't move in.

When Edward figured out I wasn't going to do anything else, he lowered his arm and stared at me. 'What the hell was that?' There was blood on his lower lip.

'I've been taking Kenpo,' I said.

'Kenpo?'

'It's sort of like Tae-kwon-do with fewer kicks and more fluid movements, a lot of hand work.'

'A black belt in Judo wasn't enough?' he asked, and it was Ted's voice asking.

'Judo's great exercise, but it's not great for self-defense. You have to close with the bad guy and grapple. This way I can stay out of reach and still do damage.'

He touched his lip and came away with blood. 'I see that. Why?'

'Why did I kick you in the face?' I asked.

He nodded, and I think he winced ever so slightly. Great.

'Why didn't you warn me about the victims? Tell me what I was up against?'

'I walked in on them cold,' he said. 'I wanted to see how you handled it cold.'

'This is not a pissing contest, Edward. Ted. I am not competing with you. I know you're better than me, tougher than me, colder than me. You win, okay? Stop with the macho bullshit.'

'I'm not so sure,' he said, softly.

'Not sure about what?' I asked.

'Who's tougher. Remember, I didn't make it through the whole room either.'

I stared at him. 'Fine, you want to go one on one, great, but not now. We are supposed to be solving a case. We are supposed to be making sure that what happened to those people doesn't happen to anyone else. When we're back on our own time, then you can get competitive. Until we solve this, cut it the fuck out, or you are going to seriously piss me off.'

Edward got slowly to his feet. I backed away out of reach. I'd never seen him use martial arts before, but I put nothing past him.

A sound made me back up farther until I could see Edward and Marks without looking away from Edward. Marks was making a small sniggering sound. It took me a moment to realize he was laughing, laughing so hard his face was purplish and he seemed to be having trouble breathing.

Edward and I both stared at him.

When Marks could finally talk, he said, 'You kick a man in the face, and that's not seriously pissed off.' He straightened, hand to his side like he had a stitch in it. 'What the fuck do you call seriously pissed?'

I felt my face going blank, my eyes going empty. For just an instant I let Marks see the gaping hole where my conscience was supposed to be. I didn't really mean to, but I couldn't seem to help it. Maybe I was more shaken up from the room and its survivors than I thought. It's the only excuse I can give.

Marks' face went from fading laughter to something like concern. He gave me cop eyes, but underneath that was an uncertainty that was almost fear.

'Smile, Lieutenant. It's a good day. No one died.'

I watched the thought spill through his face. He understood exactly what I meant. You should never even hint to the police that you're willing to kill, but I was tired, and I still had to go back into the room. Fuck it.

Edward spoke in his own voice, low and empty, 'And you wonder why I compete with you?'

I turned eyes that I knew were just as dead as his to meet his

gaze. I shook my head. 'I don't wonder why you compete with me
. . . Ted. I just told you to stop doing it until the case is solved.'

'And then?' he asked.

'Then we'll see, won't we?'

I didn't see fear on Edward's face. I saw anticipation. And that
was the difference between us. He enjoyed killing. I didn't. What
really scared me was the thought that that might be the only difference
between us now. It wasn't enough of a difference for me to throw
stones in Edward's direction. I still had more rules than Edward
did. There were still things that he would do that I wouldn't, but
even that list had been growing shorter of late. There was something
close to panic fluttering in my stomach. Not fear of Edward or
anything he could do, but wondering when I'd turned the corner
and become just another monster. I'd told Doctor Evans we were
the good guys, but if Edward and I were on the side of the angels,
then what was left to be on the other side?

Something that could skin a person alive without using a tool
of any kind. Something that would jerk the penis off a man and
the breasts off a woman with its bare hands. As bad as Edward was,
as bad as I'd become, there were worse things. And we were about
to go hunting one of them.

8

I did go back into the room, and no, I didn't learn a damn thing from the last three victims. All that wasted bravery for nothing. Well, not exactly for nothing. I proved to myself that I could go back into the room without throwing up or fainting. I didn't care if it impressed Edward or Marks. It impressed me. If you can't impress yourself, then no one else really matters.

I either impressed Doctor Evans, or he needed a restorative cup of tea because he invited me back to the doctors and nurses lounge. There's no such thing as truly undrinkable coffee, but I hoped the tea was better for Evans' sake. Though I doubted it. The coffee came out of a can, and the tea was from little bags with strings on them. There's only so much you can hope for from prepackaged tea and coffee. At home I grind my own beans, but I wasn't home and I was grateful for the bitter warmth.

I added cream and sugar and noticed that the coffee was trembling in the cup, as if maybe my hands weren't quite steady. I was also cold. Nerves, just nerves.

If Edward had nerves, you couldn't tell it as he leaned against the wall, drinking his coffee black. He'd scorned sugar and cream, tough he-man that he was. He winced as he sipped, and I don't think it was the scalding liquid. His lip was swelling slightly from where I'd kicked him. It made me feel better. Childish but true.

Marks had taken a place on the room's only couch, blowing on his coffee. He'd taken cream and sugar in his. Evans settled down into the only chair that looked halfway comfortable, sighing as he stirred his tea.

Edward watched me, and I finally realized that he wouldn't sit down until I did. Screw it. I sat down in a chair that was far too straight-backed to be comfortable, but was placed so I could watch everyone in the room, including the door. There was a small, but full-size, refrigerator against the far wall. It was an older model, done in an odd shade of brown. A small L-shaped cabinet area housed a coffee maker, a second coffee maker with nothing but hot water in it, a sink, and a microwave oven.

Doctor Evans had used the hot water for his tea. There were white plastic spoons in an open packet, and a mug of those useless little coffee stirrers. There'd been a choice of sugar, Nutrasweet, and some other artificial sweetener that I'd never heard of. There was a circle of artificial creamer that had dried into a round crusty ridge where someone had sat a mug down in it. I concentrated on the minutia of the cabinet, trying not to think. For just a few moments I wanted to sip my coffee and not think. I still hadn't eaten today, and now I didn't want to.

'You said you had some questions for me, Ms Blake.' Doctor Evans spoke into the silence.

I jumped, and so did Marks. Only Edward stayed half-leaning against the wall, unmoved, blue eyes watching us all as if he were apart from the tension and the horror. Maybe he was, or maybe it was just an act. I just didn't know anymore.

I nodded, trying to focus. 'How did they all survive?'

He tilted his head to one side. 'Do you mean technically how did they survive? Medical detail?'

I shook my head. 'No, I mean, one person surviving this much trauma, or even two, I'll buy. But most people wouldn't survive it, or am I wrong?'

Evans pushed his glasses more securely on his nose, but nodded. 'No, you aren't wrong.'

'Then how did all six of them survive?' I asked.

He frowned at me. 'I'm not sure I understand exactly what you're trying to say here, Ms Blake.'

'I'm asking what are the chances that six people of varying sex, background, physical fitness, age, etc. . . . would all be able to survive the same amount of trauma. My understanding is that all the victims that were just skinned have survived, right?'

'Yes.' Doctor Evans was watching me closely, pale eyes searching my face, waiting for me to go on.

'Why did they survive?'

'They're tough sons of bitches,' Marks said.

I glanced at the lieutenant, then back to Evans. 'Are they?'

'Are they what?' the doctor asked.

'Are they tough sons of bitches?'

He lowered his eyes as if thinking. 'Two of the men worked out regularly, one of the women was a marathon runner. The other three were just ordinary. One of the men is close to sixty, and didn't have a regular exercise routine of any kind. The other woman is in her thirties but didn't . . .' He looked at me. 'No, they aren't particularly tough individuals, not physically anyway. But I've found that it's often the people who aren't physically strong or outwardly tough that survive the longest under torture. The he-men are usually the first to cave.'

I forced myself not to glance at Edward, but it was an effort. 'Let me test my understanding, Doctor. Have any people that have been skinned like the six in that room died?'

He blinked and again looked into the distance as if remembering, then he looked at me. 'No, the only deaths have been those people torn apart.'

'Then I ask again, why are they all alive? Why didn't at least one of them die from shock, blood loss, or a bad heart, or hell, the pure terror of it.'

'People don't die from terror,' Marks said.

I glanced at him. 'Are you absolutely sure of that, Lieutenant?'

His handsome face looked petulant, stubborn. 'Yeah, I'm sure.'

I waved the comment away. I'd argue with Marks later. Right now I was chasing a point. 'How did all six of them survive, Doctor? Not why this six, but why all of them?'

Evans nodded. 'I see what you mean. How could all of them have survived it?'

I nodded. 'Exactly. Some of them should have died, but they didn't.'

'Whoever skinned them is an expert,' Marks said. 'He knew how to keep them alive.'

'No,' Edward said. 'No matter how good you are at torture, you can't keep everybody alive. Even if you do exactly the same thing to each of them, some people die and some people live. You're not always sure why some make it, and some don't.' His voice was very quiet, but it filled the hush of the room.

Doctor Evans looked at him, nodding. 'Yes, yes, even an expert can't make people survive what was done to these six. You should lose some of them. For that matter I don't know why they're all still alive. Why hasn't one of them contracted some secondary infection? They are all remarkably healthy.'

Marks stood so abruptly, he spilled coffee over his hand. He cursed, striding to the sink and throwing the cup and all in the sink. 'How can you say they're healthy?' He looked over his shoulder at the doctor while he ran his hands under the water.

'They are still alive, Lieutenant, and for their condition that is very healthy indeed.'

'Magic would do it,' I said.

Everyone looked at me.

'There are spells that can keep a person alive during torture so that the torture can be prolonged.'

Marks tore too much paper towel off the roll and turned on me, wiping his hands with small abrupt movements. 'How can you say you don't do black magic?'

'I said there are spells that will do it, not that I did the spells,' I said.

It took him three tries to get the paper towel in the waste basket. 'Just knowing about such things is evil.'

'Think what you like, Marks, but maybe one of the reasons you had to call me in is that you've kept yourself so lily white that you don't know enough to help these people. Maybe if you were more interested in solving crime than in saving your own soul you'd have wrapped this up by now.'

'Saving a soul is more important than solving crime,' he said. He was striding towards me now.

I stood up, coffee cup in my hand. 'If you're more interested in souls than crime then become a minister, Marks. What we need right now is a cop.'

He stalked towards me, and I think would have come close enough to exchange blows, but I watched him remember what I'd done out in the hall. I watched him remember caution, and he walked far around me to get to the door.

Doctor Evans glanced from one to the other of us, as if wondering what he'd missed.

Marks turned at the door, pointing a finger at me. 'If I have my way, you are going to be back on a plane tonight. You can't ask the devil to help you catch the devil.' With that he closed the door behind him.

Evans spoke into the silence. 'There must be more in you, Ms Blake, than mere toughness, something I haven't seen yet.'

I looked at him and took a drink of the cooling coffee. 'What would make you say that, doctor?'

'If I didn't know better, I'd say Lieutenant Marks is afraid of you,' he said.

'He's afraid of what he thinks I am, Doctor Evans. He's jumping at shadows.'

Evans looked up at me, his tea forgotten in his big hands. The look was a long considering one. I had an urge to squirm under such scrutiny, but fought it down. 'Perhaps you are right, Ms Blake, or perhaps he has seen something in you that I have not.'

'When you spend all your time worrying that the devil is right behind you, eventually you start seeing him whether he's there or not,' I said.

Evans stood, nodding. He rinsed his coffee mug in the sink, washing it out with a fresh paper towel and soap. He spoke without turning around. 'I do not know if I will ever see the devil, but I have seen true evil, and if there is no devil behind it, still it is evil.' He turned and looked at me. 'And we must put a stop to it.'

I nodded. 'Yes,' I said, 'we must.'

He smiled then, but his eyes stayed tired. 'I will work with my colleagues here that are more accustomed to working with the living instead of the dead. We will try and discover why these six survive.'

'And if it's magic?' I asked.

He nodded. 'Do not tell Lieutenant Marks, but my wife is a witch. She has traveled the world with me seeing such things. Sometimes what we find is more up her alley than mine, not often, mind you. People are quite able to torment one another without aid of magic. But occasionally it has been more.'

'Don't take this wrong,' I said, 'but why haven't you called her in before this?'

He took in a long breath and let it out. 'She was out of the country on another matter. Why, you may ask, didn't I call her home sooner?'

I shook my head. 'I wasn't going to ask.'

He smiled. 'Thank you for that. I reasoned that my wife was needed elsewhere, and the FBI seemed so sure it was a person.' He glanced at Edward then back to me. 'The truth is, Ms Blake, something about all this frightens me. I am not a man who is easily frightened.'

'You're afraid for your wife,' I said.

He stared at me as if he could look into my mind with those pale eyes. 'Wouldn't you be?'

I touched his arm, gently. 'Trust your instincts, doctor. If it feels wrong, send her away.'

He drew away from my touch, smiling, tossing the paper towel into the trash can. 'That would be terribly superstitious of me.'

'You've got a bad feeling about your wife's involvement with this thing. Trust your gut. Don't try to be reasonable. If you love your wife, listen to your heart, not your head.'

He nodded twice then said, 'I will think about what you said. Now I really must be going.'

I held out my hand. He took it. 'Thanks for your time, doctor.'

'My . . . pleasure, Ms Blake.' He nodded to Edward. 'Mr Forrester.'

Edward nodded in return, and we were left in the silence of the lounge. 'Listen to your heart and not your head. Damn romantic advice, coming from you,' Edward said.

'Drop it,' I said. I had my hand on the door handle.

'How would your love life be if you took your own advice?' he asked.

I opened the door and walked out into the cool white hallway without answering him.

9

Marks' offer of escorting me to the crime scene seemed to have evaporated with his temper. Edward drove me. We drove in almost complete silence. Edward never sweated small talk, and I just didn't have the energy for it. If I could have thought of something useful to say, I'd have said it. Until then, silence was fine. Edward had volunteered that we were on our way to the latest crime scene, and we'd meet his other two backups in Santa Fe. He told me nothing else about them, and I didn't press it. His lip was still swelling because he'd been too macho to put ice on it. I figured the busted lip was all the slack Edward was going to give me for one day. I'd told him in the strongest terms I could manage, short of pulling a weapon, to stop the competitive crap, and nothing would change that, least of all me.

Besides, I was still riding in a ringing bell of silence as if everything echoed and nothing was quite solid. It was shock. The survivors, if that was the word for them, had shaken me down to my toes. I'd seen awful things, but nothing quite like that. I was going to have to snap out of it before we had our first firefight, but frankly if someone had pulled a weapon on me right that second, I'd have hesitated. Nothing seemed truly important or even real.

'I know why you're afraid of this thing,' I said.

He glanced toward me with the black lenses of his eyes, then back to the road, as if he hadn't heard. Anyone else would have asked me to explain, or made some comment. Edward just drove.

'You don't fear anything that just offers death. You've accepted that you're not going to live to a ripe old age.'

'*We*,' he said. '*We've* accepted that *we* aren't going to live to a ripe old age.'

I opened my mouth to protest, then stopped. I thought about it for a second or two. I was twenty-six, and if the next four years were anything like the last four, I'd never see thirty. I'd never really thought about it in so many words, but old age wasn't one of my biggest worries. I didn't really expect to get there. My life style was a sort of passive suicide. I didn't like that much. It made me want to squirm and deny it, but I couldn't. Wanted to, but couldn't. It made my chest squeeze tight to realize that I expected to die by violence. Didn't want it, but expected it. My voice sounded uncertain, but I said it out loud. 'Fine, *we've* accepted that *we're* not going to make it to a ripe old age. Happy?'

He gave a slight nod.

'You're afraid that you'll live like those things in the hospital. You're afraid of ending up like them.'

'Aren't you?' His voice was almost too soft to hear, but somehow it carried over the rush of wheels and the expensive purr of the engine.

'I'm trying not to think about it,' I said.

'How can you not think about it?' he asked.

'Because if you start thinking about the bad things, worrying about them, then it makes you slow, makes you afraid. Neither of us can afford that.'

'Two years ago, I'd have been giving you the pep talk,' he said, and there was something in his voice, not anger, but close.

'You were a good teacher,' I said.

His hands gripped the wheel. 'I haven't taught you all I know, Anita. You are not a better monster than I am.'

I watched the side of his face, trying to read that expressionless face. There was a tightness at the jaw, a thread of anger down the neck and into his shoulders. 'Are you trying to convince me or yourself, . . . Ted?' I made the name light and mocking. I didn't usually play with Edward just to get a rise out of him, but today, he was unsure, and I wasn't. Part of me was enjoying the hell out of that.

He slammed on the brakes and screeched to a stop on the side of the road. I had the Browning pointed at the side of his head, close enough that pulling the trigger would paint his brains all over the windows.

He had a gun in his hand. I don't know where in the car it had come from, but the gun wasn't pointed at me. 'Ease down, Edward.'

He stayed motionless but didn't drop the gun. I had one of those moments when you see into another person's soul like looking into an open window. 'Your fear makes you slow, Edward, because you'd rather die here, like this, than survive like those poor bastards. You're looking for a better way to die.' My gun was very steady, finger on the trigger. But this wasn't for real, not yet. 'If you were really serious, you'd have had the gun in your hand before you pulled over. You didn't invite me here to hunt monsters. You invited me here to kill you if it works out wrong.'

He gave the smallest nod. 'Neither Bernardo or Olaf are good enough.' He laid the gun very, very slowly on the floorboard hump between the seats. He looked at me, hands spread on the steering wheel. 'Even for you, I have to be a little slow.'

I took the offered gun without taking either my eyes or my gun off of him. 'Like I believe that's the only gun you've got hidden in this car. But I do appreciate the gesture.'

He laughed then, and it was the most bitter sound I'd ever heard from Edward. 'I don't like being afraid, Anita. I'm not good at it.'

'You mean you're not used to it,' I said.

'No, I'm not.'

I eased my own gun down until it wasn't pointing at him, but I didn't put it up. 'I promise that if you end up like the people in the hospital I'll take your head.'

He looked at me then, and even with the sunglasses on I knew he was surprised. 'Not just shoot me or kill me, but take my head.'

'If it happens, Edward, I won't leave you alive, and taking your head we'll both be sure that the job's done.'

Something flowed across his face, down his shoulders, his arms, and I realized it was relief. 'I knew I could count on you for this, Anita, you and no one else.'

'Should I be flattered or insulted that you've never met anyone else cold-blooded enough for this?'

'Olaf's blood is plenty cold enough, but he'd just shoot me and bury me in a hole somewhere. He'd have never thought about taking my head. And what if shooting didn't kill me?' He took off his glasses and rubbed his eyes. 'I'd be in some stinking hole somewhere alive because Olaf would never think to take my head.' He shook his head as if chasing the image away. He slid the glasses back on, and when he turned to look at me, his face was blank, unreadable, his usual. But I'd seen beneath the mask, further than I'd ever been allowed before. The one thing I'd never expected to find was fear, and beneath that, trust. Edward trusted me with more than his life. He trusted me to make sure he died well. For a man like Edward there was no greater trust.

We would never go shopping together or eat an entire cake while we complained about men. He'd never invite me over to his house for dinner or a barbecue. We'd never be lovers. But there was a very good chance that one of us would be the last person the other saw before we died. It wasn't friendship the way most people understood it, but it was friendship. There were several people I'd trust with my life, but there is no one else I'd trust with my death. Jean-Claude and even Richard would try to hold me alive out of love or something that passed for it. Even my family and other friends would fight to keep me alive. If I wanted death, Edward would give it to me. Because we both understand that it isn't death that we fear. It's living.

The house was a two-story split-level ranch that could have been anywhere in the Midwest, in any upper-middle-class neighborhood. But the large yard was done in rock paths running high to cacti and a circle of those small flowered lilacs that were so plentiful. Other people had tried to keep their lawns green as if they didn't live on the edge of a desert, but not this house. This house, these people had landscaped for their environment and tried not to waste water. And now they were dead and didn't give a damn about environmental awareness or rainfall.

Of course, one of them could be a survivor. I didn't want to see pictures of the survivors before they'd been . . . injured. I was having enough trouble keeping my professional distance without color photos of smiling faces that had been turned into so much naked meat. I got out of the car, praying that everyone had died in this house, not my usual prayer at a crime scene. But nothing about this case so far was usual.

There was a marked police car sitting out in front of the house. A uniformed officer got out of the marked car as Edward and I walked towards the yard. He was medium build but carrying enough weight for someone taller, a lot taller. His weight was mostly in the stomach and made his utility belt ride low. His pale face was sweating by the time he'd walked the five feet to us. He put his hat on as he walked towards us, unsmiling, thumb hooked in his utility belt.

'Can I help you?'

Edward went into his Ted Forrester act, putting his hand out, smiling. 'I'm Ted Forrester, Officer . . .' he took the time to read the man's name tag, 'Norton. This is Anita Blake. Chief Appleton has cleared us both to see the crime scene.'

Norton looked us both up and down, pale eyes not the least bit friendly. He didn't shake hands. 'Can I see some ID?'

Edward opened his wallet to his driver's license and held it out. I opened my executioner's license for him. He handed Edward's back, but squinted at mine. 'This license isn't good in New Mexico.'

'I'm aware of that, Officer,' I said, voice bland.

He squinted at me, much as he had the license. 'Then why are you here?'

I smiled and couldn't quite make it reach my eyes. 'I'm here as a preternatural advisor, not an executioner.'

He handed the license back to me. 'Then why the hardware?'

I glanced down at the gun very visible against my red shirt. The smile was genuine this time. 'It's not concealed, Officer Norton, and it's federally licensed so I don't have to sweat a new gun permit every time I cross a state line.'

He didn't seem to like the answer. 'I was told to let the two of you in.' It was a statement, but it sounded like a question, as if he wasn't quite sure he was going to let us in, after all.

Edward and I stood there trying to appear harmless, but useful. I was a lot better at looking harmless than Edward was. I didn't even have to work at it most of the time. He was better at looking useful, though. Without seeming dangerous in the least he could give off an aura of purposefulness that police and other people responded to. The best I could do was look harmless and wait for Officer Norton to decide what our fate would be.

He finally nodded, as if he'd made up his mind. 'I'm supposed to escort you around the scene, Miss Blake.' He didn't look happy about it.

I didn't correct him that Miss Blake should have been Ms Blake. I think he was looking for an excuse to get rid of us. I wasn't going to give him one. Very few policemen like civilians messing around in their cases. I wasn't just a civilian, I was female, and I hunted vampires; a triple threat if ever there was one. I was a civvie, a woman, and a freak.

'This way.' He started up the narrow walkway. I glanced at Edward. He just started following Norton. I followed Edward. I had a feeling I'd be doing a lot of that in the next few days.

Quiet. The house was so quiet. The air conditioner purred into that silence reminding me of the recycled air in the hospital room. Norton came up behind me, and I jumped. He didn't say anything, but he gave me a look.

I moved out of the entry hall and into the large high-ceilinged living room. Norton followed me. In fact he stayed at my heels as I moved around the room like some obedient dog, but the message I was getting from him wasn't trust and adoration. It was suspicion and disapproval. Edward had settled into one of the room's three comfortable-looking powder blue chairs. He'd stretched himself full length, legs crossed at the ankles. He'd left his sunglasses on so he looked the picture of ease in the midst of that careful living room in that too silent house.

'Are you bored?' I asked.

'I've seen the show,' he said. He'd toned down his Ted act and was more his usual self. Maybe he didn't sweat Norton's reaction, or maybe he was tired of playacting. I knew I was tired of watching the show.

The room was one of those great rooms which meant the living, dining, and kitchen were all one shared space. It was a large space, but I'm not really comfortable with the open floor plan. I like more walls, doors, barriers. Probably a sign of my own less than welcoming personality. If the house was any clue to the family that had lived in it, they'd been welcoming and somewhat conventional. The furniture was all purchased as sets: a powder blue living room set, a dark wood dining room set to one side with a bay window and white lacy drapes. There was a new hard back southwestern cook book on the kitchen cabinet. The receipt was still being used as a bookmark. The kitchen was the smallest area, long and thin with white cabinets and a black and white cow motif down to a cookie jar that mooed when you took its head off. Store bought cookies, chocolate chip. No, I didn't eat one.

'Any clues in the cookie jar?' Edward asked from his chair.

'No,' I said, 'I just had to know if it really mooed.'

Norton made a small sound that might have been a laugh. I ignored him. Though since he was standing about two feet from me the entire time, ignoring wasn't easy. I changed direction in the kitchen abruptly, and he nearly ran into me. 'Could you give me a little more breathing space?' I asked.

'Just following my orders,' he said, face bland.

'Did your orders tell you to stand close enough to tango or just to follow me?'

His mouth twitched, but he managed not to smile. 'Just to follow you, ma'am.'

'Great, then take about two big steps back so we do this without bumping into each other.'

'I'm supposed to make sure you don't disturb the scene, ma'am.'

'The name's Anita, not ma'am.'

That earned me a smile, but he shook his head and fought it off. 'Just following orders. That's what I do.'

There was something just a touch bitter about that last. Officer Norton was on the down side of fifty or looked it. He was close to putting in his thirty years, and he was still a uniform sitting in a car outside a crime scene following orders. If he'd ever had dreams of more, they were gone. He was a man who had accepted reality, but he didn't like it.

The door opened, and a man came through with his tie at half-mast, the white sleeves of his dress shirt rolled up over dark forearms. His skin was a dark solid brown, and it didn't look like a tan.

Hispanic or Indian or maybe a little of both. The hair was cut very short, not for style, but as if it were easier that way. There was a gun on his hip and a gold shield clipped to the waistband of his pants.

'I'm Detective Ramirez. Sorry I'm late.' He smiled when he said it, and there seemed to be genuine cheerfulness, but I didn't trust it. I'd seen too many cops go from cheerful to hardcore up in your face too many times. Ramirez would try to catch his flies with honey instead of vinegar, but I knew the vinegar was there. You didn't get to be a plainclothes detective without that streak of sourness. Or maybe a loss of innocence was a better phrase for it. Whatever you called it, it would be there. It was only a matter of how far under the surface it was.

But I smiled and held my hand out, and he took it. The handshake was firm, the smile still in place, but his eyes were cool and noticed everything. I knew that if I left the room now he'd be able to describe me in detail down to my gun, or maybe up from my gun.

Officer Norton was still behind me like a pudgy bridesmaid. Detective Ramirez' eyes flicked to him, and the smile wilted just a touch. 'Thank you, Officer Norton. I'll take it from here.'

The look Norton gave him was not friendly. Maybe Officer Norton didn't like anybody. Or maybe he was white and Ramirez wasn't. He was old and Ramirez was young. He was going to end his career in uniform and Ramirez was already in plainclothes. Prejudice and jealousy are often close kin. Or maybe Norton was just in a bad mood.

Whatever it was, Norton went out like he'd been told, shutting the door behind him. Ramirez's smile went up a notch as he turned to me. I realized that he was cute in a young guy sort of way, and he knew it. Not in an egomaniac way, but I was a female, and he was cute, and he was hoping that that would cut him some slack with me. Boy, was he shopping in the wrong aisle.

I shook my head, but smiled back.

'Is something wrong?' he asked. Even the slight frown was sort of boyish and endearing. He must practice it in the mirror.

'No, Detective, nothing's wrong.'

'Please call me Hernando.'

That made me smile more. 'I'm Anita.'

The smile flashed bright and wide. 'Anita, pretty name.'

'No,' I said, 'it's not, and we're investigating a crime, not out on a blind date. You can tone the charm down just a touch, and I'll still like you, Detective Ramirez. I'll even share clues with you, honest.'

'Hernando,' he said.

It made me laugh. 'Hernando. Fine, but really, you don't have to work this hard to win me over. I don't know you well enough to dislike you yet.'

That made him laugh. 'Was it that transparent?'

'You make a good good-cop, and the little boy charm is great, but like I said, it's not necessary.'

'Okay, Anita.' The smile went down a watt or two, but he was still open and cheerful somehow. It made me nervous. 'Have you seen the entire house yet?'

'Not yet. Officer Norton was trailing a little too close for comfort. Made it hard to walk.'

The smile closed down, but the look in the eyes was real. 'You're a woman and with that black hair probably part something darker than the rest of you looks.'

'My mother was Mexican, but most people don't spot it.'

'You're in a section of the country where there's a lot of mixing going on.' He didn't smile when he said it. He looked serious and a little less young. 'The people that want to notice will.'

'I could be part dark Italian,' I said.

A small smile that time. 'We don't have a lot of dark Italians in New Mexico.'

'I haven't been here long enough to notice one way or another.'

'Your first time to this part of the country?'

I nodded.

'What do you think so far?'

'I've seen a hospital and part of this house. I think it's too early to form an opinion.'

'If we get a breather while you're here, I'd love to show you some of the sights.'

I blinked at him. Maybe the boyish charm wasn't just a cop technique. Maybe he was, gasp, flirting.

Before I could think of an answer, Edward came up behind us in his best good ol' boy charm. 'Detective Ramirez, good to see you again.'

They shook hands, and Ramirez wasted a smile on Edward that looked just as genuine as Edward's. Since I knew Edward was play-acting, it was sort of unnerving how similar the two expressions were.

'Good to see you, too, Ted.' He turned back to me. 'Please, continue looking around. Ted's told me a lot about you, and I hope for all our sakes that you're as good as he says you are.'

I glanced at Edward. He just smiled at me. I frowned. 'Well, I'll try not to disappoint anybody.' I walked back out into the living room trailed by Detective Ramirez. He gave me more room to maneuver than Norton had, but he watched me. Maybe he did want a date, but he wasn't watching me like a potential date. He was watching me like a cop to see what I did, how I reacted. It made me think better of him that he was professional.

Edward had lowered his sunglasses enough to give me a look as I passed by him. He was smiling, almost grinning at me. The look said it all. He was amused at Ramirez' flirting. I flipped him off, covering the gesture with my other hand so only he would see it.

It made him laugh, and the sound seemed at home here in this bright place. It was a place meant for laughter. The silence filled in behind his laughter like water closing over a stone, until the sound vanished into a profound quiet that was more than quiet.

I stood in the middle of the bright living room, and it was as if it were a display home waiting for the real estate agent to come through with a tour of potential home owners. The house was so new, it felt like a freshly unwrapped present. But there were things that no real estate agent would have allowed. A newspaper was spilled over the pale wood coffee table with the business section folded into fourths. The business section had *New York Times* written across the top of it, but some of the other pieces said *Los Angeles Tribune*. A business person recently moved from Los Angeles, maybe.

There was a large colored photo pushed to one corner of the coffee table. It showed an older couple, fiftyish, with a teenage boy. They were all smiling and touching each other in that posed casual way photos often use. They looked happy and relaxed together, though you can never really tell with posed photos. So easy to fool the camera.

I looked around the room and found smaller photos scattered throughout on numerous white shelves that took up almost all available wall space. The photos sat among souvenirs, mostly with an American Indian theme. The smaller more candid shots were just as relaxed, just as smiling. A happy, prosperous family. The boy and man, tanned and grinning on a boat with the sea in the background and a huge fish between them. The woman and three small girls covered in cookie dough and matching Christmas aprons. There were at least three photos of smiling adult couples with one or two children apiece. The little girls from the Christmas photo; grandchildren, maybe.

I stared at the couple and that tall, tanned teenager, and hoped they were dead because the thought of any of them up in that hospital room turned into so much pain and meat was . . . not a comfy thought. I didn't speculate. They were dead, and that was comforting.

I turned my attention from the photos to the Indian artifacts lining the shelves. Some of it was touristy stuff: reproductions of painted pots in muted shades, too new to be real; Kachina dolls that would have looked just as at home in a child's room; rattlesnake heads stretched in impotent strikes, dead before their murderer opened their mouths to appear fearsome.

But in among the tourist chic were other things. A pot that was displayed behind glass with pieces missing and the paint faded to a dull gray and eggshell color. A spear or javelin on the wall above the fireplace. The spear was behind glass and had remnants of feathers and thongs, beads trailing from it. The head of the spear looked like stone. There was a tiny necklace of beads and shells under glass with the worn edges of the hide thong that bound them together showing. Someone had known what they were collecting because every piece that looked real was behind glass, cared for. The tourist stuff had been left out to fend for itself.

I spoke without turning around, staring at the necklace. 'I'm no expert on Indian artifacts but some of this looks like museum quality.'

'According to the experts it is,' Ramirez said.

I looked at him. His face had gone back to neutral, and he looked older. 'Is it all legal?'

That earned me another small smile. 'You mean is it stolen?'

I nodded.

'The stuff we've been able to trace was all purchased from private individuals.'

'There's more?'

'Yes,' he said.

'Show me,' I said.

He turned and started walking down a long central hallway. It was my turn to play follow the leader though I gave him more room than either he or Norton had given me. I couldn't help noticing how nicely his dress slacks fit. I shook my head. Was it the flirting, or was I just tired of the two men in my life? Something less complicated would have been nice, but part of me knew that the time for other choices was long past. So I admired his backside as we walked up the hall and knew it meant nothing. I had enough problems without dating the local cops. I was a civilian surrounded by police, and a woman, too. The only thing that would earn me less respect in their eyes was to date one of them. I would lose what little clout I had and become a girlfriend. Anita Blake, vampire executioner and preternatural expert, had some ground to stand on. Detective Ramirez' girlfriend would not.

Edward trailed behind us, but far enough back that we were at the far end of the hallway when he was barely in the corridor. Was he giving us privacy? Did he think it was a good idea to flirt with the detective, or was any human better than a monster, no matter how nice the monster was? If Edward had any prejudice, it was against the monsters.

Ramirez stood at the end of the hallway. He was still smiling as if he were giving me a tour of some other house for some other purpose. His face didn't match what we were about to do. He motioned to the doors to either side of him. 'Artifacts to your left, gory stuff to the right.'

'Gory stuff?' I made it a question.

He nodded, still pleasant, and I moved closer to him. I stared into those dark brown eyes and realized that the smile was his blank-cop face. It was cheerful, but his eyes were just as unreadable as any cop's I'd ever seen. Smiling blankness, but still blankness. It was unique and somehow disquieting. 'Gory stuff,' I said.

The smile stayed, but the eyes were a little less sure. 'You don't have to play the tough girl with me, Anita.'

'She's not playing,' Edward said. He'd finally joined us.

Ramirez' eyes flicked to him then back to study my face. 'High compliment coming from you, Forrester.'

If he only knew, I thought. 'Look, Detective, I just came from the hospital. Whatever is behind the door can't be worse than that.'

'How can you be so sure?' he asked.

I smiled. 'Because even with the air conditioner on, the smell would be worse.'

The smile flashed bright and I think real for a moment. 'Very practical,' he said, voice almost laughing. 'I should have known you'd be practical.'

I frowned at him. 'Why?'

He motioned at his own face. 'No makeup,' he said.

'Maybe I just don't give a damn.'

He nodded. 'That too.' He started to reach for the door, and I beat him to it. He raised eyebrows at me, but just stepped back and let me open the door. Which also meant I got to walk in first, but hey, only fair. Edward and Ramirez had both already seen the show. My ticket was fresh and hadn't been punched yet.

11

I expected to find a lot of things in the bedroom: blood stains, signs of a struggle, maybe even a clue. What I did not expect to find was a soul. But the moment I entered that pale white and green bedroom I knew it was there, hovering near the ceiling, waiting. It wasn't the first soul I'd sensed. Funerals were always fun. Souls often hung around the bodies as if unsure what to do, but by three days' time the souls were usually gone to wherever souls were supposed to go.

I stared up at this soul and saw nothing. If a soul has a physical shape, you couldn't prove it by me, but I knew it was there. I could have sketched the outline of it in the air with my hand, knew about how much space it was taking up as it floated near the ceiling. But it was energy, spirit, and though it took up space, I wasn't entirely sure it took up the same kind of space as I did, as the bed did, as anything else did.

My voice came out hushed, as if I were to speak too loudly, I'd scare it away. 'How long have they been dead?'

'They aren't dead,' Ramirez said.

I blinked and turned to him. 'What do you mean they're not dead?'

'You saw the Bromwells in the hospital. They're both still alive.'

I looked into his serious face. The smile had vanished. I turned back to gaze at that slow hovering presence. 'Someone died here,' I said.

'No one was cut up here,' Ramirez said. 'According to the Santa Fe PD that's the method of killing that this guy is using. Look at the carpet. There's not enough blood for anyone to have been cut up.'

I looked down at the pale green carpet, and he was right. There was blood like black juice soaked into the carpet, but it wasn't much blood, just spots, dabs. The blood was from the skinning of two adults, but if someone had been torn apart limb from limb there would have been more blood, a lot more. There was still the faint rank smell where someone's bowels had let go either under torture or death. It was pretty common. Death is the last intimate thing we ever do.

I shook my head and debated on what to say. If I'd been at home with Dolph and Zerbrowski and the rest of the St Louis police that I knew well, I'd have just said I saw a soul. But I didn't know Ramirez, and most cops spook around anyone that can do mystical stuff. To tell or not to tell, that was the question, when noises from the front room brought us all around to stare behind us at the still open door.

Men's voices, hurried footsteps, coming closer. My hand was on my gun when I heard a voice yell, 'Ramirez, where the hell are you?'

It was Lieutenant Marks. I eased away from my gun and knew I wasn't telling the police that there was a soul hanging in the air behind me. Marks was scared enough of me without that.

He stepped into the doorway with a small battalion of uniforms at his back, almost as if he expected trouble. His eyes were both harsh and pleased when he looked at me. 'Get the fuck off my evidence, Blake. You're outta here.'

Edward stepped forward, smiling, trying to play peacemaker. 'Now, Lieutenant, who would give such an order?'

'My chief.' He turned to the cops behind him. 'Escort her off the property.'

I held up my hands and started moving towards the door before the uniforms could move in. 'I'll go, no problem. No need to get rough.' I was at the door almost abreast with Marks.

He hissed close to my face, 'This isn't rough, Blake. You come near me again and I'll show you rough.'

I stopped in the doorway, meeting his gaze. His eyes had turned a swimming aqua blue, dark with his anger. The doorway wasn't that big, and standing in it we were almost touching. 'I haven't done anything wrong, Marks.'

He spoke low, but it carried. 'Thou shalt not suffer a witch to live.'

I thought of a lot of things to say, and do, most of which would have gotten me dragged out by a bunch of uniforms. I didn't want to be dragged out, but I wanted to make Marks suffer. Choices, choices.

I rose on tiptoe and planted a big kiss on his mouth. He stumbled back, pushing away from me so hard that he fell into the bedroom and left me pushed into the hallway beyond. Masculine laughter filled the hallway. Two bright spots of color flamed on Marks' cheeks as he lay panting on the carpet.

'You're lying in your evidence, Marks,' I said.

'Get her out of here, now.'

I blew Marks a kiss, and left through a grinning parade of policeman. One of the uniforms offered to let me kiss him any time. I told him he couldn't handle it and left through the front door to laughter, catcalls, and masculine humor mostly at Marks' expense. He didn't seem to be a popular guy. Go figure.

Edward stayed inside for a few moments, probably trying to soothe things over like a good Ted would do. But in the end he came out of the house, shaking hands with the cops, smiling, and nodding. The smile vanished as soon as he turned so that I was his only audience.

He unlocked the car and we got in. When we were safe inside of its mud-stained windows, he said, 'Marks has gotten you kicked off the investigation. I don't know how he did it, but he did it.'

'Maybe he and the chief go to the same church,' I said. I had snuggled down into the seat, as far as the seatbelt would allow. Edward looked at me as he started the engine. 'You don't seem upset.'

I shrugged. 'Marks isn't the first right-wing asshole to get up in my face, and he won't be the last.'

'Where's that famous temper of yours?'

'Maybe I'm growing up,' I said.

He shook his head. 'What did you see in the corner of the room that I didn't? You were looking at something.'

'A soul,' I said.

He actually lowered his sunglasses so I could see his baby blues. 'A soul?'

I nodded. 'Which means that someone in that house did die, and within three days.'

'Why three days?' he asked.

'Because three days is the limit for most souls to hang around. After that they go to heaven or hell or wherever. After three days you may get ghosts, but you won't get souls.'

'But the Bromwells are alive. You saw them yourself.'

'What about their son?' I asked.

'He's missing,' Edward said.

'Nice of you to mention that.' I wanted to be angry at him for the game playing, but I just couldn't find the energy. No matter how blasé I was about Marks, it did bother me. I was Christian, but I'd lost count of the number of fellow Christians who'd called me witch or worse. It didn't make me angry anymore, just tired.

'If the parents are alive, then the boy probably isn't,' I said.

Edward pulled out onto the road, easing his way among the plethora of marked and unmarked police cars Marks had brought with him. 'But all the other murder vics were cut up. We didn't find any body parts in the house. If the boy is dead, then it's a change in the pattern. We haven't figured out the old pattern yet.'

'A change in pattern may give the police the break they need,' I said.

'You believe that?' he asked.

'No,' I said.

'What do you believe?'

'I believe that the Bromwells' son is dead, and whatever skinned and mutilated his parents took his body, but didn't cut it up. However the son was killed, it wasn't by being torn apart or there would have been more blood. He was killed in a way that didn't add blood to the room.'

'But you're sure he's dead?'

'There's a soul floating around the house, Edward. Someone's dead, and if there are only three people living in a house, and two of them are accounted for . . . You do the math.' I was staring out the car window but wasn't seeing anything. I was seeing that young tanned face smiling in the pictures.

'Deductive reasoning,' Edward said. 'I'm impressed.'

'Yeah, me and Sherlock Holmes. By the way, now that I'm persona non grata, where are you taking me?'

'To a restaurant. You said you hadn't had lunch.'

I nodded. 'Fine.' Then after a moment, I asked, 'What was his name?'

'Who?'

'The Bromwells' son, what was his first name?'

'Thad, Thaddeus Reginald Bromwell.'

'Thad,' I said softly to myself. Had he been forced to watch while his parents were skinned alive, mutilated? Or had they watched him die before they bled? 'Where's your body, Thad? And why did they want it?' There was no answer. I hadn't expected one. Souls weren't like ghosts. To my knowledge there was no way to communicate with them directly. But I would have answers and soon. It had to be soon. 'Edward, I need to see the pictures from the other crime scenes. I need to see everything the Santa Fe PD have. You said only this last case was in Albuquerque, so screw them. I'll start from the other end.'

Edward smiled. 'I've got copies at my house.'

'Your house?' I sat up straighter and stared at him. 'Since when do the police share files with bounty hunters?'

'I told you the Santa Fe police like Ted.'

'You said the Albuquerque police liked you, too,' I said.

'They do like me. It's you they don't like.' He had a point. I could still see the hatred in Marks' eyes when he hissed at me, 'Thou shalt not suffer a witch to live.' Sweet Jesus. That was actually the first time I'd ever had that particular verse quoted at me. Though I suppose someone would have gotten around to it sooner or later, being who I am and what I do. I just didn't expect it from a police lieutenant during a murder investigation. It lacked a certain professionalism.

'Marks won't be able to solve this case,' I said.

'Without you, you mean?'

'It doesn't have to be me, but someone with some expertise is going to be needed. We are not dealing with a human killer here. Normal police work is not going to do the job.'

'I agree,' Edward said.

'Marks needs to be replaced,' I said.

'I'll work on it,' he said. Then he smiled. 'Maybe with that nice Detective Ramirez that found you sooo fascinating.'

'Don't go there, Edward.'

'He does have one thing over your other two boyfriends.'

'What?' I asked.

'He is human.'

I'd have liked to argue but couldn't. 'When you're right, you're right.'

'You're agreeing with me?' He sounded surprised.

'Neither Jean-Claude nor Richard are human. As far as I can tell, Ramirez is human. What's to argue about?'

'I was teasing you, and you go all serious on me.'

'You have no idea how refreshing it would be to be with a man that just wanted me for me, without any Machiavellian plots.'

'Are you saying that Richard has been plotting behind your back, just like the vampire?'

'Let's just say I'm no longer sure who the good guys are, Edward. Richard has become something harder and more complex because his role as Ulfric, Wolf King, has demanded it of him. And God help me, partly I think because I demanded it of him. He was too soft for me, so he's become harder.'

'And you don't like it,' Edward said.

'No, I don't like it, but since it's partially my fault, it's hard to bitch.'

'Then dump them both, and date some humans.'

'You make it sound so simple.'

'It's only hard if you make it hard, Anita.'

'Just dump the boys and start dating other men, just like that.'

'Why not?' he asked.

I opened my mouth sure I had an answer, but for the life of me couldn't come up with one. Why not date other people? Because I loved two men already and that seemed one too many without adding anyone else. But what would it be like to be with someone who was human? Someone who wasn't trying to use me to consolidate his power like Jean-Claude. Both Richard and Jean-Claude huddled around my humanity like it was the last fire at the end of the world and all the rest was icy darkness. Richard especially clung to me because I was human, and having a human girlfriend had seemed to help him retain human status. Though lately how human I was, was up for debate. At least Richard had been human until he became a werewolf. Jean-Claude had been human until he became a vampire. I'd seen my first soul when I was ten at my great-aunt's funeral. I'd raised my first dead by accident when I was thirteen. Of the three of us I was the only one who had never been truly human.

What would it be like to date someone 'normal'? I didn't know. Did I want to find out? I realized with a shock that I did. I wanted to go out on a normal date with a normal guy and do normal things, just once, just for a while. I'd been vampire's lover, werewolf's mate, zombie queen, and for the last year I'd been learning ritual magic so I could control all the rest, so I guess you could add apprentice witch to the list. It had been a weird year even for me. I'd called a break to the romance with both Richard and Jean-Claude because I needed a breather. They were overwhelming me, and I didn't know how to stop it. Would one date with someone else really hurt? Would going out with someone who was just a guy really bring the world crashing down around my ears? Would it? The answer was probably no, but the very fact that I wasn't sure meant I should have run from Ramirez and any other nice guy who asked me out. I should have said no, and kept saying no, so why did part of me want to say yes?

12

It was only as Edward was searching for a parking spot on the rock-covered parking lot behind Los Cuates that I realized it was a Mexican restaurant. The name should have been a clue, but I just hadn't been paying attention. If my mother had liked Mexican food, she hadn't lived long enough to pass it on to me. Blake was an English name, but before my great-grandfather came through Ellis Island it was Bleckenstien. My idea of ethnic cuisine was wiener schnitzel and sauerbraten. So I was less than enthused as we crossed the gravel to the rear entrance of the restaurant. For someone who didn't like Mexican or southwestern cuisine, I was in the wrong part of the country.

The back entrance led through a long shadowed hall, but the main restaurant was bright with white stucco walls: bright wall hangings, fake parrots dangling from the ceiling, and strings of dried chilies everywhere. Very touristy, which usually means the food won't be authentic or very good. But a lot of the diners were Hispanic and that boded well. Whatever the food, if the actual ethnic group liked the restaurant, then the food was authentic and likely good.

A woman that actually looked Hispanic asked if we'd like a table. Edward smiled and said, 'Thanks, but I see our party.'

I looked where he was looking and saw Donna at a booth. There were two kids with her, one girl about five or six and a boy in his early teens. Call it a hunch, but I was betting I was about to be introduced to her kiddies. Introduced to Edward's potential step-children. Can you stand it? I was almost sure I couldn't.

Donna stood and gave Edward a smile that would have melted a lesser man into his socks. It wasn't the sex, though that was in there. It was the warmth, the perfect trust that only true love can give you. That first romantic love that may not last, but while it does, wow. I knew that he was probably giving as good a look as he was getting, but his wasn't real. He didn't mean it. He was lying with his eyes, something I'd only managed to learn recently, and part of me is sad about that. It's one thing to know how to lie, but to be able to lie with your eyes says you are someone not to be trusted. Poor Donna. She was with two of us.

The little girl scooted out of the booth and came running towards us, arms outstretched, chestnut braids flying. She gave a glad shriek of 'Ted!' and flung herself into his arms. Edward scooped her up and tossed her towards the ceiling. She laughed that joyous full-blown sound that children eventually grow out of, as if the world bleeds the joy from them. Unless we're very lucky, the world teaches us to laugh more quietly, more coyly.

The boy just sat staring at us. His hair was the same rich chestnut brown as the girl's, cut short with a wave of bangs that hung into his eyes. The eyes were brown and dark and not friendly. Edward had said the boy was fourteen, but he was one of those boys that look younger. He could have passed for twelve easily. He looked sullen and angry as he watched Edward and Donna hug, the little girl still in Edward's arms so it was a family hug. Edward whispered something in Donna's ear that made her laugh and pull away blushing.

He swung the girl to his other arm and asked, 'How's my best girl?'

She giggled and started talking in a high excited voice. She was telling some long complicated story about her day that involved butterflies and a cat and Uncle Raymond and Aunt Esther. I assumed they were the neighbors that had played babysitter for the day.

The boy turned his hostile eyes from Edward to me. The frown did not lessen, but the eyes went from angry to curious, as if I wasn't what he'd expected. I actually get that a lot from men of all ages. I ignored the happy family stuff and held out my hand to him. 'I'm Anita Blake.'

He gave me his hand half hesitating as if most people didn't offer. His grip was unsure as if he needed practice, but he said, 'Peter, Peter Parnell.'

I nodded. 'Good to meet you.' I would have said his mother said good things about him, but that wasn't strictly true, and Peter struck me as someone who respected truth.

He nodded vaguely, eyes flicking to his mother and Edward. He didn't like it, not one little bit, and I didn't blame him. I remembered how I'd felt when my father brought Judith home. I'd never really forgiven my father for marrying her only two years after my mother's death. I hadn't finished my grieving and he was moving on with his life, being happy again. I'd hated him for it and hated Judith more.

Even if Edward had truly been Ted Forrester, and his intentions honorable, it would have been a difficult situation. As it was, it sucked.

Becca was wearing a bright yellow sundress with daisies on it. She had yellow ribbons at the end of each neat braid. The hand she put over her mouth to smother a giggle still had that soft, round baby look to it. She was looking at Edward as if he was the eighth wonder of the world. In that moment I hated Edward, hated that he could lie to the child so completely and not understand that it was wrong.

Something must have shown on my face because Peter was giving me a strange considering look. Not angry, but thoughtful. I forced my face blank and met his eyes. He held my gaze for a few seconds, but finally had to look away. Probably not fair to bring out my full stare on one angry fourteen-year-old boy, but to do less would imply that he was less, and he wasn't, just young. And time would cure that. Donna took Becca back from Edward's arms and turned towards me smiling. 'This is Becca.'

'Hi, Becca,' I said and smiled because she was one of those children that made it easy to smile.

'And this is Peter,' she said.

'We've met,' I said.

Donna gave a funny look from me to Peter and back to me. I realized she thought we'd literally met before. 'We introduced ourselves already,' I said.

She relaxed and gave a nervous laugh. 'Of course. Silly of me.'

'You were just too busy to notice,' Peter said, and his voice held what the actual words did not: scorn.

Donna looked at him as if she didn't know what to say, and finally, said, 'I'm sorry, Peter.'

She shouldn't have apologized. It implied she'd done something wrong, and she hadn't. She didn't know that Ted Forrester was an illusion. She was holding up her end of the bargain for happily ever after. Apologizing makes you sound weak, and from the look on Peter's face Donna needed all the strength she could get.

Donna slid into the booth first, then Becca, and Edward on the outside, with one leg hanging out from the booth. Peter had already sat down in the middle of his side of the booth. I sat down beside him and he didn't move over, so I found enough seat to be comfortable and ended with the line of our bodies touching from shoulder to hip. If he wanted to play sullen teenager with Edward and his mom, great, but I was not playing.

When Peter realized I wasn't moving over, he finally scooted over with a loud sigh that let me know it had been an effort. I did feel sorry for Peter and his plight, but my sympathy is never endless, and the sullen teenager routine might use it up pretty quick.

Becca was sitting happily between her mother and Edward. She was swinging her legs, and her hands were out of sight, maybe holding a hand of each of them. Her contentment was large and complete as if by sitting between them not only was she happy, but she felt safe the way you're supposed to feel with your parents. It made my chest tight to see her so pleased with the situation. Edward was right. He couldn't just leave without some explanation. Becca Parnell more than her mother deserved better than that. I watched the little girl sit there and shine between them and wondered what excuse would be good enough. Nothing came to mind.

A waitress came to the booth, handed plastic menus all around even to Becca which pleased her, and then went away while we looked at them. Peter's first comment was, 'I hate Mexican food.'

Donna said, 'Peter,' in a warning voice.

But I added my two cents worth, 'Me, too.'

Peter looked at me sideways, as if he didn't trust my show of solidarity with him. 'Really?'

I nodded. 'Really.'

'Ted picked the restaurant,' he said.

'Think he did it just to be irritating?' I asked.

Peter was looking directly at me, eyes a little wide. 'Yeah, I do.'

I nodded. 'Me, too.'

Donna had an open-mouthed astonished look on her face. 'Peter, Anita.' She turned to Edward. 'What are we going to do with the two of them?' Her appealing to Edward for help over such a small thing made me think less of her.

'You can't do anything with Anita,' he said, and he turned cool blue eyes to Peter. 'I'm not sure about Peter yet.'

Peter wouldn't meet Edward's gaze, and the boy squirmed just a bit. Edward made him uncomfortable on more than one level. It wasn't just that Edward was doing his mom. It was more than that. Peter was just a little afraid of Edward, and I was betting that he hadn't done anything to earn it. I was betting that Edward had tried very hard to win Peter over as he'd won Becca over, but Peter wasn't having any of it. It had probably started out as just the normal resentment of anyone his mom dated, but the way he sat there now with his gaze carefully avoiding Edward's let me know it was more now. Peter was more nervous than he should have been around Ted, as if he somehow had picked up the real Edward under all the fun and games. It was both good for Peter and bad for him. If he ever guessed the truth and Edward didn't want it known . . . Well, Edward was very practical.

One problem at a time. Peter and I bent over our menus and made disparaging comments about nearly every menu item. By the time the waitress had come back with a basket of bread, I'd actually seen him smile twice. My own younger brother Josh had never been sullen, but I'd always gotten along with him. If I ever had children, not that I was planning on it, I wanted boys. I was just more comfortable with them.

The bread wasn't bread, but some fluffed pastry thing called a sopapilla. There was a plastic container of honey on the table especially for them. Donna spread honey on a small corner and ate that. Edward spread honey across one entire end of his bread. Becca put so much honey on her bread that Donna had to take it away from her.

Peter took a sopapilla. 'It's the only good part of the meal,' he said.

'I don't like honey,' I said.

'Me, either, but this isn't bad.' He spread a minute amount of honey and ate the small bite he'd spread it on, then repeated the process.

I got one and followed his example. The bread was good, but the honey was very different, stronger, and with an undercurrent that reminded me of sage. 'This honey tastes nothing like honey back home.'

'It's sage honey,' Edward said. 'Stronger flavor.'

'I'll say.' I'd never had anything but clover honey. I wondered if all honey took on the flavor of the plant the bees used. It seemed likely. Learn something new every day. But Peter was right. The sopapillas were good, and the honey wasn't bad in small, nay, microscopic amounts.

I finally ordered chicken enchilada. I mean, what could they possibly do to chicken to make it uneatable. Don't answer that.

Peter had plain cheese enchiladas. Both of us seemed to be going on the less is better plan.

I was on my second sopapilla when everyone else, including Peter, had finished their two apiece, when I saw bad guys come into the restaurant. How did I know they were bad guys? Instinct? Nope, practice.

The first one was six foot and almost obscenely broad through the shoulders. His arms swelled against the sleeves of his T-shirt as if the cloth couldn't contain him. His hair was straight and thick, tied back in a loose braid. I think the braid was for effect because the rest of him was so ethnic, he could have been the poster boy for the American Indian *GQ*. The cheekbones were high and tight under the dark skin, a slight uptilt to his black eyes, a strong jaw, slender lips. He wore blue jeans that were tight enough that you could tell his lower body had not had the workout that his upper body had. There is only one place where a man will put that much effort into his upper body and ignore his lower: prison. You don't lift weights in prison to get a balanced effect. You lift weights so you look like a complete badass and can hit with everything you got when the time comes. I looked for the next clue, and the tattoos were there. Black barbwire chased the swell of his arms just below the sleeves of the T-shirt.

There were two other men with him, one taller, one shorter. The taller one was in better shape, but the shorter had a wicked-looking scar that nearly bisected his face giving him the more sinister look. All the three of them needed was a sign above their heads that flashed 'bad news.' Why was I not surprised when they started walking toward us. I looked at Edward and mouthed, 'What's up?'

The strangest part was that Donna knew them. I could tell by her face that she knew them and was scared of them. Could this day get any stranger?

13

Peter let out a soft, 'Oh, my God.'

His face showed fear. He put his angry sullen look up like a mask, but I was close enough to see how wide his eyes were, how his breathing had quickened.

I glanced at Becca, and she had curled back into the seat between Edward and Donna. She peered out around Edward's arm with wide eyes. Everyone knew what was happening except me.

But I didn't have long to wait. The threatening threesome came right up to the booth. I tensed, ready to stand if Edward did, but he stayed seated though his hands were out of sight under the table. He probably had a gun out. I dropped my napkin accidentally on purpose and when I came out from under the table, the napkin was in one hand, and the Browning Hi-Power was in the other. The gun was under the table out of sight, but it was pointed at the bad guys. From under the table the shot probably wouldn't kill anyone, but it would make a big hole in someone's leg, or groin, depending on how tall the person was who happened to be standing in the wrong place at the wrong time.

'Harold,' Edward said, 'you brought backup.' His voice was still Ted's voice, more lively than his usual, but it was no longer a pleasant voice. I couldn't have told you what had changed in the voice, but it raised the tension level another notch. Becca scooted back until she couldn't see the men, hiding her face against Edward's sleeve. Donna reached for her, drawing her away from Edward and into her arms. Donna's face was openly fearful like the girl's. Edward's was open, almost smiling, but his eyes had gone empty.

His real eyes peeking out. I'd seen monsters, real monsters, pale under that gaze.

The short one with the scar shifted from foot to foot. 'Yeah, this is Russell,' he motioned at the Indian, 'and this is Newt.'

I almost said, 'Newt,' aloud, but figured we had enough problems without me being a smart-ass. And people say I don't know when to keep my mouth shut.

'Tom and Benny still in the hospital?' Edward asked, voice still conversational. So far we hadn't attracted too much attention. We were getting some glances but not much else, yet.

'We're not Tom and Benny,' Russell said. His voice matched the smile on his face, but I was reminded that smiling is just another way of baring teeth, another way to snarl.

'Bully for you,' I said.

His gaze swiveled to me. His eyes were so black that the iris and pupil had melted into one black hole. 'You another psychic bleeding heart trying to keep the Indian lands safe for us poor savages?'

I shook my head. 'I've been accused of a lot but never of being a bleeding heart.' I smiled up at him and thought that if I pulled the trigger, I would take out most of his thigh, and maybe cripple him for life. He was standing that close to the table. Close enough that I wanted him to back up, but I was waiting on Edward, and he seemed just fine with them towering over us.

'You should leave now,' Edward said, and his voice was beginning to sound like Edward. Ted was leaking away, leaving his face a blank, cold mask, his eyes empty as a winter sky. His voice was without inflection as if he were saying something totally different. Edward was emerging from his Ted mask like a butterfly pulling free of a chrysalis, though I wanted something less pretty, less harmless for the analogy, because what was pulling free into the light wasn't harmless, and if things went wrong it wasn't going to be pretty at all.

Russell leaned over the table, large hands spread across the top. He leaned way over so he would be close to Donna's face, ignoring both Edward and me. Either he was stupid, or he figured we wouldn't draw first blood in a public place. He was right about me, but I wasn't so sure about Edward.

'You and your friends stay out of our way, or you are going to get hurt.' He wasn't smiling when he said it. His voice was flat and ugly. 'You've got a cute little girl there. Be a shame if something happened to her.'

Donna paled and clutched Becca tighter. I don't know what Edward had planned because it was Peter who spoke: 'Don't you threaten my sister.' His voice was low and angry, no fear showed through.

Russell's gaze flicked to Peter, and he leaned over into his face. Peter sat unmoving, until their faces were inches apart but his eyes flickered back and forth like they were trying to escape. His hands gripped the seat edge as if he were literally holding on to keep from backing down.

'And what are you going to do about it, little man?'

'Ted?' I made it a question.

Russell's eyes flicked to me, then back to Peter. He was enjoying the boy's fear and the show of bravado. Hard to be tough muscle if you can't make a fourteen-year-old boy back down. He'd finish scaring Peter then turn to me. I don't think he considered me a threat. His mistake.

I couldn't see Edward through Russell's bulk, but I heard his voice, cold and empty, 'Do it.'

No, I didn't shoot him. That wasn't what I'd asked permission to do or what Edward had given the go ahead on. How did I know this? I just did. I switched the gun to my left-hand, and let out a breath, long and soft, until my shoulders were relaxed. I centered myself like I learned for years in Judo, and now Kenpo. I visualized my fingers going into his throat, through the flesh. When fighting for real, you don't visualize hitting someone. You visualize throwing the punch through them and out the other side. Though I would hold back a little. You can collapse a man's windpipe with this move, and I didn't want to go to jail over this. I dropped my right hand down to the seat beside me and brought my hand up with two fingers like a spear pointed. Russell saw the movement, but didn't react in time. I drove my fingers into his throat coming to my feet with the strength of the blow.

He gagged, hands going to his throat, half collapsing on the table. I used my right hand to drive his face into the table, once, twice, three times. Blood spurted from his nose, and he slid bonelessly across the tabletop to end up on the floor, staring up at the ceiling, gagging, trying to breathe through his injured throat and the smashed nose. I think if he could have breathed better, he'd have passed out, but it's hard to pass out when you're gagging. He rocked on the floor, gagging, eyes rolled back into his head, not focused.

I was standing beside the booth, staring down at him. My gun was still in my left hand, at my side, unobtrusive against my black jeans. Most people wouldn't even see the gun. They'd see the blood and the man on the floor.

Harold and the tall Newt were standing there, frozen, staring down at Russell. Harold shook his head sadly. 'You shouldn't have done that.'

Edward was standing beside the booth, blocking their view of Donna and Becca. He spoke softly, so his voice wouldn't carry much beyond our little circle. 'Don't ever threaten these people again, Harold. Don't come near them for any reason. Tell Riker that they are off limits, or the next time it won't just be a broken nose.'

'I see the guns,' Harold said, voice low. He bent down beside Russell. The big man's eyes still weren't focused. His blue T-shirt had turned purple with blood. Harold was shaking his head. He looked up at me. 'Who the hell are you?'

'Anita Blake,' I said.

He shook his head again. 'Don't know the name.'

'I guess my reputation does not precede me,' I said.

'It will,' Harold said.

I said, 'Peter, get some napkins.'

Peter didn't ask questions. He just got a double handful of napkins from the dispenser on the table and handed them my way. I took them with my right hand and held them out to Harold. He took them, watching my face, eyes flicking to the gun still bare against my leg.

'Thanks.'

'Don't mention it.'

He shoved the napkins against Russell's nose and took one arm. 'Get his other arm, Newt.'

There was a distant wail of sirens coming closer. Someone had called the cops.

Russell was still unsteady on his feet. They'd shoved napkins into his flattened nose, and he looked both silly and grotesque with the bloody napkins sticking out of his nose. He had to clear his voice twice before he could speak. His voice sounded rough, clogged, painful. 'You fucking bitch! I am going to hurt you so bad for this.'

'When you can stand without help and you've got your nose packed at the nearest emergency room, give me a call. I'd love a rematch.'

He spat in my general direction but didn't have the aim, so it splattered harmlessly onto the floor. Gross, but not very effective.

'Come on,' Harold said. He was trying to move the show towards the door. The sirens were very close now.

But Russell wasn't finished. He turned, forcing the other two to turn with him. 'I am going to fuck your bitch, and leave the girl and boy for the coyotes.'

'Russell is not a fast learner,' I said.

Becca was crying now, and Donna was so pale, I was worried she was going to faint. I couldn't turn around enough to see Peter's face without turning away from the bad guys, so I don't know what he looked like. But it wasn't a pretty scene.

The cops spilled in with Harold still trying to get Russell out the door. Edward and I used the confusion to put up our guns. The two uniforms were a little unsure whom to arrest, but the people actually testified to having heard Russell's threats, and seeing him 'menace' us before I hurt him. I'd never seen so much witness cooperation. Most of the time people are deaf and dumb, but having a small, pretty little girl in tears helped people's memories. Technically, Russell could press assault charges on me, but everyone was jumping over themselves to say that he'd been threatening us. One man claimed he'd seen Russell pull a knife. Amazing how quickly details are added to a story. I could not corroborate the knife, but I had enough witnesses to the threats that I didn't think I'd be going to jail. Edward pulled out his Ted ID, and the officers knew him by reputation if not by sight. I pulled out my executioner's license and my gun carry permit. Technically, I was carrying concealed when my permit wasn't for this state. I explained I'd worn the jacket to keep from distressing the children. The cops nodded, wrote it down, and seemed to accept it all.

It helped that Russell was being verbally abusive to the officers and was so obviously a badass, and I was so harmless looking, so small, so feminine, and so much less scary than he was. Edward gave them his address, said I'd be staying with him, and we were free to go.

The restaurant offered us a different table, but strangely Donna and the kids had lost their appetites. I was still hungry, but no one asked me. Edward paid for the food, and declined a takeout order. I put the tip on the bloodstained table, way overtipping to try and make up for the mess. Then we left, and I still hadn't eaten today. Maybe if I asked nicely, Edward would run through a drive-up window at McDonalds. Any port in a storm.

14

Donna started crying out in the parking lot. Becca joined her. Only Peter stayed silent and apart from the general hysteria. The more Donna cried, the more panicky the girl got, like they were feeding off each other. The girl was crying in those great hiccuppy sobs bordering on hyperventilation. I looked at Edward and raised my eyebrows. He looked blank. I finally gave him a push. He mouthed, 'Which one?'

'Girl,' I mouthed back.

He knelt by them. Donna had settled down on the bumper of his Hummer cradling Becca in her lap.

Edward knelt in front of them. 'Let me take Becca for a little walk.'

Donna blinked up at him, as if she saw him, heard him, but wasn't really understanding. He reached for Becca and started prying her from her mother's arms. Donna's arms were limp, but the girl clung to her mother, screaming.

Edward literally pried her small fingers away, and when she was free of her mother, Becca turned and clung to him, burying her face in his shoulder. He looked at me over the girl's head, and I shooed him away. He never questioned, just walked towards the sidewalk that edged the parking lot. He was rocking the girl slowly as he moved, soothing her.

Donna had covered her face with her hands, collapsing forward until her face and hands met her knees. Her sobs were full-blown, almost wails. Shit. I looked at Peter. He was watching her, and the look on his face was disgusted, embarrassed. I knew in that instant that he'd been the adult in more ways than just shooting his father's killer. His mother was allowed hysterics, but he wasn't. He was the one who held together in a crisis. Damned unfair, if you ask me.

'Peter, can you excuse us for a few minutes?'

He shook his head. 'No.'

I sighed, then shrugged. 'Fine, just don't interfere.' I knelt in front of Donna, touching her shaking shoulders. 'Donna, Donna!' There was no response, no change. It had been a long day. I got a handful of that short thick hair and pulled her head up. It hurt, and it was meant to. 'Look at me, you selfish bitch.'

Peter moved forward, and I pointed a finger at him. 'Don't.' He settled back a step, but he didn't leave. His face was angry, watchful, and I knew that he might interfere regardless of what I said if I went much further. But I didn't have to go further. I'd shocked her. Her eyes were wide, inches from mine, her face drenched with tears. Her breathing was still coming in small chest-heaving gulps, but she was looking at me, she was listening.

I released her hair slowly, and she stayed staring at me with a horrible fascination on her face as if I were about to do something cruel, and I was. 'Your little girl has just seen the worst thing she's ever seen in her life. She was calming down, taking it in stride, until you started on the hysterics. You're her mother. You're her strength, her protector. When she saw you fall apart like that, it terrified her.'

'I didn't mean . . . I couldn't help . . .'

'I don't give a shit what you feel or how upset you are. You're the mommy. She's the child. You are going to hold yourself together until she is not around to see you fall apart, is that clear?'

She blinked at me. 'I don't know if I can do that.'

'You can do it. You're going to do it.' I glanced up but didn't see Edward yet. Good. 'You are the grown-up, Donna, and you are by God going to act like it.'

I could feel Peter watching us, could almost feel him storing it away for later playback. He would remember this little scene and he would think on it, you could feel it.

'Do you have children?' she asked, and I knew what was coming.

'No,' I said.

'Then what right do you have to tell me how to raise mine?' She was angry now, sitting up straighter, wiping at her face with short harsh movements.

Sitting up on the bumper, she was taller than I was kneeling. I looked up into her angry eyes and told the truth. 'I was eight years old when my mother died, and my father couldn't handle it. We got a phone call from a state trooper that told us she was dead. My father dropped the phone and started to wail, not cry, wail. He took me by the hand and walked the few blocks to my grandmother's house, wailing, leading me by the hand. By the time we got to my grandmother's we had a crowd of neighbors, all asking what was wrong, what was wrong. I was the one who turned to my neighbors and said, "My mommy's dead." My father was collapsed in the bosom of his family, and I was left standing alone, uncomforted, unheld, tears on my face, telling the neighbors what had happened.'

Donna stared at me and there was something very close to horror on her face. 'I'm sorry,' she said in a voice that had grown soft and lost its anger.

'Don't be sorry for me, Donna, but be a mother to your own daughter. Hold it together. She needs you to comfort her right now. Later when you're alone, or with Ted, you can fall apart, but please, not in front of the kids. That goes for Peter, too.'

She glanced at him, standing there, watching us, and she flushed, embarrassed at last. She nodded her head too rapidly, then visibly straightened. You could actually see her gathering herself. She took my hands, squeezing them. 'I am sorry for your loss, and I apologize for today. I'm not very good around violence. If it's an accident, a cut, no matter the blood, I'm fine, honestly, but I just can't abide violence.'

I drew my hands gently from hers. I wasn't sure I believed her, but I said, 'I'm glad to know that, Donna. I'll go get . . . Ted and Becca.'

She nodded. 'Thank you.'

I stood, nodding. I walked across the gravel in the direction Edward had gone. I liked Donna less now, but I knew now that Edward had to get away from this family. Donna wasn't good around violence. Jesus, if she only knew who, what, she'd taken to her bed. She'd have had hysterics for the rest of her life.

Edward had walked down the sidewalk to stand in front of one of the many small houses. They all had gardens in front, well tended, well planned. It reminded me of California where every inch of yard is used for something because land is at such a premium. Albuquerque didn't look nearly as crowded and yet the yards were crowded.

Edward was still holding Becca, but she was looking at something that he was pointing at, and there was a smile on her face that showed from two houses away. A tension I hadn't realized I was carrying eased from my back and shoulders. When she turned so that her face was full to me, I saw a sprig of lilac tucked into one of her braids. The pale lavender flower didn't match the yellow ribbons and dress, but hey, it was cute as hell.

Her smile faltered around the edges when she saw me. There was a very good chance that I wouldn't be one of Becca's favorite people. I'd probably scared her. Oh, well.

Edward put her down, and they walked towards me. She was smiling up at him, swinging his arm a little. He smiled down at her, and it looked real. Even to me it looked real. You might have really believed he was Becca's adored and adoring father. How the hell were we going to get him out of their lives without screwing Becca over? Peter would be pleased if Ted went poof, and Donna . . . She was a grownup. Becca wasn't. Shit.

Edward smiled at me and said in his cheerful Ted voice, 'How are things?'

'Just dandy,' I said.

He raised eyebrows, and for a split second his eyes flinched, going from cynical to cheerful so fast it made me dizzy.

'Donna and Peter are waiting for us.'

Edward turned so that the girl was between us. She glanced up at me, and her gaze was questioning, thoughtful. 'You beat up that bad man,' she said.

'Yes, I did,' I said.

'I didn't know girls could do that.'

That made my teeth hurt. 'Girls can do anything they want to do, including protect themselves and beat up bad guys.'

'Ted said that you hurt that man because he said bad things to me.'

I glanced at Edward, but his face was all open and cheerful for the child and gave me nothing.

'That's right,' I said.

'Ted says that you'd hurt someone to protect me just like he would.'

I met her big brown eyes, and nodded. 'Yes, I would.'

She smiled then and it was beautiful, like sunshine breaking through clouds. She reached out her free hand to me, and I took it. Edward and I walked back to the parking lot, holding the child's hands while she half-walked, half-danced between us. She believed in Ted, and Ted had told her that she could believe in me, so she did. The odd thing was that I would hurt someone to protect her. I would kill to keep her safe. I looked across at Edward and for just a moment he looked back at me from the mask. We stared at each other over the child, and I didn't know what to do. I didn't know how to get us all out of the mess that he had made.

Becca said, 'Swing me.'

Edward counted out, 'One, two, three,' and swung her up and out, forcing me to swing her other arm. We moved across the parking lot, swinging Becca between us while she gave that joyous, full-throated laugh.

We sat her down laughing in front of her mother. Donna was composed and smiling. I was proud of her. Becca looked up at me, shining. 'Mommy says I'm too big to swing now, but you're strong, aren't you?'

I smiled at her, but I looked at Edward when I said, 'Yes, I am.'

15

Donna and Edward did a tender but decorous goodbye. Peter rolled his eyes and scowled as if they'd done a lot more than a semi-chaste kiss. He'd have had a cow if he could have seen them smooching earlier at the airport. Becca kissed Edward on the cheek, giggling. Peter ignored it all and got in the car as soon as he could as if afraid 'Ted' might try to hug him, too.

Edward waved until the car turned onto Lomos and out of sight, then he turned to me. All he did was look at me, but it was enough.

'Let's get in the car and get some air conditioning going before I grill you about what the hell is going on,' I said.

He unlocked the car. We got inside. He started the engine and the air conditioner, though the air hadn't had time to cool yet. We sat in the expensive hum of his engine with the hot air blowing on us, and silence filled the car.

'Are you counting to ten?' he asked.

'Try a thousand and you'll be closer.'

'Ask. I know you want to.'

'Okay, we'll skip the tirade about you dragging Donna and her kids into your mess and go straight to who the hell is Riker and why did he send goons to warn you off?'

'First, it was Donna's mess, and she dragged me into it.'

My disbelief must have shown on my face because he continued, 'She and her friends are a part of an amateur archeology society that tries to preserve Native American sites in the area. Are you familiar with how an archeological dig is done?'

'A little. I know they use string and tags to mark where an object is found, take pictures, make drawings, sort of like you do for a dead body before you move it.'

'Trust you to come up with the perfect analogy,' he said, but he was smiling. 'I've gone with Donna on weekends with the kids. They use freaking toothbrushes and tiny paint brushes to gently clean the dirt away, or dental picks.'

'I know you have a point,' I said.

'Pot hunters find a sight that is already being explored, or sometimes one that hasn't been found, and they bring in bulldozers and backhoes to take out as much as possible in the least amount of time.'

I gaped at him. 'But that destroys more than they can possibly take out, and if you move an object before its site is recorded, it loses a lot of its historical value. I mean the dirt it's found in can help date it. What is found near an object can tell all sorts of things to a trained eye.'

'Pot hunters don't care about history. They take what they find and sell it to private collectors or dealers who aren't too particular about how an object was found. A site that Donna was volunteering on was raided.'

'She asked you to look into it,' I said.

'You underestimate her. She and her psychic friends thought they could reason with Riker, since they were pretty sure it was his people behind it.'

I sighed. 'I don't underestimate her, Edward.'

'She and her friends didn't understand what a bad man Riker is. Some of the really big pot hunters hire bodyguards, goon squads, to help take care of the bleeding hearts, and even the local law. Riker is suspected of having been behind the deaths of two local cops. It's one of the reasons that things went so smoothly in the restaurant. All the local cops know that Riker's a suspected cop killer, not personally, but of hiring it done.'

I smiled, not a pleasant smile. 'I wonder how many traffic tickets he and his men have acquired since it happened.'

'Enough that his lawyer filed a harassment suit. There is no proof that Riker's people were involved, just the fact that the cops were killed at a dig that had been partially bulldozed, and an eye witness that saw a car with a partial plate that might have been one of his trucks.'

'Is the witness still among the living?' I asked.

'My, you do catch on quick.'

'I take it that's a no.'

'He's missing,' Edward said.

'So why come after Donna and her kids?'

'Because the kids were with her when she and her group formed a protest line protecting a site that was on private land that Riker had gotten permission to bulldoze. She was their spokesperson.'

'Stupid, she should not have taken the kids.'

'Like I said, Donna didn't understand how bad a man Riker was.'

'And what happened?'

'Her group was manhandled, abused, beaten. They fled. Donna had a black eye.'

'And what did Ted do about this?' I was watching his face, arms crossed over my stomach. All I could see was his profile, but it was enough. He hadn't liked it, that Donna had gotten hurt. Maybe it was just that she belonged to him, a male pride thing, or maybe . . . maybe it was more.

'Donna asked me to have a talk with the men.'

'I take it that would be the two men that you put in the hospital. I seem to remember you asking Harold if two guys were still in the hospital.'

Edward nodded. 'Yeah.'

'Only two in the hospital, and none in a grave. You must be slipping.'

'I couldn't kill anyone without Donna knowing, so I made an example of two of his men.'

'Let me guess. One of them would be the man who gave Donna the black eye.'

Edward smiled happily. 'Tom.'

'And the other one?'

'He pushed Peter and threatened to break his arm.'

I shook my head. The air had begun to cool, and it raised goose-bumps even through my jacket, or maybe it wasn't the cold. 'The second guy has a broken arm now?'

'Among other things,' Edward said.

'Edward, look at me.'

He turned and gave me his cool blue gaze.

'Truth, do you care for this family? Would you kill to protect them?'

'I'd kill to amuse myself, Anita.'

I shook my head, and leaned close to him, close enough to study his face, to try and make him give up his secrets. 'No jokes, Edward, tell me the truth. Are you serious about Donna?'

'You asked me if I loved her and I said, no.'

I shook my head again. 'Dammit, don't keep evading the answer. I don't think you do love her. I don't think you're capable of it, but you feel something. I don't know exactly what, but something. Do you feel something for this family, for all of them?'

His face was blank, and I couldn't read it. He just stared at me. I wanted to slap him, to scream and rant until I broke through his mask into whatever lay underneath. I'd always been on sure ground with Edward, always known where he stood, even when he was planning to hurt me. But now suddenly, I wasn't sure about anything.

'My God, you do care for them.' I slumped back in my seat, weak. I couldn't have been more astonished if he'd sprouted a second head. That would have been weird, but not this weird.

'Jesus, Mary, and Joseph, Edward, you care for them, all of them.'

He looked away. Edward, the stone cold killer, looked away. He couldn't or wouldn't meet my gaze. He put the car in gear and forced me to buckle my seatbelt.

I let him pull out of the parking lot in silence, but when we were sitting at the stop sign waiting for the traffic to clear on Lomos, I had to say something. 'What are you going to do?'

'I don't know,' he said. 'I don't love Donna.'

'But,' I said.

He turned slowly onto the main street. 'She's a mess. She believes in every new age bandwagon that comes along. She's got a good head for business, but she trusts everyone. She's useless around violence. You saw her today.' He was concentrating very hard on the driving, hands gripping the wheel tight enough for his knuckles to be white. 'Becca is just like her, trusting, sweet, but . . . tougher, I think. Both the kids are tougher than Donna.'

'They've had to be,' I said, and couldn't keep the disapproval out of my voice.

'I know, I know,' he said. 'I know Donna, everything about her. I've heard every detail from cradle to the present.'

'Did it bore you?' I asked.

'Some of it,' he said carefully.

'But not all of it,' I said.

'No, not all of it.'

'Are you saying that you do love Donna?' I had to ask.

'No, no, I'm not saying that.'

I was staring so hard at his face that we could have been driving on the far side of the moon for all the attention I gave the scenery. Nothing mattered more right that second than Edward's face, his voice. 'Then what are you saying?'

'I'm saying that sometimes when you play a part too long, you can get sucked into that part and it becomes more real than it was meant to be.' I saw something on his face that I had never seen before, anguish, uncertainty.

'Are you saying that you are going to marry Donna? You're going to be a husband and a father? PTA meetings, and the whole nine yards?'

'No, I'm not saying that. You know I can't marry her. I can't live with her and two kids and hide what I am twenty-four hours a day. That good an actor I'm not.'

'Then what are you saying?' I asked.

'I'm saying . . . I'm saying that part of me, a small part of me, wishes I could.'

I stared at him opened-mouthed. Edward, assassin extraordinaire, the undead's perfect predator, wished he could have not a family, but this family. A trusting new age widow, her sullen teenage son, and a little girl that made Rebecca of Sunnybrook Farm look jaded, and Edward wanted them.

When I trusted myself to be coherent, I said, 'What are you going to do?'

'I don't know.'

I couldn't think of anything helpful to say, so I resorted to humor, my shield of last resort. 'Just please tell me they don't have a dog and a picket fence.'

He smiled. 'No fence, but a dog, two dogs.'

'What kind of dogs?' I asked.

He smiled and glanced at me, wanting to see my reaction. 'Maltese. Their names are Peeka and Boo.'

'Oh, shit, Edward, you're joking me.'

'Donna wants the dogs included in the engagement pictures.'

I stared at him, and the look on my face seemed to amuse him. He laughed. 'I'm glad you're here, Anita, because I don't know a single other person who I'd have admitted this to.'

'Do you realize that your personal life is now more complicated than mine is?' I said.

'Now I know I'm in trouble,' he said. And we left it on a lighter note, on a joke, because we were more comfortable that way. But Edward had confided in me about a personal problem. In his way he'd come to me for help about it. And being who I was, I'd try to help him. I thought we would solve the mutilations and murders, eventually. I mean violence and death were our specialties. I was not nearly so optimistic about the personal stuff.

Edward did not belong in a world with a woman who had a pair of toy dogs named Peeka and Boo. Edward was not now, nor ever would be, that cutesy. Donna was. It wouldn't work. It just wouldn't work. But for the very first time I realized that if Edward didn't have a heart to lose, that he wished he had one to give. But I was reminded of the scene in *The Wizard of Oz* where Dorothy and the Scarecrow bang on the Tin Man's chest and hear the rolling echo. The tinsmith had forgotten to put in a heart. Edward had carved his own heart out of his body and left it on a floor somewhere years ago. I'd known that. I just never knew that Edward regretted the loss. And I think until Donna Parnell came along, he hadn't known it either.

16

Edward did take me through a drive-up window, but he didn't want to stop. He seemed anxious to get to Santa Fe. Since he was rarely anxious about anything, I didn't argue. I requested we go through a carwash while I ate my French fries and cheeseburger. He didn't say a word, just drove into one beside the highway that let us ride through in the car. When I was little, I'd loved watching the suds slide down the windows and the huge brushes roll by. It was still nifty, though not the thrill a minute it had been when I was five. But the carwash did mean that I had a clear view out all the windows. The dirty windows had made me feel ever so slightly claustrophobic. I'd finished my food before we left Albuquerque. I sipped on my soda as we drove out of town and towards the mountains. These were not the black mountains, but a different range that looked more 'normal.' They were jagged and rocky looking, with a string of glittering light near their base.

'What's with the light show,' I asked.

'What?' Edward asked.

'The glitter, what is it?'

I felt his attention shift from the road, but he was wearing his sunglasses, and I couldn't really see his gaze shift. 'Houses, the sun is hitting the windows on the houses.'

'I've never seen sunlight on windows glitter like that.'

'Albuquerque is at 7,000 feet. The air is thinner than you're used to. It makes light do strange things.'

I stared at the sparkling windows like a line of jewels imbedded in the mountains. 'It's beautiful.'

He moved his whole head. This time so I knew he was really looking at it. 'If you say so.'

After that we stopped talking. Edward never did idle chatter, and apparently he had nothing to say. My mind was still reeling from Edward being in love, or as close as he would probably ever get. It was just too weird. I couldn't think of a single useful thing to say so I stared out the window until I thought of something worth saying. I had a feeling it was going to be a long quiet drive to Santa Fe.

The hills were very round, covered in dry brownish grass. I had the same feeling I'd had when I stepped off the plane in Albuquerque – desolate. I'd thought the hills were close until I spotted a cow standing on one. The cow looked tiny, small enough for me to cover with two fingers held up, which meant the 'hills' were really small mountains and not nearly as close to the road as they appeared. It was late afternoon or early evening depending on how you looked at it. It was still daylight, but you could feel night looming even in the brightness. The day had worn away like a piece of candy sucked too long. No matter how bright the sunshine, I could feel the darkness pressing close. Partly it was my mood – confusion always makes me pessimistic – but it was also an innate sense of the coming night. I was a vampire executioner, and I knew the taste of night on the breeze just as I knew the feel of dawn pressing against the darkness. There had been times when my life had depended on dawn coming. Nothing like near death experiences to hone a skill.

The sunlight had begun to fade to a soft evening gloom when I'd finally had enough of the silence. I still had nothing helpful to say about his personal life, but there was the case. I'd been asked here to help solve a crime, not to play Dear Abby, so maybe if I just concentrated on the crime, we'd be okay.

'Is there anything about the cases that you've withheld from me? Anything I'm going to be pissed that I didn't know beforehand?'

'Changing the subject?' he asked.

'I wasn't aware we were on a subject,' I said.

'You know what I meant.'

I sighed. 'Yeah, I know what you meant.' I slumped in my seat as far as the seatbelt would allow, arms crossed over my stomach. My body language was not happy, nor was I. 'I don't have anything to add to the Donna situation, or nothing helpful.'

'So concentrate on business,' he said.

'You taught me that,' I said, 'you and Dolph. Keep your eye and mind on the important stuff. The important stuff is what can get you killed. Donna and her kiddies aren't a threat to life and limb so put them on the back burner.'

He smiled, his normal close-lipped, I-know-something-you-don't-know smile. It didn't always mean he knew something I didn't. Sometimes he did it just to irritate. Like now. 'I thought you said you'd kill me if I didn't stop dating Donna.'

I rubbed my neck against the expensive seats and tried to ease a tension that was beginning at the base of my skull. Maybe I had been invited here to play Dear Abby, at least in part. Shit.

'You were right, Edward. You can't just leave. It would screw up Becca for one thing. But you cannot keep dating Donna indefinitely. She's going to start asking for a date for the wedding, and what are you going to say?'

'I don't know,' he said.

'Well, neither do I, so let's talk about the case. At least with that we've got a solid direction.'

'We do?' He glanced at me as he asked.

'We know we want the mutilations and murders to stop, right?' I asked.

'Yes,' he said.

'Well, that's more than we know about Donna.'

'Are you saying you don't want me to stop seeing her?' he asked, and that damn smile was back. Smug, he looked smug.

'I'm saying I don't know what the hell I want you to do, let alone what you should do. So let's leave it alone until I get some brilliant idea.'

'Okay,' he said.

'Great,' I said. 'Now back to the question I asked. What haven't you told me about the crimes that you think I should know, or rather that I think I should know?'

'I don't read minds, Anita. I don't know what you'll want to know.'

'Don't be coy, Edward. Just spill the beans. I don't want any more surprises on this trip, not from you.'

He was quiet for so long, I thought he wasn't going to answer. So I prompted him, 'Edward, I mean it.'

'I'm thinking,' he said. He moved in his seat, shoulders tightening and loosening as if he were trying to get rid of tension, too. I guess, even for him, this had been a stressful day. Odd to think of Edward letting anything truly stress him. I'd always thought he walked through life with the perfect Zen of the sociopath, so that nothing truly bothered him. I'd been wrong. Wrong about a lot of things.

I went back to watching the scenery. There were cows scattered close enough to the road that you could make out color and size. If it wasn't a Jersey, a Guernsey, or a Black Angus, I didn't know it. I watched the strange cows standing at impossible angles on the steep hillsides and waited for Edward to finish thinking. Twilight seemed to last a long time here, as if the light of day gave up the fight slowly, struggling to remain and keep the darkness at bay. Maybe it was just my mood, but I wasn't looking forward to darkness. It was as if I could sense something out there in those desolate hills, something waiting for the night, something that could not move during the day. It could be just my own overactive imagination, or I could be right. That was the hard part about psychic abilities: sometimes you were right, and sometimes you weren't. Sometimes your own anxiety or fear could poison your thinking and make you, almost, literally see ghosts where there were none.

There were, of course, ways to find out. 'Is there a place where you can pull over out of sight of the main road?'

He looked at me. 'Why?'

'I'm . . . sensing something, and I just want to make sure I'm not imagining it.'

He didn't argue. When the next exit came up, he took it. We took a side road from the exit. It was dirt and gravel and full of huge dry potholes. The shocks on his Hummer took the road like silk flowing down hill, comfy. A soft roll of hills hid us from the main highway, but the road was very flat in front of us, giving a clear view of the road as it went almost straight towards a distant rise of hills. There were a handful of tiny houses on either side of the road, the major cluster some ways ahead with a small church sitting to one side by itself, as if it were part of the houses and not. The church had a steeple with a cross on top of it, and I assumed a bell inside of it. Though we were too far away to be sure. The town, if it were a town, looked down on its luck but not empty. There were people there and eyes to see us. Just our luck, the land had been so empty and the road we go down has a town.

'Stop the car,' I said. We were as far from the first house as we could get without backtracking.

Edward pulled over to the side of the road. The dust rose in a cloud to either side of the car, settling over the clean paint job in a dry powder.

'You guys don't get much rain up here, do you?'

'No,' he said. Anyone else would have elaborated, but not Edward. Even the weather wasn't a topic of conversation unless it affected the job.

I got out of the car and walked a little way into the dry grass. I walked until I could no longer sense Edward or the car. When I looked back, I was yards away. Edward was standing on the driver's side door, arms crossed on the roof, hat tilted back so he could watch the show. I don't think there was another person I knew who wouldn't have asked at least one question about what I was about to do. It would be interesting to see if he asked any questions afterwards.

Darkness hung like a soft silken cloth, hanging against the sky, and the dying light. It was a soft comfortable twilight, an embracing dark. A breeze blew across the open land and played with my hair. Everything felt fine, good. Had I imagined? Was I letting Edward's problems get to me? Was the memory of the survivors in their air-compressed hospital room making me see shadows?

I almost just turned around and walked back to the car, but I didn't. If it were my imagination, then it wouldn't hurt to check, and if it wasn't . . . I turned and faced away from the car, away from the distant houses, and looked out into the emptiness. Of course, it wasn't really empty. There was grass rustling in the wind, it sounded so dry, like corn in autumn just before it's harvested. The ground was covered in a thin layer of pale reddish-brown gravel with paler dirt showing through. The ground ran until it met the hills that continued on and on towards the darkening sky. Not empty, just lonely.

I took a deep cleansing breath, let it out and did two things at once: I dropped my shields and spread my arms wide, hands reaching. I was reaching with my hands, but it wasn't just my hands. I reached outward with that sense I have – magic, if you like the word. I don't. I reached outward with that power that let me raise the dead and mix with werewolves. I reached outward towards that waiting presence that I'd felt, or thought I'd felt.

There, there like a fish tugging on my line. I turned to face the direction of the road. It was in that direction, going towards Santa Fe. It – I had no better word. I felt its eagerness for the coming night and knew that it could not move in daylight. And I knew that it was large, not physically, but psychically, because we were not close to it, and yet I'd picked it up miles away. How many miles I couldn't say, but far, very far to have sensed it. It didn't feel evil.

That didn't mean it wasn't evil, just that it didn't think of itself as evil. Unlike people, preternatural entities are rather proud of being evil. They embraced their malignancy because whatever this was, it wasn't human. It wasn't physical. Spirit, energy, pick a word, but it was up ahead, and it was not contained in any physical shell. It was free floating. No, not free ... Something slammed into me, not physically, but as if a psychic truck had run me down. I was on my butt in the dirt, trying to breathe, as if someone had hit me in the chest and knocked the wind out of me.

I heard Edward's running footsteps, but I couldn't seem to turn around. I was too busy relearning how to breathe.

He knelt by me, gun in hand. 'What happened?' He was looking out into the thick twilight, not at me, searching, searching for the danger. His sunglasses were gone, and his face was very serious as he searched for something to shoot.

I gripped his arm, shaking my head, trying to talk. But when I finally had air enough, all I said was, 'Shit, shit, shit!' It wasn't helpful, but I was scared. Most of the time when I get this scared, I get cold, shocky, but not when it's psychic shit. When something goes wrong with 'magic,' I never go shocky or get cold, I stay warm. If anything it's like tingling, warm, as if I'd stuck my finger in a light socket. Whatever 'it' was, had sensed me and shut me down.

I pulled my shields around me like clutching a coat against a blizzard, but strangely it had backed off. Though if that one swat of power was any indication, it could slice me, dice me, and serve me on toast if it wanted to. It hadn't wanted to. I was glad, thrilled, but why hadn't it hurt me worse? How had I sensed it from so far away, and how had it sensed me? Usually, my greatest talent is with the dead. Did that mean whatever 'it' was, was dead, or had something to do with the dead? Or was this one of the new psychic abilities that my teacher, Marianne, had warned me might crop up. God, I hoped not. I didn't need more strange shit in my life. I had plenty.

I forced myself to stop the useless cursing, and said, 'Put up the gun, Edward. I'm all right. Besides, there's nothing to shoot and nothing to see.'

He put a hand under my arm and pulled me to my feet before I was ready. I'd have been very happy to stay sitting for a while. I leaned on him, and he started moving us back towards the car. I stumbled and finally had to tell him, 'Stop, please.'

He held me up, still searching the new dark, gun still in hand. I should have known he'd keep the gun out. It was his security blanket – sometimes.

I could breathe again, and if Edward stopped dragging me on, I might be able to walk. The fear had faded because it was useless. I'd tried a bit of 'magic,' and I hadn't been good enough. I was learning ritual magic, but I was a beginner. Power isn't enough. You've got to know what to do with it, like a gun with the safety on. It makes a fine paperweight, but that's about it unless you know what to do with it.

I slid into the car, had my door closed and locked before Edward opened his door. 'Tell me what happened, Anita.'

I looked at him. 'It would serve you right if I just looked at you and smiled.'

Something crossed his face, a frown, a snarl, quickly lost to that perfect blankness he could manage. 'You're right. I've been a secret-loving bastard, and it would serve me right. But you're the one who said we needed to stop the pissing contest and solve the crime. I'll stop if you will.'

I nodded. 'Agreed.'

'So,' he said.

'Start the car and get us out of here.' Somehow I didn't like sitting on the nearly deserted road in the freshly spilled darkness. I wanted to be moving. Sometimes movement gives you the illusion that you're doing something.

Edward started the car, turned around in the weeds and drove back towards the highway. 'Talk.'

'I've never been to this area before. For all I know what I sensed is always here, just some local bugaboo.'

'What did you sense?'

'Something powerful. Something that's miles away towards Santa Fe. Something that may be connected to the dead in some way, which would explain why it called to me so strongly. I'm going to need to find a good local psychic to see if this thing is always around or not.'

'Donna will know some psychics. Whether they're good, I can't say, and I'm not sure she can either.'

'It's a place to start,' I said. I snuggled into my seatbelt, hugging myself. 'You got any local animators, necromancers, anyone who works with the dead? If it is something connected to my type of power, then an ordinary psychic might not sense it.'

'I don't know of any, but I'll ask around.'

'Good.'

We were back out on the highway. The night was very dark, as if thick clouds hid the sky. The headlights seemed very yellow against the blackness.

'Do you think this whatever-it-is has anything to do with the mutilations?' he asked.

'I don't know.'

'You don't know a hell of a lot,' he said. He sounded grumpy.

'That's the problem with psychic shit and magic. Sometimes it's not very helpful.'

'I've never seen you do anything like what you just did. You hate the mystical crap.'

'Yes, I do, but I've had to accept what I am, Edward. This mystical crap is a part of who and what I am. I can't run from it because it is me. You can't hide from yourself, not forever, and you can't ever outrun yourself. I raise the dead for a living, Edward. Why should it be a shock that I may have other abilities?'

'It's not,' he said.

I glanced at him, but he was watching the road, and I couldn't read his face. 'It's not,' I said.

'I called you in to be backup not just because you're a shooter, but because you know more about preternatural stuff than anyone else I know, that I trust. You hate the psychics and the mediums, because you are one, but you still deal in reality, and that makes you different from the rest of them.'

'You're wrong, Edward. I saw a soul today hovering in that room. It was real, just as real as the gun in your holster. Psychics, witches, mediums, they all deal in reality. It's just not the same reality that you deal with, but it is real, Edward, it is very, very real.'

He didn't say anything to that, just let the silence fill the car, and I was content with silence because I was tired, terribly, terribly tired. I'd found that doing psychic shit sometimes exhausted me a hell of a lot faster than physical labor. I ran four miles every other day, lifted weights, took Kenpo class, and Judo, and none of it made me as tired as having stood in that field and opened myself to that thing. I never sleep in a car because I don't trust the driver not to have a wreck and kill me. That is the truth about why I don't sleep in cars, no matter what I say out loud. My mother was killed in a car accident, and I've never really trusted cars since.

I settled down in my seat, trying to find a comfortable place for my head. I was suddenly so tired, so tired my eyes burned. I closed my eyes just to rest them, and sleep dragged at me like a hand pulling me under. I could have fought it, but I didn't. I needed the rest, and I needed it now, or I wouldn't be worth shit soon. And the thought crossed my mind as I let myself relax that I did trust Edward. I really did. I slept huddled in the seat and didn't wake until the car stopped.

'We're here,' Edward said.

I struggled to sit up, feeling stiff, but rested. 'Where?'

'Ted's house.'

I sat up straighter. Ted's house? Edward's house. I was finally going to get to see where Edward lived. I was going to snoop and strip some of his mystery away. If I didn't get killed, finding out Edward's secrets would make the entire trip worthwhile. If I did get killed, I'd come back and haunt Edward, see if I could make him see ghosts after all.

17

The house was adobe and looked old or genuine, not that I was an expert, but there was a feel to the house of age. We unloaded my luggage from the back of the Hummer but I had eyes mostly for the house. Edward's house. I'd never really hoped to see where he lived. He was like Batman. He rode into town, saved your ass, then vanished, and you never really expected an invitation to see the Bat Cave. Now here I was standing in front of it. Cool.

It wasn't what I'd pictured. I'd thought maybe a high-tech condo in the city. LA maybe. This modest appearing adobe house hugging the land was just not what I'd had in mind. It was part of his secret identity, his Tedness, but still, Edward lived here, and there had to be more reason than just Ted would have liked it. I was beginning to think I really didn't know Edward at all.

The light over the front door switched on, and I had to turn away, shielding my night vision. I'd been staring right at it when it glared to life. I had two thoughts: one, who had turned on the light; two, the door was blue. The door was painted a blue-violet, a rich, rich color. I could also see the window nearest the door. Its trim was painted the same vibrant blue.

I'd seen it at the airport, though with more flowers and an addition of fuchsia. I asked, 'What's with the blue door and trim?'

'Maybe I like it,' he said.

'I've seen a lot of doors painted blue or turquoise on a lot of houses since I've been here. What gives?'

'Very observant.'

'A failing of mine. Now explain.'

'They think witches can't cross a door painted blue or green.'

I widened my eyes. 'You believe that?'

'I doubt most of the people who paint their doors believe it anymore, but it's become part of the local style. My guess is that most people who do it, don't even remember the folklore behind it.'

'Like putting out a jack o' lantern at Halloween to frighten the goblins away,' I said.

'Exactly.'

'And because I am so observant, who turned on the porch light?'

'Either Bernardo or Olaf.'

'Your other backups,' I said.

'Yes.'

'Can't wait to meet them.'

'In the spirit of cooperation, and no more surprises, Olaf doesn't like women much.'

'You mean he's gay?'

'No, and implying that to him will probably mean a fight, so please don't. If I'd known I'd be calling you in, I wouldn't have called him in at all. The two of you in the same house on the same case is going to be . . . a fucking disaster.'

'That's harsh. You think we can't play nice together.'

'I'd almost guarantee it,' he said.

The door opened, and our conversation cut off abruptly. I was wondering if it was the dreaded Olaf. The man in the doorway didn't look much like an Olaf, but then what does an Olaf look like?

The man was six foot, give or take an inch. It was hard to tell his exact height because his lower body was completely covered by a white sheet that he had clutched in one hand at his waist. The sheet spilled around his feet like a formal dress, but from the waist up he was anything but formal. He was lean and muscular with a very nice set of abs. He was tanned a lovely even brown, though some of that was natural color because he was American Indian, oh, yes, he was. His hair was waist length falling over one shoulder and across the side of his face, heavy and solid black, tousled from sleep, though it was early to be in bed. His face was a soft, full triangle, with a dimple in his chin, and a full mouth. Was it racist to say that his features were more white than Indian, or was it just true?

'You can close your mouth now,' Edward said near my ear.

I closed my mouth. 'Sorry,' I mumbled. How embarrassing. I didn't usually notice men this much, at least men I didn't know. What was wrong with me today?

The man folded the sheet over his free arm until his legs showed and he could come down the two steps without tripping. 'Sorry, I was asleep, or I'd have come out to help sooner.' He seemed perfectly at ease in his sheet, though he was going to a lot of effort to spill it over the same arm that was holding it in place, so he could grab a suitcase.

'Bernardo Spotted-Horse, Anita Blake.'

He was holding the sheet with his right hand, and he looked mildly perplexed as he dropped the suitcase and started the process of switching everything to the other hand. The sheet slipped down in front, and I had to turn my head away, fast.

I kept my head turned because I was blushing and wanted the darkness to hide it. I waved my hand vaguely behind me. 'We'll shake hands later when you're wearing clothes.'

Edward's voice. 'You flashed her.'

Great, everybody noticed.

'I'm sorry,' Bernardo said, 'truly.'

'We can get the luggage,' I said. 'Go get a robe.'

I felt someone move up behind me, and I wasn't sure how I knew, but I knew it wasn't Edward. 'You're modest. I expected a lot of things from Edward's descriptions but not modesty.'

I turned around slowly, and he was standing too close, invading the hell out of my personal space. I glared at him. 'What were you expecting? The Whore of Babylon?' I was embarrassed and uncomfortable and that always made me angry. The anger showed in my voice.

The half-smile on his face faded round the edges. 'I didn't mean any offense.' His hand came up as he said it, as if he'd touch my hair.

I stepped back out of reach. 'What's with the touchie-feelie routine?'

'I saw the way you looked at me in the doorway,' he said.

I felt the heat ride up my face, but I didn't turn away this time. 'If you want to come to the door looking like a Playgirl centerfold, don't blame me for staring. But don't make more of it than it is. You're nice eye candy, but the fact that you're coming on this strong isn't flattering to either of us. Either you're a whore, or you think I am. The first I'm willing to believe. The second I know isn't true.' I walked up to him now, invading his space, the blush gone, leaving me pale and angry. 'So back off.'

It was his turn to look uncertain. He stepped back, put the sheet into as much of a cover as it could be, and bowed. It was an old-fashioned, courtly movement, as if he'd done it before and meant it. It was a nice gesture with his hair spilling all around, but I'd seen better. Not for six months, but I had seen better.

He raised up, and his face was solemn. He looked sincere. 'There are two kinds of women that hang around with men like Edward, like me, that know what we are. The first are whores, no matter how many guns they own; the second is strictly business. I call them Madonnas because they never sleep with anyone. They try to be one of the guys.' The smile played along his lips again. 'Forgive me if I'm disappointed that you're one of the guys. I've been here for two weeks, and I'm getting lonely.'

I shook my head. 'Two weeks, poor baby.' I pushed past him and grabbed my overnight case. I looked at Edward. 'Next time remind me about everybody's little foibles.'

He raised his hand in a Boy Scout oath. 'I have never seen Bernardo do that with any woman at first meeting her, I swear it.'

My eyes narrowed, but I looked into his eyes, and believed him. 'How did I get the honor?'

He picked up my suitcase, and did smile. 'You should have seen the look on your face when he came down the steps in the sheet.' He laughed and it was very masculine. 'I've never seen you that embarrassed.'

Bernardo came up next to us. 'I really, honestly, didn't mean to flash you. I just don't wear anything to bed so I threw this on.'

'Where's Olaf?' Edward asked.

'Pouting that you're bringing her in.'

'Great,' I said. 'One of you thinks he's a Lothario, and the other one won't talk to me. That's just perfect.' I turned and followed Edward toward the house.

Bernardo called from behind us. 'Don't mistake Olaf, Anita. He likes women in his bed, and he's not nearly as particular as I am about how he gets them there. I'd be more careful of him than of me.'

'Edward,' I said.

He was just inside the door. He turned back and looked at me. 'Is Bernardo right? Is Olaf dangerous to me?'

'I can tell him about you what I told him about Donna.'

'What's that?' I asked.

We were all still in the doorway, not quite in the house. 'I told him if he touched her, I'd kill him.'

'If you come to my rescue, then he'll never work with me, never respect me,' I said.

Edward nodded. 'That's true.'

I sighed. 'I'll handle it on my own.'

Bernardo had moved up behind me, closer than I wanted him. I used the carry-on bag to accidentally move him back a step or two. 'Olaf has been in prison for rape.'

I looked at Edward and let my disbelief show on my face. 'Is he serious?'

Edward just nodded. His face had gone to its usual blankness. 'I told you in the car that I wouldn't have invited him if I'd known you were coming in on this.'

'But you didn't mention the rape conviction,' I said.

He shrugged. 'I should have.'

'What else should I know about good ol' Olaf?'

'That's it.' He looked behind me to Bernardo. 'Can you think of anything else she needs to know?'

'Only that he brags about the rape and what he did to her.'

'All right,' I said, 'you've both made your point. I only have one question.'

Edward just looked at me expectantly. Bernardo said, 'Shoot.'

'If I kill another one of your backups, do I owe you another favor?'

'Not if he deserves it.'

I dumped the bag on the doorsill. 'Shit, Edward, if you keep putting me together with fucking crazies and I keep having to defend myself, I'll be owing you favors until we're in our graves.'

Bernardo said, 'You're serious. You really killed his last backup.'

I glanced at him. 'Yeah, I'm serious. And I want permission to off Olaf if he gets out of hand, without having to owe Edward another pound of flesh.'

'Who'd you kill?' Bernardo asked.

'Harley,' Edward said.

'Shit, really?'

I walked up to Edward, invading his space, trying to read past the blank blue of his eyes. 'I want permission to kill Olaf if he gets out of hand, without owing you another favor.'

'And if I don't give it?' he asked, voice low.

'Drive me to a hotel because I'm not staying in a house with a bragging rapist if I can't kill him.'

Edward looked at me for a long slow moment, then gave a small nod. 'Done, as long as he's in this house. Outside the house, play nice.'

I would have argued, but it was probably the best I was going to get. Edward was very protective of his backups, and since I was one of them, I could appreciate the attitude. I picked up my bag from the floor, and said, 'Thank you. Now where's my room?'

'Oh, she's going to fit in just fine,' Bernardo said, and there was something in his voice that made me look at his face. His handsome face had thinned to a blankness, an emptiness that left his dark brown eyes like two burned holes in his face. It was as if he'd dropped his mask and let me see inside because I'd proven myself monster enough to handle it. Maybe I had. But I knew one thing: Olaf or Bernardo, either one, better not walk in their sleep.

18

There was a fireplace against the far wall, but it was narrow and white, formed of the same smooth whiteness as the walls. There was an animal skull mounted over the fireplace. I would have said deer, but the skull was heavier than that and the horns long and curving. Not a deer, but something close kin, and not from this country. The narrow mantlepiece held two tusks, as in elephant tusks, and smaller animal skulls. A low white couch faced the fireplace. A large block of unpolished marble sat to one side of it with a small white china lamp on it. A small alcove above the lamp held a huge chunk of white crystal. There was a black lacquered table against the far wall between two doorways. A second larger lamp sat on the table. Two chairs sat facing each other in front of the fireplace. They had carved arms with winged lions on the arms and legs. They were black leather and looked vaguely Egyptian.

'Your room is this way,' Edward said.

'No,' I said, 'I've waited a long time to see your home. Don't rush me.'

'Mind if I take your luggage through to your room while you explore?'

'Help yourself,' I said.

'Gracious of you,' he said, and put an extra touch of sarcasm into his voice.

'Don't mention it,' I said.

Edward picked up both my bags, and said, 'Come on, Bernardo. You can get dressed.'

'You didn't let us look around on our own,' Bernardo said.

'You didn't ask.'

'It's one of the joys of being a girl and not a guy,' I said. 'If I'm curious, I just ask.'

They went through a far door, though the room was small enough that 'far' was relative. There was wood to one side of the fireplace in a woven basket of pale, almost white reeds. I ran my hand down the smooth coolness of the black marble coffee table that sat nearest the fireplace. There was a black vase on the table full of what looked like either small wild flowers or large black-eyed-Susans. The deep yellow gold and the brown center didn't really match anything in the room. Even the Navajo rug that took up most of the floor was in shades of black, white, and gray. There were more flowers in an alcove between the far doorways. The alcove was large enough to be a window except it didn't look out on anything. The flowers spilled from the opening like a mass of gold and brown water, a huge riotous bouquet.

When Edward came back into the room, without Bernardo, I was sitting on the white couch with my feet stretched out underneath the coffee table. I had my hands clasped over my stomach and was trying to picture a roaring fire and a cold winter evening. But somehow the fireplace looked too clean, too sterile.

He sat down beside me, shaking his head. 'Happy?'

I nodded.

'What do you think?'

'It's not a restful room,' I said, 'and for Heaven's sake look at all the wall space. Get some paintings.'

'I like it this way.' He had settled down on the couch beside me, feet stretched out, hands on his stomach. He was mimicking me, but even that couldn't ruin my mood. I was going to see every room in detail before I left. I could have tried to be cool about it, but I didn't sweat being cool with Edward. We'd moved beyond that in our strange friendship. I really wasn't trying to play king of the hill with Edward. The fact that he was still playing the game with me just made him look silly. Though I hoped the game-playing was over for this trip.

'Maybe I'll get you a painting for Christmas,' I said.

'We don't buy Christmas presents for each other,' Edward said.

We were both staring at the fireplace as if visualizing that make-believe fire. 'Maybe I'll start. One of those big-eyed children or a clown on velvet.'

'I won't hang it if I don't like it.'

I glanced at him. 'Unless it's from Donna.'

He was very still suddenly. 'Yes.'

'Donna added the flowers, didn't she,' I said.

'Yes,' he said.

'White lilies, or an orchid maybe, but not wild flowers, not in this room.'

'She thinks they brighten up the place.'

'Oh, they do,' I said.

He sighed.

'Maybe I'll tell her how much you love those pictures of dogs playing poker and she can buy you some prints.'

'She wouldn't believe it,' he said.

'No, but I bet I could come up with something that she would believe that you'd hate just as much.'

He stared at me. 'You wouldn't.'

'I might.'

'This sounds like the opening to blackmail. What do you want?'

I stared at him, studying that blank face. 'So you're admitting that Donna and her crew are important enough for you so that blackmail would work.'

He just looked at me with those pitiless eyes, but the blank face wasn't enough now. There was a chink in his armor big enough to drive a truck through. 'They're hostages, Edward, if anyone ever thinks of it.'

He looked away from me, closing his eyes. 'Do you really think you're telling me something I haven't thought about?'

'My apologies, you're right. Like teaching your grandmother to suck eggs.'

'What?' He turned and was half-laughing.

I shrugged. 'Just an old saying. It means that I'm lecturing someone who taught me what I'm lecturing about.'

'And what have I taught you?' he asked, humor dying, face turning serious.

'You can't take all the credit. My mother's death started the lesson early, but I learned that if you care for people, they can die. If other people know you care for someone, they can use that person against you. You ask why I don't date humans. Hostages, Edward. My life is just too damn violent for cannon fodder to be near and dear to my heart. You taught me that.'

'And now I've broken the rule,' he said, voice soft.

'Yep,' I said.

'And where does that leave Richard and Jean-Claude?' he asked.

'Oh, I make you uncomfortable and now it's my turn.'

'Just answer the question.'

I thought about it for a second, or two, then answered truthfully, because I'd spent a lot of the last six months thinking about it, about them. 'Jean-Claude is so *not* cannon fodder. If anyone I've ever met knows how to take care of himself, it's Jean-Claude. I guess you can't be a four-hundred-year-old anything without being a survivor.'

'And Richard?' Edward was watching my face as he asked, studying me as I so often studied him, and I wondered for the first time if my face was empty more often than it was full, if I hid my emotions, my thoughts, even when I wasn't meaning to. How can you really tell what your own face shows?

'Richard can survive a shotgun blast to the chest with non-silver shot. Can you say the same about Donna?' It was blunt, maybe too blunt, but it was truthful.

His eyes shut down like curtains had been pulled, hiding, hiding. There was no one home. It was the face he wore when he killed sometimes, though sometimes when he killed he wore the most joyous expression I ever saw on his face.

'You told me that they huddle around your humanity. Are you saying you huddle around their monstrousness?' he asked.

I looked into that so carefully unreadable face, and nodded. 'Yeah, it took me a while to realize it and longer to accept it. I've lost enough people in my life, Edward. I'm tired of it. The chances are very good that both the boys will outlive me.' I held up my hand before he could say it. 'I know that Jean-Claude isn't alive. Trust me. I probably know that better than you do.'

'You guys look serious. Talking about the case?' Bernardo walked into the room wearing blue jeans and nothing else. He'd tied all that hair back in a loose braid. He padded barefoot towards us, and it made my chest tight. It was one of Richard's favorite ways to walk around the house. He only put shoes and a shirt on to go out or if company was coming over.

I watched a very handsome man walk towards me, but I wasn't really seeing him. I was seeing Richard, missing him. I sighed and struggled to sit up straighter on the couch. Call it a hunch but I was betting that Edward didn't have heart to heart talks with Bernardo, at least not about Donna.

Edward had also straightened. 'No, we weren't talking about the case,' he said.

Bernardo looked from one to the other of us with a smile playing on his lips. But his eyes didn't match. He didn't like the serious air and it not being about the case, and him not knowing what it was about. I'd have asked. Edward wouldn't have told me, but I'd have still asked. Sometimes it was good to be a girl.

'You said you had the files on the Santa Fe cases,' I said.

Edward nodded, standing. 'I'll bring them to the dining room. Bernardo, show her the way.'

'My pleasure,' he said.

Edward said, 'Treating Anita like a girl would be a mistake, Bernardo. It would piss me off to have to replace you this late in the game.' With that, Edward left through the far right door. There was a wash of night air and a buzz of insects before he closed the door behind him.

Bernardo looked at me, shaking his head. 'I've never heard Edward talk about any woman the way he talks about you.'

I raised eyebrows at him. 'Meaning?'

'Dangerous. He talks about you like you're dangerous.' Intelligence showed in his solid brown eyes, an intelligence that had been hiding behind his good looks and charming smile. An intelligence that didn't show when he had his monster face on. For the first time I thought that it might be a mistake to underestimate him. He was more than just a gun for hire. How much more remained to be seen.

'What, I'm supposed to say I am dangerous?'

'Are you?' he asked, still studying me with that intense expression.

I smiled at him. 'Well, you get to go down the hall first.'

He tilted his head to one side. 'Why don't we go together, side by side?'

'Because the hall's too narrow, or am I wrong?'

'You're not wrong, but do you really think I'll shoot you in the back?' He spread his arms wide and turned a slow circle. 'Do I look armed?' He was smiling when he faced me again, charming.

I didn't buy it. 'Unless I run my hands through all that thick hair and down your pants, I don't know you're unarmed.'

The smile faded a touch. 'Most people don't think about the hair.' Which meant that he did have something hidden away. If he was truly unarmed, he'd have teased and offered me a chance to search.

'It's got to be a blade. The hair isn't thick enough to hide a gun, not even a derringer,' I said.

He reached behind his head and drew out a slender blade that he'd woven through his hair. He held it up, then flipped it hilt to blade, back and forth, dancing it through his long slender fingers.

'Isn't it an ethnic stereotype that you're good with a knife?' I asked.

He laughed, but not like it was funny. He bounced the blade once more in his hand, and it made me tense. I was still standing behind the couch, but knew that if he were really good, I'd never get behind cover or draw my gun in time. He was just too damn close.

'I can cut my hair and put on a suit, but I'm still going to be an Indian to most people. If you can't change it, might as well embrace it.' He slipped the knife back into his hair, making it look smooth and easy. I'd have had to use a mirror and even then I'd have probably cut off half my hair.

'You try to play in corporate America?' I asked.

'Yeah,' he said.

'So now you don't do corporate stuff.'

'I still play in corporate America. I protect the suits that want flashy muscle. Something exotic to impress their friends about what a big shot they are.'

'You do the knife act on command?' I asked.

He shrugged. 'Sometimes.'

'I hope it pays well,' I said.

He smiled. 'It either pays well or I don't do it. I may be their token Indian, but I'm a rich token Indian. If you're as good as Edward thinks you are, you'd do better at bodyguard work than I do.'

'Why?' I asked.

'Because the majority of protective work wants their bodyguard to blend in. They want you not to be flashy or exotic. You're pretty, but it's more a girl-next-door pretty, nothing too beautiful.'

I agreed with him, but said, 'Oh, that won you a lot of brownie points.'

'You've pretty much told me I don't have a chance so why should I bother lying?'

I had to smile. 'Point taken.'

'You may be a little dark around the edges, but you can pass for white,' Bernardo said.

'I'm not passing, Bernardo. I am white. My mother just happened to be Mexican.'

'You got your father's skin?' he asked.

I nodded. 'Yeah, what of it?'

'No one's ever got up in your face about it, have they?'

I thought about it. My stepmother's hurried comments to strangers that I was not hers. No, I wasn't adopted. I was her stepdaughter. Me and Cinderella. The really rude ones would ask, 'What was her mother?'

Judith would always answer quickly, 'Her mother was Mexican.' Though lately it was Hispanic-American. No one could accuse Judith of not being politically correct on the issue of race. My mother had died long before people had worried about political correctness being in vogue. If someone asked, she always said proudly, 'Mexican.' If it was good enough for my mother, it was good enough for me.

That memory I didn't share. I'd never really shared it with my father. I wasn't about to start with a stranger. I chose another memory that didn't hurt quite so much. 'I was engaged once until his mother found out my mother had been Mexican. He was blond and blue-eyed, the epitome of WASP breeding. My future-in-law didn't like the idea of me darkening her family tree.' That was a brief, unemotional way to say some very painful things. He had been my first love, my first lover. I thought he was everything to me, but I wasn't everything to him. I'd never let myself fall so completely into anyone's arms before or since.

Jean-Claude and Richard were both still paying the bill for that first love.

'Do you think of yourself as white?'

I nodded. 'Yeah. Now ask me if I think I'm white enough?'

Bernardo looked at me. 'Are you white enough?'

'Not according to some people.'

'Like who?'

'Like none of your damn business.'

He spread his hands. 'Sorry, didn't mean to step on your toes.'

'Yes, you did,' I said.

'You think so?'

'Yeah,' I said. 'I think you're jealous.'

'Of what?'

'That I can pass and you can't.'

He opened his mouth and emotions flowed over his face like water; anger, humor, denial. He finally settled on a smile, but it wasn't a happy one. 'You really are a bitch, aren't you?'

I nodded. 'You don't pull on my chain and I won't pull on yours.'

'Deal,' he said. The smile flashed wider. 'Now, allow me to escort your lily white ass to the dining room.'

I shook my head. 'Lead on, tall, dark, and studly, as long as I get to watch your ass while we walk down the hall.'

'Only if you promise to tell me how you like the view.'

I widened my eyes. 'You mean give you a critique on your butt?'

He nodded and the smile looked happy now.

'Are you this big an egotist or just trying to embarrass me?'

'Guess.'

'Both,' I said.

The smile spread to a grin. 'You are as smart as you look.'

'Just get moving, Romeo. Edward doesn't like to be kept waiting.'

'Damn straight.'

We went down the short hallway; him leading, me following.

He put an extra glide into his walk, and yes, I watched the show. Call it a hunch, but I was betting Bernardo would actually ask me for the critique, probably out loud in front of other people. Why is it when you have a sure thing to bet on, there's never anyone around to take your money?

19

There were more heavy dark beams in the dining room, more off-white walls. If the chairs were a clue, the dining table was black and silver. But the table was hidden under a tablecloth that looked like another Navajo rug. Though this one had some color, dull red stripes running with black and white. There was even a black metal candelabrum with red candles in the middle of the table. It was nice to see some color that hadn't been added by Donna. It had taken me years to break Jean-Claude of his fixation on black and white decor. Since I was just Edward's friend and nothing more, it wasn't my business how he decorated.

There was a fireplace in the corner nearly identical to the one in the living room except for a black piece of wood set into the white stucco. I would have called it a mantel, but it didn't stick out that far. The true mantel was decorated in more red candles of every shape and size, some sitting with their waxy bottoms directly on the mantel, some in black metal holders. There were two round ones that stuck up above the rest on the kind of holders where you spear the candle to hold it into place. A silver-edged mirror that looked antique was hung behind the candles so that when they were burned, you'd get their reflection. Strange, I hadn't thought Edward was the candlelight type.

There were no windows in the room, just a molded doorway leading out the other side. The walls were utterly white and utterly blank. Somehow the lack of decoration made the room seem more claustrophobic rather than less.

A man appeared in the far doorway. He had to bend over to

keep his bald head from smacking the top of the door. He was taller than Dolph, who was six foot eight, which meant he was the tallest person I'd ever met. The only hair on his head was heavy black eyebrows and a shadow of beard along his chin and cheeks. He was wearing the draw-string bottoms of men's pajamas. They were black and looked satin. He had on slippers, the kind that have no heels and always seem in danger of falling off. Olaf, because who else could it be, moved in the slippers like they were part of his flesh. Once he got over stooping through the door, he moved like a well-oiled machine, muscles rippling under his pale skin. He was tall, but there wasn't an ounce of fat on him. It was all hard, lean, muscle. He walked around the table towards us, and I moved without thinking to keep the table between us.

He stopped moving. I stopped moving. We stared at each other across the table. Bernardo was at the end of the table, nearest the door, watching us. He looked worried. Probably wondering if he was supposed to come to my rescue if I needed one. Or maybe he just didn't like the tension level in the room. I know I didn't.

If I hadn't moved away as he walked in, would the tension level have been lower? Maybe. But I'd learned long ago to trust my gut, and my gut said, to stay out of reach. But I could try and be nice. 'You must be Olaf. I didn't catch your last name. I'm Anita Blake.'

His eyes were dark brown set deep in the bones of his face like twin caves, as if even in daylight his eyes would be shadowed. He just looked at me. It was as if I had not spoken.

I tried again. I'm nothing if not persistent. 'Hello, Earth to Olaf.' I stared into his face, and he never blinked, never acknowledged my words in any way. If he hadn't been glaring at me, I'd have said he was ignoring me.

I glanced at Bernardo, but kept my gaze on the big man across the table. 'What gives, Bernardo? He does talk, right?'

Bernardo nodded. 'He talks.'

I turned my full attention back to Olaf. 'You're just not going to talk to me, is that it?'

He just glared at me.

'You think not hearing the dulcet sounds of your voice is some kind of punishment? Most men are such jabber mouths. Silence is nice for a change. Thanks for being so considerate, Olaf, baby.' I made the last word into two very separate syllables.

'I am not your baby.' The voice was deep and matched that vast chest. There was also a guttural accent underneath all that clear English, German maybe.

'It speaks. Be still my heart.'

Olaf frowned. 'I did not agree with your being included on this hunt. We do not need help from a woman, any woman.'

'Well, Olaf, honey, you need help from someone because the three of you haven't come up with shit on the mutilations.'

A flush of color crept up his neck into his face. 'Do not call me that.'

'What? Honey?'

He nodded.

'You prefer sweetheart, honeybun, pumpkin?'

The color spread from pink to red, and was getting darker. 'Do not use terms of endearment to me. I am no one's sweetheart.'

I'd been all set to make another scathing remark, but that stopped me, and I thought of something better. 'How sad for you.'

'What are you talking about?'

'How sad that you are no one's sweetheart.'

The color that had been fading from his face flushed dark now, almost as if he were blushing. 'Are you feeling sorry for me?' His voice rose a notch, not yelling but like the low growl of a dog just before it bites. As he got more emotional, the accent got thicker. Very German, very lowland. Grandmother Blake was from Baden-Baden, on the border between Germany and France, but Great-uncle Otto had been from Hapsburg. I couldn't be a hundred percent sure, but it sounded like the same accent.

'Everyone should be someone's sweetheart,' I said, but my voice was mild. I wasn't angry. I was baiting him, and I shouldn't have. My only excuse was that all the talk of rape had made me scared of him, and I didn't like that. So I was doing something that was actually very masculine. I was pulling the tail of the beast to make myself feel braver. Stupid. The moment I realized why I was doing it, I tried to stop.

'I am no one's fool, and that means I am no one's sweetheart.' He spoke carefully, enunciating each word but his accent was thick enough to walk on. He had started to move slowly around the table, muscles tense like some big predatory cat.

I flashed my jacket on the left side, showing the gun. He stopped moving forward, but his face was furious. 'Let's start over, Olaf,' I said. 'Edward and Bernardo here told me what a big bad guy you were and that made me nervous, which made me defensive. When I'm defensive, I'm usually a pain in the ass. Sorry about that. Let's pretend that I wasn't being a smart ass, and you weren't being all big and bad, and start over.'

He stilled. That was the only word I had for it. The quivering tension in his muscles eased like water running downhill. But it wasn't gone, just shoved away somewhere. I had a glimpse into Olaf. He operated from a great dark pit of rage. That it was directed mostly at women was accidental. The rage needed some target or he'd turn into one of those people that drive their cars through restaurant windows and start shooting strangers.

'Edward has been most insistent that you are to be here, but nothing you will say can make me like it.' His words were pulling free of the accent as he regained control of his temper.

I nodded. 'Are you from Hapsburg?'

He blinked, and for an instant puzzlement replaced the sullenness. 'What?'

'Are you from Hapsburg?'

He seemed to think about it for a second or two, then gave a small nod.

'I thought I recognized the accent.'

The scowl was back full force. 'You are an expert on accents?' He managed to sound sarcastic.

'No. My Uncle Otto was from Hapsburg.'

He blinked again, and the scowl wilted around the edges. 'You are not German.' He sounded very sure.

'My father's family is; from Baden-Baden on the edge of the Black Forest, but Uncle Otto was from Hapsburg.

'You said only your uncle had the accent.'

'By the time I came along, most of the family, except for my grandmother, had been in this country so long there was no accent, but Uncle Otto never lost his.'

'He's dead now.' Olaf made it half question, half statement.

I nodded.

'How did he die?'

'Grandma Blake says Aunt Gertrude nagged him to death.'

His lips twitched. 'Women are tyrants if a man allows it.' His voice was a touch softer now.

'That's true of men or women. If one partner is weak, the other partner moves in and takes charge.'

'Nature abhors a vacuum,' Bernardo said.

We glanced at him. I don't know what the expressions were on our faces, but Bernardo held his hands up and said, 'Sorry to interrupt.'

Olaf and I went back to looking at each other. He was close enough now that I might not be able to draw the Browning in time. But if I moved away now, all my peace-making efforts would be for nothing. He'd either be insulted or see it as weakness on my part. Neither reaction would be helpful. So I stood my ground and tried not to look as tense as I felt, because no matter how calm I sounded, my stomach was in one hard knot. I had one chance to make this work. If I blew it, then the rest of this visit was going to be an armed camp, and we needed to be solving the crime, not fighting each other.

'You are either a leader or being led,' Olaf said. 'Which are you?'

'I'll follow if someone's worth following.'

'And who decides, Anita Blake, who is worth following?'

I had to smile. 'I do.'

His lips twitched again. 'And if Edward put me in charge, would you follow me?'

'I trust Edward's judgment, so yeah. But let me ask you the same question. Would you follow me if Edward put me in charge?'

He flinched. 'No.'

I nodded. 'Great, we know where we stand.'

'And where is that?' he asked.

'I'm sort of goal-oriented, Olaf. I came down here to solve a crime and I'm going to do that. If that means at some point taking orders from you, so be it. If Edward puts me in charge of you, and you don't like it, take it up with him.'

'Just like a woman to put the responsibility off on a man's shoulders.'

I counted to ten, and shrugged. 'You talk like your opinion matters to me, Olaf. I don't give a damn what you think of me.'

'Women always care what men think of them.'

I laughed then. 'You know I was starting to feel insulted, but you are just too funny.' I meant it.

He leaned towards me trying to use his height to intimidate. It was impressive, but I've been the smallest kid around for as long as I can remember. 'I will not take it up with Edward. I will take it up with you. Or don't you have the balls to stand up to me?' He gave a harsh laugh. 'Oh, I forgot, you don't have balls.' He reached for me in a quick motion. I think he meant to grope me, but I didn't wait to see. I threw myself backward into the floor and was drawing the Browning before my butt hit the floor. Drawing the gun meant I didn't have time to slap my hands down and take the impact the way you were supposed to. I hit hard and felt the shock all the way up my spine.

He'd drawn a blade as long as his forearm from somewhere. The blade was coming down, and the Browning wasn't quite pointed at his chest. It would be a race to see who drew first blood, but it was almost a guarantee that we'd both bleed. Everything slowed down to that crystalline vision, as if I had all the time in the world to point the gun, to avoid the blade, and at the same time everything was happening too fast. Too fast to stop it or change it.

Edward's voice cut through the room. 'Stop it! The first one to draw blood, I will personally shoot.'

We froze in mid-action. Olaf blinked, and it was as if time had resumed normal flow. Maybe, just maybe, we weren't going to kill each other tonight. But I had the gun pointed at his chest, and his hand was still upraised with the knife. Though knife seemed too small a word; sword was more like it. Where had he pulled it from?

'Drop the knife, Olaf,' Edward said

'Have her put up the gun, first.' I met those hard brown eyes and saw a hatred there like what I'd seen earlier in Lieutenant Marks' face. They both hated me for being things that I could not change: one for an innate God-given talent, and the other because I was a woman. Funny, how one unreasoning hatred looks so much like another.

I kept the gun very steadily pointed at his chest. I'd let all the air go out of my body, and was waiting, waiting for Olaf to decide what we'd be doing tonight. Either we'd be fighting crime, or we'd be digging a grave, maybe two if he was good enough. I knew what my vote was, but I also knew that the final vote wasn't mine. It wasn't even Olaf's. It was his hatred's.

'You drop the knife, and Anita will put up the gun,' Edward said.

'Or she will shoot me while I'm unarmed.'

'She won't do that.'

'She is afraid of me now,' Olaf said.

'Maybe,' Edward said, 'but she's more afraid of me.'

Olaf looked down at me, a glimmer of puzzlement rising up through the hatred and anger. 'I am going to shove this blade inside her. She fears me.'

'Tell him, Anita.'

I hoped I knew what Edward wanted me to say. 'I will shoot you twice in the chest. You may get a slice of me before you fall to the ground. If you're really good, you might even slit my throat, but you'll still be dead.' I hoped he made up his mind soon because it was awkward holding a shooting stance while sitting on your butt. I was going to get a crick in my back if I didn't get to move soon. The fear was fading, leaving only a dull emptiness behind. I was tired, and the night was still young. Hours to go before I'd sleep. I was tired of Olaf. I had a feeling if I didn't shoot him tonight, I'd get another chance.

'Who are you more afraid of, Anita — Olaf or me?' Edward asked.

I kept my gaze on Olaf and said, 'You, Edward.'

'Tell him why.'

It sounded like a teacher telling his student what to say, but from Edward I'd take it. 'Because you would have never let me get the drop on you like this. You would have never let your emotions compromise your safety.'

Olaf blinked at me. 'You do not fear me?' He made it a question and seemed disappointed. There was something almost little-boyish about his disappointment.

'I'm not afraid of anything I can kill,' I said.

'Edward can be killed,' Olaf said.

'Yes, but can he be killed by anyone in this room? That's the question.'

Olaf looked at me, puzzled now more than angry. He began to lower the blade, slowly.

Edward said, 'Drop it,' in a quiet voice.

Olaf dropped the blade to the floor. It hit with a ringing clang.

I got to my knees and then scuttled backwards along the edge of the table, lowering the gun as I moved. I got to my feet at the head of the table near Bernardo. I looked at him. 'Move over around by Edward.'

'I didn't do anything,' he said.

'Just do it, Bernardo. I need a little space right now.'

He opened his mouth as if to argue, but Edward cut him off. 'Do it.'

Bernardo did it.

When they were all at the other end of the room, I put the gun up.

Edward had an armful of cardboard box. It was brimming over with files. He set it down on the tabletop.

'You didn't even have a gun,' Olaf said.

'I didn't need one,' Edward said.

Olaf pushed past Edward to the hallway beyond. I hoped he was going to pack and leave, but doubted we'd get that lucky. I hadn't known Olaf for an hour, and I already knew why he was no one's sweetie.

20

A murder always breeds a lot of paper, but a serial murder, you can drown in the paperwork. Edward, Bernardo, and I were swimming upstream. We'd been at it for about an hour, and Olaf hadn't come back. Maybe he had decided to pack up and go home. Though I hadn't heard any doors or cars, but I wasn't sure how soundproof the house was. Edward didn't seem bothered by Olaf's absence, so I didn't give it much attention either. I had read one report through back to front. One to get an overview and see if anything jumped out at me. One thing did. There were slivers of obsidian in the cut-up bodies. An obsidian blade, maybe. Though we were in the wrong part of the world for it, or were we?

'Did the Aztecs ever get up this far?' I asked.

Edward didn't treat it like a weird question. 'Yes.'

'So I'm not the first one to point out the obsidian clue might mean Aztec magic?'

'No,' he said.

'Thanks for telling me that we're looking for some sort of Aztec monster.'

'The local cops talked to the leading expert in the area. Professor Dallas couldn't come up with any deity or folklore that would account for these murders or the mutilations.'

'You sound like you're quoting. Is there a report around here somewhere?'

He looked out over the mound of papers. 'Somewhere.'

'Isn't there an Aztec deity that the priests skinned someone as an offering, or is that Mayan?'

He shrugged. 'The good professor couldn't make a connection. That's why I didn't tell you. The police have been looking into the Aztec angle for weeks. Nothing. I brought you down here to think different thoughts, not follow old ones.'

'I'd like to talk to the professor all the same. If that's okay with you.' I made sure he got the sarcasm.

'Look at the reports first, try to find what we've missed, then I'll introduce you to Professor Dallas.'

I looked at him, trying to read behind those baby blues and failing as usual. 'When do I get to see the professor?'

'Tonight.'

That raised my eyebrows. 'Gee, that is quick, especially since you think I'm wasting our time.'

'She spends most nights in a club near Albuquerque.'

'She, being Professor Dallas,' I said.

He nodded.

'What's so special about this club?'

'If your career was Aztec history and mythology, wouldn't you just love to interview a real live Aztec?'

'A live ancient Aztec in Albuquerque?' I didn't try and keep the surprise out of my voice. 'How?'

'Well, maybe not live,' he said.

'A vampire,' I said.

He nodded again.

'Has this Aztec vamp got a name?'

'The Master of the City calls herself Itzpapalotl.'

'Isn't that like an Aztec goddess?' I asked.

'Yes, it is.'

'Talk about delusions of grandeur.' I was watching his face, trying to catch a hint. 'Did the cops talk to the vamp?'

'Yes.'

'And?'

'She wasn't helpful.'

'You didn't believe her, did you?'

'Neither did the cops. But she was on stage at her club during at least three of the murders.'

'So she's cleared,' I said.

'Which is why I want you to read the reports first, Anita. We've missed something. Maybe you'll find out what, but not if you keep looking for Aztec bogeymen. We raised that rock, and as much as the police would like it to be the Master of the City, it isn't.'

'So why the offer to take me down to see her tonight?'

'Just because she's not doing the murders, doesn't mean she can't have information that could help us.'

'The police questioned her.' I made it a statement.

'Yeah, but funny how vampires don't like talking to the police, and how much they like talking to you.'

'You know you could have just told me that we were seeing the Master Vamp of Albuquerque tonight.'

'I wasn't going to take you down there tonight unless you got bitchy about it. I was actually hoping you wouldn't make the Aztec angle until you'd read everything first.'

'Why?'

'I told you, it was a blind alley. We need new ideas. Things we haven't thought of, not things the police have already crossed off the list.'

'But you haven't crossed this Itza-whatever off your list, have you?'

'The goddess will let you call her by her English translation, Obsidian Butterfly. It's also the name of her club.'

'You think she's involved, don't you?'

'I think she knows something that she might share with a necromancer, but not a vampire executioner.'

'So I go down off duty, so to speak.'

'So to speak.'

'I'm Jean-Claude's human servant, one third of his little

triumvirate of power. If I go visiting the Master of this City without police credentials, then I'll have to play vamp politics. I hate vamp politics.'

Edward looked out over the table. 'When you've read your hundredth witness report tonight, you may change your mind. Even vampire politics look good after reading enough of this shit.'

'Gee, Edward, you sound almost bitter.'

'I'm the monster expert, Anita, and I don't have a fucking clue.'

We looked at each other, and again I had the sense of his fear, his helplessness, things that Edward just didn't feel. Or so I'd thought.

Bernardo came in with a tray of coffees. He must have caught something in the air because he said, 'Did I miss something?'

'No,' Edward said, and he went back to the papers in his lap.

I stood and started sorting papers. 'You haven't missed anything yet.'

'I just love being lied to.'

'We're not lying,' I said.

'Then why is the tension level so high in here?'

'Shut up, Bernardo,' Edward said.

Bernardo didn't take it as an insult. He just shut up and handed out the coffee.

I sorted out all the witness reports I could find, then spent the next three hours reading them. I'd read one report back to front and found out nothing the police and Edward hadn't known weeks ago. Now I was looking for something new, something that the police, Edward, the experts they'd called in, nobody had found. It sounded egotistical, but Edward seemed sure I'd find it, whatever it was. Though I was beginning to wonder if it was confidence in me or sheer desperation on Edward's part that made him so sure I'd find something. I'd give it my best shot, and that was all I could do.

I looked down at several stacks of witness reports and settled in to read. I know most people read each report in full, or almost in full, then move to the next, but in a serial crime you were looking for a pattern. On serial murders I'd learned to divide the files up into parts: all the witness statements, then all the forensic reports, then the pictures of the crime scene, etc. . . . Sometimes I did the pictures first, but I was putting it off. I'd seen enough in the hospital to make me squeamish. So the pictures could wait, and I could still do legitimate work on the case without having to see all the horrors. Procrastination with a purpose, what could be better?

Bernardo kept making us all coffee and continued to play host, going back and forth when the coffee ran low, offering food, though we both declined. When he brought me my umpteenth cup of coffee, I finally asked, 'Not that I'm not grateful, but you didn't strike me as the domestic type, Bernardo. Why the perfect host routine? It's not even your house.'

He took the question as an invitation to move closer to my chair until his jean-clad thigh was touching the arm, but it wasn't touching me so that was fine. 'You want to ask Edward to go for coffee?'

I looked across the table at Edward. He didn't bother to look up from the papers in his hands. I smiled. 'No, I was more thinking I'd get my own.'

Bernardo turned and leaned his butt against the table, arms crossed over his chest. Muscles played in his arms as if he were flexing just a bit for my benefit. I didn't think he was even aware he was doing it, as if it were habit.

'Truthfully?' he asked.

I looked up at him and sipped the coffee he'd brought me. 'That would be nice.'

'I've read the reports more than once. I don't want to read them again. I'm tired of playing detectives and wish we could just go kill something, or at least fight something.'

'Me, too,' Edward said. He was watching us now with cool blue eyes. 'But we have to know what we're fighting, and the answer to that is in here somewhere.' He motioned at the mounds of papers.

Bernardo shook his head. 'Then why haven't we, or the police, found the answer in all this paper?' He ran his finger down the nearest stack. 'I don't think paperwork is going to catch this bastard.'

I smiled up at him. 'You're just bored.'

He looked down at me, a little startled expression on his face, then he laughed, head back, mouth wide as if he were howling at the moon. 'You haven't known me long enough to know me that well.' Laughter was still sparkling in his brown eyes, and I wished it were a different pair of brown eyes. My chest was suddenly tight with missing Richard. I looked down at the papers in my lap, not sure if it would show in my eyes. If my eyes showed sorrow, I didn't want Bernardo to see it. If my eyes showed longing, I didn't want him to misinterpret it.

'Are you bored, Bernardo?' Edward asked.

Bernardo turned at the waist so he could see Edward with a minimum of movement. It put his bare chest facing me. 'No women, no television, nothing to kill, bored, bored, bored.'

I found myself staring at his chest. I had an urge to rise up out of my chair, spill the papers to the floor and run my tongue over his chest. The image was so strong, I had to close my eyes. I had feelings like this around Richard and Jean-Claude, but not around strangers. Why was Bernardo affecting me like this?

'Are you all right?' He was bending over me, face so close that his face filled my entire vision.

I jerked back, pushing the chair and rising to my feet. The chair crashed to the floor, papers spilled everywhere. 'Shit,' I said with feeling. I picked up the chair.

He bent down to help pick up the papers. His bare back made a firm curved line as he started shoveling the papers back into a pile. I watched the way the small muscles in his lower back worked, fascinated by it.

I stepped away from him. Edward was watching me from across the table. His gaze was heavy, as if he knew what I was thinking, feeling. I knew it wasn't true, but he knew me better than most. I didn't want anyone to know that I seemed to be unwarrantedly attracted to Bernardo. It was too embarrassing.

Edward said, 'Leave us alone for a while, Bernardo.'

Bernardo stood with a bundle of papers, looking from one to the other of us. 'Did I just miss something?'

'Yes,' Edward said. 'Now get out.'

Bernardo looked at me. He looked a question at me, but I gave nothing back. I could feel my face unreadable and empty. Bernardo sighed and handed me the papers. 'How long?'

'I'll let you know,' Edward said.

'Wonderful. I'll be in my room when Daddy decides to let me come out.' He stalked through the nearest door where Olaf had vanished through.

'No one likes being treated like a child,' I said.

'It's the only way to deal with Bernardo,' Edward said. His gaze was very steady on my face, and he looked way too serious for comfort.

I started sorting the papers in my hands. I used the cleared space on the table that I'd made hours ago when I was still leaning over the table instead of slumping in the chair to read. I concentrated on sorting and didn't look up until I felt him beside me.

I looked then and found his eyes weren't blank. They were intense, but I still couldn't read them. 'You said you hadn't been dating either of the guys for six months.'

I nodded.

'Have you been dating anyone else?' he asked.

I shook my head.

'No sex, then,' he said.

I shook my head again. My heart was beating faster. I so did not want him to figure this out.

'Why not?' he asked.

I looked away then, unable to meet his eyes. 'I don't have any moral high ground to preach from anymore, Edward, but I don't do casual sex, you know that.'

'You're jumping out of your skin every time Bernardo comes near you.'

Heat climbed up my face. 'Is it that noticeable?'

'Only to me,' he said.

I was grateful for that. I spoke without looking at him. 'I don't understand it. He's a bastard. Even my hormones usually have better taste than that.'

Edward was leaning against the table, arms crossed over his white shirt. It was exactly how Bernardo had been sitting, but it didn't move me, and I didn't think it was just the shirt. Edward just did not affect me in that way and never had.

'He's handsome, and you're horny.'

The heat that had been fading, flared until it felt like my skin would burn. 'Don't say it that way.'

'It's the truth.'

I looked at him then, and let the anger show in my eyes. 'Damn you.'

'Maybe your body knows what you need.'

I widened eyes at him. 'Meaning what?'

'A good uncomplicated fuck. That's what I mean.' He still looked calm, unmoved as if he'd said something entirely different.

'What are you saying?'

'Fuck Bernardo. Give your body what it needs. You don't have to go back to the monsters to get laid.'

'I cannot believe you said that to me.'

'Why not? If you were having sex with someone else, wouldn't it be easier to forget Richard and Jean-Claude? Isn't that part of their hold on you, especially the vampire. Admit it, Anita. If you weren't celibate, you wouldn't be missing them as much.'

I opened my mouth to protest, closed it, and thought about what he'd said. Was he right? Was part of the reason I was still mooning over them the lack of sex? Yeah, I guess it was, but it wasn't just that. 'I miss the sex, yeah, but I miss the intimacy, Edward. I miss looking at them both and knowing they're mine. Knowing I can have every inch of them. I miss Sunday after church and having Richard stay over to watch old movies. I miss watching Jean-Claude watch me eat a meal.' I shook my head. 'I miss them, Edward.'

'Your problem, Anita, is that you wouldn't know an uncomplicated fuck if it bit you on the ass.'

I wasn't sure whether to smile or be mad, so my voice was a little amused and a little angry. 'And your relationship with Donna is so uncomplicated?'

'It was at the beginning,' he said. 'Can you say that about either of yours?'

I shook my head. 'I'm not a casual person, Edward, not in anything.'

He sighed. 'I know that. When you give your friendship, it's for life. When you hate someone, it's forever. When you say you're going to kill someone, you do it. One of the things making you squirm about your boys is the fact that for you, love should be forever.'

'And what's wrong with that?'

He shook his head. 'Sometimes I forget how young you are.'

'And what does that mean?'

'It means you complicate your life, Anita.' He raised a hand before I could say it, and said it for me. 'I know I've screwed up with Donna, but I went into it meaning to be casual, meaning it to just be part of the act. You always go into everything like it's life or death. Only life and death are life and death.'

'And you think that sleeping with Bernardo would fix all that.'

'It'd be a start,' he said.

I shook my head. 'No.'

'Your final word?' he asked.

'Yes,' I said.

'Fine, I won't bring it up again.'

'Great,' I said and looked into that blank, Edward face. 'Being with Donna has made you more personal, more warm and fuzzy. I'm not comfortable with the new Edward.'

'Neither am I,' he said.

Edward went back to his side of the table, and we both started reading again. Usually, silence between us was companionable and not strained. But this quiet was full of unsaid advice: me to him about Donna, and him to me about the boys. Edward and I playing Dear Abby to each other. It would have been funny if it hadn't been so sad.

21

An hour later, I'd finished the witness reports. I stretched my lower back while still sitting in the chair, just bending slowly at the waist until my hands touched the floor or almost touched the floor. Three stretches, and I could press my palms flat to the floor. Better. I got up and checked my watch. Midnight. I felt stiff and strange, estranged from this quiet room and the peaceful surroundings. My head was filled with what I'd read, and what I'd read hadn't been peaceful.

Standing, I could see Edward. He'd moved to the floor, lying flat on the floor, holding the reports up in front of his face. If I had lain down, I'd have been asleep. Edward always did have a will of iron.

He glanced at me. I got a glimpse of what he was looking at. He'd moved on to the pictures. Something must have shone on my face because he placed the pictures face down on his chest. 'You finished?'

'With the witness reports, yeah.'

He just looked at me.

I went around the table and sat in the chair he'd started the night in. He stayed lying on the floor. I would have said like a contented cat, but there was something more reptilian about him than feline; a coldness. How could Donna miss it? I shook my head. Business, concentrate on business.

'The majority of the houses are isolated ones, mostly because of the wealth of the owners. They've got enough money to give them land and privacy. But three of the houses were located in developments like the Bromwells' with neighbors all around. Those three attacks occurred on one of the few nights that all the neighbors were gone.'

'And?' he said.

'And I thought this was going to be a brainstorming session. I want your ideas.'

He shook his head. 'I brought you down here for a set of fresh eyes, Anita. If I tell you all our old ideas, it may lead you down the same wrong paths we've already taken. Tell me what you see.'

I frowned at him. What he said made sense, but it still felt like he was keeping secrets. I sighed. 'If this was a person, I'd say he or they stake out the houses night after night, waiting for that one night when all the neighbors are out of the way. But do you know the odds of an entire street clearing out on any given night in the suburbs?'

'Long odds,' Edward said.

I nodded. 'Damn straight. A few people had plans for that night. One couple went to a niece's birthday party. Another family had their once a month dinner with the in-laws. Two couples from different crime scenes were both working late, but the rest of the people didn't have plans, Edward. They just all left home about the same time on the same night for different reasons.'

He was watching me, eyes blank, but steady, intense, and neutral at the same time. From his face I didn't know whether I was saying something he'd heard a dozen times before, or something brand new. Detective Sergeant Dolph Storr likes to stay neutral and not influence his people so I was kind of used to it, but Edward made Dolph seem positively loaded with influence.

I continued, but it was like slogging through mud without any feedback at all. 'The detective in charge of the second case, he noticed it, too. He went out of his way to ask why they left their houses. The answers are almost identical where the police take the time to ask details.'

'Go on,' Edward said, face still blank.

'Dammit, Edward. You've read all the reports. I'm just repeating what you already know.'

'But maybe you'll end up someplace new,' he said. 'Please, Anita, just finish your thought.'

'They all got restless. A spur of the moment trip to get ice cream with the kids. One woman decided to go grocery shopping at eleven o'clock at night. Some of them just got in their cars and went for a drive, no place in particular. Just had to get out for a while. One man described it as cabin fever.'

'A woman, Mrs Emma . . . shit. I've read too many names in too short a space of time.'

'Was it an unusual name?' Edward asked without a single change of expression.

I frowned at him and leaned across the table, lying on it to reach the reports. I shuffled through them until I found the one I wanted. 'Mrs Emma Taylor said, "The night just felt awful. I just couldn't stand being inside." She goes on to say, "Outside the air was suffocating, hard to breathe."'

'So?' he asked.

'So I want to talk to her.'

'Why?'

'I think she's a sensitive, if not a psychic.'

'There's nothing in the reports that say she's either.'

'If you have the gift and you ignore it or pretend it's not real, it doesn't go away. Power will out, Edward. If she's a strong sensitive or a psychic that has neglected her powers for years, then she'll be either depressed or manic. She'll have a history of treatment for mental illness. How serious will depend on how gifted she is.'

He finally looked interested. 'You're saying that having psychic ability can drive you crazy?'

'I'm saying that psychic ability can masquerade as mental illness. I know ghost hunters that hear the voices of the dead like whispers in their ears, one of the classic symptoms of psycophernia. Empaths, people who draw impressions from other people, can be depressed because they're surrounded by depressed people, and they don't know how to shield themselves. Really strong clairvoyants can spend their lives getting visions from everything they touch, unable to turn it off, again seeing things that aren't there. Psycophernia. Demonic possession can mask itself as a multiple personality. I could give you examples for the next hour matching mental illness with different types of power.'

'You've made your point,' he said. He sat up and didn't seem the least bit stiff. Maybe the floor was good for his back. 'I still don't understand why you want to talk to this woman. The report was taken by Detective Loggia. He was very thorough. He asked good questions.'

'You noticed that he took more time with why people left than the rest of the cops, just like I noticed it.'

Edward shrugged. 'Loggia didn't like the way everyone cleared out. Too damn convenient, but he couldn't come up with anything that tied the people together into a conspiracy.'

'A conspiracy?' I almost laughed then stopped at the seriousness in his face. 'Did someone actually suggest that an entire upper-middle-class to more-than-middle-class neighborhood conspired together to kill these people?'

'It was the only logical explanation for why they all left within thirty minutes of each other on the night of the murders.'

'So they investigated all these people?' I asked.

'That's where some of the extra paperwork comes from.'

'And?' I said.

'Nothing,' Edward said.

'Nothing?' I made it a question.

'A few neighborhood squabbles over kids destroying the flowers, one affair where the husband that turned up dead was banging the next door neighbor's wife.' Edward grinned. 'The neighbor was lucky that the other man got cut up in the middle of a string of serial killings. Otherwise, he'd have been the top of the hit parade.'

'Could it have been a copycat?' I asked.

'The police don't think so, and believe me they tried to make the pieces fit.'

'I believe you. The police hate to let a good motive slide since most of the time motive isn't even one of their top priorities. Most people kill over stupid things, impulse, screw motive.'

'Do you have a logical reason why all these people would vacate their houses just at the right time for the killer, or killers, to make their move?'

I nodded. 'Yep.'

He looked up at me, a slight smile on his face. 'I'm listening.'

'It's very common in hauntings for people to be uncomfortable in the area where the ghost is strongest.'

'You're saying ghosts did this?'

I waved a hand. 'Wait, wait until I'm done.'

He gave a small nod. 'Dazzle me.'

'I don't know if it's dazzling, but I think it's how it was done. There are spells that supposedly can make a person uneasy in a house or a place. But the spells I read in college were for one person or one house, not a dozen homes and twice that many people. I'm not even sure a coven working together could affect that big an area. I don't know that much about actual witchcraft of any flavor. We'll need to find a witch to ask. But I think it's moot. I just mentioned it as a possibility.'

'It's a possibility the cops haven't come up with yet.'

'Nice to know I haven't entirely wasted the last five hours of my life.'

'But you don't think it was witches,' Edward said.

I shook my head. 'Witches of almost any flavor believe in the threefold rule. What you give out comes back to you threefold.'

'What goes around comes around,' Edward said.

'Exactly, and no one is going to want this shit coming back on them three-fold. I would have said they also believe in "do what you will, only harm none," but you can have bad pagans just like you can have bad Christians. Just because your belief says something is wrong doesn't mean someone's not going to break the rules.'

'So what do you think caused them all to leave their homes just when our killer needed it?'

'I think whatever is doing this, is big enough and powerful enough to simply arrive on the spot and want the people to go, and they went.'

Edward frowned at me. 'I'm not sure I understand what you mean.'

'Our monster arrives, knows which house it wants, and he fills the rest of the houses with dread, driving the other families out. That takes a hell of a lot of power, but to then turn around and shield the murder house so that that one family doesn't flee, that's truly impressive. I know some preternatural critters that can throw a sense of unease around them. Mostly I think to keep hunters at bay. But I don't know anything that can cause this kind of controlled panic.'

'So you're saying you don't know what it is,' he said, and there was just a tinge of disappointment in his voice.

'Not yet, but if this is true, then it rules out a hell of a lot of things. I mean some vampires can throw out fear like this, but not on this large a scale, and if they could do the other houses, they couldn't shield the murder house.'

'I know a vampire kill when I see it, Anita, and this isn't one.'

I waved my hands in the air as if clearing it. 'I'm just throwing out examples, Edward. Even a demon couldn't do this.'

'How about a devil?' he asked.

I looked at him, saw he was serious, so I gave him a serious answer. 'I won't go into how long it's been since anyone saw a devil, a greater demon, above ground, but if it were anything demonic, I'd have felt it today in the house. The demonic leave a stain behind, Edward.'

'Couldn't one that was powerful enough hide its presence from you?'

'Probably,' I said. 'I'm not a priest, so probably, but whatever is mutilating these people doesn't want to hide.' I shook my head. 'It's not demonic, I'd almost bet the farm on it, but again I'm not a demonologist.'

'I know that Donna can help us locate a witch tomorrow. I don't think she knows any demonologists.'

'There are only two in the country. Father Simon McCoupen, who has the record in this century in this country for number of exorcisms performed, and Doctor Philo Merrick, who teaches at the University of San Francisco.'

'You sound like you know them,' Edward said.

'I attended a class taught by Merrick, and a talk given by Father Simon.'

'I didn't know you were that interested in demons.'

'Let's just say that I'm tired of running into them without knowing much about them.'

He looked at me, sort of expectantly. 'When did you run into a demon?'

I shook my head. 'I won't talk about it after dark. If you really want to know, ask me again tomorrow when the sun is shining.'

He looked at me for a second or two, as if he wanted to argue, but he let it go. Which was just as well. There are some stories, some memories, that if you tell them after dark, they seem to gain weight, substance, as if there are things listening, waiting to hear themselves spoken of again. Words have power. But even thinking about them is sometimes enough to make the air in a room heavy. I'd gotten better over the years at turning off my memories. It was a way to stay sane.

'The list of what our murderer isn't is getting longer,' Edward said. 'Now tell me what it is.'

'I don't know yet, but it is preternatural.' I leafed through the pages until I found the part I'd marked. 'Four of the people now in the Santa Fe hospital were only found because they wandered outside their homes at night, skinned and bleeding. Neighbors found them both times.'

'There's a transcript of the 911 call somewhere in this mess. The woman who found the Carmichaels had hysterics over the phone.'

I thought about what I'd seen in the hospital and tried to imagine finding one of my neighbors, perhaps a friend, in that condition in the middle of the street. I shook my head and chased the image back. I did not want to imagine it. I had enough nightmares of my own, thank you very much.

'I don't blame her,' I said. 'But my point is this: how could they walk around in that condition? One of the survivors attacked his neighbor when the man came to help. He bit his shoulder so badly that the man was taken to the hospital with the mutilation victims. Doctor Evans said that they have to restrain all the patients in Albuquerque or they try to get up and leave. Don't you find that strange?'

'Yes, it's all strange. Is there a point in here somewhere?' And I heard that thread of tiredness in his voice.

'I think that whatever skinned them was, is, calling them.'

'Calling them how?' he asked.

'The same way a vampire calls a person he's bitten and mind-raped. The skinning or something about it gives the monster a hold over them.'

'Why doesn't the monster just take them with him the night he skins them?' Edward asked.

'I don't know.'

'Can you prove that the skinned victims are being called by some bogeyman?'

'No, but if the doctors would okay it, I wonder where one of the survivors would go, if no one stopped him. Maybe the mutilation victims could lead us right to the thing.'

'You saw the hospital today, Anita. They are not going to let us take one of their patients and set him free. Between you and me, I'm not sure I could stand to watch it myself.'

'Well, the great Edward, afraid at last,' another voice said.

We both turned to see Olaf standing in the far doorway. He was wearing black dress slacks, and a black polo-style shirt, the shirtsleeves a little short for his long arms. I guess there just aren't a lot of choices when you wear Jolly Green Giant sizes.

He glided into the room, and if I hadn't spent so much time around vampires and shapeshifters, I'd have said he was good at gliding. For a human, he was very good.

Edward stood as he spoke. 'What do you want, Olaf?'

'Has the girl solved your mystery?'

'Not yet,' Edward said.

Olaf stopped at the edge of the table closest to us. 'Not yet. Such confidence you have in her. Why?'

'Four hours and that is the best question you can come up with,' I said.

Olaf turned to me with a snarl. 'Shut up!'

I took a step forward, and Edward touched my elbow. He shook his head. I stepped back, gave them some room. Truthfully, I wasn't up to arm wrestling Olaf, and I couldn't really shoot him just for yelling at me. It kind of limited my options.

Edward answered Olaf's question. 'When you look at her, Olaf, you see just the surface, just the small, attractive packaging. Underneath all that prettiness is someone who thinks like a killer, and a cop, and a monster. I don't know anyone else who bridges all three worlds as well as she does. And all the preternatural experts you find are specialists; they're witches, or clairvoyants, or demonologists.' He glanced at me as he said the last, then back to Olaf. 'But Anita is a generalist. She knows a little about most of it and can tell us whether we need to find a specialist, and what kind of specialist we need.'

'And what kind of magical specialist do we need?' He put a lot of sarcasm into that question.

'A witch, someone who works with the dead.' He'd remembered my earlier request about finding out what I'd sensed on the road. 'We're making a list.'

'And checking it twice,' I said.

Edward shook his head.

Olaf turned to me. 'Was that a joke?'

'A little one, yes.'

'Perhaps you should not try to make jokes.'

I shrugged.

He turned back to Edward. 'You told me all this before she came. You waxed eloquent about her abilities. But I have worked with your magical people in the past, and you never talked about them as you speak of her. What is it about her that is so goddamned special?'

Edward glanced at me, then back to Olaf. 'The Greeks believed that once there were no male and female, that all souls were one. Then the souls were torn apart, male and female. The Greeks thought that when you found the other half of your soul, your soul mate, that it would be your perfect lover. But I think if you find your other half, you would be too much alike to be lovers, but you would still be soul mates.'

I was fighting hard to keep my face from showing the growing surprise at this little speech. I hoped I was succeeding.

'What are you trying to say?' Olaf demanded.

'She is like a piece of my soul, Olaf.'

'You are mad,' Olaf said, 'a lunatic. Soul mates, bah!'

I kind of agreed with Olaf on this one.

'Then why is the thought of giving her a gun while I hunt her one of my greatest fantasies?' Edward asked.

'Because you are mad,' Olaf said.

Hear, hear, but I didn't say it out loud.

'You know that I have no greater compliment to give than that,' Edward said. 'If I wanted to kill you, Olaf, I would just do it. The same with Bernardo because I know that I'm better than both of you. But with Anita I'll never be sure unless we do go up against each other for real. If I die without knowing which of us is better, I'll regret the not knowing.'

Olaf stared down at him. 'You cannot mean to say that this girl, *die Zimtzicke* of a girl is better than Bernardo or me.'

'That's exactly what I mean.'

Die Zimtzicke meant a quarrelsome or bitchy woman. Couldn't really argue with that one. I sighed. Olaf had hated me before. Now he was going to feel forced to be competitive. This I did not need. And compliment though it was, it was not reassuring to know that Edward fantasized about killing me. Oh, excuse me, hunting me while I was armed to see which of us was better. Oh, yeah, that was much more sane.

I checked my watch. It was 1:30 A.M. 'Frankly, boys, I don't know whether to be flattered or frightened, but I do know one thing. It's late, and I'm tired. If we are really going to see the big bad vampire tonight, then it has to be now.'

'You just don't want to look at the pictures tonight,' Edward said.

I shook my head. 'No, not just before trying to sleep. I don't even want to read the forensic reports tonight. I'll look at the gory remains first thing tomorrow.'

'Afraid,' Olaf said.

I met his angry eyes. 'I need some sleep if I'm to function well while I'm here. If I see the pictures right before bedtime, I can't guarantee sleep.'

He turned back to Edward. 'Your soul mate is a coward.'

'No, she's just honest.'

'Thank you, Edward.' I went to stand closer to Olaf, so that I had to crane my neck back to see his face, and he loomed over me. There was really no way to get decent eye contact, so I stepped back to a more comfortable angle for my neck, and settled for meeting his deep-set eyes. 'If I'd been a man I'd have probably felt compelled to look at the pictures, to prove myself worthy of all Edward's praise. But one of the good things about being a woman is that my level of testosterone poisoning is lower than most men's.'

'Testosterone poisoning?' Olaf looked confused. Probably not a new sensation for him.

'Show me to my room, then explain it to him, Edward. I want to get some extras if I'm going to be interviewing vamps tonight.'

Edward led me past the brooding Olaf and out the door that everyone seemed to disappear through. The hallway was white and so unadorned it looked unfinished. He pointed out Bernardo's room as the first door and Olaf's was right beside mine.

'Do you really think Olaf and I bunking next door to each other is a good idea?'

'By putting you right beside him, it shows him I'm not afraid for you.'

'But I am,' I said.

He smiled. 'Just take some basic precautions. You'll be fine.'

'Nice to know one of us is confident. If you hadn't noticed, he outweighs me by like a ton.'

'You're talking like it would be a standup fight. I know you, Anita. If Olaf comes through your door tonight, you'll just shoot him.'

I studied his face. 'Are you setting him up so I will kill him?'

He blinked, and I saw for a moment that I'd surprised him. 'No, no. I meant what I said to Olaf. If I wanted him dead, I'd just kill him. I put you next door to him because I know how he thinks. He'll think it's a trap, too easy, and he'll behave himself tonight.'

'What about tomorrow night?'

Edward shrugged. 'One night at a time.'

I shook my head and opened the door. Edward called to me before I could go inside or even turn on the light. I turned back to face him.

'You know most women get all mushy when a man tells them they're his soul mate.'

'I'm not most women.'

His smile widened. 'Amen to that.'

I looked at him. 'You know what you said in there scares me. The thought that you fantasize about hunting me and killing me. That's creepy, Edward.'

'Sorry,' he said, but he was still smiling, still amused.

'But honestly if you'd said the soul mate stuff and meant it like lovey-dovey, that could have scared me more. I've known since we met that you might kill me some day, but fall in love with me . . . that would be just too weird.'

The smile faded a notch or two. 'You know if we could love each other, our lives would be less complicated.'

'Truth, Edward. Have you ever had a romantic thought about me?'

He didn't even have to think about it. He just shook his head.

'Me, either. I'll meet you out front by the car.'

'I'll wait for you here,' he said.

I looked at him. 'Why?'

'I don't want you smarting off to Olaf on your way out if I'm not there to stop the fight.'

'Would I do that?'

He shook his head. 'Get the extra firepower and let's start the drive. I'd like to get to bed before dawn.'

'Good point.' I went into the room, closing the door behind me. There was a knock on the door almost immediately. I opened it back up, slowly, but was pretty sure it was Edward. It was.

'We'll take you into the club as my guest, just a friend. If the vamps don't know who you are, they might be more careless around you, let something slip that would make sense to you, that wouldn't make sense to me.'

'What happens if I get outted during the evening? Think Her Worship will resent you sneaking the Executioner into her club?'

'I'll tell her that you wanted to see the best show in town and thought that they might not want the Executioner around, but that you're strictly there in an unexecution work mode.'

'Will you say it just like that, unexecution work mode?'

He smiled. 'Probably. She likes her men to be either very serious or very cute.'

'She. You talk like you know her.'

'Ted only kills rogues. He is very welcome in a lot of the local monster hangouts.'

'Edward the actor,' I said.

'I do good undercover work.'

'I know you do, Edward.'

'But it always makes you uncomfortable to see me do it.'

I shrugged. 'You're such a good actor, Edward, sometimes it makes me wonder which act is real.'

The smile faded, leaving his face blank, and empty like some of him had slithered away with his smile. 'Go get your gear, Anita.'

I closed the door with him still standing there. In some ways I understood Edward better than either of the men I had been dating. In other ways he was the biggest mystery of all. I shook my head, literally shaking it off, and looked around the small bedroom. If we came back here at dawn, I'd be tired, and tired could mean careless. I decided to make some changes now while I was fresh.

The room's only chair would go under the doorknob, but not until I was in for the night. I moved a line of miniature Kachina dolls from the dresser to the windowsill. If anyone opened the window, one or more of the dolls would fall. There was a small mirror on the wall that was framed by deer antlers. I placed it under the window, just in case the dolls didn't fall. I'd leave my suitcase to one side of the door entrance so if the door did somehow manage to open without knocking the chair over, Olaf might trip over the suitcase. Of course, I was almost as likely to trip over it trying to get to the bathroom on the way out. The moment I thought of it, I had to go. I'd hit the bathroom on the way out. Edward could stand outside and make sure Olaf didn't interrupt.

I searched through my suitcase. It was illegal for me to carry my vampire gear without a court order of execution. Carrying it without one was like premeditated murder. But no law against carrying a few extras. I had two thin vials of holy water with little rubber caps. You hit the cap with your thumb and it popped open, sort of like a grenade, but only dangerous to the vamp. Which made it a lot more user friendly than a grenade.

I slipped the holy water into each of my back pockets. They barely showed through the dark cloth. I already had my cross, but I'd had crosses ripped off of my throat before, so I had backups. I put a plain silver cross with chain in one front pocket of my jeans, and another one in the pocket of the black dress jacket. I opened the box of new ammunition that I'd packed.

I'd had to leave my apartment almost two years ago now. When I'd lived in my apartment, I'd put Glazer Safety Rounds in my guns because I didn't want my neighbors to take a stray bullet. Glazers will not go through walls, but as Edward and some of my police friends had pointed out, I'd been lucky. Glazers will shatter bone, but don't really go through bone, the difference between a shotgun and a rifle round, sort of. Edward had actually come into town just to take me out to the shooting range and test fire stuff. He'd asked me questions about specific gun fights, and what I'd learned was that the reason the Glazers had done what I wanted them to do was mostly being almost point blank every time I used them for a kill. What I needed was something that was a reliable kill from a safer distance than arm's length. It also might explain why I'd hit some older vamps from a distance, but they hadn't stopped. Maybe not.

Maybe they were just that old, but ... Edward had been very convincing. Something with more penetrating power, more stopping power, ammo meant not to wound but to kill. Because let's face it: when was the last time I'd wounded anyone that I hadn't meant to kill? Wounding was an accident for me. Killing was the goal.

I'd settled on the Homady Custom XTP handgun ammo. To be exact the 9mm Luger, 147 JHP/XTP, silver-coated of course. There were other hollow point bullets that will expand to a bigger mass, but some of them don't penetrate nearly as far into a body mass. With a vamp you need to make sure you hit something vital, not just that you make a big hole. There were even bullets that penetrated farther into a mass, which meant they'd reliably go through a body and out the other side. But all the Homady XTPs were designed to penetrate the target, but not so far as to pass through the target object and 'create a hazard.' That last was a quote from some of the Hornady Manufacturing literature. The ammo followed the FBI penetration requirements. The Feds, even more than little ol' me, have to worry about what happens when a bullet hits the bad guy and keeps traveling. Is it going to hit a kid, a pregnant woman, a nun out for her morning stroll? Once a bullet hits the mark and keeps traveling, you really never know where it will end up. So the plan is to make sure it doesn't leave the target, but that the target doesn't get up either.

Of course, Edward had made his own recipe for killing. He'd taken silver hollow points and filled the end with holy water and mercury, then sealed the top with wax. I'd been afraid that the wax would make the bullets jam in a gun, but they ran through like silk – smooth, dependable, like Edward himself. The ammo was a hell of a show. So Edward had told me. I hadn't used Edward's homemade surprise yet. I was still vaguely wary of them. He shouldn't have told me that they might jam the gun. Or maybe, I would have been nervous of them anyway. With these even if you hit in a non-lethal area, missed the heart, the head, everything vital, you still did damage. The holy water and silver mercury would explode through the vamp's body, burning where they touched. The holy water would eat through the body like acid. Hit a vamp even in a leg or arm with this shit, and they might lose all interest in killing you and just want to stop the pain.

I stared at the two boxes of ammo, and finally loaded up with the Homady XTP, Edward's specials in their box. If I did have to shoot any vamps tonight, I had no court order of execution, and carrying the homemade seemed too much like premeditation. Premeditation is the difference between first degree murder and second degree murder or even manslaughter if you had a good lawyer and a sympathetic jury. There were people in jail at this very moment for killing vamps. I did not want to be one of them. Besides, we were just going down there to ask questions, nothing major. So I told myself as I closed the suitcase and left the other bullets behind.

But I knew better than most that what should be simple always grows complex when you add a vampire. Add a Master of the City, any city, and you never really know what you're walking into. I'd killed three Masters of the City: one with a sword, one with fire, one by killing their human servant. Never just a straight-on shootout. I probably wouldn't be shooting anyone tonight, but . . . I loaded up my extra clip with the bullets. I'd only use them if I'd used up the first clip. If I emptied thirteen of the XTPs into something and it didn't go down, all bets were off. I'd worry about murder charges later, after I survived. Survival first. Try to stay out of jail second. My priorities in order, I slipped the extra clip into the right pocket of my jacket and went off to find Edward. He was, after all, the one who had taught me my priorities.

22

I was cooling my heels in the living room when Bernardo and Olaf came out of the far rooms. They had both changed clothes.

Bernardo was in white dress slacks with a sharp crease and a roll of cuff. A white vest showed off his darkly muscled arms. He'd added heavy silver arm bracelets at mid-bicep, and matching ones at each wrist. A silver saint's medallion glittered against the smooth darkness of his chest. Most of his hair fell like a black dream around all that white, except for a braid on one side. It was a thick braid because he just had that much hair, and he'd woven silver chains with tiny bells here and there in his hair, so he stalked into the room to the sound of gentle chimes. He looked at me through a curtain of blackness caressing one side of his face, the other graced by the silver on black glint of the braid. It was, to say the least, eye-catching. It was a little bit of a struggle to tear my gaze from Bernardo and look at Olaf. He had gone for a black shirt that seemed utterly sheer. To hide his shoulder holster, he'd put on a leather jacket. It was way too hot for leather. Though admittedly, with his totally shaved head, black jeans, and black boots with silver toes and heels, the leather jacket looked about the right speed. 'You guys look spiffy. What's the occasion?' 'We're going to a club,' Bernardo said, as if that explained it.

'I know that,' I said.

He was frowning now. 'You should change.' I pushed to my feet from the couch. 'Why?' He walked toward me. I caught glimpses of dark flesh above his white leather loafers and the hem of his pants, no socks. He stopped at the edge of the couch, as if I'd pulled back, or made some other sign that I wasn't happy. 'I know you can look as good as we do.' He gave a little self-deprecating smile. 'Or as good as Olaf here. Maybe not as good as me.' He smiled, and it was a good smile, meant to melt something a little lower than my heart. But I'd been working on my reaction to him. I was not a slave to my libido. Richard and Jean-Claude could attest to that.

I looked at him in all his light and dark glory. 'If I can't look as good as you, why try at all?'

The smile widened to a grin that made his face look somehow more real and less handsome. Less handsome, less practiced, but I liked it more. He took a step closer, and that teasing, practiced look was back. This was a man who knew how to flirt. But if anything will turn me off, it's a very practiced approach, as if the man has done it a thousand times before, to a lot of different women. Which always seems to imply that I am no different from all the rest. Not flattering.

'I think you might, might, be able to approach my glory, if you tried.'

Even knowing it was an act, I had to smile. 'I just don't want to work that hard, Bernardo.'

'If I am forced to change, then everyone changes,' Olaf said.

I looked at him. Was he handsome? Not really, but he was striking. If he could tone down the bad boy routine, he could probably pick up plenty of girls at the club, or maybe even if he didn't tone it down. It always amazes me how many women like dangerous men. Men who almost from the moment you meet them, you know are bad news. Me, I prefer my men kinder, gentler, nice. Niceness is highly underrated by most people.

'I don't remember anyone putting you in charge, Olaf. When Edward asks me to change clothes, I'll change.'

He took a step towards me, but whatever he was going to say or do, stopped when Edward came into the room. He was wearing a red tank top with a short-sleeved silk shirt that matched the tank. The shirt would hide his shoulder holster if he were careful. His jeans were new and black, and with his yellow hair grown out enough to have a little curl to it, he actually looked sort of cute. Edward never looked cute.

I knew when I was beaten. I raised hands in surrender and started walking towards the bedrooms. Then stopped. I turned back to him. 'I thought the point to taking me down there without cops was that the monsters might talk to Anita Blake, vamp executioner. So that means no undercover crap.'

'Why would changing clothes be undercover for you?' Bernardo asked.

I looked at him, then looked at Edward. 'If you want my services, you take whatever the hell I'm wearing. I don't dress up outside the office.'

Edward said, 'Let's go down there with you a little under wraps. Look around the club, meet the monsters, before they find out who you are.'

'Why?'

'You know the answer.'

'You want me to look around, use my expertise, before they know I have any expertise.'

He nodded.

'But you also want me to be Anita Blake and impress the monsters.'

'Yes,' he said.

'Hard to do both.'

'Be a tourist until they make you, then be yourself.'

'The best of both worlds,' I said.

'Exactly.'

I looked at him. 'Is this all your plan? No hidden agenda?'

He smiled, and it was Ted's smile, slow, lazy, innocent. 'Would I do that to you?'

I just shook my head and started for the bedrooms. 'Forget I asked. I'll change into something more . . . festive,' I said without turning around.

Edward didn't call me back and say no need to change so I kept walking. We were undercover tonight apparently. I hate undercover work. I am just so damn bad at it.

I had also not packed with an eye for club hopping. I changed into the newest, blackest jeans I had. The Nikes would have to do because I hadn't brought anything else. Except more Nikes. All my shirts were just different colors of one or two styles. If I find something comfy, I've learned to buy doubles if I really like something, and multiple colors if I really, really like a style. This means I am usually wearing last year's style long after the fashion trend has moved on, but it's not like I care.

I had a royal blue cotton tee with a scoop neck. Almost all the shirts I'd packed had a scoop neck. The blue was a little softer than the rest of the colors. I added a touch of eye shadow, enough eyeliner to be dramatic, enough mascara so that the eyeliner didn't overwhelm my eyelashes, a hint of blush, and some kiss-ass red lipstick.

I couldn't really get a good look in the room's small mirror, but at least the makeup looked good. The shoulder holster was very black against the blue shirt, but the black suit jacket took care of that. Since I couldn't take the jacket off without flashing the guys, I added my wrist sheaths with matching silver knives. If I was going to be stuck with the jacket all night, I might as well carry them. Besides, you never know when you'll need a good blade. I ran a brush through my hair and called it done.

Apparently, I looked okay because Bernardo said, 'I take it back. If you'd packed a dress, you'd be prettier than I am.'

I shook my head. 'No, I wouldn't, but thanks for saying it.'

'Let's go,' Edward said.

'She is showing too much breast,' Olaf said.

I looked at his completely sheer black shirt. 'I can see your nipples.'

His face darkened. I think he was actually blushing. 'Bitch.'

'Yeah, sure, you and the horse you rode in on,' I said.

Edward moved between us, soothing the big man. To me, he said, 'Don't tease him unless you want the trouble.'

'He started it,' I said.

He looked at both of us, his face that icy gaze that I'd seen him wear when he killed. 'I don't care who starts it, but I will finish it. Is that clear?'

Olaf and I looked at Edward, then at each other. Slowly, we both nodded. 'It is clear,' Olaf said.

'Crystal,' I said.

'Good.' His face transformed into a smiling face, somehow appearing years younger. How did he do it? 'Then let's go.'

We went.

23

Obsidian Butterfly, the club, was located between Santa Fe and Albuquerque. The club was set back from the road like one of the Indian casinos. It had high-class tourist trap written all over it. The parking lot was so full we had to circle to find a spot.

The building was done in faux-Aztec temple. Or for all I knew real Aztec temple. But the outside of the building looked like a movie set. Red neon traced square carved faces, and the name was traced in more red neon. There was a line stretching around the corner of the building and out into the hot summer dark. This was not my town. I didn't know the manager, so I couldn't jump the line. I also did not want to stand in the line.

Edward walked up the line, confident, as if he knew something I didn't. We followed him like obedient puppies. We weren't the only foursome trying to get into the club. We were the only foursome that wasn't made up of couples. To blend in we needed at least one more woman. But Edward didn't seem to be trying to blend in. He walked up to the head of the line where a large, broad-shouldered man of very Indian descent stood bare-chested, wearing what looked like a skirt but probably wasn't, and a heavy faux-gold collar that covered most of his shoulders like a mantle. He was wearing a crown covered in macaw feathers and other smaller feathers that I couldn't identify.

If this was just the bouncer at the door, I was actually interested in seeing the show. Though I hoped they had access to lots and lots of pet parrots and hadn't actually slaughtered birds just for the outfits.

'We're Professor Dallas's party. She's expecting us,' Edward said in his best hail-fellow-well-met voice.

The feather and gold bedecked man said, 'Names.' He uncrossed his arms and looked at a clipboard that had been in his hand the entire time.

'Ted Forrester, Bernardo Spotted-Horse, Olaf Gundersson and Anita Lee.' The new last name stopped me. Apparently, he was serious about me going in incognito.

'IDs.'

I tried very hard to keep my face blank, but it was an effort. I didn't have any fake ID. I looked at Edward.

He handed his driver's license to the man, then still smiling, said, 'And now aren't you glad that I didn't let you leave your license in the car.' He handed a second license to the man.

He looked at both for longer than I thought he should have, as if he suspected something. My shoulders were actually tight, waiting for him to turn to me and say, ah-hah, fake ID, but he didn't. He handed both licenses back to Edward, and turned to Bernardo and Olaf. They waited with their licenses out, as if they'd done this before.

Edward moved back to stand by me and handed me the license. I took it and looked at it. It was a New Mexico license with an address on it that I didn't know. But it was my picture, and it said Anita Lee. The height, weight, and the rest were accurate, just the name and address were wrong.

'Better put it in your pocket. I may not be around to find it next time,' he said.

I slipped it in my pocket along with my other license, a lipstick, and some money, and an extra cross. I wasn't sure whether to be flattered or insulted that Edward had set up a secret identity for me. Of course, maybe it was just the license, but knowing Edward there'd be more to it. There usually was.

The big double doors were opened by another large muscled

guy in a skirt, though he didn't have a feather crown or a nifty collar. A lesser bouncer, apparently. The doors led into a darkened room thick with an incense I didn't recognize. The walls were completely covered with heavy drapes, only another set of double doors showing the way.

Another bouncer, this one blond and tanned the color of thick honey, opened the door. He had feathers woven into his short hair. He winked at me as we went through the door, but it was Bernardo he watched the closest. Maybe he was looking for weapons, but I think he was watching Bernardo's butt. He wouldn't see a weapon from the back. Bernardo had transferred his gun to a front cross draw because the gun had showed a lump at the back. Which told you how snug the pants fit in back.

The room we entered was large, stretching out and out into the near darkness. People sat at square stone tables that looked suspiciously like altars to me. Or at least what Hollywood is always using for altars. The 'stage' took up most of the far left wall, but it wasn't a stage, not really. It was being used as a stage, but it was a temple. It was as if someone had sliced off the top of a pyramid temple and transported it here to this night club, in a city so far removed from the lush jungles where the building began that the stones themselves must be lonely.

A woman appeared in front of Edward. She looked as ethnic as the first doorman with high sculpted cheekbones, and a fall of shiny black hair that fell to her knees as she moved through the tables. She had menus in her dark hands, so I assumed she was the hostess. But her dress was red with a black design, and I knew silk when I saw it. The dress was vaguely oriental and didn't match the decor of the room, or the waitresses hurrying to and fro in odd loose dresses made of some rough material. The waitresses struggled along in loose-fitting sandals, while the hostess glided before us in high heels the same scarlet as her dress and perfectly manicured nails.

She was beautiful in a tall, slender, graceful fashion, like a model, but she was a discordant note, as if she belonged to a different theme. She showed us to a table that was in the very front with a view dead center of the temple. There was a woman at the table, who stood and offered us her hand as we sat down. Her handshake was firm, and her hand was about my size. It takes practice to have a firm handshake with hands this small.

Professor Dallas, call me Dallas, was shorter than I was, and so petite that in the right clothes she'd have looked prepubescent. She wore tan Docker pants, a white polo shirt, with a tweed jacket complete with leather elbow patches, as if she'd read the dress code for college professors and was trying to conform. Her hair was shoulder length, a baby fine, medium brown. Her face was small and triangular and as pale and perfect as God had intended it to be. Her glasses were gold wire frames and too large for the small face. If this was her idea of party clothes, someone needed to take her shopping. But somehow I didn't think the good doctor gave a shit. I like that in a woman.

A man stepped out of the odd-shaped door at the top of the temple. The moment he stepped out, silence fell in rings around him, spreading out and out into the murmuring audience until it was so quiet I could hear the pulse of my own blood. I'd never heard a crowd this large go so quiet so quickly. I'd have said it was magic, but it wasn't, not exactly. But this man's presence was a sort of magic. He could have worn jeans and a T-shirt and he'd still have commanded your attention. Of course, what he was wearing was pretty eye-catching all on its own.

His crown was a mass of thin, long feathers, a strange greenish, bluish, goldish color, so that as he moved they shifted color like a trapped greenish rainbow hovering in a fan of colors above his forehead. His cape hung nearly to his knees and seemed to be formed of the same feathers as his headdress, so that he moved in a wave of iridescence. The body that showed was strong, square, and dark.

I was sitting close enough to tell if he was handsome or not, but staring at him, I wasn't sure. It was impossible to separate his face from that presence, and so the face didn't matter much. He was attractive, not because of the length of a nose or the turn of a chin, but just because.

I found myself sitting up a little straighter in my seat, as if coming to attention. The moment I did it, I knew that even if it wasn't magic, it was something. I had to fight to tear my gaze from him and look at the others at the table.

Bernardo was gazing at him, as was Doctor Dallas. Edward was gazing out over the hushed crowd. Olaf was studying the doctor. He watched her, not as a man watches a woman, but as a cat watches a bird through cage bars. If Dallas noticed, she ignored it, but somehow I think she didn't notice. I think even with the man's presence filling the room, his rich voice riding the air, I'd have felt Olaf's gaze like a cold wind down my spine. That Dallas was oblivious to it made me worry about her, just a little, and made me very sure that I never wanted Olaf alone with her. Her survival instincts just weren't up to it.

The man, king or high priest, talked in rich tones. I caught part of it. Something about the month of Toxcatal, and a chosen one. I could not concentrate on his voice, any more than I could gaze upon him because to give him too much of my attention meant I was caught up in the spell he was weaving over the crowd. It wasn't a spell in the true sense of the word, but there was power in it, if not magic. The difference between magic and power can be very small. I'd been forced to accept that fact in the last two years.

The high priest was human, but there was a taste of ages to him. There are just not that many ways for a human to last centuries. One way is to be the human servant of a powerful master vamp. Unless Obsidian Butterfly was more generous about sharing her power than most of the Masters of the City that I'd met, the high priest belonged to her. He was too powerful an echo of his master to be endured unless she was that master. Master vamps have a tendency to either destroy or own that which is powerful.

The high priest had been powerful in life, a charismatic leader. Now centuries of practice had turned that charisma into a kind of magic. I'd had full-fledged vamps not affect me this much. If this was the servant, how scary was the master going to be? I sat there at the stone table, flexing my shoulders to feel the tightness of the shoulder holster. I was glad I'd packed an extra clip of bullets. I moved my wrists just enough to feel the knives resting against my arms. I was very glad I'd brought the knives. You can stab vamps and keep them alive, but still make your . . . point.

I was finally able to separate the power of his voice from the words. Most vamps, when they can, do tricks with their voices. The words themselves hold the key. They say *beautiful*, and you see beauty. They say *terror*, and you feel afraid. But this voice had little to do with the words. It was just an overwhelming aura of power like a great white noise hum. The audience may have thought that they were hanging on every word, but the man could have recited a grocery list with similar effect.

The words were, 'You saw him as the god Tezcathpoca in our opening dance. Now see him as a man.' The lights had been dimming as the priest spoke, until he was left in near darkness; only the iridescent gleam of feathers showed as he moved. The light came up on the other side of the stage, revealing a man, pale skin that glowed in the lights from his bare feet to equally bare shoulder. His back was to the audience and for a moment I thought he was nude. There was nothing to break up the curve of his body from the swell of his calves, to his thighs, the tight roundness of his buttocks, the lean waist, the spread of shoulders. His hair looked black under the lights, cut so close to his head that it looked shaved. He turned slowly, revealing the barest of G-strings, a color so close to his skin that you knew the illusion of nudity was a planned effect.

His face shone unadorned like a star, starkly beautiful. He looked somehow pure and perfect, which wasn't possible. No one human was perfect. But he was pretty. A line of black hair ran down the center of his chest and stomach to vanish into the thong. Our table was close enough, and his body white enough, that I could see the thin line of hair encircling his nipples to meet that thin line down his chest like the soft arms of a T.

I actually had to shake my head to clear it. Maybe it was being celibate, or maybe there was more magic in the air than just the voice of the human servant. I looked back at the stage and knew that it was only a trick of the light that made his skin seem to glow. I looked over at Professor Dallas. She had her head bent very close to Edward, talking to him in whispers. If she saw the show almost every night, it was nothing new to her, but the lack of attention that she paid the man made me turn and search the dim tables around us. Most eyes, especially the women, were turned rapt to the stage. But not all eyes. Some were drinking, holding hands with their dates, doing other things. I turned back to the stage and just looked at him, drinking in the lines of his body. Damn, it was just me. Or rather, it was just a normal human reaction to a nearly naked and attractive man. I'd have preferred a spell. At least then I could blame someone else. My hormones, my fault. I needed more hobbies, that was it, more hobbies. That would fix everything.

The lights came up slowly until the priest was visible once more. 'It was traditional that twenty days before the great ceremony, brides would be chosen for him.' I caught a glimpse of fur, and for just an instant I thought it was a line of shapeshifters in their half-human, half-beast guise. But it was men dressed in leopard skins. Not hanging loose like cloaks but as if the skins were sewn around their bodies. Some of them were too tall for the skins so that a foot or more of bare leg showed below the animal feet, or out of the clawed arms. They moved among the tables in a strangely graceful line, encased in fur with their faces framed through the open jaws of the dead animals.

A man passed within touching distance of our table, and I saw the black rosettes that decorated the golden skin more closely, and it wasn't leopard. I was spending a lot of time with St Louis' wereleopards. I'd killed the wereleopard leader because he was trying to kill me, among other things. But I'd left the leopards without a leader, and shapeshifters without a leader are anyone's meat. So I was de facto leader until we could work something else out. I'd been learning how to forge them into a stronger unit, or pard. One of the ways you did that was sheer physical closeness, not sex, but closeness. I stared at the skin, and my hand went out without thinking. The man's movement stroked my hand over the once living fur. The spots were larger. The markings weren't as neat somehow. I watched the cat heads on the men, and the heads were more square, not the rounded almost feminine line of leopard. Jaguars, they were jaguars, which made perfect sense with the Aztec motif, but, like the bird feathers, I wondered how they'd obtained the skins, and was it legal. I knew it wasn't right. I don't believe in killing for decoration. I wear leather because I eat meat, just using the whole animal. Nothing wasted.

The man turned and looked at me. His eyes were blue, his face tanned a pale gold that matched the line of belly fur just before it turned white. The moment he looked at me energy danced down my skin like a hot breath. A shapeshifter, great. There was a time, not long ago, that that much power this close would have drawn an answering energy from me, but not this time. I sat there staring at him, and I was safe behind my shield that squeezed down a layer of energy that stood between me and all the psychic shit. I gave him innocent brown eyes, and he moved off through the tables as if I was no longer interesting. Which was fine with me.

I didn't reach out for it, but the energy came here and there from them. It would have been so much worse without the shielding. They had to be werejaguars or the costumes were like the ultimate false advertising. Somehow, this didn't strike me as a show that promised anything it couldn't deliver.

The werejaguars picked women from the audience, took them by the hand and led them towards the stage. A petite blonde was pulled from her seat giggling. A short, square woman with skin the color of tanned leather was pulled solemn-faced and didn't seem to be nearly as pleased, but she let herself be led to the stage. A taller more slender Hispanic woman was next, with long black hair that shimmered as she moved like an ebony curtain. She stumbled on the steps, and only the werejaguar's arm saved her from falling. She laughed as he steadied her, and I realized she was drunk.

A figure appeared in front of me, blocking my view of the stage. I looked up into a dark face framed by snarling jaws. The jaguar's golden glass eyes rode above the man's face, as if the dead animal were staring at me, too. The man reached a square, dark hand out to me.

I shook my head.

The hand stayed, pale palm up, waiting.

I shook my head again. 'No, thanks anyway.'

Dallas leaned around Edward, across the table, having to nearly crawl on it to get close to me. It stretched her body in a long line, her long ponytail pooling on the stone. Olaf's hand hovered over that spill of hair, and the look on his face was strange enough to distract me from everything else. Her voice made me look at her face instead of Olaf's. 'They need someone your size and body type to round out the brides. Someone with long hair.' She was smiling. 'Nothing bad is going to happen.' She gave me a cheerful smile that made her look even younger.

The man leaned over me and I could smell the fur and . . . him. Not sweat, just his scent, and that made my stomach contract, made me have to concentrate on holding my shields, because the part of me that was tied to Richard and his beast wanted to respond, wanted to spill outward and wallow in that scent. The animal impulses, true animal impulses, always threw me.

The man's voice was thickly accented, and sounded unsuited to whispering. It was a voice for shouting orders. 'Do nothing that you do not wish to do, but please come to our temple.'

Maybe it was the please or the accent or the absolute seriousness in his face but I believed. I still might not have gone with him, but Edward leaned into me, and said, 'Tourist, think tourist.' He didn't say, 'Play along, Anita. Remember, we're undercover,' because with a shapeshifter this close he'd hear anything that was said at the table. But Edward had said enough. I was a tourist. A tourist would go.

I gave the man my left hand and let him pull me to my feet. His hand was very warm. Some lycanthropes seem to adopt their alter ego's body temperature. Even Richard's skin grew warmer near the full moon, but that couldn't be it tonight. We were only days away from the dark of the moon, as far from the shining fullness that called the beasts as we could get. The man was just warm. Too hot for fur.

The priest in his feathers encouraged the audience to applaud as the last reluctant bride, me, joined the grouping around the nearly naked man. The werejaguar stood me on the side with the giggling blonde. The smell of beer was strong enough that I knew the giggling wasn't just nervousness. Perfect.

I looked past the man, doing my best to ignore him, to the two women on the other side. The tall one with all the hair was swaying slightly on her spike heels. Her skirt was leather, and the blouse looked like a red camisole. The other woman was that solid that some people call fat, but it isn't. She was square and wore a loose black shirt over black pants. She caught my eye, and we shared a moment of discomfort. Audience participation was great as long as the audience wants to participate.

'These are your brides,' the priest said, 'your reward. Enjoy them.'

The solid woman and I both took a step back as if it were choreographed. The blonde and the tall one with all the hair melted into his arms, cuddling and laughing. The man played to them, but it was their hands that wandered over his body. He was very careful where he touched them. I thought at first it was just fear of being sued, but there was a stiffness, a tightening of his body when their hands wandered over his bare buttocks that said he wasn't having as good a time as it looked. From the audience you'd have never noticed. He came away from them with orange-red lipstick like a wound on his pale skin and pale pink like a patch of glitter down his face.

He reached out to us, and both of us shook our heads. We took another step back, and a step closer together. Solidarity. She offered me her hand, not to shake, but to hold, and I realized she was scared, not just nervous. I was neither, just not happy. She whispered, 'I'm Ramona.' I gave her my name, and what seemed to matter more, held her hand. I felt like Mommy on the first day of school when the bullies are waiting.

The priest's voice came. 'You are his last meal, his last caress. Do not deny him.'

Ramona's face changed, grew soft. Her hand fell away from mine. The fear was gone. I called, softly, 'Ramona.' But she moved forward as if she never heard me. She moved into the man's arms. He kissed her with more tenderness than he'd shown the other two. She kissed him back, with a passion and a strength that made anything the other two had done seem pale and watered down. The other two women had gone to their knees on either side, either because they couldn't stand upright anymore, or the better to run their hands over both the man and the new woman. It looked like a mild version of a pornographic four-way.

He drew back from Ramona, laying a second kiss on her forehead as if she were a child. She stayed unmoving, eyes closed, face slack. It was illegal to force anyone to do anything against their will by use of magic. I looked at Ramona's empty face, waiting, waiting for what came next, all decision, all choice, washed away. If I'd been myself tonight instead of whoever the hell I was supposed to be, I'd have called them on it. I should still turn them in to the cops. But truthfully, unless they did worse, I wasn't going to turn them in if the Master of the City could help us solve the mutilation murders. If the murders stopped, a few mind-games could be overlooked.

There was a time when I wouldn't have tolerated it, when I wouldn't have looked the other way for any reason. They say everyone has their price. Once I thought I was the exception to the rule, but if it was a choice of letting this nice woman be made to do some things she didn't want to do, or seeing another crime scene, another survivor, they could have the woman. Not have in the true sense of the word, but to my knowledge mind-magic by a human servant wasn't permanent. Of course, until tonight I hadn't known a human servant could do mind-rape. I really didn't know how much danger this woman was in, and yet . . . and yet I would risk her, as long as nothing worse happened. If they told her to strip, all bets were off. I had rules, limits. They just weren't the same ones they'd been four years ago, or two years, or a year ago. The fact that I let them mind-rape her and didn't complain, bothered me, but not enough.

The blonde woman leaned into the man and bit his butt, not hard but enough to make him jump. His back was to the audience, so I was probably the only one who saw the anger that showed for just a moment in that handsome face.

The priest stayed on his side of the stage, as if he didn't want to distract from the show, but I knew he'd turned his attention to me. The full force of him was like pressure against my skin.

His voice. 'A most reluctant bride to leave him lonely in his hour of need.' I felt his power and now that power was wedded to the words. When he said, 'need,' I felt need. My body tightened with it, but I could ignore it. I knew I could stand there and be unmoved, that he could do his worst and I could stand against it. But no human could have done it. Anita Blake, vamp executioner, could stand firm, but Anita Lee, undercover partygoer, well . . . If I just stood there, the game was up. At the very least they'd know I wasn't an ordinary tourist. Times like these are one of the reasons I hate undercover work.

I ignored the priest's rich voice and just walked toward the man. He was having trouble keeping the blonde's hand out of the front of his G-string. The other woman knelt in a pool of her own dark hair, hanging on his leg, one hand playing with the side strap of the G-string. Only Ramona stood there, face blank, hands at her sides, waiting for orders. But the priest was concentrating all his energies on me. She was safe until he finished with me.

The dark-haired woman got the strap to slide over the smooth bone of his hip, and the blonde used it as a chance to plunge her hand under the cloth. His eyes closed, head going back, body reacting automatically, even as his hand grabbed her hand and tried to pull her hand out of his pants. Apparently, she was hanging on, not hurting him exactly, but not letting go.

I doubted the club would have tolerated this level of abuse if the performer had been a woman and the audience member a man. Some forms of sexist double standards do not work in a man's favor. A woman, they would have rushed on stage and saved her, but he was a man, and he was on his own.

I touched Ramona's shoulders and moved her to one side like she was furniture. She moved where I put her, eyes still closed. Made me feel worse that she was that pliant. But one problem at a time. I put my hand on top of his and moved his hand away from the blonde's wrist. His hand didn't move at first, then he looked at me, really looked at me. His eyes were large, a soft pure gray with a circle of black around the iris like someone had used the same eye pencil to trace his eyes that they'd used on the sweep of eyebrow and dark lashes. Strange eyes. But whatever he saw in my eyes seemed to reassure him because he let go of the blonde. There's a nerve in the arm about three fingers down from the bend of the elbow. If you hit it right, it's pretty painful. I dug my fingers into her flesh, as if I'd find that nerve and drag it to the surface. I was pissed, and I wanted to hurt her. I succeeded.

She gave a small scream, her hand opened, and I was able to move her arm back, fingers digging into the nerve. She didn't struggle, just whimpered and stared up at me with large unfocused eyes, but the pain was chasing the liquor away. If I kept it up long enough, I could have sobered her up in, oh, fifteen minutes or so, if she didn't pass out first.

I spoke low, but my voice carried. The stage had great acoustics. 'My turn.'

The tall Hispanic woman crawled away from the man, scuttling in her tight skirt until she fell flat on her face. You have to be pretty drunk to fall from a crawling position. She got to one elbow, and her voice came thick, but panicked. 'He's yours.'

I drew the blonde a few steps farther away from the man, and slowly let go of her arm. I told her, 'Stay.' She cradled her arm against her body, huddling over it. The look she gave me was not friendly, but she didn't mouth off. I think she was afraid of me. I wasn't having a great night. First, I let the nice lady be mind-raped, then I terrorized drunken tourists. I would have said, how could the night get worse, but worse was waiting. I looked back at the nearly naked man and didn't know what to do with him.

I walked back over to him because I couldn't figure a graceful way off stage. I'd probably blown my cover as a tourist, but Edward had let me bring a gun and knives into the club. In fact, we were all loaded for bear or vampire or whatever. The bouncers, unless they were idiots, had to have seen some of the weapons. I was just not supposed to be a vamp executioner, but I've never played victim well. I should never have come on stage, but too late now.

The man and I stood facing each other, his back still to the audience. He leaned into me, breath warm against my hair. He whispered, 'My hero, thank you.'

I nodded, and that small movement brushed my thick hair against his face. My mouth was dry, and it was hard to swallow. My heart was suddenly beating too hard, too fast, as if I'd been running. It was a ridiculous reaction to a strange man. I was horribly aware of how close he was, how little he was wearing, and how my hands just hung at my sides because to move at all would mean to brush against him. What was the matter with me? I had not been noticing men this badly in St Louis. Was there something in the air in New Mexico, or was it just lack of oxygen from the elevation?

He rubbed his face against my hair, whispered, 'I am César.' That small movement put the curve of his jaw, the skin of his neck next to my face. There was a trace of the women's perfume mixing along his face, overlaying the clean scent of his skin, but underneath it all was a sharper scent. It was the smell of warmer flesh than human, slightly musky, so rich it was almost a damp smell, as if you could bathe in the scent like water, but the water would be hot, hot as blood, hotter. The scent was so strong that I swayed, and for a second I could feel the brush of fur against my face like rough piled velvet. The sensory memory poured through me, and overwhelmed all my careful control. The power poured upward in a spill of heat along my skin. I'd managed to cut the direct links to the boys so that I was alone in my own skin, but the marks were still there, coming to the surface at odd moments, like this one. Shapeshifters always recognize each other. Their beasts always know, and though I had no beast of my own, I had a piece of Richard's. That piece reacted to César. If I'd been expecting it, I might have been able to prevent it, but it was too late now. It wasn't dangerous, just a spill of heat, pulsing along my skin, a dance of energy that didn't belong to me.

César had jerked back from me as if I'd burned him, then he

smiled. It was a knowing smile like we shared a secret. He wasn't the first shapeshifter to mistake me for one of them. To my knowledge I was one of only two humans in the world that had this close a tie to a shapeshifter. The other man's tie was to a weretiger, not a werewolf, but the problems were similar. We were both part of a vampire's triumvirate, and neither of us seemed happy.

César's hands went to either side of my face, hesitating just above my skin. I knew he was feeling the push of that otherworldly energy like a veil that had to be pushed aside to touch. Except he didn't. He spilled his own power into his hands, so that he held me in a pulsing shell of warmth. It made me close my eyes, and he hadn't even touched me yet, not with his hands.

I opened my mouth to tell him not to touch me, but as I drew breath to speak his hands touched my face. I wasn't ready. He pushed his power into mine. It hit like a jolt of electricity, raising the small hairs on my body, tightening places low on my body, raising gooseflesh in a wash down my skin. The power flowed towards César like a flower turning towards the sun. I couldn't stop it. The best I could do was ride the power instead of letting it ride me.

He bent his face towards me, still cradling my face between his hands. I put my own hands on top of his as if I was going to hold on. Power poured from his mouth as he hovered over my lips. The power ran through my body and spilled out of half-parted lips like a hot wind. Our mouths met and the power flowed into each of us, mingling as it brushed like two great cats rubbing furred sides along each other's bodies. The warmth grew to heat, until it almost hurt to stay tied to his lips, as if any second now our flesh would burn into each other, melting through skin, muscle, bone, until we fell into the center of each other like molten metal cutting through layers of silk.

The energy had turned sexual, as it usually did . . . for me. Embarrassing but true. We drew back from the kiss at the same time, blinking at each other like sleepwalkers awakened too early. He gave a nervous laugh and leaned into me as if to kiss me again, but I put a hand on his chest, and held him away. I could feel his heart thudding against my palm. I could suddenly feel the blood racing in his body. My eyes were drawn to the big pulse in his throat. I watched that rapid rise and fall in the side of his neck as if it were some sort of jewel, something to watch sparkle and glitter in the lights. My mouth was suddenly dry, and it wasn't sex. I actually stepped into him, pressed my body down the front of his, brought my face close to his neck and that jumping beat of life. I wanted to go down on that soft skin, sink teeth into his flesh, taste what lay beneath. I knew with a knowledge that was not mine that his blood would be hotter than a human's. Not warm but hot, a scalding rush of life to warm cold flesh.

I had to close my eyes, turn my head, step away with my hands over my eyes. I had no direct link to either of the men, but I held their power in me. Richard's burning warmth, and Jean-Claude's cold hunger. For a space of heartbeats I had wanted to feed on César. This when I had walled up the marks, boarded them up, chained them, locked them with everything I had. When the marks were open between the three of us, the desires that ran through me, the things that I thought, were too horrible or maybe just too alien. Not for the first time I wondered what piece of me each of them held in their bodies. What dark desire or strange urge did I leave behind? If I ever talked to either of them again, maybe I'd ask, or then again, maybe I wouldn't.

I felt someone hovering close. I shook my head. 'Don't touch me.'

'Let us get backstage, then I can apologize.' It was the priest's voice.

I lowered my hands and found him standing beside me. He held out his hand to me. I didn't touch him. 'We meant no harm.' I laid my left hand in his and found his skin quiet. There was nothing but human warmth and the solid feel of him. He led me towards an area to the far left of the stage. César was already there with the three other women.

The werejaguars were there like guards, and it seemed to have made the blonde and the one with all the hair brave again. They were pawing César, and he was kissing Ramona, who was kissing him back with enthusiasm.

The priest led me towards them, and I hung back. I whispered, 'I can't.' I meant that I couldn't touch César again so soon. I didn't trust myself, and I didn't want to have to say it out loud. I didn't have to. The priest seemed to understand.

He leaned close. 'Please, just stand near them. No one will touch you.'

I don't know why I believed him, but I did. I stood near the near-orgy, trying not to look as uncomfortable as I felt. Then a large white screen came down out of the ceiling, and before it was solidly in place, the priest drew me to one side. A woman my size with hair my length appeared and moved towards the mini-orgy. I watched her join the group, and a jaguar dragged the blonde out. A woman that matched the blonde came to take her place. They replaced everyone, even César, with actors, who did a shadow orgy against the white screen, thrown large for the audience. The actresses matched all the women chosen, at least for a shadow play. Which is what Dallas had meant when she said they needed someone my size with long hair to complete the brides.

The actors weren't really doing anything, but it must have looked awful from the audience's point of view. Clothes flew and the women were topless. I wondered if the shadows looked as topless as the real thing.

The priest drew me away until we stood in a small curtain area. He spoke low but clearly, so I guess we could talk without being heard onstage. 'You would never have been chosen if we didn't think you human. Our deepest apologies.'

I shrugged. 'No harm done.'

He looked at me and there was a weight of knowledge in his eyes that I couldn't lie to. 'You are frightened of what lies inside you, and you have not made peace with it.'

That much was true. 'No, I haven't made peace with it.'

'You must accept what you are, or you will never know what your true place in the world is, your true purpose.'

'Don't take this wrong, but I don't need a lecture tonight.'

He frowned at that, and there was a flash of anger. He wasn't used to being talked to like that. I was betting that everyone was afraid of him. Maybe I should have been, but what fear I had of him or them had vanished when I realized I wanted to take a bite out of César's neck. That scared me more than anything they could do to me tonight. All right, almost anything they could do tonight. Never underestimate the creativity of a being that is hundreds of years old. Most of them know more about pain than we poor humans will ever know. Unless we are very, very unlucky. I was either feeling lucky or stupid.

He made a small motion and the werejaguar that had chosen me came to us. He dropped to one knee, head bowed. The priest said, 'You chose this woman.'

'Yes, Pinotl.'

'Did you not feel her beast?'

His head lowered even more. 'No, my lord, I did not.'

'Choose,' the priest said.

The kneeling man drew a knife from his belt. The handle was turquoise in the shape of a jaguar. The blade was about six inches of black obsidian. The man held the blade up to the priest who took it as reverently as it had been offered. The man undid some hidden catch on the jaguar skin, and pushed the hood back so that his head was bare. His hair was thick and long, tied in a long club at the back of his head. He raised a dark face that was so square and chiseled, it looked like he could have poised for

Aztec temple carvings. If you were into Meso-Americans, his profile was perfect.

He raised his face up to the priest. His face was empty of all expression, just a calm waiting.

There was a roar from the audience that made me glance at the actors, but I turned back to the priest and the man before I'd really seen anything. I had a glimpse of seminude bodies, and an impression of something large and phallic strapped around the man. Normally, that would have made me take a second glance, just to make sure I was seeing what I thought I'd seen, but no matter what was happening out there, the real show was here. It was in the serene, upturned face of the man, and the serious eyes of the priest, the dull gleam of the black blade. They could use all the props they wanted, no matter how big, but it wouldn't come close to the two men and the quiet intensity stretching between them.

I didn't know exactly what was about to happen, but I had an idea. He was being punished because he'd chosen a lycanthrope from the audience, instead of a human. But I was human, or at least not a lycanthrope. I couldn't let him get sliced up, not even if it meant admitting who I was. Could I?

I touched the priest's arm, lightly. 'What are you going to do to him?'

The priest looked at me, and his eyes seemed like deep caves, a trick of shadows. 'Punish him.'

My fingers tightened on his arm, trying to feel it through the slick softness of feathers. 'I just want to make sure you're not going to slit his throat or something really dramatic.'

'What I do with our men is my business, not yours.' The force of his disapproval was strong enough that I took my hand off his arm. But I was worried now what he was going to do. Damn Edward and his undercover idea. It never worked for me, pretending. Reality always screwed it up.

The priest laid the blade point against the man's cheek. There was no fear in his face, nothing but an eerie serenity that made my throat tight and a thrill of fear slide down my spine. God, I hated zealots, and that's what I was seeing.

'Wait,' I said.

'Do not interfere,' the priest said.

'I'm not a lycanthrope,' I said.

'Lies, to save a stranger,' nothing but contempt in his voice.

'I'm not lying.'

The priest called, 'César.'

He appeared like a well-trained dog coming to his master's call. Maybe the analogy was unfair, but I wasn't feeling particularly charitable right now. If I blew our cover, had to say who I was, I didn't know if I was going to be blowing something that Edward had planned. By saying who and what I was, I didn't know if I was endangering us. Edward hadn't shared enough of his plans, which I would take up with him when the evening was over, but my first concern was safety. Was saving a stranger from being sliced up worth our lives? No. Was keeping a stranger from being killed worth maybe risking our lives? Probably. I had so many unanswered questions and so little real information that I felt like I must be killing brain cells thinking around all the things I didn't know.

César appeared beside me, on the far side of me away from the priest. I think he'd spotted the blade. 'What has he done?'

'He picked her out of the audience and did not sense her beast,' the priest said.

'I don't have a beast,' I said.

César laughed, and it was too loud. He covered his mouth with his hand for a moment, as if to remind himself we had to be quiet. 'I saw the hunger in your face.' He said hunger like it should have been in capital letters. Great, more shapeshifter slang that I didn't know.

I tried to think of a short version that would make sense. I made

two starts, before I finally said, 'There is too much. I will sum up.'
I even threw in the bad Spanish accent.

The priest's face stayed blank and unhappy. He did not get the
movie reference. César choked back another laugh. He'd probably
seen *The Princess Bride*. 'The hunger you saw was not from some
beast,' I said.

The priest gave his full attention to the man kneeling in front
of him. It was as if I'd been dismissed. He sliced the man's cheek
open. The thin cut spread and blood welled in liquid lines down
the dark skin.

'Shit,' I said.

He placed the knife against the man's other cheek. I grabbed his
wrist. 'Please, listen to me.'

The priest turned his dark eyes to me. 'César.'

'I am not your cat to call,' César said.

The priest's dark gaze slid from me, to the man beside me. 'Be
careful that what is pretense does not become real, César.'

It was a threat, though I didn't understand exactly what the
threat had been, but I knew a threat when I heard one. César moved
up beside me. 'She merely wishes to speak, my lord Pinotl. Is that
so much to ask?'

'She also touches me.' They both stared at my hand on his wrist.

'I'll let go if I have your word that you won't cut him until
you've heard me out.'

Those eyes came back to rest fully on my face, and I felt the
force of him thundering down on me. I could almost feel his skin
vibrate under my hand. 'I can't let you bleed him for something
that wasn't his fault.'

He never said a word, but I felt movement behind me, and I
knew it wasn't César, because he turned toward the movement. I
looked back and found two of the jaguar men coming towards us.
They were probably not going to hurt me, just stop me from
interfering. I turned back to the priest, met his eyes. I let go of his

wrist. I had a few seconds to decide whether to draw a gun or a knife. They weren't trying to kill me, so the least I could do was return the favor. I slipped a knife out, holding it against my leg, trying to be unobtrusive. I'd made the decision to go for the knife and not the gun. I hoped it was the right decision.

One of jaguars was the tanned, blue-eyed one. The other was the first African American I'd seen in the club, his face very contrasting with all the pale spotted fur. They advanced on me in a roil of energy; a low growl escaped from one of their throats, the faintest of threats. That one faint sound raised the hair at the back of my neck. I backed up, putting the kneeling man between me and the two jaguars.

The priest had laid the obsidian blade against the man's right cheek. He hadn't started cutting yet. 'Are you just going to cut each cheek, is that it? Will it stop there?'

The blade tip bit into his cheek. Even in the dark I could see the first liquid drop, a faint gleam, like a dark jewel. 'If you just want to slice him up a little, fine. It's your business. I just don't want to see him mutilated or killed for something he couldn't have sensed.'

The priest sliced the other cheek, slower this time. I think I was making things worse. I asked it out loud, of everyone and no one. 'Am I making things worse?'

The cheek closest to me began to heal, the skin reknitting as I watched. I had an idea. I stepped closer to the priest and the kneeling man. I kept an eye on the two jaguars across from them, but they just stood watching. They'd backed me off; maybe that's all they were supposed to do.

I touched the kneeling man's chin, turned his face towards me. The other cheek was completely healed. I'd never seen an obsidian blade used and hadn't been a hundred percent that it didn't act like silver. But it didn't. Shapeshifters healed the damage. The priest was still holding the obsidian knife upright in his hand.

The audience broke into thunderous applause, the sound rising like thunder through the small backstage area. The actors were pouring away from the white screen. The act was almost over. Everyone had turned at the noise and the movement, even the priest. I put my finger against the tip of the obsidian knife and pressed. The tip was like glass, the pain sharp and immediate. I drew back with a hiss.

'What have you done?' the priest demanded, and his voice was too loud; it must have carried out into the crowd.

I spoke lower. 'I won't heal, not as fast as he did. It'll prove that I'm not a lycanthrope.'

The priest's anger filled the air like something hot and touchable. 'You do not understand.'

'If someone would talk to me, instead of hugging their secrets so damn close, I wouldn't be blundering into things.'

The priest handed the blade back to the kneeling man. He took the knife and bowed his forehead to it. Then he licked the blade, carefully around the sharp edges, until he came to the point and my blood. Then he slid the tip between his lips, into his mouth, sucking it down like a woman taking a man into her mouth. His mouth worked around the blade and I knew it was cutting him, as he swallowed it. I knew it was cutting him up, but he made it look as if it were something wonderful, orgasmic, as if he were having a very good time.

He watched me as he did it, and his eyes weren't serene anymore. They had filled with heat. It was the same heat you could see in any man's eyes when he was thinking about sex. But not when the man was sucking on a glass-sharp blade, cutting his mouth, tongue, throat, drinking his own blood, with a taste of my blood as a chaser.

Someone grabbed my hand, and I jumped. It was César. 'We must be on stage. You must take your seat.' He was watching the kneeling man, all the men, carefully. He eased me around the group of them, and all eyes followed me like I was some wounded gazelle.

The other three women were already in place, standing behind the now dim white screen. They'd taken off some clothing. The giggling blonde was down to pale blue bra and panties, still laughing her head off. The Hispanic had taken off her skirt and was down to a pair of crimson panties that matched the red camisole she was still wearing. She'd kept the matching red high heels. She and the blonde were leaning against each other, swaying and laughing. Ramona wasn't laughing. She still stood quietly, unmoved and unmoving.

The priest's voice came from backstage. 'Disrobe for our audience.' His voice was soft, but Ramona grabbed the bottom of her shirt and lifted. Her bra was an ordinary bra, white and simple. It wasn't meant to be lingerie, and I doubted she'd planned on anyone seeing it tonight. She let her shirt fall to the floor. Her hands went to the top button of her pants. I pulled away from César and grabbed Ramona's hands. 'No, don't.'

Her hands went slack in mine, as if even that small interference had broken the spell, but she didn't look at me. She didn't see what was in front of her, just the internal landscape that I couldn't see.

I picked her shirt back up and placed her hands over it. She clutched it automatically, covering most of the front of her.

César took my arm. 'The screen is going up. There is no time.'

The screen began to slowly lift.

'You can't be the only one dressed,' he said. He tried to slide the jacket from my shoulders, and bared the shoulder holster.

'We'll scare the audience,' I said.

The screen was to our knees. He grabbed the front of my shirt, jerking it out of my pants, baring my stomach. He dropped to his knees and was licking my stomach as the screen came up completely. I tried to grab a handful of hair to pull him off me, but there wasn't enough hair to grab. The hair was much softer than it looked, much softer than my hair would have been if you shaved it to stubble. His teeth bit gently into my skin, and I put my hand under his chin, raising his face, so that he either had to take his teeth out of my skin, or bite deeper. He let go, let me raise his face to stare upward at me. There was a look in his eyes that I couldn't read, but it was something large and more complex than you see in a stranger's eyes. Complex I didn't need tonight.

He was on his feet in a movement so liquid and graceful that I knew that Edward would spot him for what he was, not human. He went to the one with all the hair first, giving her a tonsil-cleaning kiss, as if he'd crawl into her from the mouth down. Then he spun her like a dance move, and jaguar men were there to escort her and her arm full of clothes back to her table. The blonde was next. She kissed him, running pale nails down his back. She gave a little jump and wrapped her legs around his waist, forcing him to hold her weight or fall. The kiss was long, but she was in control of it. César walked her to the edge of the stage, still clinging to his body like a limpet.

The jaguar men pried her away from his body, one pale limb at a time, until they had to carry her above their heads while she struggled, and then finally went limp, laughing as they carried her back to her table.

Ramona seemed to wake up. She blinked around her as if she'd woken and wasn't sure where she thought she should be. She stared down at her blouse clutched to the front of her and screamed. César tried to help her on with her blouse, and she slapped at him. I went to her, trying to help her, but she seemed afraid of me, too, now, as if her panic had spread to include all of us.

The jaguar men tried to help her offstage, and she fell trying to keep them from touching her. It was finally a man from her table who came and escorted her out of the lights, out of the ring of strangers.

She was crying and speaking softly in Spanish as he led her back to the table. I would have to talk to someone about her. I couldn't leave town without knowing that the mind tricks weren't permanent.

If it had been a vampire with a one on one call like that, he could have called her any time, any night, and she would answer his call. She would have no choice.

César stood in front of me. He raised my hand, I think to kiss it, but it was the hand that I'd cut to prove I wouldn't heal. Not that anyone had cared. César raised my hand and stared at the small wound in the tip of my finger. It was a small cut and didn't bleed much, but it wasn't healing either. If I'd been a lycanthrope, the small prick would have closed up and healed by now.

He looked at me over the still bleeding finger. 'What are you?' he whispered.

'Long story,' I whispered back.

He kissed the wound like a mother with a child's scrape, then his mouth slid over my finger, down to my hand. He drew it slowly back out. Fresh blood welled to the tip of my finger, bright and sparkling under the lights. His tongue flicked out, rolling the drop of blood into his mouth. He leaned close as if to kiss me, but I shook my head and moved towards the steps that would lead me off the stage and away from him.

The jaguar men were there to help me off the stage, but I looked at them, and they backed off, letting me walk down the steps by myself. Edward held my chair for me, and I let him. Food had been served while I was on stage. Edward handed me a linen napkin. I wrapped it around my finger, holding pressure to it.

Dallas actually got up from her chair and came to talk to me, hanging over the back of my chair. 'What happened back there? I've been a volunteer before, and I've never seen anyone hurt.'

I looked up at her, her face close in the dimness, all serious and concern. 'If you think no one gets hurt, then you haven't been paying attention.'

She frowned, looking puzzled.

I shook my head. It was too late, and I was suddenly too tired to try and explain. 'I cut myself shaving.'

She frowned harder, but also got the point that I didn't want to talk. She sat back down, leaving me to Edward. He leaned into me, laying his mouth against my ear and whispering so low it was like he was breathing into my ear. He knew how good a shapeshifter's hearing was, not to mention vamps. 'Do they know who you are?'

I turned, putting my mouth against his ear, having to raise on one knee in my seat, putting my body in a line against his. It looked intimate, but it allowed me to whisper to him in a voice so low I wasn't sure he would hear. 'No, but they know I'm not human, not a tourist.' I put my arm across his shoulders, one hand on his shoulder, holding him because I didn't want him to move away. I wanted the next question answered. 'What are you planning?'

He turned to me, a look on his face that was far too intimate, too teasing for the conversation. He leaned into me, mouth pressed so close to my ear that it must have looked to the others like he had his tongue down it. 'No plan, just thought you being you might scare the monsters from talking to us.'

It was my turn to whisper, 'No plan, you promise?'

'Would I lie to you?'

I jerked back from him and slugged him in the shoulder, not hard, but he got my point. Would Edward lie to me? Would the sun rise tomorrow? Yes to both.

The actors that had taken our places were finally on stage, in robes. The priest in his feathers was introducing them, getting the applause they deserved. I was glad they ruined the effect and didn't leave poor Ramona convinced she'd done terrible things. I was actually surprised that they'd spoiled the trick, like a magician revealing his secrets.

'We'll allow you to eat before the next and last act of our show.'

The lights came up, and we all turned to our meals. I'd thought the meat was beef, but when I put the first bite in my mouth the texture told me I was wrong. The waitress had brought me an extra napkin, and I used that to spit the bite into.

'What's wrong?' Bernardo asked. He was eating the meat and enjoying himself.

'I don't eat . . . veal,' I said. I took a forkful of an unrecognizable vegetable, then realized it was sweet potatoes. I didn't recognize the spices in them. Of course, cooking wasn't exactly my area of expertise.

Everyone was eating the meat except me, and strangely, Edward. He'd taken a bite, but then he concentrated on the flat bread, and the vegetables, too.

'You don't eat veal either, Ted?' Olaf asked. He put another bite in his mouth and chewed slowly, as if trying to draw every ounce of flavor.

'No,' Edward said.

'I know it's not moral indignation about the poor little calves,' I said.

'And you worry about the poor little calves?' Edward said. He gave me a long look as he asked. I couldn't read his eyes, but they weren't blank, I just couldn't read them. What else was new?

'I don't approve of the treatment of the animals, no, but truthfully I just don't like the texture.'

Dallas was watching us all as if we were doing something a lot more interesting than discussing meat. 'You don't like the texture of . . . veal?'

I shook my head. 'No, I don't.'

Olaf had turned to the other woman. He took his latest bite of meat and offered it to her on the end of his fork. 'You like veal?'

She got a strange little smile on her face. 'I eat veal here almost every night.' She didn't take his bite that he offered but took another bite from her own fork.

I felt like I was missing something, but before I could ask, the lights went down again. The final act was about to begin. If I was still hungry, surely there'd be something open on the way home. There usually was.

24

The lights went down until the room was left in darkness. A dim spotlight cut the darkness. The light was only a faint white gleam when it finally stopped at the far, far end of the darkened room.

A figure stepped into that pale gleam. A crown of brilliant red and yellow feathers was bent towards the light. A cloak of smaller feathers covered the figure from neck to the edge of the light. The crown raised, revealing a pale face. It was César. He turned his face to one side, giving profile and showing that he had earrings going from lobe to halfway up the edge of his ear. Gold glittered as he moved his head, and the light grew stronger. He lifted something in his hands and a note of music filled the near dark. A thin trilling note like a flute, but not. The song was beautiful, but eerie, as if something lovely were crying. A jaguar man lifted off the feathered cloak and vanished into the darkness. A heavy gold collar lay across his shoulders and chest. If it were real, it was a fortune in precious metal. Hands came from either side of the darkness, appearing in the light, taking the feathered crown without ever showing themselves.

César walked slowly, and halfway up the room I could see what he was playing. It looked like a panpipe, but not exactly. The song cut through the darkness, crawled through it, one moment uplifting, the next mournful. It looked like he was truly playing it, and if so it was impressive. Jaguar men stripped him of everything he was carrying: a small shield, a strange stick that looked sort of like a bow, but not, a bag of short arrows or something like them. He was close enough now that I could see the jade decoration that he wore in front of his kilt, though I knew it wasn't a kilt, but skirt wasn't right either. The front was covered in feathers; the rest, some rich cloth. More hands came into the light to undo the garment and take it and the jade away. They were close enough now that the darkness and light couldn't hide that the hands belonged to the jaguars. They stripped him down to the flesh-colored G-string he'd worn before, or one like it.

The song rose into the dimness as he neared the last few rows of tables. You could almost see the notes rising upward like birds. I don't usually wax poetic about music, but this was different. Somehow you knew it wasn't just a song, just something to listen to and forget, or hum in odd moments. When you think of ritual music, you think of drums, something with a beat to remind us of our hearts, and the ebb and flow of our bodies. But not all ritual is made to remind us of our bodies. Some of it's made to remind us of why the ritual is happening. All ritual at its heart is for the sake of divinity. All right, not all, but most. Most of it is us yelling, hey God, look at me, look at us, hope you like it. We are all just children at heart, hoping Dad or Mom likes the present we picked out.

Of course, sometimes Mom and Dad can have quite a temper.

César let the flute or pipes hang from a thong around his neck. He knelt and removed his own sandals, then handed them to a woman at the nearest table. There was a shifting in the dimness as if she wasn't sure she wanted them. Maybe after the earlier show she was afraid to take them. Couldn't really blame her on that one.

He stopped at the table just behind that one and spoke quietly to another woman. She stood and removed one of the gold earrings from his ear. Then he went from table to table, and let sometimes men, but mostly women take the last of his decoration from his body. Which probably explained why the earrings were the least expensive, least authentic pieces he'd been wearing. Except for the last earrings. A medium sized jade ball set in each earlobe, but it was the figurines that dangled beneath, moving as his head moved, swaying as he walked, that made the earrings special. Each figure was nearly three inches high, brushing his shoulders like the hair he did not have. As he got closer, you could see the green stone was intricately carved into one of those squat deities the Aztecs were so fond of.

He stopped at our table, and I was surprised because he'd carefully ignored the other 'brides' on this walk. He raised me to my feet with one hand in mine, then turned his head so I could reach the earring. I didn't want to stop the show, but they were too expensive a gift to accept unless they were fake. The moment I touched the cool stone, I knew it was real jade. It was too heavy, too smooth to be anything else.

I don't wear earrings, and I've never had pierced ears, so I was left feeling the back of his ear in the near dark, trying to figure out how to undo the earring. He finally reached up and helped me, hands doing quickly and almost gracefully what I'd been fumbling at. By watching him I realized that they unscrewed, and when he turned his head I was able to get the second one out myself. I knew enough about jewelry to know that the screws were modern. It was real jade, real gold, but it wasn't an antique, or at least the clasps were modern.

The stones rested heavy and very solid in my hands. He leaned over and whispered, breath warm against my cheek. 'I will get them back from you after the performance. Don't interfere.' He laid a gentle kiss on my cheek and walked to the bottom step. He took the flute from around his neck and broke off one of the many reeds, scattering it on the step.

I sat back down, the jade gripped in my hands. I leaned into Edward. 'What's about to happen?'

He shook his head. 'I've never seen this particular show.'

I looked across the table at Professor Dallas. I wanted to ask her what was going on, but she had all her attention on the stage.

César had broken part of the flute on every step as he walked up them. Four jaguar men were waiting at the top, grouped around a small, roundish stone. The priest was there, too, but without the cape. He was even broader through the shoulders than he'd seemed, and though not tall you got the impression of sheer strength, sheer physicality. He seemed more warrior than priest.

César had made it to the top of the temple. The four jaguar men grabbed him, by wrist and ankle, lifting him over their heads, steadying his body with their hands. They paced the stage with him held above their heads, showing him to the four corners of the stage, even the one that faced away from the audience. Then they brought him to the small round stone and laid his body across it, so that his head and shoulders leaned back, and the lowest part of his chest and upper stomach were curved over the stone.

I was on my feet before I saw the obsidian blade in the priest's hand. Edward grabbed my arm. 'Look to your left,' he said.

I glanced and found two of the jaguar men waiting. If I made a run for the stage, I bet they'd try and stop me. César had said that he'd come for the earrings after the performance. Which implied he'd be alive to do it. He'd warned me not to interfere. But dammit, they were going to cut him up. I knew that now. What I didn't know, was how badly they were going to cut him up.

Dallas had gotten up from her seat and was at my other arm, whispering, 'It's part of the show. César plays sacrifice twice a month. Not always this exact sacrifice, but it's part of his job.' She spoke low and soothingly like you talked to a crazy person on a ledge. I let her and Edward ease me back into my seat. I was gripping the jade earrings so hard the edges dug into my hands.

Dallas knelt beside me, keeping a hand on my arm, but she watched the stage. The jaguar men held him, and you could see their grip tighten, see them take in their collective breaths. César's face showed nothing, not fear, not anticipation, just waiting for it.

The priest drove the blade into the flesh just below the ribs.

César's body jerked in reaction, but he didn't cry out. The blade tore across him, digging into the meat, widening the hole. His body danced with the wound, but he never made a sound. Blood poured across César's pale skin, bright and almost unreal under the lights. The priest reached his hand into the wound nearly up to his elbow, and César cried out.

I grabbed Dallas's arm. 'He can't survive without his heart, not even a shapeshifter can survive that.'

'They won't take his heart, I swear it.' She stroked my hand where it gripped her like you'd soothe a nervous dog.

I leaned in close to her, and whispered, 'If they take his heart when I could have stopped it, I'll have your heart on a knife before I leave New Mexico. You still willing to swear?'

Her eyes had gone wide. I think she was holding her breath, but she nodded. 'I swear it.'

The funny thing was that she believed the threat instantly. Most people you tell them you're going to cut their heart out and they won't believe you. People believe you'll kill them, but get too graphic and they take it like a joke or an exaggeration. Professor Dallas believed me. You could see it in her face. Most college professors wouldn't have. Made me wonder about Dallas more than I already did.

The priest's voice came into the utter silence that had filled the room. 'I hold his heart in my hand. In the long gone days we would have torn it from his chest, but those days are gone,' and you heard, felt the regret in his words. 'We worship as we can, not as we would.' He slid his hand out slowly, and I was close enough to hear the wet, fleshy sound as his hand pulled out of the wound.

He raised a hand covered in blood above his head, and the audience cheered.

They cheered. They fucking cheered.

The jaguar men lifted César from the altar and tossed him down the steps. He tumbled bonelessly, coming to rest on the floor directly in front of the steps. He lay on his back, gasping, fighting to breathe and I wondered if the priest had damaged a lung or two when he went fishing for the heart.

I just sat there, staring at him. He did this twice a month. It was part of his job. Shit. Not only didn't I understand it, I didn't want to. If he was into pain and death, I didn't need to know anything else about him. I was eyeball deep in sadomasochistic wereleopards back home. I didn't need another one.

The priest was talking, but I didn't hear him. I didn't hear anything but a great roaring like white noise in my ears. I watched the wereleopard twitch, body jerking, blood pouring down his sides, across the floor, but even as I stared, the blood was slowing. It was hard to tell through all the blood and torn flesh, but I knew he was healing.

Two of the human bouncers came and picked him up, one taking his ankles, the other lifting under his arms. They carried him through the tables, past us. I stood, stopping them. Dallas stood with me, as if afraid of what I'd do. I stared into César's eyes. There was real pain there. He wasn't having a good time or didn't seem to be. But you don't do shit like this on a regular basis unless you enjoy it on some level. His hands were lying on his chest, as if he were trying to hold himself together. I pried one hand up. The skin was slick with blood. I pressed the jade earrings into his hand, closed his fingers around them.

He whispered something, but I didn't bend down to hear. 'Don't ever come near me again.'

I sat back down, and they carried him away. I started to reach for a napkin to wipe my hands, but Dallas grabbed my arm. 'She's ready to see you now.'

I hadn't seen anyone talk to her, but I wasn't questioning it. If she said it was time, fine. We could meet the Master of the City and get the hell out of here.

I started to reach for the napkin again, but she moved it out of reach. 'It is fitting that you meet her with the blood of sacrifice on your hands.'

I looked at her and grabbed the napkin out of her hands. She actually struggled to keep it, and we had a little tug of war before I jerked it away from her. But a woman appeared at my elbow. She wore a red-hooded cloak and came up only to my shoulder, but even before she turned her head so I could see the face that lay inside that cloak, I knew what she was. Itzpapalotl, Obsidian Butterfly, Master of the City, and self-proclaimed goddess. I hadn't felt her coming. I hadn't heard her or sensed her. She just appeared beside me like magic. It had been a long time since a vampire had been able to do that. I think I stopped breathing for a second or two as I met her eyes.

Her face was as delicate as the rest of her, her skin a milk-pale brown. Her eyes were black, not just brown, but truly black like the obsidian blade she was named for. Most master vamp's eyes are like drowning pools, things to fall into and be trapped, but her eyes were like solid black mirrors reflecting back, not something to fall into, but something to show you the truth. I saw myself in those eyes, a miniature reflection perfect in every detail like a black cameo. Then the image split, doubling, tripling. My face stayed in the center with a wolf's head on one side, and a skull on the other. As I watched, the three images grew closer until the wolf and skull were superimposed over my face, and for a split second I couldn't tell where one image left off and the others began.

One image floated above the rest. The skull rose above the first two, spilling upward through the blackness, filling her eyes until the skull filled my vision, and I was able to stumble back, nearly falling. Edward was there, catching me. Dallas had moved to stand beside the vampire.

Bernardo and Olaf were at Edward's back, and I knew in that instant that if he'd given the word, they'd have both drawn guns and fired. It was a comforting thought. Suicidal, but comforting.

Because I could feel her people now, which meant she had to have been blocking me, hiding them. I felt the vampires underneath the building, around it, through it. There were hundreds of them, and most of them were old. Hundreds of years old. And Obsidian Butterfly? I glanced at her but was careful not to meet her eyes this time. It had been years since I'd had to avoid a vampire's eyes. I'd forgotten how hard it is to look someone in the face without making eye contact, like some elaborate game. Them trying to catch my glance and bespell me, me trying to keep away.

She had a fall of straight black bangs, but the rest of her hair was pulled back from her face to reveal delicate ears set with jade ear spools. She was a delicate thing, petite even standing next to me and Professor Dallas, but I wasn't fooled by the packaging. What lay inside was a vampire not that old. I doubted she was a thousand years yet. I'd met older, much older, but I'd never met any vampire under a thousand that echoed in my head with the power that this one had. Power breathed off her skin like a nearly visible cloud, and I'd learned enough of vampires to know that the echo of power wasn't on purpose. Some of the masters with special abilities, like causing fear or lust, just gave off that power constantly like steam rising from a pot. It was involuntary, partially at least. But I'd never met one that leaked power, pure power.

Edward was talking to me, probably had been talking to me for a while. I just hadn't heard. 'Anita, Anita, are you all right?' I felt the press of a gun not pointed at my back, but drawn, using my body to shield it from the room. Things could get ugly really fast.

'I'm all right,' but my voice didn't sound all right. It sounded hollow and distant, like I was in shock. Maybe I was, a little. She hadn't exactly rolled my mind, but she knew things about me in that first contact that most vampires never figured out. I realized suddenly that she knew what kind of power I was. That was her gift, to be able to read power.

Her voice when it came was heavily accented and much deeper than that fragile throat should have held, as if the voice was an echo of that immense power. 'Whose servant are you?'

She knew I was a vampire's human servant, but not whose servant I was. I liked that, made me feel better. She read only power, not details, unless of course, she was only pretending not to know. But somehow I didn't think she'd pretend ignorance. No, this was one that liked showing off her knowledge. She breathed arrogance as she breathed power. But why not be arrogant? She was, after all, a goddess, self-proclaimed anyway. You'd have to be either absolutely arrogant or crazy to claim godhood.

'Jean-Claude, Master of the City of St Louis.'

She cocked her head to one side as if listening to something. 'Then you are the Executioner. You did not give your true name at the door.'

'Not all vampires will talk to me if they know who I am.'

'What is it you wish to speak with me about?'

'The mutilation murders.'

Again, she turned her head to one side as if listening. 'Ah, yes.' She blinked and looked up at me. 'The price for an audience is what lies on your hands.'

I must have looked as puzzled as I felt, because she elaborated. 'The blood, César's blood. I wish to take it from you.'

'How?' I asked; just call me suspicious.

She simply turned and started walking away. Her voice came like the sound to a badly dubbed film, sound long after it should have been heard. 'Follow me, and do not clean your hands.'

I glanced at Edward. 'Do you trust her?' I asked.

He shook his head.

'Me either,' I said.

'Are we going or staying?' Olaf asked.

'I vote for going,' Bernardo said. I hadn't really looked at him since the sacrifice began. He was looking a little pale. Olaf wasn't.

Olaf looked fresh and bright-eyed, as if he were enjoying the evening.

Dallas said, 'It would be a grave insult if you refuse her invitation. She rarely gives personal interviews voluntarily. You must have impressed her.'

'I didn't impress her. I attracted her,' I said.

Dallas frowned. 'Attracted her. She likes men.'

I shook my head. 'She may have sex with men, but what attracts her is power, Professor.'

She looked at me, searching my face. 'You have that kind of power?'

I sighed. 'We'll find out, won't we?' I started walking in the direction that the cloaked figure had gone. She hadn't waited for us to decide. She'd just walked away. Like I said, arrogant. Of course, we were about to follow her into her private lair. That was arrogance, too, or stupidity. Arrogance or stupidity, sometimes there's not much difference between the two.

25

I didn't know where to go, but Dallas did. She led us to a small door set to one side of the temple steps, hidden by curtains. The door was still open, like a black mouth. Steps led down. Where else? Just once I'd like to see a vamp whose major hideout was up instead of down.

Dallas walked down the steps with a spring in her step and a song in her heart. Her ponytail bounced as she skipped down the steps. If she had a single misgiving about going down into that darkness, it didn't show. Dallas confused me. On one hand she didn't see that Olaf was dangerous, and she wasn't afraid of any of the monsters in the club. On the other hand, she'd believed me when I told her I'd cut her heart out. I'd seen it in her eyes. How could she believe that threat from a total stranger and not see the other dangers? Didn't make sense to me, and I didn't like what I didn't understand. She seemed utterly harmless, but her reactions were weird, so I put a question mark by her. Which meant, I wouldn't be turning my back on her or treating her like a civilian until I was convinced that that was what she was.

I was going too slowly for Olaf. He pushed past me and followed Dallas's bouncing ponytail down the stairs. He had to stoop to keep from bumping his head on the ceiling, but he didn't seem to mind. Fine with me. Let him take the first bullet. But I followed them down into the dark. No one had offered me violence, not really, not yet. So it seemed rude to have a gun naked in my hand, but . . . I'd apologize later. Unless I knew the vampire personally, I liked having a loaded gun in hand the first time I paid a call. Or maybe it was the narrow stairs, the close press of stone as if it would close around us like a fist and crush us. Have I mentioned that I'm claustrophobic?

The stairs didn't go down very far, and there was no door at the end of them. Jean-Claude's retreat in St Louis was something of an underground fortress. The barely hidden doorway, the short stairs, no second door – arrogance, again.

Olaf blocked my view of Dallas, but I saw him reach the dimly lit doorway at the bottom. He had to stoop even farther to get through the door and hesitated before standing up on the other side. There was a sense of movement around him, or rather to either side of him. Quick, almost not there, like things you see out of the corner of your eyes. It reminded me of the hands that had stripped César as he walked between light and darkness.

He stayed just in the doorway, his body nearly filling it completely, blocking what little light there had been. I caught the faintest edge of Dallas. She led him away from the door farther into the firelit dark.

I called down, 'Olaf, are you okay?'

No answer.

Edward tried. 'Olaf?'

'I am fine.'

I glanced back at Edward. We had a moment of staring into each other's eyes, both of us thinking the same thing. This could be a trap. Maybe she was behind the murders. Maybe she just wanted to kill the Executioner. Or maybe she was a centuries-old vampire, and she just wanted to hurt us for the hell of it.

'Could she make Olaf lie?'

'You mean mind tricks?' I asked.

He nodded.

'Not this fast. I may not like him, but he's stronger than that.' I looked at him, searching his face in the dim light. 'Could they force him to lie?'

'You mean a knife at his throat?' Edward said.

'Yeah.'

He gave a faint smile. 'No, not this quick, not ever.'

'You're sure of that?' I asked.

'My life on it.'

'We're betting all our lives on it.'

He nodded. 'Yes, we are.'

But if Edward said that Olaf wouldn't sell us out on fear of death or pain, then I believed him. Edward didn't always understand why people did what they did, but he was usually right about the fact that they were going to do it. Motive evaded him, but he was seldom wrong. So . . . I kept walking down the steps.

I strained my peripheral vision, trying to see on either side of the doorway as I walked through it. I didn't have to bend over to go through. The room was square and small, maybe sixteen by sixteen. It was also packed nearly corner to corner with vampires.

I put my back against the wall to the right of the door, gun clutched two-handed, pointed at the ceiling. I wanted badly to point it at someone, anyone. My shoulders ached with the tension of not doing it. No one was threatening me. No one was doing a damn thing except standing, staring, milling around the way people do. So why did I feel like I should have entered the room shooting?

Tall vampires, short vampires, thin vampires, fat vampires, every size, every shape, and almost every race, moved around that small stone room. After what had happened upstairs with their master, I was careful not to make eye contact with any of them. My gaze swept over the room, taking in the pale faces, and getting a quick head count. When I got over sixty, I realized the room was at least twice the size I'd originally thought. It had to be just to hold this many of them. It only looked small because it was packed so tight. The torchlight added to the illusion, flickering, dancing, uncertain light.

Edward stayed in the doorway, his back to the doorframe, shoulder touching mine lightly. His gun was up like mine, his eyes searching the vamps. 'What's wrong?'

'What's wrong? Look at them.' My voice was breathy, not because I was trying to whisper – that would have been useless – but because my throat was tight, my mouth dry.

He scanned the crowd again. 'So?'

My gaze flashed to him, then back to the waiting vampires. 'Shit, Ed . . . Ted. Shit.' It wasn't just the number of them. It was my own ability to sense them that was the problem. I'd been around a hundred vamps before, but they hadn't affected me like this. I didn't know if having walled off my link to Jean-Claude made me more vulnerable to them, or if my necromancy had grown since then. Or maybe Itzpapalotl was just that much more powerful than the other master had been. Maybe it was her power that had made them so much more than most vamps. There were close to a hundred in this room. I was getting impressions from all of them, or most of them. My shields were great now; I could keep out a lot of the preternatural stuff, but this was too much for me. If I had to guess, there wasn't a vamp in the room under a hundred. I got flashes from individual ones if I looked at them too long, a slap in the face of their age, their power. The four females in the right corner were all over five hundred years old. They watched me with dark eyes, dark-skinned, but not as dark as they would have been with a little sun. The four of them watched me with patient, empty faces.

Her voice came from the center of the room, but she was hidden behind the vampires, shielded by them. 'I have offered you no violence, yet you have drawn weapons. You seek my aid, yet you threaten me.'

'It's not personal, Itz . . .' I stumbled over her name.

'You may call me Obsidian Butterfly.' It was odd talking to her without being able to glimpse her through the waiting figures.

'It's not personal, Obsidian Butterfly. I just know that once I put up the gun, chances of drawing it again before one of your brood rips my throat out are damn small.'

'You mistrust us,' she said.

'As you mistrust us,' I said.

She laughed then. Her laughter was the sound of a young woman, normal, but the strained echoes from the other vampires were anything but normal. The laughter held a wild note to it, a desperation, as if they were afraid not to laugh. I wondered what the penalty was for not following her lead.

The laughter faded away, except for one high pitched masculine sound. The other vampires went still, that impossible stillness where they seem like well-made statues, things made of stone and paint, not real, not alive. They waited like a host of empty things. Waited for what? The only sound was that high, unhealthy laughter, rising up and up like the sounds the movies have you hear in insane asylums, or mad scientists' laboratories. The sound raised the hair on my arms, and it wasn't magic. It was just creepy.

'If you put up your guns, I will send most of my people away. That is fair, is it not?'

It was fair, but I didn't like it. I liked having the gun naked in my hands. Of course, the gun only worked if shooting a few of them would stop the rest from rushing us, and it wouldn't. If she said, go to hell, they'd start digging a hole. If she told them to rush us, they most certainly would. So the guns were just a security blanket, a delaying tactic before the end. It took only a few seconds to think it through, but that awful laughter kept going like it was one of those creepy dolls with a laugh track inside of it.

I felt Edward's shoulder pressing against mine. He was waiting for me to give the answer, trusting my expertise. I hoped I didn't get us killed. I put the gun back in its holster. I rubbed my hand against my leg. I'd been holding the gun too long, and too damn tight. Me, nervous?

Edward put his gun up. Bernardo was still in the stairway, and

I realized that he was making sure nothing came down the stairs and blocked our retreat. It was kind of nice working with more than just two people and knowing everyone on your side was willing to shoot anything that moved. No bleeding hearts, no empathy, just business.

Of course, Olaf was off to one side with Dallas. He had never pulled a gun. He had waded into this many vampires, following her bouncing ponytail to destruction. Or at least to potential destruction.

The vampires drew a breath, each chest rising as one, as if they were many bodies with one mind. Life, for lack of a better term, flowed back into them. Some of them looked almost human, but many of them were pale and starved, and weak. Their faces were too thin, as if the bones of their skull would push out through the sickly skin. They were all pale, but the natural skin color of many was darker than Caucasian, so even pale, they weren't the ghostly paleness I was used to seeing. I realized with something like shock that most of the vampires I knew were Caucasian. Here, white skin was the minority. A nice reversal.

The vampires began to glide towards the door. Or some of them glided. Some of them shuffled as if they didn't have energy to pick their feet up, as if they were truly ill. To my knowledge vampires couldn't catch any disease. But these vampires looked sick.

One of them stumbled and fell at my feet, landing heavily on hands and knees. He stayed where he was, head hanging down. His skin was a dirty white, like snow that had lain too long by a busy road, a greyish white. The other vampires moved around him as if he were a bump in the road. They flowed past him, and he didn't seem to notice. His hands looked like the hands of a skeleton, barely covered with skin. His hair was a blond so light, it looked white, hanging down around his face. He raised his face up, slowly, and it was like looking at a skull. His eyes had sunk so far into his head that they seemed to burn at the end of long black tunnels. I wasn't afraid of looking in this one's eyes. He didn't have enough juice to roll me with his eyes. I could tell that just standing here. The bones of his cheeks pushed so hard against the thin skin that it looked like they should tear through.

A pale tongue slid from between thin, nearly invisible lips. His eyes were a pale, pale green, like bad emeralds. The thin walls of his nose flared as if he were scenting the air. He probably was. Vamps didn't rely on scent the way shapeshifters did, but they had a much better sense of smell than humans. He closed his eyes in the middle of drawing a deep breath. He shuddered and seemed to swoon, faint. I'd never seen a vamp act like this. It caught me off guard, and that was my fault.

I saw him tense, and my hand was going for the Browning, but there was no time. He was less than a foot away. I never even touched the gun before he slammed into me. He knocked the breath from my body. His hand was on my face, turning my head to one side, baring my neck, before I had time to breathe. I had a sense of movement even though I couldn't see him. I felt his body tense and I knew he was coming in for a strike. He made no effort to control my hands. I kept going for the gun, but I would never get it out and pointed in time. He was going to sink fangs into my neck, and I couldn't stop it. It was like a car accident. I just had time to see it coming and to think, 'I can't stop it.' There wasn't even time to be afraid.

Something jerked the vampire backwards. His hand curled in my jacket, and didn't let go. His desperate grip nearly pulled me off my feet, but I got the gun out before I worried about staying on my feet.

A large, very Aztec-looking vamp had the skeletal vamp, holding him pinned against his body, only that one arm with its clutching hand not pressed to the larger man's body.

Edward had his gun out pointed at the vampires. He'd gotten to his gun first, but then he hadn't been shoved up against a wall and manhandled. Or would that be vampire-handled?

The big vamp jerked the thin one hard enough that he nearly pulled me off my feet, but that one clutching hand stayed curled in my jacket, catching on the shirt underneath. I had the Browning pointed at the vamp's chest, though I wasn't sure if the Hornady ammo was safe to shoot at arm's distance into one target pressed directly in front of another person. I wasn't sure if the ammo would go through the first vamp and into the second. The second vamp had saved me. It really wouldn't be nice to blow a hole in him.

The other vampires were leaving the room in a hurrying line to get past us and up the stairs, out of harm's way. Cowards. But it was thinning out the ranks, which would be great. Eventually, I'd care that there weren't so damn many vamps in the room, but right now the world was narrowed down to the vamp that had hold of me. First things first.

The big vamp kept backing up, trying to get the skeletal one to let go of me. We kept moving farther into the room. Edward paced us, gun held two-handed pointed at the vampire's head. I finally put the barrel of my gun underneath the vamp's chin. I could blow his brains up without hitting the second vampire.

Obsidian Butterfly's voice slashed through the room like a whip. The sound made me wince, shoulders tightening as if it had been a blow. 'These are my guests. How dare you attack them!'

The skeletal vampire started to cry, and his tears were clear, human. Vampire's tears are tinged red. They cry bloody tears. 'Please, please let me feed, please!'

'You feed as we all feed, as befits a god.'

'Please, please, mistress, please.'

'You disgrace me before our visitors.' Then she spoke low and rapidly in a language that was sort of Spanish sounding, but it wasn't Spanish. I don't speak Spanish, but I've heard it spoken often enough to know it when I hear it, and this wasn't it. Whatever she was saying, upset both vampires.

The big one pulled so hard that he finally jerked me off my feet because the other vamp was still holding on. I ended up on my knees, my jacket and shirt dangling from the vamp's hand, one arm pulled up at an awkward angle. My gun was pressed into his stomach now, and again I wondered if at point blank range the new ammo would kill both vamps? It was a miracle that I hadn't accidentally shot his head off. Edward was still there, gun pointed at the vamp's head. The first hint I had that something else had gone wrong was a faint glow. The glow grew into something pure and white. My cross had spilled out of my shirt.

The vampire kept his grip on me, but started to scream in a high pitiful voice. The cross flared bright and brighter until I had to turn my head and shield my eyes. It was like having magnesium burning around your neck. So bright, it only got this bright when something very bad was near. I didn't think the something bad was the thing still hanging onto me. I was betting the cross was glowing for her benefit, maybe others' but mostly hers. A lot of things in the room could kill me, but nothing else in the room was worth this much of a light show.

'Let him go to his destiny,' she said.

I felt the arm that was still pulling so desperately go limp. I felt him kneeling, felt it through the barrel of the gun still pressed against him.

Edward said, 'Anita?' It was a question, but I didn't have an answer yet.

I blinked past the light, trying to see. The vampire put a hand on either side of my shoulders. His eyes were squeezed shut against the light. His face stretched wide with pain. The white white light glistened on fangs as he moved in to feed.

'Stop, or die,' I said.

I'm not sure he even heard me. His hand caressed the edge of my cheek, and it was like being touched by fleshy sticks. His hands didn't even feel real. I yelled, 'I'll kill him.'

'Do so. It's his choice.' Her voice was so matter of fact, so uncaring, that it made me not want to do it.

His hand grabbed my hair, tried to twist my face to one side. His head was drawn back for a strike, but he couldn't push past the glare of the cross. But he might work up to it. As weak as he was, he should have run screaming from this much holy light.

'Anita.' Edward's voice and it wasn't a question now, more a preview.

The vampire let out a scream that made me gasp. His head threw back, then down, and his face moved in a white blur towards me. The gun went off before I realized I'd squeezed the trigger, just a reflex. A second gun echoed so close on my shot that it sounded like a single gunshot. The vamp jerked, and his head exploded. Blood and thicker things sprayed half my face.

I knelt in a sudden deafening silence. There was no sound, nothing but a fine, distant ringing in my ears, like tinny bells. I turned in a sort of slow motion to see the vamp's body sprawled on its side. I got to my feet and still couldn't hear anything. Sometimes that's shock. Sometimes it's just gunshots going off next to your ears.

I scraped at the blood and thicker pieces on the left side of my face. Edward handed me a white handkerchief, probably something Ted would carry, but I took it. I started trying to scrape the stuff off of me.

The cross was still glowing like a captive star. I was already deaf. If I didn't stop having to squint around the light, I was going to be blind as well. I looked around the room. Most of the vamps had fled up the stairs away from the cross's glow, but what was left huddled around their goddess, shielding her, I think, from us. I blinked through the glare, and I think I saw fear on one or two faces. You don't see that often on several hundred years worth of vampire. It might have been the cross, but I didn't think that was it. I slipped the cross back into my shirt. The cross was still cool silver. It never burned unless vampire flesh touched it. Then it would flare into actual flame and burn the vamp and any human flesh that happened to be touching it at the same time. Usually, the vamp would jerk away before you got past second degree burns so I'd never gotten a scar from one of my own crosses.

The vampires stayed in front of their mistress, and the fear was still there on at least one face. The cross could keep them at bay, but that wasn't what they feared. I looked down at the body. The entrance hole was just a small red thing, with black scorch marks around it, but the exit hole was nearly a foot in diameter. There was no head on the body, only the lower jaw and a thin rim of back brain left. The rest had been blown in a wide spray across the floor and across me.

Edward's mouth was moving, and sound came back in a kind of Doppler shift, so that I heard only the end of it. '. . . ammo are you using now?'

I told him.

He knelt by the body and inspected the chest wound. 'I thought the Hornady XTP wasn't supposed to make this much of a mess going out.'

His voice still sounded like it was distant, tinny, but I could hear again. It meant that my hearing would go back to normal eventually. 'I don't think they did any firing tests at point blank range.'

'It makes a nice hole at point blank range.'

'In like a penny, out like a pizza,' I said.

'You had questions about the murders?' Obsidian Butterfly said. 'Ask them.'

She was standing in the middle of her people, but no longer shielded. I don't know if she decided we weren't going to shoot her, or if she thought it was cowardice to hide behind others, or if we'd passed some kind of test. But if she were willing to answer my questions, then I'd take it any way I could get it.

I saw Dallas and Olaf to one side of the vamps. Dallas had her face hidden against his chest, and he was holding her, comforting her, helping her not see the mess on the floor. Olaf was looking down at her as if she were something precious. It wasn't love, more the way a man will look at a really nice car that he wants to own. He looked at her like she was a pretty thing that he'd wanted but hadn't expected to get. He stroked her hair, running his fingers through the long dark ponytail over and over, playing with her hair, watching it fall against her back.

I wasn't the only one watching them. 'Cruz, take the professor upstairs. I think she's seen enough for one night.'

A short male vamp, very Hispanic, went to them, but Olaf said, 'I'll take her upstairs.'

'No,' Edward said.

'I don't think so,' I said.

Itzpapalotl said, 'That will not be necessary.'

The three of us exchanged a glance, though I didn't meet her eyes dead on. But there was an understanding between us, I think. Olaf needed to stay away from the professor. Maybe a state or two away from her.

Cruz pulled Dallas out of Olaf's reluctant arms and led the crying woman up the stairs, and away from the horror we'd stretched out on the floor. Though we hadn't made the vampire a horror, we just killed him. Itzpapalotl had starved him until he faced a glowing cross for the chance to feed. Starved him until he'd let two humans point guns at him and not even try to get away. He'd wanted to sink fangs into human flesh more than he'd wanted to live. I don't usually feel sorry for vampires that try to feed off of me, especially without permission, but this one time I'd make an exception. He'd been pitiful. Now he was dead. Pity has never stopped me from pulling a trigger, and Edward didn't feel pity. I could stare down at what was left of that skeletal body and think, poor thing, but I felt nothing about the death. It wasn't just that I didn't feel regret. I felt nothing, absolutely nothing.

I looked at Edward, and he looked at me, and I'd have given a great deal for a mirror right that second. Staring into Edward's blank face, those empty eyes that felt nothing, I realized that I didn't need a mirror. I already had one.

26

Maybe I'd have been afraid of that revelation, but the vampires began to flow out towards us. Survival first, moral issues later. Richard might say that was one of my biggest problems. Jean-Claude wouldn't. There's more than one reason why Richard and I haven't settled down to a happy ever after life, and there's more than one reason why I haven't cut Jean-Claude loose.

Itzpapalotl glided forward still shrouded in the scarlet cloak. It was so long that you couldn't see her feet and she moved so smoothly that it looked like she was on wheels. There was something artificial about her.

The four silent women moved on her left, and something bothered me about the way they moved. It took me a second or two to realize what it was. They were moving in utter unison, perfect step. One lifted a hand to brush a strand of black hair from her face, and all the others followed the movement like puppets, though there was no stray hair on their faces. From the breaths that raised their chests, to the small jerk of a finger, they imitated each other. No, not imitated, that was too mild a word. They were like one being with four bodies. The effect was eerie because they didn't look alike. One was short and square. One was tall and thin. The other two were delicate and did look something alike. All of them had paler skin than Itzpapalotl, as if in life they hadn't been much darker than they were now.

The tall vamp that had tried to pull the starving vamp off me walked to her right. He was the tallest of the ones that looked pure Aztec, six feet at least, with shoulders and muscles to match. His hair fell in a black wash down his back, held from his face by a crown of feathers and gold. His nose was pierced, though that was too mild a word for the three inches of thick gold that bisected his face. Gold earplugs stretched his earlobes to a thin line of flesh. His skin was the color that old ivory sometimes gets, not a pale gold, but a pale copper, palest bronze. It was a striking color with the coal black hair and the perfectly black eyes. He moved two steps back, at her right, and like the women, he moved as if this had always been his place.

Three male vamps moved a little distance from the man. They were all that shining ivory white that I was used to seeing. They were dressed in the same clothing as the bouncers, those skirt/thong bathing suit thingies. But they had no adornment. Their arms and legs were pale and empty. They were even barefoot. I knew servants when I saw them, or prisoners maybe.

One was medium height with curly brown hair cut short, and a darker brown line of beard and mustache outlining the perfect whiteness of the skin. The eyes were pale blue. The second man was shorter with short hair turned salt and pepper as if he'd died after the hair had gone grey. The face was lined, but strong, and the body still muscular, so that his age at death was hard to tell. Older than the others, fortyish, though I was no judge of age of death in vamps. His eyes were the dark grey of storm clouds, echoing his hair color. He held a leash in one hand, and on the end of that leash the third man crawled, not on all fours, but on his hands, and his feet, legs hunched monkey like, or like a whipped dog. His hair was short and a surprising yellow, curling soft. It was the only thing on him that looked alive. His skin was like old paper, clinging and yellowed to his bones. His eyes were sunk so far back into his head that I couldn't tell what color they were.

The end of the entourage was five very Hispanic, Aztecy bodyguards. Bodyguards are bodyguards regardless of the culture, the century, or state of life, or would that be death? I knew muscle when I saw it, and the five vamps were muscle, even carrying obsidian blades, and obsidian-edged clubs, and looking somewhat less than serious in feathers and jewelry. They exuded that aura of badass.

Olaf had moved back to stand with us, and the three of us faced them. Bernardo had stayed near the stairway, making sure our retreat wasn't cut off. So nice to work with other professionals. Olaf had his gun out now, too, and was watching the vamps with a look that wasn't neutral. It was hostile. I didn't know why, but he seemed pissed. Go figure.

The vamps stopped about eight feet from us. The dead vampire lay on the floor between us. The body had already stopped bleeding. When you take a head off of a vamp, they bleed just like a human, quarts and quarts of the red stuff. It is a freaking mess when you decapitate someone. But this vampire had bled only a small odd-shaped space on the stone floor, barely a foot across, and a second even smaller pool under the chest. Not nearly enough blood for what we'd done to him.

The silence seemed thicker than it should have, and Olaf filled it. 'You can check his pulse if you want.'

'Olaf, don't,' Edward said.

Olaf shifted, either uncomfortable, or fighting down the urge to do something worse than mouthing off. 'You're the boss,' he said, but not like he meant it.

'I doubt this one had a pulse,' I said, and I was looking at the vampires while I said it. 'It takes energy to make a vamp's heart beat and he didn't have any.'

'You feel pity for him,' Itzpapalotl said.

'Yeah, I guess I do.'

'Your friend does not.'

I glanced at Edward. His face showed nothing. It was nice to know there were still some differences between us. I felt pity. He didn't. 'Probably he doesn't.'

'But there is no regret in either of you, no guilt.'

'Why should we feel guilty? We just killed him. We didn't turn him into a crawling, starved thing.'

Even under the masking cloak, I could feel her grow still with that awful stillness that only the old ones have. Her voice came warm with the first thread of anger. 'You presume to judge me.'

'No, just stating facts. If he hadn't been starved worse than any vamp I've ever seen outside of a coffin prison, he would never have attacked me.' I also thought that they could have tried harder to get him off of me, but didn't say it out loud. I really didn't want to piss her off with eighty or so vamps waiting upstairs between us and the door. That wasn't even taking into account the werejaguars.

'And if I told my starved ones that they could feed off of you, all of them, what would they do?' she asked.

The starved vamp on the leash, looked up at that. His eyes never stayed on anyone too long, flitting from face to face to face, but he'd heard her.

My stomach jerked tight in a knot hard enough to hurt. I had to blow out a breath to be able to talk around the sudden flutter of my pulse. There'd been at least ten, fifteen of the starved ones. 'They'd attack us,' I said.

'They would fall upon you like ravening dogs,' she said.

I nodded, hand settling more securely on the butt of my gun. 'Yeah.' If she gave the order, my first bullet was going between her eyes. If I died, I wanted to take her with me. Vindictive, but true.

'The thought frightens you,' she said.

I tried to see her face in that hood, but some trick of shadow left only her small bowed mouth visible. 'If you can feel all these emotions, then you can tell a lie from a truth.'

She lifted her face, a sudden defiant movement. A look passed over her face, the barest flicker across that calmness. She really couldn't tell lie from truth. Yet she sensed regret, pity, fear. Truth and lie should have come in there somewhere.

'My starved ones are useful from time to time.'

'So you starve them deliberately.'

'No,' she said. 'The great creator god sees they are weak and does not sustain them as he sustains us.'

'I don't understand.'

'They are allowed to feed as gods feed, not as animals.'

I frowned. 'Sorry, I still don't get it.'

'We will show you how a god feeds, Anita.' She said my name like it was meant to be said, making it a rolling three syllable word, making of the ordinary name something exotic.

'Shapeshifter coming down,' Bernardo said. He had his gun up and pointed.

'I have called a priest to feed the gods.'

'Let him come down,' I said. I looked at that delicate face and tried to read what was there, but there was nothing home that I could talk to, nothing I could understand. 'I don't mean to be insulting, my apologies if I am being insulting, but we came here to talk about the murders. I would like to ask you some questions.'

'Your vast knowledge of things arcane and things Aztec has brought us to you,' Edward said.

I fought not to raise eyebrows at him, just nodding. 'Yeah, what he said.'

She actually smiled. 'You still believe I and my people are merely vampires. You do not truly believe that we are gods.'

She had me there, but she couldn't smell a lie. 'I'm Christian. You saw that when the cross glowed. That means I'm a monotheist, so if you guys are gods, then it's something of a problem for me.' That was so diplomatic, even I was impressed.

'We will prove it to you, then we will offer you hospitality as our guests, then we will talk business.'

I've learned over the years that if someone says they're a god, you don't argue with them unless you're better armed. So I didn't try and get the business moved up. She was nuts and had enough muscle backing her in this building to make her brand of craziness contagious, or even fatal. So we'd do arcane vampire shit, then when the self-proclaimed goddess was satisfied I'd get to ask my questions. How bad could it be, watching them prove they were gods? Don't answer that.

The werejaguar that came through the door was the blue-eyed blond with his golden tan that had first passed so near our table that I'd touched his fur. He came through the door with a neutral face, empty-eyed as if he wasn't entirely sure he wanted to be here.

His gaze took in the room, and hesitated over the dead vamp in the middle. But he fell to one knee in front of Itzpapalotl, his back to us and our guns, fur-covered head bowed. 'What would you have of me, holy mistress?'

I fought to keep my face blank. Holy mistress? Good grief.

'I want to show our visitors how a god is fed.'

He looked up then, looking into her face. 'Who am I to worship, holy mistress?'

'Diego,' she said.

The brown-haired vampire startled at the name, and though his face was blank, empty, I knew he wasn't happy. 'Yes, my dark goddess, what would you have of me?'

'Seth will offer sacrifice to you.' She caressed a delicate hand across the fur of the man's hood.

'As you like, my dark goddess,' Diego said. His voice was as empty as his face tried to be.

The werejaguar, Seth, crawled on all fours, mimicking the animal whose skin he wore. He pressed his forehead to his hands, lying nearly prostrate at Diego's feet.

'Rise, priest of our dark goddess, and make sacrifice to us.'

The werejaguar stood, and he was nearly half a foot taller than the vampire. He did something on the front of the jaguar skin, and it opened, enough for him to lift the headpiece over his head, so that the animal's sightless glass eyes stared back at us over the man's shoulders. The head flopped bonelessly like a broken-necked thing. His hair was a rich honey blond, sun-streaked, held back in a long club, woven back and forth so that it looked like a lot of hair, but held close to his head so the jaguar skin would slip on easily. It was just like the hairdo on the one who had gotten cut up by the priest backstage.

'Turn so our visitors can see all,' Itzpapalotl said.

The men turned so we had a side view. The werejaguar's earlobes were covered in thick white scars. He drew a small silver knife from his belt, the hilt was carved jade. He placed the sliver blade against his earlobe, steadying it with his other hand and sliced it open. Blood spilled in scarlet lines on his fingers, down the blade, to drip on the shoulders of the jaguar skin.

Diego went to the taller man, putting a hand behind his neck, and another at the small of his back. It looked oddly like a kiss, as he drew the werejaguar's head downward. The vampire's mouth sealed around the earlobe, drawing it and some of the ear into his mouth. His throat worked as he swallowed, sucking on the wound, drawing it down. The pale blue of his eyes had spread to a sparkling fire like palest sapphires sparkling in the sun. His skin began to glow as if there was white fire inside. The brown of his hair darkened, or maybe that was illusion because of how glowing white his skin had become.

The werejaguar had closed his eyes, head thrown back, breath catching in his throat, as if it felt good. One of his hands lay on the vampire's bare shoulder, and you could see the pressure of his fingers in that pale, glowing flesh.

Diego drew back, flashing fangs. 'The wound closes.'

'Another offering, my cat,' she said.

The vampire moved back just enough for the other man to use the silver blade on the other ear. Then he fell on him, like a lover long refused. He drew back, eyes sparkling with blue light. He looked blind and heavy-lidded as he drew back from him. 'The wound closes.'

It was actually interesting that the wound closed as fast as it did. Vamps had an anticoagulant in their saliva that should have kept it flowing, and silver should have forced the shapeshifter to heal human normal, but the wound was closing pretty fast, not fast enough to make me comfortable, but a lot faster than it should have. The only thing I could figure was that Itzpapalotl had somehow given her shapeshifters even more healing ability than a normal shapeshifter. Maybe normal silver bullets wouldn't work on them, not to kill them anyway. It was something to think about, just in case.

'I want them to see what it is to be a god, Diego. Show them, my cat.'

The werejaguar opened a seam on the fur that looked almost like it was Velcroed shut. He slit open the front of the fur, having to stop and undo the belt that held knives and a small pouch. The belt dropped to the floor, and he slipped the fur down his body. The golden tan was an all-over tan, complete with . . . um, you know. Nude sun bathing, how unhealthy.

The jaguar slipped out of the skin until he stood completely nude. He still had the silver knife in his hand. I didn't have a clue what he was about to use it on, but having to strip couldn't be a good sign. He cupped his own penis, and it had come out of the fur smooth and hard, excited. He put the point of the blade against that delicate skin and drew it in a thin crimson line. His breath ran out in a ragged gasp.

It was echoed by me and Olaf. Bernardo said, 'Shit!' Eeeyah. I don't think I had as much sympathy as the guys, but that had to hurt. Edward was the only one of us who hadn't made a sound. Either he knew what was coming, or nothing surprised him.

'Diego,' Itzpapalotl said, 'show them what it means to be a god.' There was a thread of warning in her voice, as if she were warning him to do his job. I wasn't sure why because Diego had seemed to thoroughly enjoy the ear sucking. Why wouldn't he do this?

Diego dropped to his knees, and his face was very close to the offered blood; all he had to do was reach out and take it. But he stayed kneeling, staring at the cut flesh with eyes that still blazed pale blue fire. He stayed kneeling until the cut began to heal, and finally vanish as if the flesh had absorbed it. I'd never seen a shapeshifter heal silver that well. Never.

Seth looked over his shoulder, one hand still around his naked penis, though it was beginning to wilt a little. 'Holy mistress, what do you wish me to do?'

'Sacrifice,' she said, and there was enough heat in that one word to make me shiver.

Seth put the blade point to his flesh again. It seemed harder to get a clean cut when he wasn't fully erect, but he managed. Blood spread in fine rivulets over his skin, staining his fingers with tiny bits of red.

Diego stayed kneeling, but made no move to feed. The fire faded from his eyes, the glow leeched out of the skin, leaving him still lovely, a contrast of pale skin, dark hair, and blue eyes, but he looked defeated somehow, hands limp in his lap.

The four women moved around behind Itzpapalotl, gliding as a unit until they stood in a half-circle behind the kneeling vampire. 'You have disappointed me again, Diego,' the goddess said.

He shook his head and bowed it, eyes closing. 'I am sorry for that, my dark goddess. I would not disappoint you for the sun and the moon itself.' But his voice was tired when he said it, like it was a memorized line but his heart wasn't in it.

The four vamps surrounding him pulled black leather bound rods from their belts, and lifted leather bags off the ends. Dozens of thin leather cords spread out from each bag like obscene flowers. Silver balls were braided in the cords so that they sparkled in the torchlight. It was a cat o' nine tails, except it had a lot more tails.

'Why do you insist on refusing this honor, Diego? Why do you make us punish you?'

'I am not a lover of men, my dark goddess, and I will not do this. I am sorry that my refusal pains you, but this one thing I will not do.' Again, his voice was tired, as if he'd said all of it before, many times before.

He was about five hundred years old, like the four women that surrounded him. Had he been turning the 'honor' down for five centuries?

The four women watched their goddess, not glancing even at the vampire at their feet. Itzpapalotl gave a small nod. Four arms went back, flaring the cat o' nine tails in a fan of silver and leather. They whirled it through the air like they knew what they were doing. They hit him in sequence, right to left, each whip landing a blow, then the next, the next, the next. The blows fell so close together it was like the sound of hard rain, except that this rain was smacking into flesh, and you could hear it thudding home. They whipped him until they drew blood, then they stood motionless around him, waiting.

'Do you still refuse?'

'Yes, my dark goddess, I still refuse.'

'When you raped these women long ago, did you dream of the price you would pay?'

'No, my dark goddess, I did not.'

'You didn't believe in our gods, did you?'

'No, my dark goddess, I did not.'

'You thought your white Christ could save you, didn't you?'

'Yes, my dark goddess, I did.'

'You were wrong.'

His head hunched between his shoulders as if he were trying to draw into himself like a turtle. The metaphor was funny. The gesture was not. 'Yes, my dark goddess, I was wrong.'

She gave another nod, and the women began to whip him in a

blur that made the whips gleam silver like lightning in their hands. Blood ran in streamers down his back, but he never cried out, never asked for mercy.

I must have made some movement, because Edward stepped close to me, not grabbing my arm, but touching it. I met his eyes, and he gave the barest shake of his head. I wouldn't really risk our lives for a vampire I didn't know, really I wouldn't, but I didn't like it.

Olaf made a small sound. He was watching it with glowing eyes like a child at Christmas who comes down to find that he'd gotten exactly what he wanted. He'd put up the gun, his big hands clasped in front of him, clasped so hard they were mottled, and a fine tremor ran up his arms. I might not like it, but Olaf did.

I glanced at Edward, sort of nodding to the big man. Edward gave the barest of nods. He saw it, too, but he was ignoring it. I tried. I caught Bernardo's eyes. He was staring at the big man, a look very close to fear on his face. He turned and concentrated on the stairs, turning his back on everything in the room. I'd have liked to join him, but I couldn't turn away. It wasn't just macho crap, you know. If Edward could stand to watch it, then so could I. Though there was a little of that. Mostly it was if Diego could endure it, I could watch it. If I wasn't going to stop it then I had to at least watch. To do nothing to help him and to turn away would have been too much cowardice for me to swallow. I'd have choked on it. The best I could do was try to watch other things around him. The way the women's arms went up and down like machines, as if they would never tire.

The five guards stood impassive, but the vamp that walked at Itzpapalotl's right side watched it with half-parted lips, eyes intent as if afraid to miss even the smallest movement. He was almost as old as the goddess herself, seven, eight hundred years, and for five hundred of those years he'd been watching this particular show, and he still enjoyed it. I knew in that moment that I never wanted to make an enemy of the creatures in this room. I never wanted to be at their mercy. Because they had none.

The other two Spanish survivors had moved back to stand against the far wall, as far from the show as they could get. The one with salt and pepper hair stared at the ground as if there was something of great interest there. The starved one on his leash had curled into a fetal position, as if he were trying to disappear altogether.

The women turned Diego's back into bloody ribbons. A red pool formed at his feet. He curled his upper body over his legs until he was like a little ball of pain. Blood began to drip down his shoulders to form a second puddle in front of him. He was weaving, even that low to the ground, as if he might pass out. I hoped he passed out soon.

I finally did take a step forward, and Edward grabbed my arm. 'No,' he said.

'You feel pity for him,' Itzpapalotl said.

'Yes,' I said.

'Diego was one of the strangers that came into our lands. He thought we were barbarians. We were things to be conquered, robbed, raped, slaughtered. Diego never saw us as people, did you, Diego?'

There was no answer this time. He wasn't exactly unconscious but close enough that he was beyond words. 'You didn't think we were people, did you, Cristobal?'

I didn't know who Cristobal was, but there was a high keening sound. It was the vampire on the leash. He unrolled from his tight fetal ball. The keening ended in that same awful laughter that I'd heard earlier. The laughter rose up and up until the vampire holding the leash jerked it tight, pulling him like you'd discipline a dog. I realized that the leash was a choke collar. Shit.

'Answer me, Cristobal.'

The vampire let up on the leash enough for the starved one to get a ragged breath. His voice, when it came, was strangely cultured, smooth and sane. 'No, we did not think you were people, my dark goddess.' Then the ragged laughter came from those thin lips, and he huddled around himself again.

'They broke into our temple and raped our priestesses, our virgin priestesses, our nuns. Twelve of them raped these four priestesses. They did unspeakable, vile things to them, forced them with pain and threats of death to do whatever the men wanted them to do.'

The women's faces never changed during the speech, as if it were about someone else. They had stopped whipping the man. They just stood there watching him bleed.

'I found them dying in the temple from what had been done to them. I offered them life. I offered them vengeance. I made them gods, and then we hunted down the strangers that had raped them, the ones that left them for dead. We took each of them, made them one of us, so their punishment would last forever. But my teyolloquanies were too strong for most of them. There were twelve of them once. Now only two remain.'

Itzpapalotl looked at me, and there was a challenge in her face, a look that demanded an answer. 'Do you still feel pity for him?'

I nodded. 'Yes, but I understand hate, and revenge is one of my best things.'

'Then you see the justice here.'

I opened my mouth. Edward's hand tightened on my arm, until it was painful. He forced me to think before I answered. I'd have been careful, but he didn't know that.

'He did a terrible, unforgivable thing. They should have their revenge.' In my head I added, though five hundred years of torment seemed a bit much. I killed people when they deserved it; anything beyond that was up to God. I just didn't think I was up to making decisions that would last five hundred years.

Edward eased up on my arm and started to let go of me, when

she said, 'So you agree with our punishment?' His hand locked back onto my arm, if anything tighter than before.

I glared up at him, hissing under my breath, 'You're bruising me.'

He let me go, slowly, reluctantly, but the look in his eyes was warning enough. Don't get us killed. I'd try not to. 'I would never presume to question the decision of a god.' Which was true. If I ever met a god, I wouldn't question their decision. The fact that I didn't believe in any god with a little 'g' was beside the point. It wasn't a lie, and it sounded perfect for the situation. When you're prefabricating as fast as you can, it doesn't get better than that.

She smiled, and she was suddenly young and beautiful like a sudden glimpse of the young woman she must have been once. It was almost more of a shock than the rest. I'd expected a lot of things, but not Itzpapalotl to have retained even a shred of her humanity.

'I am very pleased,' she said, and she looked it. I'd pleased the goddess, made her smile. Be still my heart.

She must have made some sign because the whipping continued. They beat him until the white of his spine showed through in places where the flesh had worn completely away. A human would have died long before they got that far, or even a shapeshifter, but the vampire was as alive as when they started. He had collapsed into a little ball, his forehead on the floor, arms trapped under his body, his weight resting on his legs. He was unconscious, but the body didn't fall over. It was propped up by its own weight.

Olaf was making a high-pitched hiss under his breath, fast and faster. If the circumstances had been different, I'd have said he was working up to an orgasm. If that was what he was doing, I so didn't want to know. I ignored him, or did my best to.

The werejaguar stood there through it all, nude, body going limp, the cut long healed as he watched the vampire's body be torn apart. He watched it with a neutral face, but occasionally when a blow was particularly vicious, or when the first hint of bone showed through, he winced, gaze sliding away, as if he didn't want to watch but was afraid to actually turn his head away.

'Enough.' That one word, and the whips stopped, drooping like wilted flowers. The silver balls had all turned crimson, and blood dripped from the end of the whips in slow spatters. The women's faces had never changed, as if the faces were just masks, and what lay underneath was inhuman and held all the emotions that the masks could not show. As if the monstrousness inside was more human than the human shells they wore.

The four women walked in a line to a small stone basin in the far corner. They dipped each whip into the water in turn, then ran their hands over each lash almost lovingly.

Olaf tried twice to speak, had to clear his throat, and finally said, 'Do you use saddle soap and mink oil on the leather?'

The four women turned as one toward him. Then they all looked at Itzpapalotl. She answered for them. 'You sound knowledgable about such things.'

'Not as knowledgeable as they are,' he said, and he sounded impressed, like a cellist seeing Yo-Yo Ma perform for the first time.

'They have had centuries to perfect their craft.'

'Do they use their craft just on the bodies of the men who hurt them?' he asked.

'Not always,' she said,

'Can they speak?' he asked. He was watching them as if they were something precious and lovely.

'They have taken a vow of silence until the last of their tormentors is dead.'

I had to ask. 'Are they executing them periodically?'

'No,' she said.

I frowned, and the question must have shown on my face.

'We do not execute them. We merely harm them, and if they

die of their injuries, then so be it. If they survive, then they live to see another night.'

'So you're not going to give Diego any medical attention?' I asked.

Edward's hand had never let go of me during the torture as if he truly didn't trust me not to do something heroic and suicidal. His hand dug into me again, and I'd had my fill. 'Let me the fuck go, now, or we are going to have a disagreement . . . Ted.' I wasn't feeling good about watching Diego bleed. I was feeling worse because it hadn't bothered me as much as I thought it should have. I'd have helped him if I could have, as long as it wasn't suicide. He was a stranger and a vampire. I wasn't risking our lives for him, and that was that. Had there been a time when I would have risked us all, even for a strange vampire? I just didn't know anymore.

'Diego has survived far worse than this. He is the strongest of all of them. We broke all the others before they died. They did everything we asked them in the end. Except Diego, and still he fights us.' She shook her head, as if dismissing it all. 'But we must show you how it is to be done properly. Chualtalocal, show them how the sacrifice is to be embraced.'

The vamp that stood at her right hand stepped forward. He walked around the fallen Diego as if he were a pile of trash to be avoided, and left for someone else to clean up. He faced the werejaguar as Diego had faced him, but things had changed. Seth had been all pumped up from having his ears sucked when he first stripped, hard and eager to please. Now he was just naked, and his eyes kept going to the bloody mess that Diego had become as if he was wondering when his turn was coming.

'Make your offering, my cat,' she said.

Seth was looking from Diego's body to the vampire in front of me. 'My holy mistress, I am willing, you know I am, but I . . . I seem to be,' he swallowed hard enough that I heard it even over the still faint ringing in my ears. 'I seem to be . . .'

'Make your sacrifice, Seth, or suffer my wrath.'

The four sisters weird had hung their cat o' nine tails on small hooks in the wall, all in a row like a sadomasochistic version of the seven dwarves with their identical possessions. They glided back towards us all, like sharks scenting blood in the water.

Seth seemed to know they were there. He actually grabbed himself and started trying to get some attention going, but his eyes were flicking wildly through the room as if looking for an escape. He was making the effort, but nothing was happening.

Edward wasn't holding onto my arm anymore; maybe that was it, or maybe I'd just had enough for one night. 'You've scared him shitless. It's hard to get it up when you're scared.'

She and Chualtalocal looked at me, and their black eyes held nearly identical expressions, not that I chanced looking into the eyes long, but it was still there, disdain. How dare I interfere?

Edward made as if to grab me again. I held up a hand to him. 'Don't touch me.'

He let his hand fall back, but his eyes were not happy with me. Fine, I wasn't happy with anyone right now.

'And are you offering to help him overcome his fear?' Itzpapalotl asked. The look on her face said plainly that she didn't expect me to offer.

'Sure,' I said.

I don't know who looked the most surprised, but I think it was Edward, though Bernardo was a close second from the doorway. Olaf just watched me like a fox watching a rabbit through the fence, who's just spotted a hole big enough to crawl through. I ignored him. It was probably best to always ignore Olaf, if possible. Ignore him or kill him. That was my vote.

I held my hand out to the werejaguar. He hesitated, glancing from the vamp in front of him, to me, to the goddess behind him. I wiggled my fingers at him. 'Come on, Seth. We don't have all night.'

'Go with her, do as she says, as long as you offer fitting sacrifice.'

He took my hand, tentatively, and though he was a six foot plus, naked man, there was something very little boyish on his face. Maybe it was the near panic in his baby blues. He was scared, scared that he was going to end up on the floor, meat for the four weird sisters. I didn't blame him for worrying. I think if I hadn't stepped in, that was exactly what was about to happen. But I'd had all the torture I could handle for one night. It wasn't moral outrage. It was just plain outrage. I wanted to ask my questions and get the hell out of here. Vampires can live a very long time, theoretically forever, which means their idea of getting down to business can be damn leisurely. The vamps might have had eternity. I didn't.

I led Seth the werejaguar off to the other side of the room. The easiest thing would have been to work him by hand, but I was like so not doing that. The option I was voting for wasn't that simple, but it was something I was willing to do. I was going to call that part of me that was Richard's mark. Not the connection to him — that was safely walled away. I'd packed it so tight, I wasn't even sure I could open to the mark even on purpose. But I held a part of it inside me. The same part that had recognized César, the same part that let me deal with the wereleopards back home. That electric rush of energy was a turn-on to wereanimals. I'd discovered it accidentally. Now I was going to try and do it on purpose.

But it wasn't like a switch. Maybe someday it would be, but right now it took some preparation to get it going. It was maddening that something that came out at odd moments when I didn't want it, would refuse to come out when I did, but psychic shit is like that, unpredictable. It's one of the reasons it's so hard to study in laboratory conditions. X does not always equal Y.

I put my hands on my hips and looked at him, from head to foot, and didn't know where to start. My life would be both easier and harder if I was into casual sex, but for better or worse, it wasn't my cup of tea.

'Can you undo your hair?'

'Why?' He sounded suspicious, and I didn't blame him.

'Look, I could have let her turn you over to her pet torturers, but I didn't. So work with me here.'

His hands went to the knot at the back of his head. He pulled long pins out of his hair, and finally a comb that was made of bone. The hair uncurled slowly as if it were stretching from some long sleep, sliding down his back in a heavy mass. I walked behind him and he started to turn and watch me. I touched his shoulder, made him face front. 'I'm not going to hurt you, Seth. I'm probably the only person in this room who won't.'

He kept his face front, but there was a tension to his shoulders, his back that said he didn't like it. I didn't care. We needed to do this fast. Call it a hunch but the goddess didn't strike me as patient.

I unrolled his hair, helping it slide down his back. The colors were extraordinary, bright yellow, rich gold, a pale almost white, all of it streaked together, each color blending into the next the way sea water blends one color into the next, distinct but making a whole. I ran my hands through the thick warmth of his hair until it lay spread across his back, an inch past his waist. I grabbed two handfuls of hair and pressed it to my cheek. There was the close smell of sweat and the scent of the fur he'd worn. He had a cologne, faint on his skin, something so sweet, it smelled like candy. I spread the hair apart until I could see the skin of his back, and laid my face against the warmth of him. He smelled warm, as if you could sink your teeth into him like something fresh from the oven. I walked around him, hands trailing lightly over his skin, touching mostly the fall of that sun-streaked hair.

I came to stand in front of him, looked up into those wide, still half-afraid eyes, but a glance down his body showed that I'd made some progress, not enough, but some.

I didn't look at the vampires, or Edward, or anybody. I concentrated just on the man in front of me. To look elsewhere was to lose ground. I took his hand, and that pale golden tan looked darker against the paleness of my skin. I lowered my face over his hand as if I'd kiss it, but I brushed my lips barely against his skin, moving up his arm, breathing in the scent of his skin. I opened my mouth, laying my breath like a warm touch just above the skin of his arm. It raised the pale hairs on his arm in a march of goosebumps.

He flexed the hand I was holding, rolling me into his body with my back resting against the front of him. His other arm wrapped around from the other side, enfolding me in the warmth of his body. He laid his face on the top of my head, and a spill of his hair fell across me like a warm sweet scented curtain. The firelight danced through the gold of his hair, turning it into an amber cage, carved of light. He kissed the top of my head, then laid a gentle kiss against my temple, the top of my cheekbone, my cheek. He was so tall that in bending over he enveloped me in his body, covering me in the feel of him. The candy smell of his cologne breathed along his skin, and my body constricted with it. The smell was the key. The power spilled upward in a warm liquid rush that brought me to tiptoe, made me luxuriate against his body like a cat with catnip, wanting to roll my body in the scent. My body writhed against his as the power rode in almost painful waves, so warm, it was almost hot, rising off my body like invisible steam.

One hand stayed around my waist, the other touched my chin, turning my face back to meet his mouth. He kissed me, and for a second I stiffened, but I'd learned that if you called the power, you didn't fight it. You embraced it. If you fought it, then you had less control. I kissed him back. I expected the power to push out my mouth into his like it had with César, but it didn't. The kiss was nice, but it was just the feel of his lips on mine. His warmth pushed against mine, his power like a trembling shadow spilling along mine. We stood wrapped in a curtain of his hair, a circle of arms, and a vibrating blanket of that skin-dancing power that was all shapeshifter.

He shuddered against me, arms hugging me close. I could tell he was ready for sacrifice without looking, but I had to glance down anyway. He was ready. I pulled free of him, gently. 'You're ready to go back to the vamps, Seth. I think you're ready to make a sacrifice.' I made myself look him in the eyes.

He bent and kissed my forehead, gently. 'Thank you.'

'You're welcome.'

We walked back to the vamps hand in hand. But it wasn't the vampires that made me uncomfortable as we crossed the room. It was the humans. Bernardo looked like he was reconsidering my status as untouchable Madonna. Olaf had an almost hungry look on his face. It was closer to the way werewolves looked at you on the night of full moon than the way a man looks at a woman. Edward had a slight frown between his eyes, which for him meant he was bothered by something. The vampires looked about like I'd expected. Itzpapalotl looked serious, as if she hadn't known I could call the power up on purpose. It's why they'd apologized for dragging me up onstage earlier.

I gave Seth over to Chualtalocal like a father handing the bride to the groom. Then I moved back to stand by Edward. He looked at me, as if he was the one trying to read me for a change, and failing. It was almost worth it, if I could confuse Edward.

'Did you enjoy yourself, my cat?' the goddess asked

'Yes, holy mistress, I did.'

'Are you ready to make sacrifice?'

'Yes, holy mistress.'

'Then do so.' She looked past him to me, as if she didn't like what she saw. Something about what I'd done with Seth had disturbed her. Had she expected me to take him off in the corner and just do him by hand like a fluffer in a porno movie? Had the fact that I'd used power as well as mild sex disturbed her? Or had she seen something I hadn't, or understood something I did not? No way of knowing short of asking, and admitting that kind of ignorance to master vamps is a good way to get killed. So no questions about magic, just eventually, hopefully about the case.

Seth picked up the small silver blade again. He cradled his flesh in his hand and set the tip of the blade against himself. I caught Bernardo turning back towards the door. The blade tip bit into flesh, and I looked away. I think we all did, except for Olaf. It might have startled him the first time, but he was over the shock. Blood was being spilled, flesh being cut. Olaf couldn't miss that.

He watched the cutting, but then I caught him turning away out of the corner of my eye, and I had to look. I had to see what was bad enough for Olaf not to be able to stomach it.

The vampire had gone to his knees. I guess maybe I'd expected him to just lick the blood off, but he wasn't. He was sucking at it the way that Diego had sucked at Seth's ears, except this wasn't an ear. The vampire had covered almost every inch of Seth with his mouth. Seth's eyes were closed, and there was a look of concentration on his face.

I looked away again and found myself meeting the dead eyes of the four fallen nuns. Those empty, angry faces were almost harder to stare at than a vampire going down on someone. I literally turned my back on all of them and found that Olaf had done the same thing. He was hugging himself and staring at nothing. His discomfort rose off of him in almost visible waves. Even with his back turned, the sounds carried. I wished for the ringing in my ears to get worse.

Soft, sucking sounds, wet sounds, the sound of flesh in flesh, and the sharp intake of breath that was probably Seth. His breath came in three fast pants, and he spoke, 'Please, holy mistress, I am not sure of my control tonight.'

'You know the punishment,' she said. 'Surely, that is incentive enough to hold yourself in check.'

I glanced back then and found that Seth was staring back over his shoulder at the four women in the corner. When he turned back, he looked scared. The vampire was still feeding, sucking, throat swallowing. Surely, the wound had healed by now, unless they'd made a second wound while I was being embarrassed and not looking.

Seth dug his fingernails into the palms of his hands. His hands paled with the force of squeezing nails into his own flesh. He threw his head back suddenly, breath coming fast, faster, fastest. The vampire pulled off of him, leaving him hard and still intact. 'The wound has closed.'

Chualtalocal stood and went back to his mistress. The moment there was room, Seth collapsed to his knees, opening his hands slowly as if they hurt. There were bloody half-moons where his nails had bitten into his palms. But it had worked. Any distraction to keep him out of the clutches of the goddess's pet freaks.

'I offer you hospitality, to you and your friends. You may have Seth if you like and finish him as his body seems to so badly need.'

I suddenly knew what she meant by hospitality. Somehow I didn't think that was Aztec culture, though if I remembered correctly, hadn't some of the Aztecs sent Cortes and his men women along with food and gold? Maybe this wasn't any different. But I didn't want to mess with it.

'Dawn is coming. I can feel it pressing against the darkness like a weight about to tear the night apart.'

She turned her head to one side and seemed to think, or maybe she was sensing the night, the air, something. 'Yes,' she said, 'I feel it, too.'

'Then if it isn't too large an insult, can we skip the hospitality for tonight and get to the murders?'

'Only if you give me your word that you will return and taste our hospitality before you go back to Saint Louis.'

I glanced at Edward. He shrugged. I guess it was up to me. What else was new when it came to monsters? 'I don't agree to having sex with your people, but I'll agree to a return visit.'

'You seemed to like Seth. I would offer you César, who your

power seemed to like even more, but he does not make sacrifice, nor does he act as hospitality. It is his price for letting us come so near killing him twice a month.'

'You mean because he lets you nearly tear his heart out twice a month, he doesn't have to make sacrifice or all the other stuff?'

'That is what I mean.'

It made me think better of ol' César. I'd seen his show, and now I'd seen some of the behind the scenes stuff, and I had to say that it was a close call which was worse. Letting someone cut your chest open and touch your still beating heart, or letting vamps suck blood off of tender body parts and be offered for sex to strangers. No, come to think of it, I'd have rather had my chest cut open, as long as I knew I'd heal completely every time.

'It's not that Seth isn't lovely to look at. I'm sure it would be a pleasure to be with him, but I don't do casual sex. Thanks for thinking of me though. I know the police spoke with you.'

'They did. I do not think they learned anything of value from me.'

'Maybe they didn't ask the right questions,' I said.

'And what are the right questions?'

I was about to do something that the police wouldn't like at all. I was about to tell the monsters, someone they had suspected at one point of being the murderer, details of the crime. But she needed specific details or how was she to recognize the marks of some Aztec bogeyman? I knew how the cops had done it. They'd been so general, it was almost useless to show up. I understood why they did it that way. Once I opened my mouth and let out details to Itzpapalotl, then she was contaminated. They'd never be able to slip her up in an interrogation, because she got the secret details from me.

What I knew and the police couldn't was that they'd never interrogate the truth out of her. She was the kind of vamp that could sit in a dark room and watch the colors on the inside of her own eyeballs and be content. The only thing they could threaten her with was the death penalty, and if she was behind the murders, it was already a death penalty. One of the downfalls to a swift and certain punishment was that it took a lot of the give and play out of an interrogation. Once someone knows they are going to be executed, you can't bargain with them.

'Can we clear the room out a little?'

'What do you mean?'

'Can we have fewer of your people in here? I'm going to share confidential police information with you, and I don't want it to get out.'

'Whatever you say in this room remains in this room. No one here will talk of it to anyone else. I can promise you this.' She was utterly sure of herself, arrogant. But why not? All of her people were terrified of her. If what happened to Diego was commonplace, then think what the exotic stuff must be. If she dictated that the secrets were safe, they were safe.

Edward stepped close to me. He lowered his voice though he didn't try and whisper. 'Are you sure about this?'

'I'm sure, Edward. She can't help if she doesn't have enough information.' We looked at each other for a few seconds, then he gave a small nod. I turned back to the waiting vampire. 'Okay,' I said, and I told her about the survivors, and the dead.

I don't know what I expected, maybe for her to be titillated, or to go, a-ha, and recognize the monster responsible. What I got was serious attention, good questions at the right places, and a glimpse at a very intelligent mind behind all the games. If she wasn't a delusional, sadistic, megalomaniac, would-be goddess, she might have been likable.

'The skins of men are valuable to Xipe Totec and Tlazolteotl. The priests would flay the sacrifice and wear the skin. The heart had many uses for the gods. Even the flesh was used, at least in part. Sometimes, the insides of a sacrifice would have some strange thing inside it, and be an omen. Then the other organs might be kept for a time and studied, but it was rare.'

'Can you think why they would cut out the tongues?'

'To keep them from speaking the secrets they have seen.' She said it, like of course that was the reason. It made sense ritually, I guess.

'Why cut off the eyelids?'

'So they can never not see the truth, even though they cannot speak it. I do not know if this is why they have done these awful things.'

'Why would someone remove the outward secondary sex characteristics?'

'I do not understand,' she said, and she was holding the cloak close about her, as if she were cold. We'd been talking long enough, I had to remind myself not to look directly in her eyes.

'The genitalia on the men, the breasts on the women, were removed.'

She shuddered, and I knew something I hadn't before. Itzpapalotl, the goddess of the obsidian blade, was frightened. 'It sounds like some of the things the Spanish did to our people.'

'But the flaying and taking the organs, that's more Aztec, than European.'

She nodded. 'Yes, but our sacrifices were messengers to the gods. We caused pain only for sacred purposes, not for cruelty or a whim. All blood was holy. If you died at the hand of a priest, you died knowing it served a greater purpose. Literally, your death helped the rain to fall, the maize to grow, the sun to rise in the sky. I do not know of any god that would flay people and leave them alive. Death is necessary for the messenger to reach the gods. Death is part of the worship of the deity. The Spaniards taught us to kill for the sake of killing, not as a sacred trust, but just for slaughter.' She stared past me at the four women that waited patiently for her to notice them, for her to give them a purpose. 'We have learned the lesson well, but I would rather have stayed in a world where it was not true.' I saw in her face that she had some clue to what she'd lost, to what her vampires had lost when she decided they would become as cruel as their enemies. 'The Spaniards killed so many of our people along the road to Acachinanco that they tied white handkerchiefs over their noses because of the stench of rotting bodies.'

She looked at me then, and the hatred in those eyes burned along my skin. After five hundred years, she still carried a grudge. You had to admire someone who could hold on to hate like that. I thought I knew how to hold a grudge, but looking into her face, I realized I was wrong. There was room in me for forgiveness. In Itzpapalotl's face there was room for only one thing, hatred. She'd been angry about the same thing for over five hundred years. She'd been punishing people for the same crimes for five hundred years. It was impressive in a psychotic sort of way.

I hadn't learned much more about the murders than when I'd stepped through the doors. I'd mostly learned negatives. A genuine Aztec didn't recognize the murders as the work of any god or cult associated with the Aztec pantheon. It was good to know, something to cross off the list. Police work is mostly negatives. Finding out what you don't know, so you can decide what you do. I didn't know anything positive about the murders, but I knew one thing for absolute certain as I listened to the outrage in her voice about atrocities older than the entire country we were sitting in. I never wanted this woman mad at me. I'd told people that I'd chase them into hell to have my vengeance, but I probably didn't mean it. Itzpapalotl would mean every word.

27

It was still dark as Edward drove us homeward. Still night, true dark, the vampires still roamed, but that soft edge in the air let you know the light was coming. If we hurried, we'd make it into bed before true dawn. If we dawdled, we'd get to see the sun come up. None of us seemed to be dawdling. We sat in the car in a silence that no one seemed willing to break.

We left the club behind and drove out into the hills beyond, towards Santa Fe. Stars spread like a blanket of cold fire across the soft black silk of the sky. The sky had that larger than life, empty quality it gets over large bodies of water or in the desert.

Olaf's voice came out of the darkness, low and strangely intimate the way voices can be in a car at night. 'If we'd accepted their hospitality, do you think I could have had the vampire they whipped?'

I raised an eyebrow. 'Define have?' I said.

'Have, to do with as I liked.'

'What would you have done with him if they had?' Bernardo said.

'You don't want to know, and I don't want to hear it,' Edward said. He sounded tired.

'I thought you liked women, Olaf.' Bernardo said it. I didn't say it, honest.

'For sex I like women, but so much blood. It shouldn't have gone to waste.' He sounded wistful.

I turned in my seat and tried to see his face in the dark. 'So it's not just women who have to be careful around you, is that it? Does it just have to bleed to be attractive?'

'Leave him alone, Anita. About this, leave him the fuck alone.'

I turned to look at Edward. He rarely cussed, and he rarely sounded as tired and almost overwhelmed as he did now. 'Okay, I mean, sure.'

Edward glanced in the rearview mirror. There wasn't a car in either direction for miles. I think he was looking at Olaf. He stared into the mirror a long time. I think they had some major eye contact going.

He finally blinked and went back to staring at the road, but he didn't seem happy.

'What aren't you telling me?'

'Us,' Bernardo said. 'What isn't he telling us?'

'All right, what aren't you telling us?'

'It's not my secret to tell,' Edward said, and that was all he'd say. He and Olaf had a secret, and they weren't willing to share.

We finished the rest of the drive in silence. The sky was still black, but it was a paler black, the stars dim in it. Dawn was tremblingly close when we went into the house. I was so tired, my eyes burned. But Edward took me by the arm and led me down the small hallway away from the bedrooms. He kept his voice low. 'Be very careful of Olaf.'

'He's big and bad. I get it.'

He dropped his hand from my arm, shaking his head. 'I don't think you do.'

'Look, I know he's a convicted rapist. I saw the way he looked at Professor Dallas tonight, and I saw his reaction to the blood and torture. I don't know what you're not telling me, but I know that Olaf would hurt me if he could. I know that.'

'You're afraid of him?'

I took a breath. 'Yeah, I'm afraid of him.'

'Good,' Edward said. He hesitated, then said, 'You fit his vic profile.'

'Excuse me?'

'His favorite victims are petite women, usually Caucasian, but always with long dark hair. I told you I would never have brought him in on this case if I'd known you were coming down, too. It isn't just because you're a woman. You're his physical ideal for a victim.'

I stared at him for a few seconds, mouth opened, then closed it, and tried to think what to say. 'Thanks for telling me, Edward. Shit. You should have told me this up front.'

'I was hoping he could hold his act together, but I saw him tonight, too. I'm worried that he'll snap. I just don't want you to be the one in the way when it happens.'

'Send him back to wherever he came from, Edward. We don't need him if he adds to the problem.'

He shook his head. 'No, he's got a specialty that's perfect for this case.'

'And that specialty would be?'

He gave that small smile. 'Go to bed, Anita. It's already dawn.'

'No,' I said, 'almost, but not quite.'

He studied my face. 'You can really feel the sunrise without looking?'

I nodded. 'Yep.'

He looked at me, and it was as if he were trying to read me now. For the first time I felt that maybe, just maybe, Edward was as puzzled by me as I was by him, sometimes. He escorted me to my room and left me at the door like an overprotective date.

I was glad I'd prepared the room for safety before I left. If someone came through the window, they'd knock the dolls over or step on the mirror with its antlers. The door would have a chair and the suitcase in front of it. The room was as safe as it was going to get. I undressed, putting the guns and knives on the bed until I could decide exactly what was staying where for overnight. A man's extra large T-shirt that hung past my knees came out of the overnight bag. I'd started keeping one change of clothes, nightclothes, and toiletries in the overnight bag ever since the airline lost my luggage on a business trip. The last thing I pulled out of the overnight bag was my toy penguin Sigmund. I used to only sleep with Sigmund every so often, but lately, he'd been my constant companion under the sheets. A girl needs something to cuddle with at night.

The Browning Hi-Power was my other constant companion. At home it stayed in a holster I'd rigged to my headboard. Here I put it under my pillow, making very sure the safety was on. It always made me slightly nervous to put a loaded gun under my pillow. Seemed less than safe, but not nearly as unsafe as being unarmed if Olaf came through the door. I had brought four knives with me. One of them went between the mattresses. I put the Firestar back into the suitcase. I wanted something bigger than a handgun. I had a sawed-off shotgun and a mini-Uzi. Normally, I'd have brought more big guns, but I knew Edward would have more and better, and he would share. I finally decided on the mini-Uzi with a modified clip that held thirty rounds with enough oomph to cut a vampire in half. It was a gift from Edward so the ammo was probably illegal, but then so was the gun. I'd been almost embarrassed about carrying it at first, but one night last August I used it for real. I'd pointed it at a vampire, pulled the trigger, and cut him in half. It had looked like his body was torn in half by some giant hand. His upper body had fallen slowly to one side. His lower body collapsed to its knees. I still had the vision of it like a slow motion image. There was no horror or regret. It was just a memory. The vampire had come with a hundred of his friends to kill us. I'd tried to kill one of them as messily as possible to get the rest to leave us alone. It hadn't worked, but that was only because the vampires were more afraid of their Master of the City than of me.

Maybe the Uzi was overkill for a human being, but if by some chance I emptied the Browning into Olaf's chest and he didn't go down, I wanted to make sure he didn't reach me. I'd cut him in half and see if the pieces could crawl.

28

It was after five when I finally closed my eyes. Sleep sucked me under like a roll of black water, dragging me deep, and instantly into a dream. I stood in a dark place. There were small stunted trees everywhere, but they were dead. All the trees were dead. I could feel it.

Something crashed over to my right, something large moving through the trees, and a sense of dread rode before it like a wind. I ran, hands up to protect my face from the dry branches. I tripped over a root and went sprawling. There was a sharp pain in my arm. It was bleeding. Blood poured down it, but I couldn't find a wound.

The thing was getting closer. I could hear tree trunks snapping with sharp explosions. It was coming. It was coming for me. I ran, and ran, and ran, and the dead trees stretched out forever and there was no escape.

A typical chase dream, I thought, and the moment I thought it, I realized it was a dream, and the dream changed, faded into another dream. Richard standing in nothing but a sheet, one tanned muscled arm reaching out to me. His brown hair falling in a froth of waves around his face. I reached for him, and as my fingertips brushed his, a smile curving his lips, the dream shattered, and I woke.

I woke, blinking into a patch of sunlight that spilled across the bed. But it hadn't been the light that had woken me. There was a light tapping on my door. A man's voice. 'Edward says get up.'

It took me a moment to realize it was Bernardo's voice. It didn't take Freud to analyze the dream at the end with Richard in a sheet.

I was going to have to be careful around Bernardo. Embarrassing, but true.

I sat up in bed, yelling through the door, 'What time is it?'

'Ten.'

'Okay, I'm coming.'

I listened but didn't hear him walk away. Either the door was more solid than it looked, or Bernardo was quiet. If it had just been Edward, I'd have thrown on a pair of jeans under the over-sized T-shirt, and had some coffee. But there was company in the house and it was all male. I managed to get into the bathroom and dress without meeting anyone in the hallway. I was wearing dark blue jeans, a navy blue polo shirt, white jogging socks, and my black Nikes. Normally, I'd left the guns off until I went out into the big bad world, but at Edward's house the big bad world was staying in the next room, so I put the Firestar 9mm in an inner pants holster, set for a right-handed cross draw. Brushed, cleaned, and armed, I wandered toward the smell of bacon.

The kitchen was small and narrow and white. But all the appliances were black, and the starkness of the contrast was almost too much first thing in the morning. There was another bouquet of wild flowers in the middle of a small white wooden table. Donna had struck again, but truthfully I agreed with her. The kitchen needed something to soften it.

The two men sitting at the table did nothing to humanize the room. Olaf had shaved so that the only hair left were the black lines of his eyebrows. He wore a black tank top, black dress slacks. Couldn't see the shoes, but I was betting on a monochromatic look. He was also wearing a black shoulder rig with a big automatic of some kind. I didn't recognize the brand. A black-hilted knife was in a holster under his left arm.

Shoulder holsters chaff when you wear them with tank tops, but hey, it wasn't my problem.

Bernardo wore a white short-sleeved T-shirt and black jeans.

He'd pulled the top layer of his hair back on either side with a large multi-colored barrette. There was still plenty of hair to fall down past his shoulders, stark and black against the pure whiteness of his shirt. He was wearing a ten mil Beretta just in back of his right hip. I couldn't see a knife on him, but I was betting it was there.

Edward was at the stove, emptying a pan of scrambled eggs onto two plates. He was also wearing black jeans with matching cowboy boots, and a white shirt that was a twin of the one he'd worn yesterday.

'Gee, guys, do I have to go back to my room and change?'

They all looked at me, even Olaf. 'What you're wearing is fine,' Edward said. He carried the plates to the table and put one in front of each of the empty chairs. There was a plate of bacon in the center of the table beside the flowers.

'But I don't match,' I said.

Edward and Bernardo smiled. Olaf didn't. Big surprise. 'You guys look like you're in uniform,' I said.

'I guess we do,' Edward said. He sat down in one of the empty chairs.

I sat in the other one. 'You should have told me there was a dress code.'

'We didn't do it on purpose,' Bernardo said.

I nodded. 'Which is what makes it funny.'

'I am not changing clothes,' Olaf said.

'No one's asking you to,' I said. 'I was making an observation.' My eggs had bits of green and red things in them. 'What's in the eggs?'

'Green peppers, red chilies, and diced ham,' Edward said.

'Gee, Edward, you shouldn't have.' I liked my scrambled eggs the way God intended them, plain. I pushed the eggs around with my fork, and reached for the bacon. Half the plate was barely cooked, the other half done to a crisp. I went for the crisp.

The bacon on Olaf's plate was the crispy kind, too. Oh, well.

I said grace over the food. Edward kept eating, but the others hesitated, uncomfortable with their mouths full. It's always fun to say grace at a table with people who don't. That uncomfortable silence. The panic while they wonder whether to keep chewing or to stop. I finished praying and took a bite of bacon. Yum. 'What's the game plan for today?' I asked.

'You haven't finished looking at the files,' Edward said.

Bernardo groaned.

'I think it is a waste of time,' Olaf said. 'We have gone over the files. I do not believe that she will find anything new.'

'She's already done that,' Edward said.

Olaf looked at him, a piece of bacon halfway to his mouth. 'What do you mean?'

Edward told them.

'That is nothing,' Olaf said.

'It's more than you came up with,' Edward said, quietly.

'If I am such a burden on this job, maybe I should leave,' Olaf said.

'If you can't work with Anita, maybe you should.'

Olaf stared at him. 'You would rather have her as backup instead of me?' He sounded astonished.

'Yes,' Edward said.

'I could break her in half over my knee,' Olaf said. The astonishment was turning to anger. I suspected that most emotions turned into anger for Olaf.

'Maybe,' Edward said, 'but I doubt she'd give you the chance.'

I held up my hand. 'Don't make this a competition, Edward.'

Olaf turned to me, slowly. He spoke very slowly, very clearly. 'I do not compete with women.'

'Afraid you can't measure up?' I asked. The moment I said. it, I wished I hadn't. The momentary satisfaction wasn't worth the look on his face as he rose from his chair. I leaned into the table and drew the Firestar, pointing it in his general direction under the table.

Olaf stood, looming over me, like a muscular tree. 'Edward has spent the morning talking to me about you. Trying to convince me that you are worth listening to.' He shook his head. 'You are a witch and I am not. The thing we hunt may be magical and we need your expertise. Maybe this is all true, but I will not be insulted by you.'

'You're right,' I said. 'I'm sorry. It was a cheap shot.'

He blinked at me. 'You are apologizing?'

'Yes, on the rare, rare occasions when I'm wrong, I can apologize.'

Edward was staring at me across the table.

'What?' I asked.

He just shook his head. 'Nothing.'

'Olaf's hatred of women is sort of a handicap, and I try not to make fun of people with handicaps.'

Edward closed his eyes and shook his head. 'You just couldn't leave it alone, could you?'

'I am not a cripple.'

'If you hate anyone or anything with an unreasoning, uncompromising hatred, then you are blind where that hatred is concerned. The police kicked me out of a crime scene yesterday because the cop in charge is a right-winger squeaky-clean Christian, and he considers me devil spawn. So he'd rather more people get killed and mutilated than have me help him solve the case. He hates me more than he wants to catch this monster.'

Olaf was still standing, but some of the tension had drained away. He seemed to actually be listening to me.

'Do you hate women more than you want to catch this monster?'

He looked at me, and for once his eyes weren't angry. They were thoughtful. 'Edward called me because I am the best. I have never walked away from a job until the quarry was dead.'

'And if it takes my preternatural expertise to help kill the monster, can you deal with that?'

'I don't like it,' he said.

'I know that, but that's not what I asked. Can you handle my expertise helping you kill the monster? Can you take my help if it is the best thing for the job?'

'I don't know,' he said. At least he was being honest, even reasonable. It was a start.

'The question, Olaf, is which do you love more: the kill or your hatred of women?'

I could feel Edward's and Bernardo's stillness. The room held its collective breath waiting for the answer.

'I would rather kill than do anything else,' Olaf said.

I nodded. 'Great, and thank you.'

He shook his head. 'If I take your help, it does not mean that I consider you my equal.'

'Me either,' I said.

Someone kicked me under the table. I think it was Edward. But Olaf and I nodded at each other, not exactly smiling, but I think we had a truce. If he could control his hatred, and I could control my smart-ass impulses, the truce might last long enough for us to solve the case. I managed to reholster the Firestar without him noticing, which made me think less of him. Edward had noticed, and I think, so had Bernardo. What was Olaf's specialty? What good was he if he didn't know where the guns were?

29

After breakfast we headed back into the dining room. Bernardo had volunteered to do the dishes. I think he was looking for any excuse to get out of the paperwork. Though I was beginning to wonder if Bernardo had been as badly spooked by the mutilations as Edward had been. Even the monsters were afraid of this one.

Last night I'd been ready to look at the forensic reports next, but in the clear light of day I could admit that it was cowardice. Reading about it was not as bad as seeing it. I so did not want to look at the photos. I was afraid to see them, and the moment I admitted that to myself, I moved them to the top of the list.

Edward suggested we stick all the pictures on the walls of the dining room.

'And put pin holes in your nice clean walls,' I said.

'Don't be barbaric,' Edward said. 'We'll use sticky putty.' He held up a small packet of the pliable yellow rectangles. He peeled off some and handed it to Olaf and me.

I squeezed the stuff between my fingers, rolling it into a ball. It made me smile. 'I haven't seen this stuff since elementary school.'

The three of us spent the next hour putting the pictures up on the wall. Just handling the sticky putty made me remember fourth grade and helping Miss Cooper hang Christmas decorations on the walls.

We'd hung cheerful Santas, fat candy canes, and bright balls. Now I was hanging vivisected bodies, close-ups of skinless faces, shots of rooms full of body parts. By the time we had one wall covered I was mildly depressed. Finally, the pictures took up almost all the empty white wall space.

I stood in the center of the room and looked at it all. 'Sweet Jesus.'

'Too harsh for you?' Olaf asked.

'Back off, Olaf,' I said.

He started to say something else but Edward said, 'Olaf.' It was amazing how much menace he could put into one ordinary word.

Olaf thought about it for a second or two, but in the end he let it go. Either Olaf was getting smarter or he was afraid of Edward, too. Guess which way I was voting.

We'd grouped the photos by crime scene in large clusters. This was my first glimpse of the bodies that had been torn apart.

Doctor Evans had described the bodies being cut by a blade of unknown origin, then disjointed by hand. But that had been a very clean description of what had actually been done.

At first, all my eyes could see was blood and pieces. Even knowing what I was looking at, my mind refused to see it at first. It was like looking at one of those 3-D pictures where at first it's just colors and dots, then suddenly you see it. Once you see it, you can't unsee it. My mind was trying to protect me from what I was looking at by just simply not allowing me to make sense of it. My mind was protecting me, and it only does that when it's bad, really, really bad.

If I had just walked out now before my eyes made sense of it, I might escape the full horror of it all. I could turn on my heel and march out of here. I could just refuse to take one more terror into my brain. Probably a good idea for my own sanity, but it wouldn't help the next family that this thing got hold of. It wouldn't stop the mutilations, the deaths. So I stood there and made myself stare up at the first picture, waiting to see what was really there.

The blood was brighter than movie blood, a cherry red. They'd gotten to this scene before the blood had started to dry.

I spoke without turning around. 'How did the police find the bodies so quickly in this house? The blood is still fresh.'

Edward answered, 'The husband's parents were supposed to meet them for an early breakfast, before work.'

I had to look away from the picture, at the floor. 'You mean his parents found him like this?'

'It gets worse,' Edward said.

'How could it possibly get worse?' I asked.

'The wife told her best friend she was pregnant. The breakfast meeting was to tell the husband's parents they were about to be grandparents for the first time.'

The rug swam in my vision, like looking at it through water. I reached back for a chair and eased my way into it. I put my head between my knees and breathed very carefully.

'You all right?' Edward asked.

I nodded without raising up. I waited for Olaf to make a sarcastic remark, but he didn't. Either Edward had warned him off or he thought it was horrible, too.

When I was sure I wasn't going to throw up or faint, I spoke with my head still between my knees. 'When did the parents arrive at the house? What time?'

I heard paper rustle. 'Six-thirty.'

I rested my cheek against my knee. It felt good. 'When did the sun come up?'

'I don't know,' Edward said.

'Find out,' I said. Gee, the rug on the floor was kind of pretty.

I raised up slowly, still practicing nice even breaths. The room did not swim. Good. 'The grandparents-to-be arrived at six-thirty. It takes what, ten minutes, less, for them to recover enough to call the cops. Then uniforms arrive on the scene first. It could take thirty minutes or an hour, more, for a crime scene photographer to arrive, and yet the blood is still fresh. It hasn't dulled yet, let alone started to brown.'

'The parents nearly walked in on it,' Edward said.

'Yeah,' I said.

'What difference does that make?' Olaf asked.

'If dawn was close to six-thirty, then the critter can be out in daylight, or it went to a hole close to the murder scene. If it wasn't close to dawn, then it may be limited to darkness.'

Edward was smiling down at me like a proud parent. 'Even with your head between your knees, you're still thinking about the job.'

'But what does it gain us,' Olaf said, 'if the creature is limited to darkness or daylight?'

I looked up at him. He was looming over me again, but I kept sitting down. Wouldn't look very macho if I stood up and fell down. 'If it's limited to darkness, then it may help us figure out what kind of critter it is. There really aren't that many preternatural creatures that are limited exclusively to darkness. It would help narrow the list.'

'And if it holed up near the first murder scene,' Edward said, 'we might find some traces.'

I nodded. 'Yeah.'

'The police tramped over that area within an inch of its life,' Olaf said. 'Are you saying you can find something that they can't?' His arrogance was showing.

'With the first murder, especially, the police were looking for a human perpetrator. If you're looking for a human being, you look for different things than if it's a monster.' I smiled. 'Besides, if we didn't all think we could find things that the police couldn't, we wouldn't be here. Edward wouldn't have called us in, and the police wouldn't have shared the files with him.'

Olaf frowned. 'I have never seen you smile like this, Edward, unless you are pretending to be Ted. You look like a proud teacher whose pupil is doing well.'

'More like Frankenstein with his monster,' I said.

Edward thought about it for a second, then nodded and grinned, pleased with himself. 'I like that.'

Olaf frowned at both of us. 'You did not create her, Edward.'

'No,' I said, 'but he helped make me the woman I am today.'

Edward and I looked at each other, and the smiles faded from both our faces, leaving us solemn. 'Am I supposed to apologize for that?' he asked.

I shook my head. 'Do you feel like apologizing for it?'

'No,' he said.

'Then don't. I'm alive, Edward, and I'm here.' I stood and didn't sway at all. Life was good.

'Let's find out if any of the killings took place after daylight. When I've looked at all this shit, let's go see some murder scenes.' I looked at Edward. 'If that's all right with you. You is the boss.'

He gave a small nod. 'That's fine, but to keep Ted working with the Santa Fe PD, we'll need to include them at the murder sites.'

'Yeah,' I said, 'police don't like civvies mucking up their murder scenes, makes them testy.'

'Besides, you're already persona non grata in Albuquerque,' Edward said. 'We've got to keep some of the cops willing to talk to you.'

'And that's really bugging me,' I said. 'I'm barred from the freshest crime scenes, the newest evidence. I don't need another handicap on a case like this.'

'You don't know what it is either, do you?' Edward said.

I shook my head, and sighed. 'Not a damn clue.' Bless his chauvinistic heart, but Olaf didn't say, I told you so.

I went back to staring at the pictures, and suddenly I could see it. I let out a breath, and said, softly, 'Wow.' The room seemed hot. Dammit, I was not going to have to sit down again. I put my fingertips on either side of the wall, steadying myself, but it must have looked like I was trying for a closer look. Trust me, I was as close as I ever wanted to get. I finally had to close my eyes for just a few seconds. When I opened them, I was okay or as okay as I was likely to be.

Body parts scattered like flower petals, stirred into a red mess. My eye flicked from one blood-covered lump to another. I was almost sure that was a forearm, and the ball of a knee joint showed whitely amid all the red. I'd never seen so many pieces before. I'd seen bodies torn apart before, but that had been for food or punishment. But there was a terrible completeness to this . . . destruction. I moved on to a shot of the same image but from a slightly different angle. I tried to put the body together in my head, but kept coming up short on parts.

I finally turned around. 'There's no head and no hands.' I pointed at small lumps in the blood. 'Unless those are fingers. Was the body completely disjointed even down to the finger bones?'

Edward nodded. 'Every victim has been almost completely dismembered down to the joints.'

'Why?' I asked. I looked at Edward. 'Where's the head?'

'They found it down the hill behind the house. The brain was missing.'

'How about the heart?' I asked. 'I mean there's the spine, almost intact, but I don't see any viscera. Where are all the internal organs?'

'They didn't find them,' Edward said.

I leaned back, half-sitting on the table. 'Why take the internal organs? Did they eat them? Is it part of some magical ritual? Or is it just part of the ritual of the killing itself, a souvenir?'

'There are a lot of organs in the body,' Olaf said. 'You put them all in one container and they can be heavy, bulky. They also rot very quickly unless you put them in some form of preservative.'

I looked at him, but he wasn't looking at me. He was looking at the pictures. He hadn't given a lot of detail, but something in the way he said it made him sound like he knew what he was talking about.

'And how do you know how heavy the internal organs of a human body can be?'

'He could have worked in a morgue,' Edward said.

I shook my head. 'But he didn't, did you, Olaf?'

'No,' he said, and now he was looking at me. His eyes had been turned into two dark caves by the deep set of his face and a trick of light, or would that be darkness. He stared down at me, and without seeing his eyes I could feel the intensity of that stare, as if I were being studied, measured, dissected.

I kept my gaze on Olaf, but asked, 'What is his specialty, Edward? Why did you call him in on this particular case?'

'The only person I've ever seen do anything close to this, is him,' Edward said.

I glanced at him, and his face was calm. I turned back to Olaf. 'I was told you went to jail for rape, not murder.'

He looked right at me and said, 'The police arrived too soon.'

A cheerful voice called out from the front of the house. 'Ted, it's us.' It was Donna, and the 'us' could only mean the kids.

Edward left at a goodly walk, trying to head her off. I think Olaf and I might have still been staring at each other when she walked in on us, but Bernardo came in, and said, 'We're supposed to hide the pictures.'

'How?' Olaf asked.

I took the candelabrum off the table and said, 'Put the tablecloth over the door.' I stood aside and let Bernardo drag it off the table.

Olaf said, 'Aren't you going to help him? You are one of the boys, after all.'

'I'm not tall enough to hold it up over the entire door,' I said.

He gave a small smile, derisive, but he moved up to help Bernardo block the open doorway with the tablecloth.

I was left standing behind them with the black iron candelabra in my hands. I stared at the tall, bald man and was half-regretful that I wasn't tall enough to smash the heavy iron candelabra into his skull. Just as well. I'd owe Edward another favor if I killed one of his backups just because he'd scared me.

30

I could hear Edward in his best consoling Ted voice, trying to convince her that she didn't need to say hi to everyone. She argued, polite, but firm, that of course she did. The more he tried to keep her away, the more she wanted to see. Call it a hunch, but I was betting it was me she wanted to see. The house was arranged so that you couldn't enter the three guest bedrooms without going through the dining room. Donna wanted to make sure where I was, and that I hadn't been in anyone's bed but my own. Or at least not in Ted's. Did she think that I was racing ahead of them to my room to throw clothes over my nakedness? Whatever the motive, she was coming this way. I heard Becca's voice.

Shit. I ducked under the rug across the door and nearly ran into them. Donna stopped walking with a small oomph of surprise. Her eyes were wide as she looked at me as if I'd scared her. Peter was watching me with cool brown eyes, as if it was all too boring for words, but underneath the perfect teenage boredom was a light, an interest. Everybody wondered why the tablecloth was in front of the doorway.

It was Becca who said it. 'Why is the rug in front of the door?' I kept calling it a tablecloth because that's what Edward was using it for, but it still looked like a rug. Kids stick to the basics.

Donna looked at Edward. 'Yes, Ted, why is the tablecloth in front of the door.'

'Because we're holding it,' Bernardo said from behind the improvised curtain.

She stepped close to the cloth. 'And why are you holding it?'

'Ask Ted,' Bernardo and Olaf said together.

Donna turned back to Edward. I usually know what Edward will say, but with Donna I was out of guesses.

'We've got the pictures from the case spread all over the room. They aren't something I want you or the kids to see.' Gee, he went for the truth. It must be true love.

'Oh,' she said. She seemed to think about it for a second or two, then nodded. 'Becca and I will take the goodies through to the kitchen.' She lifted a white, string-wrapped box, took Becca by the hand and went towards the kitchen. Becca was straining backwards, saying, 'But, Mommy, I want to see the pictures.'

'No, you don't, sweetie,' Donna said, and very firmly led the child away.

I thought that Peter would follow but he stood there, looking at the doorway, then glanced at Edward. 'What kind of pictures?' he asked.

'Bad ones,' Edward said.

'How bad?'

'Anita,' Edward said.

'Some of the worst I've seen, and I've seen some awful stuff,' I said.

'I want to see,' Peter said.

I said, 'No.'

Edward said nothing, just looked at him.

Peter scowled at us. 'You think I'm a baby.'

'I wouldn't want your mom to see them either,' Edward said.

'She's a wimp,' he said.

I agreed with him, but not out loud.

'Your mother is who she is,' Edward said. 'It doesn't make her weak. It just makes her Donna.'

I stared at him, trying very hard not to gape, but I wanted to. I'd never heard him cut anyone any slack for anything. Edward was not just judgmental. He was a harsh judge. What chemical alchemy did the woman have to have won him over? I just did not get it.

'I think what . . . Ted is trying to say is that it isn't your age that makes us not want to show you the pictures.'

'You think I can't handle it,' Peter said.

'Yeah,' I said, 'I think you can't handle it.'

'I can handle anything that you can handle,' he said, arms crossed over his thin chest.

'Why? Because I'm a girl?'

He actually blushed, as if embarrassed. 'I didn't mean that.'

But of course he had. But, hey, he was fourteen. I'd let it slide.

'Anita is one of the toughest people I've ever met,' Edward said.

Peter squinted at him, arms still hugging his chest. 'Tougher than Bernardo?'

Edward nodded.

'Tougher than Olaf?' And I thought more of the kid that he'd put the two men in that order. He knew instinctively which was the scariest man, or maybe it was just Olaf's size. No, I think Peter had a feel for the bad guys. It's something you either have or you don't. It can't really be taught.

'Even tougher than Olaf,' Edward said.

There was a disgruntled sound from behind the rug. The sound of Olaf's ego getting bruised.

Peter looked at me, and the look had changed. You could almost see him thinking, trying to put my petite female self in the same category as Olaf's aggressive male presence. He finally shook his head. 'She doesn't look as tough as Olaf.'

'If you mean arm wrestling, I'm not.'

He frowned and turned back to Edward. 'I don't understand.'

'I think you do,' Edward said, 'and if you don't, I can't explain it to you.'

Peter's frown deepened.

'Part of the problem with the tough-guy code,' I said, 'is that a lot of it can't be explained.'

'But you understand it,' Peter said. He sounded almost accusatory.

'I've spent a lot of my time around very tough guys.'

'That's not it,' Peter said. 'You're different from any girl I've ever met.'

'She's different from any girl you will ever meet,' Edward said.

Peter looked from one to the other of us. 'Mom's jealous of her.'

'I know,' Edward said.

Bernardo's voice came from inside the room. 'Can we lower the rug now?'

'Don't tell me you tough he-men are getting tired,' I said.

'Lactic acid builds up in everybody's muscles, chickie,' Bernardo said.

I'd started the name calling so I let the 'chickie' comment go. 'You need to join your mom and Becca in the kitchen,' I said.

'Do I?' He was looking at Edward, and I realized he was appealing to Edward, asking permission.

'Yes,' I said and looked at Edward, trying to tell him with my eyes, not to do this.

But he had eyes only for the boy. They stared at each other, and something passed between, some knowledge, something. 'Drop the cloth,' Edward said.

'No,' I said and grabbed Peter's arm. I spun him around, so his back was to the door. I'd caught him by surprise, so he didn't struggle. Before he could decide what to do about me, Edward spoke. 'Let him go, Anita.'

I looked at him around Peter's shoulder and realized he was taller than me by a few inches. 'Don't do this.'

'He wants to see. Let him see.'

'Donna won't like it,' I said.

'Who's going to tell her?'

I looked into Peter's dark eyes. 'He will when he gets mad enough at you or her or both.'

'I wouldn't do that,' Peter said.

I shook my head. I didn't believe him, and that more than anything made me let go of his arm and back off. If Edward showed Peter this little corner of hell and word got back to Donna, it might be enough to break them up permanently. I was willing to trade some of Peter's innocence for that. Harsh, but true.

The rug fell away on Olaf's side first, then Bernardo was left holding the rug in his arms like a limp child. He looked at Edward and shook his head, but he stepped back beside Olaf and let Peter walk into the room. I followed behind him and Edward.

Olaf had moved back near the far door. Bernardo laid the cloth on the table and stepped back to the far end of the table. I took up station at the far wall, almost mirroring Olaf, but at the opposite door. We'd all moved to separate corners of the room, and all of us tried to separate ourselves from what was happening. I don't think even Olaf approved.

Peter took in all the pictures, turning around and around. He paled, and his voice was a little breathy. 'Are those people?'

'Yes,' Edward said. He stayed right beside Peter, not touching, not too close, but very definitely with him.

Peter walked to the nearest wall, to the pictures I'd just been looking at. 'What happened to them?' he asked.

'We don't know yet,' Edward said.

Peter looked at the pictures, eyes flicking from one horrible image to another. He didn't walk the room or study any one picture as closely as I had, but he looked, he saw what was there. He didn't scream or faint or throw up. He'd proven his point. He wasn't a wimp. I wondered if I should warn him about the possibility of nightmares. Nay, he'd either have them or he wouldn't.

He was still pale, with a light dew of sweat on his upper lip, but he was mobile, and his voice was breathy, but calm. 'I better help Mom in the kitchen.' He walked out still hugging his arms around himself as if he were cold.

No one said a word as he walked out. When I was pretty sure he was out of ear shot, I walked up to Edward. 'Well, that went better than I thought it would.'

'It went about the way I thought it would,' Edward said.

'Shit, Edward, the kid is going to have nightmares.'

'Maybe, maybe not. Pete's a tough kid.' He was looking out through the doorway as if he could still see the boy. His gaze was faraway.

I stared at him. 'You're proud of him. Proud of the fact that he looked at this,' I motioned at the pictures, 'and didn't freak.'

'Why shouldn't he be proud?' Olaf asked.

I looked at him. 'If Edward were Peter's dad, maybe. But he's not.' I turned back to Edward. I stared at him. His face was its usual blankness, but there was a flinching around the eyes.

I touched his arm, and the touch was enough. He looked at me. 'You're treating him like a prospective son.' I shook my head. 'You cannot have this family.'

'I know that,' he said.

'I don't think you do,' I said. 'I think you're actually beginning to think about doing it, for real.'

He dropped his gaze, not meeting my eyes.

'Shit, Edward, shit.'

'I hate to admit it, but I agree with her,' Olaf said. 'If it was just the boy, then I would see no problem. I think you can make of him what you will, but the woman and the girl . . .' He shook his head. 'It will not work.'

'I don't understand why you even want a family,' Bernardo said.

'For different reasons. Neither of you believe in marriage,' Edward said.

'True,' Olaf said, 'but if men like us do marry, it should not be a woman like Donna. She is too . . .' he struggled for a word, and finally said, 'innocent. And you know that I do not say that about many women.'

'Maybe that's one of her attractions,' Edward said, and he seemed as truly puzzled as the rest of us.

'You're already screwing her. Why marry her?' This from Bernardo.

'If all I wanted was sex, I'd have gone elsewhere,' Edward said.

'She any good?' Bernardo asked.

Edward just looked at him, one long look.

Bernardo raised his hands. 'Sorry, sorry, just curious.'

'Don't be curious about Donna,' Edward said. He turned to me. 'You believe in marriage. Underneath all that toughness is a midwestern girl that still believes in the white picket fence.'

'I do believe in marriage, but not for people like us, Edward.'

I don't know what he would have said to that, because the phone rang and he went to answer it.

'Saved by the bell,' I said.

'He intends to marry this woman,' Olaf said.

I nodded. 'I'm afraid so.'

'If he wants to marry her, it's his business,' Bernardo said.

Olaf and I stared at him until the smile on his face faded to a look of puzzlement.

'What?'

'Olaf may be a serial rapist, Bernardo, or even a serial killer, but in his own twisted way he has more scruples than you do. Doesn't that worry you?'

Bernardo shook his head. 'No.'

I sighed.

Edward came back into the room. His face was back to his normal 'Edward face,' as if all the near revelations of just a minute ago had never happened. 'The monster did another couple in Albuquerque last night.'

'Shit,' I said. 'Are you going without me?'

Edward was watching my face just a little too closely, so I knew there was a surprise coming. 'Your presence has been requested on site.'

I could feel the surprise on my face. 'Is Lieutenant Marks not in charge anymore?'

'It was him on the phone.'

'You're kidding me,' I said.

Edward shook his head and smiled.

'I don't get it.'

'I'd guess that someone up the feeding chain chewed his ass for kicking you out. They probably gave him a choice of working with you, or being off the case.'

I had to smile. 'A case like this can make a career.'

'Exactly,' Edward said.

'Well, we know Marks' price now.'

'Price?' Bernardo asked. 'You guys bribed him?'

'No,' I said, 'but his principles that he so kindly spat in my face yesterday weren't as precious to him as his career. Always nice to know how strong a person's convictions are.'

'Not that strong,' Edward said.

'Apparently not,' I said.

I heard Donna coming down the hallway, talking loudly to Becca, but I think it was to warn us that they were coming. The men grabbed the rug and went for the doorway. Edward said in his loud, cheerful Ted voice, 'Saddle up, boys and girls. We got work to do.'

I went for my room. If we were going to go outside the house, I needed more weapons.

31

I sat in the front seat beside Edward. It was probably my imagination but I could feel someone staring at the back of my neck. If I wasn't imagining it, I was betting on Olaf.

I'd added the shoulder holster complete with Browning Hi-Power. Usually, it was the only gun I wore until someone tried to kill me, or some monster showed in the flesh. But I'd kept the Firestar in its inner pants holster. Too many pictures of dismembered corpses for comfort. I even took all the knives, which tells you how insecure I was feeling. Being stared at hard enough to bore a hole through my flesh was beginning to get on what nerves I had left. It wasn't my imagination. I could feel it.

I turned in the seat and met Bernardo's eyes. There was a look on his face when I turned around that was nothing I wanted to see. I had an uncomfortable thought that he was fantasizing and I just might be in the starring role.

'What are you staring at?' I asked.

He blinked, but it seemed to take a long time for his eyes to really focus on me rather than whatever was inside his head. He gave a slow, almost lazy smile. 'I wasn't doing anything.'

'Like hell,' I said.

'You can't tell me what to think, Anita,' he said.

'You're presentable enough. Go get a date.'

'I'd have to wine and dine her, and then I couldn't count on sex at the end of the evening. What good is that?'

'Then get a hooker,' I said.

'I would if Edward would let me out on my own.'

I turned and looked at Edward.

He answered the question without me having to voice it. 'I've forbidden Olaf from . . . dating while he's here. Olaf resented it, so I told Bernardo the same thing.'

'Very even-handed,' I said.

'It is totally unfair to punish me because Olaf is a psycho,' Bernardo said.

'If I cannot meet my needs, then why should you be able to?' Olaf said. There was something in his voice that made me look at him. He was staring straight ahead, no eye contact to anyone.

I turned around in my seat and looked at Edward. 'Where do you come up with these people?'

'The same place I find vampire hunters and necromancers,' he said.

He had a point. Enough of a point that we finished the drive to Albuquerque in silence. I felt I had enough moral high ground to throw stones, but evidently Edward disagreed. Since he knew Olaf better than I did, I wasn't going to argue. At least not now.

People talk of ranch-style houses, but this really was a ranch. A ranch as in cowboys and horses. It was a dude ranch for tourists so whether it counted as a really real ranch, I wasn't sure. But it was the closest thing to an actual working ranch that I'd ever set foot on.

The ranch really wasn't in Albuquerque, but in the middle of nowhere. In fact the house and corrals sat in the middle of a whole lot of nothing. Empty space with bunches of dry grass and strange palish soil stretching out and out to the horizon. Hills ringed the ranch like smooth piles of rock and brush. Edward drove us under an entrance that had a cow's skull nailed to it and said, 'Dead Horse Ranch.' It was so similar to a hundred western movies I'd seen on television that it seemed vaguely familiar.

Even the corral full of horses spilling in an endless nervous circle seemed stage-managed. The house wasn't exactly what I had pictured, being low to the ground and made of white adobe much like Edward's house but newer. If you could have just erased the plethora of police cars, emergency units, and even some fire rescue equipment, it would have been picturesque in a lonesome down-on-the-prairie sort of way.

A lot of the police cars had revolving lights, and the crackle of police radios was thick in the air. I wondered if it was the lights, the noise, or just this many people making the horses nervous. I didn't know much about horses, but surely rushing back and forth around their pen wasn't normal behavior. I wondered if they had been running in circles before the cops came or after. Were horses like dogs? Could they sense bad things? Didn't know, didn't even know who to ask.

We were stopped just inside the gate by a uniformed cop. He took our names and went off to find someone who would let us pass, or find someone to tell him to kick us out. I wondered if Lieutenant Marks was here. Since he'd issued the invite, it seemed likely. What kind of threat to his career had they used to get him to invite me back?

We waited. None of us spoke. I think we'd all spent a lot of our adult lives waiting for one uniform or another to give us permission to do things. It used to get on my nerves, but lately I just waited. Maturity, or was I just getting too worn down to argue over small stuff? I'd have liked to say maturity, but I was pretty sure that wasn't it.

The uniform came back with Marks trailing behind him. Marks' pale tan suit jacket flapped in the hot wind, giving a glimpse of his gun riding just behind his left hip. He stared at the ground as he walked, briskly, all business, but he was careful not to look at us, at me, maybe.

The uniform got to us first, but he stood a little back from the open driver's side door and let the lieutenant catch up. Marks finally got there, and he looked fixedly at Edward, as if he could exclude me by just not looking at me.

'Who are the men in the back?'

'Otto Jefferies, and Bernardo Spotted-Horse.' I noticed that Olaf had to use an alias, but Bernardo got to keep his real name. Guess who was wanted for crimes elsewhere.

'What are they?'

I wouldn't have known how to answer that question but Edward did. 'Mr Spotted-Horse is a bounty hunter like myself, and Mr Jefferies is a retired government worker.'

Marks looked at Olaf through the glass. Olaf looked back. 'Government worker. What sort of government worker?'

'The kind that if you contacted the state department, they'd confirm his identity.'

Marks tapped on Olaf's window.

Olaf rolled the window down with the nearly silent buttons on the door handles. 'Yes,' he said in a voice that was totally devoid of his usual German burr.

'What did you do for the state department?'

'Call them and ask,' Olaf said.

Marks shook his head. 'I have to let you and Blake inside my crime scene, but not these two.' He jerked a thumb at the back seat. 'They stay in the car.'

'Why?' Bernardo said.

Marks looked at him through the open window. His blue-green eyes were mostly green right now, and I was beginning to realize that meant he was angry. 'Because I said so, and I've got a badge and you don't.'

Well, at least it was honest.

Edward spoke before Bernardo could do more than make inarticulate noises. 'It's your crime scene, Lieutenant. We civilians are just here on your sufferance, we know that.' He twisted in his seat to give the two men direct eye contact, but turned so Marks couldn't see his face well. I could, and it was cold and full of warning. 'They will be happy to stay in the car. Won't you, boys?'

Bernardo slumped in his seat, arms crossed on his chest, sulking, but he nodded. Olaf just said, 'Of course, whatever the good officer says.' His voice was mild, empty. The very lack of tone was frightening, as if he were thinking something very different from the words.

Marks frowned but stepped back from the car. His hand hovered around his body as if he had a sudden desire to touch his gun, but didn't want to appear spooked. I wondered what had been in Olaf's eyes when he spoke those mild words. Something not mild, that I was certain of.

The uniformed cop had detected something in Marks. He stepped closer to his lieutenant, one hand on the butt of his gun. I didn't know what had changed in Olaf, but he was suddenly making the cops nervous. He hadn't moved. Only his face was turned towards them. What was he doing with just his facial expression that had them so jumpy?

'Otto,' Edward said softly, so that the sound didn't carry outside the car. But as he had in the house when he said, Olaf, that one word carried a menace, a promise of dire consequence.

Olaf blinked and turned his head slowly towards Edward. The look on his face was frightening, feral somehow, as if he'd let down his mask enough to show some of the madness inside. But as I looked at him, I thought this was a face to deliberately frighten people, a sort of tease. Not the real monster, but a monster that people could understand and fear without thinking too hard.

Olaf blinked and looked out the far window, face bland and as inoffensive as it got.

Edward turned the car off and handed his keys to Bernardo. 'In case you want to listen to the radio.'

Bernardo frowned at him, but took the keys. 'Gee, thanks, Dad.'

Edward turned back to the police officers. 'We're ready to go when you are, Lieutenant.' He opened his door as he said it. The door swinging open made Marks and the uniform take a step or so back.

I took it as my cue and got out on my side. It wasn't until I came around the front of the Hummer in full sight that Marks finally paid attention to me. He stared at me, and his face was harsh. He could manage not to show outright hatred in his face, but he couldn't manage neutral. He didn't like me being here. He didn't like it one little bit. Who had twisted his tail in a knot hard enough to force him to let me back on board?

He opened his mouth as if he'd say something, closed it, and just started walking towards the house. The uniformed officer followed at his heels, and Edward and I trailed behind. Edward had his good ol' boy face on, smiling and nodding to the police officers, the emergency workers, everyone and everything in his path. I just stayed at his side, trying not to frown. I didn't know anybody here, and I'd never been comfortable greeting strangers like long-lost friends.

There were a lot of cops outside in the yard. I spotted at least two different uniforms, enough plainclothes to open up a discount men's store, and some plainclothes detectives that stood out. I don't know what they do during FBI training that is different from anywhere else, but you can usually spot them. The clothes are slightly different, more uniform, less individual than with regular cops, but it's more an aura about them. An air of authority as if they know that their orders come straight from God and yours don't. I used to think it was insecurity on my part, but since I'm rarely insecure, that can't be it. Whatever 'it' was, they had it. The Feds had arrived. That could speed things up, be a big help, or slow things to a crawl and fuck up what little progress had already been made. It depended almost entirely on how the police in charge got along with each other, and how protective everyone was of their turf.

These crimes were gruesome enough that we might actually see some cooperation between jurisdictions. Miracles do happen.

Usually, when there's a body on the ground, the police of

whatever flavor are inside at the scene walking on the evidence. But there were too many people out here. There couldn't possibly be that many more inside the house. The house was big, but not that big.

Only one thing would keep them out in the New Mexico heat. The scene was a bad one. Gory, piteous, frightening, though no one will admit out loud to that one. Pick an adjective, but the police milled around the yard in the heat with their ties, the women in high heels on the loose gravel. Cigarettes had appeared in a lot of hands. They talked in small hushed voices that didn't carry above the crackle of radios. They huddled in small groups, or sat alone on the edge of cars, but not for long. Everyone kept moving, as if to remain still was to think and that was a bad thing. They reminded me of the horses nervously running in circles.

A uniformed police officer was sitting at the open doors of the ambulance. The emergency medical technician was bandaging his hand. How had he gotten hurt? I hurried to catch up with Marks. If he were the man in charge, he'd know what had happened. Edward just fell into step behind me, no questions, just following my lead. He had ego problems with me sometimes, but on the job there was nothing but the job. You left the shit outside the door. You could always pick it up on your way back out.

I caught up with Marks on the long narrow wraparound porch. 'What happened to the uniform that's getting his hand bandaged?'

Marks stopped in mid-stride and looked at me. His eyes were still a hard, pitiless green. You always think of green eyes as being pretty or soft, but his were like green glass. He had a big hate on for me, a big one.

I smiled sweetly and thought, fuck you, too. But I'd learned lately to lie even with my eyes. It was almost sad that I could lie with my eyes. They really are the mirror to the soul, and once they go, you are damaged. Not beyond repair, but damaged.

We stared at each other for a second or two, his hatred like a fine burning weight, my pleasant smiling mask. He blinked first, like there'd been any doubt. 'One of the survivors bit him.'

My eyes widened. 'Are the survivors still inside?'

He shook his head. 'They're on their way to the hospital.'

'Anybody else get hurt?' When you ask that at a scene where vics are down, you almost always mean other cops.

Marks nodded, and some of the hostility drained from his eyes leaving them puzzled. 'Two other officers had to be taken to the hospital.'

'How bad?' I asked.

'Bad. One nearly got his throat ripped out.'

'Have any of the other mutilation vics been that violent?'

'No,' he said.

'How many vics were there?'

'Two, and one dead, but we're missing at least three other people, maybe five. We've got a couple unaccounted for, but other guests heard them talking about a picnic earlier. We're hoping they missed the show.'

I looked at him. He was being very helpful, very professional. 'Thank you, Lieutenant.'

'I know my job, Ms Blake.'

'I never said otherwise.'

He looked at me, then at Edward, then finally settled his gaze on me. 'If you say so.' He turned abruptly and walked through the open door behind him.

I looked at Edward. He shrugged. We followed Marks in, though I noticed we'd lost the uniformed officer somewhere in the walk across the yard. No one was spending more time inside than they had to.

The living room looked as if someone had taken white liquid and poured it down to form the sloping walls, the curved doorways leading away into the house, the freeform fireplace. There was a bleached cow skull above the fireplace. A brown leather couch wrapped a huge nearly perfect square in front of the cold fire. There were pillows with Native American prints on them. A huge rug that looked almost identical to one of Edward's took up most of the center of the floor. In fact the entire place looked like an updated version of Edward's place. Maybe I still hadn't seen Edward's sense of style. Maybe this was just a type of southwestern style that I'd just never seen.

There was a large open section that had been a dining room area. The table was still there. There was even a chandelier formed of what looked to be deer antlers. There was a pile of white, red-soaked cloth to one side of the table. Blood was seeping out of the bottom of the cloth bundle, leaking across the polished hardwood floor in tiny rivulets of crimson and darker fluids.

A photographer was snapping pictures of something on the table. My view was hidden by three suit-covered backs. Panic clawed at my throat, and it was suddenly harder to breathe. I didn't want the men to move. I did not want to see what was on the table. My heart was pounding in my throat, and I had to take a deep, shaking breath, clearing my throat. The deeper breath had been a mistake. The smell of fresh death is like a cross between an outhouse and a slaughterhouse. There was an acrid stink, and I knew the intestines had been perforated. But there was another smell under the almost sweet smell of too much blood. A smell of meat. I'd tried to find other words for it, but it was the closest I could come to describing it. It was like drowning in the scent of raw hamburger. Meat, a person reduced to so much meat.

That one smell made me want to run. To just turn on my heel and walk away. This was not my job. I was not a cop. I was here as a favor to Edward. If I left now, he could bill me. But of course, it was too late. Because I wasn't here just because of a favor to anyone now. I was here to help stop this from happening again. And that was more important than any nightmares I was about to accumulate.

A thin heavy line of liquid oozed off the edge of the table and fell slowly to the floor with a sparkle of crimson from the bright chandelier. The short man in the middle turned and caught a glimpse of us. His face was grim, but when he caught sight of us, of me, something close to a smile curled his lips. He left the others grouped around the table and came towards us. He was short for an FBI agent, but Special Agent Bradley Bradford walked with a confident swinging stride that covered ground and made taller men sometimes have to hurry to keep up.

We'd met over a year ago in Branson, Missouri, on a vampire case that had turned out to be vampires plus a little something older and less local. People had died, but mostly the monsters had died. Bradford must have been happy with my performance because he kept in touch. I knew that he was now assigned to the new FBI preternatural division. Last I heard they were calling it the Special Research Section, just like the Serial Killer Profiler unit was now called Investigative Support. The FBI tries to avoid sensational buzzwords like serial killer or preternatural or monster. But call it what you like, a spade's a spade.

He started to put his hand forward to be shaken, then stopped. His hands were encased in plastic gloves splattered with blood, and a spot on one side that was too black, too thick, to be blood. He smiled an apology as he lowered his hands.

I knew who had twisted Marks' tail and gotten me back in the ball game. I took shallow, even breaths and tried not to embarrass him. I hadn't thrown up at a murder scene in nearly two years. Be a shame to spoil my record now.

'Anita, it's good to see you again.'

I nodded and felt myself smile. I was happy to see Bradley, but . . . 'We really need to start meeting when there aren't bodies on the ground.' See, light joking, I could be cool. I was also delaying the final walk to what lay on the table. I could do semi-clever repartee all damn day if I just didn't have to see what was bleeding in the dining room.

Why was this one getting to me so badly? No answer, but it was.

Another agent joined us. He was tall, slender, skin actually dark enough to be called black. His hair was cut close to his head in a low, well-groomed wedge. He straightened his tie, and settled his coat in place with long-fingered hands that seemed to dance even in these small movements. I'm not one of those women who notices hands usually, but there was something about his that made me think poet, musician, as if he did other things with them besides shooting practice.

'Special Agent Franklin, this is Ted Forrester and Anita Blake.'

He shook hands with Edward, but didn't answer the Ted smile with one of his own. He turned serious eyes to me. His hand was enough longer than mine that shaking was a little awkward, but we managed. But it was somehow an unsatisfying handshake as if we still didn't have the measure of each other. Some men still use a handshake as a way of sizing you up.

'How long have you been in the house, Ms Blake?' he asked.

'Just got here,' I said.

He nodded as if it were important. 'Bradford has painted a glowing picture of you.' There was something in his voice that made me say . . .

'I take it you don't share Bradford's opinion of me.' I smiled when I said it.

He blinked and looked startled, then his shoulders relaxed just a touch, and a very small smile played across his lips. 'Let's say I'm skeptical of civilians with no special training coming into a crime scene.'

I raised eyebrows at the 'no special training.' Edward and I exchanged glances. The Ted face was slipping, letting some of his own natural cynicism leak into those blue eyes, that nearly boyish face.

'Civilians,' he said softly.

'We don't have badges,' I said.

'That must be it,' he said, voice still soft, and vaguely amused.

Franklin frowned at us. 'Are we amusing you?'

Bradford stepped between us almost literally. 'Let's let them look at the scene, then we'll decide things.'

Franklin's frown deepened. 'I don't like it.'

'Your objection has been noted, Franklin,' Bradford said, and there was a tone in his voice that said he'd had enough of the younger man.

Franklin must have heard it too, because he smoothed his perfect tie once more and led the way towards the dining room. Bradford followed him. Edward looked at me, asking a question with his eyes.

'I'm coming,' I said. Once I'd tried being more macho than the police. Nothing phased me. I was heap-big-vampire-slayer. But lately, I just didn't give a crap. I didn't want to do this anymore. It was almost a shock to realize that I really didn't want to be here. I'd seen too many horrors in too short a space of years. I was burning out, or maybe I'd already burned out and hadn't realized it.

Panic tightened my stomach into a hard knot. I had to get it under control. I had to separate myself from the task ahead, or I was going to lose it. I tried to take a few calming breaths, but the smell came thick on my tongue. I swallowed, wished I hadn't, and stared at the tips of my shoes. I stared at the ends of my Nikes as they touched the fringe of the dining room rug until the knot in my gut eased, and I felt calm. There was still a soft flutter in my chest, but it was the best I could do. Agent Franklin said, 'Ms Blake, are you all right?' I raised my eyes and saw what lay on the table.

32

I let out a low, 'Wow.'

'Yes,' Bradford said, 'wow is good.'

The table was pale natural pine, a pale, almost white wood. It matched the walls and the rest of the decor and made a dramatic showpiece for the thing on the table. Thing, it, no other pronouns would do. Distance, distance, mustn't think that this was once a human being.

At first all I could see was the blood and pieces of meat. It was like a jigsaw puzzle with pieces missing. The first thing I was sure of was the neck. I could see the broken edge of the spine sticking up above the flesh of the neck. I looked around for the head, but none of the blood-covered lumps was the right size. But there was a leg nearly perfectly whole, only ripped away from the hips, but it was intact. It had not been disjointed. Once I saw that, I found a hand lying on its back, fingers cupped as if cradling something.

I bent closer, hands in my pockets because I'd forgotten my own surgical gloves back in St Louis. How unprofessional of me. I leaned over the hand and I wasn't smelling the stink anymore. I wasn't thinking oh, my, God, how awful. The world narrowed down to a nickel-sized lump cupped in the hand. I saw what was there. The hand had long, carefully groomed fingernails, some broken off, as if she'd struggled. She. I looked to the ring finger and found a wedding band set that looked heavy and expensive, though to be sure I'd have to move the hand and I wasn't ready for that yet. I registered all the information as if from a great distance because

I'd found a clue. I concentrated on that like it was a lifeline, and maybe it was.

'There's something in her hand. It may be only a piece of cloth, but . . .' I bent so low over it that my breath caressed the skin and brought a scent up from it to me. Musty, an animal smell. My breath did one other thing. It moved the edge of the thing in her hand. The one tiny edge wasn't as blood-logged, and it moved as I blew across the hand.

I straightened. 'I think it's a feather.' I looked around the room trying to see where it could have come from. Except for the antler chandelier nothing else in the room seemed made of animals.

Bradford and Franklin looked at each other. 'What?' I asked.

'What made you say her?' Franklin asked.

'The nails, the wedding ring set.' I glanced up at the rest of the body. The only other clue that this had been a woman was maybe the size of the neck, dainty. 'She was small, about my size, maybe a little smaller.' I heard myself say it and felt nothing. I felt empty like a shell thrown up on the sand, empty and echoing. It felt a little bit like being in shock, and I knew that later I'd pay for it. Either I'd have screaming hysterics once I had some privacy, or . . . I'd broken something in myself that might never come back, might never fix.

'Besides the fact that it's female, what else do you see?' Franklin asked.

I didn't like being tested, but somehow I just didn't have the energy to bitch about it. 'The other vics were disjointed down to their finger bones. This one isn't. When I first heard that survivors were being carefully skinned, then mutilated, and that the dead were all torn apart, I thought we might be dealing with a pair of killers. One very organized and in charge, the other disorganized and following. But the bodies weren't torn up. They were very carefully dissected. It was organized, very thought out. But this . . .' I motioned at the thing on the table. 'This was not organized. Either our organized killer is beginning to dissolve and become less coherent, or we have two killers like I originally thought. If we have two killers, then the organized one in charge has lost control over his follower. This murder was not well planned. That means mistakes, which will help us. But it may also mean that anyone that crosses paths with this thing is dead. Higher body count from here on out, more frequent kills maybe, maybe not.'

'Not bad, Ms Blake. I even agree with you on most of it.'

'Thank you, Agent Franklin.' I wanted to ask what parts didn't he agree with, but was pretty sure where we disagreed. 'You still think this is a human serial killer?'

He nodded. 'I do.'

I looked at the remains like lumpy red paint tossed across the table. The bloodstains had spread until I was standing in the edge of it. The cops hated to have you tracking blood everywhere. I stepped back, and the stain spread out towards me. I took another step back. My foot crunched in something. I knelt and found salt on the floor. Someone had gotten messy during lunch. I stood up.

'This is fresh kill, Agent Franklin, real fresh. How long would it take a person, even two people, to reduce another human being to this?'

His long hands played over his tie again. I wondered if he knew he did that when he was nervous. If he didn't, I'd play poker with him any day. 'I really couldn't give an estimate, not and be accurate.'

'Fine. Do you really think a person is strong enough to tear someone apart like this quickly enough to have the blood this fresh? The damn thing's bleeding like it's still alive, it's so damn fresh. I don't think a human being could do this much damage this quickly.'

'You are entitled to your opinion.'

I shook my head. 'Look, Franklin, it was logical for you to assume the killer, or killers, were human. It usually is human in your line of work. I'm assuming you're with the Investigative Unit.'

He nodded.

'Great. See, you hunt people. That's what you do. They are monsters but not real monsters. I don't hunt people. I hunt monsters. That's just about all I do. I don't think I've ever been called into a case where the perp was human, or at least where magic wasn't involved.'

'Your point,' he said, very stiff, eyes angry.

'My point is that if they had thought this was a monster to begin with, they'd have sent it over to Bradford's new unit. But they didn't, did they?'

His eyes were a little less angry, more uncertain. 'No, they didn't.'

'Everyone thought it was human, so why shouldn't you assume the same thing? If they'd dreamt that it was non-human, they wouldn't have sent it to you, right?'

'I suppose so.'

'Great. Then let's work together, not at cross purposes. If we split our manpower between looking for people and looking for monsters, it will cost time.'

'And if you're wrong, Ms Blake, if it is a human being doing these terrible things and we stop investigating down that avenue it could cost more lives.' He shook his head. 'It's not my initial report I'm standing by, Ms Blake. It's the chance that it is a human perpetrator. We will continue to treat this as a normal investigation.' He looked at Bradford. 'That is my final recommendation.'

He turned to Edward. 'And you, Mr Forrester, are you going to dazzle me with your profiling abilities?'

Edward shook his head. 'No.'

'What do you offer to this investigation then?'

'When we find it, I'll kill it.'

Franklin shook his head. 'We are not judge, jury, and executioner, Mr Forrester. We are the FBI.'

Edward looked at him, and most of Ted's good ol' boy charm seemed to have seeped out of his eyes, leaving them cold and uncomfortable to meet. 'I have two men with me out in the car, one of them an expert on this type of crime. If this was done by a person, then he'll be able to tell us how it was done.' His voice had gone bland, smooth, and empty.

'Who is this expert?' Franklin asked.

'Why is he still out in the car?' Bradford said.

'Otto Jefferies, and because Lieutenant Marks wouldn't let him in,' Edward answered.

'By the way,' I said, 'thanks for getting me back on the case, Bradley.'

Bradley smiled. 'Don't thank me. Help us solve the damn thing.'

'Who is Otto Jefferies?' Franklin asked.

'He's a retired government worker,' Edward said.

'How does a retired government worker have expertise on this type of killing?'

Edward looked at him until Franklin began to fidget, smoothing his hands down not just his tie but his suit coat. He even checked his cuffs, though to make the movement really effective you needed cufflinks. Buttons just didn't do it.

'I'm sure you are implying something by your so pointed gaze, but my question stands. What kind of government worker would have this kind of expertise?'

Franklin may have been nervous but he was also stubborn.

'Call the state department,' Edward said. 'They'll answer your questions.'

'I want you to answer my questions.'

Edward gave a small shrug. 'Sorry, if I told you the truth, I'd have to kill you.' He said the last with a good ol' boy smile, and an awe-shucks shine to his eyes. Which probably meant he was serious.

'Bring your men in,' Bradley said.

'I must protest involving more civilians in this case,' Franklin said.

'Duly noted.' Bradley looked at Edward. 'Bring them in, Mr

Forrester. I'm agent in charge on site.' Edward went for the door.

'For now,' Franklin said.

Bradley looked up at the taller man. 'I think you need to be elsewhere, Franklin.'

'Where would I be of better use than overseeing the crime scene?'

'Anywhere that is away from me,' Bradley said.

Franklin started to say something, then looked at both of us in turn, and finally at Bradley. 'I won't forget this, Agent Bradford.'

'Nor will I, Agent Franklin.'

Franklin turned abruptly and walked out, hands sliding over his clothes. When he was out of earshot, I said, 'He doesn't seem to like you.'

'Making a new division for preternatural crimes wasn't a popular move with everyone. Until now the Investigative Division has been handling them.'

'Gee, and I thought the FBI was above such petty disputes.'

Bradley laughed. 'God, don't I wish.'

'This is a really, really fresh scene, Bradley. I don't mean to tell you your job, but shouldn't we be searching the area for the creature?'

'We did a ground search, turned up nothing. We've still got the helicopter up. We also sent off for geology maps of the ranch in case there's a cave we missed.'

'Would a geology survey cover man-made ruins?' I asked.

'What do you mean?'

'This area of the country is supposed to be lousy with ruins. Just because nothing's visible from above ground doesn't mean there won't be something buried. A room, or even a kiva.'

'What's a kiva?' Bradley asked.

'A sacred underground room for ceremonial magic. It's one of the few things that most of the southwestern tribes, or pueblos, have in common.'

Bradley smiled. 'Don't tell me you're also an expert on Native American religious practices, too?'

I shook my head. 'Nope. I had a brief overview in my comparative religion class in college, but I didn't take Native American as one of my electives. Knowing that kiva do exist and their general use pretty much exhausts my knowledge of the southwestern tribes. Now if you need to know details about the Sioux sun-worshipping rituals, those I remember.'

'I'll check with the surveying company and see if they mark man-made structures.'

'Good.

'The locals called in some tracking dogs. The dogs wouldn't come in the house. They refused to track.'

'Were they bloodhounds?' I asked.

Bradley nodded. 'Why?'

'Bloodhounds are a very friendly breed. They are not attack dogs. Sometimes on the preternatural bad stuff they refuse the trail. You need some trollhunds.'

'Troll-what?' Bradley asked.

'Trollhunds. They were originally bred to hunt the Greater European Forest Trolls. When the trolls went extinct, the breed almost died out. They're still a rare breed, but they are the best you can find for tracking preternatural bad guys. Unlike the bloodhound they will attack and kill what they trail.'

'How do you know so much about dogs?' Bradley said.

'My dad's a vet.'

Edward had reentered with Olaf and Bernardo at his back. He'd heard the last. 'Your dad, a doggie doctor. I didn't know that.'

He was looking intently at me, and I realized that Edward didn't really know much more about me than I did about him.

'Are there any trollhunds in this area?' Bradley asked it of Edward.

He shook his head. 'No. If there were I'd know it. I'd have used them.'

'You knew about troll-whatsits, too?' Bernardo asked.

Edward nodded. 'If you're a varmint hunter, so should you.'

Bernardo frowned at the criticism, then shrugged. 'I do more bodyguard work than critter killing these days.' He was looking at everyone, everything but the table and contents.

'Maybe you should go back to guarding other people's bodies,' Edward said. I don't know what I'd missed, but Edward was angry with him.

Bernardo looked at him. 'Maybe I should.'

'No one is stopping you.'

'Damn you, . . . Ted,' and Bernardo walked out.

I looked at Olaf, as if for a clue to what had just happened, but Olaf had eyes only for the remains. His face was transformed. It took me a few seconds to realize what the expression on his face was, because it was wrong. It did not match what was happening. He stared down at the remains of that woman with enough raw lust in his eyes to burn down the house. It was a look that should have been saved for privacy, to be shared between your beloved and yourself. It was not a look for public consumption, when you were looking at the bleeding remains of a woman you did not know.

Staring into Olaf's face, I was cold, cold all the way down to my Nikes. Fear, but not of the monster, or rather not of that monster. If you had given me a choice between whatever was doing these killings or Olaf, right that moment I wouldn't have known who to pick. It was sort of like choosing between the tiger and the tiger.

Maybe I was standing too close, I don't know. He just suddenly turned his head and looked full at me. And just like I'd known in the car what Bernardo was thinking, I knew that Olaf was looking for a star in his own little fantasy.

I held my hands up, shaking my head, and backed away from him. 'Don't even go there, . . . Otto.' I was beginning to really hate all these aliases.

'She was almost exactly your height.' His voice had a soft, almost dreamy quality.

Drawing a gun and shooting him was probably overkill, but I

certainly didn't have to stand there and help his imagination. I turned
to Bradley. 'Someone said there were other bodies. Let's go see.'
Five minutes ago, you'd have had to drag me into the next chamber
of horrors. Now I grabbed Bradley's arm and half pulled him, half
let him lead me deeper into the house. I could feel Olaf's gaze
against my back like a hand, hot and close. I didn't look back.
Nothing ahead of me could be worse than watching Olaf paw
through the woman's remains, knowing that he was thinking of me
while he did it.

33

Bradley led me to a door that had been half-torn out of its hinges. Something big had pushed through here. Bradley had to use both hands to get the door to one side. It seemed to have settled into the carpet, wedging itself. He jerked back, and I jumped, pulse in my throat.

'Damn splinters.' He held up the palm of his gloved hand and there was a small crimson spot on the plastic. He jerked the glove off. The splinter seemed to have come off with the glove, but it was bleeding freely.

'Some splinter,' I said.

'Dammit.' Bradley looked at me.

'You better let somebody look at it.'

He nodded, but didn't turn to go. 'Don't be insulted, but not everyone is happy with me forcing you back on this case. I can't leave you alone in here with evidence. If there were ever questions raised, it would be hard to explain.'

'I've never pocketed evidence from a crime scene in my life.'

'I'm sorry, Anita, but I can't take the chance. Will you follow me out to the ambulance?'

He was having to cup one hand under the other to catch the blood so it didn't reach the carpet. I frowned, but nodded. 'Fine.'

He started to say something, then turned and walked back to the living room. We were about a fourth of the way through the room when Edward asked, 'Otto wants to open the tablecloth and see what's inside.'

'I'll send the photographer and Agent Franklin in to oversee it.'

Bradley kept going for the door having to hurry a little to keep his own blood from contaminating the scene.

Neither Edward nor Olaf nor the uniform that had magically appeared to watch them fondle the evidence, asked how he'd hurt his hand. Maybe no one cared.

I followed Bradley across the gravel turnaround to the ambulance. There were still too many people milling around outside. Shouldn't they be out searching for the creature? It wasn't my job to tell them their job, but this was the freshest crime scene yet, and there just didn't seem to be enough frantic activity to suit me.

Bradley sat down at the end of the ambulance and let the techs treat his wound. Because it was a wound. Splinter, my ass. He'd stabbed himself. I tried to be a good girl and just stand there, but I think my impatience showed, because Bradley started talking.

'We did send people out to search when we arrived, and we arrived damn quick.'

'I didn't say anything.'

He smiled, then grimaced as the EMT did something to his hand that hurt. 'Walk far enough away from the house to give a 360 look. Then come back and tell me what you see.'

I looked at him. He motioned me off with his good hand. I shrugged and started walking. The heat was like a weight across my shoulders, but without humidity it just wasn't as bad. The gravel crunched under my feet, louder than it should have been. I walked in the opposite direction from the horse corral. The horses were still running in their endless chase like a maniac merry-go-round. I threaded my way through the cars, marked and unmarked. The fire truck had driven away. I wasn't sure why it had been here in the first place. Though sometimes when you call 911, you get more emergency vehicles than you need, especially if the caller panics and isn't specific enough.

I stopped beside the silent revolving lights of a car. Who had called the police? Did we actually have a witness? If we did, why hadn't anyone mentioned it? If we didn't, then who had called for help?

I walked until the hot dry wind rustling through the clumps of grass was louder than the electric squawk of radios. I stopped and turned back towards the house. The cars were small enough that I could have covered one of them with my hand. I'd probably walked farther out than I needed to go. Far enough out that if I yelled for help, they might not hear me. Not bright. I should walk farther in, but I needed to be clear of it for awhile. I needed to be out in the wind alone. I compromised. I drew the Browning and put off the safety, pointing the barrel at the ground, one-handed. Now I could enjoy the solitude and still be safe. Though, truthfully, I wasn't sure if what we were chasing gave a damn about bullets, silver or otherwise.

Bradley had said to look. I looked. The ranch lay in a large round valley or maybe a plateau, since we'd had to drive up some hills to get here. Whichever, the land stretched flat and smooth for miles to the rim of distant hills. Of course, I'd been surprised by distances here, so maybe the hills were really mountains, and the land stretched for a very long way in every direction. There were no trees. There was almost no vegetation above thigh height to me. Whatever had taken that door out had been big, bigger than a man, though not by much. I turned in a slow circle, scanning the ground, and there was nowhere for something that large to hide. They'd walked this ground when they first arrived, full of confidence that the creature couldn't have gotten far. They marched out, and out, and out, and found nothing. The helicopter buzzed overhead, high enough that it didn't disturb the wind, but low enough that I was pretty sure it was looking at me. They were looking for anything unusual, and I was standing out here by myself, unusual enough.

The helicopter circled a few times, then buzzed off to search somewhere else. I looked out at the empty land. There was nowhere to hide. Where had it gone? Where could it have gone?

Underground, maybe, or it flew away. If it flew away, I couldn't help them find it, but if it went underground . . . Caves, or an old well, maybe. I'd suggest it to Bradley, and probably be told that they'd checked it. But hey, I was here to offer suggestions, wasn't I?

I heard someone behind me and whirled. I had the gun halfway up when I recognized Detective Ramirez. He had his hands up and to each side, away from his gun. I let out the breath I'd been holding and holstered the gun. 'Sorry.'

'That's okay,' he said. He was wearing another white dress shirt with the sleeves rolled back over dark, strong forearms. The tie was a different color, but it still hung loose like a necklace, and the top two buttons of his shirt were open so that you could see the smooth hollow of his throat.

'No it's not. I'm not usually this jumpy.' I hugged myself, not because I was cold. Far from it. But because I badly wanted someone to hold me. I wanted to be comforted. Edward had many uses. Comfort was not one of them.

Ramirez came up beside me. He didn't try and touch me, just stood very close and looked out over the land where I was looking. He spoke, still staring out in the distance. 'The case getting to you?'

I nodded. 'Yeah, I don't know why.'

He gave a sharp laugh and turned to me, face halfway between astonishment and humor. 'You don't know why?'

I frowned at him. 'No, I don't.'

He shook his head, smiling, but his eyes were gentle. 'Anita, this is an awful case. I've never seen anything this bad.'

'I've seen things as bad as the vivisected victims, the ones that died.'

His face sobered. 'You've seen things that bad before?'

I nodded.

'What about the mutilations?' he asked. His face was very serious now. His smooth nearly black-brown eyes watched my face.

I shook my head. 'I've never seen anything like the survivors.' I laughed, but it wasn't a happy sound. 'If survivor is the word for them. What kind of life are they going to have, if they live?' I hugged myself tighter, staring at the ground, trying not to think.

'I've been having nightmares,' Ramirez said.

I looked up at him. Police don't admit things like that often, especially not to civilian consultants that they've just met. We looked at each other, and his eyes were so gentle, so genuine. Unless he was a much better actor than I thought he was, Ramirez was letting me see the real him. I appreciated it, but didn't know how to say it out loud. You don't verbalize something like that. The best you can do is return the favor. The trouble was, I wasn't sure what the real me was anymore. I didn't know what to put in my eyes. I didn't know what to let him see. I finally stopped trying to pick and choose, and think I settled for confused, bordering on scared.

He touched my shoulder lightly. When I didn't say anything, he moved into me, wrapping his arms across my back, holding me against him. I stayed stiff in his arms for a second or two, but didn't pull away. I relaxed against him in inches, until my head rested in the curve of his neck, my arms tentatively around his waist.

He whispered, 'It will be all right, Anita.'

I shook my head against his shoulder. 'I don't think so.'

He tried to see my face but I was standing too close, at too awkward an angle. I pulled back so he could see my face, and suddenly I felt awkward standing there with my arms around a stranger. I pulled away, and he let me go, only keeping the fingers of one hand grasped in his. He gave my hand a little shake. 'Talk to me, Anita, please.'

'I've been doing cases like this for about five years. When I'm not looking at the messily dead, I'm hunting vampires, rogue shapeshifters, you name it.'

His was holding my hand solidly now, wrapped in the warmth of his skin. I didn't pull away. I needed something human to hold onto. I tried to put into words what I'd been thinking for awhile now. 'A lot of cops never use their guns, not in thirty years. I've lost count of how many people I've killed.' His hand tightened on mine, but he didn't interrupt. 'When I started out, I thought vampires were monsters. I really believed it. But lately I'm not so sure. And regardless of what they are, they look very human. I could get a call tomorrow that would send me down to the morgue to put a stake through the heart of a body that looks every bit as human as you and me. Once I've got a court order of execution, I am legally sanctioned to shoot and kill the vampire or vampires in question, and anyone that stands in my way. That includes human servants or people with just a bite on them. One bite, two bites, they can be healed, cured. But I've killed them to save myself, to save others.'

'You did what you had to do.'

I nodded. 'Maybe, maybe, but that doesn't really matter anymore. It doesn't matter whether I'm right to do it, or not. Just because it's a righteous kill, doesn't mean it doesn't affect you. I used to think that if I was right, it would be enough, but it's not.'

He drew me a little closer with his hand. 'What are you saying?'

I smiled. 'I need a vacation.'

He laughed then, and it was a good laugh, open and joyous, nothing special about it but his own astonishment. I'd heard better laughs but none when I needed it more. 'A vacation, just a vacation?'

I shrugged. 'I don't see myself taking up flower arranging, Detective Ramirez.'

'Hernando,' he said.

I nodded. 'Hernando. This is part of who I am.' I realized we were still holding hands, and I drew away from him. He let me, no protest. 'Maybe if I take a break, I'll be able to do it again.'

'What if a vacation isn't enough?' he asked.

'I'll cross that bridge when I come to it.' It wasn't just the brutal day in and day out of the job. My reaction to Bernardo's body and letting a perfect stranger comfort me were so unlike me. I was missing the guys, but it was more than that. When I left Richard, I left the pack, all my werewolf friends. When I left Jean-Claude, I lost all the vamps, and strangely one or two of them were friends. You can be friends with a vampire as long as you remember that they are monsters and not human beings. How you can do both at the same time, I can't really explain, but I manage.

I hadn't just cut myself off from the men in my life for six months. I'd cut myself off from my friends. Even Ronnie, Veronica Sims, one of my few human friends had a new hot romance. She was dating Richard's best friend which made socializing awkward. Catherine, my lawyer and friend, had only been married two years, and I didn't like to interfere with her and Bob.

'You're thinking something very serious,' Ramirez said.

I blinked and looked at him. 'Just realizing how isolated I am even back home. Here, I am so . . .' I shook my head without finishing it.

He smiled. 'You're only isolated if you want to be, Anita. I've offered to show you the local sights.'

I shook my head. 'Thanks, really. Under other circumstances, I'd say yes.'

'What's stopping you?' he asked.

'The case for one. If I start dating one of the local cops, then my credibility goes down the tubes, and I'm not too high on some lists already.'

'What else?' He had a very gentle face, soft, as if he would be very gentle in everything he did.

'I've got two men waiting back home. Waiting to see who I'm going to choose, or if I'm dumping both of them.'

His eyes widened. 'Two. I'm impressed.'

I shook my head. 'Don't be. My personal life is a mess.'

'Sorry to hear that.'

'I can't believe I just told you all that. It isn't like me.'

'I'm a good listener.'

'Yeah, you are.'

'May I escort you back?'

I smiled at the old-fashioned phrasing. 'Can you answer some questions first?'

'Ask.' He sat down on the ground in his dark brown pants, lifting the pants legs so they wouldn't bunch.

I sat down beside him. 'Who called the police?'

'A guest.'

'Where is he or she?'

'Hospital. Severe shock brought on by trauma.'

'No physical injuries?' I asked.

He shook his head.

'Who were the mutilation vics this time?'

'The wife's brother and two nephews, all over twenty. They lived and worked on the ranch.'

'What about the other guests? Where were they?'

He closed his eyes, as if visualizing the page. 'Most of them were off on a planned outing, an overnight camping trip into the mountains. But the rest borrowed the ranch cars that are kept for the guests' use and left.'

'Let me guess,' I said. 'They just felt restless, jittery, had to get out of the house.'

Ramirez nodded. 'Just like the neighbors around all the other houses.'

'It's a spell, Ramirez,' I said.

'Don't make me ask you again to use my first name.'

I smiled and looked away from the teasing look in his eyes. 'Hernando, this is either a spell or some sort of ability the creature possesses to cause fear, dread, in the ones it doesn't want to kill or hurt. But I'm betting on a spell.'

'Why?'

'Because it's too selective to be a natural anxiety like a vampire's ability to hypnotize with its eyes. A vamp can bespell one person or a room full of people, but it can't do an entire street except for one house. It's too exact. You need to be able to organize your magic for this, and that means a spell.'

He picked one of the rough-looking blades of grass, running it between his fingers. 'So we're looking for a witch.'

'I know something about wiccan and other flavors of witchcraft, and I don't know any way a lone wiccan, or even a coven could do this. I'm not saying there isn't a human spell worker involved somewhere, but there is definitely something otherworldly, nonhuman, at work here.'

'We got some blood traces off the broken door.'

I nodded. 'Great. I wish someone would tell me when we find a clue. Everyone, including Ted is playing it so close to the chest, I've spent most of my time going over ground that someone else has already figured out.'

'Ask me and I'll tell you anything you want to know.' He tossed the grass blade to the ground. 'But we better be getting back before you get a worse reputation than just dating me.'

I didn't argue. Put any woman in an area run mostly by men and rumors will fly. Unless you make it very clear that you are off limits, there is also a certain competitiveness that sets in. Some men are either trying to run you out of town or get into your pants. They don't seem to know any other way to deal with a woman. If you're not a sexual object, you're a threat. Always makes me wonder what kind of childhoods they had.

Hernando stood, brushing grass and dirt off the back of his pants. He seemed to have had a dandy childhood, or at least he'd turned out well. Congrats to his parents. Someday he'd bring home a nice girl and have nice children in a nice house with yard work on the weekends, and every Sunday dinner at one set of grandparents or another. A nice life if you can get it, and he still got to solve murders. Talk about having it all.

What did I have? What did I really have? I was too young for a mid-life crisis, and too old for an attack of conscience. We started walking back towards the cars. I was hugging my arms again, and had to force myself to stop. I lowered my arms to my sides and walked along beside Ramirez . . . ah, Hernando, like nothing was wrong.

'Marks said that one of the first cops on the scene had his throat nearly bitten out. How did that happen?'

'I wasn't here for the first rush. The lieutenant waited to call me in.' There was a trace of harshness in his voice. He was gentle, but not if you pushed him. 'But I heard that the three living victims attacked the cops. They had to subdue them with batons. They just kept trying to take pieces out of them.'

'Why would they do that? How would they do it? I mean you skin most people and rip off pieces, they aren't going to feel like fighting.'

'I helped pick up some of the earlier survivors, and they didn't fight. They just lay there and moaned. They were hurt and they acted hurt.'

'Have they ever traced down Thad Bromwell, the son of the first scene I saw?'

Hernando's eyes widened. 'Marks didn't call you?'

I shook my head.

'He is such a shithead.'

I agreed. 'What? Did they find the body?'

'He's alive. He was away on a camping trip with friends.'

'He's alive,' I said. Then whose soul had I seen hovering in the bedroom? I didn't say it out loud because I'd forgotten to mention the soul to the police. Marks had been ready to chase me out of town. If I'd started talking about souls floating near the ceiling, he'd have gotten matches and a stake.

But someone had died in that room, and the soul was still confused about where to go. Most of the time if the soul hovers, it hovers over the body, the remains. Only three people lived in the house, two of them mutilated, and the boy somewhere else.

I had an idea. 'These new mutilation victims, they kept fighting, kept trying to take bites out of the officers?'

He nodded.

'Are you sure about the bites, not just hitting, but like they were trying to feed?'

'I don't know about feeding, but it was all bite wounds.' He was looking at me strangely. 'You've thought of something.'

I nodded. 'I may have. I have to see the other body, the one behind the door first, but then I think it's time to go back to the hospital.'

'Why?'

I started walking again, and he grabbed my arm, turned me to face him. There was fierceness in his eyes, an intensity that trembled down his arm. 'You've only been here a couple of days. I've been dealing with this for weeks. What do you know that I don't?'

I looked at his hand until he let me go, but I told him. He was having nightmares about this shit, and I hadn't gotten to that point yet. 'I'm an animator. I raise zombies for a living. My specialty is the dead. One thing that the living dead have in common with one another from zombie, to ghoul, to vampire, is that they must feed off the living to sustain themselves.'

'Zombies don't eat people,' he said.

'If a zombie is raised and the animator that raised it can't control it, then it can go wild. It becomes a flesh-eating zombie.'

'I thought that was just stories.'

I shook my head. 'No, I've seen it.'

'What are you saying?'

'I'm saying that maybe there are no survivors. Maybe there are just dead and the living dead.'

He actually went pale. I touched his elbow to steady him, but he stood straight. 'I'm all right. I'm all right.' He looked at me. 'What do you do with a flesh-eating zombie?'

'Once it's gone amok, there isn't anything anyone can do except destroy it. The only way to do that is fire. Napalm is good, but any fire will do.'

'They'll never let us roast these people.'

'Not unless we can prove what I'm saying is true.'

'How can you prove it?' he asked.

'I'm not sure yet, but I'll talk to Doctor Evans and we'll come up with something.'

'Why would the earlier vics be docile and these new ones be vicious?'

'I don't know, unless the spell or the monster is changing, maybe growing stronger. I just don't know, Hernando. If I'm right about there being no survivors, then I've had my brilliant idea for the day.'

He nodded, face very serious. He stared at the ground. 'Jesus, if they are all dead, then that means that this thing we're after is making more of itself?'

'I'd be surprised if it was ever human but maybe. I don't know. I do know that if it is growing stronger and the skinned ones are growing more violent, then the creature may be controlling them.'

We looked at each other. 'I'll call the hospital and get more men down there.'

'Call the Santa Fe hospital, too.'

He nodded and broke into a half-run across the gravel, moving through the cars like he had a purpose. The other cops were watching him, as if wondering what the rush was. I hadn't asked Hernando if they'd checked for underground hiding places. Shit. I went to find Bradley and ask him. Then I'd go back into the house one last time, see the last body, and then . . . off to the hospital to answer the age-old question: what is life and when is death a sure thing?

34

The man's face stared up at me, eyes wide, glazed, unseeing. His head was still attached to his spine, but the chest had been split open as though two great hands had dug into his rib cage and pulled. The heart was missing. The lungs had been ripped, probably when the rib cage gave. The stomach had been punctured, giving a sour smell to the smaller room. The liver and intestines lay in a wet heap to one side of the body as if they had all spilled out at the same time. The lower intestine still curled down inside the lower end of the body cavity. By smell alone I was pretty sure that the intestines hadn't been pierced.

I sat back on my heels beside the body. Blood had splattered the lower half of the man's face, drops of it scattering across the rest of his face and into his graying hair. Violent, very violent, and very quick. I stared into his sightless eyes and felt nothing. I was back to being numb and I was not complaining. I think if I'd seen this body first, then I'd have been horrified, but the remains in the dining room had just used me up for the day. This was awful, but there were worse things, and those things were in the next room.

But it wasn't the body that was interesting. It was the room. There was a circle of salt around the body. A book lay within the circle covered so thickly in blood that I couldn't read the pages it was opened to. They'd taken all the pictures and videos they were going to in this room so I used borrowed gloves to raise the book up. It was bound with embossed leather, but there was no title. The middle half of the book had soaked so much blood up that the pages were sticking together. I didn't try and pry them apart.

The police and the Feds had technicians for delicate work. I was careful not to close the book and lose the place the man was probably reading from. For all I knew the book had been on the desk that the man shoved against the door, and it had simply fallen to the floor, opening on its own. But to think that meant we had no clue, so we'd all pretend we were sure that the man had deliberately opened the book. In the middle of being chased by a monster that had just butchered his wife, he went for this book, opened it, started to read. Why?

The book was handwritten and I read enough to know that it was a book of shadows. It was the spell book, sort of, of a practicing witch. One that followed an older or more orthodox tradition than the neo-pagan movement. Gardian or Alexandrian, maybe. Though again I couldn't be sure. I'd had one semester in college on comparative witchcraft, though now I'm sure they called it comparative wiccan. Of the wiccan practitioners I knew personally, none of them practiced anything this traditional.

I put the book carefully back where'd I'd found it and stood. The bookshelves against the near wall were full of books on psychic research, the preternatural, mythology, folklore, and wicca. I had some of the same books at home, so the books alone weren't proof of much. But the clincher was the altar. It was an antique wooden chest with a silk cloth over the top. There were silver candlesticks with partially burned candles in them. The candles had runes carved into them. Other than the fact that they were runes, I couldn't read them.

There was a round mirror with no frame sitting flat between the candles. There was a small bowl of dried herbs to one side, a larger bowl of water, and a small carved box tightly shut.

'Is that what I think it is?' Bradley asked.

'An altar. He was a practitioner. I think that book is his book of shadows, his spell book for lack of a better term.'

'What happened here?'

'There's salt on the floor of the dining room.'

'That's not unusual,' Bradley said.

'No, but a salt circle is. I think he was somewhere farther back in the house. He heard his wife screaming or heard the monsters. Something alerted him. He didn't come running with a gun, Bradley. He came running with a handful of salt. Maybe he had something else in his hands or on his person, some charm or amulet. I don't see it, but that doesn't mean it's not here.'

'Are you saying he threw salt at this thing?'

'Yes.'

'Why, for god's sake?'

'Salt and flame are two of our oldest purifying agents. I use salt to bind a zombie back into its grave. You can throw it on fairies, fetches, a whole host of critters, and it will make them hesitate, maybe not much more.'

'So he threw salt and maybe some charm at the creature, then what?'

'I think that's why the monster stopped, and why the tablecloth full of trophies is still sitting by the table.'

'Why didn't the monster go back and get the trophies after he killed the man?'

'I don't know. Maybe he finished the spell before he died. Maybe he drove it from the house. I'd like to get a real wiccan in here to look over the scene.'

'Wiccan, you mean witch.'

'Yes, but most of them prefer the term wiccan.'

'Politically correct,' Bradley said.

I nodded. 'Yeah.'

'What could a real wiccan tell us that you can't?'

'She might know what spell he used. If the spell drove the thing from the house, then we might be able to use a version of the same spell to trap or even destroy it. Something this man did drove the creature out of this house before it was ready to go. He forced it to leave behind its goody bag and to leave without gutting his body. It's the first weakness we've seen in this thing.'

'Franklin won't like bringing in a witch. Neither will the locals. If I force everyone to bring this wiccan in, and it doesn't work or she talks to the media, then the next time you see me I won't be an FBI Agent.'

'Aren't you supposed to try every angle to solve this crime? Isn't that your job?'

'The FBI doesn't use witches, Anita.'

I shook my head. 'How the hell did you get me in then?'

'Forrester had already brought you in on the case. All I had to do was stand up to Marks.'

'And Franklin,' I said.

He nodded. 'I outrank Franklin.'

'Then why is he so snotty?'

'It seems to be a natural talent of his.'

'I don't want to get you fired, Bradley.' I went to the overturned desk and started opening the drawers. There was a gun cabinet in the living room. Most people who had a cabinet full of them kept one for personal protection.

'What are you looking for?' he asked.

I opened the larger bottom drawer, and there it was. 'Come here, Bradley.'

He came to peer into the drawer. The gun was a 9mm Smith and Wesson. It lay on the side of the drawer where it had fallen when the desk tipped over. Bradley stared down at the gun. 'Maybe it's not loaded. Maybe he had the ammo locked in the living room.'

'Can I touch it?'

He nodded.

I lifted it, and just by the weight I was pretty sure it was loaded, but it wasn't a gun I was familiar with, so I popped the clip and showed it to Bradley.

'Full,' he said, voice soft.

'Full.' I slid the clip back inside the gun, hitting it sharply with the palm of my hand to make it click. 'He had a loaded 9mm in his desk, but he grabbed salt and his book of shadows. He didn't waste time grabbing for the gun. He either knew what the thing was, or he sensed something about it and knew the gun wouldn't work, and that the spell would.' I raised the gun up so that Bradley looked at it, the barrel pointed at the ceiling. 'The spell worked, Bradley. We need to know what it was, and the only way to know that is to get a witch in here.'

'Can't you take the book and just show her pictures?'

'What if the position of the book is important? What if there are clues to the spell in the circle itself? I don't practice this kind of ritual magic, Bradley. For all I know if you get someone in here, they may be able to sense something that I can't. Do you really want to take the chance that pictures and just seeing the book in their own home will be just as good as seeing it here like this?'

'You're asking me to risk my career.'

'I am asking you to risk your career,' I said, 'but I'm also asking you not to risk any more innocent lives. Do you really want to see this done to another couple, another family?'

'How can you be so sure that this is the key?'

'I'm not sure, but it's the closest thing we've seen to a break in this case. I'd hate to lose it because of career jitters.'

'It's not just that, Anita. If we use anything more exotic than psychics and we fail, then the entire unit could be disbanded.'

I placed the gun in his hand. He stared at it. 'I trust you to do the right thing, Bradley. That's why you're one of the good guys.'

He shook his head. 'And to think I blackmailed Marks to get you back on the case.'

'You knew I was a pain in the ass when you fought to get me back on the case. It's one of my many charms.'

That earned me a weak smile. He was still holding the gun flat across his hand. His fingers tightened around it. 'You know any witches in the area?'

I grinned at him. 'No, but I bet Ted does.' I shook my head. 'I've never hugged an FBI agent, but I'm tempted.'

That made him smile, but his eyes stayed cautious, unhappy. I was asking a lot from him. I touched his arm. 'I wouldn't ask you to bring in a witch if I didn't think it was our best shot. I wouldn't ask just on a whim.'

He gave me a long look. 'I know. You are one of the least whimsical people I've ever met.'

'I would say you should see me when I'm not neck deep in corpses, but it doesn't really matter. I don't get much lighter than this.'

'I've checked the cases you've helped the St Louis PD solve, Anita. Gruesome stuff. How old are you now?'

I frowned at the question then answered it. 'Twenty-six.'

'How long have you been helping the police?'

'About four years.'

'The Bureau switches its agents off the serial killer shit about every two years. Whether they want to transfer or not. Then after a break, they can come back.'

'You think I need a break?'

'Everyone burns out eventually, Anita, even you.'

'Actually, I'm thinking about a vacation when I get home.'

He nodded. 'That's good.'

I looked up at him. 'Do I look like I need a break?'

'I've seen it before in other agents' eyes.'

'Seen what?' I asked.

'Like your eyes are a cup, and every horror you see is another drop added. Your eyes are full of the things you've seen, the things you've done. Get out while there's still some room for things that don't bleed.'

'That is damn poetic for an FBI agent.'

'One friend stayed with it until he had a heart attack.'

'I think I'm a little young for that,' I said.

'Another friend ate his gun.'

We stared at each other. 'I'm not the suicidal type.'

'I also don't want to see you in jail.'

My eyes widened. 'Whoa. I do not know what you're talking about.'

'The state department confirmed Otto Jefferies is a retired government worker, but they couldn't access the rest of his file at the present time. I've got a friend at the state department with a level two secret clearance. He couldn't access Otto Jefferies' files either. He's a total blackout, which means he's a spook of some kind. You do not want to get involved with the spooks, Anita. If they try to recruit you, say no. Don't try to find out who Otto really is, or what he did. Don't get nosy or you'll end up in a hole somewhere. Just work with him, leave him alone, and move on.'

'You sound like you're talking from personal experience,' I said.

He shook his head. 'I'm not going to talk about it.'

'You brought it up,' I said.

'I told you just enough to get your attention, I hope. Just trust me on this. Stay the fuck away from these people.'

I nodded. 'It's okay, Bradley. I don't like . . . Otto. And he hates women, so don't worry. I don't think it would occur to him to try and recruit me.'

'Good.' He put the gun back in the desk drawer and closed it.

'Besides,' I said, 'what would the top secret set want with me?'

He looked at me, and it was a look that I wasn't used to getting. The look said, I was being naive. 'Anita, you can raise the dead.'

'So?'

'I can think of a half a dozen uses for that one talent alone.'

'Like what?'

'Prisoner dies in interrogation. Doesn't matter. Raise him up again. A world leader is assassinated. We need a few days to get our troops ready, raise the leader for a few days. Give us time to control the panic, or stop the revolution.'

'Zombies are not alive, Bradley. They couldn't pass for a country's leader.'

'From a distance, for two or three days, don't even try and say you couldn't pull that off.'

'I wouldn't do it,' I said.

'Even if it meant that hundreds of lives could be saved, or hundreds of Americans could be evacuated in safety.'

I looked at him. 'I . . . I don't know.'

'No matter how good the cause seems at the beginning, Anita, eventually it won't be. Eventually, when you're so far in you can't see daylight, they'll ask things of you that you won't want to do.'

I was hugging myself again, which irritated me. No one had approached me to do anything on an international level. Olaf thought I was good for only one thing and that did not include helping the government. But it did make me wonder how Edward had met him. Edward was spooky, but was he a spook?

I looked up at Bradley's so serious face. 'I'll be careful.' Then I had a thought. 'Did someone approach you about me?'

'I was thinking about offering you a job with us.' I raised eyebrows at him.

He laughed. 'Yeah, after looking through your file, it was decided that you're too independent, too much a wild card. It was decided that you would not thrive in a bureaucratic setting.'

'You got that right, but I am flattered you thought of me.'

His face went back to serious, and there were lines in his face that I hadn't seen before. It made him look forty plus. Most of the time he didn't. 'Your file got flagged, Anita. It got moved up the line. I don't know where to or who asked for it, but there is government work out there for the independent wild card if they have specialized enough skills.'

I opened my mouth, closed it, and finally said, 'I'd say you were joking, but you're not, are you?'

He shook his head. 'I wish I was.'

Edward had said that he wouldn't have brought Olaf in if he'd known I was coming. It made it sound like Olaf had been invited in, not volunteered, but I'd ask Edward. I'd make sure.

'Thank you for telling me, Bradley. I don't know much about this stuff, but I know you're taking a chance telling me at all.'

'I had to tell you, Anita. You see it was me that pulled your file in the first place. I was the one that pushed to get you invited in. I brought you to someone's attention. For that I am heartily sorry.'

'It's okay, Bradley. You didn't know.'

He gave a small shake of his head, and the look on his face was bitter. 'But I should have.'

I didn't know what to say to that. It turned out I didn't have to say anything. Bradley walked out of the room. I waited a second or two, then followed him out. But I couldn't shake the unease. He'd meant to scare me, and he'd succeeded. It was all Big Brother watching and paranoia. He already had me wondering if Olaf had invited himself, or even if Edward could have been asked to recruit me. It wouldn't surprise me that Edward worked for the government, at least part time. He took money from anyone.

It would have seemed silly if I hadn't seen the look on Bradley's face. If he hadn't told me about my file. He said file, like everyone had a file. Maybe they did. But someone had requested my file. I had a sudden image of my life, my crimes, all printed in neat type crossing one shadowy desk after another until it reached, where? Or would the question be who?

Blake, Anita Blake. It even sounded funny. Of course, the federal government has never been known for its sense of humor.

35

Edward let me drive his Hummer to the hospital. He stayed behind to wait for the witch. She was Donna's friend so he'd play Ted and hold her hand through the crime scene. It would be her very first crime scene. Talk about being thrown in at the deep end to sink or swim. Even I'd had a gentler introduction to police work than this.

Olaf stayed to commune with the bodies. Fine with me. I did not want to be in a car, or any small confined space with Olaf without Edward along to chaperone. I think the police and the Feds would have gladly given him to me for the ride, though. All he'd really done was confirm my supposition that the killer would not have willingly left his trophies behind, though Olaf knew less about magic than I did. He didn't know why the killer left. I was the only one with a scenario for that, and even I would be relieved if the wicca practitioner seconded my opinion. If she didn't, then we were truly out of guesses.

In fact, almost no one wanted to go with me. Franklin thought I was nuts. What did I mean, the survivors weren't survivors, but the living dead? Bradley wasn't willing to leave Franklin as the ranking agent on site. The geology maps were on the way, and I don't think he wanted Franklin in charge of the search. Marks wouldn't leave the scene to the Feds, and he also thought I was nuts. Ramirez and one uniform followed me in an unmarked car.

I didn't really think they'd find the monster. There had been no tracks. No tracks meant either it could fly or it dematerialized. Either way they weren't going to find it, not on foot, not with maps. So I felt free to go to the hospital.

Another reason to go into Albuquerque was that Edward had found me a name. A man who was known as a brujo, a witch. Donna had only given 'Ted' the name on the condition it would not be used to harm the man. She'd only been given the name on the strict understanding that no harm would come to him. The one who gave up the name didn't want the brujo to come back and hurt her. He would work evil spells for money, as well as personal vengeance. If you could prove in court that he performed real magic for nefarious purposes, it was an automatic death sentence. His name was Nicandro Baco, and he was supposed to be a necromancer. If he was, he'd be the first one, other than me, that I'd ever met. The name came with one other warning. Be careful of him. He was much more dangerous than he looked. Just what I needed – a necromancer with an attitude. Oh, wait, I was a necromancer with an attitude. If he got shitty with me, we'd see who was the bigger fish. Was that a chip on my shoulder or overconfidence? We'd see.

Oh, and Bernardo went with me. He sat in the passenger seat slumped down until the seatbelt I'd insisted he wear cut across his neck. His handsome face was set in a scowl, arms crossed over his chest. I think he'd have crossed his legs if he'd had room. Words like *closed-off*, *brooding*, came to mind.

Shadows stretched across the road, though there were no trees or buildings to cast them. It was like the shadows just spilled out of the earth itself to lie across the road like a promise of the night to come. If you went by the watch on my wrist, it was early evening. If you went by the level of daylight, it was late afternoon. We had about three hours of daylight left. I drove through the gathering shadows with a feeling of urgency pressing against me. I wanted to be at the hospital before dark. I didn't know why, and I didn't question it. We were being followed by a police car. Surely, they could fix the ticket.

It was frightening how quickly and smoothly the car went over eighty without me noticing it. There was something about the roads and the way they spilled out and out across the empty landscape that made lower speeds seem like crawling. I kept it at a solid eighty, and Ramirez kept up with me. He seemed to be the only one who believed me. Maybe he felt the urgency, too.

The silence in the car wasn't exactly companionable, but it wasn't uncomfortable either. Besides, I had enough problems without playing crying shoulder for one of Edward's sociopathic friends.

Bernardo broke the silence. 'I saw you and that detective getting it on out there in the grass.'

I frowned at him. He was watching me with hostile eyes. I think he was trying to pick a fight, though I didn't know why. 'We were not "getting it on,"' I said.

'Looked pretty cozy to me.'

'Jealous?' I asked.

His face hardened, thinning into angry lines. 'So you do sleep around. Just not with us bad guys.'

I shook my head. 'It was a comforting hug, not that it's any of your business.'

'Didn't think you were the comforting hug type.'

'I'm not.'

'So,' he said.

'So this case is getting to me.'

'I hear that,' he said.

I glanced at him. His face was turned away, only a thin rim of profile showing through his hair like the moon just before it goes dark.

I turned back to the road. If he didn't want eye contact, fine with me. 'I thought you were avoiding the pictures and forensic stuff,' I said.

'I've been here two weeks longer than you have. I've seen the pictures. I've seen the bodies. I don't need to see it all again.'

'What exactly did you and Edward quarrel about today?'

'Quarrel,' he said and gave a low chuckle. 'Yeah, you could say we quarreled.'

'What about?'

'I don't know why the hell I'm here. Tell me what or who to shoot, and I'll do it. I'll even guard bodies if the price is right. But there's nothing to shoot at. Nothing but dead bodies. I don't know shit about magic.'

'I thought you were a licensed bounty hunter that specialized in preternatural critters.'

'I was with Edward when he cleaned out a nest of lycanthropes in Arizona. Fifteen of them. We mowed them down with machine guns and grenades.' He had an almost wistful tone to his voice. Ah, the good ol' days. 'Before that I'd killed two rogue lycanthropes, but afterwards I got a lot of calls for this shit. I took the ones that were basically just hits. The only difference was that the vic wasn't human. Those I could handle, but I am not a detective. Call me in when the kill is in sight, and I'll be there, but not this. This fucking waiting around, looking for clues. Who the hell looks for clues? We're assassins, not Sherlock Holmes.'

He shifted in his seat, and struggled to sit up straighter, arms still holding himself tight. He did the headshake to get the hair back away from his face. The headshake is a very feminine gesture. A man has to be muy macho for it not to be. Bernardo managed.

'Maybe he assumed that since you helped him out with the shapeshifters that you'd be useful with this.'

'He was wrong.'

I shrugged. 'Then go home.'

'I can't.'

I glanced at him. I could see most of his profile, and it was a nice one. 'You owe him a favor, too?'

'Yes.'

'Mind me asking what sort of favor?'

'Same as you.'

'You killed one of his other backups?'

He nodded, and had to run his hands through his hair to slide it back from his face.

'Want to talk about it?'

'Why?' He looked at me, and his face, for one of the few times, wasn't teasing, but serious, even solemn. He looked less handsome without the smile and glow in his eyes, but he also seemed more real. Being real will get me into trouble faster than any amount of charm. 'Do you want to talk about how you killed Harley?' he asked.

'Not really.'

'Then why did you ask?'

'You seem uptight. I thought it might help to talk, or is that just a girl thing?'

He smiled, and it almost reached his eyes. 'I think it's a girl thing because I don't want to talk about it.'

'Okay, let's talk about something else.'

'What?' He was staring out the far window now, one shoulder pressed against the glass. The road went down between two hills, and the world was suddenly dark gray. We were literally running out of daylight. But this last attack had most definitely been a daylight attack. So why was I so worried about the coming night? Maybe it was just years of hunting vampires, where darkness meant that we humans no longer had any advantage. I hoped it was just old habits, but the fluttering in my stomach didn't think that was it.

'How long have you known Edward?' I asked.

'About six years.'

'Shit,' I said.

He looked at me then. 'What's wrong?'

'I've known him for five. I was hoping you'd known him longer.'

He grinned at me. 'Wanting to pump me for information, eh?'

'Something like that.'

He turned in the seatbelt until most of his body was facing me, one leg drawn up into the seat. 'Let me pump you, and you can pump me all you want.' His voice had dropped a notch or two. His head was to one side, the hair sweeping across the seat like black fur.

I shook my head. 'You're horny, and I'm available. That isn't very flattering, Bernardo.'

He moved back in his seat, sweeping his hair back to his side of the seat. 'Now that is a girl thing.'

'What is?'

'Complicating things, needing the sex to be about something more than sex.'

'I don't know. I know a guy or two that make it just as complicated.'

'You don't sound happy with him or them.'

'Did Edward call you before Olaf or after?' I asked.

'After, but you're changing the subject.'

'No, I'm not. Edward is an expert on people. He knows who to call for any given situation, for any kill. Olaf makes sense. I make sense. You don't make sense. He knows that this isn't your type of crime.'

'You lost me.'

'Edward encouraged me to sleep with you.'

Bernardo looked at me, shocked, I think. Nice to know he could be. 'Edward matchmaking. We are talking about the same Edward, right?'

'Maybe Donna has changed him,' I said.

'Nothing changes Edward. He's a mountain. He's just there.'

I nodded. 'True, but he wasn't encouraging me to pick out curtains with you. He said, and I quote, "What you need is a nice uncomplicated fuck."'

Bernardo's eyebrows went up into his hair. 'Edward said that?'

'Yeah, he did.'

He was looking at me now. I could feel his gaze on me even while watching the road. It wasn't sexual now. It was intense. I had his attention. 'Are you saying that Edward brought me on to tempt you?'

'I don't know. Maybe. Maybe I'm wrong. Maybe it's just a coincidence. But he's not happy with my choice of lovers.'

'First, there are no coincidences when it comes to Edward. Second, who could you possibly be sleeping with that would bother Edward? He wouldn't care if you were doing your dog.'

I ignored the last comment, because I couldn't think of a comeback for it. Though notice I didn't disagree. Usually, Edward just wanted to know if you could shoot. Anything else was not important. 'I'll answer your question, if you answer mine first.'

'Try me.'

'You may look like the cover boy for the Native American GQ, but there's no sense of you coming from a different culture?'

'Too white for you?' and his voice was angry. I'd touched the chip on his shoulder.

'Look, my mother's family is Mexican American, and you have a sense of their culture when you interact with them. My father's family is German, and they'll say things, do things that are sort of European or have a foreign flavor to them. You don't seem to have any specific culture or background. You talk like generic middle America, like television or something.'

He looked at me, and he was angry now. 'My mother was white. My father was Indian. I'm told he died before I was born. She gave me up at birth. No one wanted a little mixed baby, so I went from one foster home to another. When I was eighteen, I joined the army. They found out I could shoot. I killed things for my country for a few years. Then I went freelance. And here I am.' His voice had grown increasingly bitter until it almost hurt to hear it.

Saying I was sorry would have been insulting. Saying I understood would have been a lie. Thanks for answering the question seemed wrong, too.

'Nothing to say?' he asked. 'Shocked? Sorry for me? Give me a little pity sex.'

I looked at him then. 'If someone has sex with you, it isn't out of pity, and you damn well know it.'

'But you don't want to have sex with me.'

'It's not because of your ethnicity, or lack thereof, or your background. I've got two guys waiting for me at home. Two is one too many. Three would be ridiculous.'

'Why doesn't Edward like them?' Bernardo asked.

'One's a werewolf and the other is a vampire.' My words were bland, but I watched his face long enough to see the reaction. He gaped at me.

He finally closed his mouth, and said, 'You're the Executioner, scourge of the undead. How can you be doing a vampire?'

'I'm not sure I can answer that question, even to myself. But currently, I'm not doing him at all.'

'Did you think the werewolf was human? Was he trying to pass?'

'At first, but not for long. I knew what he was when I took him to my bed.'

He let out a low whistle. 'Edward hates the monsters. But I didn't think he'd give a damn if one of his backups slept with them.'

'He cares. I don't know why, but he does.'

'So he thought what? That one night with me would change your religion? Make you swear off the monsters?' He was staring at me now, studying my face. 'I've heard that shapeshifters can change the shape of their bodies at will. Is that true?'

'Some of them can,' I said. We were in the outskirts of Albuquerque. Strip malls and fast food restaurants.

'Can your boyfriend?'

'Yes.'

'Can he change the shape of all his body, at will?'

I felt the blush roll up my neck into my face and couldn't stop it.

Bernardo laughed. 'I guess he can.'

'No comment.'

He was still laughing softly to himself, a very masculine chuckle. 'Is your vampire an old one?'

'Four hundred years and counting,' I said. We'd left the strip malls behind and turned into a residential area. We were coming up to the first landmark on the directions Edward had given me. We'd used up nearly an hour of daylight. I almost drove past the turnoff to Nicandro Baco's place, but if I was right, if the thing we were dealing with was another type of undead from any that I'd ever heard of, then another necromancer might be nice to have around. For all I knew, this type of undead was a regional specialty, and Baco would know more than I did. I turned, checking the rearview to see that Ramirez was still behind me. We were actually all going the speed limit.

'Can you read the directions to me?' I asked.

He didn't answer, just picked the piece of paper up off the dashboard, and began reading off street names. 'You're safe on the directions for a little bit. Let's get back to our little talk.'

I frowned at him. 'Do we have to?'

'Let me get this straight,' Bernardo said. 'You've been shacking up with a shapeshifter that has such fine control of his body that he can make any one part of it . . . bigger.'

'Or smaller,' I said. I was counting streetlights, under my breath. Didn't want to miss the turn. We had time to see this guy and get to the hospital before dark, but not if we got badly lost.

'No man makes things smaller during sex. I don't care what he is, he's still male.'

I shrugged. I was not going to discuss Richard's size with Bernardo. The only person I had discussed it with had been Ronnie, and that had been over much giggling, while she shared embarrassing facts about her boyfriend, Louie. It has been my experience that women tell more intimate details to their friends than men do. Men may brag more, but women will talk the nitty-gritty and share the experience more.

'So, where was I?' Bernardo said. 'Ah, you're doing this shapeshifter that has such fine control of his body that he can make any part bigger or smaller at will.'

I squirmed in the seat, but finally nodded.

Bernardo smiled happily. 'And you're doing a vampire that has been having sex for over four hundred years.' He suddenly sounded faux-British. 'Can one assume that he is well-skilled by now?'

The blush that had been fading came back with a burn. I'd almost have welcomed darkness to hide behind. 'Yes,' I said.

'Shit, girlfriend, I may be good, but I'm not that good. I am just a poor mortal boy. I can't compete with the lord of the undead and the wolfman.'

We were in a section of town that seemed nearly deserted. Gas stations with bars on the windows and graffiti spread across everything like a contagious disease. The storefront across from it had boarded-up windows and more graffiti. The afternoon was still thick with reflected sunlight, but somehow the light didn't quite reach the street, as if there was something here that kept it at bay. The skin on my back crept so hard, I jumped.

'What's wrong?' Bernardo asked.

I shook my head. My mouth was suddenly dry. I knew we had arrived before he called out, 'There it is, Los Duendos, the dwarves.'

The air was thick and oppressive with the weight of magic. Death magic. Either they had just killed something to gain power for a spell or they were actively working with the dead right at this very moment. Since the sun was still up, that was a trick. Most animators couldn't raise the dead until after dark. Theoretically, I am powerful enough to raise the dead at high noon, but I don't. I was told once that the only reason I couldn't do it was that I believed I couldn't do it. But Nicandro Baco didn't seem to share my doubts. Maybe I wouldn't be the biggest fish after all. Now I got an attack of the doubts. Too late to get Edward down here for backup. If Baco got a whiff of police, he'd either run, be uncooperative, or try to hurt us. His power breathed along my body, and I was still sitting in the car. What was he going to be like in person? Bad. How bad? As the old saying goes, only one way to find out.

36

I'd pulled into a deserted parking lot about two blocks down and around the corner from the bar. Ramirez had pulled in beside me, and he and the uniform, Officer Rigby, walked over to us. Rigby was medium height, well built, and moved like he worked out. He had an easy confidence, and a ready smile that went all the way to his eyes. He was entirely too comfortable in his own skin, as if nothing really bad had ever touched him. He lacked entirely that air that most policemen have of having been ridden hard and put up wet. He looked older than I was, but his eyes were younger, and I resented that.

Ramirez had spent his drive time checking out Nicandro Baco, alias Nicky Baco. He was suspected of murders, but witnesses had a strange way of disappearing or forgetting what they'd seen. He was associated with a local biker gang, ah, club. Biker gangs now preferred the more politically correct term of club, according to Ramirez. The local 'club' was called Los Lobos. 'Not to be confused with the music group,' Ramirez said.

I'd blinked at him. Then I got the joke. 'Oh, yeah, Los Lobos, the music group.'

He looked at me. 'Are you all right?'

I nodded. Even two blocks away I could feel a touch of Baco's magic. I was betting if someone took the time, they'd find spells, charms, wards, set up here and there in the surrounding area. I didn't think he was aware of me yet. I think the only reason I'd sensed him so strongly was he was in the middle of a spell. The charms were scattered around the neighborhood to give off a certain unease. He might have literally driven the other businesses out of business. Illegal, as well as unethical. Of course, why he'd want to destroy the entire economy of the area surrounding his bar was a mystery to me. I'd worry about it later. Murder and mayhem first. Possible real estate scam later. Some days you just have to prioritize.

'The Lobos are small and local, but they've got a bad rep,' Ramirez said.

'How bad?' I asked.

'Drug running, murder, murder for hire, assault, assault with a deadly, attempted murder, rape, kidnapping.'

Bernardo said, 'Kidnapping?' As if the other crimes were to be expected but not the last.

Ramirez looked at him, and his eyes went from friendly to cool. He didn't like Bernardo for some reason. 'We think they abducted a teenage girl, but nobody ever surfaced, and the only witness just saw her being dragged into a van that looked like one that their leader, Roland Sanchez, owned at the time. But a lot of people own gray vans.'

'Have you had a lot of disappearing teenage girls?' I asked.

'Our share, but no, we haven't noticed a pattern of young women being abducted by the gang. I'm not saying they won't do it, but they're not making a habit of it.'

'Glad to hear it,' I said.

Ramirez smiled. 'You're armed, and . . .' He handed me a slender cell phone. 'Press this button and it'll call this phone.' He held up a matching phone. 'Rigby and I will come running with backup.'

My eyes flicked to Rigby, who actually tipped his hat at me. 'At your service, ma'am.'

Ma'am? Either he was five years younger than he looked, or he used ma'am for all women. I turned from his peaceful eyes to Ramirez. His eyes were kind, but they weren't peaceful. He'd seen too much of life for true tranquility. I liked his eyes better. 'You're not going to try and argue me out of just Bernardo and I walking into the bar?'

'We suspect Baco of using magic to kill people. That is an automatic death sentence. If he gets a whiff of police, then he'll clam up and start asking for a lawyer. If you want information from him, you'll have to play ordinary citizen. Now, if you planned to go in there alone without Bernardo or some man with you, then I'd argue.'

I frowned at him. 'I can take care of myself.'

He shook his head. 'In the world that this gang runs in, women do not exist except through men.'

My frown deepened. 'You've lost me.'

'All women are either someone's mother, daughter, wife, sister, girlfriend, lover. They would not know what the hell to do with you, Anita. Go in as Bernardo's girlfriend.' He had his hand up, stopping me from interrupting before I could even open my mouth and try. 'Trust me on this. You need to have some sort of status that they can grasp quickly and easily. Flashing your animator's license is too close to a badge. No woman in her right mind would just wander in there for a drink. You have to be something.' He glanced at Bernardo not like he was happy. 'I'd go in with you as your boyfriend, but like it or not, I look like a cop, or so I've been told.'

I looked at him. I wasn't sure what it was about most policemen, but after a while they really did look like cops, even off duty sometimes. It was partially the clothes, partially some indefinable air of authority or bad attitude or something. Whatever 'it' was, Ramirez had it. Rigby was in uniform, and I wouldn't have taken him as backup anyway. He made me nervous with his air of contentment. Policemen should never be that well pleased with themselves. It means they haven't had much experience yet.

I looked at Bernardo's smirking face. 'Agreed, under protest.'

'Good,' Ramirez said, but he was looking at Bernardo, too, like he didn't like the look on his face. He held a finger up near the taller man's face. 'You get out of line in there with Anita, and I will personally make you sorry for it.'

Bernardo's eyes drifted from amused to cool. It reminded me of the way Edward's eyes lost emotion until they were empty and somehow harsh.

I stepped between them, enough to get both of them looking at me. 'I can take care of myself when it comes to Bernardo, Detective Ramirez. Thanks anyway.' I'd used his title to remind Bernardo who and what he was. Even Edward treaded soft around the cops.

Ramirez's face had closed down, empty. 'Suit yourself, Ms Blake.'

I realized that he thought I'd used his title because I was angry with him. Shit. Why was I always ass deep in male egos in the middle of any given crisis? 'It's okay, Hernando. I just like to remind everyone that I'm a big girl.' I touched his arm lightly.

He looked at me, and his eyes softened. 'Okay.' That was male shorthand for apology and apology accepted. Though truthfully if one of the parties involved hadn't been female, the shorthand would have been shorter.

I stepped away from both of them and changed the subject. 'Amazing how many bad guys and monsters will talk to me and not the police.'

He nodded, face still serious. 'Amazing. That's one word for it.' The look he gave me was so studied, so searching, that I wondered if he'd been checking me out as well as Baco.

I didn't ask. I didn't really want to know. But he was right about Baco. If he was what people said, then he wouldn't want the police anywhere near his home or his work area. They were not kidding about the automatic death penalty. The last execution in this country of a spell caster had been two months ago. It had been in California, which is not a death penalty state for any other crime.

They'd tried and convicted a sorcerer, or would that be sorceress, of trafficking with the demonic. She'd used a demon to kill her sister so she'd inherit the parents' estate. They suspected she'd also killed her parents, but they couldn't prove that. And who cared? They could only kill her once. I'd read some of the trial transcript. She'd been guilty. I had no doubt on that point. But it had been three months from arrest, to conviction, to the carrying out of the sentence. It was unheard of in the American justice system. Hell, it usually takes longer than that to get a hearing date, let alone a full-blown trial. But even California had learned its lesson a few years back. They'd arrested a sorcerer for very similar crimes. They'd tried to give the sorcerer the usual wait for a trial because some congressman or other was arguing that the death penalty shouldn't be allowed even in cases of magical assassination.

That sorcerer had called a greater demon in his cell. It killed every guard on the cellblock, and some of the prisoners. He'd finally been tracked down with the help of a coven of white wiccans. The death total had been forty-two, forty-three, something like that. He was killed during the capture attempt. He took thirty slugs, which meant people had emptied their clips into his body once it went down. For none of the police to get caught in the crossfire, they must have been standing over him, pointing down. Overkill, you bet, but I didn't blame them. They never did find all the body parts of the guards at the prison.

New Mexico was a death penalty state. I was betting that they would be able to beat California's three months turnaround from arrest to completion of sentence. I mean, after all, in this state they might actually put you to death for a good old-fashioned murder. Add magic to it, and they'd be scattering your ashes to the wind faster than you could say Beelzebub.

The actual method of execution is the same for everyone. America does not allow burning at the stake for any crime. But after you're dead, they burn the body to ash if you were convicted of a crime involving magic. Then they scatter the ashes, usually into running water. Very traditional.

There are parts of Europe where it's still legal to burn a 'witch' at the stake. There's more than one reason that I don't travel outside the country much.

'Anita, are you still with us?' Ramirez asked.

I blinked. 'Sorry, just thinking about the last execution in California. I don't blame Baco for being worried.'

Ramirez shook his head. 'Me, either. Be very careful. These are bad people.'

'Anita knows about bad people,' Bernardo said.

The two men looked at each other, and again I got that hint that Ramirez didn't like him. Bernardo seemed to be teasing him. Did they know each other?

I decided to ask. 'Do you guys know each other?'

They both shook their heads. 'Why?' Bernardo asked.

'You guys seem to have some sort of personal shit going on.'

Bernardo smiled then, and Ramirez looked uncomfortable. 'It's not personal with me,' Bernardo said.

Rigby turned away, coughing. If I hadn't known better, I'd have said he was covering a laugh.

Ramirez ignored him, all attention for Bernardo. 'I know Anita knows how to handle herself around the bad guys, but a knife blade in the back doesn't care how good you are. The Lobos pride themselves on using blades instead of guns.'

'Guns are for sissies,' I said.

'Something like that.'

I had the black suit jacket on over the navy blue polo shirt. If I buttoned two buttons, the jacket hid the Firestar in front and still left me plenty of room to reach for it, and the Browning. In fact the slender cell phone swinging in the right side-pocket was more noticeable than the guns. 'I just love taking a gun to a knife fight.'

Bernardo had thrown a black short-sleeved dress shirt over his white T-shirt. It fanned in back and covered the Beretta 10 mil on his hip. 'Me, too,' he said and smiled. It was a fierce smile, and I realized that this may have been the first time in weeks that he was going up against something flesh and blood and killable.

'We're going in for information, not to do the OK Corral. You do understand that?' I said.

'You're the boss,' he said, but I didn't like the way his eyes looked. They were anticipatory, eager.

I'd felt paranoid this morning when I slipped the knife in its spine sheath. Now I moved my head a little back and forth feeling the handle against my neck. It was comforting. I almost always carried the wrist sheaths and their matching knives, but the spine sheath was optional. One minute you're paranoid and packing too much hardware, the next you're scared, and under-armed. Life's like that, or my life's like that.

'Do you know what los duendos are?' Ramirez asked.

'Bernardo said it meant the dwarves.'

Ramirez nodded. 'But around here it's folklore. They're small beings that live in caves and steal things. But they're supposed to be angels that got left suspended between Heaven and Hell during Lucifer's revolt. So many angels were leaving Heaven that God slammed the gates shut and los duendos got trapped outside of Heaven. They were suspended in limbo.'

'Why didn't they just go to Hell?' Bernardo asked.

It was a good question. Ramirez shrugged. 'The story doesn't say.'

I glanced at Rigby standing behind Ramirez. He was standing so easy, ready, prepared like a grown-up Boy Scout. He didn't seem worried about anything. It made me nervous. We were about to go into a bar that was thick with bikers, bad guys. There was a necromancer inside so powerful that it made my skin crawl from blocks away. The rest of us looked confident, but it was a confidence born of having been there and done that and survived. Rigby's confidence struck me as false, not false confidence, but based on a false assumption. I couldn't know for sure without asking, but I was betting that Rigby had never really been in any situation where he thought he might not come out the other side. There was a softness to him despite the lean muscles. I'd take a few less muscles and more depth to the eyes any day. I hoped that Ramirez didn't have to come in with Rigby as his only backup. But I didn't say it out loud. Everyone loses their cherry sometime, somewhere. If things went wrong, tonight might be Rigby's night.

'Did you tell us that little story for a reason, Hernando? I mean you don't really think that Baco or this biker gang are los duendos?'

He shook his head. 'No, I just thought you might want to know. It says something about Baco to name his bar after fallen angels.'

I opened the driver's side door of the Hummer. Bernardo took the hint and went for the passenger side door. 'Not fallen angels, Hernando, just caught in limbo.'

Hernando leaned into the open window of the car. 'But they're not in Heaven anymore, are they?' With that last cryptic comment he stepped back and let me raise the window. He and Rigby watched us drive off. They looked sort of forlorn standing there in the abandoned, broken parking lot. Or maybe it was just me feeling forlorn.

I looked at Bernardo. 'Don't kill anyone, okay?'

He slid back in his seat, snuggling against the leather. He looked more relaxed than I'd seen him in hours. 'If they try to kill us?'

I sighed. 'Then we defend ourselves,' I said.

'See, I knew you'd see things my way.'

'Don't start the fight,' I said.

He looked at me with eager brown eyes. 'Can I finish it?'

I looked back at the road searching for a parking space. Whatever spell Baco had been working was over. The atmosphere was a little easier to breathe. But there was still something in the air like close lightning waiting to strike. 'Yeah, we can finish it.'

He started humming under his breath. I think it was the theme from 'The Magnificent Seven.' To quote an overused movie line, I had a bad feeling about this.

37

By the time I found a parking space, Bernardo and I had a plan. I was an out of town necromancer wanting to talk shop with one of the only other necromancers I'd ever heard of. If it hadn't been so damn close to the truth, it would have been a lousy cover story. Even being the truth, almost, it sounded weak. But we didn't have all day, and besides, I don't think being sneaky was a strong suit for either of us. We were both more comfortable with the bust-the-door-down-and-start-shooting school, than the concoct-a-good-cover-story-and-infiltrate.

Bernardo reached his hand out for me just before we crossed the street. I frowned at him.

He waggled his hand at me. 'Come on, Anita, play fair.' He was holding his right hand out to me. I stared at the offered hand for a heartbeat, but finally took it. His fingers slid around my hand a little slower, and a little more proprietarily than necessary, but I could live with it. Lucky for us that I was right-handed, and Bernardo was left-handed. We could hold hands and not compromise either of our gun hands. Usually, I was the only one armed when I was cuddling, so it was only my gun hand we had to worry about.

I've dated men that I couldn't walk hand in hand with, like an awkward rhythm between us. Bernardo was not one of those men. He slowed his pace to let me catch up to his longer legs, until he realized I was a step ahead of him, tugging on his hand. I have a lot of tall friends. No one ever complains that I can't keep up.

The door to the bar was black and blended so well with the building's facade that you almost missed it. Bernardo opened the door for me, and I let him. It might blow our cover to argue over who got to hold the door for who. Though if he had been my real boyfriend, we'd have had the discussion. Ah, well.

The minute I stepped inside the bar, no, the second I stepped inside the bar, I knew we were not going to blend in. So many things had already gone wrong. We were not so much overdressed as wrongly dressed. If Bernardo had ditched the black dress shirt and just worn the white T-shirt, and if it hadn't looked fresh out of the box, then he might have mingled. I was *so* the only suit jacket in the room. But even the polo shirt and jeans seemed a little much beside what some of the women were wearing. Can you say, short-shorts?

A girl near us, and I meant girl – if she was eighteen, I'd eat something icky – looked at me with hostile eyes. She had long brown hair that swung past her shoulders. The hair was clean and shiny even in the dim light. Her makeup was light but expertly applied. She should have been deciding who to take to the prom. Instead, she was wearing a black leather bra with metal studs on it and matching shorts that looked like they'd been painted over her narrow hips. A pair of those clunky platform high-heels completed the look. Those platform shoes had been ugly in the seventies and eighties, and they were still ugly two decades later, even if they were back in style.

She was hanging all over a guy that had to be thirty years or more her senior. His hair and ragged beard were gray. At first glance you'd think he was fat, but he was fat the way an offensive lineman was fat, flesh with muscle under it. His eyes were hidden behind small round sunglasses, even though the bar was cast in permanent twilight. He sat at the table closest to the door, big hands resting on the wood. He was totally at rest, but you still got a sense of how very large he was, how physically imposing. The girl was slender and shorter than I was. I hoped she was his daughter, but doubted it.

He stood, and a wave of energy moved off of him in a curling, almost visible roil of power. It was suddenly hard to breathe, and it wasn't the cigarette smoke rolling like a low fog through the room. I'd come in expecting to meet a necromancer. I had not expected a werewolf. I couldn't be a hundred percent sure of the type of animal, but call it a hunch — los lobos — had to be werewolves.

I looked out over that room full of people, and felt their power raise like invisible hackles. Bernardo put his right hand on my shoulder and drew me towards the bar, slowly. It took almost all the restraint I had not to reach for one of the guns. They had not offered us violence. They probably always did this show to unwanted tourists. Almost anyone would get the message and leave. Leaving actually sounded like a really good idea. Unfortunately, we had business, and a really good threat display was not reason enough to stop us. Pity. Because they would not like the fact that we didn't leave. What if this afternoon's little display wasn't the norm? What if they were trying to chase us away because something illegal was going down? Worse and worse.

The long wooden bar had cleared out as we moved towards it. Fine with me. I didn't want to be outflanked. The bartender was a woman, surprise, and a dwarf, ah, little person. I couldn't see over the bar, but she had to have something she was standing on. She had short, thick hair, dark, shot through with strands of white. Her face was the typical rough square, but her eyes were as hard as any I've ever seen. Her face was heavily lined not with age, but with wear and tear. One eyebrow was bisected by a heavy white scar. All she needed was a sign above her head that said, 'I've had a hard life.'

'What do you want?' she asked. Her tone matched the rest of her, harsh.

I half expected Bernardo to answer, but his attention was all for the room and the growing air of hostility. 'We're looking for Nicky Baco,' I said.

Her eyes never flickered. 'Never heard of him.'

I shook my head. Her answer had been automatic. She didn't even have to think about it. I could have asked to see anyone in the room and the answer would have been the same. I lowered my voice, though I knew most of the things in the room would hear even the barest whisper. 'I'm a necromancer. I heard that Baco is one, too. I've met a lot of zombie raisers, but never another necromancer.'

She shook her head. 'Don't know what you're talking about.' She started to rub the top of the bar with a stained rag. She wasn't even looking at me now, as if I'd become something totally without interest.

They'd stall for a while, then they'd get impatient and try to kick us out. Unless we were willing to start shooting people, they'd succeed. When in doubt, tell the truth. Not my usual ploy, but hey, I'll try anything once.

'I'm Anita Blake,' and that was all I got out before her gaze snapped upward, and she really looked at me for the first time.

'Prove it,' she said.

I started to reach inside the jacket for my ID. I heard the gun click underneath the bar, as she pulled the hammer back. Just from the sound I'd say it was an old-fashioned shotgun, sawed off or it wouldn't have fit under the bar.

'Slowly,' she said.

I caught Bernardo's movement out of the corner of my eye. Turning towards us, maybe going for a gun. 'It's okay, Bernardo. It's under control.'

I don't think he believed me.

I said, 'Please.'

I didn't say please often. Bernardo hesitated but finally turned back to watch the gathering werewolves. He hissed, 'Hurry up.'

I did what the lady with the shotgun pointed at my chest said, I moved very, very slowly, and handed her my ID.

'Lay it on the bar.'

I laid it on the bar.

'Hands flat on the bar. Lean into it.'

The bar top was sticky, but I kept my hands on it and leaned into it, in a sort of push-up position. She could have just asked me to assume the position. It was a leg width away from it.

'Him, too,' she said.

Bernardo had heard her. 'No,' he said.

Something passed through her eyes that would have made Edward proud. I knew she'd do it. 'Either do what she says or get the fuck out of here,' I said.

He moved so he could watch the room at large, and see me and the lady behind the bar. He was beside the outer door. One quick move and he could be out in the afternoon sunlight. He didn't go for the door. He looked at me. His eyes flicked to the woman behind the bar. I think he saw in her face what I'd seen because he sighed enough that his shoulders slumped. He shook his head, but he moved towards the long bar. He moved stiffly, as if each small movement pained him. His posture, his face, all screamed that he didn't like doing this, but he leaned beside me against the bar.

'Legs farther apart,' she said. 'Lean into it like you want to see that pretty face in the polish.'

I heard Bernardo take a hissing breath, but he spread his legs and leaned close enough to see the varnish on the scarred bar. 'Can I just say now that this is a bad idea?' he said.

'Shut up,' I said.

The woman opened the ID on the bar top, one hand still hidden under the bar. They had the shotgun attached underneath the bar somehow. I wondered what other surprises they had.

'Why do you want to see Nicky?' she asked.

She hadn't told me to stop leaning, so I didn't. 'I told the truth. I want to talk to another necromancer.'

'Why didn't you tell me who you were up front?'

'I work with the cops sometimes. I thought it might make you nervous.' I had to roll my eyes up to see her face. I was rewarded with a smile. It looked almost awkward on her harsh features, but it was a start.

'Why do you want to talk to another necromancer?'

I let the truth spill out of my mouth without concentrating on the fact that I planned to stop before I'd told all of it. I mean Nicky Baco was a necromancer, and if necromancy was involved in the killings . . . So only part of the truth until I knew whether he was a bad guy. 'I've got a little problem that involves the dead. I wanted a second opinion.'

She laughed then, a harsh sound like the caw of a crow. I jumped, and I swear I could feel the werewolves behind me flinch. If I hadn't known better, I'd have said they were just a little afraid of this small woman. I know I was.

'Nicky'll love that. The famous Anita Blake coming to consult him. Oh, he will just fucking love this.' She motioned with her head. 'Who's he?'

'This is Bernardo, he's . . . a friend.'

Her eyes hardened. 'How good a friend?'

'Close, very close,' I said.

She leaned across the bar, putting her face next to mine, her hand still under the bar on the shotgun. 'I should kill you. I can feel it. You'll hurt Nicky.' I looked into her eyes from inches away. I expected to see anger or even hatred, but there was nothing. It was the very emptiness that clued me in. If she pulled the trigger on me, it wouldn't be the first time.

My pulse was suddenly thudding in my throat. Blown away by a psychotic dwarf bartender, how ironic. I kept my voice low and even the way you talk to jumpers on ledges, and people with guns pointed at you. 'I don't plan to hurt Nicky. I honestly just want to consult with him, one necromancer to another.'

She just kept looking at me, not even blinking. She raised up slowly. 'If you move, I'll kill you. If he moves, I'll kill you.' The way she said it promised that whatever was about to happen, was something we weren't going to like.

She turned her gaze to Bernardo and leaned down so that her head was sideways looking at him, her ear almost pressed to the bar. 'Did you hear me, boyfriend?'

'I heard you,' he said, and his voice was low and calm, too. He'd seen it, too. She wanted an excuse to kill me. I'd never met her before, so it couldn't be personal. But personal or not, I'd be just as dead.

'We don't let outsiders bring guns into our house.'

'No disrespect intended,' I said. 'I always go armed. Nothing personal.'

She leaned back down next to Bernardo's face. 'How 'bout you? You always go armed?'

'Yes,' he said. He frowned, then went back to staring at the bar. My hands felt like they were becoming permanently glued to the wood.

'Not in here you don't,' she said.

It was the big man in front who searched us. Somehow I'd known it would be. His power beat against my back like a nearly solid wall of power. Shit. He patted me down like he'd done it before. He found the knives at my wrist and back, as well as the guns. He also found the cell phone but placed it on the bar in front of me instead of taking it.

You could see the effort it took for Bernardo to let the man touch him, pat him down, take his gun. He also took a knife out of one of Bernardo's boots. Anything was an improvement over the last crime scene, but the day really wasn't going well.

'Can we stand up now?' I asked.

'Not yet,' she said.

Bernardo gave me a look that said plainly if he died, he was coming back to haunt me because it was all my fault.

I kept my voice calm, tried to make sense. 'You know I'm Anita Blake. You know why I'm here. What else do you want?'

'Harpo, check the man's wallet. Find out who he is,' she said.

Harpo? The big man, the vibrating mountain of mystical energy was named Harpo. I said none of this out loud. I really am getting smarter.

Harpo took out Bernardo's wallet. He'd stuffed Bernardo's ten mil down the side of his pants and my Browning on the other side. I didn't see the Firestar or the knives. Maybe he'd stuffed them in his pockets. 'The driver's license says, Bernardo Spotted-Horse, but there ain't no credit cards, no pictures, no nothing.'

The woman's eyes had gone back to pitiless. 'You say he's a close friend?'

'Yes,' I said. I was beginning to get scared again.

'He your lover?' she asked.

If she hadn't had a shotgun pointed at me, I'd have told her to go to hell, but she did, so I answered. 'Yeah.' I was trusting that Ramirez knew what he was talking about, that I needed to belong to a man. I hoped the lie was the right answer.

'Prove it,' she said.

I raised eyebrows at her. 'Excuse me?'

'Excuse me,' she mimicked, and that brought low rumbling laughter from the rest of the room.

'Is he circumcised?' she asked.

I hesitated. I couldn't help it. The question caught me too far off guard. I swallowed, and said, 'Yes.' I had a fifty-fifty chance, and being American and under forty I had a better than even chance.

She smiled, but it left her eyes like empty glass. 'You can stand up now.'

I fought the urge to wipe my hands on my pants. Didn't want to insult her cleanliness, but I also wanted desperately to wash my hands. I moved closer to Bernardo, as if I wanted a hug. I even put my left arm around his waist, though I wondered if I was getting his nice white shirt dirty. His arm slid over my shoulders, but I'd really just wanted out of the line of fire of the damned shotgun. I was betting it was on a stationary mount and not a swiveling one. I hoped I was right.

Her hands were back in plain sight. A good sign. 'Drop your pants, Bernardo,' she said.

I felt him tense beside me. We both looked at her. I started to say excuse me again, but Bernardo said, 'Why?'

I'd have asked her to repeat it, just to make sure I'd understood her. He just asked why, as if this had happened to him before.

'So we can see if you're circumcised.'

I moved my hand out from behind Bernardo's back, standing close together but not entangled in each other's arms. We might be in for a fight after all. 'I said he was. Isn't that enough?'

'No. You see, you're right. You do work with the cops a lot. You alone might have been okay to see Nicky, but him, we don't know anything about him. If he's your lover, then fine, but if he's not, then maybe he's a cop.'

Bernardo laughed, and the sound startled all of us, I think. 'Now that is a new one. Me being mistaken for a cop.'

'What are you, if you're not a cop?' she asked.

'Sometimes I'm a bodyguard. Sometimes I'm someone you need to guard the body against. Depends on who's paying better.' His voice sounded very sure of itself, very matter of fact.

'Maybe you are, and maybe you're not. Drop the pants, and we'll see.'

He started unbuckling his belt. I moved away from him, though not too far. Didn't want to get back in front of the shotgun again.

'What's wrong? You've seen him without his pants before,' she said. I was beginning to think she didn't believe me.

'Not in a crowd, I haven't,' I said. I let the righteous indignation blaze in my voice. It got more laughter from the crowd.

The women were starting to chant, 'Take it off, take it all off,' and worse. The girl that had been hanging on Harpo was just behind him, watching the show with glittering excited eyes.

Bernardo didn't complain or blush. He just undid his pants and pushed them to about mid thigh, and stood there. My look away was automatic. The women screamed and whistled. One voice yelled, 'Big daddy, yes!' The men joined in. The men were congratulating him and speculating on how we did it without hurting me.

I had to look. I just couldn't help myself. I had to know if I'd guessed right, and frankly I just had to look. Embarrassing but true. It took me a few seconds to register that he was circumcised because what I saw first was sheer size. He was well, well endowed.

I was blushing, and I couldn't help that. But I knew if I just stood there and gaped that the lies would all be for nothing. I tried to act as if it were Richard or Jean-Claude standing there. What would I have done? I'd have covered them up.

I moved to stand in front of him, though was careful not to touch. I admit though that I couldn't seem to look anywhere else. Richard was impressive. Bernardo had passed impressive and gone over to scary. I shielded him from view with my body, putting my hands on either side of his waist to steady myself. I was blushing so hard, I was dizzy.

I looked at her, still shielding him from the room. 'Good enough?' I asked. Even my voice sounded strangled with discomfort.

'Give him a kiss,' she said.

I looked at her. 'Let him put his pants up and I will.'

She shook her head. 'I didn't say kiss his lips.'

If I blushed any harder, my head was going to explode. I turned around so I couldn't see him anymore. 'We are so not doing this.'

'I think you'll do anything we want,' she said.

I don't know what I would have said to that because a man's voice sounded. 'Enough games, Paulina. Give them back their weapons, and let them go.'

We all turned. Coming from the dim back of the room was another dwarf, little person. He was maybe half a head taller than the bartender, Paulina, and he was more obviously Hispanic and younger. His hair was a rich black, his skin tanned and unlined. He looked twenty-something, but the aura of power that spread outward from him like an overwhelming perfume felt older.

'I am Nicandro Baco, Nicky to my friends.' The crowd parted for him like a curtain being drawn back. He held his hand out to me, and I took it, but he didn't shake hands. He raised my hand to his lips and kissed it. But he kept his eyes rolled up to see my face as he did it, and something about the way his eyes looked, his mouth on my skin, reminded me of much more intimate places for a man's mouth to be. I took my hand back as soon as I could and still be polite.

'Mr Baco, thank you for seeing me.' It sounded so businesslike, as if Bernardo wasn't standing behind us with his pants around his thighs.

'Get dressed,' he said. He barely glanced at Bernardo. But I heard him pulling up his pants, struggling to get everything back in place, though frankly I was surprised his jeans could fit over everything.

'Why are you here, Ms Blake?'

'I really did want to talk to another necromancer.'

'It sounds like you've changed your mind,' he said. He watched me minutely, studying my face. When I moved a hand to touch my hair, his eyes tracked it.

'The grandstanding has taken up all my time. I've got an appointment with the police that I can't really miss.' I'd added the police part on purpose because I had a feeling that Baco had known exactly what was happening out here. They hadn't really hurt us, just embarrassed us or me. He came in just in the nick of time. Yeah, right.

'Like the two policemen that are waiting outside for you.'

I felt the knowledge flinch across my face, not much of a reaction, but it was enough. 'Do you blame us for backup?'

'Are you saying you are afraid of us?' That brought a low rumble through the room, as if they had all drawn a breath together.

'I would be a fool if I wasn't,' I said.

He cocked his head to one side in an almost bird-like movement. 'And you are not a fool, are you, Anita?'

'I try not to be.'

He motioned to the woman still standing behind the bar. 'Paulina does not like you. Do you know why?'

It was my turn to shake my head. 'Nope.'

'She's my wife.'

I must have still looked blank. 'Sorry, I don't understand.'

'She knows I have a weakness for women with power.'

I frowned at him. 'She doesn't have to worry. I'm sort of taken.'

He smiled. 'No more lies, Anita. You and he are not lovers.' He took my hand again and gazed up at me with those black eyes. I realized for the first time that he considered himself a ladies' man. And that his wife had reason to worry, not about me, but about other women. It was there in his eyes, the way he stroked my hand.

I drew my hand away from him and moved back to stand with Bernardo. I actually reached out my hand, and he took it. Both our hands were sticky from the bar, but I clutched at him.

Baco was half a body-length shorter than I was, but he made me nervous. Part of it was the push of his magic like a thick curtain filling the room. But part of it was the way any man can make you nervous. I didn't like how blatant he was, with us unarmed. I glanced at Paulina, and her harsh face was stricken. Was it a game he played with her? Tormenting her? Who knew, but I wanted out of here.

'I need to be somewhere before dark. If you don't want to talk to me, fine. We'll go.' I started moving backwards, using my body to push Bernardo behind me towards the door.

'Without your weapons?' Baco made it a question, his voice lifting upward.

Bernardo and I froze. We were close enough to the door that we could have made a rush for it, probably made it, but . . . 'Our weapons would be nice,' I said.

'All you had to do was ask,' Baco said.

I said, 'May we have our weapons back?'

He nodded. 'Harpo, give them back.'

Harpo never questioned it, just gave us back the guns, the knives. Then he stepped back to join the rest of the silent watchers. The guns and wrist knives were easy to slide into place. The knife in its spine sheath was another matter. I had to use my left hand to feel for the sheath, then feel the blade's tip at the mouth of the sheath. I'd gotten in the habit of closing my eyes so that all I concentrated on was touch. It actually took only a few seconds now to put it away. The real trick was not chopping off a hunk of my hair as the blade slid home.

When I opened my eyes, Baco was looking at me. 'So nice to see a woman who doesn't rely exclusively on sight. Touch is such an important sense for intimate occasions.'

Maybe being armed again made me brave, or maybe I was just tired of the tension level. 'Men who turn everything into a sexual come-on are such bores.'

Distaste, anger filled his face, turning his charming eyes to black mirrors, like the eyes of a doll. 'Too good to fuck a dwarf?'

I shook my head. 'It's not your height that's the problem, Baco. Where I come from, you don't do shit like this in front of your wife.'

He laughed then, and it sparkled through his eyes, his face. 'The sacrament of marriage? You're offended for my wife's sake? You are a funny girl.'

'Yeah, me and Barbra Streisand.'

The humor faded a little from his face. I don't think he got the joke. Strangely, it was the young girl in her short-shorts who met my eyes. I think she got the joke. If she liked early Streisand movies, maybe she wasn't a completely lost soul.

Bernardo touched my shoulder, and I jumped. 'We're leaving now, Anita.'

I nodded. 'I'm with you.'

'You never asked your questions,' Baco said.

'Have you felt it?' I asked.

His face was suddenly serious. 'There is something new here. It is like us. It deals in death. I have felt it.'

'Where?' I asked.

'Between Santa Fe and Albuquerque, though it began closer to Santa Fe.'

'It's moving closer to Albuquerque, to you,' I said.

For the first time he looked uncertain, not quite afraid, but not happy either. 'It knows that I am here. I have felt that, too.' He stared up at me, and now there was no teasing in his eyes. 'It knows that you are here, too, Anita. It knows you are here, too.'

I nodded. 'We might be able to help each other, Nicky. I've seen the bodies. I've seen what this thing does. Trust me, Nicky. You don't want to go out that way.'

'What do you propose?' he asked.

'That we pool our resources and see if we can stop this thing before it gets here, to you. And that we stop playing games. No more teasing. No more power plays.'

'Just business between us?' he said.

I nodded. 'We don't have time for anything else, Baco.'

'Come back later tonight, and I will do what I can to help you. Though the police will not want you to share information with me. I am a very bad man, you know.'

I smiled. 'You're a bad man, Nicky, but not a stupid one. You need me.'

'As you need me, Anita,' he said.

'Two necromancers are better than one,' I said.

He nodded, face solemn. 'Come back tonight when you are finished with your police business. I will be waiting.'

'It may be late,' I said.

'It is already later than you think, Anita. Pray, if you are the praying sort, that it is not too late.'

'Anita?' Bernardo said.

'We're going.' I let Bernardo back us out the door, his hand on my shoulder guiding me backwards. I got to watch the room, trusting him to make sure nothing was coming up behind us through the door. The werewolves just watched us, not happy, but willing to take orders. Baco had to be their vargamor, their resident witch. I'd just never met a pack that feared its vargamor before.

It was Paulina's face that stayed with me. She was staring at Baco, and the hatred on her face was raw. I knew in that instant that once she had loved him, really loved him, because only true love could twist to such hatred. I'd looked into Paulina's eyes across the barrel of a gun. I think Nicky Baco had more problems than just monsters in the desert. If I were him, I'd be sleeping with a gun.

38

We arrived at the hospital with the world wrapped in a heavy blue dusk. A twilight so solid it was like cloth, something you could wrap around your hands or wear like a dress. I'd called ahead using Ramirez's cell phone. How do you prove that someone is really dead? I'd seen the 'survivors.' They drew breath. I assumed they had a heartbeat or the doctors would have mentioned it. Their eyes looked at you and seemed to be aware. They reacted to pain. They were alive.

But what if they weren't? What if they were only vessels for a power that made Nicky Baco and I look like backstreet charlatans? There might have been a spell to prove it, but you couldn't take the results of a spell to court and get permission to burn the bodies. And that was what I wanted.

I finally came up with brain waves. I was betting that the higher functions of the brain weren't working. It was the only thing I could think of that might show that something was wrong with the survivors other than not having skin and missing body parts.

Unfortunately, Doctor Evans and company had done monitored brain-wave activity long ago. They all had higher brain functions. So much for my brilliant idea. Doctor Evans had wanted to talk in the doctor's lounge, but I'd insisted we talk closer to the survivors' room than that. We talked in low tones in the hallway. He wouldn't let me talk in front of the survivors about the fact that they might be dead. Because if I was wrong, it might cause them distress. He had a point. But I didn't think I was wrong.

The survivors already at the hospital had become agitated and violent, snapping at the hospital staff like dogs on chains. No one had been hurt, but the timing coincided with the last murders. Why had the skinned ones been more violent? Was it the spell used to banish whatever it was from the home? Had that upped the ante somehow? Maybe frightened the creature that we were on to it? I didn't know. I just didn't know.

All I did know was that I could feel the darkness pressing like a hand about to crush us all. It was a heaviness in the air like before a thunderstorm, but worse, closer, harder to breathe through. Something bad was coming, and it was tied to the darkness. I wasn't able to convince Doctor Evans that his patients were dead, but my urgency must have been persuasive because he did give permission for the two officers that were already at the hospital to guard inside the room instead of out. The only proof I had that there were cops inside the room was a hat lying on one of the chairs outside the door.

I wanted to go into the room myself, but by the time I got suited up in gown and mask it would be full dark. It was that close, like a trembling line. So I stood in the hall and pretended that I was okay with it, because there was nothing else I could do.

Since Officer Rigby and Bernardo were new, they got the standard lecture about not shooting inside an oxygen atmosphere. It would be bad, though it wouldn't explode, which is what I thought it would have done. It would be the flash fire to end all flash fires, turning the room into a lower circle of hell for the few moments it took to use up all the oxygen or fuel in the room. But it wouldn't explode in a shower of glass and plaster. Nothing too dramatic, just deadly.

Rigby asked, 'And if they try to eat us, what are we supposed to do? Spit on them?'

'I don't know,' Evans said. 'All I can tell you is what you shouldn't do, and you shouldn't fire a gun into a room full of oxygen.'

Bernardo drew a knife from somewhere. He hadn't bent down

near his boot, which meant it was a different knife, and one the werewolf in the bar had missed. He held the blade up to the light, letting it gleam. 'You cut them.'

Darkness fell like a lead curtain, almost clanging in my head like the roll of thunder. I waited for the door to the room to open. I waited for the screaming to start because that's what I was expecting. Nothing happened. Then the pressure that had been building for hours vanished. It was as if something had swallowed it up. I was just suddenly standing in the hallway feeling light, empty, better. I didn't understand the change, and I don't like what I don't understand.

We all waited for a few tense heartbeats, then I couldn't stand it. I spilled a knife into my own hand and reached for the door. The door swung outward. I jumped back. The male nurse that I'd been introduced to earlier paused in the door staring at the naked blade in my hand.

He never took his eyes off me, but he talked to Evans. 'Doctor, the patients are quiet, quieter than they've been all day. The police officers are wanting to know if they can step out of the room for a while.'

'The survivors are quieter than they've been all day?' I asked.

Ben the nurse nodded. 'Yes, ma'am.'

I took two steps back from the door, and let out the tension in my body in a long breath.

'Well, Ms Blake?' Evans asked. 'Can the officers come out?'

I shrugged and looked at Ramirez. 'Ask him. He's ranking officer on site. But truthfully, I guess so. Whatever I've been feeling seemed to fade when darkness fell. I don't understand it.' I slid the knife back into its sheath. 'I guess there's not going to be a fight.'

'You sound disappointed,' Bernardo said. His knife had vanished to wherever he'd gotten it from.

I shook my head. 'Not disappointed, just confused. I felt a great deal of power building for hours, and it just vanished. That much power doesn't just vanish. It went somewhere. Apparently, not into the survivors, but it's off somewhere tonight doing something.'

'Any ideas what it's doing and where?' Ramirez asked.

I shook my head. 'Not really.'

He turned to the doctor. 'Tell the men they can come outside.'

Ben the nurse looked to Doctor Evans for confirmation. Evans nodded. The nurse ducked back inside, the door closing slowly behind him.

Evans turned to me. 'Well, Ms Blake, looks like you hurried over here for nothing.'

I shrugged. 'I thought we'd be ass deep in man-eating corpses by now.' I smiled. 'It's nice to be wrong once in a while.'

We all smiled at each other. The tension spilled out of all of us. Bernardo gave that nervous laugh you sometimes give when the emergency is over, or the bullet passed you by.

'I'm very glad you were wrong, this time, Ms Blake,' Evans said.

'Me, too,' I said.

'Me, three,' Bernardo said.

'I'm happy, too,' Ramirez said, 'but it is disappointing to find out you're not perfect.'

'If you don't know I'm not perfect after forty-eight hours of working with me on a police investigation, then you are not paying attention.'

'I'm paying attention,' Ramirez said, 'close attention.' There was a weight to his gaze, an intensity to his words that made me want to squirm. In trying not to squirm I caught Bernardo's eyes. He was smiling at me, enjoying my discomfort. Glad someone was.

'If you were wrong about this, you may be wrong about them being dead,' Evans said.

I nodded. 'Maybe.'

'You admit you may be wrong, just like that?' Evans seemed surprised.

'This is magic, not math, Doctor Evans. There are very few

hard and fast rules. There are even fewer rules the way I do it. Sometimes I think two and two is going to add up to five, and I'm right. Sometimes all you get is four. If it lowers the body count, I don't mind being wrong.'

The door opened, and two men came out dressed in Albuquerque uniforms. They'd headed for the door as soon as Ben the nurse told them they could go. I didn't blame them one bit.

Their eyes looked haunted. The tallest one was blond and built all of squares. Broad shoulders, thick waist, heavy legs, not fat, just solid, strong. His partner was shorter and almost completely bald except for a ring of brown curls low on his head. Apparently, it was his hat sitting on the chair by the door.

Doctor Evans said, 'Excuse me.' He moved past them into the room.

The short one said, 'He can have it.'

The blond looked at me, eyes narrowing, not friendly. 'Well, if it isn't the wicked witch of the Midwest. I hear we have you to thank for us sitting in there for the last hour.'

I didn't recognize him, but apparently he knew me on sight. 'I suggested it, yes.'

The blond moved closer, using his size to intimidate me, or he tried. Size just isn't as impressive as most men think it is. 'Maybe Marks was right about you.'

Ah hah. He must have been one of the officers on site when Marks kicked me out. I felt Ramirez start to move up, probably to step between us. I put my hand on his shoulder. 'It's all right.'

Ramirez didn't move back the step he'd taken, but at least he didn't move forward. It was probably the best I would get out of him. But it meant that I was sandwiched between the two men. The blond's eyes flicked to Ramirez behind me. The look on his face was enough. He wanted a fight and didn't really care who it was with.

He was glaring at Ramirez now, and I could almost feel the testosterone rising on every side. Enough testosterone to get the officer in trouble, maybe suspended when all he needed was to blow off some steam. He was trying to cleanse himself of the horrors in that room.

Both his partner and Bernardo were staying back. I didn't know what the partner was doing, but Bernardo was enjoying the show.

'You must have been one of the officers that helped Marks throw me out,' I said. I was looking way up at the man, and he was looking over me at Ramirez.

It took him a second to blink and look at me. He frowned at me, and it was a good frown. I bet it made a lot of bad guys run like hell.

His partner came up behind him. 'Yeah, Jarman and I were both there.' The partner sounded calm, and I think worried about his partner. Good partners look after more than just your physical health.

'And you are?' I asked. I asked it like his partner, Jarman, wasn't about to pick a fight with everyone in the hallway.

He introduced himself like everything was normal, too. 'Jakes.'

'Jarman and Jakes?' I made it a question.

He nodded, smiling. 'J and J at your service.'

I felt the tension easing in the big man in front of me. Hard to stay pissed when you're being ignored, and everyone else is behaving themselves. I pressed my back into Ramirez, trying to urge him to back off. He took the hint, stepping back a little.

Officer Rigby came bounding down the hallway. He'd gone to the car to get something less explosive than his gun. What he was carrying was a Tazer gun. It would send a charge of 30,000 to 60,000 volts through a suspect. Theoretically, it could put someone down for the count without the danger of killing him. Unless you get very unlucky, like the perp has a pacemaker.

Ramirez was shaking his head. 'What the hell is that for?'

Rigby looked at the Tazer. 'I can't use my gun so I'll use this.'

'Rigby,' Jarman said, 'a Tazer makes a spark.'

Rigby looked puzzled. 'So?'

'If the spark when we fire a gun will set off the oxygen in the room, so will the spark from a Tazer,' Ramirez said.

'Go back to the car and find something else,' Jarman said.

Jakes and I had moved to one side, watching Ramirez and Jarman ream the rookie. No one was mad anymore, derisive, condescending, but not mad. When Rigby had disappeared through the doors at the far end of the hall, Jarman turned to Ramirez. 'Is Rigby all Marks gave you for backup?'

Ramirez nodded, then shrugged. 'He'll learn.'

'And get someone killed doing it,' Jarman said.

Jakes held his hand out low, palm up. He was smiling. I gave him a low five. I was smiling, too, but not because his partner hadn't belted a detective. I was just happy that I'd been wrong. I'd had my fill of corpses for the day. Hell, for the year.

Bernardo was leaning against the opposite wall. He seemed puzzled by my interaction with the cops. I doubt it ever occurred to Bernardo to make friends with them.

The two uniforms had batons stuck in their utility belts. Ramirez looked unarmed except for his gun. 'Where's your baton, Hernando?'

'Oooh, Hernando,' Jakes said.

'Yeah, Hernando,' Jarman said, rolling the name off his tongue, 'where's your baton?' That they were willing to give Ramirez shit meant that under normal conditions he and Jarman got along. There is a different flavor to teasing when it's hostile. Rigby's teasing was close to hostile, not quite, as if they weren't sure if he were really one of them yet.

Ramirez took a short metal rod out of his hip pocket. He made a small sharp movement with his wrist, and the rod telescoped into a solid piece of metal about two feet long.

'An asp,' I said. 'I didn't notice you carrying one when we met. I'm usually pretty aware of weapons.'

He flicked the rod back into its compact size. 'An asp is pretty small when it's put away. How do you know I wasn't carrying one?'

I opened my mouth, then closed it, and looked at him. He was grinning at me. I debated on whether to rise to the bait, or let it pass. Hell, this was the most fun I'd had all day. 'Are you implying that I was staring at your butt?'

'How else would you know I didn't have something about the size of a pen in my back pocket?' His eyes were sparkling like dark jewels, shiny with humor.

I shrugged. 'Just checking for weapons.'

'That's what they all say.'

Jarman said, 'Wanna check me for weapons?'

I looked at him. 'I can see your weapon from here, Jarman.'

He puffed his chest out a little, managing to strut without moving his feet an inch. 'When you're my size, it's hard to miss.'

I looked at every man in turn and had to really fight the urge to linger on Bernardo. I was willing to bet that his 'weapon' was the biggest in the hallway. 'Oh, I don't know, Jarman. You know what they say. It's not size that matters. It's talent.' Again, I had to fight the urge to stare at Bernardo.

Jarman smiled happily. 'Trust me, baby. I've got the talent and the size.'

'Easy to brag when you know you'll never have to prove it,' I said, and yes, I was baiting him.

Jarman swept his hat off and gave me a look. I think it was supposed to be a come hither look. His scary frown was better than his sexy look, but hey, I bet he got a lot more opportunity to practice scary than sexy.

'Let's find some privacy, babe, and I will prove it.'

I shook my head, smiling. 'And what would your wife say about you taking me out for a test drive. Nice wedding band, by the way.'

He laughed, a good-natured rumble.

Jakes answered for him. 'His wife would feed him his dick on a stick.'

Jarman nodded, still chuckling. 'Yeah, my Bren has a temper, that she does.'

He said it like it was a good thing, a thing he valued. He looked at me. 'My Bren would have kicked Marks in the balls, not kissed him.'

'I thought about it,' I said.

'Why didn't you hit him?' Ramirez asked. The humor still sparkled in his eyes but his face was more serious. I think he wanted a real answer, not a joke.

'He was expecting me to hit him. Maybe even wanted me to hit him. He could have pressed assault charges, gotten me behind bars for awhile.'

I expected one of the three men to say Marks wouldn't do that, but no one did. I looked from one suddenly serious face to another. 'No one going to defend the lieutenant's honor? Protest that he wouldn't do such a dastardly thing?'

Jarman said, 'Nope.'

Jakes said, 'Dastardly. You talk real pretty for a devil-worshipping assassin.'

I blinked at him. 'Pass that by me again, slowly.'

Jakes nodded. 'According to the lieutenant, you're suspected in the disappearances of several citizens, as well as dancing naked in the moonlight with the devil himself.'

'Marks didn't say that last part.'

Jakes grinned. 'Can't blame a man for wishful thinking.' He wiggled his eyebrows at me.

I laughed. They laughed. A good time being had by all. Except Bernardo, who leaned against the wall apart from the general goodwill. He was watching me as if he'd never really seen me before. I'd surprised him in some way.

'Marks tried to get you arrested for magical malfeasance, so the rumor mill says,' Jarman said.

I stared at him. Magical malfeasance could carry a death sentence. I stared at Ramirez. 'Did you know he was trying to do that?'

Ramirez touched my arm. We moved down the hallway to the distant rumble of masculine laughter. The two officers were probably still giving each other good-natured shit. From the caliber of the laughter, if it was about me, it was probably something I didn't want to hear. There is always a line to the teasing that must be carefully avoided. I wanted to be a female one of the guys, not get a reputation for being a slut. A thin line to walk sometimes.

Probably best to be out of earshot, but I didn't want to be alone with Ramirez right now. It bothered me that he hadn't told me what Marks had said about me. He was a virtual stranger. He didn't owe me anything, but it made me think less of him.

An African-American nurse walked past us and went into the room. Since all I'd seen were her eyes the first time, I couldn't be sure if she was the same nurse I'd glimpsed earlier in the room. She was small, about the right size, but in full surgical scrubs, who knew?

The men had fallen silent as she walked past. As soon as the door closed safely behind her, the laughter sounded again.

Ramirez looked at me with that honest face, a line of concern between his eyebrows like a tiny wrinkle of discontent. He looked even younger when he frowned. 'Doesn't that bother you?' he asked.

'What?' I asked.

He glanced back at the two officers. They were still smiling. 'Jakes and Jarman.'

'You mean the teasing?'

He nodded.

'When I kissed Marks in front of all of them, I sort of invited a little teasing. Besides, I sort of started it, or rather you did.' I shrugged. 'It blows off steam, and we all need that right now.'

'Most women don't see it that way,' Ramirez said.

'I'm not most women. But frankly, one reason a lot of women

don't stand for any teasing is that some men don't know when teasing crosses the line to harassment. If I had to work day in and day out with them, I might be more careful. But I don't, so I can afford to push the line a little.'

'What is your line, Anita?' He was standing just a little too close for comfort.

'I'll let everyone know when they've reached it. Don't worry.' I stepped back from him, giving myself the distance I wanted.

'You're mad at me.' He sounded surprised.

I half-smiled. 'Believe me, Detective, when I'm mad at you, you'll know it.'

'Detective. Not even Ramirez. Now I know you're upset. What did I do?'

I looked at him, studying that open, honest fact. 'Why didn't you tell me what Marks said about me? What he was telling the other cops about me? It could carry a death sentence.'

'No way was Marks going to push that through, Anita.'

'You still should have told me.'

He looked puzzled for a moment, then shrugged. 'I didn't know I was supposed to.'

I frowned. 'I guess not.' But I wasn't happy with his answer.

He touched my arm again, ever so lightly. 'I didn't believe that Marks could get you arrested. I was right. Isn't that enough?'

'No,' I said.

He let his hand fall away from me. 'What good would it have done to tell you? You'd have worried for nothing.'

'I don't need my feelings protected. I need to feel that I can trust you.'

'You don't trust me because I didn't tell you everything that Marks said?'

'Not as much as I trusted you before.'

The first hint of anger hardened his eyes. 'And you told me everything that happened in Los Duendos? You didn't hold anything back about your interview with Nicky Baco?' His eyes weren't kind now. They were cool and searching, cop eyes.

I looked down once, then fought to maintain eye contact when what I desperately wanted to do was duck my head and say, aw shucks, you caught me. Push me into a corner, and I usually get angry. But somehow looking into his deep brown eyes, I couldn't pull up much moral indignation. Maybe it was having no moral high ground to stand on. Yeah, that might be it.

'I didn't kill anybody, if that's what you're implying.' It was one of my usual comments with less than my usual force.

'That's not what I'm implying and you know it, Anita.'

There was something familiar, almost intimate about the conversation. We'd known each other for two days, and yet we interacted as if we'd known each other much longer. It was unnerving. I didn't usually bond this quickly with people or monsters.

But if it had been my longtime police friend Sergeant Rudolph Storr himself standing in front of me, I'd have lied. If Nicky Baco got a whiff of cops, he'd back off, and he'd never trust me again. People like Baco don't give second chances when it comes to the police.

'Baco knew you and Rigby were outside the bar, Hernando. He has the entire area wired with magical . . .' I waffled my hand back and forth, seeking the right word '. . . wards, spells. He knows what happens in his streets. If I go back in with police as backup, no matter how distant, he won't help us.'

'Are you so sure he can help?' Ramirez asked. 'He may just be stringing you along, trying to find out what you know.'

'He's scared, Hernando. Baco is scared. Call it a feeling, but I don't think much frightens him.'

'You've just told me you're withholding information from an ongoing murder investigation.'

'If you wire me up or insist on sending someone undercover with me, we'll lose Baco. You know I'm right on this.'

'We may lose Baco, but you're not right,' he said, and the anger was back. A frustrated anger that I'd seen before in other men that I'd known longer and in more intimate ways. That anger that I can't just be a good girl and play by their rules, and be what they want me to be. It made me tired to hear that thread in Ramirez's voice after only two days.

'The most important thing to me right this second is stopping these murders. That is my goal. That is my only goal.' I thought about what I'd said, and added, 'And staying alive. But other than that I don't have any other agenda. Stop the bad guys. Stay alive. It makes things simple, Hernando.'

'You told me earlier that you wanted your life to change, to be more than blood and horror. If you want that to change, you are going to have to complicate your life, Anita. And you are going to have to start trusting people, really trusting them again.'

I shook my head. 'Thanks for using my moment of weakness against me. Now I remember why I don't confide in strangers.' I was finally angry myself. It felt good. It felt familiar. If I could just stay angry, I could stop being so damned confused.

He grabbed my arm, and the grip wasn't gentle this time. It didn't hurt, but I could feel the press of his fingers in my flesh. For the first time since I'd met him, he let me see the hardness underneath. That core of harshness that you either have or acquire if you stay with the cops. Without that core to protect yourself, you may stay on the job, but you won't thrive.

I smiled. 'What next, rubber hoses and bright lights?' It was meant to be a joke, but my voice wasn't light when I said it. We were both angry now. Underneath all those smiles and mild manners was a temper. We'd see whose was worse, his or mine.

He spoke low and carefully, the way I do sometimes when to do anything else will start me yelling. 'I could just tell Marks about the meeting. Tell him you're holding out on us.'

'Fine,' I said, 'do it. Marks will probably have him arrested, search his bar. He might even find enough magical paraphernalia to get him jailed on suspicion of magical malfeasance. And what will that get us, Detective? Baco in jail, and a few days from now more people dead. More bodies gutted.' I leaned into his angry face and whispered, 'How will your dreams be then, Hernando?'

He let me go so abruptly that I stumbled. 'You really are a bitch, aren't you?'

I nodded. 'If the situation warrants it, you bet.'

He shook his head, rubbing his hands up and down his arms. 'If I hold out on this and it goes wrong, it could be my career.'

'Just say you didn't know.'

He shook his head. 'Too many people know I was your police escort.' He managed to make the last two words heavy with irony. 'You've got another meeting planned with him, haven't you?'

I tried to keep the surprise off my face, but a blank face was just as bad. It was like when you were asked if you were sleeping with someone, and you refused to answer. Not answering was as good as a yes.

He stalked from one side of the hallway to the other. 'Dammit, Anita, I can't sit on this.'

I realized he meant it. I stood in his path, so he had to stop pacing and look at me. 'You can't tell Marks. He'll screw it up. If he thinks I'm dancing with the devil, he'll have hysterics when he meets Nicky Baco.'

The anger was beginning to leak from his eyes. 'When's the meeting?'

I shook my head. 'Promise first that you won't tell Marks.'

'He's in charge of the investigation. If I don't tell him and he finds out, I might as well hand in my badge.'

'He doesn't seem very popular around here,' I said.

'He's still my superior.'

'He's your boss,' I said. 'He is in no way your superior.'

That earned me a smile. 'Flattery will get you nowhere with me.'

'It's not flattery, Hernando. It's the truth.'

He was finally quiet, standing there looking at me. His expression was almost his normal one, or what I thought was normal for him. For all I knew he dissected puppies in his spare time. All right, I didn't believe that, but I didn't really know him. We were strangers, and I was having to remind myself of that. I kept wanting to treat him like a friend or better. What was the matter with me?

'When is the meeting, Anita?'

'If I won't tell you, then what?'

A shadow of that hardness seeped into his eyes. 'Then I tell Marks you're withholding evidence.'

'And if I tell you?'

'Then I'll go with you.'

I shook my head. 'No way.'

'I promise not to show up looking like a cop.'

I looked at him from shined shoes to short, clean hair. 'In what alternate reality would you NOT look like a cop?'

I heard the door open behind us, but neither of us turned. We were too busy making major eye contact.

Jarman yelled, 'Ramirez!'

There was a tone in that one word that whirled us both around. Doctor Evans was leaning against the wall, holding his wrist upright. Blood gleamed like a scarlet bracelet around his arm.

Ramirez and I started running at the same time down that short space of hallway as if we had farther to go and less time to get there. Jarman and Jakes were disappearing through the door. Bernardo hesitated at the door, holding it open long enough for the screams to cut through the hospital silence. Low and wordless and panicked, and I knew without knowing that it was a man screaming. I was almost at the door, almost to Bernardo, Ramirez pacing me like a shadow.

Bernardo said, 'This is a bad idea.' But he went through the door, a heartbeat before we reached it. God, I hated being right all the time.

39

The white sterile room had been a quiet corner of hell. Now it was a loud, chaotic corner of hell. A skinless hand snatched at me. I slashed at it with the big blade that I'd pulled from the spine sheath. The hand bled and jerked back. They could feel pain. They bled. Good.

I had the blade raised for a neck blow as the corpse came at me again. Ramirez blocked my arms. 'They're civilians!'

I looked at him, then back at that raw thing that was held to the bed only by one last wrist restraint. It launched at me again, slashing the air with its bloody hand, screaming wordlessly, butchered tongue flopping like a worm in the lipless ruin of its mouth.

'Just stay out of reach,' he said and pulled me past it.

I had time to say, 'They're corpses, Ramirez, just corpses.'

He held up the asp. 'Don't kill them.' He moved into the fight, though it wasn't a fight yet. Most of the corpses were still restrained to the beds. They struggled, screaming, wailing, jerking their ruined flesh to bloodier ruin against the restraints, bodies bucking as they thrashed to free themselves.

Ben the nurse was beating at the head of one patient. It had sunk teeth into his arm so deeply that he couldn't free himself. Jarman was with him, beating the thing's head with his baton from far back like you'd hit a baseball. You could hear the soft, melon-like thunk even over the screaming.

Jakes and Bernardo were at the last bed near the windows. The African-American nurse was held in the embrace of a corpse that still had one hand and one ankle attached to the bed. Its head was buried into her chest. Blood plastered her gown to her body like someone had spilled a can of red paint down her. Where the thing was gnawing shouldn't have been a killing spot, but there was too much blood. It had reached something vital.

Jakes was beating at the thing's head so hard that he was rising on tiptoe, his body almost leaving the ground with each blow. The corpse's head was bleeding, cracking, but it wasn't letting go. Its head was buried into her chest like a monstrous child, feeding.

Bernardo was stabbing the corpse in the back over and over. The blade came free in a spray of blood, but it didn't matter. The one by the door had reacted to pain, but once they started feeding, they were just meat. You couldn't hurt meat, and you sure as hell couldn't kill it.

I walked between the beds with the corpses screaming, bodies writhing, and all the eyes looked the same. It was as if there was only one personality looking out of every pair of eyes. Their master, whatever that was, watched me walk between the beds, watching me go to the far bed, away from Ramirez, and his cautions. He still didn't understand what was about to happen when they all freed themselves. We had to be out of this room before that happened.

I moved in beside Bernardo, moving him back a step. I wiggled the blade underneath the thing's jaw. I took a deep breath, centered myself the way you do in martial arts class just before you break something big and permanent-looking. I pictured the blade coming out the top of the skull, and that's what I tried for. I tried to shove it through its head. The blade went through the soft tissue under the jaw with a sharp, wet movement, then the tip hit the bone at the roof of the mouth, and kept going. The blade didn't come out of the top of its head, but I felt it shove into the strange emptiness of the sinus cavities.

It reared back from the woman, its jaws trying to open around the gleam of the blade. It clawed at its mouth with the one free hand, letting the nurse fall back onto the bed. We got our first glimpse of the wound. There was a hole in the middle of her chest. Broken ribs jutted outward like the broken sides of a frame. The hole was just the size for a human face to shove deep. I stared down into that dark, wet hole, and half her heart was gone, eaten away.

'Oh, God!' Jakes said.

The thing in the bed had freed its other hand. It was tugging at the hilt of the blade, trying to pull it free. Jakes, Bernardo, and I exchanged a look between us. One look, no words, and we turned towards the rest of the room with one goal in mind: get to the door any way we could. There was nothing human in this room but us.

I looked up and found Ramirez and Jarman at the far door with the male nurse sagging between them. Great. I yelled, 'Run!'

We tried. I sensed movement and turned in time for the corpse to hit me full on and send us both crashing to the floor. I stabbed for the jaw, trying to pin its teeth like I had the other one, but it moved and I only got the throat. Blood splashed across my face in a hot liquid rush. It blinded me for a second. I could feel it moving over my body, legs straddling my waist. I kept my hand pushed into raw shoulder, holding it back, while it strained over me. I wiped the blood out of my eyes with the back of my hand that held the knife. It snapped at me like a dog, and I screamed. I cut its cheek so deep the blade scraped on teeth. It screamed and sank its teeth into my hand. I screamed as it shook its head like a dog with a bone. My hand opened, and the knife fell.

It came at me, mouth open, pale blue eyes so impossibly wide. It went for my throat. There was no time to try for the last knife. I went for its eyes. I plunged my thumbs into its eyes, and its own momentum pushed them deeper than I could have gotten them. I felt the eyeballs rupture, exploding in warm fluid and thicker things.

It screamed, whipping its head back and forth, hands clawing at its face. Bernardo was suddenly there, pulling it backwards, throwing it one-armed across the room to skid into the wall. Amazing what you can do when you're terrified.

I was on my knees, drawing the last knife. Bernardo dragged me to my feet, and we were almost to the door. Rigby was there with an ax, hacking at the corpses. Hands and less identifiable bits littered the ground around him. Ramirez shoved his asp into one's mouth, so hard the dull tip showed through the back of its throat.

Jakes was dragging Jarman by his wrists, leaving a thick red trail behind him. Jarman's body was wedged in the door. Rigby's ax had chopped two of the corpses into enough pieces that they were down. Two of the corpses were still held to the bed with one last restraint. Ramirez was wrestling with the one that was trying to swallow his asp. A corpse threw itself at Rigby, and the ax sliced air.

I heard the scrambling behind me before Bernardo yelled, 'Behind . . .'

I was on the way down to the floor with the thing riding my back, before I heard Bernardo yell, '. . . you.'

I tucked my head, trying to protect my neck. Teeth bit through my shirt, drawing blood, but had trouble gnawing through the strap of the shoulder holster and spine sheath. It dug its teeth into my flesh, but the leather straps acted like a sort of armor. I drove the knife back into its thigh, once, twice. It didn't care.

Suddenly, there was a wash of air, and a heavy blow, blood spilled across my hair, shoulders, and back, in a scalding wash. I scrambled out from under the corpse and found it was headless.

Rigby stood over it with the bloody ax and a wild look in his eyes. 'Go, get out. I'll cover your back.' His voice was high-pitched, fear dripping from it, but he stood his ground and started moving us all towards the door.

One of the corpses was on Bernardo's back, but it wasn't trying to eat him. It pounded his head twice into the floor, hard. It looked up at me. There was something in its eyes that hadn't been in any of the others. It was afraid. Afraid of us. Afraid of being stopped. Afraid, just maybe, of dying.

It scrambled through the open glass doors and brushed past Jakes, as if it had somewhere to go and something else to do. And I knew it had to be stopped, knew if it escaped that it would be very bad. But I put a hand under Bernardo's arm and started dragging him for the door. Ramirez took his other arm and it was suddenly easy to drag him through that glass door.

There was a sudden rush in the room behind us. Rigby stumbled back against the button that closed the door. It slid closed with Ramirez beating on it. I saw Rigby swing the ax, then a corpse came in from both sides. Ramirez reached for the button to open the door, but either Rigby's weight had jammed it or something else had.

Ramirez screamed, 'Rigby!'

There was a gigantic whoosh of air as if a giant had drawn a breath, and the room filled with fire. Flames licked the glass like orange-gold water through the glass of an aquarium. I could feel the heat beating against the glass. Fire alarms went off with a high-pitched scream. I threw myself to the floor on top of Bernardo, covering my face, waiting for that tremendous heat to crack the glass and spill over all of us.

But it wasn't heat that spilled over me. It was coolness, water. I raised my head to the sprinklers that were filling the room. The glass was blackened, and smoke and steam curled against the glass like fog as the water killed the fire.

Ramirez reached for the button, and the doors opened in a sound of rushing water. The alarm was louder now, and I realized that it was two different alarms now, mixing together in one nerve-jangling screech. Ramirez stepped into the room, and I heard his voice over the maddening noise. 'Madre de Dios.'

I stood with the water pounding me, soaking my hair, clothing. I didn't follow him into the room. Rigby was beyond any help I could give him. We still had one more corpse on the run. I laid my fingertips on Bernardo's neck just under the jaw. The screech of the fire alarms seemed to make it hard to feel his pulse, but it was there, strong and sure. He was down for the count, but he was alive. Jakes was kneeling beside Jarman, tears streaming down his face. He was trying to stop a wound in Jarman's neck with his bare hands. The pool of blood that had spilled to either side of Jarman's head was being washed away by the sprinklers. His eyes were fixed and staring, unblinking as the water poured down on him.

Shit. I should have grabbed Jakes and said, 'He's dead. Jarman is dead.' But I couldn't do it. I got to my feet. 'Ramirez.'

He was still staring into the room at whatever was left of Rigby.

'Ramirez!' I yelled it, and he turned, but his eyes were unfocused as if he wasn't really seeing me.

'We've got one more corpse to catch. We can't let it get away.'

He stared at me with dull eyes. I needed some help here. I took those few steps to stand in the doorway by him, and I slapped him hard enough that my hand stung with the blow. Harder than I'd meant to hit him.

His head whipped back, and I braced for him to hit me back, but he didn't. He stood there, hands in tight fists, shaking with the urge, eyes blazing with a rage that was just looking for someone to rain all over. It wasn't me hitting him. It was everything.

When he didn't slap me back, I said, 'The bad thing went that way.' I pointed at the door. 'We need to go after it.'

He started to talk very rapidly in Spanish. I couldn't understand the majority of it, but the anger came through just fine. I caught one word that I did know. He called me a bruja. It meant witch.

'Fuck this!' I opened the door, having to edge around Jarman's body. The sprinklers were on in the hallway, too. Evans was still sitting with his back to the wall. He'd pulled his mask down, as if he couldn't get enough air.

'Where did it go?' I asked.

'Down the fire stairs, end of the hall.' He had to raise his voice over the sound of fire alarms, but his voice was dull, distant. Maybe later if I was good, I could go into shock, too.

I didn't hear the door open behind me, but Ramirez yelled, 'Anita!'

I half-turned as I ran for the door. 'I'm taking the stairs, you take the elevators.'

He yelled, 'Anita!'

I turned, and he tossed one of the cell phones to me. I caught it one-handed awkwardly against my chest.

'If I get to ground and haven't found it, I'll call,' he said.

I nodded, jamming the phone into my back pocket, running for the door. I found it. I had the Browning out now. There was no oxygen-filled room now. We'd see if bullets worked as well as knives. I pushed the heavy fire door with my whole body, until it was flat against the wall, and I knew the thing wasn't behind the door. Then I hesitated on the concrete landing. The sprinklers were going in here, too, like waterfalls down the concrete steps. The fire alarms filled the space with high-pitched echoes. I looked up at the rising stairs, then down. I had no idea which way it had gone. It could have gotten off on any floor above or below me.

Dammit, I needed to find this thing. I wasn't sure why it felt so urgent that it not get away, but I'd been right about the coming dark and the corpses. I'd trust my judgment. They were just animated corpses, just a kind I'd never seen before. But they were dead, and I was a necromancer. Technically, I could control any form of the walking dead. I could sometimes sense a vampire when it was near. I took a breath and centered myself in a solid line, drew my power in, flung it out, searching, my back to the door, the water pouring down on me, the scream of the fire alarms so piercing it was hard to think. I sent that 'magic' outward, up the stairs, down the stairs like an invisible line of fog.

I jerked upright. I'd felt something like a pull on the end of a fishing line. Down, it had gone down. If I was wrong, there was nothing I could do about it. But I didn't think I was wrong. I started running down the wet cement steps, one hand on the banister to catch myself when I slipped, the other with the gun pointed upward. There was a woman crumpled outside the next landing, lying across the door, motionless, but breathing. I turned her face to the side so she wouldn't be drowned in the sprinklers, and kept going. Down, it was going down, and it wasn't taking time to feed. It was running, running away from us, running away from me.

I got to my feet, sliding on the wet steps, only my death grip on the slippery metal banister catching me before I fell. I lost my connection to the creature when I slipped. I just couldn't hold the concentration and do everything else. The sprinklers stopped abruptly, but the fire alarms went on and on, more piercing without the water to muffle it. I pushed to my feet and started running again. Very distant, far down below, there was a scream. I vaulted the next turn of banister, sliding down the wet metal, almost going head first over the next turn of railing. I was going as fast as I could, faster than was safe. I ran and slid and stumbled down the stairs, and all the time the growing sense that I was going to be too late. That no matter how fast I ran, I wouldn't get there in time.

40

I couldn't regain the link with the thing without stopping and concentrating. I made the decision to keep chasing, and hoped I didn't miss it as I ran past the doors. Besides, on the 19th floor there was a huddled group of water-soaked patients with a nurse. They all pointed wordlessly down. At 17 there was a man with a bouquet of flowers with a bloody lip that babbled at me and pointed down. The door opened on 14, and a nurse in a pink smock rushed out and ran into me. She screamed, jerking back against the wall, staring at me with huge eyes. She had a baby in each arm, in those little blankets. One even had its little pink knit hat still in place. Both babies were screaming, their high cat-like wails competing with the fire alarm.

The nurse just stared at me, unable to speak or afraid to. Maybe it was the gun, or maybe not all the blood had washed away in the sprinklers. I raised my voice above the noise, 'Is it on this floor?'

She just nodded. She was mumbling something over and over. I had to lean into her to understand it. 'It's in the nursery. It's in the nursery. It's in the nursery.'

I didn't think my adrenaline could get any higher. I was wrong. I could suddenly feel the blood rushing through my body, feel my heart like a painful thing in my chest. I opened the door, scanning the hallway with the Browning. Nothing moved. The corridor stretched long and empty with too many closed doors for comfort. The fire alarm was still screaming, making my skin tight with the noise. But even over the screech of the alarm I could hear the babies . . . crying . . . screaming.

I slipped the phone out of my pocket, hit the button he'd told me to hit earlier, and started jogging down the hallway towards the sounds. Ramirez answered it in the middle of the first ring. 'Anita?'

'I'm on maternity. It's the 14th floor. A nurse says the thing is in the nursery.' I was at the first corner. I threw myself against the far wall, but didn't really stop. I'm usually more cautious around corners, but the crying was getting closer, more piteous.

'I'm on my way,' Ramirez said.

I hit the button that cut us off, but still had it in my hand when I came around the next corner. There was a body pushed through a pane of wired safety glass. I could tell it was a man, but that was about all. The face looked like hamburger. I stepped on a stethoscope on the floor below him. Doctor or nurse. I didn't check for a pulse. If he was alive, I didn't know how to help him. If he was dead, it didn't matter. One last door, then a long expanse of window. But I didn't need to see the long window to know it was the nursery. I could hear the babies crying. Even over the fire alarm the sound of those panicked cries made my heart flutter, made me want to run and help them. A hard wiring response that I hadn't even known I had made me reach for the door. I still had the phone in my left hand, and made one attempt to shove it in my pocket. The bite on my left hand made me awkward. The phone slipped, and I let it fall to the floor.

The handle turned, but the door stopped just inches open. I put my shoulder into it, and realized it was a body, an adult body. I backed off and hit it again, moving it by painful inches. There was a woman screaming, not just the babies. I couldn't open the door. Dammit!

Then the window crashed outward in a spray of glass and a body. A woman hit the ground and lay there sprawled and bleeding. I left the wedged door and went for the window. There were shards of glass like small swords on the bottom of the break. But I'd taken falls in Judo higher than this. I'd practiced falling for years. I glanced in to check one thing. The herd of little plastic cribs was pushed to either side. I had room. I took a running leap at it and threw myself over the broken glass, rolling as I fell. I only had one free hand to slap the floor with and take the impact of the fall, but I wanted the gun in my hand ready to fire. I hit the floor, and the force of my blow, the jump, whatever, was still there, still rolling me. I used it to come to my feet before I even knew what was in the room.

I didn't so much see what was happening as take pictures of isolated things. I registered the overturned cribs: a tiny, tiny baby lying on the floor like a broken doll, the center of its body eaten away, like the center sucked out of a piece of candy; cribs still standing upright splattered with blood, some with tiny twisted bodies inside, some empty except for the blood; then in the far corner was the monster.

It held a tiny blanket-wrapped bundle. Tiny fists waving in the air. I couldn't hear it crying. I couldn't hear anything. There was nothing but sight, and that skinless face bending over the baby. My first bullet took it through the forehead, the second through the face as its head was thrown back by the impact of the first shot. It raised the struggling baby up in front of its face, and our eyes locked over the tiny form. It looked at me. The bullet holes in its face filled in like soft clay. I fired into its stomach because that's what I could hit without endangering the baby. It jerked back, but it threw itself to the floor. It didn't fall. I hadn't really hurt it. It took cover behind a row of tiny cribs. They were all on thin-legged wheels. I dropped to a crouch and sighted through that forest of thin metal legs, and saw it crouching, bringing the baby to its mouth.

There was no clear shot. I fired anyway, shooting into the wall beside it. It flinched, scuttling away, but didn't drop the baby. I fired through the legs of the wheeled cribs, keeping it moving. Where was Ramirez?

It stood and ran straight at me. I fired into its body. It shuddered but kept coming. The baby was naked except for a little diaper now, but it was alive. The thing threw the baby at me. It wasn't even a decision. I just caught it, cradling it to my chest, both hands compromised. The monster smashed into me. The momentum took us all back through the window I'd come through. We landed with the monster on the bottom as if we'd flipped in midair. My gun barrel was pressed into its stomach, and I started pulling the trigger with my right hand before I even started cradling the baby tight with my left.

The creature jerked like a broken-backed snake. I got to my knees beside it, firing until the gun clicked empty. I dropped the Browning and went for the Firestar. I had it almost pointed when it hit me with the back of one hand, and the blow sent me crashing into the wall. I'd tried to protect the baby from the impact and had taken more of it than was good for me. I was stunned for a second, and it grabbed me by the hair, turning me towards it.

I fired into its chest and stomach. Each bullet made the body jerk, and somewhere around the sixth or seventh shot, it let go of my hair. A bullet later and the Firestar clicked empty. It stood over me, and that lipless mouth smiled.

The fire alarm stopped. The sudden silence was almost frightening. I could hear my heart pounding in my head. The baby in my arms was suddenly piercingly loud, more frantic sounding. The thing tensed, and I knew a second before it came that it was going to rush me. I used that second to try and put the baby on a clear piece of floor. I was half-turned when it picked me up and flung me into the opposite wall. I didn't have the baby to worry about anymore. I slapped my hands and arms into the wall taking as much of the impact as I could. When it closed the distance, I wasn't stunned. It grabbed one upper arm, and I struggled to keep it from grabbing the other.

I knew how to grapple, but not with something that was slick and skinless. There was nothing to grab onto. It picked me up by my shirt, the other hand under my thigh, and dead lifted me like a barbell. I hit the wall as though it had tried to throw me through it. I tried to protect myself, but I slid to the floor, stunned, unable to breathe or think for a space of heartbeats.

It knelt beside me, tearing my shirt out of my pants, baring my stomach and my bra. It put a hand under my back and lifted me almost gently, bowing my back, raising me up, and lowering its face towards my bare flesh, as if it meant to kiss me. I heard a voice in my head. It whispered, 'I hunger.' Everything seemed distant, dreamlike, and I knew that I was close to passing out. I raised my hand and almost didn't feel like it was mine. But I moved it. I caressed that slick, fleshless face. And it rolled those strange lidless eyes up at me as it lowered its mouth to feed. My thumb slid along the flesh, feeling, feeling for the eye. It didn't stop me. It bit into my upper stomach, as my thumb slid into its eye. We both screamed.

It reared back, dropping me to the floor. It was a short fall, and I was on my knees, edging away from it when the first bullet whirled it around. Ramirez came down the hallway from the direction of the fire stairs, firing in a two-handed stance as he advanced down the hall.

The body jerked, but the wounds were closing faster and faster, as if the more we shot it, the better the flesh was at healing the damage. I expected the thing to attack Ramirez or me, or escape, but it didn't. It leaped into the broken window of the nursery. And I knew what it meant to do. It wasn't trying to escape. It was trying to take as many lives as it could before we destroyed it. Its master was feeding off the deaths.

Ramirez went to the door that I'd tried earlier. I left him banging against it with his shoulder. I pulled myself up to the window. It was tearing the blanket off of another baby, like unwrapping a present. I didn't know where my guns were. I had nothing left to throw at it. It turned in silhouette, and the baby was grabbing for the air with tiny matchstick arms. The monster's mouth widened showing a mouth already red with blood.

Ramirez had gotten the door open enough to slip inside. He shot at its legs and lower body, afraid to try a head shot so close to the baby. The monster ignored him, and everything slowed down to a crystalline crawl. The face lowered, mouth wide to take that tiny heart. I screamed, and I put all my rage, all my helplessness into that shout. I pulled that power that let me raise the dead, I pulled it around me like a shining thing and flung it outward. I could actually see it in my mind like a thin white rope of fog. I threw my aura, my essence around the thing. I was a necromancer, and all this fucking thing was, was a corpse.

I screamed, 'Stop!'

It froze in mid-motion, the baby almost at its mouth. I felt the power that animated it. I felt it inside that dead shell. Its master's power was like a dark flame inside it. I had a hand outstretched as if I needed it to point my power. I opened my hand and flared that white rope over the corpse. I covered it in my aura like growing a new body. I closed my aura like a fist around the thing and severed it from the power that made it move. The corpse shuddered, then collapsed instantly like a puppet whose strings had been cut.

I felt its master. I felt him like a cold wind across my skin. I felt him coming for me, following the line of my own aura towards me, like a string through a maze. I tried to pull it back, tried to fold it into myself again, but I'd never tried anything like this before, and I wasn't fast enough. Your aura is your magical shield, your armor. When I lashed out at the corpse, I'd opened myself to anything and everything. I thought I'd understood the risks, but I was wrong.

The master's power lashed out at me like fire following a trail of gasoline, and when it hit, there was a moment where I threw back my head, and I couldn't breathe. I felt my heart flutter and stop. I felt my body fall to the floor, but it didn't hurt, as if I were already numb. My vision went gray, then black, and there was a voice in the blackness. 'I have many servants. That you stopped this one is nothing to me. I will feed through others. You die in vain.'

I tried to form words to answer that voice and found that I could. 'Fuck you.'

I felt his anger, his outrage that I could defy him.

I tried to laugh at him, at his impotence, but there wasn't enough left of me to laugh. The darkness became something thicker. I passed beyond the master's voice, beyond my own, then there was . . . nothing.

41

The first hint I had that I wasn't dead was pain. The second was light. My chest was burning. I jerked back to consciousness, gasping for air, trying to pull the burning things off of me. I blinked up into a burning white light, then voices.

'Hold her down!'

Weight on my arms and legs, hands holding me down. I tried to struggle, but couldn't feel my body enough to be sure I was moving at all.

'BP sixty over eighty and dropping fast.'

I saw shapes, blurred with light moving around me. A sharp jab in my arm, a needle. A man's face swam into view, blond, wire-framed glasses. His face slid back out of sight into a white-rimmed fog.

Gray spots slid like greasy streamers across my vision, and I felt myself sinking backwards, downwards, outwards.

A man's voice, 'We're losing her!'

Darkness rolled over me taking the pain, and the light. A woman's voice floated through the dark. 'Let me try.' Then silence in the dark. There was no alien voice this time. There was nothing but the floating dark and me. Then there was just the dark.

42

I woke up smelling sage incense. Sage for cleansing and ridding you of negativity, or so my teacher Marianne was fond of telling me when I complained about the smell. Sage incense always gave me a headache. Was I in Tennessee with Marianne? I didn't remember going there. I opened my eyes to see where I was, and it was a hospital room. If you wake up in enough of them, you recognize the signs.

I lay there blinking into the light, happy to be awake. Happy to be alive. A woman came to stand by the bed. She was smiling. She had shoulder-length black hair, cut blunt around a strong face. Her eyes seemed too small for the rest of her face, but those eyes stared down at me like she knew things I didn't, and they were good things or at least important ones. She was wearing something long and flowing, violet with a hint of red in the pattern.

I tried to talk, cleared my throat. The woman got a glass from the small bedside table, her many necklaces clinking as she moved. She bent the straw so I could drink. One of the necklaces was a pentagram.

'Not a nurse,' I said. My voice still sounded rough. She offered the water again, and I took it. I tried again, and this time my voice sounded more like me. 'You're not a nurse.'

She smiled, and the smile turned an ordinary face into something lovely, just as the burning intelligence in her eyes made her striking. 'What was your first clue?' She had a soft rolling accent that I couldn't place; Mexican, Spanish, but not.

'You're too well dressed for one thing, and the pentagram.' I tried to point at the necklace, but my arm was taped to a board with an IV running into my skin. The hand was bandaged, and I remembered the corpse biting me. I finished the gesture with my right hand, which seemed unharmed. My left arm seemed to have a sign over it that said cut here, bite here, whatever here. I moved the fingers of my left hand to see if I could. I could. It didn't even really hurt, just tight, as if the skin needed to stretch a little.

The woman was watching me with those eyes of hers. 'I am Leonora Evans. I believe you've met my husband.'

'You're Doctor Evans' wife?'

She nodded.

'He mentioned you were a witch.'

She nodded again. 'I arrived at the hospital in the . . . how do you say, nick of time, for you.' Her accent thickened when she said, how do you say.

'What do you mean?' I asked.

She sat down in the chair beside the bed, and I wondered how long she'd been sitting there, watching me. 'They restarted your heart, but they couldn't keep life in your body.'

I shook my head, and the beginnings of a headache were starting behind my eyes. 'Can you put out the incense? Sage always gives me a headache.'

She didn't question it, just got up and moved to one of those little folding tables on wheels that they have in hospitals. There was incense stuck in a small brazier, a long wooden wand, a small knife, and two candles burning. It was an altar, her altar, or a portable version of it.

'Don't take this wrong, but why are you here and a nurse isn't?'

She spoke with her back to me as she quenched the incense. 'Because if the creature that attacked you tried to kill you a second time, the nurse would probably not even notice it was happening until it was too late.' She came and sat back down by the bed.

I stared at her. 'I think the nurse would notice if a flesh-eating corpse came into the room.'

She smiled and it was patient, even condescending. 'You and I both know that as horrible as its servants are, the true danger is in the master.'

My eyes widened. I couldn't help it. Fear thudded in my throat. 'How did you . . . know that?'

'I touched his power when I helped cast him out of you. I heard his voice, felt his presence. He was willing you to die, Anita, draining you of life.'

I swallowed, my pulse still too fast. 'I'd like a nurse now, please.'

'You're afraid of me?' She smiled when she said it.

I started to say no, but then . . . 'Yeah, but it's not personal. Let's just say after my brush with death, I'm not sure who to trust, magically speaking.'

'Are you saying I saved you because this master allowed me to save you?'

'I don't know.'

She frowned for the first time. 'Trust me on this, Anita. It was not easy to save you. I had to encircle you with protection, and some of that protection was my own power, my own essence. If I had not been strong enough, if the names I called on for aid had not been strong enough, I would have died with you.'

I looked up at her and wanted to believe her, but . . . 'Thank you.'

She sighed, settling the skirt of her dress with fingers aglitter with rings. 'Very well, I will fetch you a familiar face, but then we must talk. Your friend Ted told me of the marks that bind you to the werewolf and the vampire.'

Something must have shown on my face because she said, 'I needed to know in order to help you. I'd saved your life by the time he arrived here, but I was trying to fix your aura, and I couldn't.' She passed a hand just above my body and I felt that trail of warmth that was her power caressing over mine. She hesitated over my chest, over my heart. 'There is a hole here as if there is a piece of yourself missing.' Her hands slid farther down my body and hesitated low on my stomach, or high on my abdomen depending on how you looked at it. 'Here is another hole. They are both chakra points, important energy points for your body. Bad places to have no ability to shield from magical attack.'

My heart was back to beating faster than it should have. 'They are closed. I've worked for the last six months to close them up.'

Leonora shook her head, taking her hands gently back from me. 'If I understand what your friend told me of this triumvirate of power you are a part of, then these spaces are like electrical sockets in the wall of your aura, your body. The two creatures have the plugs that fit their respective sockets.'

'They aren't creatures,' I said.

'Ted painted a very unflattering picture of them.'

I frowned. It sounded like something Edward would do. 'Ted doesn't like the fact that I'm . . . intimate with monsters.'

'You are lovers with both then?'

'No. I mean . . .' I tried to think of a quick version. 'I was sleeping with them at separate times. I mean for a little while I was . . . dating them both at the same time, but it didn't work out.'

'Why did it not work?'

'We were invading each other's dreams. Thinking each other's thoughts. Every time we had sex, it was worse, as if the sex was tying the knots tighter and tighter.' I stopped talking, not because I was finished, but because the words weren't enough. I started over. 'One night the three of us were alone, just talking, trying to work things out. A thought popped into my head, and it wasn't mine, or I didn't think it was mine, but I didn't know whose thought it was.' I looked up at her, trying to will her to understand the moment of sheer terror that had been for me.

She nodded, as if she did, but her next words said she'd missed the point. 'That frightened you.'

'Yeah,' I said, making the word two syllables so she'd catch the sarcasm.

'The lack of control,' she said.

'Yes.'

'The lack of individual privacy.'

'Yes,' I said.

'Why did you take on these marks?'

'They would have died if I hadn't done it. We might all have died.'

'So you did it to save your own life.' She sat there, hands crossed in her lap, perfectly at ease while she probed my psychic wounds. I hate people who are at peace with themselves.

'No, I couldn't lose them both. I might have survived losing one, but not both, not if I could save them.'

'The marks gave you all enough power to overcome your enemies.'

'Yes.'

'If the thought of sharing your life with them is so terrifying, then why did their deaths loom so large?'

I opened my mouth, closed it, tried again. 'I loved them, I guess.'

'Past tense, loved, not love?'

I was suddenly tired. 'I don't know anymore. I just don't know.'

'If you love someone, then your freedom is curtailed. If you love someone, you give up much of your privacy. If you love someone, then you are no longer merely one person but half of a couple. To think or behave any other way is to risk losing that love.'

'It's not like having to share the bathroom, or argue over which side of the bed you get to sleep on. They're trying to share my mind, my soul.'

'Do you really believe that last about your soul?'

I settled into the pillow, and closed my eyes. 'I don't know. I guess not, but it . . .' I opened my eyes. 'Thank you for saving my life. If I can ever return the favor, I will, but I don't owe you an explanation of my personal life.'

'You're quite right.' She straightened her shoulders as if pulling herself back, and suddenly she seemed less intrusive, more businesslike. 'Let's return to my analogy of the holes being like light sockets, and the men being the plugs that fit them. What you did was spackle over the holes, cover them with plaster. When the master attacked you, his power tore off the plaster and reopened the holes. You cannot close these holes with your own aura. I cannot imagine the amount of effort it took to put patches over them. Ted said you were learning ritual from a witch.'

I shook my head. 'She's more psychic than witch. It's not a religion, just natural ability.'

Leonora nodded. 'Did she approve of you closing the holes the way you did?'

'I told her I wanted to learn how to shield myself from them, and she helped me do that.'

'Did she tell you it was a temporary repair?'

I frowned at her. 'No.'

'Your hostility flares every time we approach the fact that you have given these two men in effect the keys to your soul. You cannot block them permanently, and by trying to you weaken yourself, and probably them as well.'

'We'll all just have to live with it,' I said.

'You almost didn't live with it.'

She had my attention now. 'Are you saying that the reason the master was able to almost kill me was the weakness in my aura?'

'He would have hurt you badly, even without them, but I believe the holes made you unable to resist him, especially with them freshly opened as they were. Think of them, perhaps, as wounds, freshly opened wounds that any preternatural infection can enter you through.'

I thought about what she was saying. I believed it. 'What can I do?'

'The holes are meant to be filled by only one thing, the auras of the men you loved. Your auras must now be like jigsaw puzzles with pieces missing, and only the three of you together are a whole now.'

'I can't accept that.'

She shrugged. 'Accept it or not, but it is still the truth.'

'I'm not ready to give up the fight just yet. Thanks anyway.'

She stood, frowning. 'Do as you will, but remember that if you come up against other preternatural powers, then you will not be able to protect yourself from them.'

'I've been like this for a year. I think I can manage.'

'Are you that arrogant, or just that determined not to talk about it anymore?' She looked down at me as if she expected an answer.

I gave her the only one I had. 'I don't want to talk about it anymore.'

She nodded. 'Then I will get your friend, and I'm sure the doctor will want to speak with you.' She turned and walked out.

The room was very quiet, full of that hush that hospitals are so fond of. I looked at her makeshift altar and wondered what she'd had to do to save me. Of course, I only had her word for that. The moment I thought it, I was sorry. Why was I so distrustful of her? Because she was a witch, the way Marks hated me because I was a necromancer? Or was it just that I didn't like the truth she was telling me? That I couldn't shield myself from magical critters until the holes in my 'aura' had been filled in. It had taken me most of the last six months to fill up those holes. Six months of effort, and they were raw again. Shit.

But if they were open, why didn't I sense Jean-Claude and Richard? If the marks were truly unshielded again, then why wasn't there a burst of closeness? I needed to call my teacher Marianne. I trusted her to tell me the truth. She'd warned me that simply blocking off the marks was only temporary. But she helped me do it because she felt I needed some time to adjust, to accept. I wasn't sure I had another six months of meditative prayer, psychic visualization, and celibacy in me. It had taken all that and power, energy. Hers and mine.

Of course, Marianne had taught me other things, and one of those meant I could check myself. I could run my hand down my own aura and see if the holes were there. The trouble was I needed my left hand for that, and it was wrapped in bandages, strapped to a board with a tube in it.

Now that I was alone and not being pestered with hard questions, I began to feel my body. It hurt. Every time I moved my back, it hurt. Some of it was the dull ache of bruises, but there were two spots that had the sharp bite of things that had bled. I tried to remember how I could have cut my back. The glass in the window when the corpse took us back through it, that had to be it.

My face ached in a line from jaw to forehead. I remembered the corpse hitting me backhand. It had been almost casual, but it had knocked me half-senseless. Just once I'd like to meet a type of walking dead that wasn't stronger than a living person.

I lifted the loose neck of my hospital gown and found little round pads stuck to my chest. I glanced at the heart monitor beside the bed, giving that reassuring sound that said my heart was still working. I had a sudden memory of the moment when my heart had stopped, when the master had willed it to stop. I was suddenly cold, and it wasn't the overly ambitious air conditioner. I'd come very close to dying yesterday . . . today? I didn't know what day it was. Only the sunshine pressing against the drawn blinds let me know it was day and not night.

There were red patches on the skin of my upper body like bad sunburns. I touched one, gently. It hurt. How the hell had I gotten burns? I lifted the gown until it made a cave and I could see down the line of my body, at least until mid-thigh where the weight of the covers hid me from view. There was a bandage just below my rib cage. I remembered the thing's mouth opening over my skin while he cradled me, gently. The moment when he bit down . . . I pushed the memory away. Later, much, much later. I checked my left shoulder, but the scrape marks from teeth had already scabbed over.

Scabbed over? How long had I been out?

A man came into the room. He seemed familiar, but I knew I did not know him. He was tall with blond hair and silver-framed glasses. 'I'm Doctor Cunningham, and I am very glad to see you awake.'

'Me, too,' I said.

He smiled and started checking me over. He used a penlight and made me follow the light, his finger, and kept staring into my eyes so long, he had me worried. 'Did I have a concussion?'

'No,' he said. 'Why? Does your head hurt?'

'A little but I think it's from the sage incense.'

He looked embarrassed. 'I am sorry about that, Ms Blake, but she seemed to think all this was very important, and frankly I don't know why you almost died to begin with, or why you didn't just keep on dying. I let her do what she wanted.'

'I thought my heart stopped,' I said.

He tucked his stethoscope into his ears and pressed it to my chest. 'Technically, yes.' He stopped talking, listening to my heart. He asked me to breathe deeply a couple of times, then made some notes on the chart at the foot of my bed. 'Yes, your heart did stop, but I don't know why it stopped. None of your injuries were that serious, or for that matter, that kind of injury.' He shook his head and came back to stand by me.

'How did I get the burns on my chest?'

'We used the defibrillator to start your heart. It can leave mild burns.'

'How long have I been here?'

'Two days. This is your third day with us.'

I took a deep breath and tried not to panic. I'd lost two days. 'Have there been any more murders?'

The smile wilted on his face, leaving his eyes even more serious than they had been. 'You mean the mutilation murders?'

I nodded.

'No, no new bodies.'

I let out the breath. 'Good.'

He was frowning now. 'No more questions about your health? Just about the murders?'

'You said you don't know why I almost died, or why I didn't go ahead and die. I assume that means Leonora Evans saved me.'

He looked even more uncomfortable. 'All I know is that once we allowed her to lay hands on you, your blood pressure started to go back up, your heart rhythm steadied out.' He shook his head. 'I simply don't know what happened, and if you knew how hard it is for a doctor, any doctor, to admit ignorance, you'd be much more impressed with me saying that.'

I smiled. 'Actually, I've been in the hospital before. I appreciate you telling me the truth and not trying to claim credit for my miraculous recovery.'

'Miraculous is a good word for it.' He touched the one thin knife scar on my right forearm. 'You have quite a collection of war injuries, Ms Blake. I believe you have seen a lot of hospitals.'

'Yeah,' I said.

He shook his head. 'You're what, twenty-two, twenty-three?'

'Twenty-six,' I said.

'You look younger,' he said.

'It's being short,' I said.

'No,' he said, 'it isn't. But still to have these kinds of scars at twenty-six is not a good sign, Ms Blake. I did my residency in a very bad section of a very big city. We used to get a lot of gang members. If they lived to see twenty-six, their bodies looked like yours. Knife scars . . .' He leaned across the bed and raised the sleeve of the gown enough to touch the healed bullet wound on my upper arm. '. . . bullet wounds. We even had a shapeshifter gang, so I've seen the claw marks and bites, too.'

'You must have been in New York,' I said.

He blinked. 'How did you know?'

'It's illegal to purposefully give lycanthropy to a minor even with their permission, so the gang leaders were put under a death sentence. They sent in special forces along with New York's finest to wipe them out.'

He nodded. 'I left the city just before they did that. I'd treated a lot of those kids.' His eyes were distant with remembering. 'We had two of them shapechange during treatment. Then they wouldn't let them in the hospital anymore. If you wore their colors, you were left to die.'

'Most of them probably lived anyway, Doctor Cunningham. If the initial wound doesn't kill them immediately, they probably aren't going to die.'

'Are you trying to comfort me?' he asked.

'Maybe.'

He looked down at me. 'Then I'll tell you what I told all of them. Get out. Get out of this line of work or you will not live to see forty.'

'I was actually wondering if I was going to make it to thirty,' I said.

'Was that a joke?'

'I think so.'

'You know the old saying, half in jest, all in seriousness?' he asked.

'Can't say I've heard that one.'

'Listen to yourself, Ms Blake. Take it to heart and find something a little safer to be doing.'

'If I was a cop, you wouldn't be saying this.'

'I have never treated a policeman that had this many scars. The closest I've ever seen outside the gangs was a marine.'

'Did you tell him to quit his job?'

'The war was over, Ms Blake. Normal military duty just isn't that dangerous.'

He looked at me, all serious. I looked back, blank-faced, giving him nothing. He sighed. 'You'll do what you want to do, and it's none of my business anyway.' He turned and walked towards the door.

I called after him. 'I do appreciate the concern, Doctor. Honestly, I do.'

He nodded, one hand on either side of his stethoscope like it was a towel. 'You appreciate my concern, but you're going to ignore my advice.'

'Actually, if I live through this case, I'm planning to take some time off. It's not the injury rate, doctor. It's the erosion of the ethics that's beginning to get to me.'

He tugged on the stethoscope. 'Are you telling me that if I think you look bad, I should see the other guy?'

I gazed down, sort of taking it all in. 'I execute people, Doctor Cunningham. There are no bodies to look at.'

'Don't you mean you execute vampires?' he said.

'Once upon a time, that's what I meant.'

We had another long moment of looking at each other, then he said, 'Are you saying you kill humans?'

'No, I'm saying that there's not as much difference between vamps and humans as I used to tell myself.'

'A moral dilemma,' he said.

'Yeah,' I said.

'I don't envy you the problem, Ms Blake, but try to stay out of the line of fire until you figure out the answer to it.'

'I always try and stay out of the line of fire, Doctor.'

'Try harder,' he said and walked out.

43

Edward came in the door before it had time to swing closed. He was wearing one of those short-sleeved shirts with little pockets on the front. If it had been tan, I'd have said he looked dressed for a safari, but the shirt was black. So were his freshly pressed jeans, the belt that encircled his narrow waist, down to the black-over belt buckle, so it wouldn't shine in the dark and give you away. The belt buckle matched the shoulder holster and gun that outlined his chest. There was a line of white undershirt at the open neck of the shirt, but other than that it was unrelieved blackness. It made his hair and eyes look even paler. It was the first time I'd seen him without the cowboy hat out of doors since I arrived.

'If you're dressed for my funeral, it's too casual. If it's just street clothes, then you must be scaring the tourists.'

'You're alive. Good,' he said.

I gave him a look. 'Very funny.'

'I wasn't being funny.'

We looked at each other. 'Why so serious, Edward? I asked the doc, and he said there hadn't been any more murders.'

He shook his head and came to stand at the foot of the bed, near the makeshift altar. I ended up looking down the length of the bed at him, and it was awkward. I found the button controls with my right hand and raised the head of the bed slowly. I'd been in enough hospital beds to know where everything was.

'No, there haven't been any more murders,' he said.

'Then what's with the long face?' I was paying attention to my body while the bed raised, waiting for it to hurt. I ached all over, which you tend to do after being thrown into walls. My chest hurt, and it wasn't just the burns. I stopped when I was sitting up enough to see him without straining.

He gave a very small smile. 'You nearly die, and you ask what's wrong?'

I raised eyebrows at him. 'I didn't know you cared.'

'More than I should.'

I didn't know what to say to that, but I tried. 'Does this mean you won't kill me just for sport?'

He blinked, and the emotion was gone. Edward was standing there staring at me, his usual amused blankness showing on his face. 'You know I only kill for money.'

'Bullshit,' I said. 'I've seen you kill people when you weren't getting a paycheck.'

'Only when I'm with you.'

I'd tried to play it tough and guylike. He wasn't having any of it. I tried for honesty next. 'You look tired, Edward.'

He nodded. 'I am.'

'If there haven't been any more murders, why do you look so beat?'

'Bernardo only got out of the hospital yesterday.'

I raised eyebrows at him. 'How bad was he hurt?'

'Broken arm, concussion. He'll heal.'

'Good,' I said.

There was still an air to him of strangeness, more than normal Edward strangeness, as if there was more to tell and he didn't want to tell it. 'Drop the other shoe, Edward.'

His eyes narrowed. 'What do you mean?'

'Tell me what's got you all bothered.'

'I tried to see Nicky Baco without you or Bernardo.'

'Bernardo tell you about the meet?' I asked.

'No, your detective friend, Ramirez, told me.'

That surprised me. 'Last time I talked to him, he was sort of insisting that he go along with me to meet Baco.'

'He still wanted to come along, but Baco wouldn't see any of us. He insisted that you and Bernardo, or at least you, had to be there.'

'You're not upset just because Nicky wouldn't dance with you,' I said. 'Just tell me.'

'Do you really need Baco, Anita?'

'Why?'

'Just answer the question.' I knew Edward well enough to know he meant it. I answered his question or he wouldn't answer mine.

'Yeah, I need him. He's a necromancer, Edward, and whatever this thing is, it is just a form of necromancy.'

'But you're a better necromancer than he is, stronger.'

'Maybe, but I don't know much about ritual necromancy. What I do is actually closer to voodoo than traditional necromancy.'

He gave a dim smile, shaking his head. 'And what exactly is traditional necromancy, and how are you so sure that Baco practices it?'

'If he was an animator, I'd have heard of him. There just aren't that many of us. So he doesn't raise zombies. But you and everyone else in the metaphysical community in and around Santa Fe say that Baco works with the dead.'

'I only know his reputation, Anita. I've never seen him do shit.'

'Fine, but I've met him. He doesn't do vaudun, voodoo. I've seen that enough to know the trappings and the feel of it. So if he's not a zombie raiser or a vaudun priest, and people still call him a necromancer, then he must do ritual necromancy.'

'Which is?' Edward said.

'To my knowledge it's raising the spirits of the dead for sort of divination purposes or to get questions answered.'

Edward shook his head. 'Whatever Baco does, it has to be worse than raising a few ghosts. People are scared of him.'

'Nice of you to mention that before I met him the first time,' I said.

He took a deep breath, hands on hips, not looking at me. 'I was careless.'

I looked at him. 'You're a lot of things, Edward. Careless isn't one of them.'

He nodded and looked up at me. 'How about competitive?'

I frowned at him, but said, 'Competitive, I'll give you. But what does that have to do with Baco?'

'I knew that his bar was the hangout for the local were-wolves.'

I stared at him, just stared at him. When I closed my mouth, I said, 'You competitive shit. You let Bernardo and me walk in there unprepared. You could have gotten us killed.'

'You're not even going to ask why I let you walk in blind?' he asked.

'Let me take a wild guess. You wanted to see how I'd handle it cold, or maybe how Bernardo would handle it, or maybe both.'

He nodded.

'Fuck, Edward. This isn't a game.'

'I know that.'

'No you don't. You've been keeping things from me from the moment I stepped off the plane. You keep testing my nerve to see if it's better than yours. It is so junior high, so damned . . .' I struggled to find the right word, '. . . such a guy thing to do.'

'I'm sorry,' he said, and his voice was soft.

The apology stopped me, drained some of the righteous indignation. 'I've never heard you apologize for anything, Edward, not to anyone.'

'It's been a long time since I said I was sorry to anyone.'

'Does this mean the games are over, and you'll quit trying to see who is the biggest, baddest person?'

He nodded. 'That's what it means.'

I lay there and looked at him. 'Is it just being with Donna, or is something else starting to open you up?'

'What do you mean?'

'If you don't stop all this sentimental shit, I'll begin to think you're just a mere mortal like the rest of us.'

He smiled. 'Speaking of immortals,' he said.

'We weren't,' I said.

'I'm changing the subject,' he said.

'Okay.'

'If this monster really is an Aztec boogey-man, then it is a hell of a coincidence that the Master of the City, who just happens to be an Aztec, doesn't know anything about it.'

'We talked to her, Edward.'

'Do you think a vamp, even a master vamp, could do all the things we've been seeing?'

I thought about it, but finally said, 'Not just from vampiric powers, no, but if she were some kind of Aztec sorcerer in life, she might retain her powers after death. I just don't know that much about Aztec magic. It doesn't come up a lot. She was different from any vampire I've ever met. It could mean that she was a sorcerer in life.'

'I think you need to see her again.'

'And what, ask her if she's involved in the murder and mutilation of some twenty people?'

He grinned. 'Something like that.'

I nodded. 'Okay. When I get out of the hospital, a visit to vampire central goes up to the head of my list.'

His face went very blank.

'What is it, Edward?'

'Do you really need Baco?' he said.

'I sensed this thing the first night I arrived or first day. It sensed me right back, and it shielded itself. I haven't picked it up that strongly since, and I've driven past the spot where I felt it. Baco can sense it, too, and he's afraid of it. So yeah, I want to talk to him.'

'You don't think he's behind it?'

'I've felt this thing's power. Baco is powerful, but he's not that powerful. Whatever this thing is, it's not human.'

He sighed. 'Fine.' He said it like he'd made a decision. 'Baco says you have to meet him before ten this morning or don't bother coming.'

I searched the room until I found the clock on the wall. It was eight. 'Shit,' I said.

'The doc says you need at least another twenty-four hours in here. Leonora says that if the monster tries for you again, you won't make it.'

'You have a point to make,' I said.

'I almost didn't tell you.'

I was beginning to get pissed. 'I don't need you to protect me, Edward. I thought you of all people knew better than that.'

'Are you sure you're up to it?'

I almost just said yes, but I was so tired. It was a bone weariness that had nothing to do with lack of sleep. I was hurt, and it went beyond the bruises and cuts that I could feel. 'No,' I said.

He blinked. 'You must feel like shit to admit that.'

'I've felt better, but something's scaring Baco. If he says meet before ten this morning, we meet. Maybe the great bad thing is coming to get him at eleven today. Can't miss that, can we?'

'I've got a bag of fresh clothes out in the hall for you. They cut your shoulder holster off of you in the emergency room, and the spine sheath.'

'Shit,' I said, 'that spine sheath was a custom job.'

He shrugged. 'You can order a new one.' He went to the door, stepped out a moment, then came back in with a small overnight bag. He came around to the side of the bed that Leonora's chair was on. The other side of the bed was a little too crowded with equipment for visitors to stand.

He opened it and started laying out the clothes. His button-down black shirt didn't fit perfectly smooth around his ribs. He laid out the clothes in neat piles: black jeans, black polo shirt, black socks, even the underwear and bra matched the theme. 'What's with the funerary color scheme?'

'The dark blue polo shirt and jeans were trashed. All you had left was black, red, and purple for shirts. We need something dark today, authoritative.'

'Why are you in black, then?' I was watching the way the shirt lay when he moved. It wasn't a gun. I didn't think it was knives. What was under his shirt?

'White shows blood.'

'What's under your shirt, Edward?'

He smiled and unbuttoned the middle buttons. He had what looked like a modified belly band holster strapped across his upper body. But it wasn't a gun. It was metal pieces, too big to be ammo, and too oddly shaped on the end I could see. They looked like teeny-tiny metal darts . . . 'Are those some sort of itty-bitty throwing knives?'

He nodded. 'Bernardo said that if you took out an eye the flayed ones didn't like it.'

'I poked out eyes on them twice, and each time it seemed to hurt and disorient them. Truthfully, I didn't think Bernardo noticed what I was doing.'

He smiled and started buttoning his shirt up. 'You shouldn't underestimate him.'

'Could you really hit an eye throwing one of those things?' He slipped one out of its little holster and threw it into the wall in one flick of his hand. He pierced one of the tiny designs on the wallpaper across the room.

'I can't hit shit with something like that.'

He retrieved it from the wall and replaced it on his chest, and walked back to me. 'You can even have your very own flamethrower, if you want it.'

'Gee, and it isn't even Christmas.'

He smiled. 'Not Christmas, more like Easter.'

I frowned up at him. 'I don't get the Easter reference.'

'You came back from the dead, or didn't anyone tell you?'

I shook my head. 'Tell me what?'

'Your heart stopped three times. Ramirez kept it going with CPR until the doctors got to you. But they lost you twice. You were going down for the third time when Leonora Evans convinced them to let her try and save you with some of that good old time religion.'

My heart was suddenly beating too hard, and I could have sworn that the inside of my ribs hurt with each beat. 'Are you trying to scare me?'

'No, just explaining the Easter reference. You know, Christ rose from the dead.'

'I get it, I get it.' I was suddenly scared and angry. I am rarely one without being the other.

'If you still believe in it, I'd light a candle or two,' he said.

'I'll think about it,' I said, and my voice sounded defensive even to me.

He was smiling again, and I was beginning to distrust his smile almost as much as the rest of him. 'Or maybe you should talk to Leonora and ask her who she asked for help to get you back. Maybe it's not a church candle you need to light. Maybe you need to slaughter a few chickens.'

'Wiccans do not kill things to raise power.'

He shrugged. 'Sorry, they don't teach comparative religion or metaphysics in assassin school.'

'You've scared me, reminded me how hurt I am, and now you're yanking my chain, teasing me. Do you want me to get up out of this bed and meet Baco or not?'

His face was all serious, the last of the humor draining away like ice melting down a hot plate. 'I want you to do whatever you need to do, Anita. I thought I wanted to get this son of a bitch at any price.' He touched my right hand where it lay on the sheet. He didn't hold it, just touched it, then pulled away. 'I was wrong. Some things I'm not willing to pay.'

Before I could think of anything to say, he turned and left. I wasn't sure which was confusing me more: this case, or the new and more emotional Edward. I caught sight of the clock. Shit. I had an hour and forty minutes to get dressed, check out of the hospital against doctor's orders, and drive to Los Duendos. I was betting arguing with Doctor Cunningham was going to take longer than either of the other two.

44

I pressed the button to slowly raise the bed. The closer I got to a sitting position, the more I hurt. My chest ached as if the muscles around my ribs had been overused. The cuts on my back did not like sitting up and would probably like walking even less. There was a certain tightness to the skin, like a shoe laced too tightly, that said I had stitches on my back. They would be a pain all their own when I insisted on moving. Nothing feels quite like stitches. I wondered how many I had in my back. It felt like a lot.

When I was in a sitting position, I waited for a few seconds listening to my body complain. I usually don't get this hurt until the end of a case. I hadn't even met the great-bad-thing face to face yet. It had nearly killed me from a nice supposedly safe distance.

I let myself think about that for a few minutes. I'd almost died. Seems like I should get a few days of grace before having to crawl back into the trenches. But crime and tide wait for no woman, or something like that. I'll admit I thought about just staying put, just letting someone else be heroic for a change. But the moment I seriously thought it, I flashed on the nursery and those red-splashed cribs. I couldn't just lie here and trust that everyone would muddle through without me. I just couldn't do it.

I had my gown halfway down my arms when I realized I couldn't just yank the sticky pads that connected me to the heart monitor. Just yanking them off would give the hospital staff just a little too much excitement.

I finally pressed the nurse call button. I had to get unplugged from all the drips and machines.

The nurse came almost immediately, which either meant the hospital had more nurses on staff than most hospitals could afford these days, or I was really hurt and they were paying extra attention to me. I was hoping for a surplus of nurses, but wasn't betting on it.

The nurse was shorter than I am, very petite, with blond hair cut short and sort of bouncy. Her professional smile wilted when she saw me sitting up with the gown obviously coming off.

'What are you doing, Ms Blake?'

'Getting dressed,' I said.

She shook her head. 'I don't think so.'

'Look, I'd prefer help getting all the tubes and wires off me, but it is all coming off because I'm checking out.'

'I'll get Doctor Cunningham.' She turned and walked out.

'You do that,' I said to the empty room. I got a death grip on the little wires that attached to the sticky pads and pulled. It felt like I'd pulled a foot worth of skin off with them, a sharp, grinding ache, like it would hurt to touch the skin. The high pitched scream of the machine let people know my heart was no longer going pitty-pat on the other end of the wires. The sound reminded me uncomfortably of the fire alarm, though it was much less obnoxious.

The pads had left large circular welts on my skin, but they were not nearly as big as they felt. The fact that the welts hurt enough to rise above all the other aches and pains lets you know how raw my skin felt.

Doctor Cunningham came through the door while I was still working on the tape that bound my hand to the IV board. He turned the screaming heart monitor off.

'What do you think you're doing?' he asked.

'Getting dressed.'

'Like hell you are.'

I looked up at his enraged face and just didn't have any anger to throw back at him. I was too tired and too hurt to waste energy on anything but the process of getting up and getting out of this bed.

'I have to go, Doctor.' I kept picking at the tape and wasn't making much progress. I needed a knife. 'Where are my weapons?'

He ignored the question, and asked one of his own. 'Where could you possibly need to go badly enough to climb out of this bed?'

'I need to get back to work.'

'The police can handle things for a few days, Ms Blake.'

'There are people who will talk to me that won't talk to the police.' I'd gotten an edge of tape up.

'Then your friends in the hallway can talk to them.' Doctor Cunningham got points for realizing that Edward and company were the kind of men that people who avoided the police might talk to.

'This particular person won't talk to anyone but me.' I finally stopped picking at the tape. 'Can you please get this off of me?'

He took a breath, to argue, I think, but what he said was, 'I'll help you check out if you let me show you something first.'

I must have looked as suspicious as I felt, but I nodded.

'I'll be right back,' and he left the room. Everyone seemed to be doing that today. He was gone long enough that Edward came in to see what the holdup was. I lifted the taped arm, and he produced a switchblade from his pocket. The blade cut through the tape like paper. Edward always did take good care of his tools.

I was still left with having to peel the tape off my arm, and the IV itself had to come out, mustn't forget that.

'If you want it fast, I'll do it,' Edward said.

I nodded, and he ripped the tape off my arm along with the IV. 'Ow!'

He smiled. 'Sissy.'

'Sociopath.'

Doctor Cunningham came in carrying a large hand mirror. His

gaze flicked to Edward and my now free arm. It was not a friendly look. 'If you'll step back for a moment, Mr Forrester?'

'You're the doctor,' Edward said, moving back to the foot of the bed.

'Nice of you to remember that,' Doctor Cunningham said. He held the mirror in front of my face.

I looked startled, eyes too wide and so dark they looked black. I'm naturally pale, but my skin was ghost-white, ethereal like flexible ivory. It was what made my eyes look even darker than normal, or maybe it was the bruise.

I'd known my face hurt, and I'd even known why. Being hit hard enough to slam into a wall should leave a mark.

The bruise went up to the edge of my cheek, just under the eye, and catty-corner down to my jaw line just under the ear. My skin was a rainbow of purple-black with a core of red skin with darker red scattered across it. It was one of those really deep bruises that probably hadn't even shown much of a mark for the first day, but it would go through all the color changes once it started. I had shades of green, yellow, and brown to look forward to. If I hadn't had three vampire marks on me, I'd have had at least a broken jaw, or maybe a broken neck.

There were moments when I'd give almost anything to be free of the marks, but staring at the bruise, knowing that I healed faster than normal for a human and it still looked this bad, was not one of them. I was grateful to be alive.

I said a brief silent prayer while I stared at my face. 'Thank you, dear God, for me not being dead.' Aloud, I said, 'Nasty,' and handed the mirror to the doctor.

He frowned; obviously it wasn't the reaction he'd wanted. 'You've got over forty stitches in your back.'

My eyes went wide before I could stop them. 'Gee, that's a record even for me.'

'This isn't a joke, Ms Blake.'

'It might as well be funny, doctor.'

'If you start moving around, you're going to rip the stitches open. Right now, if you're careful, the scars won't be bad, but if you start moving around, you'll scar.'

I sighed. 'It'll have plenty of company, doctor.'

He stood there, shaking his head slowly, face set in harsh lines. 'Nothing I can say is going to make any difference, is it?'

'No,' I said.

'You're a fool,' he said.

'If I stay in here until I'm healed, what am I going to say to myself when I'm staring down at the next round of bodies?'

'Saving the world is not your job, Ms Blake.'

'I'm not that ambitious,' I said. 'I'm just trying to save a few lives.'

'And you truly believe that only you can solve this case?'

'No, but I know that I am the only one that . . . this man will talk to.' I'd almost said Nicky Baco, but I didn't want Doctor Cunningham calling the police and telling them where we were going. Not that he would do that, but better safe than sorry.

'I told you that I'd check you out if you looked at your injuries. I keep my word.'

'I appreciate that in a person, Doctor Cunningham. Thank you.'

'Don't thank me, Ms Blake. Don't thank me.' He moved towards the door, giving both the makeshift altar and Edward a medium-wide berth, as if both made him uncomfortable. At the door he turned. 'I'll send a nurse in to help you dress because you will need the help.' He walked out before I could say thank you again. Probably just as well.

Edward stayed until the nurse arrived. It was a different nurse, tall, light brunette, if that wasn't an oxymoron. Her gaze stayed on my bruised face longer than was politic, and when she helped me slip out of the gown, she gave a low hiss at my back. It was unprofessional and sort of unnurselike. They were usually blankly cheerful to the point of nausea when you were hurt, or blunt. Anything to cover that what had happened to you bothered them.

'You'll never be able to wear a bra over the stitches in your back,' she said.

I sighed. I hated to go without a bra. It always made me feel underdressed no matter what else I was wearing. 'Let's just get the shirt on.'

She held it and helped me slip it over my head. Putting my arms up to go through the sleeves made the pain in my back sharp and immediate, as if the skin would pull apart if I moved too quickly. I wondered if that would have been the analogy that I'd have chosen if Doctor Cunningham hadn't warned me about the stitches pulling apart. I'd have shrugged if I hadn't been sure it would hurt.

'I normally work in the nursery,' the nurse said as she helped me straighten the shirt, buttoning the first two buttons.

I looked up at her, not sure what to say. But I didn't need to worry. She knew exactly what to say. 'They called me in after you destroyed the monster. For the . . . cleanup.' She helped me sit on the edge of the bed. I sat there for a few seconds with my legs dangling off the edge, letting my body adjust to the fact that we were getting dressed, we were going to stand . . . in just a second.

'I'm sorry you had to see it,' I said, because I had to say something. I wasn't even comfortable with her saying I'd 'destroyed' the monster. It made it sound entirely too heroic, and what it had felt like was desperate. Desperation is the true mother of invention, at least for me.

She started to help me into the black panties, but I took them from her hands. If I couldn't even put on my own underwear, I was in serious trouble. And if I was truly that hurt, I needed to know it. It would cut down on my urge to be heroic.

I started to simply bend at the waist, but it just wasn't that easy. I lowered myself downward a little bit at a time, and I was still nowhere near low enough.

'Let me start them up your legs, so you don't have to bend all the way down,' the nurse said.

I finally let her, and even pulling them only part way up my body turned my back into one great big hurt. I leaned against the bed when they were on, and didn't even argue when she bent down to put on my socks. She never argued that I was too hurt to be leaving. It was too obvious to argue about it.

'I'd worked with Vicki for two years. It was Meg's first job.' Her eyes were dry, wide, and I noticed the dark circles under them like purplish smudges, as if she hadn't slept much in the last three days.

I remembered the body that had blocked the door into the nursery, and the nurse that had been thrown through the window. Vicki and Meg, though I'd probably never know which had been which, not that it mattered. They were dead and didn't care, and the nurse helping me slip into a pair of black jeans looked too fragile for questions. My job was to listen, and make encouraging noises where needed.

I slipped the jeans over my butt without help, buttoned them and zipped them all by myself. Things were looking up. I'd tried tucking the shirt into my pants out of habit, but that required more back movement than I thought. Besides, untucked, my braless state would be a little less noticeable. I was really too well endowed to go without, but my modesty wasn't worth the pain, not today.

'Every time I close my eyes, I see the babies.' She was kneeling with one of my shoes in her hands, when she looked up. 'I keep thinking I should be dreaming about my friends, but I only see the babies, their little bodies, and they cry. Every time I close my eyes, I hear the babies screaming. I wasn't there, and I hear them, every night.' The tears were finally there, sliding soundlessly down her face as if she didn't know she was crying. She slid the shoe on my foot and looked down, paying attention to what she was doing.

'See a counselor or a priest or whoever you trust,' I said. 'You'll need help.'

She got my other shoe off the bed, and gazed up at me, the tears drying in tracks down her pale cheeks. 'I heard that there's some sort of witch making these corpses, causing them to attack people.'

'Not a witch,' I said. 'What's behind all this isn't human.'

She slipped the shoe on me, frowning. 'Is it immortal like a vampire?'

I didn't do my usual lecture about how vamps aren't immortal, only hard to kill. She didn't need that particular lecture. 'I don't know yet.'

She laced my shoe solid, but not too tight, as if she did this regularly. She looked up at me with those strange empty eyes of hers, tear tracks still visible on her face. 'If it's not immortal, kill it.'

Her face held that absolute trust that is usually reserved for small children or people that are not quite all there. There was no questioning in her shocked eyes, no doubt in that pale face. I answered that trust. Reality could wait until she was ready for it. I said what she needed to hear. 'If it can die, I'll kill it.'

I said it because she needed to hear it. I said it because after what I'd seen it do, that was the plan. Maybe it had been the plan all along. Knowing Edward it probably had been. He said solve the case when what he usually meant was kill them, kill them all. As a plan, I'd heard worse. As a way of life, it lacked a certain romance. As a way to stay alive, it was just about perfect. As a way to keep your soul intact, it sucked. But I was willing to trade a piece of my soul to stop this thing. And that was perhaps my biggest problem. I was always willing to compromise my soul if it would take out the great evil. But there always seemed to be another great evil coming down the road. No matter how many times I saved the day and took out the monster, there was always another monster, and there always would be. The monster supply was unlimited. I was not. The parts of myself that I was using up to slay the monsters was finite, and once I used it all up, there would be no going back.

I'd be Edward in drag. I could save the world and lose myself. And staring down into the woman's face, watching that perfect faith fill her lost eyes, I wasn't sure the bargain was a good one, but I was sure of one thing. I couldn't say no. I couldn't let the monsters win, not even if it meant becoming one of them. God forgive me if it was arrogance. God protect me if it wasn't. I got up out of bed and went in search of monsters.

45

I was buckled into the front seat of Edward's Hummer, holding myself stiff and careful, glad the ride was smooth. Bernardo and Olaf were in the back seat, dressed in someone's idea of assassin chic. Bernardo was in a leather vest. His cast looked very white and awkward, right arm at a forty-five degree angle, a white strap going from arm to around his neck. His long hair was done in a vaguely oriental style, with one large, deceptively loose knot held back with what looked like two long gold chopsticks. It held back the sides of his hair, but left most of the length swinging free down his back. Black jeans of a looser cut with holes worn through across his knees, and the black boots I'd seen him wear since I arrived. But who was I to complain? I had three pairs of black Nikes, and I had brought all three with me.

There was a swollen bump to the side of his forehead and bruises like a pattern of modern art tattoos down one side of his face. His right eye was still puffy around one edge. But he managed not to look pale or ill like I did. In fact, if you could ignore the cast and bruises, he looked dandy. I hoped he felt as good as he looked, because I looked like shit and felt worse.

'Who did your hair?' I asked, because with only one good arm, I knew he hadn't.

'Olaf,' he said, and that one word was very bland, very empty.

I widened my eyes and looked over at Olaf.

He sat beside Bernardo on the side behind Edward, as far from me as he could get and still be in the car. He hadn't spoken a word to me since I walked out of the hospital room and the four of us walked to the car. It hadn't bothered me at the time because I'd been too busy trying to walk without making small pain noises under my breath.

Whimpering while you walked was always a bad sign. But now I was sitting down and as comfortable as I was likely to get for a while. I was also in a momentously bad mood because I was scared. I felt physically weak and not up to a fight. Psychically, my hard-won shields were crap again, full of holes, and if the 'master' tried for me again, I was in very deep shit.

Leonora Evans had given me a woven silk cord with a little drawstring bag on it. The little bag was lumpy, packed full with small hard objects that felt like rocks, and dry crumbling things that were probably herbs. She'd told me not to open the bag because that would let all the goodness out. She was the witch, so I did what she told me.

The bag was a charm of protection, and it would work without my believing in its power. Which was good since, except for my cross, I didn't believe in very much. Leonora had been making the charm for three days, since she saved me in the emergency room. She had not intended it to be a cure-all for the holes in my defenses, but it was all she had to give me on such short notice. She was almost as angry with me as Doctor Cunningham had been for leaving the hospital early.

She had taken one of her own necklaces and placed it over my head. It was a large piece of polished semiprecious stone. A strange dark gold color. Citrine for protection and to absorb negativity and magical attacks directed at me. To say that I wasn't a big believer in crystals and the new age was an understatement, but I took it. Mainly because she was so angry and so sincerely worried about me out in the world with my aura hanging open for the bad guys to munch on. I knew I had holes in my aura. I could feel them, but it was all just a little too hocus pocus for me.

So I turned in my seat, feeling the stitches in my back tighten, adding a little push to the pain I was already feeling, and stared at Olaf. He was staring out the window as if there was something fascinating in the rows of small houses on that side of the car.

'Olaf,' I said.

He never moved, just watched the passing scenery.

'Olaf!' It was almost a yell in the small confines of the car. His shoulders twitched, but that was all. It was like I was some kind of insect buzzing around him. You might wave a hand at it, but you wouldn't talk to it.

It pissed me off. 'Now I understand why you don't like women. You should have just said you were homosexual, and my feelings wouldn't have been so hurt.'

Edward said, softly, 'Jesus, Anita.'

Olaf turned very slowly, almost in slow motion as if each muscle in his neck were pulling him around in small jerks. 'What – did – you – say?' Each word was rage-filled, hot with hatred.

'You did a great job on Bernardo's hair. You made him look very pretty.' I didn't believe that particular sexual stereotype, but I was betting that Olaf did. I was also betting that he was homophobic. A lot of ultramasculine men are.

He undid his seatbelt with a noticeable click and eased forward. I pulled the Firestar out of the holster that was sitting in my lap. The pants that Edward had brought to the hospital were a little too tight for my innerpants holster. I watched Olaf's hand vanish underneath the black leather jacket. Maybe he hadn't understood the movement when I'd unholstered the gun. Maybe he expected me to raise the gun and sight along the back of the car. I pointed the gun between the small space between the seats. It wasn't a perfect angle, but I had my gun pointed first, and that counted in a gunfight.

He'd pulled his gun out from under the jacket, but it wasn't pointed yet. If I'd meant to kill him, I'd have won.

Edward slammed on the brakes. Olaf slammed into the back of the seat, gun at a bad angle, driving his wrist backwards. It wasn't being thrown into the seatbelt, and nearly the dashboard that hurt. It was the being flung backwards into the seat. My breath went out in a sharp gasp. Olaf's face ended up very close to the space between the seats, and he saw the gun barrel pointed, now, at his chest. I was hurting so bad that my skin twitched with the need to writhe, but I kept my hand tight around the gun, using my free hand to brace myself and make sure I didn't move. I had the drop on him, and I was keeping it.

The Hummer skidded to a stop against the curb. Edward had his seatbelt off and was whirling around in his seat. I caught the flash of a gun in his hand and had a heartbeat to decide whether to try and take the gun off Olaf and try for Edward, or keep the gun where it was. I kept the gun on Olaf. I didn't think Edward would shoot me, and Olaf might.

Edward shoved the barrel of his gun against the back of Olaf's bald head. The tension level in the car skyrocketed. Edward went to his knees, gun never moving from Olaf's head. I could see Olaf's eyes rolled up. We looked at each other, and I saw that he was afraid. He believed that Edward would do it. So did I, though I didn't know why, and with Edward there was always a why, even if it was only money.

I had a sense of Bernardo sitting very stiff on his side of the seat, trying to pull back from the mess that was about to spill all over the car.

'Do you want me to kill him?' Edward asked. His voice was quiet and empty, as if he'd asked, did I want him to pass the salt. I could do an empty uninterested voice, but not like Edward. I could never be that dispassionate, not yet anyway.

I said, 'No,' automatically, then added, 'not like this.'

Something passed through Olaf's eyes. It wasn't fear. It was more like surprise. Surprise that I hadn't said, yeah, shoot him, or surprise about something else I couldn't fathom. Who knew?

Edward took the gun from Olaf's hand, then clicked the safety off on his own gun, and leaned back still on his knees in the driver's seat. 'Then stop baiting him, Anita.'

Olaf sat back in his seat, slowly, almost stiffly as if afraid to move too quickly. Nothing like having a gun to your head to teach you caution. He smoothed his hands down the leather jacket, which still looked like way too much to wear in the heat. 'I will not owe my life to any woman.' His voice was sort of subdued, but it was clear.

I eased the Firestar back out from between the seats, and said, 'Consistency is the hobgoblin of little minds, Olaf.'

He frowned at me. Maybe he didn't get the quote.

Edward looked at both of us, shaking his head. 'You're both scared, and that makes you both stupid.'

'I'm not scared,' Olaf said.

'Ditto,' I said.

He frowned at me. 'You just crawled out of a hospital bed. Of course you're scared. Wondering if the next time you meet the monster will be your last.'

I looked back at him, and it was not a friendly look.

'So you picked a fight with Olaf because you'd rather fight him than be scared.'

'Just like a woman to be so irrational,' Olaf said.

Edward turned to the big man. 'And you, Olaf, you're afraid that Anita is tougher than you are.'

'I am not!'

'You've been quiet ever since we saw the mess at the hospital. Ever since you heard what Anita did, how much damage she took and survived. You're wondering just how good is she? Is she as good as you are? Is she better?'

'She is a woman,' Olaf said, and his voice was thick with some dark emotion as if he was choking on it. 'She cannot be as good as I am. She cannot be better than I am. That is not possible.'

'Don't make this a competition, Edward,' I said.

'Because you will lose,' Olaf said.

'I'm not going to arm wrestle you, Olaf. But I will stop picking on you. I'm sorry.'

Olaf blinked at me as if he couldn't quite follow the conversation. I didn't think I'd overstepped his English, more like his logic circuits were overloading. 'I do not need your pity.'

I moved up from being 'she' or 'a woman' to a neuter pronoun. It was a start. 'It's not pity. I acted badly. Edward's right. I'm scared, and fighting with you is a nice diversion.'

He shook his head. 'I don't understand.'

'If it's any consolation, you confuse me, too.'

Edward smiled, his Ted smile. 'Now kiss and make up.'

We both frowned at him and said simultaneously, 'Don't push it,' and 'I do not think so.'

'Good,' Edward said. He looked at Olaf's gun in his hand for a second, then handed it back with a lot of heavy-duty eye contact. 'I need you to be my backup, Olaf. Can you do that?'

He nodded once and took the gun slowly from Edward's hand. 'I am your backup until this creature is dead, then we will talk.'

Edward nodded. 'I look forward to it.'

I glanced at Bernardo, but his face told me nothing, nothing except that it had gone blank and empty and confirmed what I was thinking. Olaf had just warned Edward that when the case was over, he would try and kill him. Edward had agreed to it. Just like that.

'Just one big happy family,' I said into the thick silence that had filled the car.

Edward turned around in his seat and buckled back in. He gave me sparkling Ted eyes. 'And just like family we'll fight among ourselves, but we're much more likely to kill an outsider.'

'Actually,' I said, 'the vast majority of murders are done by your nearest and dearest blood relatives.'

'Or spouse, don't forget the spouse,' Edward said and put the car in gear, pulling carefully out into the sparse traffic.

'Like I said, your nearest and dearest.'

'But you said blood relative, and there's no blood between husband and wife.'

'Sharing one body fluid or another doesn't seem to matter. We kill those we're closest to.'

'We are not close,' Olaf said.

'No, we are not close,' I said.

'But I hate you all the same,' he said.

I spoke without turning around. 'Right back at you.'

'And I thought the two of you would never agree on anything,' Bernardo said. His voice was cheerful, joking. No one laughed.

46

The black-painted front of the bar looked tired in the morning sunlight. You could see where the paint was cracked and beginning to peel. The front of the bar looked almost as neglected as the rest of the street. Maybe Nicky Baco hadn't tried to run the other businesses off. Maybe it had been an accident. Standing there in the soft heat of morning, I felt something I hadn't felt at night. It was as if the street had been used up in a mystical sense. I'd felt very strongly when I'd been here last time that Baco had drained the street of vitality, caused this to happen, but if that were true, then it hadn't been enough energy to sustain him. Or maybe all that negativity was finally coming home to roost. Most systems of magic or mysticism have rules of conduct, things you do and things you do not. You break the rules at your peril. The wiccans call it the threefold law: what you do to others comes back to you threefold. Buddhists call it karma. Christians call it answering for your sins. I call it what goes around comes around. It really does, you know.

I had the Firestar tucked into the front of my pants, minus the innerpants holster, because the gun could ride higher and not dig in as much. Edward had loaned me a paddle holster for the Browning, and I had ended up with it in front, so that I looked like one of those wild west gunslingers with two guns crossed over my hips. Though actually the black polo shirt came down low enough to hide both guns. Untucked, most shirts are too long on me. It looked sloppy, but it did hide the guns if you weren't looking too close. The polo shirt was a little too close to the body not to show telltale lumps, though Edward had been thoughtful enough to bring my black suit jacket, which helped camouflage the lumps. Last time I'd been here with guns I'd had the police backing me, but now we were taking guns into a bar, very illegal in New Mexico. Strangely, it wasn't a big worry, but I did hope the cops didn't choose today for a raid.

I still had the wrist sheaths plus knives on my wrists. Ramirez had collected all my knives from the inferno and given them to Edward, who had scrubbed, cleaned, oiled, and sharpened them to an inch of their lives. I'd had to leave the big blade in the car because I couldn't figure out how to carry it concealed, and carrying what amounted to a small sword barehanded seemed a little too aggressive.

Edward had even given me an incendiary grenade for my jacket pocket. It helped balance out the derringer in my right-hand pocket so that the jacket didn't swing too funny as I walked. The derringer had been his idea, too, though I had brought it with me from St Louis. I wasn't sure I really needed it today, but I'd learned never to argue with Edward when he gave me a weapon. If he thought I might need it, I almost certainly would. Scary thought on the grenade, isn't it?

At some unknown signal, Olaf moved up and tried the bar door. It was locked. He knocked twice hard enough to rattle the door. He also stood right in front of the door. After staring down a sawed-off shotgun the last time I came to the bar, I might not have stood facing front at that black door. Either Olaf hadn't heard about the shotgun, or he didn't care. Maybe he was trying to be muy macho for my benefit or maybe for his own benefit. If he'd been more secure in himself, then he wouldn't have been so easy to piss off.

Even standing off to one side, the sound of the locks being drawn back was loud. Good, solid locks just from the sound of it. The door pushed open, slowly, showing a thick slice of darkness like a cave pressing against the sunlight. The door continued to push slowly open as if on its own power. Only at the very last did a large beefy arm come into view, spoiling the illusion.

Harpo stood in the doorway peering out at us, eyes hidden behind the same small black sunglasses he'd been wearing the first time I saw him. He had changed clothes, though. He was wearing a jean vest open over a very hairy chest and stomach. He looked more like a bear than a werewolf. He looked like a great big sleepy bear that had rolled out of bed, pulled on some clothes and rumbled out to the door. Even his otherworldly energy seemed dimmer than last time.

But he blocked the door with his bulk, and growled out, 'Anita, but not the others.'

I moved around Olaf, and he actually moved back so I could face Harpo. Either Olaf was being nicer, or he figured better me than him in the door. 'Nicky said I could bring some friends.'

Harpo peered down at me. 'Looks like you need better friends.'

I didn't touch the bruise. It wouldn't help. 'Let's just say I was relying on police backup and they were late.' Which was true, and I still wanted to know where the hell Ramirez had been while I'd been playing lone ranger. I like policemen, but I knew the comment would please Harpo.

It did. He smiled a quick baring of teeth that flashed wolf fangs in the thickness of his beard. He had definitely been spending too much time in wolf form. There was a low murmuring voice, male. Harpo turned to look over one massive shoulder towards the voice. Then he turned back to me. The smile was gone.

'Boss says you were invited but not the others.'

I gave a very small shake of my head because a big one would have hurt. 'Look, Nicky invited me here. He said I could bring friends. I brought them. I'm here before ten in the fucking morning. I came down here to talk about our common problem, not to be dicked around at the door.'

'This ain't dicking around,' Harpo said, hand cupping his groin. 'I can show you dicking around.'

I held up a hand. 'Fine, my mistake for using the wrong word. I didn't come down here to be stopped at the door.'

He was still rubbing himself, getting into it or trying to piss me off. He'd succeeded on the last. I was so not standing here with forty-plus stitches in my back watching some werewolf ape jack off before I'd even had coffee.

'I am too tired for this shit,' I said.

He started to get a little body language into it, smiling at me.

I raised my voice so it would carry into the open door of the bar. 'I am not going anywhere today without my friends here. If you're waiting for me to give in on that point, then we're wasting each other's time.'

There was no answer from inside the bar. Harpo had gotten a little hip action into his show. I'd had enough. 'When the monster sucks your life out, Nicky, don't worry. It doesn't really hurt. Have a nice day.'

I turned to my friends. 'They're not going to let us see Nicky.'

Edward nodded. 'Then let's go.' He made a small motion, and Bernardo and Olaf moved off down the sidewalk. Edward lagged a little behind with me. I think we were both hoping that Harpo would call my bluff. Except it was only partially a bluff. We could have forced our way in there with weapons, but Nicky wouldn't talk at the end of a gun. I needed a dialogue, not an interrogation.

I started walking away. Edward fell into step behind me, but kept an eye on our backs. I wasn't flexible enough to do much back trailing without turning my entire body around which was awkward. Besides I trusted Edward to watch our backs.

I admit there was a tension between my shoulder blades, waiting for Harpo to come running out and say come back, let's talk. But he didn't. So I kept walking. Olaf and Bernardo were beside the Hummer waiting for Edward to unlock the doors.

We were actually getting in the car when Harpo appeared on

the sidewalk and started to walk towards us. He looked unarmed, but not happy.

I sat in the seat, and closed the door. 'Start the engine,' I said. Edward did what I told him.

Harpo started jogging towards us waving those big arms. Some shapeshifters run like their animal counterparts, all grace and God-given motion. Harpo was not one of those. He ran awkwardly, as if he hadn't done it in a while, at least not in human form. It made me smile.

'You just wanted to see him run,' Edward said. 'Petty.'

'Yeah, it's petty. Fun though,' I said.

He put the car in gear, and Harpo put on a burst of awkward speed. He got to the car as Edward was starting to pull away. He actually slammed a big meaty hand on the hood.

Edward stopped. My window glided down, and I looked up at Harpo. There was sweat beading on his naked chest. His breath came harsh and too quick. 'Fuck,' he said.

'Did you want something?' I asked.

'Boss says – that you can all – come inside.' He was leaning his hands against the Hummer while he got his breath back.

'Okay,' I said.

Edward pulled the car back into the curb while Harpo moved so there was room. We all got back out of the car. Harpo was still not breathing right. 'Aerobic exercise is the key to good cardiovascular health,' I said, sweetly, as we waited for him to start walking back to the bar.

'Fuck you.'

I thought about getting back in the Hummer, but I'd played the game as far as I was willing to go. I wanted to talk to Baco, but only with backup. Harpo had said I could do both. I'd achieved my goal. Anything else was pure childishness. I was feeling petty, but not that petty.

When he recovered, he was once again the sunglass-wearing

muscle man, face impassive. He strode back, hands in loose fists, doing his best impression of a moving mountain of flesh. His otherworldly energy prickled along my skin. Just a whisper of power, as if it were leaking out without him meaning for it to. Which probably meant he was pissed. Strong emotions made it harder to hold all that vibrating energy inside.

None of us spoke on the short walk back. Men are usually not good at useless small talk or don't see a need for it, and I was just too busy concentrating on walking normally without giving away just how much it hurt to sweat chitchat.

Harpo held the door for us. I glanced at Edward. He gave me blank eyes back. Fine. I walked inside and the others followed. Three days ago I'd have been nervous stepping into that dark with the vibrating energy of werewolves rising like an invisible tide. But that was three days ago, and there just wasn't that much fear left in me. My body hurt, but the rest of me was oddly numb. Maybe I'd finally crossed that line that Edward seemed to live behind. Maybe I'd never really feel anything again. When even that thought didn't scare me, I knew I was in trouble.

47

It took a second for my eyes to adjust to the dark interior, but it wasn't my eyes that told me something was wrong. It was the skin on the back of my neck. I didn't argue with it. I had my hand on the Browning underneath the shirt and didn't care if it gave away the fact that I was carrying a gun. They'd be fools to think we'd come in here unarmed. Los Lobos Biker Club might have a lot of faults, but being that kind of fool wasn't one of them.

Nicky Baco was lying on the bar with his hands tied to his ankles so that the ropes formed a sort of handle like he was some kind of carry-on bag. His face was bloody and bruised, and the injuries were a lot fresher than mine.

I had the Browning out, and I felt rather than saw the other three fan out until we were the corners of a box, and each corner held a gun. Each corner watched its section of the room, and whether we liked each other or not, I trusted all of us to take care of our sections of the room, even Olaf. It was good to be sure.

My part of the room included the bar with Nicky on it; a tall man with a beard, and a curl of waist-length ponytail over one shoulder; two wolves the size of ponies; and a man's body staring sightless at the room, his throat cut like a second mouth, red and screaming.

I had a peripheral sense of how full the room was of crowding bodies. The energy was thick enough to choke on. I heard a noise to the right and did three things almost simultaneously. I pointed the Browning at the noise, drew the Firestar left-handed to point at the man with the ponytail, and let my eyes flick to the side to see what I'd heard. Good that I'd been practicing left-handed firing drills. The heavy slithering sound came again from behind the bar. The bar was in my section of the room. It was my ball, so to speak. I felt the others surging forward like a trembling tide about to swallow us all. We could shoot a lot of them, but there had to be over a hundred in this room and we were dead if they all came at once.

Fear tightened my stomach, jerking my pulse into my throat. Just like that the numbness was gone, chased away by adrenaline, and the musky scent of wolves. There were more wolves than just the two in front of me out in that packed, darkened room. I could smell them. My stomach jerked again, but not from fear. The mark that tied me to Richard, tied me to his pack, was alive again. It flared in my body like a tiny flame reborn, waiting to be fed so it could grow. Great, just great. I had to worry about it later. My concentration was all used up.

The ponytailed man just stood there smiling. He was handsome in a rough around the edges, tattooed prisoner sort of way. Even in the dimness his eyes flashed wolf amber, not human. I also knew what, or would that be who, I was looking at. This was their Ulfric, their wolf king. He stood in a space of emptiness with most of the pack huddled farther back into the room, and yet his power made up for theirs. His power filled the nearly empty side of the room with a flesh-creeping energy like thunder just before it strikes.

The tension was thick enough that I had to swallow some of it before I could speak. 'Greetings, Ulfric of the Los Lobos clan. What's shaking?'

He threw his head back and laughed, a big hearty, good-natured sound that ended with a howl that crawled out of his human throat and down my spine.

'Nice effect,' I said, 'but this is an official police investigation into the mutilation murders. I'm sure you've heard about them.'

He turned those startling pale eyes to me. 'I've heard.'

'Then you know that we aren't investigating your pack.'

He laid a casual hand on Nicky, who whimpered even though I don't think it really hurt. 'Nicky is my vargamor. If the police wish to speak with him, then they must ask me first.' He smiled, and I was close enough to notice that his teeth were human, no fangs for the Ulfric.

'Sorry. The only other pack I've ever met that had a vargamor doesn't make you talk to the Ulfric first. My apologies on the oversight.' I hoped whatever we were doing was going to be over soon, because I couldn't keep up the gun in each hand stance for long. I'd practiced left-handed, but it was still my weak hand, and the bite in it was already starting a faint tremble in the muscles. I had to be able to lower my hand soon or it would begin to shake.

'If you were the police, then I would accept your apologies. We are always ready to help the police.' That last brought a wave of snickers from the packed house. 'But I don't see any police in this room.'

'I'm Anita Blake. I'm a vampire executioner . . .'

He cut me off. 'I know who you are. I know what you are.'

I didn't like that last, made me nervous. 'And just what am I?'

'You are the lupa of the Thronnos Roke clan, and you have come to my clan for help, but you have not honored me or my lupa. You enter my lands without permission. You contact my vargamor without talking to me first, and you give us no tribute.' His power grew with every sentence until it was like standing in warm water up to your chin, knowing that if it got much deeper you'd drown.

But I understood the rules now. I'd insulted him, and he had to wipe out that insult. I'd try sweet reason, but I didn't have much hope for it. Besides, my left arm was getting tired. Hell, so was my right. Whatever was behind the bar moved in a huge roll of motion that you could feel and hear. It sounded bigger than a werewolf.

'I flew down here on police business. I did not enter your lands as lupa of the Thronnos Roke clan. I came down here as Anita Blake, the Executioner, that's all.'

'But you contacted my vargamor.' He slapped Nicky's thigh, and that did seem to hurt, because he closed his eyes and writhed at the touch, straining through his gag to scream.

'I didn't know Nicky was your vargamor until after I'd talked to him. No one told me that this bar was your lair. You're Ulfric. You can smell that I'm not lying.'

He gave a small nod. 'You tell the truth.' He looked at the small man on the bar, running his hand over his body the way you'd stroke a dog, though the dog doesn't usually wince and try to pull back. 'But he knew that he was my vargamor. Nicky knew that you were a lupa of another clan. It was the hot topic for a while, a human lupa.'

'Lupa's often just another word for the Ulfric's girlfriend,' I said.

He turned those golden eyes to me, more gold because of the heavy black eyebrows that framed them. 'Nicky agreed to help you without asking me later, or even telling me about your visit.' He gave a low growl that refreshed the fading goosebumps on my skin. 'I am Ulfric. I lead here.' He slapped Nicky and fresh blood trickled from his nose.

I badly wanted to put a stop to the abuse, just out of principle, but I didn't want it badly enough to die for it, so I waited and watched Nicky Baco bleed. I didn't like it, but I let it happen. My left hand was beginning to cramp. I needed to either start shooting people or put my guns up. Even holding my arms out for this long was putting a strain on my back and chest.

'Anita,' Edward said, and just the tone of my own name was enough. He was quietly telling me to hurry it up.

'Look, Ulfric, I didn't mean to walk into some inner pack squabble. I'm just trying to do my job. Trying to keep more innocent people from being killed.'

'Humans are fun,' he said. 'Sex and a meal and you never have to leave your car. But-you-do-not-make-them-your-queen!' His voice rose until with the last word he was screaming. Howls echoed him from the mob that was pressing close and closer.

'Anita,' Edward said, and this time there was more of a warning to his voice.

'I'm working on it, Edward.'

'Work faster,' he said.

'You're a racist, Ulfric,' I said.

He stared at me. 'What?'

'I'm human so I'm good enough to fuck, good enough to kill but not good enough to be your equal just because I'm human. You're a racist chauvinistic big bad wolf.'

'You come into my lands, ask aid of my pack, give no tribute to me or my lupa, and now you're calling me names.' I don't know if he made some kind of psychic signal or his anger was enough, but the two giant wolves at his feet began to stalk forward on stiff legs.

My left hand was beginning to shake, visibly. Whatever was behind the bar thrashed, sounding large and bestial. My left hand was threatening to give out completely, and I needed both hands. 'You die first, Ulfric,' I said.

'What?' and he sort of laughed when he said it.

'The first thing that jumps any of us, and I shoot you. No matter what else happens today, you'll be dead. Your two pony wolves better stop right where they are.'

'Your hand is shaking so badly, I don't think you've got it in you to kill anyone.'

It was my turn to laugh. 'You think my hand is shaking because I feel remorse about the thought of shooting you. Boy, have you got the wrong girl. Look at my right hand, Ulfric. It's not shaking. A walking corpse took a bite out of my left hand a couple of days ago, so I'm a little shaky with my left, but trust me. I hit what I aim at.' This is usually when I give my victim full eye contact and let them know I'm not bluffing, but I was divided between the Ulfric and his entourage, and the bar. 'How many of your wolves are you willing to sacrifice for your wounded pride?'

'If we fight, Anita, you and your friends will die.'

'And you'll die, and some of your best people, so wouldn't it be nice to avoid the carnage and have you tell me what the hell you want from me. You know I'm telling the truth. I didn't know that I was stepping on your toes. If Nicky is making some kind of power play behind your back, I didn't know it. So, tell me what you want to make this . . . social gaffe okay between us. Tell me before my left hand starts spasming so badly that I start shooting things just because I have to.'

He was watching me very narrowly, and I saw intelligence behind all the bragging and pride. There might be somebody home to bargain with. If there wasn't, then we were going to die. We were going to die, not because of the case but because I had been at one time Richard's girlfriend. It was a stupid reason to die.

'Tribute, I want the lupa of the Thronnos Roke Clan to give me tribute.'

'You mean a gift,' I said.

He nodded. 'If it's the right kind of gift, yeah.'

If I'd been coming to Albuquerque with Richard on personal business I'd have expected to make a gift to the local pack. The gift was usually a freshly killed animal, jewelry for the lupa, or something mystical. Death, jewelry, or magic. I didn't have any jewelry on me except Leonora's necklace, and I wasn't exactly sure what it would do for someone other than me. For all I knew it might be harmful, if it was just handed out. I didn't have enough information. The charm was so not leaving my body.

I lowered my left hand. One, it was twitching so badly, I wasn't a hundred percent sure I could hit anything with it. Two, I couldn't keep pointing guns if we weren't going to kill people. Three, my hand was hurting.

'Your word that if I give you a suitable gift, we all leave here in safety.'

'You'd take the word of an ex-con, drug dealing, biker gang leader?'

'No, but I'll take the word of the Ulfric of the Los Lobos clan. That I'll take.' There were rules, and if he broke his word as Ulfric, he lost brownie points. He had to be on shaky ground anyway for a human, no matter how magically powerful, vargamor to have challenged his authority. He wouldn't give his word and break it, not in front of his pack.

'I am Ulfric of the Los Lobos clan, and I give my word that you will all go in safety, if your gift is worthy.'

I didn't like the wording on that last. 'I didn't have time to stop at Tiffany's and pick up something for the little lady. Didn't get to hunt on the way here from the hospital. Cops frown on you shooting animals in town. The mystical shit is beyond me today.'

'Then you have nothing worthy,' he said, but he looked puzzled as though he was sure I had a gift of some kind.

'Let me see what's behind the bar, and I'll put up my guns and make tribute.' I'd tried to put up the Firestar, but my left hand was shaking so badly that I couldn't raise the shirt and slide it inside my pants. I needed two hands for it. Which meant I needed to be able to holster the Browning.

'Done,' he said. 'Monstruo, rise, greet our guest.'

It rose above the bar in a thin line of pale flesh like the rising of a crescent moon, then a face came into view. It was a woman's face with one eye gone stiff and dry like some kind of mummy. Face after face, rose brown and withered like a string of monstrous beads, strung together with pieces of body, arms, legs, and thick black thread like gigantic stitches holding it all together, holding the magic inside. It rose up and up until it towered against the ceiling, curving like a giant snake to stare down at me. I estimated forty heads, more, before I lost count, or lost heart to count anymore.

The werewolves had moved back farther into the room like the tide retreating backwards. They feared the thing. I didn't blame them.

I heard Bernardo say, 'Fuck.'

Olaf said something in German, which meant he wasn't watching his part of the room. Only Edward remained silent and on the job, ever vigilant. I have to admit that if the werewolves had wanted to jump me while that thing rose above me like some demented snake I would have been slow. It was too much horror to leave room for anything else.

I'd only seen something like it once before. That monster had been made by the most powerful vaudun priestess I'd ever met. But hers had been formed of fresh zombies and pulled seamlessly together into one monstrous ball of flesh. Pure magic. This had been stitched together like Frankenstein's monster, and the bodies being dead like that, dried, deliberately mummified, or an aftereffect of the spell.

I dragged my gaze from the thing to Nicky Baco still lying on the bar, gagged and bound and bloody. I heard my voice like a distant thing, 'Why, Nicky, you bad, bad boy.' I'd made a joke, when what I wanted to do was put a gun to his head and blow him away. Some things you did not do. Some things you simply did not do.

'You see why he's still alive,' the Ulfric said.

'Too powerful to get rid of,' I said, voice still oddly detached, as if I wasn't really concentrating on what I was saying.

'I used him as my threat. He would lay his magic on a wolf that was misbehaving, and they would be turned into what you see. And he would stitch them into the monstruo. But my wolves fear him now more than they fear me.'

I was nodding over and over because I couldn't think of a good thing to say. Alive, they were alive when Nicky did his magic. I had a truly awful thought. Somehow it seemed wrong to be putting away the guns, but I needed my hands for other things. I raised the shirt and slid the Browning home, though it wasn't as smooth as it would have been if the holster had been familiar. But my left hand was pretty much gone. I had to raise the shirt with my right and very carefully tuck the Firestar into the front of my pants. Even after the hand was empty, it continued to twitch uncontrollably. There was nothing I could do but wait for it to calm down on its own. I cradled the hand against my body and walked towards the monster.

I stood on the other side of the bar from it, looking at one of those dried faces. The mouth had been sewn shut on this one. I didn't know why. I took a few deep cleansing breaths, and there was an odor of herbs to it, but mostly just a dry smell like tanned leather and dust. I reached out with my left hand. Even with the bandages and the muscle cramps this was still my power hand, the hand to sense magic with. Most people have a hand that is better for sensing stuff, usually the opposite hand from the one you write with. I have no idea what ambidextrous people do.

There was an amazing amount of power pushing out from the thing, but the bar was wide and I was hurt so my concentration wasn't good, and I still couldn't answer the one question I needed answered. I used my right hand to sort of jump-sit on the bar, then got onto my knees. There was a face at eye level with me, and this one had eyes. A man's face, I think, with pale grey wolf eyes trapped in a dried mummy face. Those eyes stared out at me, and there was someone home. The walking dead don't show fear. I knew what I'd feel before I stretched my hand out toward the face. There was Nicky's power like a warm blanket of worms, squirming over my skin. It was some of the most uncomfortable magic I'd ever felt, unclean, as if the power itself would eat your flesh if you stayed too close to it for too long. This was where Nicky's energy had gone, and this was why no matter how much energy he gathered, it would never be enough. Magic this negative, this evil, is like a drug. It takes more and more energy to get the same result with worse and worse effect on the spellcaster.

I sent my own magic into that mess, not to empower, but seeking. I felt the cool brush of a soul, and before I could pull back, my power ran up that column of trapped flesh, and the souls glowed behind my eyelids with cool white light. None of them had been dead when he did this to them. I wasn't a hundred percent sure they were dead now.

I opened my eyes and pulled my hand back from the thing. His power sucked at my hand like invisible mud. I pulled free with an almost audible pop. The man's face moved its withered mouth, and made a long dry sound, twice. 'Help,' it said, 'help.'

I swallowed a wave of nausea and was very glad I'd missed breakfast. I crawled on one arm and my knees to Nicky. I bent over him and whispered, 'Would burning it free their souls?'

He shook his head.

'Can you free their souls?'

He nodded.

I think if he'd said yes to the first question, I'd have put the Browning to his head and killed him. But I needed him to free them, and I added that to my list of things to do before I left town. But there was nothing I could do for them today, except stay alive, and strangely, keep Nicky Baco alive. One of life's little ironies, that last.

I sat on the bar with my legs dangling over the edge, hand cradled to my chest, dazed with the sheer evil of it. I'd seen my share, but this was near the top. This was near the top after what I'd seen in the hospital. At least the corpses were just eating bodies, not souls.

'You look like you've seen a ghost,' the Ulfric said.

'You're closer than you know,' I said.

'Where is our gift?' he said.

'Where's your lupa?'

He stroked the head of one of the wolves by his legs. 'This is my lupa.'

'I can't share the gift with anyone in animal form,' I said.

He frowned, and it was very close to being angry. 'You must honor us.'

'I plan to.' I rolled the sleeve of my jacket back over my left arm. The wrist sheath had to go. I undid the straps, propping the blade, sheath and all between my legs. The monster hovered behind me, peering curiously. It was distracting me. I couldn't save them today, and didn't want to see it anymore until I could fix it.

'Can you order it to leave the room?'

He looked at me. 'Scared?'

'I can feel the souls crying out for help. It's sort of distracting.'

He looked at me, and I watched the color drain from his face. 'You mean that.'

I smiled, but not like it was funny. 'You didn't know that he's trapping their souls in that thing?'

'He said he was.' His voice had gone softer.

'You didn't believe him,' I said.

The Ulfric was gazing up at the thing as if he'd never seen it before. 'You wouldn't believe something like that, would you?'

'I would.' I shrugged, wished I hadn't, and said, 'But then this is my line of work. Can you please send it away?'

He nodded, and spoke rapidly in Spanish. The thing folded down on itself and crept away on arms and legs and bodies like a broken centipede. Sitting on the bar, I could see it go down a trap door behind the bar. When the last segment of it had slithered out of sight, I turned back to the Ulfric. He still looked pale.

'Baco is the only one who can free their souls. Don't kill him until he's done that.'

'I didn't plan to kill him,' the man said.

'That was before you knew. I don't know you well enough to know if when I leave, you'll get all self-righteous and try to end this evil. Don't, please, or you condemn them all to an eternity of that.'

He swallowed like he was having a little trouble keeping down his own breakfast. 'I won't kill him.'

'Good.' I drew the knife from between my knees right-handed. 'Now gather round, boys and girls, because I'm only going to do this trick once.'

There was a general movement as the wolves moved forward. I spared a glance for the boys I'd come in with. They hadn't put their guns up, but they had them pointed at the floor or the ceiling. Edward was watching the wolves. Bernardo was watching the wolves, too, though he looked pale. Olaf was watching me. I really, really, didn't like him.

'I give honor to the Ulfric and lupa of the Los Lobos clan. I give the most precious of gifts to the Ulfric, but not being true lukoi, I cannot share this gift with the lupa in her present form. For that, I apologize most sincerely. If I come back this way, I'll shop better.' I sat the blade on the bar and leaned over the edge until I could reach a clean glass. One of those thick chunky ones that people are so fond of putting scotch in. It was a strain to get back into a sitting position on the bar, but I managed it with the glass in one hand. I put the glass beside me on the bar and picked the knife up. I laid the blade against my left arm, just above the wrist, and stared at the whole, pale, unscarred flesh. There were scars just above it where a shapeshifted witch had clawed me, and the cross-shaped burn scar that was now a little crooked from the claw marks, but this one patch was still pure. I hoped it didn't scar, but what was one more.

I took in a deep breath and sliced the blade down my skin. A sigh ran through the watching werewolves, and whimpers from a few of the furrier throats. I ignored them. I'd known it would get a crowd reaction. I kept looking at my flesh and the damage I'd just done to it. The wound didn't bleed immediately. It was just a thin red line, then the first drop spilled from the wound, and the rest of the wound spilled in crimson rivulets down my arm. Deeper than I'd wanted it, but probably about what was needed. I held the wound over the glass. Some of it splashed around the edges, trailing down the sides, but I managed to get it going into the cup. I didn't even need to squeeze the wound much to encourage the flow. Deeper than I wanted it, oh yeah.

The Ulfric had moved closer, close enough that he was standing with his body touching my legs. The wolf that he'd introduced as his lupa moved up to nuzzle at my knee, and he hit her. He backhanded her the way you'd hit a dog you didn't like much. Where was women's lib when you needed it? She went to her belly, crying in doggy fashion, telling him she hadn't meant any harm with her tail tight curled to her rump.

No one else tried to move forward. If the lupa couldn't share, the rest of them knew better than to try.

The Ulfric stayed pressed against my legs. 'Let me take it out of your arm.' He stared at my bleeding arm like I'd stripped for him, something beyond sex, beyond hunger, and yet a little of both. I raised the arm so the blood trickled down it in fast little streams of red, splashing down into the glass. His gaze followed the movement like a dog after a piece of food.

The truth was that letting people lick a wound directly tended to distract me. Through the marks I was bound to a werewolf and a vampire. Both of which found blood exciting. The thoughts that filled me when I shared blood with anyone were too primitive, too overwhelming. Especially now with my shields in ruins, I couldn't risk it. 'Is the gift worthy?' I asked.

'You know it is,' and his voice had that peculiar hoarseness that men get when sex is in the air.

'Then drink, Ulfric, drink. Don't waste it.' I held the bloody glass out to him. He took it reverently in both hands. He drank, and I watched his throat convulse as he swallowed my blood. It should have bothered me more, I guess, but it didn't. The numbness was back, a distant, almost comfortable feeling. I fished under the bar until I found a stack of clean napkins and pressed them to my arm. The napkins soaked crimson in moments.

The Ulfric had waded into the pack with my blood in his hands. They surrounded him, touching him, caressing, begging for him to share. He dipped his fingers in the nearly empty cup and held them down for the wolves to lick.

Edward came to stand near me. He said nothing, just helped me put pressure on the wound, got more napkins from under the bar and a clean cloth to tie it tight. Our eyes met, and he just shook his head, the faintest of smiles playing on his face. 'Most people pay money for information.'

'Money doesn't interest most of the people I deal with.'

The Ulfric called back to me through the reaching werewolves. His mouth was bloodstained, his neat beard and mustache thick with my blood. He stared at me with his golden eyes and said, 'If you want to talk to Nicky, help yourself.'

'Thank you, Ulfric,' I said. I hopped down off the bar, and Edward had to catch me or I'd have fallen. Fresh blood loss on top of everything else was not what I had needed. I waved him away, and he didn't argue.

Edward undid Nicky's gag, and took a step back. The werewolves had pulled back, giving us the illusion of privacy, though I knew that every werewolf in the room would hear us, even if we whispered.

'Hi, Nicky,' I said.

He had to try twice before he said, 'Anita.'

'I was here before ten.' I put my hands on the bar and propped my chin on them so he wouldn't have to strain. The movement hurt my back, but somehow I wanted to be on eye level with him. The bulky makeshift bandage seemed to be in the way, but I wanted to keep the arm elevated. Nicky looked even worse up close. One eye was completely closed, blackened and blood-filled. His nose looked broken, blood bubbling from it when he breathed.

'He came back into town early.'

'I figured as much. You've been a very bad boy, Nicky. Pissing off your Ulfric, power play behind his back when you're just human, not even a werewolf, and that thing. That's not voodoo. How the hell did you do that?'

'Older magic than voodoo,' he said.

'What kind of magic?' I asked.

'I thought you wanted to talk about the monster that's killing innocent citizens.' His voice was strained, pain-filled. Normally, I'm against torture, but I just couldn't find much pity in my heart for Nicky. I'd seen his creation, and I felt the torment of its parts. Nope, I just couldn't spare much sympathy for Nicky. He'd never take enough damage to make up for what he'd done, not at least while he was alive. Hell might be a very nasty place for Nicky Baco. I trusted the divine to have a better sense of justice and irony than I did.

'Okay, what do you really know about the thing that's out there?' I asked.

He lay there on the bar, wrists and ankles bound together, blood trickling from his mouth, and talked as if he were sitting behind a desk. Except for the little pain sounds he made every once in a while, which spoiled some of the effect.

'I felt it years ago, maybe ten. I felt it wake.'

'What do you mean wake?'

'Have you had it in your mind yet?' he asked, and this time I heard the fear in his voice.

'Yeah,' I said.

'It was sluggish at first, as if it had been asleep or imprisoned, dormant for a very long time. It grew stronger every year.'

'Why didn't you tell the police?'

'Ten years ago the police didn't have any psychics or witches working for them. And I already had a criminal record.' He coughed and spat blood and a tooth out on the bar. It made me raise my head up, which forced Nicky to roll his head a little. 'What was I going to tell them? That there was this thing out there somewhere, this voice in my head, and it was getting stronger. I didn't know what it could do at first. I didn't know what it was.'

'What is it?'

'It's a god.'

I raised eyebrows at him.

'It was worshipped as a god once. It wants to be worshipped again. It says that gods need tribute to survive.'

'You got all this from just a voice in your head?'

'I've had ten years with the thing whispering in my head. What have you learned in less than that many days?'

I thought about that. I knew it was killing to feed, not just for sport. Though it enjoyed the slaughter, that I'd felt, too. I knew it both feared me and wanted me. It feared another death worker on the opposite side, but it wanted to drink my powers and would have if Leonora hadn't stopped it.

'Why has it just started to kill people now? Why after a decade?'

'I don't know,' he said.

'Why does it slaughter some and skin others?'

'I don't know.'

'What is it doing with the body parts that it takes away from the scenes?' Which was a detail that the police would not like me sharing with someone outside the investigation, but I wanted answers more than I wanted to be cautious.

'I don't know.' He coughed again, but didn't spit out anything. Good. If he'd continued to spit blood, I'd have worried about internal injuries. I didn't want to have to persuade the pack to take him to the hospital. I didn't think I'd have much luck.

'Where is it?'

'I've never been there. But understand that what's been killing people is not the god. He's still trapped wherever he started. His servants have done all the murders, not him.'

'What are you saying?'

'I'm saying that if you think you've got trouble now, you ain't seen nothing yet. I can feel him in the dark, lying like some kind of bloated thing, filling up with power. When he's full enough, he'll rise, and it'll be hell to pay.'

'Why didn't you tell me all this before?'

'You had the police with you the first time. If you turn me over to them, I'm dead. You've seen what I do. There wouldn't even need to be a jury.'

He had a point. 'When this is over, you have to dismantle it. You have to free their souls, agreed?'

'When I can walk again, agreed.'

I glanced at his legs and saw that there was a lump under his pants leg. It was the bone of the leg, a compound fracture. Jesus. Some days there are so many stones to throw in so many different directions that I don't even know where to start.

'Does this god have a name?'

'He calls himself the Red Woman's Husband.'

'That can't be an original English phrase.'

'I think he knows what his victims know. By the time he came to me, he spoke in English.'

'So you think he's been here a long time.'

'I think he's always been here.'

'What do you mean, always? Like eternity, or a really, really long time.'

'I don't know how long he's been here.' Nicky closed his good eye, as if he were tired.

'Okay, Nicky, okay.' I turned to the Ulfric. 'Is he telling the truth?'

The man nodded. 'He didn't lie.'

'Great. Thank you for your hospitality and please don't kill him. We may need him in the next few days to help kill this thing, not to mention freeing the souls of your pack mates.'

'I'll lay off on the beating.'

It was the closest thing I was going to get to a 'yes, we are going to let him go and make sure he isn't hurt anymore.' 'Great, I'll be in touch.'

Edward stayed near me as we walked to the door. He didn't offer me his arm, but he stayed close enough that if I stumbled he'd be there. Bernardo already had the door open. Olaf just watched us walk towards them. I stumbled a little up the two steps to the door, and Olaf caught my arm. I looked up into his eyes, and it wasn't pride or honor or respect that I saw. It was . . . hunger, a desire so great it was a physical need, a hunger.

I pulled away from him and left a smear of blood on his hand. Edward was at my back, helping me towards the door. Olaf raised his hand to his mouth and pressed it to his mouth like a kiss, but he was doing the same thing that the wolves did. He was tasting my blood and liked it. There are all kinds of monsters. Most of them crave blood. Some for food, some for pleasure, but you're dead either way.

48

Everyone was quiet in the car. Olaf consumed by his own thoughts, which I wanted no details about. Bernardo had finally said, 'Where to?'

'My house,' Edward said. 'I don't think Anita's up to anything else today.'

For once, I didn't argue. I was so tired, I was nauseated. If I could have found a comfortable position, I think I could have slept.

We drove out of Albuquerque and headed towards the distant mountains, bright and cheerful in the morning light. I wished for a pair of sunglasses, because I suddenly was neither cheerful nor bright.

'Did you learn anything worth getting out of the hospital early?' Edward asked.

'I learned that the thing has a name, the Red Woman's Husband. It is hiding someplace that it can't move from, which means if we can track it, we can kill it.' I added, because just in case, they needed to know. 'Nicky says it was worshipped as a god once, and that it still thinks it is one.'

'It can't be a god,' Bernardo said, 'not a real one.'

'I'm the wrong person to ask,' I said. 'I'm a monotheist.'

'Edward?' Bernardo made a question of his name.

'I've never met anything that was truly immortal. It's just a matter of figuring out how to kill it.'

I actually had met a few things that seemed immortal. Maybe Edward was right, but I'd seen things that I still couldn't figure out how to kill. Lucky me, the naga had been a crime victim and not a bad guy, and the lamia had been converted to our side. But as far as I knew they were both immortal. Of course, I'd never shoved an incendiary grenade down their pants or tried to set them on fire. Maybe I just hadn't been trying hard enough. For all our sakes, I hoped Edward was right.

We pulled onto the long road that led, as far as I could tell, just to Edward's house. It had a steeper drop off than I'd noticed at night, enough of a drop off that being an all-terrain vehicle didn't mean anything unless you could fly. A white truck pulled in behind us and started following us.

'Do you know them?' Olaf asked.

'No,' Edward said.

I managed to turn in the seat far enough to watch the truck. It didn't try and overtake us or anything. There was nothing wrong with the truck except for the fact that it was on the road to Edward's house and he didn't recognize it. Add to that that all four of us were paranoid by profession, and it made for tension.

Edward pulled into the turnaround in front of his house. 'Everybody into the house until we find out who it is.'

Everyone was quicker out of the car than I was, but then I'd just managed to get the bleeding on my arm stopped. Lucky for me, Edward had a heavy duty first-aid kit in the back seat. I had a nice big bandage taped to my arm, and the wrist sheath shoved in my pocket.

Edward was at the door, unlocking it. Olaf was behind him. Bernardo had actually waited for me, as if he would have liked to offer to help me out of the car, but was afraid to. I was actually feeling rough enough that I didn't mind the babysitting, which told you how truly bad I felt.

There was a small, sharp sound, a bolt being drawn back on a rifle, and everything happened at once. Edward had his gun out and pointed at the sound. Olaf's gun was out but not pointed. Bernardo had his gun pointed, using the door as a brace. I have to admit my gun was in my hand but not pointed. I just wasn't used to the new holster, and having to lift the shirt with a wounded left hand. Damn, I was slow.

Harold of the scarred face was leaning at the far end of Edward's house with a high-powered rifle pointed at Edward. He had most of his body hidden behind the house, and held the rifle like he knew what he was doing. If he'd wanted to drop Edward, he could have done it before Edward got the drop on him. That Harold hadn't shot anyone yet meant they had come for more than just killing. Probably.

Harold said, 'Nobody panics, nobody gets hurt.'

'Harold,' Edward said, 'when did you guys make bail?' He was still staring down the barrel of his Beretta at Harold. I could almost guarantee he was sighting on the top of the other man's head, his best killing target from what little he had to shoot at. Edward did not shoot to wound.

'Only Russell got arrested,' Harold said, rifle settled comfortably against his shoulder.

Speak of the devil. Russell came around the corner behind Harold. His nose was packed with white cotton and covered in a hard bandage. I'd broken his nose. Great.

'I thought terrorizing women and children carried more time than this,' I said. I kept the gun behind the open door. I didn't want to give anyone an excuse to start shooting.

The tall silent Newt came around the other side of the house with a large shiny revolver in his hands. He held it two-handed and moved in a cross-foot glide that said he knew what he was doing. There was a woman beside him, moving like a smooth oiled shadow. She was six foot if she was an inch, and the tank top she was wearing showed off shoulders and arms that made most of the men look puny. Only her breasts pressed against the shirt showed her braless and very much a girl.

Olaf pointed his gun at them. Bernardo moved up with his gun, and the woman turned to him. Olaf turned as Newt moved across in front of him like a long distance dance. The woman and Bernardo were more practical. They just stood a little bit apart and stared at each other over their guns.

Only Russell kept walking and didn't pull a gun. I tried pulling mine and pointing it at him. He did stop, but his smile got wider and the look in his eyes got worse, as if he had plans for me, and they were all about to come true.

'You shoot me and they shoot your friends. You're the only one our boss wants,' Russell said.

'But we're not here to kill anyone,' Harold said, very quickly, as if he wanted to be clear on that. If I were staring down a gun barrel that Edward was holding, I'd want to be clear, too.

Russell started walking towards me, even though I had the Browning pointed at his chest.

'Our boss just wants to talk to you, that's all,' Harold said. 'I promise he just wants to talk to the girl.'

I was backing up with the gun held out. Russell was still walking forward very confident. Unless I was willing to shoot him, he wasn't stopping. I did not want to be the one who fired the first shot. People were going to die, and I couldn't control which people that would be.

I could hear the truck now, crunching over the gravel. I did the only thing I could think of, I turned and ran. I heard a surprised, 'Hey,' from behind me. But I was over the edge of the slope and down the other side. I suddenly wasn't worried about tearing my stitches up, or how tired I was. My heart was in my throat, and I found that not only could I walk without falling down, I could run. My mind seemed to be working faster and faster. I saw a dry wash at the base of the slope and a clump of trees to one side. I slid into the wash in a rush of small stones. I landed on all fours, heavy, and was scrambling to my feet before I felt the first trickle of blood down my back. I was behind the trees as I heard Russell slither down the slope behind me.

I couldn't shoot him, but there were other options. I was aiming for the clump of trees. But say what you like about Russell, he could run, because I could hear him doing it. He wasn't going to give me enough time to hide. I ran past the trees and knew that I couldn't outrun him. The adrenaline was already beginning to fade, and the heat folded around me like a hand. I just wasn't up to a long chase today. I had to end it, soon.

I slowed, just a little, one to save energy, and one to let Russell catch up sooner. I took a big breath and prepared. I knew what I wanted to do. But my body had to do it. I couldn't hesitate because my back or my arm or anything else hurt. I risked a glance back, and Russell was almost there, almost on me. I kicked him, full out, straight in the balls. I did it without hesitating, almost without setting up for it, letting his own momentum carry him into me. The shock sent me hopping backward, and I did what I still wasn't smooth at in class, I did a reverse roundhouse kick, to where I thought his face would be, and it was. He'd crumbled, clutching himself, and he went to his knees with the kick. He stayed on all fours shaking his head, but he didn't go down. Dammit!

A voice yelled from up the slope. 'I don't see them.'

There was a long piece of bleached wood on the floor of the wash. I picked it up and hit him twice, hard. He finally slumped on the ground and didn't move. I didn't have time to check for a pulse. The wash stretched straight for about a hundred yards before brush filled the end of it. There was a place in the bank that had washed away more than the rest. It was like a shallow cave. I had a split second to decide which way to go. I took the knife sheath out of my back pocket, and threw it knife and all as far as I could towards the brush. I went for the cave, scrambling on feet and hands like a monkey, keeping low. I was in the cooler shade of the depression when I heard the men coming down the slope.

'I don't see them,' the first man said.

'They went this way,' a woman's voice. Could there be two

female bad guys? I didn't think so. Did that mean that there was one less gun up with Edward and the others? I let the thought go. I had my own problems.

Rocks cascaded down over the overhang like a dry waterfall. At least one of them was coming down directly on top of me. Would the ceiling of the little cave hold the weight? I was already regretting hiding. But the wash stretched open and straight for too far. I'd have never made it to the place where it emptied and there was brush. I just wasn't that fast today. If they thought I'd gone that way and didn't see me, then it would be a good plan. If they turned and spotted me, it was a bad plan. I heard them coming, but the man's voice was right above me. It made me jump. He had to be standing just to the right of the roof. 'Jesus, there's Russell.' He jumped into the wash and started running towards the fallen man.

The woman was more cautious, sliding down into the wash, searching up and down the wash. She was so close, I could have reached out and touched the leg of her jeans. My heart was thundering in my throat, but I'd stopped breathing. I was holding my breath, willing her to go to the men, to walk away, and not look back.

'He's alive,' the man said. Then he was up and moving towards the sheath I'd thrown. 'She went this way.' He went for the brush.

The woman walked towards him.

He was already at the brush, pushing into it.

'Maury, dammit, don't go in there.' She had to jog to have any chance of catching him. She didn't look back to see me crouched in the hole. When her broad back vanished into the brush, and I heard the man curse, I crawled out of the hole and started up the slope on all fours. If the woman and Maury came out now, I would be caught like a black speck on a white sheet of paper. But they didn't come, and I made the top of the slope down from where I'd first entered, crawling on my belly to lie under the sage bushes that edged Edward's front yard.

Something slithered off to my right, and it wasn't human. A snake. A snake had slithered away deeper into the bushes. Shit. Thank you, dear God, that it left. One more problem and I was out of solutions. Of course, now every noise seemed to be reptilian, and crawling on my belly through the thick bushes, the smell of sage thick in the hot air, was a little slice of nightmare. I kept waiting to hear that dry rattle that would tell me I'd used up all my luck. Every twig that brushed my leg seemed to have scales. The only thing that kept me from screaming was the knowledge that someone would probably shoot me before they knew it was me.

By the time I crawled to the very edge of the bushes one painful inch at a time, I was sweating and it was only partially from heat. The sweat stung on my back, and I knew that some of the thicker trickles were blood and not sweat. I could see the yard through the last screen of sage. Things had not improved.

The woman and the new man, Maury, had left the yard, but three others had taken their places. They had the men on their knees. Olaf had his hands laced on his bald head. Bernardo had his one good hand on his head, and his cast raised as high as he could. Edward was the closest to me. Newt was so close I could have put the knife into his foot. Harold was talking into a cell phone. He was waving one hand and had the rifle slung over one arm. He put the phone away from his mouth, and said, 'He says search the house.'

'What for?' one of the new men said. He had dark hair and a revolver.

'For an artifact, something the girl used against the monster.'

'What kind of artifact?' the dark man asked.

'Just do it,' Harold said.

Dark hair grumbled, but he motioned and the two men left to go into the open door of the house. Edward must have unlocked it for them. What the hell had been happening while I was crawling through the bushes?

The three men went into the house. Harold was still talking on the phone. That left just Newt with his .45, and he wasn't even pointing it at anyone's head. It would never get better than this. Any second now the others would come back up the wash or out of the house. I'd have liked to have at least gotten to my knees and plunged the knife into a vital area, but the bushes were too thick. I'd never push to my knees without making all kinds of noise.

If I fired a gun, I'd alert all the others. Shit. I had two knives. I had one idea. I slipped the blade out of my right arm sheath, making sure my left hand had a good grip. Newt's foot was still so temptingly close. I took the invitation. I stabbed the right-hand knife into the foot opposite from his gun. I felt the blade sink into the ground underneath his shoe, as he screamed. I was on my knees behind him, as he tried to twist and bring the gun on me, but he had the gun pointed for someone standing on his left side, and I wasn't there. I plunged the other knife up into his pants, into the front of his pants, my hand between his legs, and I missed. I didn't hit flesh. Fuck. I twitched the blade to the side and felt him, but he wasn't cut. But he was very, very still.

I hissed, 'Don't move.'

He didn't move. He stayed like some kind of awkward statue.

Harold started walking towards us. 'What's wrong, Newt?'

Newt swallowed, and said, 'N – nothing. Thought I saw a snake.'

I whispered, 'Good boy, Newt. If you want to keep the family jewels intact, very quietly hand me your gun.' He let the .45 fall into my hand. I was close enough to whisper to Edward, 'What do you want me to do?'

'Call Harold over.'

'You heard him, Newt,' I said.

The man never argued. 'Hey, Harold, can you come over here a second?'

Harold sighed, snapping the cell phone shut. 'What is it now, Newt?' He was almost even with Edward when he noticed that Newt's gun was gone. I was still hidden behind the larger man's body; even the blade was hidden in the cloth of his pants. 'What the hell?'

Bernardo pulled one of the gold chopsticks out of his hair, and it was a blade that ended in Harold's arm. Edward hit him in the gut, doubled him over, and disarmed him. He stood over him with the rifle. Olaf and Bernardo were on their feet. I don't know what the plan would have been next because we heard the sirens. Police sirens.

'Did you call the cops, Harold?' Edward asked.

'Don't be an ass,' Harold said.

'Anita,' Edward said.

'I didn't call them. I've still got a .45 pointed at you, Newt. Don't get cute.' But I withdrew the blade very carefully and stood up. I kept his gun pointed at his back, but I was beginning to doubt I'd have to shoot anybody. The sirens were almost here.

The three guys came out of the house with their guns in plain sight. They looked to Harold, saw him on the ground, and Edward had the rifle to his shoulder and was sighting down the barrel at them. Their eyes flicked to the cops coming at a fast pace, and back to Edward. They threw their guns down and laced their fingers on their heads without being told. I doubted it was the first time they'd had to do it.

It was an unmarked car with a marked car following it. They skidded to a stop on opposite sides of the black truck and four cops spilled out. Lieutenant Marks, Detective Ramirez, and two uniforms I didn't know. They had guns pointed but looked a little unsure who the bad guys were. Couldn't blame them. We had all the guns.

'Detective Ramirez,' I said. 'Thank God.'

'What's going on?' Marks said, before Ramirez could answer me.

Edward told them that Harold and his men had jumped us and were trying to question us about the mutilation murders. Marks found that fascinating. Edward had known he would. Yes, Ted

Forrester would press assault charges. Any good citizen would. There were enough handcuffs to go around, barely.

'There are two more out there somewhere,' Edward said in his best helpful voice.

'There's one unconscious in the wash that way,' I said.

Everyone looked at me. I didn't have to pretend to be uncomfortable. 'He was chasing me. I thought they were going to kill the others.' I shrugged and winced. 'He's alive.' It sounded like an excuse even to me.

They called for more men to search the area. They called for an ambulance for Harold, Newt, and Russell, when they found him. I'd sat down on the ground, waiting for everyone to do their jobs. I was using both hands to prop myself up. Now that the emergency seemed to be over, I wasn't feeling so good.

Marks was yelling at me. 'You left the hospital against doctor's orders! I don't give a damn, but I want a statement. I want to know exactly what happened at that hospital.'

I looked up at him, and he seemed to be taller than he was, farther away somehow. 'Are you saying that all the lights and sirens were because you were mad at me for not giving a statement before I left the hospital?'

A flush spread up his face, and I knew that that was exactly it. One of the uniforms called, 'Lieutenant.'

'I want that statement today.' He turned and walked away. I hoped he stayed there.

Ramirez knelt beside me. He was wearing his usual, shirtsleeves rolled back, a striped tie at half-mast, around an open collar. 'You all right?'

'No,' I said.

'I went to the hospital today, and you were already gone. That night, the elevator had been turned off because of the fire alarms. I had to double back and get the stairs, and come up behind you. That's why I was late. That's why I wasn't there for you.' For it to be almost the first thing out of his mouth, it must have been bugging him. I liked that.

I managed something close to a smile. 'Thanks for telling me.' I was so hot. The yard seemed to be swimming in heat, as if I were looking at the world through rippling glass.

He touched my back, I think to help me up. He drew his hand away from my shirt. His hand was bloody. He went on all fours, using one hand to raise my shirt. It was so blood-soaked that he had to peel it away from my skin. 'Jesus and Joseph, what the hell have you done to yourself?'

'It doesn't even hurt anymore.' I heard myself saying it from a long way away, then I was sliding over into his arms, his lap. I heard someone call my name, and I finally passed out.

I woke up in the hospital. Doctor Cunningham was bending over me. I thought, 'We have to stop meeting like this,' but didn't even try to say it out loud.

'You've lost blood and had your stitches redone. Do you think you can stay in here long enough for me to actually release you this time?'

I think I smiled. 'Yes, Doctor.'

'Just in case you got any funny ideas about leaving, I've doped you up with enough painkillers to make you feel really good. So sleep, and I'll see you in the morning.'

My eyes fluttered shut once, then opened. Edward was there. He bent over me and whispered, 'Crawling through bushes on your belly, threatening to cut off a man's balls. Such a hard ass.'

My voice came faintly even to me. 'Had to save your ass.'

He bent over me and kissed me on my forehead, or maybe I dreamed that part.

49

Some time during the second day in the hospital they lowered the meds, and I started having the dreams. I was wandering in a maze made up of high green hedges. I was wearing a long, heavy dress, made of white silk. There were heavy things under it, weighting it down. I could feel the tightness of a corset under the dress, and I knew it wasn't my dream. I would never dream of clothing that I had never worn. I stopped running through the green maze, looked up into a flawless blue sky, and shouted, 'Jean-Claude!'

His voice came, rich, seductive. He could do things with his voice that most men couldn't do with their hands. 'Where are you, ma petite? Where are you?'

'You promised to stay out of my dreams.'

'We felt you dying. We felt the marks open. We worried.'

I knew who 'we' was. 'Richard isn't invading my dreams, just you.'

'I have come to warn you. If you had picked up a phone to call us, this would not be necessary.'

I turned and there was a mirror in the middle of the grass and the hedges. It was a full-length mirror with a gilt-edged frame. Very antique, very Louis XIV. My reflection was startling. It wasn't just the clothes. My hair was in some kind of complicated mound, with thick curls hanging down here and there. There was also more of it, and I knew at least some of it was a wig or at least hairpieces. There was even one of those beauty marks on my cheek. I expected to look ridiculous, but I didn't. I looked delicate, like a china doll, but it wasn't ridiculous. My reflection wavered, then grew taller, and it was Jean-Claude in the mirror, and my reflection had vanished.

He was tall, slender, dressed head to foot in white satin, in a suit that matched my dress. Gold brocade glittered down his sleeves, the seams of the pants. White boots rode over his knees tied with huge white and gold ribbons. It was a foppish outfit, sissy to use a modern word, but he didn't look foppish. He looked elegant and at ease like a man who'd pulled off his tie and slipped into something more comfortable. His hair fell in long black banana curls. Only the delicate masculinity of his face and his midnight blue eyes looked normal, familiar.

I shook my head, and the weight of the hair made it awkward. 'I am so out of here,' and I started to reach out to shred the dream.

'Wait, please, ma petite. Truly, I have a warning for you.' He looked up as if seeing the mirror as a sort of prison. 'This is to let you know that I will not touch you. I come only to talk.'

'Then talk.'

'Was it the Master of Albuquerque who harmed you?'

It seemed an odd question. 'No, Itzpapalotl didn't hurt me.'

He winced at her name. 'Do not use her name aloud within this dream.'

'Okay, but she didn't hurt me.'

'But you have seen her?' he asked.

'Yes.'

He looked puzzled, and he lifted a white hat and slapped it against his leg like it was a habitual gesture, though I'd never seen him do it before. But then I'd only seen him in clothes like this once before, and we'd been fighting for our lives, so there really hadn't been time to notice the small stuff.

'Albuquerque is taboo. The high council has declared the city off limits to all vampires and their minions.'

'Why?'

'Because the Master of the City has slain every vampire or minion that has entered her city in the last fifty years.'

I stared at him. 'You're joking.'

'No, ma petite, I do not joke.' He looked worried, no, scared.

'She didn't try anything hostile, Jean-Claude, honest.'

'Then there was a reason for it. Were the police with you?'

'No.'

He shook his head, slapping the hat against his leg again. 'Then she wants something from you.'

'What could she want from me?'

'I do not know.' He slapped the hat against his leg again and stared out at me through the glass wall.

'Has she really killed any vampire that just happened to be passing through?'

'Oui.'

'Why hasn't the council sent someone to kick her ass?'

He looked down, then up, and the fear was in his eyes again. 'The council fears her, I believe.'

Having met three of the council members personally, that raised my eyebrows as far as they would go. 'Why? I mean I know she's powerful, but she's not that powerful.'

'I do not know, ma petite, but I do know they decreed her territory taboo, rather than fight her.'

That was just plain scary. 'It would have been nice to know that before I got here.'

'I know you value your privacy, ma petite. I have not contacted you in all these long months. I have respected your decision, but it is not merely our romance, or lack of it, that is important between us. You are my human servant whether you will or no. It means that you cannot simply enter another vampire's territory without some diplomacy.'

'I'm here on police business. I thought I could enter anyone's territory as long as it was police business. I'm here as Anita Blake, preternatural expert, not as your human servant.'

'Normally, that is true, but the Master whose lands you are in does not obey council decrees. She is a law unto herself.'

'What does that mean for me here and now?'

'Perhaps she fears human law. Perhaps she will not harm you for fear of the humans destroying her. Your authorities can be very effective at times. Or she simply wants something from you. You've met her. What do you think?' he said.

It came to my lips before I thought about it. 'Power, she's attracted to power.'

'You are a necromancer.'

I shook my head, and again the hairpieces made it awkward. I closed my eyes in the dream, and when I opened them, my hair just hung around my shoulders like normal. 'The hair was heavy.'

'It could be,' he said. 'I am happy that you left the dress. I cannot tell you how long I have wished to see you in something like it.'

'Don't push it, Jean-Claude.'

'My apologies,' and he did a sweeping bow, using the hat in the gesture, so that it swept across his chest.

'I think it's more than the necromancy. She figured out that I was part of a triumvirate the first moment she met me. I felt her sift through the three of us, like unwinding a string. She knew. I think that's what she wants. She wants to figure out how it works.'

'Could she repeat it?' he asked.

'She's got a human servant and jaguars are her animal to call. Theoretically, I guess she could, though can you make it a three-way when you've already got marks on a human, and no animal?'

'If the marks are recent, perhaps.'

'No, not recent. They've been a couple a long time.'

'Then no, her human's marks will be too entrenched to stretch for a third.'

'So she may be interested in me for a power she can't have? If she finds out then I can't be of help to her?' I said.

'It would perhaps be best if she did not learn that, ma petite.'

'You think she'd kill me.'

'She has killed all that crossed her path for half a century. I do not see why she should change her ways now.'

. I was standing very close to the mirror now. Close enough that I could see the gold buttons on his jacket, and the rise and fall of his chest as he drew breath. This was the closest I'd been to him in months. It was just a dream, but we both knew it wasn't just a dream. He'd put the mirror barrier between us because once we'd used our dreams to enter each other's fantasies. He'd come like a demon lover in my dreams, in my sleep. We'd done the real thing, too, but the dreams had been sweet, sometimes a prelude to the real thing, sometimes an end in themselves.

The glass grew thinner, as if the glass were wearing away. It was like a thin pane of spun sugar. He touched fingertips to it, and the glass moved like clear plastic, giving at his touch.

My fingertips touched his, and the thin barrier vanished. Our fingers touched, and it was startling, electric. His fingers slid over mine, entwining, our palms touching, and even that one chaste touch sent my breath racing.

I stepped back but didn't let go of his hand, so the movement drew him out of the mirror. He stepped out of the golden frame and was suddenly standing in front of me, our hands still raised in front of us. I could feel his heart beating through his palm, feel the rise and pulse of his body through my hand as if all of him were contained in that one pale hand where it lay pressed against mine.

He leaned down towards me, as if to kiss me, and I started to pull away, afraid, but the dream shattered, and I was suddenly awake, staring up at the hospital ceiling. A nurse was in the room, checking my vitals. She'd woken me. I wasn't sure whether I was glad or sad.

The marks had been open for less than a week, and Jean-Claude was already pushing me. Okay, okay, I needed the warning, but . . . Oh, hell. My teacher, Marianne, had told me that I couldn't just ignore the boys, that that would be dangerous. I thought she meant ignoring the power that bound us, but maybe she meant more than that. I was Jean-Claude's human servant, and that made things complicated when I traveled. Each vampire's territory was like a foreign country. Sometimes you had diplomatic treaties between them. Sometimes you didn't. Occasionally, you just had a couple of master vamps that were enemies pure and simple, so if you belonged to one, you stayed the hell out of the other one's lands. By refusing to contact Jean-Claude, I could screw up, get myself killed or held hostage. But I'd thought I was safe as long as I was on police business or animating zombies. That was work. It had nothing to do with Jean-Claude and vampire politics. But I could always be wrong, like now.

Why, you may ask, did I believe Jean-Claude and his warning? Because it gained him nothing to lie about it. I'd also felt his fear. One of the things about the marks, you could usually tell what the other person was feeling. Sometimes that bugged me. Sometimes it was helpful.

The nurse shoved a thermometer with a little plastic sheath on it under my tongue. She took my pulse while we waited for the thermometer to beep. What really bugged me about the dream was how attracted to him I was. When I had the marks closed off, I'd have never touched him in the dream. Of course, I hadn't let him enter my dreams when I had the marks blocked off. With the barriers up, I'd policed my dreams, kept him and Richard out. I could still keep them out, but it took more work to do it. I was out of practice. I was going to have to get back into practice, fast.

The thermometer beeped. The nurse read the little monitor on her belt, gave me an empty smile that could have meant anything, and made a note. 'I hear you're getting out of here today.'

I looked up at her. 'I am? Great.'

'Doctor Cunningham will be in to see you before you leave.' She smiled again. 'He seems to want to oversee your release personally.'

'I'm one of his favorite patients,' I said.

The nurse's smile slipped just a touch. I think she knew exactly what Doctor Cunningham thought of me. 'He should be in to see you soon.'

'But I am definitely getting out of here today?' I asked.

'That's what I hear.'

'Can I call a friend to come pick me up?'

'I can call them for you.'

'If I'm getting out today, can't I have a phone?' The good doctor had made sure there was no phone in my room because he didn't want me trying to do work, any work, not even business phone calls. When I'd promised not to use the phone if he'd just give me one, he'd just looked at me, made some kind of note in his file, and left. I don't think he trusted me.

'If the doctor says you can have a phone, I'll bring you one, but just in case, give me the number and I'll contact your friend.'

I gave her Edward's number. She wrote it down, smiled, and left.

There was a knock on the door. I expected Doctor Cunningham, but it was Detective Ramirez. His shirt today was a pale tan. The half-mast tie was deep brown with a small white and yellow design on it. But he'd also kept on a brown suit jacket that matched his pants. It was the first time I'd seen him with an entire suit on at once. I wondered if the sleeves were rolled up underneath the jacket sleeves. He had a bouquet of shiny Mylar balloons with cartoon characters on them. The balloons said things like 'get well soon,' and 'oh, bother.' That was the Winnie the Pooh balloon.

I had to smile. 'You already sent flowers.' There was a small, but nice arrangement running long to daisies and miniature carnations on the bedside table.

'I wanted to bring something in person. I'm sorry I wasn't here sooner.'

My smile wilted around the edges. 'This level of apology is usually reserved for boyfriends or lovers, detective. Why are you feeling so guilty?'

'I keep having to remind you to call me Hernando.'

'I keep forgetting.'

'No, you don't. You keep trying to distance yourself.'

I just looked at him. It was probably true. 'Maybe.'

'If I was your lover, I'd have followed you to the hospital and been by your side every minute,' he said.

'Even with a murder investigation going on?' I asked.

He had the grace to shrug and look sheepish. 'I'd have tried to be here every minute.'

'What's been happening while I've been in here? My doctor has made sure I haven't found out anything.'

Ramirez put the balloons beside the flowers. The balloons had one of those little weights on them to keep them from drifting away. 'The last time I tried to see you, your doctor made me promise not to talk about the case.'

'I didn't know you were here before.'

'You were pretty out of it.'

'Was I awake?'

He shook his head.

Great. I wondered how many other people had paraded through here while I was passed out cold. 'I'm getting out today, so I think it's safe to talk about the case.'

He looked at me, and the expression was enough. He didn't believe me.

'Doesn't anyone trust me?'

'You're like most of the cops I know. You never really get off work.'

I raised my hand in the Boy Scout's salute. 'Honest, the nurse told me I'm being released today.'

He smiled. 'I saw your back, remember. Even if you're being let out, you won't be going back on the case, not in person anyway.'

'What? I'm going to look at pictures and listen to the clues that other people find?'

He nodded. 'Something like that.'

'Do I look like Nero Wolfe? I am not a staying at home, out of the firing line, kind of girl.'

He laughed, and it was still a good laugh. A nice normal laugh. It had none of Jean-Claude's touchable sex appeal, but in some ways I liked it better for its very normalcy. But . . . but as nice and warm as Ramirez was, I had the memory of Jean-Claude's dream in my head. I could feel the touch of his hand on mine, a touch that lingered on my skin the way an expensive perfume will linger in a room long after the woman who wears it is gone.

Maybe it was love, but whatever it was, it was hard to find a man who could compete with it, no matter how much I wanted to find one. It was as if when he was with me, all other men just faded into the background, except Richard. Was that what it meant to be in love? Was it? I wish I knew.

'What are you thinking about?' Ramirez asked.

'Nothing.'

'Whatever that nothing is, it makes you look very serious, almost sad.' He'd moved very close to the bed, fingers touching the edge of the sheet. His face was gentle, questioning, very open. I realized in a way that Ramirez had my ticket. He knew what punched my buttons, partly just coincidence, partly he read me well. He read what I liked and what I hated in a man better than Jean-Claude had for years. I liked honesty, openness, and a sort of little boy charm. There were other things that led to lust, but for my heart that was the way. Jean-

Claude was almost never open about anything. He always had a dozen different motives for everything he did. Honesty was not his best thing, and his little boy charm . . . nope. Jean-Claude had gotten there first, and for better or worse that was the way things were.

Maybe a little honesty would work here, too. 'I'm wondering how different my life would be if I'd met you or someone like you first.'

'First, that implies that you've already met someone.'

'I told you I had two guys back home.'

'You also said you couldn't decide between them. My grandmother always said that the only reason a woman hesitates between two men is that she hasn't met the right one.'

'Your grandmother didn't say that.'

He nodded. 'Yes, she did. She was being courted by two men, sort of halfway engaged to both, then she met my grandfather and she knew why she'd been hesitating. She didn't love either of the two men.'

I sighed. 'Don't tell me I've got caught up in some family folklore?'

'You never said you were taken. Tell me I'm wasting my time and I'll stop.'

I looked up at him, really looked at him, let my eyes follow the smiling line of his face, the shining humor in his eyes. 'You're wasting your time. I am sorry, but I think you are.'

'Think?'

I shook my head. 'Stop it, Hernando. I'm taken, okay.'

'You're not taken until you make a final choice, but that's okay. I'm not the one. If I were, you'd know it. When you meet him, you won't have any doubts.'

'Don't tell me you believe in true love, soul mate kind of stuff.'

He shrugged, fingers running up and down the edge of the sheet. 'What can I say? I was raised on stories about love at first sight. My grandmother, both my parents, even my great-grandfather said the same thing. They met that special person, and no one else existed after that.'

'You're descended from a family of romantics,' I said.

He nodded happily. 'My great-grandfather, Poppy, talked about my great-grandmother like they were still school kids right up until he died.'

'It sounds nice, really, but I don't believe in true love, Hernando. I don't believe that there's only one special person for your whole life's happiness.'

'You don't want to believe it,' he said.

I shook my head. 'This is about to go from cute to irritating, Hernando.'

'At least you're using my first name.'

'Maybe because I don't see you as a threat anymore.'

'A threat? Just because I like you? Just because I asked you out?' He frowned when he said it.

It was my turn to shrug. 'Whatever I mean, Hernando, just cut the juice. It ain't going nowhere. Whatever I decide, it's between the two guys I have waiting for me back home.'

'It sounds like you weren't sure of that until just now.'

I thought about that for a heartbeat, or two. 'You know, I think you're right. I think I've been looking around for someone else, anyone else. But it's no good.'

'You don't sound happy about that. Love should make you happy, Anita.'

I smiled and knew it was wistful. 'If you think love makes you happy, Hernando, you've either never been in love, or never been in love long enough to have to start compromising.'

'You're not old enough to be this cynical.'

'It's not cynicism. It's reality.'

His face was soft and sad. 'You've lost your sense of romance.'

'I never had a sense of romance. Trust me, the guys at home will back me on it.'

'Then I'm even sorrier.'

'Don't take this wrong, but hearing you go on about true love and romance, makes me sorry for you. You are setting yourself up for the big fall, Hernando.'

'Not if it works out,' he said.

I smiled and shook my head. 'Isn't it against the rules for homicide detectives to be naive?'

'You think it's naive?' he asked.

'I know it is, but it's sweet. I wish you luck finding your Ms Right.'

The door opened and it was Doctor Cunningham. Ramirez asked, 'Does she really get out today, Doctor?'

'Yes, she does.'

'Why doesn't anyone believe me?' I asked.

They both looked at me. Funny how quickly people caught onto certain aspects of my personality. 'I want to do one more check on your back, then you're free to go.'

'You got a ride out of here?' Ramirez asked.

'I asked the nurse to call Ted, but I don't know if she did, or if he's home.'

'I'll wait around to give you a ride.' Before I could say anything, he added, 'What are friends for?'

'Thanks, and this means you can fill me in on the case on the way out.'

'You never give up, do you?'

'Not about a case,' I said.

Ramirez walked out shaking his head, giving the doctor and me some privacy. Dr Cunningham poked and prodded, and finally just ran his hands over my back. It was nearly healed. 'It's just impressive. I've treated lycanthropes before, Ms Blake, and you're healing almost that fast.'

I flexed my left hand, stretching the skin where the bite mark still showed where the flayed one had bitten me. The bite was pale pink, settling into a nice ordinary scar, only weeks ahead of schedule. I wondered if the scar would eventually disappear, or if it would be another permanent one.

'I've done a blood workup on you. I even snuck some of your blood down to the genetics department and had them look for something not human.'

'Genetic work takes weeks or months,' I said.

'I've got a friend in the department.'

'Some friend,' I said.

He smiled and it was warmer than it should have been. 'She is.'

'So I'm free to go?'

'You are.' His face got all serious again. 'But I'd still like to know what the hell you are.'

'You wouldn't believe human?'

'Forty-eight hours after your second injury, we had to remove the stitches from your back because the skin was starting to grow over them. No, I won't believe human.'

'It's too long a story, Doc. If it was something I could teach you to use on other people, I'd tell, but it's not that kind of thing. You might call the healing a bonus for some other less pleasant shit that I put up with.'

'Unless the other shit is really awful, the healing makes up for it. You'd never have survived the original injuries if you'd been human.'

'Maybe.'

'No maybe,' he said.

'I'm glad to be alive. I'm glad to be nearly healed. I'm glad it didn't take months to recover. What more do you want me to say?'

He draped his stethoscope over his shoulders, holding onto the ends, frowning at me. 'Nothing. I'll tell Detective Ramirez that he can tell you about the case now and that you are getting out today.' He glanced at the flowers and the balloons. 'You've been here, what, five days?'

'Something like that.'

He touched a balloon, making them bounce on their strings. 'You work fast.'

'I don't think it's me that works fast.'

He gave the balloons one more whack so they bobbed and weaved like some underwater creature. 'Whatever, enjoy your stay in Albuquerque. Try to stay healthy.' With that he left, and Ramirez came back in.

'Doctor says I can talk about the case with you again.'

'Yep.'

'You're not going to like it.' He looked all serious.

'What's happened?'

'There's been another murder, and not only are you not invited to the scene, neither am I.'

50

'What are you talking about?'

'Marks is in charge of the case. He has the right to use his resources as he sees fit.'

'Stop talking political rhetoric and tell me what the little shithead has done now.'

He smiled. 'Okay. The men assigned to the case are one of those resources. He decided that I was best used at the police property room going over the items that we've confiscated from the victims' homes, and matching them to the pictures and video we have of some of the houses before the murders.'

'Pictures and videos for what?' I asked.

'Insurance purposes. A lot of the houses hit had enough rare and antique pieces that they insured them, and that meant they needed proof that they had the pieces to begin with.'

'What pieces did you find in the last scene I was at, the one on the ranch?'

The smile didn't change, but the eyes did. They went from pleasant to shrewd. 'It's not just that you're cute. I like the way you think.'

'Just tell me.'

'There were a lot of similar pieces since most of the people had collected things from this area, or the southwest in general, but nothing out of the ordinary. Except for this.' He reached behind his back underneath the suit jacket and pulled a manila envelope out that must have been inside his belt underneath the jacket.

'I knew you had to be wearing the suit jacket for some reason.'

He laughed. He unfolded the envelope and spilled out pictures into my lap. Half of them were semiprofessional shots of a small carved piece of turquoise. A glance and I wanted to say Mayan, Aztec, something like that. I still couldn't tell the difference at a glance. The second set were a few better shots of the object in the study of the man that had been killed. The one that had used salt to interrupt the critter. Then a series of Polaroids, taken from every angle.

'You took the Polaroids?' I asked.

He nodded. 'This afternoon after he decided my best use was not at the murder site.'

I lifted one of the first series of pictures. 'These are sitting on a wooden surface, much better light, natural, I think. Insurance pictures?'

He nodded.

'Who did it belong to?'

'The first house you saw.'

'The Bromwells',' I said.

He lifted another picture. 'This one was from the Carsons', and that's it. Either no one else owned one, or they didn't think to get it insured.'

'Did the people who didn't try to get it insured, try to insure their other pieces?'

'Yes.'

'Shit,' I said. 'I don't know much about this stuff, but I know that it's valuable. Why wouldn't they try to insure it, if they owned one?'

'What if they thought it was hot?'

'Illegal? Why would they think that?' I asked.

'Maybe because of the two houses we can prove had it, their history of the piece – where they got it and when – isn't real.'

'What do you mean?'

'Something like this doesn't just show up. It has to have a history if you want it insured. They gave their papers, what they'd been given to the insurance company, and just a little investigation showed that the people that were supposed to have unearthed the piece, sold the piece, had never heard of it.'

'They refused to insure it,' I said.

'Yes.' There was something in his face, a suppressed excitement like a kid with a secret.

'You're holding something back. What is it?'

'You know what Riker is?'

'He's a pot hunter, an illegal dealer in artifacts.'

'Why would he be so interested in you and this case?'

'I have no idea.' I looked at the pictures in my lap. 'You're saying that he sold these to the victims?'

'Not him personally, but Thad Bromwell, the teenage son, he was with his mother when she purchased it. It was a present for Mr Bromwell's birthday. They bought it from a shop that is a known associate of Riker. It takes pieces and makes them look legit.'

'Have you talked to the shop owner?'

'Unless you've got a ouija board, we're not going to be talking to him.'

'He's the newest victim,' I said.

Ramirez nodded, smiling. 'You got it.'

I shook my head. 'Okay, Riker is unusually interested in the case. He wanted to see me specifically about it. At least two of the victims are people who bought one of his pieces. The shop owner that sold it is dead now, too.' I looked up at him. 'Is it enough for a warrant?'

'We already searched his house. Riker's men are suspected in the killing of two local cops. It wasn't hard to find a judge that would give us a warrant on the crap they pulled out at Ted's house.'

'What the hell did the warrant give you permission to search for? They didn't mention stolen artifacts at Ted's house. They just pointed guns at us and said Riker wanted to talk about the case.'

'The warrant was to search for weapons.'

I shook my head. 'So even if you found stolen artifacts, you wouldn't be able to use them in court.'

'It was just an excuse to search the house, Anita. You know how that goes.'

'Did you find anything?'

'A few guns, two without license, but the warrant didn't allow us to knock down walls or destroy things. We couldn't pull up carpet or pull down shelves. Riker has a secret cache of artifacts, but we didn't find it.'

'Was Ted with you on the search?'

'Yes, he was.' He was frowning now.

'What's wrong?'

'Ted wanted to take a sledge hammer to some of the walls. He seemed pretty certain there was a hidden room in the lower areas, but we couldn't find a way to open it.'

'And the warrant didn't allow you to tear up things,' I said.

'No.'

'What did Riker think of all the fun?'

'He had his lawyer screaming about harassment. Ted got up in his face, not yelling, but in his face, speaking real quiet. The lawyer said he threatened Riker, but Riker wouldn't back it up. He wouldn't say what Ted had said to him.'

'You think he threatened him?'

'Oh, yeah.'

It wasn't like Edward to threaten anyone, especially in front of the police. The case really was getting to him. 'So what the hell are these little figures?'

'No one knows. According to experts, they are Aztec, but very late period like after the conquest.'

'Wait a minute, you mean these were carved after the Spanish came and kicked the Aztecs' butts?'

'Not after, but right about the same time.'

'Who was your expert?'

He mentioned a name I wasn't familiar with at the university. 'Does it matter who it was?'

'I thought you were using Professor Dallas.'

'Marks thinks she's spending too much time with the unholy demons.'

'If he means Obsidian Butterfly, then I agree. Marks and I agreeing on anything. Jeez, that's almost scary.'

'So you think she's a contaminated source, too.'

'I think Dallas thinks the sun shines out of Itzpapalotl's butt, so yeah. Have you shown any of these pictures to Dallas?'

He nodded. 'The ones from the Bromwells'.'

'What did she say?'

'That it was a fake.'

I raised eyebrows at him. 'What's the other expert think?'

'That he understands why someone would think it was a fake just from pictures. The figure has rubies for eyes, and the Aztecs didn't have access to rubies. So just from pictures, you might assume it was a fake.'

'I hear a "but" coming,' I said.

'Doctor Martinez got to hold it in his hand, look at it up close, and he thinks it's authentic, something made after the Spaniards arrived.'

'I didn't think anything was made after the Spaniards arrived. Didn't they destroy everything?'

'If these are authentic, then apparently not. Doctor Martinez says that he'll need more tests to be a hundred percent sure.'

'Cautious man.'

'Most academics are.'

I shrugged. Some were. Some weren't. 'So let's say for argument's sake that Riker found these things, and he sold them to some people who knew they were hot, or suspected they were, and sold some to shops that passed them off as legit. Now something is killing off the customers and following the trail back to Riker. Is that what he's afraid of?'

'Sounds reasonable,' Ramirez said.

I started looking through the Polaroids. They were back and front shots, not great pics, but from every angle. It looked like the figure was wearing armor, sort of. Its hands held long thick strings of things. 'What did Martinez say this figure's holding?'

'He wasn't sure.'

There were people curled around its feet, but they were thin and sticklike, not fat and square like the figure itself. The eyes were rubies, the mouth open and full of teeth. There was a long tongue coming out of the mouth, and what looked like blood pouring from the mouth. 'Nasty looking.'

'Yeah.' He picked up one of the pictures from the sheet, staring at it as he spoke. 'Do you think this thing is out there killing people?'

I looked at him. 'An Aztec god, as in the real deal, out there slaughtering people?'

He nodded, still staring at the picture.

'If you mean a real god with a capital G, then I'm a monotheist, so no. If you mean some kind of preternatural nasty associated with this particular god, then why not?'

He looked up then. 'Why not?'

I shrugged. 'You were expecting a definitive yes or no? I don't know much about Aztec pantheon stuff, except that most of the deities were big and bad and required sacrifice, usually human. They don't have much in their pantheon that isn't a major god. Something big and bad enough that you don't fight it, you just try and stop it with magic or sacrifice, or you die. And whatever this thing is that's been doing the killings, it's not that bad.'

I remembered what Nicky Baco had said, that the voice in his head was still trapped, that what had been doing the killings was just a minion, not the real deal.

'You're all serious again. What did you just think of?' Ramirez asked.

I looked up at him and tried to decide how much of a cop he was, and how much of a player he would be. I could never have told Dolph. He'd have used the info for strict cop stuff. 'I have information from an informant that I don't want to name right now. But I think you need to know what was said.'

His own face was solemn now. 'Did you obtain this information legally?'

'I did nothing illegal to obtain this information.'

'Not exactly a no,' he said.

'Do you want it or not?'

He took a deep breath and blew it out slow. 'Yeah, I want it.'

I told him what Nicky had said about the voice and the thing being trapped. I finished with, 'I don't believe in a real god, but I do believe there are things out there so terrible that once upon a time they were worshipped as gods.'

'Are you saying that we haven't seen the worst of it?'

'If what is doing the killings is just a minion, and the master isn't up and around yet, then yeah, I'm saying the worst is yet to come.'

'I'd really like to talk to this informant.'

'You would be dandy, but Marks would have this informant up on charges so fast, we'd never find out what this person knew. Once you slap an automatic death sentence on someone, they tend not to cooperate.'

We looked at each other. 'There's only one person you've talked to that has a rep to get himself an automatic death sentence. That's Nicky Baco.'

I didn't even blink. It wasn't like I hadn't known he'd figure it out. I was ready for it, and I'd gotten much better at lying. 'You have no idea who I've talked to since I arrived. I've talked to at least three people that could be put up on charges with a death sentence attached.'

'Three?' He made it a question.

I nodded. 'At least.'

'Either you are a better liar than I thought you were, or you're telling the truth.'

I just looked up at him, giving him a blank but earnest face. Even my eyes were quiet and able to meet his gaze, no flinching. There had been a time, not long ago, when I couldn't have pulled it off. But that was then, and I wasn't the same person anymore.

'All right, if there is some sort of Aztec god out there, what do we do about it?'

There was only one answer. 'Itzpapalotl should know what this is.'

'We questioned her about the killings.'

'So did I.'

He looked at me long and hard. 'You went without police backup, and you didn't share what you found.'

'I didn't find anything about the murders. She told me about what she told you, nothing. But when I talked to her, she stressed that no deity she knew of would flay people and keep them alive. Later I figured out that they were dead. She stressed that only through death could the sacrifice be a suitable messenger to the gods. She repeated almost word for word that she didn't know a being or god that would flay people and keep them alive. Maybe we should go back and ask her if she knows of any deity or creature that would flay people and not keep them alive.'

'Oh, you're inviting the police now.'

'I'm inviting you,' I said.

He started picking up the pictures and shoving them back in the envelope. 'I took the pictures out of the property room, but I signed for them. I brought Doctor Martinez in to see the statue, but it was official. I haven't done anything wrong, yet.'

'Marks is going to be so pissed that you found out important stuff when he meant to just get you out of the way.'

Ramirez smiled, but it wasn't exactly a pleased smile. 'I've got better than that. Marks will take credit for the brilliant idea of putting one of his senior detectives on special detail to investigate the relics.'

'You're kidding me.'

'He did send me to the property room to look at what we took from the victims' houses.'

'But he did it to humiliate you and get you out of the way.'

'But that's not what he said out loud. Out loud it's going to make him seem inspired.'

'He's done shit like this before, I take it.'

Ramirez nodded. 'He's a very good politician, and when he's not on his right-wing high horse, he's a good detective.'

'Fine. You mentioned that I wasn't allowed on the murder scene either. What gives there?'

'Well, we all thought you were still out of the game, but he got Ted and company excluded by getting the powers that be to agree that Ted hadn't been a big help on the case, and that without you, his newest expert, Ted wasn't necessary on the murder scene.'

'Oh, I bet Ted's going to love that.'

Ramirez nodded. 'He was very . . . unprofessional, or unlike himself when we searched Riker's place. I've never seen Ted so . . .' Ramirez shook his head. 'I don't know, he just seemed different, close to the edge.'

Edward had let a little of his real self peek out where the police could see. He had to be under immense pressure to be screwing up like that, or he thought that it was necessary. Either way, things were bad when Ted started losing focus and Edward's real self came through, accident or on purpose.

The door opened, no knock. It was Edward.

'Speak of the devil,' I said.

His Edward face had been on, and I watched it move like liquid into Ted, smiling, but still weary around the eyes. 'Detective Ramirez, I didn't know you were here.'

They shook hands. 'I was just filling Anita in on some of the things she's missed.'

'You tell her about the search at Riker's?'

Ramirez nodded.

Edward hefted a gym bag. 'Clothes.'

'You didn't have time to drive from your house to here since the nurse called.'

'I packed the bag the night you went in the hospital. I've been riding around with it in my Hummer ever since.'

We looked at each other, and there was a weight of things unsaid and unsayable in front of company. Maybe it showed, or maybe Ramirez just felt it. 'I'll leave you two alone. You probably have things to talk about. Mystery informants and things like that.' He went for the door.

I called after him. 'Don't go far, Hernando. When I'm dressed, we'll go see Obsidian Butterfly.'

'Only if it's official, Anita. I go in, and we call for uniform backup.'

It was our turn for solid eye contact and the weight of wills. I blinked first. 'Fine, we go in with the cops like good little boys and girls.'

He flashed that warm smile that he could draw from his bag anytime he wanted, or maybe it was real and my cynical nature was showing. 'Good, I'll wait outside.' He hesitated, then walked back and handed the envelope to Edward. He looked at me one more time then walked out.

Edward opened the envelope and looked inside. 'What is this?'

'The link, I think.' I explained what Ramirez and I had been discussing, about Riker and why he might be interested in the case on a very personal level.

'That would mean that Obsidian Butterfly lied to us,' he said.

'No, she never lied. She said she knew of no deity or creature that would flay people and keep them alive. They aren't alive. They're dead. Technically, it wasn't a lie.'

Edward smiled. 'That is cutting it very thin.'

'She's a nine hundred, nearly a thousand-year-old vampire. They tend to cut the truth pretty thin.'

'I hope you like what I picked out for you to wear.'

The way he said it made me start pulling things out of the gym bag. Black jeans, black scoop-neck T-shirt, black jogging socks, black Nikes, a black leather belt, my black suit jacket, the worse for being folded for two days, black bra, black satin panties – Jean-Claude had been a bad influence on my clothing – and under it all was the Browning, the Firestar, all the knives, an extra clip for the Browning, two boxes of ammo, and a new shoulder rig. It was one of the lightweight nylon ones with the holster itself angled for the front carry, downward draw that I favored. I always needed one with a very sharp downward angle to avoid scraping my breast every time I drew the gun. I'd found that the millisecond I lost from the angle was made up for from the second I lost every time I went past my breast and had the flinch reaction. Concealed carry is the art of compromise.

'I know you like leather, but most of those would have to be tailored down for you. The straps on the nylon ones can be adjusted down smaller,' Edward said.

'Thanks, Edward. I was missing my rig.' I looked at him, trying to read past the neutral baby blues. 'Why this much ammo?'

'Better to not need and have it,' he said.

I frowned at him. 'Are we going someplace where I'll need this much ammo?'

'If I thought that, I'd have packed the mini-Uzi and the sawed-off shotgun. This is just the normal stuff you carry.'

I drew the big blade that would have normally rode down my back. 'When they cut off the shoulder holster, they cut through the rig for this, too.'

'Was it a specialty item?'

I nodded.

'I thought it must be because I asked around and no one had a sheath for concealment of something that large for the back, especially not when you throw in how damn narrow you are through the shoulders.'

'It was a custom job.' I laid the big knife back in the bag, almost sadly. 'There's no way to conceal this thing without a rig for it.'

'Did the best I could.'

I smiled at him. 'No, it's great. I mean it.'

'Why are we taking the police in with us to Obsidian Butterfly?'

I told him what Jean-Claude had told me, though not how the message had gotten through. 'With the police at our backs, she'll know it's not vampire politics and we'll probably be able to walk out without a fight.'

He was leaning against the wall, arms crossed. The white shirt didn't quite lay smooth over the front of him. His gun was showing but only if you knew what you were looking for. A paddle holster or a clip holster because the gun was riding outside the pants. It explained why the white shirt wasn't tucked in, and the fact that he was wearing a T-shirt under the shirt probably meant that he had something on him that would chafe without cloth between it and his skin.

'You still carrying that band of throwing darts?' I asked.

'You can't see it, not with the shirt untucked.' He didn't even try to deny it. Why should he?

'Because you're wearing an undershirt, and because the shirt is untucked. I know, it's partially to hide the gun, but you never wear an undershirt, so you've got to be wearing something under the shirt that would chafe without the undershirt.'

He smiled, and it was a pleased smile, almost proud, as if I'd done something smart. 'I'm carrying two more guns, a knife, and a garrote. Tell me where they are and I'll give you a prize.'

My eyes had gone wide. 'A garrote. Even for you that's a little Psychos 'R Us.'

'Give up?'

'No. Is there a time limit?'

He shook his head. 'We've got all night.'

'If I guess wrong, is there a penalty?'

He shook his head.

'What's the prize if I figure out where everything is?'

He smiled that close, secretive smile that said he knew things that I didn't. 'It's a surprise prize.'

'Get out so I can get dressed.'

He touched the belt where it lay on the bed. 'This buckle didn't come black. Who painted it?'

'I did.'

'Why?'

He knew the answer. 'So that if I'm out after dark, the buckle doesn't catch the light and give me away.' I lifted the tail of his white shirt exposing the large ornate silver belt buckle. 'This is like a freaking target after dark.'

He looked down at me, making no move to lower the shirt. 'It just clips on over the real buckle.'

I let the shirt slide back. 'The buckle underneath?'

'It's blacked,' he said.

We smiled at each other. It went all the way to our eyes. We did like each other. We were friends. 'Sometimes I think I don't want to be you when I grow up, Edward, sometimes I think it's too late, I'm already there.'

The smile faded, leaving his eyes the color of winter skies and just as pitiless.

'Only you decide how far gone you are, Anita. Only you can decide how far you'll go.'

I looked at the weapons and the black clothing like funeral clothes, even down to the things that touched my skin. 'Maybe it would be a start if I bought something pink.'

'Pink?' Edward said.

'Yeah, you know, pink, like Easter Bunny grass.'

'Like cotton candy,' he said. 'Or almost everything women give each other at baby showers.'

'When were you at a baby shower?' I asked.

'Donna's taken me to two of them. It's the new thing, couples baby showers.'

I looked at him, eyes wide. 'You, at a couples baby shower, Edward.'

'You in something the color of children's candy and baby doll clothes.' He shook his head. 'Anita, you are one of the least pink women I've ever met.'

'When I was a little girl, I'd have given a small body part to have a pink canopy bed, and ballerina wallpaper would have been perfect.'

He gave me wide, surprised eyes. 'You, in a pink canopy bed with ballerina wallpaper.' He shook his head. 'Just trying to imagine you in a room like that gives me a headache.'

I looked at the things spread on the bed. 'I was pink once, Edward.'

'Most of us start off soft,' he said, 'but you can't stay that way, not and survive.'

'There's got to be someplace I won't go, something I won't do, some line I won't cross, Edward.'

'Why?' That one word held more curiosity than he usually allowed himself.

'Because if I don't have any lines, limits, then what kind of person does that make me?' I asked.

He shook his head, moving the cowboy hat low on his head. 'You're having a crisis of conscience.'

I nodded. 'Yeah, I guess I am.'

'Don't go soft, Anita, not on my dime. I need you to do what you do best, and what you do best isn't soft or gentle or kind. What you do best is what I do best.'

'And what is that? What is it that we do best?' I asked, and I knew the anger came through in my voice. I was getting angry with Edward.

'We do what it takes, whatever it takes, to get the job done.'

'There's got to be more to life than the ultimate practicality, Edward.'

'If it makes you feel any better, we have different motives. I do what I do because I love it. It's not just what I do. It's who I am. You do the job to save lives, to keep the damage down.' He looked at me with eyes gone as empty and bottomless as any vampire's. 'But you love it, too, Anita. You love it, and that bothers you.'

'Violence is one of my top three responses now, Edward, maybe my number one.'

'And it's kept you alive.'

'At what price?'

He shook his head, and now the blankness was replaced by anger. He was just suddenly moving forward. I caught his hand going under the shirt, and I was rolling off the bed, with the Browning in my hand. I had a round in the chamber and was falling back onto the floor with the gun pointed up, eyes searching for movement.

He was gone.

My heart was thudding so loudly that I could barely hear, and I was straining to hear. A movement, something. He had to be on the bed. It was the only place he could have gone. From my angle I couldn't see anything on top of the bed, just the corner of the mattress and the trail of sheet.

Knowing Edward, the ammo in the Browning was probably his homemade brew, which meant that it would pierce the bottom of the bed and go up into whatever lay on top of the bed. I felt the last of the air in my body slide outward, and I sighted on the underneath of the bed. The first bullet would either hit him or make him move, then I'd have a better idea of where he was.

'Don't shoot, Anita.'

His voice made me move the gun barrel just a touch more right. It would take him mid-body because he was crouched up there, not lying down. I knew that without seeing it.

'It was a test, Anita. If I wanted to come against you, I'd warn you first, you know that.'

I did know that, but . . . I heard the bed creak. 'Don't move, Edward. I mean it.'

'You think you can just decide to turn all this off. You can't. The genie is out of the bottle for you, Anita, just like it is for me. You can't unmake yourself. Think of all the effort, all the pain, that went into making you who you are. Do you really want to throw all that away?'

I was lying flat on my back, gun pointed two-handed. The floor was cold where the gown had gaped at my back. 'No,' I said, finally.

'If your heart starts bleeding for all the bad things you do, it won't be the last thing that bleeds.'

'You really did this to test me. You son of a bitch.'

'Can I move now?'

I took my finger off the trigger and sat up on the floor. 'Yeah, you can move.'

He eased back off the other side of the bed as I stood up on this one. 'Did you see how fast you went for the gun? You knew where it was, you had the safety off and a round chambered, and you were looking for cover, and trying to target me.' Again there was that pride, like a teacher with a favorite student.

I looked across at him. 'Don't ever do anything like that again, Edward.'

'A threat?' he asked.

I shook my head. 'No threat, just instinct. I came so close to putting a bullet through the bed and into you.'

'And while you were doing it, your conscience wasn't bothering you. You weren't thinking, "It's Edward. I'm about to shoot my friend."'

'No,' I said. 'I wasn't thinking anything but how to get the best shot possible before you had time to shoot me.' It didn't make me happy to say it. It felt like I'd been mourning dead pieces of myself, and Edward's little demonstration had confirmed the deaths. It made me sad, and a little depressed, and not happy with Edward.

'I knew a man once who was as good as you are,' Edward said. 'He started second-guessing himself, worrying about whether he was a bad person. It got him killed. I don't want to see you dead because you hesitated. If I have to bury you, then I want it to be because someone was just that good or that lucky.'

'I want to be cremated,' I said, 'not buried.'

'Good little Christian, fallen Catholic, practicing Episcopalian, and you want to be cremated.'

'I don't want anyone trying to raise me from the dead or stealing body parts for spells. Just burn it all, thanks.'

'Cremated. I'll remember.'

'How about you, Edward? Where do you want the body shipped?'

'It doesn't matter,' he said. 'I'll be dead, and I won't care.'

'No family?'

'Just Donna and the kids.'

'They are not your family, Edward.'

'Maybe they will be.'

I put the safety on the Browning. 'We don't have time to discuss your love life and my moral crisis. Get out so I can get dressed.'

He had his hand on the door when he turned. 'Speaking of love life, Richard Zeeman called.'

That got my attention. 'What do you mean Richard called?'

'He seemed to know that something bad had happened to you. He was worried.'

'When did he call?'

'Earlier tonight.'

'Did he say anything else?'

'That he'd finally called Ronnie and had her track down Ted

Forrester's unlisted number. He seemed to think that you leaving a forwarding number with him would be a good idea.' His face was utterly blank, empty. Only his eyes held a faint hint of amusement.

So both the boys had finally grown frustrated at my silence. Richard had turned to my good friend, Ronnie, who happened to be a private investigator. Jean-Claude had taken a more direct route. But they'd both finally gotten hold of me on the same night. Would they compare notes?

'What did you tell Richard?' I laid the gun on the bed with the rest.

'That you were all right.' Edward was looking around the room. 'Doctor Cunningham still not allowing you a phone in here?'

'Nope,' I said. I had managed to untie the back of the gown.

'Then how did Jean-Claude contact you?'

I stopped in mid-motion. The gown slid off one shoulder and I had to catch it with my hand. It caught me off guard and I'm never as good a liar on the spur of the moment. 'I never said it was a phone call.'

'Then what was it?'

I shook my head. 'Just go, Edward. The night's not getting any younger.'

He just stood there, looking at me. His face had gone all cold and suspicious.

I got the bra in one hand and turned my back on him. I let the gown slide to my waist, leaned back against the bed to hold it in place, and slipped the bra on. There was no sound from behind me. I got the panties and slipped them on underneath the gown. I had the jeans halfway up my legs under the cover of the gown when I heard the door hush open and close.

I turned and found the doorway empty. I finished dressing. I had my toiletries in the bathroom all ready, so I threw them in the gym bag along with the big knife, and the boxes of ammo. The new shoulder holster felt odd. I was used to a leather one which fit tight and secure. I guess nylon was secure, but it was almost too comfortable, as if it seemed less substantial than my leather one had. But it beat the heck out of sticking it down my jeans.

The knives went in the wrist sheaths. I checked to see what kind of ammo the Firestar had in it. Edward's homemade stuff. I checked the Browning, and it was his stuff, too. The backup clip for the Browning was the Homady XTP Silver-Edge. I changed the clip. We were going into the Obsidian Butterfly as cops, which meant if I had to shoot someone, I'd have to explain it to the authorities later. Which meant I didn't want to go in there with some possibly illegal homemade shit in my gun. Besides I'd seen what the Homady Silver-Edge could do to a vampire. It was enough.

The Firestar went into an Uncle Mike's inner pants holster, though truthfully the jeans were too tight for an inner pants holster. Maybe I wasn't spending enough time in the gym. I had been on the road more than I'd been home. The Kenpo was neat stuff, but it wasn't the same thing as a full workout with weights and running. Another thing to pay more attention to when I got back to St Louis. I'd been letting a lot of things slide.

I finally transferred the Firestar to the small of my back and hated it, but it dug in something fierce in front. I have a slight sway to my back so there's always more room for a gun there, but it wasn't a quick place to draw from. Something about a woman's hip structure makes a gun at the small of the back not the best idea. That I kept the gun at the small of my back tells you just how tight the jeans were. Definitely going to have to get back into a regular gym schedule. The first five pounds are easy to get rid of, the second five are harder, and it gets even harder from there. I'd been chunky in junior high, close to fat, so I knew what I was talking about. So that no teenager out there will get the wrong idea and go all anorexic on me, I was a size thirteen in jeans, and that was at five foot nothing. See, I really was chunky. I hate women who complain about being fat when they're like a size five. Anything under size five isn't a woman. It's a boy with breasts.

I stared at the black jacket. Two days folded in a gym bag and it desperately needed to go to the dry cleaners. I decided to carry it folded over one arm, on the theory it would unwrinkle a little. I didn't really need to hide the weapons until we got to the club. The knives were illegal if I'd been a cop or a civvie, but I was a vampire executioner, and we got to carry knives. Gerald Mallory, the grandfather of our business, had testified before a senate subcommittee, or something like that, at how many times knives had saved his life. Mallory was well liked in Washington. It was his home base. So the law got changed to let us carry knives, even really big ones. If someone challenged me, all I had to do was whip out my executioner's license, and I was legal. Of course, that predicated on them knowing the loophole in the law. Not every cop on the beat is going to know. But my heart is pure because I'm legal.

Edward and Ramirez were waiting for me in the hallway. They both smiled and the smiles were so close to identical it was unnerving. Will the real good guys please stand up? But Edward's smile never faltered as I walked towards them. Ramirez's did. His gaze hesitated on the wrist sheath. The jacket hid the other one. I walked up to them smiling, and my eyes were shiny, too. I put a hand around Edward's waist and brushed my arm along the gun I'd thought was there at the small of his back.

'I've called for backup,' Ramirez said.

Edward had given me a quick Ted hug and let me go, though he knew I'd found the gun. 'Great. It's been a long time since I visited a Master of the City with the police.'

'How do you usually do it?' Ramirez asked.

'Carefully,' I said.

Edward turned his head away and coughed. I think he was trying not to laugh, but you can never tell with Edward. Maybe he just had a tickle in his throat. I watched him walk and wondered where in the world he was hiding the third gun.

51

One of the things I liked about working with the police was that when you went into a business and asked to speak with the manager or owner, no one argued. Ramirez flashed his badge and asked to speak with the owner, Itzpapalotl, also known as Obsidian Butterfly.

The hostess, the same darkly elegant woman that had shown Edward and me to a table last time, took Ramirez's business card, showed us all to a table, and left us. The only difference was this time we didn't get any menus. The two uniforms stayed at the door, but kept us in sight. I'd put the wrinkled jacket on to cover the guns and knives, but I was glad the club was dark, because the jacket had seen better days.

Ramirez leaned over and asked, 'How long do you think she'll keep us waiting?'

Funny how he didn't ask if she would keep us waiting. 'Not sure, but a while. She's a goddess and you've just ordered her to appear before you. Her ego won't let her be quick.'

Edward was leaning in on the other side. 'Half hour, at least.'

A waitress came. Ramirez and I ordered Cokes. Edward got water. The lights on the stage dimmed, then came up brighter. We settled back for the show. César had probably healed by now, but not by much. So it would either be a different wereanimal or a different show altogether.

There was what looked like a stone coffin propped up on the stage, sitting on its end with the carved lid staring out at the audience. Our table wasn't as good as last time. I spotted Professor Dallas at her usual table, alone this time. She didn't seem to mind.

The stone lid was carved in a crouching jaguar with a necklace of human skulls. The high priest Pinotl came onto the stage. He was dressed only in that skirt thing, a maxtlatl, that left the legs and most of the hips bare. I'd asked Dallas what the skirt was. His face was painted black with a stripe of white across the eyes and nose. His long black hair had been formed into individual strands curling at the ends. He wore a white crown, and it took me a second to realize it was made of bones. The stage lights flickered over the white bones, making them shimmer, and almost bleed white color when he moved his head. Finger bones had been restrung and formed a fan above the main band, reminiscent of the feathers I'd seen him wearing the first time. His ear spools of gold had been replaced by bones. He looked totally different from the first time, and yet the moment he stepped out onstage I knew it was him. No one else had had that aura of command.

I leaned into Ramirez. 'You wearing a cross?'

'Yes, why?'

'His voice can be a little overwhelming without a little help.'

'He's human, isn't he?'

'He's her human servant.'

Ramirez turned his face full into mine, and we were too close. I had to move back to keep from bumping noses. 'What?'

Did he really not know what a human servant was for a vampire? I didn't have time to give him a preternatural lesson, and this wasn't the place anyway. Far too many listening ears. I shook my head. 'I'll explain later.'

Two very Aztec-looking bouncers came onstage and lifted the lid of the coffin off. They moved to one side with it, and the way they shuffled, muscles in their arms and back working, it looked heavy. There was a cloth-draped body in the coffin. I didn't know for certain that it was a body, but it was shaped like a body. There just aren't that many things that are body-shaped.

Pinotl began to speak. 'Those of you who have been with us

before, know what it is to make sacrifice to the gods. You have shared in that glory, taken the offering into yourselves. But only the bravest, the most virtuous, are fit sacrifices. There are those that are not fit to feed the gods with their lives, but they, too, may serve.' He drew the cloth off in one large movement, sending the black and sequined draped cloth spreading wide like a fisherman's net. As that glittering cloth fell to the stage, the contents of the coffin were revealed. Gasps, screams spread through the audience like ripples in a pool.

There was a body in the coffin. It was dried and wizened, as if the body had been buried in the desert and had mummified naturally. No artificial preservatives. The spotlight on the coffin seemed very bright, harsh. It showed every line in the dried skin. The skeletal shadow of bones underneath was painfully clear.

We were only three rows back, close enough to see more detail than I cared to see. At least this time they wouldn't be cutting anyone up. I really wasn't in the mood to see inside anyone's chest tonight. I was searching the crowd, trying to see if she was coming or if we were about to be surrounded by werejaguars.

I turned and looked. The dead mummy's eyes were open. I looked at Edward. He answered the question without me having to say it. 'Its eyes just opened. Nobody touched it.'

I stared at that skull trapped under dry parchment skin. The eyes were full of something dry and brown. There was no life to the eyes, but they were open. The mouth began to open slowly, as if the mouth were on a stiff hinge. As the mouth opened a sound came out of it, a sigh that grew into a scream. A scream that echoed through the room, reverberated off the ceiling, the walls, the inside of my head.

'It's a trick, right?' Ramirez said.

I just shook my head. It wasn't a trick. Dear God, it wasn't a trick. I looked at Edward, and he just shook his head. He'd never seen this particular act either.

The scream died, and there was a silence so thick you could have dropped a pin and heard it bounce. I think everyone was holding their breath, straining to hear. To hear what I didn't know, but I was doing it, too. I think I was trying to hear it breathe. I studied that skeletal chest, but it didn't rise and fall. It didn't move. I said a silent prayer of thanks.

'This one's energy went to feed our dark goddess, but she is merciful. What was taken shall be given back. This is Micapetlacalli, the box of death. I am Nextepeua. In legend I was the husband of Micapetlacalli, and I am still married to death. Death runs through my veins. My blood tastes of death. Only the blood of one consecrated to death will free this one of torment.'

I realized that Pinotl's voice was just a voice, a good voice, like a good stage actor, but nothing more. Either he wasn't trying to bespell the audience, or I wasn't as susceptible tonight. The only change that I knew for certain was the marks. They were wide open now. I'd been told by my teacher and by Leonora Evans that the marks made me more vulnerable to psychic attack, but maybe on some things having a direct link to the boys helped me. Whatever it was, his voice didn't move me tonight. Great.

Pinotl drew an obsidian blade from behind his back. He'd probably been carrying it the way Edward and I were carrying guns, at the small of his back. He held his arm over the open coffin, over that gaping mouth. He drew the blade across his skin. It wasn't clear to the audience what he'd done. It would have been much better theater for Pinotl to slash his arm where the audience could see that first crimson slash. For him to hide it, there had to be some ritual significance, some importance, to those first drops of blood going into the corpse's mouth.

He dripped blood on the top of the thing's skull, dabbed it in the middle of that skull forehead, touched it to the throat, the chest, the stomach, the abdomen. He went down the line of chakras, energy points, of the body. I'd never believed in chakras until this year, when I'd found they were real, and they seemed to work. I hated all this new age stuff. I hated it worse when it worked. Of course, this wasn't new age stuff. This was very old stuff. With each touch of blood to that dried thing I felt magic. Each drop of blood made it grow, until the air hummed with it and my skin crept in waves of goosebumps.

Edward sat unmoved, but Ramirez was rubbing his arms, chasing goosebumps. 'What's happening?'

He was at the very least a sensitive. I guess I couldn't possibly be attracted to a totally normal human being. I whispered, 'Magic.'

He looked at me, eyes showing too much white. 'What kind?'

I shook my head. That I didn't know. I had a few clues, but I really had never seen anything like it, not exactly.

Pinotl walked around the coffin in a counter-clockwise motion, bleeding arm and bloody knife held apart, palm up while he chanted. The power built and built in the air like close thunder until my throat closed with it, and I was having trouble breathing. Pinotl came back to the front of the coffin where he'd begun. He made some kind of sign with his hands, then flung a spray of blood onto the body, and began to back slowly away. The lights dimmed until the only light was the harsh white light on the thing in the coffin.

The power had built to a screaming pitch. My skin was trying to crawl off my body and hide. The air was too thick to breathe, as if it had grown more solid, thick with magic.

Something was happening to the body. The power broke like a cloud bursting with rain, and that invisible rain broke over the body, over the room, over us all, but the focus was that dried thing. The skin began to move, to twitch. It filled out as if water flowed beneath it. Something liquid moved under that dry, wasted skin, and where it flowed the skin began to stretch. It was like watching one of those blow-up dolls fill up. Flesh, flesh was flowing under the skin. It plumped like some obscene kind of dough. The body, the man, began to thrash and twist against the sides of the coffin.

The chest finally rose, drawing in a great draught of air, as if he were struggling back from the dead. It was like the opposite of that death rattle where the breath flows away for the last time. Of course, that was exactly what it was: life returning, the last breath being drawn back in. When he had air to breathe, he began to scream. One long ragged shriek after another. As fast as his healing chest could bring in the air, he screamed.

The dry hair on his head turned curly, brown, and soft. His skin was tanned and young, smooth and flawless. He'd been under thirty when he went into the coffin. Who knew how long he'd been in there? Even after he looked human again, he kept shrieking, as if he had been waiting a very long time to scream.

A woman near the front screamed and took off running for the door. The vampires had moved up quietly through the tables. I hadn't sensed them over the suffocating flow of magic, and the sheer horror of the show. Careless of me. A vampire caught the running woman, held her, and she grew instantly still. He led her quietly back to her table, to the man that was standing, wondering what he should do. The vampires moved through the crowd touching someone here, stroking a hand there, soothing, soothing, telling the great lie. It was safe, it was peaceful, it was good.

Ramirez watched the vampires. He turned to me. 'What are they doing?'

'Soothing the crowd so they don't all bolt for the exits.'

'They aren't allowed to use one on one hypnosis.'

'I don't think it's personal, more like crowd hypnosis.' I looked back to the stage and found the man had collapsed onto the stage, pushing his way out of the coffin as soon as he got the strength. He was trying to crawl away.

Pinotl appeared in the growing circle of light. The man screamed and held his hands up in front of his face as if to ward off a blow. Pinotl spoke, and he didn't yell, so he must have been using a microphone of some kind. 'Have you learned humility?' he asked.

The man whimpered and hid his face.

'Have you learned obedience?'

The man nodded his head over and over, still hiding his face. He started to cry, great sobs that made his shoulders shake. Three rows out and I could hear him sobbing.

Pinotl motioned and the two bouncers that had opened the coffin walked onstage. They lifted the weeping man up, carrying him between them. His legs didn't seem to move yet, so they carried him, with an arm on either of their shoulders, his feet dangling off the floor. He wasn't a small man, and again you got that sense of how strong the two men were. They were human, too, not wereanything.

Two werejaguars walked onstage in their spotted skin clothes, and between them they held another man. No, not a man, a wereanimal. It was Seth. He'd been stripped down to a G-string that left very little to the imagination. His long yellow hair was unbound, streaked with light and color. He didn't struggle as they brought him up onstage. The jaguar men had him kneel in front of Pinotl.

'Do you acknowledge our dark goddess as your one and true mistress?'

Seth nodded. 'I do.' His voice didn't have the resonance of the other man's, and I doubted that the people in the back could hear him.

'She has given you life, Seth, and it is right that she should ask you give that life back to her.'

'Yes,' Seth said.

'Then I will be her hand, and take that which is hers.' He cradled Seth's face between his hands. It was gentle. The two jaguar men let go of Seth and backed away. But they stayed close, almost as if afraid that he might run. But his face was turned upward with a near beatific expression on it, as if this were wonderful. He'd been so afraid of being tortured by Itzpapalotl's four sisters weird, and yet now he seemed at peace with what they were about to do. I thought I knew, and I hoped I was wrong. Just once when I expect something truly hideous is about to happen, I'd like to be wrong. It would be a nice change.

It wasn't flashy. There was no fire or light or even a shimmer of heat. Lines appeared on Seth's twenty-something skin. The muscles under his skin began to shrink as though he had a wasting disease, but what should have taken months was happening in seconds. No matter how willing the sacrifice, it can still hurt. Seth started screaming as fast as he could draw breath. His lungs were working better than the other man's, and he drew breath so fast, it was like one continuous shriek. The skin darkened as it drew in and in like something were sucking him dry. It was like watching a balloon shrivel. Except there was muscle and when the muscle vanished, there was bone, and finally there was nothing but dried skin over bones, and still he screamed.

I've become something of a connoisseur of screams over the years, and I've heard some good ones. Some of them have even been mine, but I'd never heard anything like this. The sound stopped being human and became like the high-pitched sound of some wounded animal, but underneath it all you knew, knew at a level that you couldn't even explain, that it was a person.

Finally, there was no more air for screaming, but that dry, empty mouth kept opening and closing, opening and closing. Long after the screaming stopped, that skeletal thing was still writhing, still flinging its head from side to side.

Pinotl kept his hands pressed to Seth's face. He held him, and it looked gentle the whole time, but he had to be gripping with all the strength he had because he never lost his grip. While the flesh of that handsome face shriveled and died between his hands, Pinotl never moved. And through it all, Seth never once raised his hands up to save himself. He struggled because he couldn't not struggle, it hurt that much, but he never raised his hands against the other man. A willing sacrifice, a fit sacrifice.

My throat was tight, and something burned behind my eyes. I just wanted it over now. I just wanted it to stop. But it didn't stop. The skeletal thing that had been Seth kept twitching, opening and closing its mouth, as if trying to talk.

Pinotl looked up, breaking eye contact with Seth for a heartbeat. The two jaguar men that had escorted him onto the stage came into the light. One of them held a silver needle with black thread on it. The other held a pale green ball, tiny, the size of a marble maybe. If I'd been sitting much farther out, I'd have never known what it was. Jade, I think, a jade ball. They placed it in that gaping mouth, and the mouth closed. The other jaguar began to sew his mouth shut, driving the silver needle through the dry lipless flesh, tugging it tight.

I looked at the table too, resting my forehead on the cool stone of the table. I would not faint. I never fainted. But I had a sudden flash of the creature that Nicky Baco had created out of the werewolves. Some of them had had their mouths sewn shut. I'd never seen a power like this. It was too big a coincidence that two people in one town could do it and not be connected.

Ramirez touched my shoulder. I raised my head and shook it. 'I'm all right.' I looked up and they were putting Seth in the coffin. I knew without trying to sense it that he was still in there. Still aware. He could not have understood what he was letting them do to him. He couldn't have. Could he?

Pinotl turned to the audience, and his eyes glowed with black fire the way a vampire's does when their power is high. Black flames licked around his eye sockets, and his skin seemed to glow with the power.

The thing that Seth had become was covered with the same black glittering cloth that had covered the last body. The jaguar assistants closed the coffin, securing the heavy lid. A collective sigh ran through the audience as if they were all relieved that it was covered. I wasn't the only one that didn't want to see it anymore.

Itzpapalotl glided on stage. She was wearing the same crimson cloak as before. Pinotl went to one knee in front of her, extending his hands. She put her delicate hands on his strong ones, and I felt the rush of power like the brush of bird's wings.

Pinotl stood, holding her hand, and they turned to the audience and now both of them had eyes of black flame, spreading over their faces like a mask.

Soft spotlights filled the darkness of the tables like giant, soft fireflies. Each light found one of the vampires. They were pale and wan, hungry, fasted maybe, because I wasn't the only one who could tell they hadn't fed. You heard the exclamations through the audience, how pale, how frightening, oh, my god. No, she wanted everyone to see them for what they truly were.

She and Pinotl stared off into that soft-lit dark and again I felt the rush of power, like a chittering flight of birds, brushing across my face, my skin, as if I had no clothes, and the swift passing of feathered things caressed my body. I felt it almost like a series of physical blows as the power hit each vampire, and their eyes filled with black fire. They became shining things with skin of alabaster, bronze, copper, all glowing, all beautiful with eyes filled with the light of black stars.

Then they fell into line and began to sing. A song of praise to her, their dark goddess. Diego, the vampire we'd seen whipped senseless, passed by our table with a leash in his hand. On the end of that leash was a tall, pale-skinned man with curly yellow hair. Was it Cristobal, one of the starved ones? There were no starved ones in line. All of them were glowing and well fed and filled to bursting with a dark, sweet power like overripe berries before they fall to the ground, when they are poised between the sweetest of ripeness and rotting. Life is often like that, the best balancing on a knife edge with the worst.

The vampires left the stage still singing her praises. Pinotl and she walked hand and hand down the steps, and I knew where they were coming, and I didn't want them near me. I could still feel the power as though I were standing in the middle of a cloud of butterflies, and they were beating at my skin with soft wings, beating at me, trying to come inside.

They came and stood in front of our table. Her face was smiling, soft as she gazed down at me. The black flames had quieted, but her eyes were still an empty blackness with a flicker of light in their depths. Pinotl's eyes echoed hers like a mirror, but it wasn't black flame. It was the blackness of endless night, and there were stars in her eyes, an endless fall of stars.

Edward had my arm. He had turned me to face him. We were both standing, though I didn't remember getting up. 'Anita, are you okay?'

I had to swallow twice to find my voice. 'I'm okay, I think. Yeah, I'm okay.' But the power was still beating against me like frantic wings, birds crying that they've been shut out in the dark and they want inside to the light and the warmth. How could I leave them crying in the dark when all I had to do was open and they would be safe?

'Stop it,' I said. I turned to face them. They were still smiling, still welcoming. She held her hand out to me, the other still holding Pinotl's hand. I knew if I took that hand that all this power would flow into me. That I could share it with them. It was an offering to share. But at what price, because there was always a price?

'What do you want?' I asked. I wasn't even sure who I was asking.

'I want the knowledge of how your triad of power was achieved.'

'I can tell you that. You don't need to do this.'

'You know that I cannot tell truth from lie. It is not one of my powers. Touch me and I will gain the knowledge from you.'

The wings were flowing over my skin as if the flying things had found a current of air just above my body. 'What do I gain?'

'Think of one question, and if I have the answer, you will draw it from my mind.'

Ramirez was standing. He motioned and I knew without looking that the uniforms were coming this way. 'I don't know what's happening, but we're not doing it.'

'Answer one question first,' I said.

'If I can,' she said.

'Who is the Red Woman's Husband?'

Her face showed nothing, but her voice was puzzled. 'The Red Woman was another term for blood among the Mexicanas, among the Aztecs. I truly do not know who the Red Woman's Husband would be.'

I'd half reached out to her. I didn't really mean to. Three things happened almost together. Ramirez and Edward both grabbed me to pull me back, and Itzpapalotl grabbed my hand.

The wings erupted into a torrent of birds. My body opened, though I knew it didn't, and the winged things, only half-glimpsed spilled into that opening. The power flowed into me, through me, and out again. I was part of some great circuit, and I felt the connection with every vampire she'd touched. It was as if I flowed through them, and they through me like water coming together to form something larger. Then I was floating in the soothing dark, and there were stars, distant and glittering.

A voice, her voice came. 'Ask one question, and it shall be yours.'

I asked, though my mouth never moved, still I heard the words. 'How did Nicky Baco learn to do what Pinotl did to Seth?' With the words came the image of Nicky's creature so clear I could smell the dryness of it, and hear that voice whispering, 'Help me.'

Images then, and they had force to them like things slamming into my body. I saw Itzpapalotl standing on the top of a pyramid temple surrounded by trees, jungle. I could smell the rich greenness of it, and hear the night call of a monkey, the scream of a jaguar. Pinotl knelt and fed from the bloody wound on her chest. He became her servant, and he gained power. Many powers, and one of them was this. And I understood how he'd taken Seth's essence. More than that I understood how it was done, and how it was undone. I knew how to unmake Nicky's creature, though what he'd done to them might mean that to bring them back to flesh would kill them. We didn't need Nicky to undo the spell; I could do it. Pinotl could do it.

She didn't ask if I understood. She knew when I had it all. 'Now for my question.' And before I could say or think 'Wait,' she was inside my head. She drew the memories from me: images, pieces, and I couldn't stop her. She saw Jean-Claude mark me, and she saw Richard, and she saw the three of us calling power on purpose for the first time. She saw that last night when I'd taken the second and third mark to save our lives, all our lives.

I was suddenly back in my own skin, standing on one side of the table, still holding her hand. I was gasping, fast and faster, and I knew if I didn't get control, I was going to hyperventilate. She released my hand, and all I could do was concentrate on my own breathing. Ramirez was yelling at me, was I all right. Edward had his gun out, pointed at her. She and Pinotl just stood there, peaceful. I could see everything as though I were looking through crystal. The colors seemed darker, more vivid. Things stood out in bold relief, and it wasn't the things I would normally have noticed. The way the band in Edward's hat had a small ridge in it, and I knew where the garrote was.

When I could finally talk, I said, 'It's all right. It's all right. I'm not hurt.' I touched Edward's hand, lowering the gun to point at the table. 'Chill, okay, I'm all right.'

'She said it would harm you if we forced you to let go early,' Edward said.

'It might have,' I said. I'd expected to feel badly, drained, tired, but I didn't. I felt energized, exhilarated. 'I feel great.'

'You don't look great,' Edward said, and there was something in his voice that made me look at him.

He grabbed my hand and started leading me through the tables towards the door. I tried to slow down and he jerked me with him, pulling me along.

'You're hurting my wrist,' I said.

He pushed through the doors with the gun still naked in his hand, my wrist gripped in his other hand. He hit the lobby doors with his shoulders. I remembered it being darker in the lobby, but it wasn't dark now. It wasn't exactly light. It just wasn't dark. He pushed one of the wall hangings apart, and there was the men's room door. He pushed it open before I could say anything. The urinals stretched empty, and I was grateful. The lights were bright, made me squint.

Edward whirled me around to face the mirrors. My eyes were a solid shining black. There was no pupil, no white, nothing. I looked blind, yet I could see everything, every crack in the wall, the smallest dint on the edge of the mirror. I walked forward, and he let me go. I reached out until I could touch my reflection. I jumped when my fingers met the cool glass, as if I'd expected my hand to keep on going. I stared at my hand, and I could almost see the bones under my skin, the muscles working as I moved my fingers. Underneath that, I could see the flow of blood under my skin. I turned and looked at Edward. I looked at him slowly, and I could see the slight difference in the pants leg where the hilt of the knife was sticking out of his boot. There was the faintest line where the second knife was strapped to his thigh, and he could reach through his pants pocket and touch the hilt. There was a bulge in his other pocket, small, but I knew it was a gun, a derringer probably, but that last bit of knowledge was my knowledge. The rest was this extraordinary vision. It was like some fantasy spell of true seeing.

If this was how all vampires saw the world, then I should just stop trying to hide weapons. But I'd fooled vampires before, master-level vampires. So this was how she saw the world, but not necessarily how they all saw the world.

'Say something, Anita.'

'I wish you could see what I'm seeing.'

'I don't want to,' he said.

'The garrote is in the band of your hat. You've got a knife in a sheath in your right boot, and a knife on your left thigh. You reach the hilt through your pants pocket. There's a derringer in your right pants pocket.'

He paled, and I saw it. I saw the pulse in his throat beat faster. I could see the small changes in his body as the fear rushed through it. No wonder she'd been able to read me so easily. But it should have worked like a lie detector for her. That's what other vamps and wereanimals pick up on, the minute changes we all make when we lie. Even the smell changes, so Richard said. So why couldn't she tell if someone were lying?

The answer came in a wave of clarity that you usually have to meditate to have. She couldn't read things she didn't have inside herself. She wasn't a goddess. She was a vampire, not like any vampire I'd ever known before, but that was what she was. Yet she believed she was Itzpapalotl, the living personification of the sacrificial knife, the obsidian blade. She was lying to herself, and thus she couldn't see a lie in someone else. She didn't understand what truth was, so she couldn't recognize that either. She was fooling herself on a cosmic scale, and it weakened her. But I wasn't going to march out there and point out the error of her ways. She was just a vampire and not a goddess, but I'd had a taste of her power and I did not want to be on her dirty list.

With her power flowing through me like a rising wind, warm and smelling of flowers that I did not recognize, I didn't even want to burst her bubble. I hadn't felt this good in days. I turned back to the mirror, and my eyes were still that spreading blackness. I should have been scared or screaming, but I wasn't scared, and all I could think was, cool.

'Shouldn't your eyes go back to normal?' he asked, and again I felt that tightness of fear in him.

'Eventually, but if we really want answers to our questions, we need to go back and ask her.'

He gave one quick nod, after you, and I realized that Edward didn't trust me at his back. He thought that she had possessed me. I didn't argue with him. I just walked through the door first and went back to talk to Itzpapalotl. I hoped Ramirez hadn't tried to put handcuffs on her. She wouldn't like that, and what she didn't like, her followers didn't like, and there were a hundred and two vampires. I had no idea how many werejaguars she had. This was a feeding not meant for them. But it was a small army, and Ramirez hadn't brought that much backup.

52

Ramirez hadn't put cuffs on anyone, but he had called for more backup. There were four more uniforms in the room, and about twenty werejaguars. The audience was watching it all as if it were part of the show. I guess if they could sit through what had been done to Seth, they could sit through a little police action.

I was ahead of Edward as we came into the room. He fell a step behind me, the way we often did when one of us was going to be in charge of the next few minutes. Maybe my eyes were glowing black pits, but Edward still trusted me to calm the situation. Good to know.

The werejaguars were moving through the tables, trying to flank the cops. The uniforms had their hands on their guns. The holsters were unbuckled. It wasn't going to take much to get a gun drawn and the shit to hit the fan. Be a shame to push this big a button when the vampires weren't trying to hurt anybody.

One of the jaguars was moving again, trying to close the circle around the police. I touched his arm. His power trembled over my hand, and it was more than just my own power, or the marks, that flared and answered that rush. He looked down at me and saw the eyes or felt her power, whatever it was, when I said, 'Back up, go stand with the others.' He did it. Progress. Now if only the police would be as reasonable.

I turned to the police and started walking towards them. One of the new uniforms said, 'Shit,' hand on gun, other hand out like a traffic stop. 'Don't come any closer.'

'Ramirez,' I said, and made sure my voice carried.

'It's okay. She's with us,' he said.

'But her eyes,' the uniform said.

'She's with us. Let her through, now.' Ramirez's voice was low, but the anger carried.

The uniforms parted like a curtain, very careful not to touch me as I went past. I guess I couldn't blame them, though I wanted to. I was finally at the table with Edward behind me, and the nervous uniforms beyond him. I faced Itzpapalotl across the table. Pinotl was at her side, but they were no longer holding hands. His eyes were still as black as mine, but hers were normal. Strangely, with the hood pushed back to show that delicate face and those normal seeming eyes, she looked the most human of the three of us.

Ramirez had laid some of the pictures on the table. 'Tell me what this is.' It sounded like a question he'd asked before.

She looked at me.

'Do you know what it is?' I asked.

'No, I truly do not. It does look like one of our artisans could have made it, but the eyes are stones that came with the Spaniards. I do not recognize all the elements of the symbolism.'

'But you recognize some of them,' I said.

'Yes.'

'What do you recognize?'

'The bodies around the base could be the ones you drink.'

'You mean like you did with Seth tonight?'

She nodded.

'What is it holding in its hands?'

'It could be many things, but I think it is the lesser things of the body. The heart is spoken for, as are the bones, and many other parts, but no god feeds on the . . .' she frowned, searching for the word, '. . . intestines, and other viscera.'

'That makes sense,' I said.

I felt Ramirez shift beside me, as if he badly wanted to say it does. But he kept quiet because he was a good cop, and she was talking to me. Did it really matter why? Not right that second it didn't.

'You saw the creature that . . .' it was my turn to hesitate. If the police knew what Nicky had done, it was an automatic death sentence. But frankly, he deserved it. The werewolves that he had sucked dry hadn't been willing sacrifices. And he'd cut them up, knowing they were still alive, he'd cut them up and sewn them into that monster behind the bar. It was one of the worst things I'd come across, and that was saying a lot.

I made my decision and knew that it would eventually cost Nicky his life. 'You saw the creature that Nicky Baco made?'

She nodded. 'I saw. It is a corruption of a great gift.'

'Does his master gain power through it just like you do?'

'Yes, and Nicky Baco gains power through it, much as Pinotl does. As you have.'

'Can he pass that power to others, like maybe a werewolf pack?'

She seemed to think about that, head to one side, then finally nodded. 'It would be possible to share with wereanimals if you had some bond with them of a mystical nature.'

'He's vargamor for the local pack,' I said.

'I am not familiar with the word vargamor.'

It was a wolf term. 'It's their witch, their brujo, and they are bound to the pack.'

'Then certainly he could share the power with them.'

'Nicky said he didn't know where this god lay.'

'He lies,' she said. 'You do not gain this power without the touch of your god's hand.'

I'd gotten that from the images that had filled me, but I wanted it confirmed.

'Then Nicky should be able to take us to the place where the god is hiding?'

She nodded. 'He knows.'

'Do you have a problem with us hunting down and killing a god from your pantheon?'

A look crossed her face that I didn't understand. 'If it is a god, then you cannot kill it, and if you can kill it, then it is not a god. I do not mourn the death of false gods.'

It was kind of funny coming from her, but I let it go. It wasn't my job to convince her what she was, or what she wasn't. 'Thank you for your help, Itzpapalotl.'

She gave me a long look, and I knew what she wanted, but . . . 'You are indeed a goddess, but I cannot serve two masters,' I said.

'His power is lust, and you deny him his power.'

I felt the heat rush up my face and wondered what a blush looked like with glowing black eyes. It wasn't what she'd said. It was me knowing what she'd seen in my head. She knew more intimate details than my best friend. Just as I'd shared what she and Pinotl considered a very private and intimate moment of their sharing. Fair is fair, but somehow I didn't think Itzpapalotl blushed.

'I thought I was just denying him sex.'

She looked at me the way you'd look at a child that was deliberately misunderstanding a point. 'Tell me, Anita, what is the base of my power?'

The question surprised me, but I answered it; the time for lying between us was past. 'Power, you feed off of pure power regardless of the source.'

She smiled, and that thread of power in me smiled with her, made me feel glowy all over. 'Now, what is your master's base of power?'

I'd been running from this particular truth for a very long time. Not all master vampires had a secondary power base, another way to draw energy, other than blood or human servants or animals to call. But some did, and Jean-Claude was one of them.

'Anita,' she said, as if reminding me that I was supposed to be saying something.

'Sex, his base of power is sex,' I said.

Again, she smiled happily at me, and I felt that warm answering glow. It was good to be truthful. It was good to be smart. It was good to please her. And that of course was one of her dangers. If you stayed near her long enough, it might become an end in itself to please her. Even thinking it, I couldn't be afraid of her. Good that I didn't live in Albuquerque.

'By denying him and your wolf, you cripple not just the triad of power, but him. You have crippled him, Anita. You have crippled your master.'

I heard myself say, 'I'm sorry.'

'It is not me that you must be sorry to. It is him. Go home and beg his forgiveness, lay yourself at his feet and feed his power.'

I closed my eyes, because what I really wanted to do was nod and just agree. I was pretty sure the spell would wear off before I got home to St Louis, but putting this woman and Jean-Claude together as a team would have been my undoing. Even now, I was glad he was hundreds of miles away, because I nodded, eyes still closed.

She took the nod as assent. 'Good, very good. If your master is grateful for my aid in this matter, let him contact me. I know that we can come to an understanding.'

And for the first time since she'd zapped me, I felt a thrill of fear. I looked at her through a veil of her power and was afraid of her.

She read it in me. 'You should always be afraid of gods, Anita. If you are not afraid, then you are a fool and you are not a fool.' She looked past me to Ramirez. 'I believe that I have helped you all that I can, Detective Ramirez.'

He said, 'Anita?'

I nodded. 'Yeah, it's time to go see Nicky Baco.'

'If Nicky lied to us, then so did his pack leader,' Edward said, 'because he said Nicky was telling the truth about not knowing where the monster was.'

'If Nicky can share this kind of power with the werewolves, then I know why the pack lied.'

'The werewolves will fight to protect Nicky,' Edward said.

We looked at each other. 'It'll be a bloodbath if the police go in force.' I shook my head. 'But what choice do we have?'

'Nicky isn't at the bar,' Ramirez said.

We turned to him, said in unison, 'Where is he?'

'In the hospital. Someone beat the shit out of him.'

Edward and I exchanged glances, and we both smiled. 'Back to the hospital, then,' I said.

He nodded. 'Back to the hospital.'

I looked at Ramirez. 'If that's all right with you?'

'Can you prove what you've been saying about Baco?' he asked.

'Yes,' I said.

'Then it's a death sentence. He'll know that. I've seen Baco in an interrogation. He's tough, and he knows that he has nothing to gain and everything to lose by telling us the truth.'

'Then we'll have to find something that he's more afraid of than being executed.' I couldn't help it. I turned and looked at Itzpapalotl. I met her eyes and there was no pull to them now. Her own power protected me from her. No stars, no endless night, just a dark knowledge of what I was thinking, and her approval of the plan.

'We can't do anything illegal,' Ramirez said.

'Of course not,' I said.

'I mean it, Anita.'

I looked at him, and watched him flinch when he met my eyes. 'Would I do that to you?'

He searched my face as if trying to decipher it. It was the way

I looked at Edward sometimes, or Jean-Claude. Finally, he said, 'I don't know what you'd do.' And that, for better or worse, was the truth.

53

Edward got his sunglasses out of the glove compartment and handed them to me before we went inside the hospital. My eyes hadn't changed back, though I knew the effect was beginning to wear off, because the fact that my eyes were still black and glowy was beginning to worry me. It was a good sign.

Nicky Baco was not in a private room. The police had his roommate moved to a different room. Nicky was in traction, and wasn't going anywhere. He lay in the bed and looked smaller than I knew he was. The leg that had been badly broken was in a cast from toe to thigh. Little pulleys and cords held his leg up at an odd angle that must have been hell on the back.

Ramirez had been questioning Nicky for about thirty minutes and was getting nowhere. Edward and I leaned against the wall and watched the show. But Nicky had done exactly what we'd feared he'd do. He'd grasped his situation and his options right away. He was going to die. So why should he help us?

'We know where the monster you made is, Nicky. We know what you did. Help us stop this thing before it kills again.'

'And what?' Nicky said. 'I know the law. There's no life in prison for a witch that uses magic to kill. It's an automatic death sentence. You got nothing to offer me, Ramirez.'

I pushed away from the wall and touched Ramirez's arm. He looked at me, and the frustration was already showing. He'd been informed that Lieutenant Marks was on the way. He wanted to crack Baco before Marks arrived so he would get credit and not his lieutenant. Political, but the reality in most police work.

'Can I ask a few questions, Detective?'

He took a breath, let it out slow. 'Sure.' He stepped back to let me stand beside the bed.

I looked down at Nicky. Someone had handcuffed one of his wrists to the bed rail. I wasn't sure it was necessary with the traction, but it made a nice point. 'What would the Red Woman's Husband do if he knew you gave away his secret hideout?'

He stared up at me, and even through the sunglasses I could see the hate in his eyes. I could also see the fast rise and fall of his chest, the thud of the pulse in his neck. He was scared.

'Answer me, Nicky.'

'He'd kill me.'

'How?'

That made him frown. 'What do you mean, how?'

'I mean what method of death would he use? How would he kill you?'

Nicky shifted in the bed, trying to find a comfortable spot. The leg pulled tight, and he jerked on the handcuffed wrist, making it rattle up and down the bar. There was no comfortable position for Nicky tonight.

'He'd probably send his monster after me. It'd cut me up and gut me like it's done to the others.'

'His minion slaughtered all the witches or psychics, and skinned the mundanes. That's it, isn't it?'

'If you're so smart, you don't need to ask me. You have all the answers.'

'Not all of them,' I said. I touched the bed rail that he was cuffed to, wrapped my hands around it on either side of the cuff so he couldn't slide it without hitting one of my hands. 'I've seen the bodies, Nicky. It's a bad way to go, but there are worse things.'

He gave a harsh laugh. 'Being gutted alive – doesn't get much worse than that,' he said.

I took the sunglasses off and let him see the eyes.

He stopped breathing for a heartbeat. He just stared up at me, eyes growing wide, breath trapped in his throat.

I touched his hand, and he screamed. 'Don't touch me! Don't you fucking touch me!' He was jerking on the handcuff frantically, over and over, as if that would help.

Ramirez came to stand on the other side of the bed across from me. He looked a question at me.

'I didn't hurt him, Hernando.'

'Get her the fuck away from me.'

'Tell us where the monster is, and I'll send her out of the room.'

Nicky looked from one to the other of us, and the fear showed on his face now. You didn't have to have vampire vision to see it. 'You can't do this to me. You're the cops.'

'We're not doing anything to you,' Ramirez said.

Nicky's eyes flicked back to me. 'You're the cops. You can execute me, but you can't torture me. That's the law.'

'You're right, Nicky. The police aren't allowed to torture prisoners.' I leaned in close and whispered, 'But I'm not the police.'

He started tugging on the chain again, rattling it up and down the bar. 'Get her away from me, now! I want a lawyer. I want a fucking lawyer.'

Ramirez turned to the two uniformed cops waiting by the door. 'Go call Mr Baco a lawyer.'

The two cops looked at each other. 'Both of us?' one asked.

Ramirez nodded. 'Yeah, both of you.'

They exchanged another look and went for the door. The taller one asked, 'How long you think this phone call should take?'

'A while, and knock before you come back in.'

The uniforms left, and it was just Edward, Ramirez, Nicky, and me. Nicky was staring up at Ramirez. 'You're a good cop, Ramirez. I've never heard any dirt on you. You won't let her hurt me. You're a good guy. You won't let her hurt me.' His voice was high and frantic, but each time he said it, he seemed more sure of himself, more certain that Ramirez's goodness would be his shield.

He was probably right on one thing. Ramirez wouldn't let me hurt him, but I was willing to bet that Ramirez would let me scare him.

I reached out like I'd stroke Nicky's face. He jerked back, out of reach.

'Ramirez, shit, please, don't let her touch me.'

'I'll be over there if you need me, Anita.' He walked away from the bed and went to sit in a chair at the end of the room near Edward.

Nicky screamed after him, 'Ramirez, please, please!'

I touched his mouth with fingertips, and he froze under that gentle touch. His eyes moved slowly, so slowly until he was looking up into mine. 'Shhh,' I said and lowered my face towards his, as if I'd kiss his forehead.

He opened his mouth, drew a breath, and shrieked. I grabbed his face between my hands the way I'd seen Pinotl do, but I knew that it didn't have to be the hands. I could suck him dry with a kiss. 'Shut up, Nicky, shut up!'

He started to cry. 'Please, oh, god, please don't.'

'Did the werewolves beg like this?' I asked. 'Did they, Nicky?' I pressed my hands into his face until the skin puckered.

'Yes,' he said, voice squeezed by how tight I was holding his face. I had to force myself to release his face, or I was going to leave red marks. Couldn't mark him up. Couldn't give Marks a reason to punish Ramirez.

I leaned my arms on the bed rail that he was chained to. He pulled his hand to the length of the chain, but didn't struggle. He watched me the way mice watch cats when they know there's no way out. I leaned towards him. It was a very casual movement, but it put my face close to his, not close enough to touch but close enough that he got an up close look at the eyes.

'You see, Nicky, there are worse things.'

'You need me to bring the others back. You do me, and I can't give them back their lives.'

'You see, Nicky. I don't need you anymore. I know how to bring them back all by myself.' I leaned over, balancing on tiptoe and my arms on the rail, leaning in, as if to whisper in his ear. 'Your services are no longer needed.'

'Please,' he whispered.

I spoke with my mouth so close to his face that I could feel my breath coming back from his skin in a warm pulse. 'The doctors will certify you dead, Nicky. They'll bury you in a box somewhere, and you'll hear every shovel full of dirt as it hits the coffin lid. You'll lie there in the dark and scream in your head, and no one will hear you. Maybe we'll have to put a jade bead in your mouth and sew it shut to make you lie still.'

Tears trailed from his eyes, but his face was blank, as if he didn't know he was crying.

'Tell them where your master is, Nicky, or I swear I will do worse than kill you.' I kissed him on the forehead, very gently.

He whimpered.

I kissed the tip of his nose, the way you do with children. I hovered over his mouth. 'Tell them, Nicky.' I lowered my mouth over his, our lips brushed, and he turned his head.

'I'll tell you. I'll tell you anything you want to know.'

I moved away from the bed and let Ramirez move up to take his turn.

A phone rang, and Edward pulled his cell phone from his back pocket. He opened the door and went into the hall to take the call.

Ramirez's voice was not happy. 'What do you mean you can't tell me how to get there?' He had his notebook open, his pen poised, and nothing written down.

I started to walk back towards the bed.

Nicky held his hands up as if to ward me off. 'I swear to you that I can take you to it, but I can't give you directions and be sure you'll find it. I don't want to send you out into the dark, and have you not find it. You'd blame me, and it wouldn't be my fault.'

Ramirez looked at me.

I nodded. He was too scared to lie, and it was too stupid a story to be made up.

'I can take you to it. If I'm there, I can take you to it.'

'Of course, if you're there, you can warn your master,' I said.

'I wouldn't do that.' But I saw the change in his skin color, the rise in breathing, the flick of his eyes.

'Liar,' I said.

'All right, but I'd be a fool not to try and get away. They're going to kill me, Anita. Why shouldn't I try to get away?'

I guess I couldn't blame him on that one. 'Call Leonora Evans. She's a witch. Have her ward him, make sure that he can't contact his master by anything other than yelling.'

'And the yelling?' Ramirez said.

'Gag him when the time comes,' I said.

'You trust Leonora Evans to do this?'

'She saved my life, so I guess I do.'

Ramirez nodded. 'Okay, I'll call her in.' He looked at the traction ropes. 'The doctors aren't going to want him going anywhere tonight.'

'Talk to them, Hernando. Explain what's at stake. Besides, what good does it do to heal him if you're just going to turn around and execute him?'

Ramirez looked at me. 'That was harsh.'

'Yeah, it was, but it's still true.'

Edward knocked and came in the door just far enough to say, 'I need you out here.'

I glanced at Ramirez. 'I think we can take it from here, thank you,' he said.

'My pleasure.' I slipped the sunglasses back on as I followed Edward out into the hall. The moment I looked at Edward's face,

I knew something bad had happened. He didn't show it the way a normal person would, but it was there, the tightness around his eyes, the way he held himself, carefully, as if he were afraid to move too suddenly or he'd break. I don't think I'd have seen it without the vampire vision.

'What's wrong?' I stepped in close, because something told me this was not for police consumption. With Edward it so seldom was.

He took me by the arm down the hallway, farther away from the uniforms that were staring our way. 'Riker has Donna's kids.' His grip tightened, and I didn't tell him it hurt. 'He has Peter and Becca. He's going to kill them if I don't bring you to him now. He knows we're at the hospital. He's given me an hour to make the drive, then he starts torturing them. If I'm not there in two hours, he'll kill them. If I bring the police in, he'll kill them.'

I touched his arm. If it had been almost any other friend, I'd have hugged him.

'Is Donna okay?'

He seemed to realize he was digging into my arm and let me go. 'This is Donna's night at her group. I don't know if the babysitter's still alive, but Donna won't even be home for two, maybe three hours. She doesn't know.'

'Let's go,' I said.

We turned and started walking down the hallway. Ramirez yelled behind us.

'Where are you two going? I thought you'd want to be in on it.'

'Personal emergency,' Edward said, and kept walking.

I turned around, walking backwards, trying to talk at the same time. 'In two hours call Ted's house. The call will be forwarded to his cell phone. We'll join you on the monster hunt.'

'Why two hours?' he asked.

'The emergency will be taken care of by then,' I said. I had to touch Edward's arm, to keep walking backwards and not fall.

'Everything could be over two hours from now,' Ramirez said.

'I'm sorry.' Edward was at the doors that led into the next section of hallway. He pulled me through; the doors shut behind us. He was already punching numbers on the cell phone. 'I'll have Olaf and Bernardo meet us at the turnoff to Riker's place.'

I don't know which of them answered, but he gave a long list of things to bring, and he made them write it down. We were out of the hospital, through the parking lot and getting into his Hummer before he clicked the telephone off.

Edward drove, and all I had to do was think. Not a good thing. I was remembering last May when some bad guys kidnapped Richard's mother and younger brother. They'd sent us a box with a lock of his brother's hair, and his mother's finger in it. Everyone that had touched them was dead. Everyone that had hurt them would never hurt anyone again. I only had two regrets: one, that I hadn't gotten there in time to save them from being tortured; two, that the bad guys hadn't suffered enough before they died.

If Riker hurt Peter and Becca . . . I wasn't sure I wanted to see what Edward would do to him. I prayed as we rode through the darkness, 'Please, God, don't let them be hurt. Let them be safe.' Riker could be lying. They could already be dead, but I didn't think so. Maybe because I needed them to be alive. I remembered Becca in her sunflower dress with that sprig of lilacs in her hair, laughing in Edward's arms. I saw Peter's sullen resentment when Edward and his mother touched. I remembered the way Peter had stood up to Russell in the restaurant when he threatened Becca. He was a brave kid. I tried not to think about what could be happening to them right this second.

Edward had gone very, very quiet. When I looked at him, the dark crystal vision showed me further into him than I'd ever seen before. I didn't have to guess whether he cared for the children. I could see it. He loved them. As much as he was capable of it, he loved them. If someone hurt them, his vengeance was going to be a thing of great and awesome terror. I wouldn't be able to stop him no matter what he wanted to do to them. All I would be able to do was stand and watch and try not to get too much blood on my shoes.

54

It was a dark night. It didn't seem to be cloudy, just dark, as if something besides clouds was blocking the moon. Or maybe that was just my frame of mind. The one thing I'd wanted to avoid while I was doing my favor for Edward was dealing with Edward at his most illegal. We'd picked up Olaf and Bernardo at a crossroads in the middle of nowhere with those empty rolling hills stretching out and out into the darkness. There had been no cover except some scrub bushes, and when Edward stopped the car and cut the engine, I thought we'd have a wait ahead of us.

'Get out. We'll need to suit up.' He'd gotten out without waiting to see if I was getting out or not.

I got out. The silence seemed as big as the sky overhead, an immense emptiness. A man stood up not five feet in front of me. I had the Browning pointed before the man held a flashlight under his face and I realized it was Bernardo.

Olaf had magically appeared on the other side of the road. There was no ditch on either side of the road. There was nothing on the side of the road. What was even more impressive was that they began lifting large black bags of equipment out of that same nowhere. If we'd had the time, I'd have asked how they did it, though I doubt I'd have understood the answer. Training probably. Training I didn't have, though it might be nice to get it.

Of course, most of the things I hid from could have heard Bernardo's and Olaf's heartbeat no matter how well hidden they were. It was almost a relief to be up against mere humans. It meant you could at least hide in the dark.

Twenty minutes later we were on the road again, and Edward hadn't been joking on the suiting up part. I'd had to strip to my bra and put on a Kevlar vest. It was my size.

Which meant it had to be a special purchase because Kevlar doesn't come in my size off the rack.

'It's your prize for spotting all the weapons,' Edward said. He always knows just what to buy me.

I needed to adjust the shoulder holster after putting on the vest, but I was told to do it in the car. I didn't argue. We had less than ten minutes to get to Riker's place. My T-shirt didn't quite fit over the body armor. I mean it did fit, but not well. Bernardo handed me a black, long-sleeved, man's shirt. 'Put it on over the T-shirt. Button it up part way after you've got your holsters adjusted.'

The shoulder holster was just a matter of readjusting straps. The inner pants holster just didn't work once the vest was on. I put the Firestar down the front of my jeans and angled it until I was as happy as I was going to get with the way it fit. It still dug into my stomach, but I wanted it where I could get it fast. I could live with bruises tomorrow.

I practiced drawing the Browning through the half open shirt a few times, though it's hard to practice drawing from a sitting position, but we didn't have time for me to get out and practice standing.

'You guys are making me nervous, putting me in Kevlar.'

'You didn't argue,' Bernardo said.

'We don't have time to argue. Tell me what to do, I'll do it. But why the Kevlar?'

'Olaf,' Edward said.

'Riker employs twenty men, ten are just hired muscle. We've met half of them already. But he's got ten that he keeps close to him. Three ex-seals, two ex-army rangers, one ex-police, and four guys who have black files. Which means whatever they do or did, it's top secret and maybe rogue.'

I remembered what FBI Agent Bradford had said about Olaf.

That he had a black file. 'Isn't this a little too commando raidish for a pot hunter?'

Olaf continued like I hadn't said anything. Bernardo started showing me the contents of a large leather purse at the same time. I listened to Olaf and watched Bernardo.

'Riker has connections in South America that supply him with contraband. Suspicions are that he's running more than just artifacts. Maybe drugs. The locals have no idea how big a bad guy they've got here.'

'When did you find all this out?'

'After they came to the house,' Edward said.

'How did you find all this out?' I asked.

'If we told you, we'd have to kill you,' Olaf said.

I started to smile, thinking it was a joke, but I caught a glimpse of his face as the only car we'd seen passed by, flashing lights over us as it passed. He didn't look like he was joking.

Bernardo said, 'This looks like a can of hair spray. You can even squirt out a small amount of cresol.' He demonstrated. 'But lift here.' He did and revealed a second layer of metal. 'This is the pin. This is the depressor. It's an incendiary grenade. You pull the pin, let up on the depressor, and you have three seconds to get a minimum of fifty feet away from it. It's got white phosphorus in it. This shit burns underwater. If you get a tiny piece on your sleeve, it will eat through the cloth, your skin, bone, all the way to the other side.'

He clicked the secret compartment shut and handed it to me. 'Damned heavy for hairspray,' I said.

'Yeah, but how many ex-navy whatevers are going to notice?'

He had a point. Next was a small thing of breath freshener that was really heavy-duty mace. A key ring that when you hit the button on it, a four-inch blade popped out.

There was a heavy ink pen that actually wrote, that if you pressed the little switch, a six-inch blade came out the end. There was real perfume with a higher than normal alcohol content. 'Go for the eyes,' was the advice. A disposable lighter, because you never know when you might need some fire, and a package of cigarettes to explain the lighter. There was a transmitter in the collar of the black shirt that would allow them to find me inside the buildings or at least find the shirt. I was beginning to feel like I'd been shanghaied into a James Bond movie.

I lifted out a hairbrush with a heavier than normal handle. 'What's this?'

'It's a hairbrush,' Bernardo said.

Oh. I looked at Edward. The only thing he'd changed was putting a white Kevlar vest under his undershirt and white shirt. He was even still wearing his cowboy hat. Olaf and Bernardo were both dressed in commando black, and had backpacks that looked full. They were bristling with weapons, blacked so they didn't show up at night, but not hidden.

'I take it that the guys here aren't going in the front door with us,' I said.

'No,' Edward said. He hit the brakes, and Olaf and Bernardo slipped out of the car and into the darkness. Because I knew what I was looking for, I could see them in a running crouch going over the hill. But if you hadn't been looking, you'd have missed them.

'You're scaring me, Edward. I'm not like a commando raid, James Bond kind of girl. Where the hell did you get a hairspray grenade?'

'A lot of female secret service now. It's a prototype.'

'Nice to know where my tax dollars are going.'

We were going down a long gravel driveway. There was a big house sitting up on a hill. Lights blazed out of the windows as if someone had gone through and hit every light, as if they were scared of the dark. If Riker really thought the monsters were coming, the analogy was accurate.

Edward outlined his plan as we drove the last few yards. I

was to pretend to do a spell of protection for Riker. While I delayed, Olaf and Bernardo would try to find the kids. If they couldn't find them or couldn't get them out, Olaf was supposed to find a man and kill him as messily as possible in a short space of time, leave the body where it would be found, and hope to make Riker think the monsters had already gotten inside. They might take us to the point where the monster kill had been found to get my expert advice, which would put us and whoever was with us, hopefully Riker, near where Olaf and Bernardo could help us kill them. If that failed, Bernardo would start blowing things up. Which would create panic and hopefully allow us to find the kids. Unless Bernardo decided the structure wasn't sturdy enough to blow up and not cave in around us. Then we'd need another plan.

Edward stopped the car at a gravel turnaround near the crest of the hill. Men armed with automatic submachine guns walked towards the car. None of them were Harold or Russell. They moved like Olaf and Edward moved, like predators.

'You don't believe they're going to give back the kids, do you?'

'Do you?' he asked. He'd put his hands on the steering wheel at ten and two, in plain sight.

I raised my hands in the air where they could be seen. 'No,' I said.

'If the kids are okay, we'll do as little killing as possible, but if the kids aren't okay, it's zero survivors.'

'The police are going to find out about this one, Edward. You will blow your Ted "Good ol' boy" Forrester image all to hell.'

'If the kids don't make it out, I don't give a damn.'

'How will Olaf and Bernardo know whether to kill or not?'

'There's a wire worked into my vest. They've both got ear pieces, so they'll be able to hear.'

'You're going to tell them to kill,' I said.

'If I have to.'

The machine-gun-toting men were at either side of the car. They made motions for us to get out. We did what they wanted, being sure to keep our hands in sight. We wouldn't want any misunderstandings.

55

The machine gun guy on my side wasn't that tall, five foot eight or maybe shorter, but his arms were corded with so much muscle that veins stood out against his skin like snakes. Some people vein up if they lift even a little, but most of the time you don't get that much popping up without some major effort. It was as if he was trying to make up for the lack of height by being obscenely strong. Most muscle-bound guys are slow and rarely know how to fight. They rely on sheer strength and just being a bully. But this one moved smoothly, almost gliding on his feet, sort of sideways, which hinted at some martial art training. He moved well, and his bicep was bigger than my neck. He was also pointing a very modern looking submachine gun at me. Muscle bound, trained fighter, and better armed than me – weren't there rules against that?

'Lean on the hood, assume the position,' he said.

I put my hands on the hood and leaned. The engine was still warm, not hot, but warm. Muscle man kicked my legs. 'Farther apart.' I did what he asked. I looked across the hood and met Edward's eyes. He was getting the same treatment on his side from a taller, slender man who wore silver frame glasses. Edward's eyes were at their empty, pitiless best. But somehow I knew he wasn't pleased. When I realized that, I realized I still had the sunglasses on, and my vision was still good through dark lenses at night. Funny, how neither Olaf nor Bernardo had asked in the car. There hadn't been time for many questions.

The vampire vision had toned down, but it was still there or I'd

have been night blind with the glasses on. Wondered what Muscle
Man would think of the eyes.

He kicked my right leg again, hard enough that it hurt. 'I said,
lean!' He had that drill sergeant voice going.

'If I lean any farther, I'll be lying down.'

I felt him move behind me and had my head turned to the side
when he slapped me in the back of the head, hard enough that my
cheek hit the hood. It would have hurt if it had been the front,
nose, mouth. He'd meant it to hurt.

'Do what you're told, and you won't get hurt.'

I was beginning not to believe him, but I leaned, cheek pressed
to the hood, arms out flat like I was being nailed down, feet spread
so far that one good foot sweep would have dumped me to the
ground. But it was nice and unsteady, the way he wanted it apparently.
In a way it was flattering. He was treating me as a dangerous
person. A lot of bad guys don't. Usually, they live to regret it, but
not always. If muscle man died tonight, it wasn't going to be because
of carelessness.

He searched me, top to bottom, even running his fingers through
my hair. He'd have found Bernardo's stiletto hairpins that the others
had missed at the house. He took the sunglasses off and looked at
them as if looking for things that I would never have thought to
find in a pair of sunglasses. He didn't really look at my face, didn't
catch the eyes, or maybe they weren't glowing black anymore. Muscle
Man found everything but the transmitter that was sewn somewhere
in the shirt and the contents of the purse. He did dump it out on
the ground and shine a flashlight on every item. He made sure the
ink pen wrote, that the hairspray sprayed, and took the breath
freshener mace as if he recognized it on sight. But that was all he
took out of the purse, though once it was empty, he kneaded it with
his left hand, the right still holding the submachine gun.

'This wouldn't be one of those with a compartment for a gun,
would it?'

I'd raised my head enough to watch him empty the purse, so we could look at each other while he held the gun on me and glanced down at things. 'No, it wouldn't be.'

'I was betting it would be,' he said.

'Nope,' I said.

He finished by standing on the purse and stomping it flat. Glad it wasn't really my purse. 'I guess there's no gun,' he said.

'Told ya.'

He took three big steps back, out of reach. He was treating me like I was dangerous. Darn. I sometimes counted on passing for harmless, but I guess I'd been packing too much hardware to pass for anything but dangerous.

'You can stand up.'

I stood up.

He tossed the sunglasses to me. I caught them. My eyes were in the light from the house now, but he never flinched. Apparently, the glowy stuff had faded. He motioned with the gun for me to pick up the contents of the purse. I put everything back inside and almost put the sunglasses in, but decided to put them back on. Two reasons: one, when the night got too dark to wear them, I'd know the vampire stuff had left me completely; two, knowing Edward, they were probably expensive, and I didn't want to get them scratched up.

He motioned with the gun, and said, 'Just walk slow, straight to the house, and it'll be all right.'

'Why don't I believe you?' I asked.

He looked at me with eyes as dead and empty as a doll's. 'I don't like smart mouths.'

'You'll have to wait until I do the spell before you can shoot me,' I said.

'So they tell me. Get moving.'

The slender guy with glasses who had Edward at gunpoint was waiting for Muscle Man to get me moving. When I started walking,

Glasses moved Edward forward. They kept us walking side by side, telling us to stay together. They kept us together so that if they had to start shooting they could kill us both with one spray of bullets. True professionals. I hoped Olaf and Bernardo were as good as they were supposed to be. If they weren't, we were in deep trouble.

The house was one of those nouveau architect homes that people with more money than taste are always hiring people to build. It looked like a giant had dumped white concrete in a free form slide putting windows and doors here and there like raisins in an oatmeal cookie. A nice surprise, but never where you expect to find them. The mismatched windows made the house look deformed. The door was off center but round, like a wide open mouth. The windows were not only round and mismatched, but the number of windows didn't seem to match the floor plan as if some of the windows looked into blank walls where no room could possibly be.

White steps led up to the round door like one of those cartoon tongues that spill out of mouths and go tumbling downstairs. The steps weren't wide enough for us to walk side by side, so Edward moved a couple of steps ahead. Neither of the men behind us protested, so we kept moving.

It had been so long since I carried a purse instead of a fanny pack that it felt awkward on my shoulder. I had to keep a hand on it to keep it from swinging around. I'd put it on the left shoulder, leaving my right hand uncompromised out of habit. Not that I had anything left to draw or pull or whatever. But it was always good to have your strong hand empty, just in case. So Edward and Dolph had always told me.

At the top of the porch in a spill of bright yellow light, they told us to stop. We stopped. They moved up to flank us and move a little back to either side. I didn't understand what they were doing at first, until the door opened and another man pointed the same kind of submachine gun at us. Muscle Man and Glasses had moved out of his line of fire and moved so they wouldn't catch him in their fire line. It is not easy to use three submachine guns in that small a space without crossing your own men, but they made it look easy, very smooth. The other men had carried an extra clip for the sub guns in a thigh holster, but this one had two clips at his waist.

The man in the door was African American and tall, like Olaf's height, very six foot plus. He was also completely bald just like Olaf. If they ever met, they'd look like light and dark versions of each other.

'What took so long?' he asked; his voice matched the body, deep.

'They were carrying a lot of hardware,' Muscle Man said.

The new guy was smirking at me. 'From the way Russell talked I expected you to look like Amanda. You're just a little bitch.'

'Amanda the Amazon that came to Ted's house?' I asked.

He nodded.

I shrugged. 'I wouldn't believe much that Russell said.'

'He said you broke his nose, kicked him in the balls, and beat his head in with a piece of wood.'

'Everything but the last bit. If I'd beaten his head in, he'd be dead.'

'What's the holdup, Simon?' Muscle Man asked.

'Deuce is having some trouble locating the wand.'

'Deuce would have trouble keeping track of his head if it wasn't attached,' Muscle Man said.

'True, but we still wait.' He was looking at both of us, the gun held easily in his big hands. 'What's with the sunglasses, bitch?'

I let the name calling go. They had all the guns. 'They look cool,' I said.

He laughed then, a warm growly sound. A nice laugh if he hadn't been armed.

'What about you, Ted? I hear you are a bad dude.'

Edward transformed into Ted, like a magician deciding he was going to have to perform after all. 'I'm a bounty hunter. I kill monsters.'

Simon looked at him, and there was something about the way he did it that said the Ted act wasn't fooling him. 'Van Cleef recognized your picture, Undertaker.'

Undertaker?

Ted smiled and shook his head. 'I don't know anybody named Van Cleef.'

Simon just looked at Glasses. Edward had time to turn his head so he took the blow on his shoulder. He moved a step, but didn't fall. Simon gave another look. Glasses hit his knee, and Edward collapsed onto one knee.

'We only need the girl up and running,' Simon said. 'So I'll ask you this just once, do you know Van Cleef?'

I stood there, not sure what to do. We were so totally covered by the guns, and the priority had to be getting the children out. So no heroics until they were safe. If we died, I wasn't a hundred percent sure that Bernardo and Olaf would risk their lives to get them out. So I stood there and looked at Edward kneeling on the porch, waiting for him to give me some kind of sign what I was supposed to do.

Edward looked up at Simon. 'Yes.'

'Yes, what, asshole?'

'Yes, I know Van Cleef.'

Simon smiled broadly, obviously happy with himself. 'Boys, this is the Undertaker, the man that still has the highest body count of anyone Van Cleef ever trained.'

I felt, rather than saw, the two men twitch. The information not only made sense to them, but it scared them. It made them afraid of Edward. Who the hell was Van Cleef, and when had he trained Edward, and for what? I wanted to know the answers, but not badly enough to ask. Later, if we survived, I'd ask Edward. Maybe he'd even tell me. 'I don't know you,' Edward said.

'I came in just after you left,' Simon said.

'Simon?' Edward made the name a question, and the big man seemed to understand what was being asked.

'As in whatever the fuck Simon says, you damn well better do.'

How colorful, I thought, but didn't say out loud.

'Can I get up now?' Edward asked.

'If you can stand, then help yourself.'

Edward got to his feet. If it hurt, it didn't show. His face was empty, eyes like bits of pale blue ice. I'd seen him kill with that face.

Simon's smile faltered around the edges. 'You're supposed to be one mean son of a bitch.'

'Van Cleef never said I was mean.' He sounded very sure of that.

Simon's smile disappeared altogether. 'No, he didn't. He said you were dangerous.'

'What would Van Cleef say about you?' Edward asked.

'Same thing,' Simon said.

'I doubt that,' Edward said.

They looked at each other, and there was a weight and a testing like something nearly visible in the air between them. Muscle Man's nerve broke first. 'Where the hell is Deuce with the wand?'

Simon blinked, and switched very cold brown eyes to the man behind me. 'Shut up, Mickey.'

Mickey? It didn't have quite the ring to it that the other nicknames did. Of course, Simon hadn't sounded too tough until it was explained.

'Van Cleef didn't recognize her picture.'

'No reason he should,' Edward said.

'The newspapers call her the Executioner.'

'That's what the vampires call her.'

'Why do they call her that?'

'Why do you think?'

Simon looked at me. 'How many vampire kills you got, bitch?'

If I had a chance tonight, I was going to teach Simon some manners, but not right now. 'I don't know exactly.'

'Guess.'

I thought about it. 'I stopped keeping track around thirty.'

Simon laughed. 'Hell, every man on this porch has more kills than that.'

More kills than thirty? Who the hell were these guys? I shrugged. 'I didn't know it was a competition.'

'Did you count the human kills?' Edward asked.

I shook my head. 'He asked about vampire kills, not human.'

'Add those in,' he said.

That was harder. 'Eleven, twelve maybe.'

'Forty-three,' Simon said, 'you got Mickey beat, but not Rooster.' Apparently, Rooster was Glasses.

'Add in the shapeshifters,' Edward said.

It had turned into a competition. I wasn't really sure that I wanted to seem as dangerous as I really was, but I trusted Edward's judgment. 'Oh, hell, Edward, I don't know.' I started counting in my head. Finally, I said, 'Seven.'

'So fifty,' he said.

Just hearing it out loud made me want to cringe. It sounded so Psychos 'R Us.

'I've still got you beat, bitch,' Simon said.

He was beginning to get on my nerves. 'The fifty only counts the people I did personally with a weapon.'

'You mean it doesn't count the ones you killed barehanded?' He smiled when he said it, like he didn't believe it.

'No, I counted those.'

The smile got positively condescending. 'Then what didn't you count, little bitch.'

'Witches, necromancers, things like that.'

'Why not count them?' This from Mickey.

I shrugged.

'Because using magic to kill is an automatic death sentence,' Edward said.

I frowned at him. 'I never said anything about magic.'

'We aren't friends,' Simon said, 'but you can be honest tonight, bitch. We won't tell the cops. Will we, boys?' He laughed and they laughed with him, with that same sort of nervous mirth that Itzpapalotl's vampires had had, like they were afraid not to laugh.

I shrugged. 'Most of the fifty are sanctioned kills. The cops already know about them.'

'You ever been on trial?' This from the until now silent Rooster.

'No.'

'Fifty legal kills,' Simon said.

'Give or take,' I said.

Simon looked at Edward. They had another one of those weighted staring contests.

'Would Van Cleef like her?'

'Yes, but she wouldn't like him.'

'Why not?'

'She's not big on orders and listening to people just because they've got an extra stripe on their shoulder.'

'Not disciplined,' Simon said.

'She's disciplined. You just got to have more than rank to get her to listen to you.'

'She listens to you,' Simon said. 'She didn't want to talk about her kills, but she took your lead.'

His saying that meant Simon was very observant, too observant for comfort actually. I'd underestimated him. Stupid of me. No, not stupid, careless.

Another man came up with the identical gun in his hands. He was just shy of six feet, but seemed smaller, delicate somehow. The hair was a deep brown, cut short, curly. The face was pretty in a girlish kind of way. His skin was that dark tan that isn't really tan at all. He had a set of small headphones around his neck, with wires connecting them to a metal box and a small flat . . . wand attached with a cord to the box. It had to be Deuce and the wand.

I didn't know what it was, but Edward went very still. He knew what it was, and he didn't like it. Not a good sign.

'Where the fuck have you been?' Mickey said.

'Mickey,' Simon said, and he said 'Mickey' the way that Edward could say 'Olaf' and get perfect obedience. There was no more comment from the backup players. Simon looked at Deuce. 'Do it.'

Deuce slipped the headphones on, hit a switch and some knobs on the box, and a light went on on the box. He got a distracted inward look on his face as if he were listening to things we couldn't hear. He started at Edward's hat and worked down, hesitated over the chest area, then continued the sweep. He knelt on the ground beside Edward and waved the wand up the backside of Edward. He was careful to stay out of the line of fire of all three guns. His own gun was on a sling that he pushed far behind his back, keeping it out of the way with a well-placed elbow as he moved.

He stood, slipped the headphones off, and unplugged them from the box. 'Listen to this.' He waved the wand over Edward's chest. It beeped frantically.

'Take off the shirt,' Simon said.

Edward didn't argue. He unbuttoned the shirt and handed it to Deuce, who waved the wand over it. The thing stayed silent.

Deuce waved the wand over Edward's chest again, and the wand beeped. He ran the wand over the shirt in his hand, no noise. Deuce shook his head.

'The undershirt,' Simon said.

Edward had to take his hat off. He handed it to me, then lifted the undershirt over his head. The Kevlar looked very artificial and white. He handed the undershirt to Deuce, and we went through the same routine again.

'Take the vest off,' Simon said.

'Tell me one thing first,' Edward asked. 'Are the kids all right?'

'Why the fuck do you care about some bitch's kids?'

Edward just looked at him, but there was something in that look that made Simon take a step back. He noticed what he'd done and took the step back, pointing the gun very solidly at Edward's chest. 'Take off the damn vest.'

'It's too hot for body armor anyway,' Edward said. It seemed an odd thing to say for Edward, man of few words, but you had to know Edward to know it was odd. I had the feeling that Edward had just put the word out for zero survivors. He undid the Velcro, slipped it over his head and handed it to Deuce.

Edward stood there naked from the waist up. He looked fragile beside the musclebound Mickey or the very tall Simon, but they saw in him what I saw in him because unarmed and half-naked they were still scared of him. It was there in the way Simon reacted to him. The way the others, except Deuce, kept their distance. Deuce didn't seem to be working on the same instincts as the rest, though he never once crossed the fire line. He made Edward stretch out his hand, or he knelt under the direct line of fire. None of them were careless. It wasn't a good sign.

He ran the wand over the vest. When the wand beeped, he handed it to Simon. Then he ran the wand over Edward's bare chest. Silence. Good, because I think Simon would have said, 'Skin,' in the same voice he'd said shirt, undershirt, vest. Just because Edward made him nervous didn't mean he wasn't scary all of his own.

'In the body armor, that's good,' Simon said. 'Most people, even if they have you strip, don't check the armor.'

Edward just looked at him.

'Her next.'

Deuce duck-walked in front of us. Just in case someone started shooting, he was safe. No one shot anyone. Of course the night was young. He stood on the other side of me. He didn't bother to put the earphones back on, just ran the wand over me. It beeped. 'Hand the hat back to him, please.'

Please – refreshing after hearing myself called bitch about a dozen times. 'My pleasure,' I said and handed Edward's hat back to him.

Deuce had looked up when I spoke, as if he wasn't used to politeness in others either. The wand ran over me, and it beeped at chest level.

'Take the shirt off, bitch,' Simon said.

I untucked the shirt and started unbuttoning it. 'My name's Anita, not bitch.'

'Like I give a fuck,' he said.

Fine, I'd tried being nice. I handed the shirt to Deuce and his magic wand. It beeped, but when he ran it back over me, nothing. He laid the box gently on the ground, the wand on top of it, and started looking at the shirt. In less than a minute he'd found a small wire with a slightly thicker head sewn into the collar of the shirt. 'Looks like a transmitter, maybe a homing beacon.'

Simon tossed the vest to Deuce. 'Cut it open, find out what's inside.'

Deuce pulled a gravity knife from his back pocket, did one of those quick wrist movements that spilled the blade open. He went over the vest with his hands first, eyes closed, then he started cutting. It was a longer wire, with a little box attached. 'It's a receiver. Someone out there is hearing everything we say.'

'Destroy the homer.'

Deuce crushed mine under his heel. When it was a little metallic and plastic slimy place on the porch, he smiled up at us as if he'd done a good thing. Deuce was a few bricks shy of a load. Funny how many people that Edward introduced me to were.

'Who's out there, Undertaker?' Simon asked.

Edward had put his hat back on. It looked funny with the shirt gone, but he seemed perfectly at ease. If he was nervous, you couldn't tell it.

'I am going to ask you this one more time nice, then it won't be so nice.' He seemed to square his shoulders as if he were the one about to take a beating. 'Who was on the other end of this wire? Who's out there?'

Edward shook his head.

Simon nodded.

Rooster hit him in the back, and it must have been hard because it drove him to his knees. Something on the butt of the gun broke the skin in two small cuts. He stayed on all fours for a few seconds as if it had stunned him, then he got up on his feet and faced Simon.

'Answer the question, Undertaker.'

Edward shook his head, again. He was ready for the next blow. It staggered him, but he didn't go down. There was a third small cut. The cuts weren't anything, but they showed how much force was being used. He was going to be bruised all to hell come morning.

'Maybe she knows,' Mickey said.

'I don't know who they are,' I said, and the lie fell smoothly off my tongue. 'Edward said we needed backup. He found some.'

'You'd come into a situation like this with unknown people at your back? You don't seem that stupid,' Simon said.

'Edward vouched for them,' I said.

'And you trust him?'

I nodded.

'You trust him with your life?'

'Yes,' I said.

Simon looked at me, then back to Edward. 'She your squeeze?'

Edward blinked, and I knew that was him trying to buy time to think what answer would be the least painful. 'No.'

'I'm not sure I believe you, either of you, but if we start beating up the bitch, and she gets too hurt to do the spell, Riker'd be pissed.'

'Why don't you have Undertaker ask the backup to come in?' Deuce said.

Everyone sort of froze, then looked at him. Simon said, 'What did you say?'

'If they can hear us, why not have him ask them to come up, hands up, that sort of thing.'

Simon nodded, then turned back to Edward. 'Tell them to come up to the house. Hands where we can see them.'

'They won't come,' Edward said.

'They'll come or we'll blow your fucking head off.' Simon put the short-butted gun to his shoulder, and put the barrel against Edward's forehead. 'Ask them to come into the house. Hands up. Throw their guns down.'

It was funny how Simon had never once thought it might be the police out there, as if he didn't believe the Undertaker would bring the police to the party.

Edward stared down the barrel of that gun, looked past it, into Simon's eyes, and the look was his usual look. His eyes were cold and empty as winter skies. There was no fear. There was no anything. It was like he wasn't there at all.

Edward may have been calm, but I wasn't. I'd seen enough bad men to know that Simon meant it. More than that, he wanted to do it. He'd feel safer if Edward were dead. I was out of ideas, but I couldn't just stand here and watch it happen.

'Tell them, Undertaker, or I will blow your head all over this porch.'

'Even if I asked, they wouldn't come.'

Simon pressed the barrel in, so that Edward had to brace his feet against it to keep from being pushed backwards. 'You better hope they come. We don't need you alive, just her.'

'I need him alive,' I said.

Simon's eyes flicked to me, then settled back on Edward. 'Lying bitch.'

'Are you a witch, Simon?' I asked, though I knew the answer. I'd have spotted it if he had been a practitioner.

'What the fuck does that matter?'

'Then you don't know what I need to do this spell, do you? Your boss would be pissed if you blew away someone I needed to keep him safe from the monsters.'

'Why do you need him?' Deuce asked.

I swallowed and tried to think; nothing good was coming. I tried for truth. When I'm out of other options, it still works. 'Riker said he wouldn't hurt the kids. He said he wouldn't hurt us. He said he just wanted me to save him from the monster. If you blow . . . Ted's brains into the next county, then I'm not going to believe any of Riker's other promises. The second I think that Riker is going to kill the kids and us once I do the job, then I don't have any incentive to help him.'

Simon's eyes flicked to me again. 'We can give you incentive.' I didn't see him nod, but I felt Mickey moving behind me. I've never been good at taking a blow. I moved without thinking and he missed my shoulder, but I'd been right. He knew how to fight. I was turning towards him to do what, I'm not sure, when the butt of the gun caught me on the chin. I think I'd made him mad by ducking because he hit me hard.

The next thing I knew I was on the ground, looking up. Deuce was kneeling by me, stroking my face. I had the impression he'd been petting me for awhile, as if I'd passed out. I didn't remember passing out. The sunglasses were gone. I didn't know if Deuce took them off, or if they flew off when my head went back.

'She's awake,' Deuce said, voice sort of dreamy. He gave me a gentle smile and kept stroking my face.

Simon knelt by me, blocking out the light. 'What's your name?'

'Anita, Anita Blake.'

'How many fingers?'

I watched his hand move back and forth, following it with my eyes. 'Two.'

'Can you sit up?'

It was a good question. 'With help, maybe.'

Deuce put his arm behind my back and lifted me. I let him take a lot of the weight, not because it was necessary, but because them thinking I was more hurt than I was might make them think I was less of a threat. We needed some sort of edge.

I rested against Deuce's shoulder. He was humming something tuneless under his breath, his hand cupping my face, stroking the skin, over and over. I was finally able to see everything. Edward was on his knees with his hands clasped on top of his cowboy hat. Rooster had a gun touching his head. Edward didn't look hurt. More like they'd done it to keep him from doing anything heroic.

Mickey had a bloody lip. He was carefully not making eye contact with anyone.

'Can you stand?' Simon asked.

'With help, yeah.'

'Deuce.'

Deuce helped me to my feet, and the world wavered. I clung to Deuce, hands digging in as the world tried to slide out my ear. Maybe I wasn't pretending to be hurt.

'Shit,' Simon said. 'Can you walk if Deuce helps you?'

I started to nod, and that made me nauseated. I had to breathe through it before I could answer him. 'I think so.'

'Good. Let's go.' He backed into the house, eyes watching the darkness beyond, though with all the lights his night vision was probably shit. Deuce and I went next. He had Edward's wire hung around his neck like a doctor's stethoscope. Edward was next, hands still firmly on top of his head. Rooster, then Mickey bringing up the rear. They staggered us so that if someone started shooting, there was room to maneuver.

Simon started up a flight of stairs. I looked up the long flight and the world swam. Deuce called, 'Simon, I'm not sure she's up to stairs.'

'Mickey.' The man in question moved up to the foot of the stairs. 'Carry her.'

'I don't want him touching me,' I said.

'I didn't ask you, either of you,' Simon said.

Mickey gave his gun to Simon, then took my arm. He pulled me too fast and I was suddenly airborne on his shoulder, my head hanging down. I couldn't breathe. The world was spinning, and I was going to be sick.

'I'm going to throw up.'

He dumped me unceremoniously back to my feet, and I fell. It was Simon who caught me. 'Are you too hurt to do the spell?'

I knew the answer to that one — no. Because if Riker thought I couldn't help him, he would kill us all. 'I can do it if Mickey here doesn't dangle me over his shoulder with my head hanging down. I need to stay upright, or it's not going to get any better.'

'Carry her in your arms, not over your shoulders,' Simon said. 'All those muscles got to be good for something.'

Mickey picked me up in his arms like you'd carry a small child. He stood there like I weighed nothing. He was strong, but carrying like this is harder than it looks. We'd see how he did if there was more than one floor to climb. Here's hoping he didn't drop me.

I put my arm around his shoulders. I'd have clasped hands around his neck to be more secure, but I couldn't reach around his deltoids without straining. 'How much do you bench press?'

'Three-ninety.'

'I'm impressed,' I said.

He preened a little. Mickey was dangerous, but if I could keep him from hitting me, he was the weak one. Rooster followed orders too well. Simon was Simon. Deuce seemed harmless, but there was something in those dreamy eyes that was a little scary. Maybe I was wrong, but I'd try Mickey before I tried Deuce, for trickery anyway. Arm wrestling, I'd take Deuce.

Mickey walked up the stairs with me in his arms, effortlessly. I could feel the muscles in his legs pushing, working. Again, I had the sense of immense physical potential and quickness.

'What's Mickey mean?' I asked.

'Nothing.'

'Simon explained his nickname, I'm just wanting to know what yours means.'

Deuce answered. 'It's for Mickey Mouse.'

'Shut up, Deuce.'

'He's got a tattoo of Mickey on his butt,' Deuce said as if Mickey hadn't spoken.

Mickey's face darkened, and he turned to glare at the other man. I just fought to keep my face blank. What kind of moron would have Mickey Mouse tattooed on his butt? But not out loud, not with those tree trunk arms wrapped around my tender body. If I hadn't had the marks on me, he'd have probably killed me with that one blow. No, I didn't want Mickey angry with me.

There was a landing, and a second flight of stairs. Mickey didn't even hesitate on the landing. He just went for the next set of stairs. His legs moved as easily up the second set as the first. He never paused to catch his breath. In fact, his breathing barely sped up. Whatever you could complain about Mickey, being out of shape wasn't part of it.

I told him so. 'How far you jog a day?'

'Five miles, every other day. How'd you know?'

'A lot of body builders would be having trouble by now. They neglect the aerobic stuff, but you move like some kind of well-oiled machine. You're not even breathing hard.' There was something very intimate about being carried in someone's arms like this, a reminder of childhood and your parents' arms maybe.

Mickey's hands tightened on me; the one on my thigh began to massage my leg. I didn't tell him not to. It's been my experience that if a man is interested in having sex with you, they hesitate to kill you before they've had the sex. This rule is not always true, but more often than not. The trick is to get the man thinking more about sex than violence, so he's a little confused. We needed a little confusion among our enemies right now.

We were in a wide white hallway that ran the length of the top of the house. There were white doors with silver knobs. Nothing differentiated one door from the other. Simon went to the farthest door, and Mickey followed with me in tow. I could see Deuce following, and Edward just topping the last stairs with Rooster behind him, walking well back out of arm's or leg's length. These guys were good. I'd gotten to where I counted on the bad guys not being this good. Even if they were vampires and werewolves they'd be unprofessional. But I'd never been around professional bad guys that were this professional. It cut our options from bad to worse.

Simon opened the door. We were here. We were still alive. The night still had possibilities.

56

Mickey sat me down near the middle of a very nice Persian rug. He kept an arm around my shoulder, as if it had been his idea to carry me. I gave his arm a squeeze before I stepped away from him. Didn't want to be slutty, but wanted him hopeful in case it was useful. The room looked like the study of a prosperous academic. There were antique maps framed on the walls. Shelves lined almost every extra space of wall, a lot of books that looked well read and well used. There were books open on the big leather-topped desk with bookmarks in them and sticky notes covered in writing, as if we'd interrupted someone's research.

A man sat behind the desk. He was a big man, both tall and wide. Not fat exactly but headed that way. He rose from his chair with a smile and walked towards us, hand outstretched. He moved with a confident, easy stride, like an ex-athlete going soft with normal living. His dark hair was cut very short and mostly bald on top. His hands were big, and the new weight showed in the hands where a college ring was beginning to cut into his flesh. He had calluses on his hands like he wasn't afraid to do the real work himself, but the calluses were losing that hard edge, softening, smoothing back into his skin. He'd probably done some of his dirty work once, but no more.

He gripped my hand with both of his, when one of his hands could have swallowed both of mine. 'So glad you're here, Ms Blake.' He said it like I'd been invited instead of blackmailed.

'I'm glad one of us is glad I'm here,' I said.

The smile widened, and he let my hand go. 'I am sorry for our little theatrics. Simon called up and said he thought Mickey had broken your neck. So happy that he exaggerated.'

'Not by much, Mr Riker.'

'Are you feeling well enough to do the spell? We could have some tea first, let you rest.'

I managed a smile. 'I am grateful that we're being all civilized, and coffee would be great, but where are the children?'

His eyes flicked past me to Edward. He still had his hands clasped on top of his hat, but at least they hadn't made him kneel again. 'Ah, yes, the children.'

I didn't like the way he said it, like it was going to be bad news.

'Where are they?' Edward asked, and Rooster hit him in the back with the gun again. It staggered him, and he had to wait for it to pass before he straightened up. His hands never left his head, as if he knew they were looking for an excuse to hurt him again.

'You promised us that they wouldn't be harmed,' I said.

'You were late,' Riker said.

'No,' Edward said.

'Don't,' I said, as Rooster raised his arm back for another blow. He did it anyway. Fuck. I turned back to Riker. 'Every cruel thing you do helps convince me that you have no intention of any of us getting out of here alive.'

'I assure you, Ms Blake, that I intend to let you go.'

'What about the others?'

He gave a small shrug, and walked back behind his desk. 'Unfortunately, my men think that Mr Forrester is too dangerous to be allowed to live. I do regret that.' He sat down in his nice swivel chair, elbows on the chair arms, thick fingers steepled. 'But he will serve a useful purpose before he dies. If you are reluctant, we will take it out on Mr Forrester. Since we intend to kill him anyway, we can do anything we want to him, and it doesn't really matter.'

My stomach was a hard knot, my pulse beating in my throat hard enough that I had to try twice to talk. 'What about the kids?'

'Do you really care?'

'I'm asking, aren't I?'

He reached behind the desk and pressed something. The rear walls of the room slid open, revealing enough equipment to make NASA proud. There were four blank TV screens, but somehow I didn't think this was Riker's new Digital Television system.

'What the hell is all that for?' I asked.

'That is not really your concern. I have signaled for additional men to be brought up. When they arrive, then I will show you the children.'

'Why the additional men?' I asked.

'You'll see,' he said.

We didn't have long to wait. Four men came through the door. Two I recognized: Harold of the scarred face and Newt who I'd nearly made a soprano. Harold had a shotgun, and Newt his big nickel-plated .45. But it was the two men behind them that were the problem.

One was tall and planed down to nothing but muscle and dark, burnished skin. He didn't have Mickey's bulk, but he didn't need it. He entered the room surrounded by a cloud of his own violent potential. He set my lizard sense screaming, as if it knew here was someone to avoid. He had the same gun the other pros were carrying, but he'd added knives. At his forearms, his upper arms, both hips, and even hilts sticking up from behind his shoulders. It was very primitive somehow and very effective. If he'd walked into a cell, you might have dropped to your knees and begged for mercy.

The other one was just medium height, medium brown hair cut short, not too dark, not too light, not too anything. He had a face that you wouldn't remember two seconds after you saw it, because he was not handsome enough or ugly enough to stand out. He was one of the most unmemorable people I'd ever seen, and yet when his brown eyes swept over me, met mine for a second, I felt a jolt all the way down to my feet. One flash, and I knew that of the two men, he would kill you quicker.

He had the same submachine gun the others had, but paired with what looked like a .10 mil automatic. I didn't recognize the brand. My hands aren't big enough for a .10 mil so I don't pay that much attention.

'Simon, I want two men on both of our guests.'

'Make it four on him,' Simon said.

'I bow to your expertise.'

Rooster made Edward get on his knees. Simon made Mickey go to Edward. I guess he didn't want to risk the Muscle Man hitting me again. If they killed Edward early, they still had the kids to blackmail with. Simon sent the medium man to Edward, and Simon himself took up a post by Edward. They thought he was a very dangerous man, and they were right.

The nausea had been fading, but all the preparations were making me nervous. I was afraid of what we were going to see. If they hadn't been afraid to show us, they wouldn't have had four men on Edward. I was left with Deuce and the knife guy. Harold and Newt stayed near the door. Harold seemed nervous.

Deuce touched my arm, tracing the mound of scar tissue at my elbow. 'What did it?'

'Vampire.'

He raised his shirt up, and his stomach was a mass of white scars. 'Mortar round.'

I wasn't sure what I was supposed to say. But I was saved from the decision because the knife guy grabbed my arm and turned me to look at Riker. He kept his hand on my arm, and since his hand completely encircled my upper arm, it wasn't going to be easy to get away.

'Show time,' Riker said. He hit another switch, and two of the monitors flickered to life. Black and white film of cells. At first, all I saw was Russell's back in one room, and the Amazon Amanda's back in the other room. Then my eyes saw legs sticking out from around the woman. Legs in jeans and jogging shoes, ankles tied together. Too big for Becca. Had to be Peter.

She'd stripped down to the waist, and that broad muscular back made everyone in this room look frail except for Mickey. It was only the length of her hair that made me guess her. She leaned forward, revealing more of Peter's body. She'd pulled his jeans and underwear down to his knees. She was playing with him.

I looked at the floor, then back up.

She tried to kiss him, and when he turned his head away, she slapped him twice hard, first one cheek then the other. There was already blood on his mouth as if it wasn't the first time she'd hit him. She leaned back in for the kiss, revealing small tight breasts to the camera. She kissed him and this time he let her. Her hand never stopped working on his body.

I turned slowly to look at the other monitor. Please, God, please, don't let Russell be doing the same thing to Becca. He wasn't, and I was grateful. He'd turned with her on his lap, as if he knew he had an audience to play to now. He cradled her like you'd hold any small child, but he'd pinned one small arm, and two of the fingers on the tiny hand were at a bad angle. He broke a third finger while we watched, and her mouth opened in a soundless scream.

'Shall we have sound?' Riker asked.

Becca was screaming high and piteous. Russell cradled her and murmured soothing things. He stroked her hair and looked directly at the camera. His nose was still packed and bandaged. He knew we were there.

Peter's voice came high. He'd never sounded more like a little boy. 'Please, don't. Please stop!' His arms were tied behind his back, but he was still struggling.

She slapped him. 'It'll feel good, I promise.'

I looked at Edward. Simon had the gun against his head. The hat was on the ground. The medium-looking man had conjured a knife from somewhere and had it pressed to Edward's throat. A trickle of blood slid down his skin. I met his eyes, and I knew that everyone in this room, everyone in this house was dead. They just didn't know it yet.

Edward started to say something, but Simon said, 'No, no talking from you or Shooter will slit your throat.'

The medium guy must be Shooter. The name didn't suit him. He looked more like a Tom, Dick, or Harry.

They wouldn't let Edward talk, so it was my play, but we both knew where the game would end. Sudden death.

'Get them out of there, Riker.'

'The children?' He gave a questioning lilt to his voice.

'Order them to leave the kids alone, now.'

'And if I don't?'

I smiled. 'Then the monster is going to come in here and gut you.'

His eyes flinched. That bothered him. Good. 'Knowing what is happening to them should speed up the spell of protection, I think.'

'If you don't stop it, Riker, there won't be anything left to salvage.'

'I don't know. I think the boy is enjoying himself, from the sound of things.'

I'd been trying not to hear, but Peter's breath was coming faster and faster, frantic, but it wasn't the sound of pain. He screamed, 'Don't, please don't.'

I looked and I wished I hadn't. Some sights cut through your mind leaving a scar behind that never really heals. Watching Peter writhe caught between his first pleasure and the horror of it all, was one of those sights. I pride myself on never flinching. If someone is being tortured I don't look away. To look away only saves me pain, not them. If I can't save them the pain, then I watch as a kind of respect and as a punishment for myself, to remind me what happens to people when I fail them. But I failed Peter twice because

I looked away just before a wordless scream tore from his mouth. It wasn't the sound of pain.

I turned away, and maybe I moved too fast for the head injury, or maybe it was something else, because the room swam in streamers of color. I tried to go to my knees, and the knife man jerked my arm, kept me on my feet. Fine, I threw up on him.

He jerked back, actually let go of my arm. I fell to my knees grateful to be low to the ground. Throwing up had brought a roaring headache. Riker's voice came through the next wave of nausea.

'Amanda, Russell, be so good as to leave the children alone. Our Ms Blake is too squeamish to do her work while she fears for their safety.'

I looked up at the monitors to make sure they actually left the rooms. Russell kissed Becca on the head, then left her huddled in the corner, crying for her mommy. Amanda blindfolded Peter while he begged her not to. She whispered something in his ear that caused him to curl into a ball. She left his pants down, picked up her shirt from the floor and walked out.

I huddled into my own version of a ball on the floor. I stayed on my knees while I tried to decide whether I was going to throw up again or not. Nausea like this is usually a sign of a concussion. The headache was another. But I think sheer nerves had pushed me over the edge. I used to throw up at crime scenes quite a bit. Apparently, there were still things I couldn't handle, like child abuse. Dear God, please give us some help here. Help us get them out of here safe.

There was a beeping, and Riker hit another button on his desk. 'What is it?'

'We've got two dead down here. They were fucking butchered.'

Riker went pale. 'The monster.'

'Knives, some kind of fucking big knife.'

'You're sure of that?' Riker asked. 'You are positive?'

'Yes, sir.'

'It seems we have intruders.' He looked at Simon. 'What are you going to do about our company, Simon?'

'Kill them, sir.'

'Then do it.'

'Shooter, Rooster, stay with him and kill him as soon as Riker gives the word. Mickey, you're with me.' He looked across at the two men by me. 'You stay with her. Make sure no one else hits her. Harold, Newt, come with me.'

Then they were gone, and we were down to two bad guys a piece, and Riker. It would never get better than this.

'Is there a bathroom?' I asked.

'Are you going to be ill again?'

'It's a thought.'

'The two of you take her. And Deuce, if you can come up with something creative that won't leave a mark or physically harm Ms Blake in any way, but will convince her that the children and Mr Forrester are not the only ones that can be hurt, do so. Perhaps you can show her your namesake. You've got thirty minutes.'

There aren't a lot of things you can do to a person that fulfilled Riker's requirements. The ones I could think of were mostly sexual. Usually, the talk of my impending rape upsets me, but all I could think of now was that I had thirty minutes with two men who might want to fuck me more than kill me. All I wanted to do was kill them. It made my options easier. But I said, 'Is there a reason for torturing me, too, or is it just a hobby?'

He smiled, pleasant, confident. 'I thought you would be worthy of my men, but I find you weak, Ms Blake. Weakness should be punished. But it must be done carefully, so you can still do the spell, because I do want that.'

'Isn't the line, these things must be done delicately or you injure the spell?'

Deuce laughed. Riker frowned at me. 'It's from *The Wizard of Oz*,' Deuce said. 'The Wicked Witch of the West says it to Dorothy.'

'Take her away, Deuce,' he wrinkled his nose, 'and clean yourself up, Blade. You're welcome to help in the punishment, but Deuce is in charge. I don't want her damaged.'

Deuce grabbed my arm almost gently and helped me to my feet. The guy I'd thrown up on, Blade, followed us by a few steps. Evidently, he was taking no chances. At the door a man appeared. He was darkly Hispanic with longish hair, a shoulder holster, complete with .9mm automatic. He looked like local hired muscle, but he wasn't. He vibrated with power. A shimmering energy flowed off of him. Psychic or maybe more.

'Ms Blake, meet our resident expert on the supernatural, Alario. He was in charge of the protection spells on all my establishments. His art failed him recently at one of my shops, and my workers are dead. You will succeed where he has failed.'

Alario watched me with cool dark eyes. His power flared over mine as Deuce led me past him. We recognized each other as powers, but there wasn't time for anything else, but there would be later. Which was what I was afraid of. Alario was the real deal, a practitioner of the arts. He'd figure out pretty quickly that I didn't know shit about spells of protection, at least not the kind Riker wanted.

Deuce led me down the white hall, with Blade trailing us. We were out of time. I couldn't go back into that room and fake a spell. Olaf had failed to make his kills horrendous enough to fool the bad guys. The only good thing he'd done was divide their forces, and I had to take advantage of that while it lasted. Which meant that if at all possible only one person was coming back from the bathroom. Hopefully, it would be me.

57

It was one of those bathrooms with a double sink separate from the rest of the bathroom. Deuce led me into the little bathroom area, complete with shower. I managed to do some dry heaving, but that was the best I could do, and even that made my head ache. It hurt so much I closed my eyes trying to keep my brains from leaking out through them. If it wasn't a concussion, it was a hell of an imitation.

Deuce wet a washcloth and gave it to me.

'Thanks.' I put it over my face and tried to think. So far, Deuce hadn't touched me. Blade was trying to clean up in the sink area, but he'd want the shower soon.

'I loved the look on Blade's face when you puked on him. It was priceless.'

I put the wash rag to the back of my neck. I was thinking furiously about what was in the purse and what options I had. But my voice was calm, point for me. 'Blade? As in the comic book character?'

He nodded. 'Yeah, the vampire killer. They both carry knives.'

'And they're both African American,' I said.

'Yeah.'

I looked into his face, wash cloth that he'd so kindly given me still on my neck. I tried to read behind those pleasant, slightly dreamy, brown eyes, but it was like trying to read Edward. I just couldn't read between the lines.

'I think that Blade actually used wooden knives and like a crossbow in the comic books,' I said.

Deuce shrugged. 'You're either very brave, or you don't think I'll hurt you.'

'I believe you'll hurt me, if you want to.'

'Then you're brave,' he said. He was leaning against the wall, fingers playing lightly with the gun on its sling at his shoulder.

It was my turn to shrug. 'Yeah, but it's not really bravery that's keeping me calm.'

He looked interested for the first time. 'What is?'

'After what I saw being done to Becca and Peter, I just can't get too excited about myself.'

Blade banged on the door. 'We don't have all night, and I want a shower.'

Deuce and I both jumped when he banged on the door. We shared one of those embarrassed smiles, then he opened the door and ushered me through.

Blade had tried to scrub at his clothes in the sink, but it hadn't helped. He tried to go through the door, and Deuce stepped in his way. 'Riker won't like you taking a shower.'

'He told me to get cleaned up.'

'Simon told us to keep two people on her. We can't do that if you're in the shower.'

Blade looked at me. 'I think Simon overestimated her. Anyone that throws up after seeing mild torture like that, I'm not afraid of. Now get out of my way, Deuce.'

Deuce moved to one side, moving just ahead and to one side of him. Blade brushed past us without a word, his anger trailing behind him like a loose coat. He slammed the door behind him.

I went to the sink and rewet the wash cloth. He was watching me in the mirror now. His eyes were still pleasant, but something else had crept in. Something that promised pain, the way the wind can bring the smell of rain against your skin just before it starts to pour.

I started fishing in the purse. 'I've got some breath stuff in here somewhere.'

'I could lock you in the room with Blade. He strips real pretty, and he's not very happy with you right now.'

My hand closed on the pen with its hidden blade.

'You really think he could control himself enough to just rape me and not do other damage? Like you said, he's not very happy with me.'

'You never asked about my nickname,' he said.

The conversation was moving too fast for me. 'I assumed it was some kind of card-playing thing.'

He shook his head while I watched him in the mirror. Then he started unzipping his pants. He was too far away to touch me, or for me to fight back. All I could do was wait for him to come to me.

He slipped inside his open fly and lifted himself out in a smooth practiced movement. He was huge, impressive even limp and soft. If I hadn't seen Bernardo earlier, I'd have been more impressed. Of course, you could never be a hundred percent sure how big a man got when he was erect. Some barely changed size. Some grew a lot. Maybe he'd been very impressive. Then I realized he had a tattoo on it.

I had to turn and look, rather than trust to the mirror. 'Am I supposed to run screaming or ask to touch it?' I wasn't even scared. It was too bizarre.

'Which do you want to do?'

I admit I was having a hard time looking at his face and not his penis because it was growing, and I could see the tattoo more clearly. 'Can't rape the willing, hey?'

He smiled, as if this approach had worked before with women. It was certainly something a girl didn't get offered everyday. 'I won't tell, if you don't.'

'Is that the two of hearts on your . . . penis?'

His smile widened.

'Didn't that hurt?'

'Not as much as it's going to,' Deuce said. He moved slowly towards me, so I could get a good look. He had a flair for theatrics, did Deuce. I didn't want him using his flair or anything else on me. I turned and stumbled on purpose. He caught me, as he'd caught me all the other times. I put the pen against his chest, just under the sternum, angled upward. I was a vampire hunter. If there was one thing I knew how to do, it was to find the heart with the first blow.

I pressed the button the second I touched him. There was no upward movement, no feel of shoving the blade, because the blade did its own work.

His eyes went wide, mouth opened, but no sound came out. I twisted the blade left, then right, making sure he'd never draw breath to warn the man in the other room.

Deuce started to slide down the cabinets. I caught him and lowered him gently to the floor, glad he was one of the smaller men. I'd have had trouble wrestling Mickey's body around. The water was still running in the shower. Blade probably wouldn't have heard the sound of the body hitting the ground over the shower, but better safe than sorry.

Deuce lay there on the floor, the blade sticking out of his chest, his pants still unzipped, his namesake naked to the world. He looked very sad lying there dead. If I had time before I left, I'd zip him up, but first Blade. I got the gun off Deuce's shoulder and put the sling around my shoulder. I checked to make sure I knew where the safety was, and that it was off. The switch on the side had three settings, not just two like the Uzi. I put the setting on high. Logic said it would make the most bullets come out in the shortest space of time. I got Deuce's extra clip for the sub gun. A clip only holds twenty rounds. Normally, that sounded like a lot, but not tonight. There wasn't enough ammo in the world to make me feel safe tonight. I put the extra clips for both sub guns and the hand guns in the purse and crossed the purse straps across my chest.

Deuce's backup was a .9mm Glock. Personally, I find Glocks awkward to shoot, though I know people that swear by them, once the learning curve was over at the firing range. But I was happy to see this one.

The guns were great, but they would make a lot of noise. If I shot Blade, it would bring the rest of the bad guys down on me, and worse yet, they might kill Edward before coming after me. They had three hostages. They only needed one.

I needed something quiet. Trouble was I didn't think I could take Blade with a blade. Hand to hand, forget it. That left me with the contents of the purse.

I pulled the blade out of Deuce's chest. Blood welled up darker than most, like heart blood is supposed to be. I cleaned the blade automatically on a sleeve of his shirt and slipped it into my front pocket.

One of his hands was lying against the cabinet doors far under the sink. Maybe I did have more than just what was in the purse. I moved his arm and looked. It's amazing how much lethal stuff peopie keep in their bathroom cabinets. Almost everything has hazardous warning labels, yelling poison, caustic agent, if accidental contact with eyes, flush with water immediately. But there was a pile of big, fluffy towels, and I had Deuce's handgun. Homemade silencer. But I was going to have to hold the gun at about waist level, close into my body, to keep the towels tight enough to act as a muffler. Holding the gun that way meant I'd want to get in close before I fired. If Blade were as good as the rest of them, he'd have his gun close. I'd only get one shot, and it had to count.

How do you get that close to a well-armed man? Answer – take off some clothes. I took off the T-shirt and the vest. It wouldn't stop a knife, and the idea was that he wouldn't get a shot off, right? Besides, I was trying for romance or at least lust. Kevlar just lacks that certain something.

I kept the bra. My nerves weren't that good. Besides, if he

demanded I take some clothes off, it left me something besides my pants. It was like playing strip poker. More clothes give you more to work with.

The shower went off. Shit. My time had just run out. My heart was suddenly in my throat. But I had to get in there, before he came out here. If he saw the body, it wasn't rape I had to worry about.

I tucked the gun down the front of my pants, towels clutched to my chest and stomach, and opened the door. I closed the door with me leaning against it. Blade looked up. His dark skin was beaded with water, and Deuce had been right. Blade stripped real pretty. Under other circumstances, it would have been a pleasure to see him. Now, I was so scared I was having trouble breathing.

He reached for the gun that had been propped against the tub. His knife sheaths were draped across the back towel rack like you'd hang a wash rag, to keep them dry but handy. He stopped in mid-motion, fingers trailing on the gun.

'What do you want?'

'Deuce said to bring you towels.' I let the fear slide into my voice, making it breathy.

'How'd he get you to strip down?'

I looked down, an embarrassed head bob. 'He gave me a choice of him or you.'

Blade laughed, and it was a purely masculine sound. 'He show his deuce?'

I nodded. I didn't have to pretend to be embarrassed. I just didn't try and hide it.

'Take off the bra.' He straightened up, hand going farther away from the big gun, but still too close to the knives and his handgun on the towel rack.

I slid out of the straps, and pressed the towels to my chest, reached back and undid the snaps. I lifted the towels away from my body just enough to pull the bra out and let it fall to the floor.

I kept the towels tight against me, for modesty's sake, and to hide the gun in my waistband.

He stepped out of the tub and started to take those three steps that would close the distance. I turned my body, sort of sideways, getting the gun out, still held behind the towels.

He was right in front of me, three steps away from all his weapons. He curled his fingers over the top of the towel and pushed them lower, exposing my breasts an inch at a time. He was less than ten inches away from me. His hand stroked the upper mound of my breast, and I fired. His body jerked, and I think he said, 'Fuck.' I kept pulling the trigger until he collapsed to his knees, eyes rolled back. His stomach and lower chest were a red ruin. The towels were shredded, and covered in black powder stains. The shots had been muffled, but not silenced. I waited there in the small room, the shots seeming to echo in the walls. I waited for cries of alarm. Nothing.

I picked up my bra, but didn't take time to put it on, before I opened the connecting door and listened. Silence. Great. I got dressed and took all the weapons. Blade's handgun was a Heckler and Koch. Nice gun. I tucked it in the front of my pants where the Firestar would have normally gone. I put both the big guns over the same shoulder, and the knife sheaths I draped over the other shoulder. I brought the sub-gun around, clicked the safety off, and I was as ready as I was going to be.

The last time I'd seen Edward, he'd been on his knees. His two guards had been standing. If I was careful and the gun didn't kick too much, I could take them out over Edward's head. My plan was to spray the room. As plans went, it was crude, and secrecy would be very lost if we were within hearing of anyone, but once I knew the noise wasn't going to get Edward killed, I didn't care as much. They'd have killed Edward because he was a threat, and they'd want to take out the threat at their back before turning to face a new threat. The kids weren't a threat. If Riker was dead and couldn't give the order to hurt them, then they'd be okay until we reached them. That was the theory, and it was the best one I had.

Bristling with weapons, I listened at the outer door. Nothing. I opened it just a little. The hallway was empty. Better. I locked the door behind me so that when I shut it, people might assume it was occupied by more than dead people. The knives moved too much slung over my shoulder, so I set them down in a pile against the wall, being as quiet as I could. The corridor that had seemed so long, now seemed short because this was one of those plans that was either going to work really well or be a total disaster. In less than two minutes, I'd be at the door, and we'd see.

58

The gun had a short stock, but I braced it against my shoulder, and my arms were short enough that it was probably easier for me than the men I took them off. I was only steps from the open study door. Voices came out into the hallway.

'What do you mean that Antonio and Bandit are missing?' That was Riker. 'I thought your men were good, Simon.'

Shit. Was Simon back in the room? It didn't matter. It didn't change the plan. But I'd have preferred that Simon be elsewhere, at least until Edward was safe and armed. But Simon's voice came tinny and staticy. It was the intercom system. Shit, I didn't want them to hear the shots. The best I could do was wait until I didn't hear him using it. The longer I lurked in the hallway, the less chance the plan had. Someone was going to come up the stairs or out of the room or out of the study. If I lost surprise, it was over.

I was scared, really scared, not about killing or being killed, but about accidentally shooting Edward. I had an unfamiliar submachine gun in my hands. I'd never even seen one like this used. If you aim too high with a machine gun, more the full machine guns, but the subs, too, you can actually miss. If I fired into that room and missed everyone, I guess I deserved to get shot. I took the last deep breath and eased around the door frame. I know people always stand in the middle of the freaking door in the movies, but that's a good way to get killed. Use cover when you have it.

I had a split second to see the room. Rooster and Shooter had Edward covered, still on his knees. Alario the Witch had moved beside Riker's desk. I started firing almost before I'd finished looking.

The sound was enormous, but the gun had almost no recoil. I had to adjust my aim because I'd been expecting to have to fight the gun, but it was smooth, for a sub gun. Shooter actually got a burst off, but it was angled wrong and took out the ceiling above me. Rooster turned, but that was it. Seconds for both of them to go down, seconds to move the gun in a continuous spray that took out the control panels and monitors, and Riker, sitting behind his desk. Alario was the farthest away, and he had time to dive to the floor.

I went for the floor, too, hitting on my stomach as I aimed for him. I was angled away from Edward. I didn't have to be careful. I kept the trigger down and hit Alario before he could get a shot off. His body danced with the slap of bullets. There was something fascinating about the way the bullets shredded him, or maybe I just couldn't let go of the trigger.

I caught movement out of the corner of my eye and rolled on one shoulder, gun pointed. I let off the trigger just in time. Edward was kneeling with a gun in his hand by the bodies of his guards. He had a hand out as if to ward off the bullets, as if he hadn't been sure I'd remember in time.

We stayed that way for a frozen second, me on my side, the sub-gun pointed at him, finger still on the trigger, but not pressing down. Him with his hand out, the automatic pistol in his hand but pointed down.

His mouth moved, but I couldn't hear him. Part shock, adrenaline, and part firing a submachine gun without ear protection in a closed room. I eased to a kneeling position and stopped pointing the gun at him. He seemed to realize I was having trouble hearing because he held up two fingers and did thumbs down. Rooster and Shooter were dead. Hurrah.

I knew Alario was dead. I'd gone way overboard on him. I looked across the room at Riker. He was sitting in his chair, mouth gaping open and closed like a landed fish. The front of his nice white shirt and suit jacket were stained red in a row across the entire front of his body, including his arms. He was sitting so that I could see his hands clearly. I don't know if the force of the shots had pushed the wheeled chair back or he'd started that way.

Edward pointed at Riker, and I heard one word of the sentence, 'Guard.' He wanted me to guard Riker, not kill him. Of course, we needed to know where the children were being held. I hoped he didn't die before he told us.

My hearing came back in stages. I could hear Riker saying, 'Please, don't.' It was what Peter had been saying on the monitor. It pleased me that Riker was begging. Edward came back from checking the hallway. He had one of the sub-guns in his hands. He'd closed the door so that if we had company, we'd get a little warning.

By the time he started asking Riker questions, I could hear, but there was a ringing echo in my head that didn't seem to want to go away.

'Tell me where to find Peter and Becca,' Edward said. He was leaning on the back of Riker's chair, face very close to his.

Riker rolled his eyes to look at him. There was bloody foam at his lips. I'd pierced at least one lung. If it had been both, he was dying. If only one, then maybe he could survive if he got to the hospital soon enough.

'Please,' he managed to say again.

'Tell me where the children are being kept, and I'll let Anita call an ambulance.'

'Promise?' he said, in a voice thick with things that should never be in a throat.

'I promise, just like you promised me,' Edward said.

Either Riker didn't get the double entendre, or he didn't want to. People will believe a lot of things when they're afraid they're dying. He believed we'd call an ambulance because he gave directions in that thick wet voice. He told us where they were being held.

'Thank you,' Edward said.

'Call now,' Riker said.

Edward put his face almost next to Riker's. 'You want to be safe from the monster?'

Riker swallowed, coughed blood, and nodded.

'I'll keep you safe from the monster. I'll keep you safe from everything.' And he shot Riker in the head with the Beretta .9 mil he'd reclaimed from Rooster's body. My guns were still on Mickey somewhere out there.

Edward felt for Riker's pulse and didn't find it. He looked at me across the man's body. I'd always thought Edward killed with coldness, but his baby blues held a fine, heated rage, like a forest fire barely under control. He was still in control of himself, but for the first time I wondered if there would come a point tonight where he'd lose it. You can only stay cool and collected when things don't matter. And Peter and Becca mattered to Edward. They mattered more than I'd have ever thought anyone would matter to him. Them and Donna, his family.

He told me to reload the sub gun. I did what he asked. If Edward said I'd nearly emptied an entire clip in just a few seconds, I believed him. I added the extra clip from the dead man to the purse.

Edward went for the door, and I followed him. I'd thought that nothing could be scarier than Edward at his most cold. I was wrong. Edward the family man was downright terrifying.

59

Hours later, though my watch said thirty minutes, I was plastered to a wall, crouched as low as I could get, trying not to get shot. I knew that I originally started out to rescue the kids, and I still planned to do that, but my immediate plan was just to avoid catching a bullet. That had been the plan for about five minutes. I'd heard the expression a hail of bullets, but I'd really never understood what it meant. It was as if the very air had turned into a moving, spattering thing, where tiny fast-moving objects peppered the air around you, bit into the solid rock wall beyond and left holes. There were two submachine guns down the hall, pinning us in cross fire. I'd never been shot at by fully automatic machine guns before. I was so impressed, I hadn't done anything in the last five minutes except hug the wall, and keep my head down.

The secret panel had been exactly where Riker said it would be. Edward had killed the guard on the other side with a knife, quick, efficient. We'd killed two more men before Simon and his crew, or what was left of it, found us and started fighting back. I'd thought I was good at killing people. I'd thought I was good in a gunfight. I was wrong. If what was happening to me now was a gunfight, then I'd never been in one before. I'd shot people and been shot, but that had been one on one with semi-auto pistols. The bullets whined by me in a near constant stream of noise and percussion. I was so *not* putting my face out there.

It was pure luck that I hadn't been shot before we got this far. The only thing I'd been doing right that had helped my chances was using every freaking bit of cover offered. The one comfort to my new-found cowardice was that Edward was crouched with me, though he kept peeking around the corner and firing short bursts at the shooters that had us pinned.

He reached around me, firing. I could feel the vibration of the gun against my body, the tremble of his arms as he held it. He darted back behind the wall, and a fresh burst of bullets thundered down at us. Edward held his hand out and I handed him another clip from the purse. I felt like a surgical nurse.

I leaned close to Edward's ear and whisper-screamed, 'You want the vest? I'm not using it.'

'I've got a vest on.' Deuce had kindly left Edward's vest in the study.

'You could put mine on your head,' I said.

He actually smiled at me as if I'd been joking. He motioned for me to scoot over, an acknowledgment from both of us that I wasn't doing much. He took up my post at the corner of the wall, and I flattened my back where he'd been. He went to his belly, firing around the corner. It only took seconds for him to peek around the corner, fire and come back, but while he was staring down the corridor I saw the tiniest corner of a head peek round the bend of the stairs just above us. The head ducked back out of sight.

I started to touch Edward, to let him know we had company, when something came sailing through the air. Something small and roundish. I don't remember thinking about it. I was just on my knees, letting the sub-gun dangle. I caught the object in my hands and threw it back up the stairs, before my brain even had time to form the word grenade. I threw myself back to the floor, touching Edward's leg, and then there was an explosion. The world shuddered, and the stairway collapsed in a shower of rock and dust. Rock rained down on my arms where I'd curled them over my head. I thought that if the bad guys came running down the hall now, I wouldn't be much help, which made me raise my head enough to see the corner and Edward.

He had his head covered by one arm, but was looking round the corner, gun in one hand. Of course, nothing would make Edward forget the bad guys, certainly not a little thing like an explosion and the ceiling about to come down on us.

The silence came gradually full of creaks and groans from the stones around us. The dust lay like a thin mist in the air. I started to cough, and Edward's hand was just suddenly on my mouth. How had he known? He gave a small shake of his head.

I got the idea that he wanted me to be quiet, but I didn't know why. Of course, I didn't need to know.

We lay quiet, and the silence seemed to build. Finally, I heard the first scrape of a footstep coming down the hall. I tensed, and Edward's hand pressed on my shoulder. Easy, he was saying, easy. I swallowed as quietly as I could and tried to relax. Quiet I could do. Relaxed was not happening.

The movements were stealthy, very quiet. Someone was creeping down the hallway towards us. Wondering if we'd gotten blown up. We were pretending that we had, but once the man got down here, the jig would be up. We could kill him, but there was another man at the end of the hall. If he didn't run out of ammo, he could hold the hall against us. He didn't want to come to us, and we needed to go down that hall. Becca and Peter were in cells in the hall. The bad guys had the upper hand because we needed to move forward, and all they needed to do was hold position.

Of course, one of them was coming to us.

Edward pantomimed for me to go forward and lie down. I knew he wanted me to play dead, but that far out from the wall was kill zone. If they started firing, even flat on the ground, I might be hit. But ... I crawled forward through the debris, being very, very careful not to scrape any weapons or the purse against the floor or make the rocks roll. I was farther out than I wanted to be when I looked back, and Edward gave one nod. I lay down on the floor, quietly. I lay face down because my acting abilities aren't up to playing dead. My hair flung across my face and I left it there, the better to peek through. I kept the sub-gun in my hand, but Edward shook his head. I let the gun go, moved my hand minutely away from it, and played dead. If Edward were wrong, I wouldn't be playing for long. I'd never get to the gun in time. Once the man cleared the corner, it was over.

I lay there and strained to hear movement. Mostly, what I heard was the thudding of my heart. Whoever it was, was being even quieter than before. Maybe he'd chickened out. Maybe he wasn't coming at all, and they'd start shooting again. I had to fight to keep still, not to move, not to breathe too much. I willed myself to relax into the floor, and I'd almost succeeded when I caught movement in the hallway. I was far enough out from Edward that I had a better view at the end of the hall. Would he see the shine of my eyes through my hair? I took in a deep breath, closed my eyes, and held it. Either Edward would kill him, or he'd kill me. I trusted Edward. I trusted Edward. I trusted Edward.

Noises, soft, slithering noises, the brush of cloth. Then a sharp exhale of breath. Nothing you'd hear from the other end of the hallway. Silence so thick it was frightening, but if Edward hadn't won, there would have been gunfire. I opened my eyes a slit, then wider, because Edward was kneeling over Mickey's body, searching it.

I must not have been the only one who thought the silence was a long one because a man's voice sounded, 'Mickey, you okay?'

Edward answered, and it didn't sound like his voice. It wasn't a perfect imitation but it was good. 'All clear.'

'What's the roger?' the man asked. I didn't recognize the voice. One of Simon's men we had yet to meet face to face.

Edward looked at me and shook his head. I didn't know what a roger was, but apparently, we couldn't fake it, though Edward tried. 'Get the fuck down here and help me search the bodies.'

The answer to that was gunfire. I was already as low as I could get to the ground, but I tried to get lower. The bullets sprayed over me into the wall beyond, and the only thing that kept me from screaming was pride.

Edward gave one abrupt motion. I thought I knew what he wanted. When the shots ended, I belly crawled back towards the wall. I was actually almost there when he fired again. I froze in place, face to the ground. The firing ended, and I put my back to the wall on the other side of Mickey's body from Edward.

Mickey was still carrying my guns. I took them back.

Edward had a canister in his hand that looked suspiciously like the incendiary grenade they'd put in my purse, minus the camouflaging hairspray can. My eyes widened. He shook his head, as if reading my mind, and mouthed, 'Smoke.'

Okay.

He leaned over the body, and I leaned into him. He whispered, 'Cover me while I throw it. Belly crawl down the hall. When you see anyone through the smoke, shoot them.' Then he leaned back, pulled the pin on the smoke grenade, and stood with the wall still hiding him.

I crawled to him, hugging the wall and his legs, sub-gun clutched tight. My heart was inside my head, pounding away. I had time to think, 'Gee, the headache's gone,' then Edward said, softly, 'Now.'

I peeked around the corner, my finger on the trigger, spraying down the hallway. Edward threw the smoke grenade. He jerked back around the corner, and so did I. Thick white smoke filled the hallway. I dropped to my belly, behind the wall, waiting for the smoke to find me. Edward motioned that he'd take the other side, but he pointed forward for me. He combat crawled and was almost immediately lost to the thick smoke. The smoke was bitter, like burning cotton soaked in something bad.

I crawled with the wall on my left, the sub-gun held out in front of me. I had two guns shoved down the front of my jeans now, and it wasn't comfortable for crawling, but nothing could have persuaded me to stop and adjust them. The purse stayed solid against my back like a bulky backpack. The world had narrowed down to soft rolling smoke, the feel of the floor under my arms and legs, the brush of the wall against my left elbow when I moved too close to it. There was nothing but me moving down the hall, eyes trying to see anything in the white mass of clouds.

Nothing moved but me.

Then bullets ripped through the smoke, and I was close enough to see the flash of the gun through the smoke. I was almost on top of him, and he was firing chest high into the smoke. I was about ankle high and looking up at him. I could actually see him like a shadowy figure above me when I pressed the trigger and watched that shadow jerk. I rolled onto my side to sweep my fire line up his body, still afraid to stand or even kneel until I knew he wasn't firing back.

He collapsed to his knees, face suddenly looming out of the smoke. I fired nearly point blank into his chest, and he fell backwards half vanishing in the fading smoke, like he'd fallen into clouds. I stayed low and realized I could see his feet. The smoke was almost gone at floor level, which was one of many reasons that Edward had had us crawl.

'It's me,' Edward said, before he crawled out of the smoke. He was wise to have warned me. My finger was still on the trigger, and I was beginning to appreciate how you could accidentally shoot your friends in a combat situation, unless you were very careful.

He moved a little way, and the smoke was thinning enough that I could see him check the man's pulse. 'Stay here,' and he was gone into the dying smoke.

It pissed me off, but I stayed on the floor by the man I'd killed and waited. I might have been pissed off, but we were in a kind of fighting that I knew almost nothing about. I'd somehow fallen into Edward's other life, and he was better at surviving here than I was.

I was going to do what I was told. It was pretty much my only hope for getting out alive.

Edward came back, walking instead of crawling. Probably a good sign. 'The area's clear, but it won't be for long.' He held the keys we'd taken from Riker. 'Let's do it.'

He unlocked the cell that was supposed to be Peter's and went across the hall to Becca's before he did more than push the door open. I guess I was getting Peter. I dropped to one knee and pushed the door open until it was flat against the wall. See, no one hiding behind it. If there had been someone in the room, they'd have probably shot over my head. Kneeling, I was a lot shorter than most people. But a glance showed the room was empty except for the narrow bed with Peter on it.

I stood, debated for a second whether to shut the door and risk someone locking it behind me, or leave it open and risk someone coming up behind me with a gun. I left it open, not because it was the best option, but because I just didn't want the door shut on me in the cell. Part claustrophobia, part just having been locked in too many places waiting for things to eat me. Sometimes I think that last part contributes to the claustrophobia.

It had been bad on the black and white monitor, but it was worse in person. Peter was curled into the tightest ball he could manage. His hands tied behind his back, tied ankles tucked up tight to his bare butt. His clothes were still bunched around his knees, and the expanse of pale flesh looked incredibly vulnerable. She'd meant to humiliate him, leaving him like this. The blindfold was still in place, cutting a bright patch of color across his dark hair. His mouth was stained with drying blood, his lower lip already swollen, bruises beginning to spread across his face like ugly lipstick from an overzealous kiss.

I didn't try to be quiet. I tried to hurry. He heard me coming because he started talking through the gag. I could understand him. 'Please don't, please don't.' He kept saying it over and over in a progressively more frantic voice until his voice broke, not from adolescence, but from fear.

'It's me, Peter,' I said.

He didn't seem to hear me, just kept begging over and over.

I touched his shoulder, and he screamed. 'Peter, it's Anita.'

I think he stopped breathing for a heartbeat, then he said, 'Anita?'

'Yeah, I'm here to get you out.'

He started to cry, thin shoulders shaking. I drew one of Blade's blades and fitted it carefully between his wrists, jerking upward. The cord sliced clean under the sharp, sharp blade. I tried to lift the blindfold off of him, but it was too tight.

'I'm going to have to cut the blindfold off, Peter. Don't move.'

His breathing slowed, and he held still while I slid the blade between the cloth and the side of his head. It was harder to cut than the rope because it was tighter to his skin and just a bad angle. But the blade finally sliced through it, and the cloth fell away. I had an impression of red marks in his skin where the blindfold had marked him. Then he flung himself on me, hugging me.

I hugged him back, knife in one hand.

He whispered, 'She said she was going to cut it off when she came back.' He didn't start crying again. He just held on. I rubbed his back with my free hand. I wanted to give him comfort, but we had to get out of here.

'She won't hurt you anymore, Peter. I promise that, but we've got to get out of here.' I pulled back from his desperate arms until I could see his face and he could see mine. I held his face in my hands, the knife carefully pointed up. I looked into his eyes. They were wide and shocky, but there wasn't much I could do about it now.

'Peter, we have to go. Ted's getting Becca, and we're leaving.'

Maybe it was his sister's name, but he blinked and gave a small nod. 'I'm okay,' he said, which was the best lie I'd heard all night.

But I accepted it and said, 'Good.' I had to stand to reach the ropes at his ankles. He was just that tall or I was that short. The hug had put him facing forward, and he seemed suddenly aware that he was exposed. He started grabbing at his underwear and pants while I tried to cut his ankles free.

I had to pull the knife back. 'If you don't hold still, you're going to end up cut.'

'I want my clothes on,' he said.

I stood at the foot of the bed, and said, 'Get dressed.'

'Don't look,' he said.

'I'm not looking.'

'But you're looking at me,' he said.

'But I'm not *looking* at you.' But I couldn't explain it to him, so I turned and looked at the door while he struggled into his pants.

'You can look now.'

He had everything zipped and buttoned, and just that had taken some of the raw terror out of his eyes. I cut his ankles free, sheathed the knife, and helped him to his feet. He jerked away from me, then almost fell because the ankles had been tied too tight for too long, and he didn't have all the feeling back. Only my hand on his arm kept him upright.

'You need to walk a little with help before you can run,' I said.

He let me help him to the door, but he wouldn't look at me. His first reaction had been that of a child, grateful to be saved, wanting to hold on to someone, but his second reaction was older. He was embarrassed now. Embarrassed at what had happened, and probably at me seeing him nearly naked. He was fourteen, a trembling age between child and adult. Somehow, I think he'd been younger when he went into the cell than when he came out.

Edward met us in the hallway with Becca held in his arms. She looked pale and sick. Bruises had already started blooming on her face. But it was her hand that made me want to cry. That tiny hand that I'd held only days ago, while Edward and I swung her in the air. Three of the fingers looked crippled, at unnatural angles. They were swelling, the skin discolored. It was early for that, which meant they were bad breaks and wouldn't heal easily.

She said, 'Anita, you came to save me, too.' Her voice was high and thin. It made my throat tight.

'Yeah, sweetie, I came to save you, too.'

Peter and Edward stood staring at each other. It was Edward that reached out first, just his hand, because the arm was underneath Becca's legs. Peter took that hand and hugged them both. His fingers hovered over Becca's hand, and fresh tears fell down his face, but there was no sobbing now, just tears so quiet you wouldn't have known he was crying if you hadn't seen them.

'She'll be all right,' Edward said.

Peter looked up at him, as if he wasn't sure he believed, but he wanted to. But he stepped away from them, rubbed the tears from his face with his hands. 'Can I have a gun?'

I opened my mouth to say, no, but Edward spoke first. 'Give him your Firestar, Anita.'

'You're kidding,' I said.

'I've seen him shoot. He can handle it.'

I'd been following Edward's orders for a while. He was usually right but . . .

'If we go down, I want him armed.' Edward looked at me, and the weight in his eyes was enough. He didn't want Peter and Becca taken again. If he put a gun in Peter's hand, they'd kill him not torture him. If the worst happened, Edward had decided how the boy would go out. And, God help me, I agreed.

I pulled the gun out of the band of my jeans. 'Why the Firestar?'

'Smallest grip.'

I handed it to Peter, feeling vaguely like a child molester myself, or maybe a corrupter. 'It holds nine if you carry one in the chamber. It's only holding eight. Safety's here.'

He took the gun and popped the clip out to check it, then looked vaguely embarrassed. 'Ted says to always check if something's loaded.' He popped the clip back in, put a round in the chamber so it was ready to fire.

'Try not to shoot any of us,' I said.

He clicked the safety on. 'I won't.'

Looking into his eyes, I believed him.

'I want to go home,' Becca said.

'We're going home, honey,' Edward said.

Edward led the way around the corner still carrying Becca. Peter went next, and I brought up the rear. I didn't burst anyone's bubble, but I knew we were a long way from safe. We had Simon and the rest of his men to get through, not to mention Harold and Newt and the local guys. Where were Russell and Amanda? I was really hoping to see them before we left. I'd promised Peter that she would never hurt him again. I always keep my promises.

60

The hallway spilled out into a large open space. Edward stopped, and Peter and I did, too. Becca was still being carried, so she didn't have much choice. I kept an eye on our back trail and waited for Edward to decide what to do. I couldn't see how big the open space was, so I figured it was big enough for Edward to worry about us being out in that much open. He finally moved slowly forward, hugging the left-hand wall. When I could see the room clearly, I realized why he'd hesitated. It wasn't just this huge open space. There were three tunnels leading off to the right, dark mouths where anything might lurk, like Simon and the rest of his men. But there was a fourth opening with stairs leading up. Up was what we needed.

I walked with my back to the solid wall behind me, trying to keep an eye on the hall we'd come out of and the three tunnels to the right. I left the stairs to Edward.

The stairway was narrow, barely broad enough for two slender people to walk abreast. It wound upward and had a sharp angle at the top, a blind corner. I kept watching behind us, because I knew that if shooters came up behind us, and in front of us at the same time, we were dead. It was a perfect place for an ambush.

Peter seemed to feel the tension because he moved closer to Edward, almost touching him as they moved up the stairs. We were about three fourths of the way up to that first blind corner, when Edward hesitated, staring down at the steps. Peter took one extra step. Edward hit him with his shoulder, knocking him back. He dropped Becca to the steps, still holding her good arm, trying to save her from the full fall. I think if he'd just dropped Becca, he might have gotten them all out of harm's way, but that last effort cost him the second he needed.

I saw a blur of movement, and there was a wooden stake sticking out of Edward's back. I started to go to him, but he said, 'Up the stairs, now. Shoot them.'

I didn't ask questions. I went up the last few steps as fast as I could go and threw myself around the corner on my side, and was shooting down the hallway before I saw what I was shooting at.

Harold, Russell, Newt, and Amanda were running down another level of stairs. I fired up into them, fighting the angle to make the spray pattern hit them. The three men went down, but Amanda turned and darted back around the corner they'd come from. I made sure the men weren't getting up, firing into their down bodies, then I got to my feet and ran up the stairs after her. I crouched at the corner, but the stairs were empty. Fuck. I didn't dare pursue her and leave the kids and Edward alone.

I went back down the steps and slipped on blood so that I ended up sitting down hard on the steps; my elbow hit Harold's body, and the body grunted.

I put the barrel of the gun against his chest as his eyes fluttered open. 'Didn't make the ambush site in time. Simon's going to be pissed,' he said, and the tone of his voice said he was hurting.

'I don't think you have to worry about Simon anymore, Harold. You're not going to be around to answer to him.'

'Never approved of hurting kids,' he said.

'But you didn't stop it,' I said.

He took a breath and that seemed to hurt, too. 'Simon called someone on the radio. Said he'd failed. Said they needed to clean up the mess. I think they're coming to kill us all.'

'Who's coming?'

He opened his mouth, and I think he'd have told me, but his breath ran out in a long sigh. I felt for the pulse in his neck, but it wasn't there. I'd known he was dead, but still you check. I checked Russell and Newt just to be sure, but they were dead. I actually left everyone's guns because I just couldn't carry any more.

I heard voices as I neared the bend that would take me back to Edward. Fuck. Then I recognized one of the voices. It was Olaf.

I came around the corner and found Olaf and Bernardo kneeling by Edward. Peter was sitting on the steps holding Becca. She was crying. He wasn't. He was staring at Edward, face white with shock.

Bernardo spotted me first. 'Are they dead?'

I nodded. 'Russell, Newt, and Harold. Amanda got away.'

Peter's eyes flicked to me, and they were huge and dark in his pale, pale face. The bruised mouth stood out against his skin like it was makeup, too bright to be real.

Edward made a small sound, and Peter turned back to him. 'I'm sorry, Ted,' he said. 'I'm sorry.'

'It's all right, Pete. Just next time follow my lead better.' His voice was strained, but Peter seemed to take heart from talk of a next time. I wasn't so sure.

Olaf and Bernardo had turned him so that you could see the sharpened end of the stake that had pierced his chest. It was upper chest, close to the left shoulder. It had missed the heart or he'd be dead, but it could have pierced the sack around the heart, and blood could be spilling into that sack as we watched. Or it could have missed it entirely. It was high enough up that it had probably missed the lungs. Probably.

'How'd you know that they were coming?' I asked.

'Heard them,' and his voice reminded me of Harold's, pain stressed.

I was suddenly cold, and it wasn't the temperature. I started to kneel by them all, but Edward said, 'Watch our backs.'

So I stood up, put my back to the wall, and let my peripheral vision try to keep track of both up and down the stairs. But my eyes kept going back to him. Was he dying? Please, God, not like this. It wasn't just Edward. It was the look on Peter's face. If Edward died, Peter would blame himself. The boy was having a bad enough night. That kind of guilt he did not need.

'Give me your T-shirt,' Olaf said.

I looked at him.

'We need to pack the wound and keep the stake from moving around. We can't remove it here. It's too close to his heart. He will need a hospital.'

I agreed with that. 'Someone else watch for bad guys while I undress.'

Bernardo stood up and took my place at the wall. I noticed there was a blade sticking out of his cast like a spearhead. The blade was stained black with blood.

I pulled off my T-shirt and handed it to Olaf. He'd already stripped down to his black Kevlar vest, shoving his own shirt around the wound.

'Do you need mine?' Peter asked.

'Yes,' Olaf said.

Peter moved Becca forward on his lap and took off his shirt. His upper body was thin and pale. He was tall, but the rest of him hadn't caught up. Olaf used pieces of Bernardo's shirt to hold the makeshift bandage in place. The wound looked terrible, but it wasn't bleeding much. I didn't know if that was a good sign or a bad one.

'We caught the other half of your ambush on its way to the stairs,' Bernardo said.

'I wondered why there weren't more,' I said. I remembered what Harold had said. 'Before Harold died, he said that Simon called someone. Told them he'd failed and they needed to clean up the mess. Does that mean what I think it means?'

Edward looked up at me, as Olaf used more shirt strips to bind his left arm tight, so he wouldn't move it and risk jarring the stake into something vital. 'They'll kill everything they find.' His voice was almost normal, only slightly breathy, a touch tight. 'They'll burn the place to ash. Maybe they even salt the earth.' I think that last was the wound talking, but you never know with Edward.

Olaf lifted Edward to his feet, but the height difference was too much. Edward couldn't keep his arm over the big man's shoulders. 'Bernardo will have to help you.'

'No, Anita can do it.'

Olaf opened his mouth to argue, I think, but Edward said, 'Bernardo only has one good arm. He needs that to shoot.'

Olaf closed his mouth into a tight line, but he handed Edward over to me. Edward's arm went around my shoulders. I put my left arm around his waist. We tried a couple of steps, and it worked okay.

Olaf led the way. I came next with Edward, then Peter, carrying Becca wrapped around his body like a sad little monkey. Bernardo brought up the rear. Olaf looked at the bodies of the dead men as he passed. He spoke without looking back at me. 'You did this?'

'Yeah.' I'd have usually come up with something sarcastic like, 'you see anyone else?' but I was too worried about Edward to waste the effort. Sweat had popped out on his face, as if it was taking a lot to keep going. Trouble was, a fireman's carry would disturb the stake, and if any of us could carry him just in his arms, it was Olaf, but it would mean not being able to shoot. We needed the gun.

'You okay, Edward?' I asked.

He swallowed before he said, 'Fine.'

I didn't believe him, but I didn't ask again. This was probably as good as it was going to get for awhile.

Edward tried to turn and say something to the kids, but it hurt, and I had to turn for him, moving us both to face backwards. 'Cover Becca's eyes, Peter.'

Peter had Becca bury her face against his shoulder and kept his hand pressed to the back of her head. He didn't have the Firestar in his hands. I wondered where it was but not enough to ask.

I turned Edward back around, and we started up the stairs again. Olaf was almost at the next bend in the stairs, when he stopped. He was looking down at the steps. I froze and said, 'No one move.'

'Is it a trap?' Edward asked.

'No,' Olaf said.

I saw it then, thin rivulets of blood sliding down the steps towards us. It snaked around Olaf's feet and dripped its way toward Edward and me.

Peter wasn't that far behind us. He asked, 'What is that?'

'Blood,' Olaf said.

'Please tell me that this is your handiwork, Olaf,' I said.

'No,' he said.

I watched the blood flow around my Nikes and knew that our problems had just gotten worse.

61

I leaned Edward up against the wall. He wanted me free to shoot if Olaf told me to. Olaf got to scout ahead and see what the problem was. He vanished around that corner, and I pressed myself to the wall and gave the briefest of looks ahead. The stairs ended just up ahead. The electric lights showed a cave, I think. The lights glistened on blood and bodies.

Olaf backed up, and came down to us again. 'I can see the exit.'

'What are the bodies?'

'Riker's men.'

'What killed them?'

'I think it is our murderous beast. But there is no other way out. The other entrance has been blocked by an explosion. We must go out this way.'

I figured if the murderous beast was up there waiting for us, Olaf would have been more excited. So I went back to Edward. His skin was the color of bad paste. His eyes were closed. They opened when I touched him, but they were brighter than they should have been. 'We're almost out,' I said.

He didn't say anything, just let me settle his arm over my shoulder. He was still holding onto me, but every step we took, my arm around his waist was taking more and more of his weight. 'Hold on, Edward, just a little farther.'

His head jerked as if he'd just heard me, but his feet kept moving with me. We were going to make it, all of us. The blood got thicker the farther up we walked. Edward slipped in it, and I had to catch him and barely managed to keep us both standing.

But it was a sudden movement, and he let out a small sound of pain. Shit.

'Watch your step, Peter,' I said. 'It's slippery.'

Olaf was waiting for us at the bodies. There were only three of them. One was a man I didn't recognize, but I recognized the gun near his body. He was one of Simon's men. Simon was lying in a pool of blood and darker fluids. The entire lower chest, stomach, abdomen were open. His intestines trailed out onto the cave floor, but his eyes were still blinking upward, still alive.

The third body was Amanda, and she was still moving, too. But Olaf had her covered, so I kept my attention on Simon. He smiled up at us. 'At least I killed the Undertaker.'

'He's not nearly as dead as you are,' I said.

'You're all dead, bitch.'

'We know you invited company,' I said.

His eyes looked uncertain. 'Fuck you.' His hand inched towards his gun that was still lying beside him. Gutted, dying, in more pain than I could imagine, and he tried to go for his gun. I stepped on his hand, pinning it to the earth. Harder to do than normal with Edward hanging on me, but I managed. 'Peter, you and Becca go up with Bernardo to the front of the cave.'

Peter didn't argue. He just carried Becca past us, Bernardo trailing behind.

I pointed the gun barrel at Simon's head. I couldn't leave him behind because I didn't trust him at my back. Even this wounded, I wasn't willing to take the chance.

'I hope the monster guts you, bitch.'

'That's Ms Bitch to you,' I said and pulled the trigger. A short burst, but more shots echoed mine. I whirled, gun up, and found Peter standing over Amanda's body. He emptied the Firestar into her body while I watched. Olaf was just watching him do it. I looked for Bernardo and found him holding Becca near the cave mouth.

Edward started to slide to his knees. I knelt with him, trying to keep him upright. He whispered, 'The kids, out, get them . . . out,' and he fainted.

Olaf was there without me asking. He lifted Edward in his arms like a child. If the monster came now, we all had our hands full. Shit.

Peter had run out of bullets, but he was still squeezing the trigger, over and over and over. I went to him. 'Peter, Peter, she's dead. You killed her. Ease down.'

He didn't seem to hear me. I touched his hands, tried to lift the gun from him. He jerked away, violently, eyes wild. He kept dry-firing into the woman's body. I shoved him back against the rock wall, hard, one arm across his throat, the other pinning his hands still wrapped around the Firestar. His eyes were wide and frightened, but he looked at me. 'Peter, she's dead. You can't kill her anymore dead than she already is.'

His voice shook when he said, 'I wanted her to hurt.'

'She did hurt. Being torn apart is a bad way to die.'

He shook his head. 'It's not enough.'

'No,' I said, 'it isn't enough, but you killed her, Peter. That's as good as revenge gets. Once you kill them, there isn't any more.'

I took the Firestar out of his hands, and he let me. I tried to hug him, but he pushed me away, then walked away. The time for that kind of comfort was past, but there were other kinds of comfort. Some of them came from the barrel of a gun. There is some comfort in killing that which has hurt you, but it is cold comfort. It'll destroy things inside of you that the original pain wouldn't have harmed. Sometimes it's not a question of whether a piece of your soul is going to go missing, only which piece it's going to be.

Peter carried Becca. Olaf carried Edward. Bernardo and I took the lead. We searched the spring darkness with our guns, back and forth, back and forth. Nothing moved. There was just the sound of wind in the tall line of sage bushes that bordered the back of the cave. The air felt so good against my face, and I realized that I'd not really expected to get out, not alive. Pessimism, it wasn't like me.

Bernardo led the way back to circle the house. We'd try for Edward's car, but we wanted to make sure no one or no thing was waiting to eat us when we went for the car. Olaf went second, carrying a very still Edward. I was praying hard that he'd be okay, though strangely it felt odd to pray to God for Edward, as if I were praying in the wrong direction. Peter and Becca were just ahead of me. He stumbled as we headed into the thicker brush. He had to be tired, but I couldn't afford to carry Becca. I needed to have my hands free to fight.

I felt the prickling brush of magic. I called, 'Guys, something's out here.'

Everyone stopped and started searching the darkness. 'What did you see?' Olaf asked.

'Nothing, but something out here is doing magic.'

Olaf made a noise in his throat like he didn't believe me. Then the first wave of fear washed over us. So much fear that it closed the throat, sent the heart thundering, made the palms of your hands sweat. Becca started struggling violently in Peter's arms.

I took two steps to help Peter control her, but she struggled free, fell to the ground, and ran like a rabbit into the brush. Peter yelled, 'Becca!' and went after her.

'Peter, Becca! Oh, shit!' I ran into the brush after them. What else could I do? I heard them just up ahead, crashing through the brush, Peter calling Becca's name. I had a sense of movement to my right, and I saw something. It was bigger than a man, and even by moonlight you could see it was different colors. I fired into it as it opened a huge razored mouth, but the claw kept coming towards me, as if the bullets were nothing. The closed claw slammed into my head. It knocked me off my feet, and I hit the ground hard. Darkness swirled across my vision, and when I could see again, the thing was right above me. I kept my finger on the trigger, until it clicked empty. The monster never hesitated. It filled my vision with a face that was almost birdlike, and I had a moment to think it was pretty before it hit me again, and there was nothing but darkness.

62

I woke instantly, my skin jumping with a rush of magic that left me gasping. My body strained, writhing as the power rode over and through my body in a burning surge that just kept growing. My hands and legs strained against the chains that held me down. Chains? I turned and stared at my wrists, head still thrashing, my body jerking as the power roared through me. My arms and legs jerked, not because I was struggling against the chains but as a reaction to the power.

The magic began to fade, leaving my breath coming in pants. One thing I knew. If I didn't get my breathing under control, I was going to hyperventilate. Passing out again would be bad. Heaven knew what I'd wake up to a second time. I concentrated on my breathing, forcing myself to be calm, and take deep, even, normal breaths. It's hard to be totally panic-stricken when you're doing breathing exercises. It poured a false calm over my body, and my mind. But it let me think, which was good.

I was lying on my back, chained to a smooth stone surface. There was a curve of cave wall beside me, and a ceiling lost to sight in the darkness above. I'd have loved to believe that Bernardo and Olaf had rescued me and we were back in the cave entrance, but the chains sort of ruined that pleasant thought. This cave was much taller, and without looking it just felt bigger. Firelight bounced in orange shadows along the cave, like being in a ball of darkness and gold light.

I finally turned my head to the right and let myself see what was there. At first I thought it was Pinotl, Itzpapalotl's human servant. I had a few seconds of cursing myself for believing her when she said she didn't know about the monster, then I realized it wasn't him. It looked like him. Same square, chiseled face, dark, rich skin, and the black hair cut long and oddly square, but this man was narrow through the shoulders, thin, and there was no air of command to him. He was also wearing a pair of loose-fitting shorts instead of the nifty clothes that Pinotl wore.

There was a smooth rounded stone like the one at the Obsidian Butterfly. There was a body draped over that stone. Foreshortened legs and arms, short dark hair, and for a moment I thought it was Nicky Baco, then I saw the naked chest more clearly, and it was Paulina, Nicky's wife. There was a hole under her ribs like a great gaping mouth. They'd torn out her heart. The unknown man stood there holding the heart in his hands, above his head like an offering. His eyes looked black in the uncertain light. He lowered his arms, walking towards me with the heart cupped in his hands. His hands were so thick with blood that it looked like he was wearing red gloves. There were four men standing at attention around the altar. They were wearing some sort of soft leather on their bodies, hoods up and covering them from head to foot almost. There was something wrong with what they were wearing, but my eyes couldn't make sense of it, and I had other more immediate problems than what people were wearing.

I was still wearing the Kevlar vest and all the rest of my clothes. If they meant to take my heart, they'd have taken the clothes. It was a very comforting thought as the man, the priest, walked towards me with the heart in his hands. He held the heart over my chest and began to chant in a language that sounded like Spanish, but wasn't.

Blood dripped from the heart, splatted on the vest. It made me jump. The calm of the breathing exercises was wearing off. I did not want him to touch me with that thing. It wasn't even logic, fear of some spell or magic. It was pure revulsion. I did not want to be touched by a heart that had just been torn out of someone's body. I've put my share of stakes through hearts. I've even cut a few out for burning, but somehow this was different. Maybe it was being chained and helpless, or maybe it was Paulina's body lying limp over the altar, looking like a broken doll. The only time I'd met her she'd been so strong, threatening me with a gun, but lots of people had done that. Edward used to do that all the time. Starting out a relationship on the end of a gun didn't mean you couldn't be friends down the road. Unless one of you died. No friendship now. No nothing for Paulina.

The man ended the chant and began to lower the heart towards me.

I strained against the chains though I knew it was useless, and I said, 'Don't touch me with that.' It sounded sure and strong, but if he understood English, I couldn't tell it because he just kept lowering his bloody hands, closer and closer. He laid the heart on my chest, and I was almost as grateful that the Kevlar kept me from feeling that thing next to my skin as I'd been for the extra protection from bullets earlier.

The heart lay on my chest like so much meat. There was no magic to it. It was just dead. Then the heart took a breath, or that's what it looked like. The skin rose and fell. It sat on my chest, naked and attached to nothing and pulsed. I was suddenly aware of my own heartbeat. The moment I noticed my heartbeat, Paulina's heart stuttered, then began to beat in time with mine. And the moment the rhythms were shared, I could hear a second heartbeat. Except that Paulina's heart had no blood to pump, no chest to resonate in. It should have been a pale sound compared to the real thing, but it was a solid pulsing beat. It was as if the sound reached through the vest, through my skin, my ribs, and pierced my heart. The pain was sharp and immediate, stealing my breath, bowing my spine.

'Hold her,' the man yelled.

The men who'd been standing by the altar ran to me, strong

hands pressing on my legs, pinning my shoulders. My spine tried to bow with the pain, and a third set of hands pressed down on my thighs, three of them pinning me to the stone, forcing me to ride the pain and not struggle.

Paulina's heart was beating faster and faster, speeding, speeding, towards some grand climax. My heart thundered against my ribs, as if it were trying to tear loose of the tissue. It was as if a fist were beating on the inside of my chest, trying to smash its way out. I couldn't breathe, as if all of my chest was caught up in the frantic race, and there was no time for anything else.

The pain was centered in my chest, but it spread down my arms, my legs, filled my head until I thought that it might not be my heart that exploded. It might be the top of my head.

I could feel the two hearts like lovers separated by a wall, tearing it down between them until they would be able to touch. There was a moment when I felt them touch, felt the thick wet sides of the two organs slide into each other. Maybe it was just the pain. Then the heart stopped like a person caught in mid-motion, and my heart stopped with it. For a breathless moment my heart sat in my body and did nothing, as if waiting. Then it gave one beat, then another, and I drew air into my lungs in a frantic rush, and as soon as I had air, I screamed. Then I lay there, still listening to my heartbeat, feeling the pain begin to fade like the memory of a nightmare. Minutes later, the pain was gone. My body didn't even hurt. In fact, I felt energized, wonderful.

The heart on my chest had shriveled into a gray, used up piece of flesh. It wasn't recognizable as a heart, just a dry ball smaller than my palm. I blinked up and saw the face of the man holding my shoulders down. I'm sure he'd been looking down at me for a while, but I hadn't seen him or hadn't understood what I was seeing.

He wore a mask over his face. Only his lips, eyes, and ears showed through the thin covering. His neck was bare, then a ragged bow neck of the same material of the mask covered him. I think part of me knew what I was looking at, before the rest of me would accept it. It wasn't until I turned my head as far as I could to one side, and saw the hands that I knew what he was wearing. The empty hands bunched at his wrists like limp, fleshy lace. It was human skin. I'd finally found out what had happened to some of the skin the flayed ones had lost.

The eyes that stared out of that horrible thing were brown and very human. I looked down the line of my body and found that the other two men holding my legs wore the same thing, but the skins weren't all the same colors. One dark, two light. The chests had thick cord sewn across it where the breasts and nipples would have been, so there was no clue to whether the skin had been male or female.

The first man I'd seen stepped forward. 'How do you feel?' His English was heavily accented but clear.

I just looked at him for a second. He had to be kidding. 'How am I supposed to feel? I just woke up in a cave where you just performed a human sacrifice.' I glanced at the men still holding me down. 'I'm being held down by men wearing flayed human skin suits. How the hell am I supposed to feel?'

'I am asking after your bodily health. Nothing more,' he said.

I started to say something else sarcastic, but stopped and really thought about his question. How did I feel? Actually, I felt good. I remembered that rush of energy and well-being that had spread over me when the spell finished. It was still there. I felt better than I'd felt in days. If it hadn't required human sacrifice, it would have been a great medical treatment.

'I feel okay.'

'No pain in the head?'

'No.'

'Good,' he said. He motioned, and the skin guys moved away from me. They moved back to stand against the wall by the fourth man who hadn't been needed to hold me down. They stood there like good soldiers, waiting for their next orders.

I turned back to look at the other guy. Everyone in the room was scary, but at least he wasn't wearing someone else's skin. 'What did you do to me?'

'We have saved your life. Our master's creature was over-zealous. There was bleeding in your head. We needed you alive.'

I thought about that. 'You used Paulina's life force to heal me.'

'Yes.

'I'm glad to be alive, honest.' I looked past him at Paulina's body lying broken and forgotten. 'But she didn't volunteer to trade her life for mine, did she?'

'Nicky Baco began to suspect what price he would have to pay for our master's blessing. She was a hostage to make sure he came to this our last meeting,' the man said.

'Let me guess. He didn't show,' I said.

'He no longer answers our master's call.'

Apparently, Ramirez had taken my advice of having Leonora Evans do some sort of magical barrier around Nicky so he couldn't contact his master. Good to know it was working, but you try to do the right thing and it ends up getting someone else killed. Why is that always the way it works? But I admit that I was happier for me than sorry for Paulina. Not about her trading her life for mine, but if Nicky was being protected by magic, then he and the police were on their way. All I had to do was stall and keep them from doing whatever it was they had planned for me.

'So when Nicky didn't show up, you didn't need to keep her alive.' My voice sounded calm, but better than that, I was calm. Not normal calm, but the cool distant calm that you either learn to do during the really bad stuff, or you run screaming. I'd done all the screaming I planned on doing tonight.

'Her life did not matter. Yours does.'

'I'm glad to be alive, and don't take this wrong, but why do you give a damn if I live or die?'

'We need you,' a male voice said from behind me. I had to arch my neck and crane my head backward to see the owner of that second voice. I didn't see the man at first because he was surrounded by the flayed ones. I'd known that Edward was worried that they'd missed some bodies. He had no idea. There must have been twenty-five, thirty-five animated corpses standing behind me. They'd been standing so quietly, I hadn't heard them or sensed them. They stood there now like robots with the switch turned off, waiting for life to return. Zombies never got that still, never went that empty. At the end, when they started to rot and you had to put them back in the grave before they melted into little puddles, they were more alive than this. I realized in that instant that the bodies were raised, but the person inside that body wasn't raised. The master ate that which made them individuals. He ate that which made them more than so much muscle and skin. He didn't eat the souls because I'd seen one of them in a house where two flayed ones had been made. But he took something out of their bodies, some memory or remnant that I left in when I raised the dead. They stood like rocks carved of flesh, utterly empty. At least the ones in the hospital had pretended to still be alive. There was no pretense here.

My eyes finally found the man. He wore a steel helmet and breastplate like the history books are always showing the conquistadors wearing, but the rest of the outfit was straight out of a nightmare.

He wore a necklace of tongues, and they were all still fresh and pink as if they'd just been cut out seconds ago. He wore a skirt of intestines that writhed and twisted like snakes, as if each thick glistening strand had an independent life of its own. His arms were bare, strong and muscled, and covered in the missing eyelids of the victims. As he moved close, the eyelids opened and closed. He came to stand beside me, next to the first man. The eyelids blinked at me and there were eye-shaped holes underneath every lid that I saw. The holes held darkness and the cold light of stars.

I turned away because I was remembering Itzpapalotl's starry eyes. I didn't want to fall into these eyes. At that second if you had given me a choice, I'd have taken the vampire in town to the thing that was standing in front of me.

After what I'd seen at the murder scene, I expected to feel evil emanating from him, but there was no evil. There was power like being next to a battery the size of the Chrysler building. The energy hummed along my skin, but it was neutral energy. Neither good nor bad in and of itself, the way a gun is neither good nor bad but can be turned to evil purposes.

I stared up the line of his body, and the tongues were moving as if still trying to scream. He took off the helmet and showed a slender, handsome face that reminded me of Bernardo's, not the pure Aztec ethnicity I'd been expecting. He had turquoise ear spools in his lobes, and they matched the blue green of his eyes. He smiled down at me, looking like a fresh-faced twenty-something. I could feel the weight of the ages in his gaze like some vast weight pressing down on me, as if just being this close made it hard to breathe.

He reached out to touch my face, and I jerked back from him. That one movement seemed to break his hold over me. I could move. I could breathe. I could think. I'd been on the receiving end of enough magical glamour to know it when I felt it. You're either a god, or you're not. He was not. And it wasn't just my monotheism showing. I'd felt the magic of monsters and preternatural beasties of all sorts, and I knew one when I saw one. Power doesn't make you a deity. I don't know exactly what does, but power ain't it. Some spark of the divine was missing from the being that gazed down upon me. If he was just another monster, maybe we could deal.

'Who are you?' And I was happy that my voice was confident, normal.

'I am the Red Woman's Husband.' He gazed down at me with eyes so patient, so kind. You think angels must have eyes like that.

'The Red Woman is the Aztec phrase for blood. What does it mean that you're blood's husband?'

'I am the body, and she is the life.' He said it like it answered my question. It didn't.

Something wet and slimy touched my hand. I jerked back, but the chain didn't let me go far. The length of animated intestine followed my hand, nuzzling it like some obscene worm. I swallowed a scream, but I couldn't keep my pulse from speeding up.

He laughed at me.

It was a very ordinary laugh for a would-be god, but it was nicely condescending and maybe that's how would-be gods laughed. But it was a peculiarly masculine condescension, long gone out of style. The laugh says, 'Silly little girl, don't you know I'm the big strong man, and you know nothing, and I know everything?' Or maybe I'm just too sensitive.

'Why intestines?' I asked.

The smile faded around the edges. His handsome face looked puzzled. 'Are you making fun of me?' The intestine dropped away from my hand like a date that I'd rebuffed. Fine with me.

'No. I just wondered why intestines. You can obviously animate any body part. You can keep detached parts from decaying like the skins your men are wearing. With all that to choose from, why people's guts and not something else?' People love to talk about themselves. The bigger the ego, the more they enjoy it. I was hoping that the Red Woman's Husband was the same as everyone else, at least in this one thing.

'I wear the roots of their bodies so that all that see me will know that my enemies are empty shells and I have all that was theirs.'

Ask a silly question. 'Why the tongues?'

'So that the lies of my enemies will not be believed.'

'Eyelids?'

'I will open the eyes of my enemies so that they may never again close their eyes to the truth.'

He was answering questions so nicely that I decided to try for more. 'How did you skin the people without using a tool of some kind?'

'Tlaloci, my priest, called the skin from their bodies.'

'How?' I asked.

'My power,' he said.

'Don't you mean Tlaloci's power?'

He frowned again. 'All his power derives from me.'

'Sure,' I said.

'I am his master. He owes all to me.'

'Sounds like you owe him.'

'You do not know what you are saying.' He was getting angry. Probably not what I wanted. I tried another more polite question.

'Why take the breasts and penises?'

'To feed my minion.' He did nothing, but suddenly I felt the air in the cavern move, and it was as if the shadows themselves drew apart like a curtain revealing a tunnel about thirty feet from the foot of where I lay. Something crawled out of that tunnel. The first impression was of a brilliant iridescent green. The scales changed color at every turn of the light. First green, then blue, then blue and green all at once, then a pearl white glitter that I thought I must have imagined, until it turned its head and flashed a white underbelly. The green scales went closer to true blue as the color moved up towards the head, until the square snout was a clear pure blue the color of sky. There was a fringe of delicate feathers in a rainbow of colors around that face. It turned and stared at me, fanning the feathers around its scaled head into a display that would have been the envy of any peacock. Its eyes were round and huge, taking up most of its face like the eyes of a bird of prey. A pair of slender wings was folded along its back, rainbow colors of the fringe, but I knew without seeing that the underside of the wings would be white. It pushed forward on four legs. Counting the wings, it was a six-limbed animal.

It was a Quetzalcoatl Draconus Giganticus, or at least that was the last Latin classification I was aware of. Sometimes they were classed as a subspecies of dragons, sometimes as a subspecies of gargoyles, and sometimes they had their own group all to themselves. Whatever classification, the Giganticus was the biggest and supposedly extinct. The Spaniards had killed a lot of them to dishearten the natives to whom they were sacred, and because it was just the European thing to do. See a dragon, kill it. It was not a complex philosophy.

I'd only seen black and white photos, and the stuffed one in the Chicago Field Museum. The photos hadn't come close to doing it justice, and the stuffed one, well, maybe it was a bad taxidermy job.

It glided into the room in a shimmering roll of color and muscle. It was literally one of the most beautiful things I'd ever seen. It was also probably what had been gutting people. It opened that sky-blue snout and yawned, showing rows of saw-like teeth. The sound of its claws clattered over the stone floor like some nightmarish dog.

Red Woman's Husband laid his Spanish helmet on the stone by my legs and went to greet the creature. It lowered its head to be petted, very like a dog. He stroked it just above the eye ridges and it made a low, rolling sound, eyes closing to slits. It was purring.

He sent it away with a playful push against one muscular shoulder. I watched it vanish back through the tunnel like it wasn't real. 'I thought they were extinct.'

'My minion helped bring us to this place, then it slept a magic sleep, waiting for me to awake.'

'I didn't know Quetzalcoatls could hibernate.'

He frowned at me again and came to stand by my head. 'I know what your word hibernate means, but it was a magic sleep, done by the last of my warrior priests. The priest sacrificed himself, putting all of us in an enchanted sleep, knowing that there was no one to aid him, and that he would die alone in this alien place long before I rose.'

Enchanted sleep. Sounded like Sleeping Beauty. 'That's true loyalty, sacrifice yourself for the better good.'

'I'm so glad you agree. It will make what has to happen much easier.'

Didn't like the sound of that. Maybe flattery wasn't the way to go. I'd try something more normal for me – sarcasm – and see if that led us away from the topic of my impending doom. 'I don't owe you any loyalty. I am not one of your followers.'

'Only because you do not understand,' he said, and those smiling eyes gazed down at me with a look of almost perfect peace.

'That's what Jim Jones said just before he gave every one the Kool-Aid.'

'I do not know this name, Jim Jones.' Then he turned his head to one side, and it reminded me of Itzpapalotl when she listened to voices I could not hear. Now I realized that it might just be a way to access other people's memories. 'Ah, I know who he is now.' He looked down at me with those calm, beatific eyes. 'But I am no madman. I am a god.'

He was getting distracted, as if it mattered to him for me to believe he was a god. If he had to convince me that he was divine before he killed me, then I was safe. He could kill me, but he'd never convince me he was a god.

He frowned. 'You do not believe me.' He sounded surprised again. And I realized that for all his power, he seemed young. The ages raged through the eyes on his arms as though you could see back through to the beginning of creation, but he, himself, seemed young. Or maybe he just wasn't used to people who didn't drop down and worship him. If that's all you'd known in your entire existence, then anyone not worshipping you might be a shock.

'I am a god,' he repeated, and his voice had that condescending tone again.

'Whatever you say.' But I made sure my doubt showed in my voice.

The frown deepened, and again I was reminded forcibly of a pouting child. A spoiled, pouting child. 'You must believe that I am a god. I am the Red Woman's Husband. I am the body that will be revenged on those that destroyed my people.'

'You mean the Spanish Conquistadors?'

'Yes,' he said.

'There aren't a lot of conquistadors in New Mexico,' I said.

'Their blood still runs in the veins of their children's children's children.'

'No offense, but you didn't get those turquoise blue eyes from anyone local.'

He frowned again, and little lines formed between his eyes. If he kept talking to me, he was going to get frown lines. 'I am a god created by my people's tears. I am the power that is left of the Aztecs, and I am the Spaniard's magic made flesh. We will use their own power to destroy them.'

'Isn't it a little late to destroy them? About five hundred years too late.'

'Gods do not reckon time as men do.'

I believed that he believed what he was saying, but I also thought he was rationalizing. He'd have kicked the Spaniards' butts five hundred years ago if he'd been able to do it.

Maybe it showed on my face because he said, 'I was a new god then, and I did not have the strength to defeat our enemies, so the Quetzalcoatl brought me here to wait until I grew strong enough for our purpose. I am ready to lead my army forward now.'

'So you're saying that it took five hundred years for you to go from being a wee little god to a big bad god, the way soup needs to simmer for a really long time before it's soup?'

He laughed. 'You think very strangely. I am sad that you will be dead soon. I would make you the first of my concubines, and the mother of gods, for children born of you would be great sorcerers, but sadly, I have need of your life.'

We were back to killing me, and I didn't want to be there. His ego seemed pretty fragile for a deity. I'd see how fragile. 'The offer doesn't sound very appealing, no offense.'

He smiled down at me, fingers trailing along my arm. 'That we will take your life is not an offer. It is a fact.'

I gave him my best innocent eyes. 'I thought you were offering to make me your concubine, the mother of gods?'

He frowned at me harder. 'I did not offer you a chance to be my concubine.'

'Oh,' I said. 'Sorry. I misunderstood you.'

His fingers were still touching my arm, but they were still now, as if he'd forgotten he was touching me. 'You would refuse my bed?' He sounded truly perplexed. Great.

'Yeah,' I said.

'Is it your virtue you are protecting?'

'No, it's just your particular offer doesn't appeal to me.'

He was really having trouble with the concept that I didn't find him attractive. He ran his fingers down my bare arm in a tickling brush. I just lay there and looked at him. I was giving him some of the best eye contact I'd given anyone this trip because if I looked anywhere else, I kept seeing severed body parts wiggling on their own. Hard to be tough as nails when you wanted to start screaming. He touched my face, and I let him this time. His fingers traced my face, delicately, gently. His eyes no longer looked peaceful. No, definitely disturbed.

He leaned into me as if he'd kiss me, and the eyelashes on his arms fluttered in butterfly kisses along my body. I gave a little shriek.

He drew back. 'What is wrong?'

'Oh, I don't know. Severed eyelids fluttering against my skin, intestines that writhe like snakes around your waist, the necklace of tongues trying to lick me. Pick one.'

'But that should not matter,' he said. 'You should see me as beautiful, desirable.'

I did the best shrug I could with my hands chained higher than my shoulders.

'Sorry, but I just can't get past what you're wearing.'

'Tlaloci,' he said.

The man in shorts came forward, and dropped to one knee before him. 'Yes, my lord.'

'Why does she not see me as wonderful?'

'Apparently, the aura of your godhood docs not work on her.'

'Why not?' And there was anger now in his voice, in that once peaceful face.

'I do not know, my lord.'

'You said she could replace Nicky Baco. You said she was a nauhuli as he was. You said she had been touched by my magic, and it was the scent of my magic that drew the Quetzalcoatl to her. But she lies under the touch of my hands and does not feel for me. That is not possible if my magic clings to her.'

I thought, what if it's not his magic, but I didn't say it out loud. What if it was Itzpapalotl's? The being standing in front of me had nearly killed me from a distance. He'd roared over my mind and taken me, and I hadn't been able to stop him. Now, he was touching me, and evidently trying things on me, and it wasn't working. The only thing that had changed was Itzpapalotl's power filling me for awhile. Had that made the difference?

Tlaloci stood, head still bowed. 'There must be powerful magic at work here, my lord. First Nicky Baco is lost to us, and now this one is closed to your vision.'

'She must be open to my power or she cannot be the perfect sacrifice,' Red Woman's Husband said.

'I know, my lord.'

'You are the magician, Tlaloci. How can I undo this magic?'

The magician put some serious thought into it. Several minutes passed while he thought. I just lay there trying not to draw their attention back to me. Finally, Tlaloci looked up. 'To believe in your vision, she must believe in you.'

'How do I convince her to believe that I am a god if she cannot feel my power?'

It was a good question, and I waited patiently for Tlaloci to answer it. The longer he thought about it, the more delay time I was getting. Ramirez was coming. I had to believe that because my options were limited unless I could figure out a way to get them to untie me.

I could feel the pen still in my pocket with its hidden blade. I was armed, if I could get my hands free, and if steel could hurt him. Of course, there were the four helpers, and Tlaloci, and a small army of flayed ones. So even if the god could die, I'd have to do something about everyone else. They'd probably be pissed if I killed their god. I just wasn't sure how to get out of this one.

If Ramirez didn't arrive with the cavalry, I was in deep shit. Edward wasn't out there looking for me this time. For the first time since I came to, I wondered if Edward was alive. Please, God, let him be alive. But alive or not, Edward was out of the rescuing game for tonight. I admitted I needed help on this one, and the only hope I could count on was Ramirez and the police. He'd been late in the hospital. If he were late tonight, I probably wouldn't be around to complain.

Tlaloci motioned for his god to follow him a little away from me. I think they were whispering things they didn't want me to know. Why did it matter if I overheard them or not? What could they possibly be talking about that they needed to hide from me? They'd cheerfully told me they were going to kill me. It wasn't like they were trying to protect my feelings. So what was going on?

The Red Woman's Husband unfastened the necklace of tongues and handed it to the priest. He took off the steel breastplate and one of the skin guys came and took it from him, kneeling in front of him. He took off the skirt of intestines, and another skin guy hurried forward to take it. The 'god' never asked them to help him, just sort of assumed that someone would be there to help. He was almost perfectly arrogant, but his ego was fragile, an arrogance that had never been tested in the outer world. He was like one of those fairy tale princesses that had been raised in an ivory tower with only people who told them how beautiful they were, how smart, how good, until the witch comes and lays her curse. Maybe I could be the witch, though truthfully I wouldn't have known a curse if it bit me on the butt. Maybe I could be the prince that comes and takes him away. At this point I wasn't picky.

The 'god' was wearing a maxilatl like everyone at the Obsidian Butterfly had worn. But this one was black with a heavy fringe of golden thread hanging in front. He wore black sandals set with turquoise, which strangely I hadn't noticed when he was wearing all the severed body parts. Funny how you don't concentrate on the small details when you're scared.

He walked towards me, confidence showing in every step. The maxilatl left his lower body bare on the sides from waist to sandals. It was a nice length of thigh, but you know what they say. Pretty is as pretty does.

'Is this better?' he asked, his voice light, almost teasing, his eyes back to that peaceful contentment, as if things had always gone his way, and he didn't see why now should be different. Itzpapalotl had been arrogant, but not peaceful.

'Much better,' I said. I thought about remarking on how much I liked seeing nearly naked men, but didn't want to take it to such an obviously sexual tone unless I ran out of other options.

He came to stand beside me again. The eyelids were still on his arms, blinking at me like the winking lights of fireflies, random, and alien.

'It's a big improvement,' I said. 'You can't do anything about the eyes on your arms, can you?'

He frowned again. 'They are part of me.'

'I see that,' I said.

'But they are nothing to fear.'

'If you say so.'

'I want you to know me, Anita.' It was the first time he'd used my name. I hadn't thought he knew it, until then. Of course, Paulina had known who I was. The Red Woman's Husband reached down to my right wrist, and he undid that little piece of metal that held the manacle closed.

The skinned man who was still standing on the other side of the stone took a step forward, hand on the knife at his belt. I froze, not sure if I was really going to be allowed to have my hand free.

The 'god' lifted my hand free of the chain and laid his lips on the back of my hand. 'Touch them. See that they are nothing to fear.' It took me a second to figure out that 'them' meant the eyes on his arms. I was relieved to realize he didn't mean anything below his waist, and so not happy that he meant all those eyes. I did not want to touch them. I wanted nothing to do with anything that had been carved off of a dead body, especially while that person had still been alive.

He held my wrist and tried to bring my hand over his arm, but I kept a tight fist. 'Touch them, Anita, gently. They will not harm you.' He began to pry my fingers open, and I couldn't fight him. I could have fought harder, maybe make him break a finger or two, to persuade me, but in the end I was going to lose this wrestling match, so I just let him spread my hand open. I didn't want anything broken if I could avoid it.

He guided my hand just above his arm, and the eyelids fluttered under my touch. I jumped every time one of them blinked, but the eyelids moving against my skin in a line of butterfly kisses weren't as scary. The lids felt full, as if there was an eye behind them, and there wasn't. I'd seen that.

'What's inside them?' I asked.

'Everything,' he said. Which told me nothing. 'Explore them, Anita.' He pressed one of my fingertips to the edge of an eye. Then he urged me to put the finger inside the eye.

I pushed my finger into that empty seeming eye, and there was a resistance like pushing against something thin and fleshy, then my finger was through and I could touch what was inside. Warm, a warmth that flowed through my hand, up my arm, and spread like a blanket over my body. I felt safe, warm. I stared up at him and wondered why I hadn't seen it before? He was so handsome, so kind, so . . . My finger was cold, so cold that it hurt. It had that stinging pain that you get just before you lose all feeling in the limb, and frostbite settles in and spills over your body, and you fall into that last gentle sleep, never to wake. .

I jerked my hand back, and blinked awake, with a gasp. 'What is wrong?' he asked, and leaned over me, touching my face.

I jerked away from him, cradling my hand against my chest, staring up at him, afraid. 'You're cold inside.'

He took a step back from me, and the surprise showed on his face. 'You should feel safe, warm.' He leaned over me, trying to get me to gaze into his blue-green eyes.

I shook my head. Feeling was coming back into my finger in a stinging rush, the way circulation comes back after frostbite. The throbbing ache helped me think, helped me avoid his gaze. 'I'm not safe,' I said, 'and I'm not warm.' I looked away from him, which put me gazing at the skin-clad guy. But truthfully even that was better than staring at the 'god.' Itzpapalotl's touch was helping me, but it had limits. If I fell into his eyes, wherever they might be, they'd just kill me, and I might go willingly, eagerly into that last dark.

'You are making this difficult, Anita.'

I kept my gaze on the far wall. 'Sorry that I'm ruining your night.'

He stroked the curve of my face. I flinched as if he'd hurt me. I'd thought what I was trying to delay was my death. Now I realized that I was trying to delay falling into his power. They'd kill me after that, but I'd be gone before the knife fell. Had Paulina gone like that, willingly, eager to please the 'god?' I hoped so, for her sake. For mine, I wasn't so sure.

'I want you to believe that your death will be for a great purpose.'

'Sorry, not buying swampland today.'

I could almost feel his puzzlement like a play of energy along my skin. I'd felt anger, lust, fear dance along my skin from vampires and wereanimals, but I'd never felt puzzlement before. I hadn't felt his emotions before I touched that damned eye. He was sucking me down a piece at a time.

He grabbed my hand.

'No.' I said it through gritted teeth. He could break my fingers this time, but I wasn't just opening up and touching him again. I couldn't just cooperate with him anymore, not even to buy time. I had to start fighting him now, or there'd be nothing left of me. I'd had vampires roll my mind before, but I'd never felt anything like him. Once he got a really good hold on my mind, I wasn't a hundred percent sure I'd come back. There are a lot of ways to die. Being killed is only one of the more obvious ones. If he rolled my mind and there was nothing left of who I was, then I was dead or would wish I was.

I flexed my arm, hugging it to my chest, straining my muscles to keep it there. He lifted the wrist and my whole upper body with it, but I held the arm, fingers closed into a fist.

'Do not make me hurt you, Anita.'

'I'm not making you do anything. Whatever you do, it's your choice to do it, not mine.'

He laid me back down, gently. 'I could crush your hand.' It sounded like a threat, but his voice was still gentle.

'I won't touch you again, not like that, not voluntarily.'

'But lay your hand upon my chest, above my heart. That is not a hard thing, Anita.'

'No.'

'You are a very stubborn woman.'

'You're not the first one to say it,' I said.

'I will not force you.'

The skinned man moved forward until he was directly against the stone, mirroring his 'god.' He drew an obsidian blade and bent over me. I tensed, but I didn't say anything. I could not touch him again and promise I'd come out the other side. If I was going to die anyway, I'd die whole, not possessed by some would-be god.

But he didn't stab me. He slipped the tip of the blade under the shoulder of the Kevlar vest. Kevlar isn't meant to stop a stabbing motion, but it's not an easy thing to cut through, especially with a stone knife. The empty skin hand that decorated his wrist wobbled back and forth, back and forth, as he sawed. I stared past him at the far wall, but my peripheral vision just couldn't get rid of that flopping hand. I finally had to stare up at the ceiling, but it was just darkness. It's hard to stare into the dark when there are other things to look at, but I tried.

I almost asked them if they knew what Velcro was, but didn't. It would take them a while to cut the vest off with an obsidian blade. Hell, I might not have to do anything else to delay them. It'd be morning by the time the obsidian cut through the material. Unfortunately, I wasn't the only one who figured that out.

The skin man put the blade back in his sheath and pulled a second knife out from a sheath behind his back, the way you'd carry a backup gun. When he raised it into the firelight, it glimmered silver, steel. With or without high silver content, it would still cut through the vest a lot quicker than the obsidian.

He slipped the tip under the shoulder seam of the vest. I finally had to say something. 'You just planning to cut my heart out?'

'Your heart will remain in your chest where it belongs,' the 'god' said.

'Then why do you want the vest off?' I finally turned my head and looked at him, though not at any of his eyes.

'If you will not touch my chest with your hand, there are other parts of your body that can feel,' he said.

It was almost enough to make me give him my hand, almost. I didn't trust what he might consider other parts of my body that could feel. But it would take time to get the vest off, and if I just gave up my hand, that wouldn't take any time at all. I needed the time.

The vest came off quicker than you'd think. It was not designed to stand up to a sawing blade. They pulled the pieces of the vest off me, tugging the last from under my back.

The Red Woman's Husband climbed up beside me. He knelt, staring down at me, and he wasn't staring at my face. He traced the outline of my bra with the tip of one finger. Trailing, oh, so lightly, along my skin. 'What is this?' He traced under the bra back and forth, back and forth.

'Underwire,' I said.

He traced the black lace at the top of the bra. 'So many new things to learn.'

'Glad you like it,' I said. He didn't get the sarcasm. Maybe he was immune to it.

He did what I'd thought he'd do. He climbed on top of me. But he didn't get into a standard missionary position. He scooted lower until his chest was pressed against mine. With our height differences, that put his groin safely below mine. So it wasn't rape that we were doing. Maybe it was just me that worried so much about that. But somehow the knowledge that it wasn't sex he was after scared me more. There were worse things he could take from me than sex, like my mind.

His chest pressed against mine, smooth, warm, very human. Nothing bad happened. Funny, that didn't slow the frantic beat of my heart, or make me look him in the eyes.

'Do you feel it?' he asked.

I just kept staring at the far wall of the cave. 'I don't know what you mean?'

His chest pressed harder against me. 'Do you feel my heart beating?'

It wasn't the question I'd been expecting, so I actually thought about it. I tried to feel the answering beat of his heart against me, but all I could feel was my own panicked pulse.

'Sorry, all I can feel is mine.'

'And that is the problem,' he said.

I actually looked up at him then, getting a brief glimpse of his face, leaning so close below mine, the startling glimpse of his blue-green eyes in that dark face. I looked back to the wall. 'What do you mean?'

'My heart does not beat.'

I tried to feel his heart then, tried to sense the pulse of his life through the warm flesh of his chest. Concentrating on it slowed my own heart. You aren't always aware of a man's heart beating against your body, but when they're lying chest to chest, you usually feel it. But his chest pressed quiet above mine. I moved my free hand slowly toward him. He raised up, supporting himself with his hands, so I could press my hand against his chest.

His skin was warm and smooth, almost perfect, but nothing beat under my hand. Either he had no heart, or it wasn't beating.

'I am only a body. The Red Woman does not live in me. My heart is not a fit sacrifice without her touch.'

That made me look back at him. I looked into his peaceful eyes. 'Sacrifice? You're going to sacrifice yourself?'

His eyes stayed gentle and hopeful. 'I will be a sacrifice to the creator gods. They need to feed on the blood of a god as they did at the beginning of time.'

I tried to read something in that peaceful handsome face. Some doubt, fear, anything I could understand.

'You're going to let your priest cut you up?'

'Yes, but I will be reborn.'

'You're sure of that?' I said.

'My heart will be strong enough to beat outside my body, and when it is placed back within me, the old gods will return from the exile that your white Christ has cast them into.' His face, more than his words, said that he did believe it.

I'd read enough of the conquest of Mexico by the Spanish to doubt that Christ had much to do with it, no matter how many things had been done in His name. 'Don't blame Jesus Christ for what the Spanish did to your people. Our god gave us free choice, and that means we can choose evil. I believe that that's what happened to the men who conquered your people.'

He looked down at me, and he was puzzled again. 'You believe that. I can tell you believe that.'

'With all my heart,' I said. 'No pun intended.'

He sat up, sitting across my waist. 'Most of the people I have taken as offerings did not believe in much of anything. The ones who did believe, did not believe in your white Christ.' He touched my face. 'But you do.'

'Yeah,' I said.

'How can you believe in a god that would allow you to be brought to this place and sacrificed to a foreign god?'

'If you only believe when it's easy, you don't really believe,' I said.

'Is it not ironic that you, a follower of the god that destroyed us, will be what allows me to come into my power. When I have taken your essence, I will be strong enough to make the precious liquid, and I will be free of this place at last.'

'What do you mean, take my essence?' I'd stopped being afraid because we'd just been talking so long, or maybe I just can't sustain fear for that long. Eventually, if you don't kill me or hurt me, I stop being afraid.

'I will but kiss you and you will become as light and dry as the aged maize. You will feed me as the corn feeds men.' He began to lie down beside me on my right side, near my free hand.

I was suddenly scared again. I hoped I was wrong, but I was pretty sure I'd already seen what he meant to do to me at the Obsidian Butterfly. 'You mean you'll suck the life out of me and I'll end up looking like a dried mummy.'

He stroked a finger down my cheek, his eyes sad now, regretful. 'It will hurt a great deal, and I am sorry for that, but even your pain will go to strengthen me.' He leaned his face towards mine. I had a free hand and a knife in my pocket, but if I went for it too soon and failed, I was out of options. Where the hell was Ramirez?

'You're going to torture me. Great,' I said.

He drew back from me, just a little. 'It is not torture. It is the way all my priests waited for my waking.'

'Who brought your priests back?' I asked.

'I wakened Tlaloci, but I was weak and I had no more blood to give the others. Then before we could raise the others the man you call Riker disturbed our place of rest.' He stared off into space, as if he were seeing it over again. 'He found what you called the mummies of my priests. Many were torn apart by his men, searching for jewels inside them.' Anger darkened his face, stole the peacefulness from his eyes. 'The Quetzalcoatl was not yet awake or we would have killed them all. They took things that belonged to my priests. It forced me to find a different way to give them back their lives.'

'The skins,' I said.

He looked down at me. 'Yes, there are ways to make them give life.'

'So you hunted down the people who desecrated your . . . sleeping place, and the people who bought the things that belonged to your people.'

'Yes,' he said.

I guess from a certain point of view it was fair. If you had no ability to feel mercy, then it was a dandy plan. 'You killed and took the organs from the people who were gifted,' I said.

'Gifted?' he made it a question.

'Witches, brujos.'

'Ah, yes, I did not wish to leave them alive to hunt us before I came into my power.' He was touching my face again, stroking it. I think he was getting back on track to give me his 'kiss'.

'What exactly does coming into your power mean?' I asked. As long as I could keep him talking, he wouldn't be killing me. I could think of questions all night long.

'I will be mortal and immortal.'

I widened eyes at him. 'What do you mean mortal?'

'Your blood will make me mortal. Your essence will make me immortal.'

I frowned at him. 'I don't understand what you mean.'

He cupped my face in his hands like a lover. 'How could you possibly understand the ways of gods.' He held out his hand, and the skin-man handed him a long bone needle. Maybe I didn't know what he was going to do.

'What's that for?'

He held the needle, maybe four inches long, twirling it slowly between his fingers. 'I will pierce your ear lobe and drink your blood. It will be a small pain.'

'You keep saying you want me to believe in you, but you're the only one who never seems to be in pain. Your priests, the people who stole from you, all the sacrifices, everybody hurts but you.'

He propped himself up on one elbow, his body snug against mine. 'If my pain will convince you of my sincerity, then so be it.'

He jabbed the needle into his finger, deep, deep enough to touch bone. He drew the needle out slowly, making it hurt as much as he could. I waited for blood to come to the surface, but it didn't. He held the finger so I could see the hole the needle had left, but the hole was empty, no blood. As I watched, the wound closed like water smoothing, perfect once more. The knife wasn't going to do me any good, not against him.

'Does my pain make your pain less?' he asked.

'I'll let you know,' I said.

He smiled, so patient, so kind. So full of it. He started moving the needle towards my left ear. I could have fought him with my free hand, but if all he was going to do was pierce my ear lobe like I'd seen at the nightclub, then he could do that. I didn't like the idea, but I wasn't going to fight him. If I fought now, they might chain my hand back up. I wanted the free hand more than I wanted to keep him from sucking on my ear.

Truth is, I don't like needles, not just doctor needles, any of them. I have a phobia about small pointed things in my body. Knives don't seem to bother me, but needles do. Go figure. It was a phobia. To keep from struggling, I finally had to close my eyes because otherwise I'd have fought. I just couldn't help it.

The pain was sharp and immediate. I gasped, opening my eyes, watching his face lean over me. For a second I thought I'd blown it. I thought he was going straight to the kiss, then his mouth passed by my mouth. He turned my face to the right, gently, exposing the ear, and the long line of my neck. It reminded me of vampires, except that this mouth licked my ear, one quick movement. He made a small sigh, as he swallowed the first blood, then his mouth closed over my ear lobe, mouth working at the wound, tongue coaxing blood from the wound. He pressed his body the length of mine, one hand cupping my turned head, the other playing down the line of my body. Maybe it was just blood, but I never stroked my steak while I was eating it.

The line of his jaw was pressed to my face. I could feel his mouth moving as he swallowed. I'd had vampires take blood without me being under their spell, so it had hurt. This didn't hurt nearly as much. It was more like an overzealous lover with an ear fetish. Disturbing, but not really painful. His hand moved from my face to slide inside my bra. That I didn't like.

'I thought you said you weren't offering sex.'

He drew his hand out of my bra and drew back from my ear. His eyes were wide and unfocused and drowning in turquoise glow like the eyes of any vampire when its bloodlust is up. 'Forgive me,' he said, 'but it has been so very long since I felt life in my body.'

I thought I understood what he meant, but I was asking every question I could think of tonight. Anything to keep him talking. 'What do you mean?'

He laughed and rolled on his side to prop himself up on his elbow again. He jabbed the needle into his finger again, and gasped. Blood welled up from the wound, crimson blood. He laughed again. 'Your blood runs through my body, and I am mortal once more, with all the appetites of a mortal man.'

'You need blood to have blood pressure,' I said. 'You've got your first hard-on in centuries. I get it.'

He looked down at me with drowning eyes. 'You could have it.' He moved so that his body was pressed against mine, and I could feel him pressed against my jeans, eager, and ready.

I started to say my usual, no, then stopped. If my choices were being raped or being killed, when I thought that help was on the way . . . I debated, and I really don't know what I would have said, because another of the skin-men ran in from behind us where the silent flayed ones waited.

I heard the man's running footsteps and turned to watch him push his way through the flayed ones. He dropped to one knee in front of the Red Woman's Husband. 'My lord, armed strangers are approaching. The little brujo is with them, leading them this way.'

The Red Woman's Husband looked at him. 'Kill them. Delay them. When I have come into my power, it will be too late.'

The skin-men got weapons out of a chest and went running. I turned my head to watch the flayed ones trail after them. Only Tlaloci the priest stayed behind. It was just the three of us. Ramirez was coming. The police were coming. Surely, I could delay a few more minutes.

Fingers touched my face, moving me to look at him. 'You could have been the first woman in centuries for me, but there is no time.' He began to lower his face towards me. 'I am sorry that I must take you as an unwilling sacrifice because you have not harmed me or mine.'

I slipped my hand into my pocket. Fingers closed on the pen. I turned my head to the side so he couldn't kiss me, but I was really looking to see where Tlaloci was in the room. He'd moved back to the altar. He'd thrown Paulina's body off to one side like so much garbage. He was cleaning the altar, preparing I think for his god's death.

The Red Woman's Husband stroked my face, trying to turn me gently towards him. He whispered, breath warm against my face. 'I will wear your heart on the necklace of tongues, so that all my followers may remember your sacrifice for all eternity.'

'How romantic,' I said. I started easing the pen out of my pocket.

'Turn to me, Anita. Do not make me hurt you.' His fingers closed on my chin and began to turn my face slowly towards his. I felt his strength in his fingers and knew he could crush my jaw with only a flexing of his hand. I couldn't keep him from turning my face up to him. I couldn't stop it, but I had the pen in my hand now. I had my finger on the button that would release the blade. I just had to make sure it was over his heart.

Gunfire sounded from outside the cave, and it sounded close, as if the entrance wasn't that far away. Then there was a sound like a roaring, and I knew what it was because I'd heard it before. The police had brought flame-throwers or found some National Guard to join the party. I wondered whose idea it had been. It was a good one. I hoped they all burned.

I stared up at him, his fingers keeping my face looking at him. 'Does your heart really beat for me?' I asked.

'My heart beats. Blood runs through this body. You have given me life, and now you will give me immortality.'

The Red Woman's Husband leaned over me like Prince Charming about to bestow the kiss that would make everything all right again. His mouth hovered an inch above mine. The memory of how Seth's body had dried, died, was too vivid. I must have rushed to get the pen in position just above his heart. He pulled back a fraction of an inch, eyes questioning. I hit the button, and the blade took him through the heart.

His eyes flew wide, all that turquoise fire fading, leaving his eyes human looking. 'What have you done?'

'You're just another kind of vampire. I kill vampires.'

He rolled off the stone, fell to the floor. He held a hand out to Tlaloci. The priest rushed over to him. I didn't wait to see if there was a cure for the 'god.' I undid my left wrist and reached down for my ankles.

The Red Woman's Husband collapsed to his knees, and the priest collapsed with him. He was crying. 'No, no, no.' He pressed his hands around the hilt, trying to stop the blood from pouring out. His 'god' fell into convulsions on the floor. He tried to hold his hands over the wound, to staunch the blood.

I got my ankles freed and rolled off to the other side of the stone. Call it a hunch, but I thought that Tlaloci would be upset with me.

He rose to his feet, bloodstained hands held out in front of him. I'd never seen anyone look so horrified, so desolate, as if I had destroyed his world. And maybe I had.

He never said a word, just drew the obsidian blade at his waist and stalked towards me. But the rock I'd been chained to was the size of a large dining-room table, and I kept it between him and me. I kept the distance between us even, and he couldn't catch me. The gunfire was coming closer. He must have heard it, too, because he suddenly rolled over the stone to slash at me with the knife. I ran away from the stone, out into the open, which was what he wanted.

I turned and faced him. He came for me in a crouch, knife held loose but firm, as if he knew what he was doing. I'd left the blade in the vampire. I faced him hands out from my body, not sure what to do, except not get cut. I thought of one thing. I screamed, 'Ramirez!'

Tlaloci rushed me, blade slashing. I turned, feeling the rush of air as the blade passed. There were screams from the stairs, the sounds of in-close fighting. Tlaloci slashed at me like a madman. All I could do was keep backing up, trying to stay out of reach. I was bleeding from both arms, and one cut on my upper chest, when I realized he'd backed me up by the altar.

I tripped over Paulina's body about the second I started looking for it, to avoid it. I went down on my side, her body trapped under my legs. I kicked out at him without looking to see where he was, anything to keep him at a distance.

He grabbed my ankle, pinning my leg against his body. We stared at each other, and I saw my death in his face. He tossed the knife one-handed so that the grip changed from slashing, to a downward stab. He had my left leg pinned, but my right leg was still on the floor. I braced my upper body with my arms, leaned my shoulders downward and drew back my right leg. I lined up his kneecap. Tlaloci started the downward stroke. I kicked the downward edge of his kneecap with everything I had. I saw the kneecap slide sideways, dislocated. His leg crumbled, he cried out in pain, but the blade kept coming.

Tlaloci's head exploded in a shower of brains and bone. The

pieces rained down on me, and the body fell to one side, obsidian blade scraping along the stone floor as the hand convulsed around the hilt.

I stared across the cave and saw Olaf standing at the foot of the stone steps. He was still standing in his shooting stance, one-handed, gun still pointed at where the priest had been standing. He blinked, and I watched the concentration leave his face, watched something close to human spill across his face. He started walking towards me, gun at his side. The other hand held a knife, bloody to the hilt.

I was wiping Tlaloci's brains off my face when Olaf came to stand in front of me. 'I never thought I'd say this, but damn I'm glad to see you.'

He actually smiled. 'I saved your life.'

That made me smile. 'I know.'

Ramirez came down the stairs with what looked like a SWAT team in full battle gear behind him. They spilled out to either side, nasty-looking guns pointed at every inch of the cavern. Ramirez just stood there, gun in hand, looking for something to shoot. National Guardsmen in flame-thrower gear came next, nozzles of the flame-throwers pointed up at the ceiling.

Olaf cleaned his knife on his pants, sheathed it, and offered me a hand. The hand was stained red, but I took it. His skin was sticky with blood, but I squeezed his hand and let him pull me to my feet.

Bernardo came into the room with more cops behind him. His cast was red with blood, the blade sticking out of it so dark with blood, it looked black. He said, 'You're alive.'

I nodded. 'Thanks to Olaf.'

He gave a small pressure to my hand, then let me go.

'I was late again,' Ramirez said.

I shook my head. 'Does it matter who saves the day, as long as it gets saved?'

The other cops were starting to relax as they realized there was no one to shoot.

'Is this all?' one of the black-decked cops asked.

I looked back at the far tunnel. 'There's a Quetzalcoatl down that tunnel.'

'A what?'

'A . . . dragon.'

Even through the battle gear you could see them all exchange glances.

'Monster, if you like the word better, but it's still down there.'

They got into ranks and went past me to the tunnel at a crouched run. They hesitated at the tunnel entrance, then slipped through one at a time. For once I let them go. I'd done my part for one night. Besides, they were a hell of a lot better armed than I was. One of them ordered Ramirez and some of the other more civvie looking policemen to escort the civilians to the surface.

Ramirez came to stand in front of me. 'You're bleeding.' He touched the cut on my arm.

I turned so he could see some of the other cuts. 'Pick one.'

Bernardo and the other cops that had been ordered to stay behind came to look at the two dead men. 'Where's this Red Woman's Husband that the little creep kept talking about?' one of the cops asked.

I pointed at the body with the blade sticking out of its chest.

Two of the cops went to stand over the body. 'He doesn't look much like a god.'

'He was a vampire,' I said.

That got everyone's attention. 'What did you say?' Ramirez asked.

'Let's concentrate on the important details here, boys. We need to make sure that body doesn't get back up. Trust me. He is one powerful son of a bitch. We want him to stay dead.'

A cop kicked the body, which rolled limply as only the true dead move. 'Looks dead to me.'

Watching the body roll limply made me jump, as if I expected him to sit up and say, just kidding, I'm not really dead. The body stayed still, but it hadn't done my nerves any good.

'We need to take the head and cut out his heart. Then we burn them separately and scatter the ashes over different bodies of water. Then we burn the body to ash, and scatter it over a third body of water.'

'You've got to be kidding,' one of the cops said.

'The flayed ones just fell down and stopped moving,' Ramirez said. 'Did you do that?'

'Probably when I put the knife through his heart.'

'Bullets hadn't worked on any of them until the flayed ones fell down, then the bullets killed everything.'

'She did that?' the cop asked. 'She made our bullets work?'

'Yes,' Ramirez said, and probably he was right. Probably it had been me. Regardless, I wasn't going to raise any doubts. I wanted them to listen to me. I wanted to make sure that the 'god' stayed dead.

'How exactly do we chop off the head?' the same cop asked.

Olaf went to the chest that the men had gotten their weapons out of and lifted a large flat club with bits of obsidian embedded in it. He holstered his gun and walked to the body.

'Shit, that's one of those damn things they used on us,' the cop said.

'Nicely ironic to use it on their god, don't you think?' Bernardo asked.

Olaf knelt beside the body.

'Hey, we didn't say you could do that,' the cop said.

Olaf looked at Ramirez. 'What do you say, Ramirez?'

'I say we do whatever Anita says.'

Olaf whirled the club as if getting the feel for it. It also made the cops back up. He looked at me. 'I'll take the head.'

I pulled the knife out of Tlaloci's hand. He wasn't going to be needing it anymore. 'I'll take the heart.' I walked toward him, blade in hand. The cops kept backing away from us.

I stood over the vampire. Olaf knelt on the other side, looking up at me. 'If I'd let you get killed, Edward would have thought I failed.'

'Edward's alive then?'

'Yes.'

A tightness left my shoulders that I hadn't even realized was there. 'Thank God.'

'I don't fail,' Olaf said.

'I believe you,' I said.

We stared at each other, and there was still something in his eyes that I couldn't read or understand, a step beyond whatever I'd become. I stared into his dark eyes and knew that here was a monster, not as powerful as the one that lay on the ground, but just as deadly in the right circumstances. And I owed him my life.

'You take the head first.'

'Why?'

'I'm afraid if I take the knife out while the body's still intact that he'll sit up and start breathing again.'

Olaf raised eyebrows at me. 'You are not joking me?'

'I never joke about vampires,' I said.

He gave me another long look. 'You would have made a good man.'

I took the compliment because that's what it was, maybe the best compliment he'd ever given a woman.

'Thank you,' I said.

The SWAT team came back out of the far tunnel. 'There's nothing down there. It's empty.'

'Then it got away,' I said. I looked at the body still lying there. 'Take the head. I want out of this damn cave.'

The SWAT team leader didn't like us cutting up the body. He and Ramirez went into a yelling match. While everyone was watching the argument, I nodded to Olaf and he beheaded the corpse in one blow. Blood gushed out onto the cave floor.

'What the fuck are you doing?' one of the SWAT cops asked, bringing his gun pointed at us.

'My job,' I said. I put the tip of the blade under the ribs.

The policeman brought the gun up to his shoulder. 'Get away from the body until the captain tells you it's okay to do it.'

I kept the knife against the body. 'Olaf.'

'Yes.'

'If he shoots me, kill him.'

'My pleasure.' The big man turned his eyes to the policeman, and there was something in that gaze that made the heavily armed man take a step back.

The captain in question said, 'Stand down, Reynolds. She's a vamp executioner. Let her do her job.'

I plunged the blade into the skin, and it slid home. I cut a hole just below his ribs and reached into the hole. It was tight and wet and slick, and it took two hands to get the heart out, one to cut it free of the connecting tissue, and one to hold onto it. I drew it from the chest, bloodstained to my elbows.

I caught Ramirez and Bernardo both looking at me, with nearly identical looks on their faces. I didn't think either of them would be wanting a date any time soon. They'd always remember watching me cut a man's heart out, and that memory would stain anything else. With Bernardo, I didn't give a shit. With Ramirez, it hurt to see that look in his eyes.

A hand touched the heart. I stared at that hand, then looked up to meet Olaf's eyes. He wasn't repulsed. He stroked the heart, hands sliding over mine. I pulled away, and we looked at each other over the body we'd butchered. No, Olaf wasn't repulsed. The look in his eyes was that pure darkness that only fills a man's eyes in the most intimate of situations. He raised the severed head up by the hair and held it almost as if he'd let me kiss it. Then I realized he was holding it over the heart, like a matched pair.

I had to turn away from what I saw in his face. 'Does anyone have a bag that I can carry this in?'

Someone finally found an empty equipment bag and let me spill the heart into it. The policeman told me I could keep the bag. He didn't want it back.

No one offered Olaf a bag, and he never asked.

63

They found my guns in the chest with the rest of the weapons, though the holsters were missing. I just couldn't keep a holster intact on this job. But I stuffed the guns down my jeans. The knives weren't in the chest. Ramirez drove me personally to a crematorium so that I could see the heart and head burned down to ash. When I had two little containers of ash, it was almost dawn. I fell asleep in the seat beside him, or he'd have had a fight about taking me to the hospital. But he insisted that the doctors check me out. Amazingly enough, none of the cuts were even deep enough for stitches. I wouldn't even have any new scars. Miraculous.

One of the men had given me a jacket that said FBI on it to cover my nearly naked upper body. Several of the uniforms and most of the hospital staff assumed I was a federal agent. I kept having to correct people, and I finally realized that the emergency room doctor thought my denial meant I had a concussion and didn't know who I was. The more I argued the more concerned he got. He ordered a series of head X-rays, and I couldn't talk him out of it.

I was actually sitting in a wheelchair waiting to be escorted to X-ray when Bernardo came up. He touched the FBI jacket. 'You're moving up in the world.'

'When the nurse comes back, he'll be taking me down to X-ray.'

'You okay?'

'Just precautionary,' I said.

'I just came back from checking on the invalids.'

'Olaf said Edward would live.'

'He will.'

'How are the kids?'

'Peter is okay. They put Becca in a room. She's got a cast to her elbow.'

I stared at his cast stained a dirty brown. 'That thing is going to start stinking with all that blood dried into it.'

'The doc wants me to get a new cast, but I wanted to check on everyone first.'

'Where's Olaf?'

Bernardo shrugged. 'I don't know. He disappeared once the monsters were all dead and Ramirez had you in his car. He said something about the job being done. I guess he went back under whatever rock Edward found him under.'

I started to nod, then remembered something that Edward had said. 'Edward told you that you couldn't have a woman because he'd forbidden Olaf to have women, right?'

'Yeah, but the job's over, babe. I am headed for the first open bar.'

I looked at him, nodding. 'Maybe that's where Olaf is.'

He frowned at me. 'Olaf's at a bar?'

'No, he's out getting his ashes hauled, his way.'

We both looked at each other, and there was a moment when horror dawned on Bernardo's face, and he whispered, 'Oh, my god, he's out killing someone.'

I shook my head. 'If he's just out killing at random, there's no way to find him, but what if it's not random?'

'What do you mean?'

'Remember how he looked at Professor Dallas?'

Bernardo looked at me. 'You don't think . . . I mean he wouldn't . . . oh, shit.'

I got up out of the wheelchair and said, 'I've got to tell Ramirez what we're thinking.'

'You don't know he's there. You don't know he's doing anything wrong.'

'Do you believe he just went home?' I asked.

Bernardo seemed to think about that for a second, then shook his head.

'Neither do I.'

'He saved your life,' Bernardo said.

'I know.' We went to the elevator.

The elevator doors opened and Lieutenant Marks was standing there. 'Where the fuck do you think you're going?'

'Marks, I think that Professor Dallas is in danger.' I got into the elevator.

Bernardo followed.

'You think I'd believe anything you say, witch?' He hit the button that kept the doors open.

'Hate me if you want, but don't let her die.'

'Your pet FBI agent kept me out of the big raid.'

I didn't know what he meant, but I was pretty sure who he meant. 'Whatever Bradley did, he did without me knowing, but that's not the point.'

'I can make it the point.'

'Did you hear that Dallas is in danger? Did you hear that part?' I asked.

'She's as corrupt as you are.'

'So it's okay that she dies a horrible death,' I said.

He just looked at me. I moved as if to go towards the buttons. Bernardo caught his clue. He hit Marks in the head with his cast. The man went down, and I hit the door close button. The doors hushed closed as Bernardo lowered Marks to the floor.

'You want me to kill him?' Bernardo asked.

'No.' But now if I went to Ramirez for help, Marks would think he'd been in on it. Shit. 'Do you have Edward's car?'

'Yeah.'

'How did Olaf drive off, then?'

Bernardo looked at me. 'If he's really doing this, he'll steal a car and ditch it away from the murder scene. He won't chance using Edward's car.'

'He'll go back to Edward's house for his goody bag,' I said.

The doors opened on the floor that he'd parked on. We got out. 'What do you mean goody bag?'

'If he's going to cut her up, then he'll want the tools he normally uses. Serial murderers are very anal when it comes to how the victims are treated. They spend a lot of time planning exactly what they'll do and how.'

'So he's at Edward's?'

'How long has he been gone?'

'Three hours, maybe three and a half.'

'No, he'll be at Dallas's, if that's where he is at all.'

Bernardo opened the car, and we got in. I had to take the Browning out of my pants. The barrel's just too long for sitting down like that. I ended up holding it in my lap. I watched Bernardo drive with his cast-wrapped arm. 'You need me to drive?'

'I'm fine. Just tell me where Dallas lives, and I'll drive us.'

'Shit!'

He put the car in park and looked at me. 'The police would know the address.'

'When Marks wakes up, we'll be lucky to stay out of jail,' I said.

'We don't even know that Olaf's at her house,' he said.

'I got a better one. How to explain that we know he was a serial murderer and didn't warn the police sooner.'

'Do you have Edward's cell phone?' I asked.

He didn't argue, just leaned across and opened the glove compartment. I got the phone out.

'Who you going to call?'

'Itzpapalotl. She'll know the address.'

'She'll eat Olaf's face.'

'Maybe, maybe not. Either way you better get us out of the parking area before Marks wakes up and starts screaming.'

He drove us out of the parking lot and started slowly down the street. I dialed information, and the operator was happy to dial The Obsidian Butterfly for me. It was daylight. I knew better than to ask for Itzpapalotl herself, so I asked for Pinotl and told them it was an emergency and it was Anita Blake. I think it was my name that got me through, as if they'd been expecting the call.

Pinotl came on the line with his rich voice. 'Anita, my mistress said you would call.'

I was betting that she'd been wrong on the why, but . . . 'Pinotl, I need the address for Professor Dallas's house.'

Silence on the other end of the phone.

'She's in danger, Pinotl.'

'Then we will take care of it.'

'I'm going to have to call the police in on this, Pinotl. They'd shoot your werejaguars on sight.'

'You are worried about our people?' he said.

'Give me the address, and I'll take care of it for you, Pinotl.'

Silence except for his breathing.

'Tell your mistress, thanks for her help, Pinotl. I know I'm alive now because she helped me.'

'You are not angry that she did not tell you all she knew?'

'She's a centuries old vampire. They can't help themselves sometimes.'

'She is a goddess.'

'We're just arguing semantics, Pinotl. We both know what she is. Please give me the address.'

He gave it to me. I read the directions to Bernardo, and off we went.

64

I called the police on the way. I made it an anonymous call. Saying I'd heard screams. I hung up without giving my name. If Olaf wasn't there, then they'd scare the hell out of Dallas, and I'd apologize. I'd even pay for any busted locks.

'Why didn't you tell them the truth?' Bernardo asked.

'What? I think that some serial killer is there murdering her. And how do you know this, ma'am? Well, officer, you see it's like this. I've known he was a serial killer for days now, but our mutual friend Ted Forrester had forbidden him from attacking women while he was here helping us solve the mutilation murders. You've heard of the mutilation murders. Who is this? It's Anita Blake, the vampire executioner. And what does an executioner know about serial murderers? More than you'd think.' I looked at Bernardo.

'All right, all right. They'd still be asking questions when we arrived at the house.'

'This way they'll send an Albuquerque PD car there ASAP. They'll get there before we can even come close.'

'I didn't think you even liked Dallas when we met her.'

'It doesn't matter if I like her or not.'

'Yes, it does,' he said.

'If I don't like her, then we just let Olaf butcher her, is that it?'

'He saved your life. He saved mine. We don't owe this woman anything.'

I looked at him, trying to read his face from just the profile. 'Are you saying that you won't back me on this, Bernardo? Because if you're not on my side on this, then I need to know because if we go up against Olaf, and you hesitate, then you're going to get yourself killed, and maybe me.'

'If I go in, I'll go in ready to kill him.'

'If?' I said.

'I owe him my life, Anita. While we were at Riker's, we saved each other's lives. We counted on each other and knew the other one would be there. I don't owe this Dallas chick anything.'

'Then stay in the car.' A thought occurred to me. 'Or are you saying that you're on his side, really on his side?' I had the Browning out in my hand already. I clicked the safety off, and he heard it. I saw him stiffen.

'Well, that's not fair. If I take my left hand off to pull a gun, then we wreck.'

'I didn't like the way the conversation was going,' I said.

'All I'm saying, Anita, is that if we can save Dallas and let Olaf get away we should let him go. It'd make things even between us all.'

'If Dallas is unharmed, I'll think about it. That's the best I can do. But let me remind you, if you plan on killing me to help Olaf, that Edward is going to live. He'd hunt you both down, and you know it.'

'Hey, I never said anything about pulling down on you.'

'Just trying to test the limits of our misunderstanding, Bernardo, because trust me, you don't want me to misunderstand you.'

'There's no misunderstanding,' Bernardo said, and there was no teasing in his voice, just a dry seriousness that reminded me of Edward. 'I think it's shitty to turn Olaf in to the cops.'

'They'll already be there, Bernardo.'

'If there's only two uniforms, we can help him get away.'

'Are you talking about killing the policemen?'

'I didn't say that.'

'Don't. Don't go there because not only will I not follow you, I'll bury you there.'

'For two cops you don't even know.'

'Yeah, for two cops I don't even know.'

'Why?' he said.

I shook my head. 'Bernardo, if you have to ask that, you wouldn't understand the answer.'

He glanced at me. 'Edward said that you were one of the best shooters he'd seen, quick to kill. He said you only had two faults. You got too up close and personal with the monsters, and you thought too much like an honest cop.'

'An honest cop, I like that,' I said.

'I've seen you, Anita. You're as much a killer as Olaf, or me. You're not a cop. You never were.'

'Whatever I am, we are not killing the cops on sight. If Dallas is unhurt, we'll discuss letting Olaf go, but if he's hurt her, then he pays. If you don't like the plan, then give up your weapons and wait in the car. I'll go in alone.'

Bernardo looked at me. 'What's to keep me from lying to you, keeping my guns, and shooting you in the back?'

'You're more afraid of Edward than you are grateful to Olaf.'

'You know that for a fact,' he said.

'I know that Olaf has more rules of honor than you do. If you'd really felt all that damn grateful you'd have said something before I called the cops. Being protective of Olaf wasn't your first thought, or your second, or even your third.'

'Edward said you were one of the most loyal people he'd ever met. So why aren't you protecting Olaf?'

'He preys on women, Bernardo. He preys on them not because he's paid to or owes them vengeance, but because that's what he does. He's like a vicious dog that keeps attacking people. Eventually, you have to put it down.'

'You're going in there planning to kill him,' Bernardo said.

'No, no I'm not. Remember, if I kill either of you, I'll either owe Edward another favor, or I'll have to draw a gun on him and finally find out which of us is better. I don't think I'll survive the latter, and I have not had a good time honoring Edward's favor. I got a glimpse of his other life at Riker's place. I don't want to be in another firefight. It's not my cup of tea.'

'It's not anyone's cup of tea,' Bernardo said. 'You just get used to it.'

'You don't get used to shit like that.'

'Like you don't get used to cutting out people's hearts? You did that like an old pro.'

I shrugged. 'Practice makes perfect.'

'This is the street,' Bernardo said.

The street had that just past dawn silence. The cars still sat unmoved in their driveways, but there were people standing in their driveways peering out at the marked police car that was sitting in front of Dallas's house. One of the doors was open, filling the quiet neighborhood with the radio squawk. The lights rotated pale and underdone like a child's toy in the heavy morning light.

Professor Dallas's house was a small ranch with those faux adobe walls that everyone was so fond of here. In the earlier morning light it looked almost golden, as if it glowed. Bernardo parked by the road.

'Well?' I asked.

'I'm with you.' But before we could draw guns, the two uniforms came out of the house with Dallas in a robe. We sat there staring at her, smiling at the policemen while they apologized for bothering her. She looked up, noticed us. She looked puzzled but waved at us.

'Anita, look at the mailbox,' Bernardo said,

Our car was almost right in front of the mailbox. There was a white envelope pinned to the front of the mailbox with a knife. My first name was printed in block letters on the front of the envelope. No one had noticed it yet, but us.

Edward's car was tall enough to hide it from the neighbors. 'Can you help me hide it from the cops?'

'My pleasure.'

I got out of the car, leaving the Browning on the seat because I couldn't figure out a way to put it down my pants without the police noticing me doing it, and I didn't have any ID on me. I might be able to fake being a Fed, but then again maybe not. And it's a federal offense to impersonate a federal agent. Bernardo and I had assaulted a police officer. We didn't need any more charges.

Bernardo pulled the knife out, making the movement look natural. The envelope dropped into my hand, and I walked up to the house hitting my thigh with the envelope, as if I'd carried it from the car.

Neither of the cops yelled, 'Halt, thief!' so I kept moving. I didn't know what Bernardo had done with the knife. It had just vanished. 'Hi, Dallas, what's up?'

'Someone made a prank phone call about screams coming from my house.'

'Who'd do such a dastardly thing?' Bernardo asked.

I frowned at him.

He smiled at me, pleased with himself.

'Did you get a call, too?' she asked.

'I got it,' Bernardo said. 'They called Edward's cell phone, said you were in danger.'

The uniform cops made the same mistake that the hospital staff had made. They introduced themselves by rank and name, and shook hands. I said, 'Anita Blake. This is Bernardo Spotted-Horse.'

'He's not a . . .' The policeman looked uncomfortable as soon as he started to say it.

'No, I'm not a federal agent,' Bernardo said. There was bitterness in his voice.

'It's the hair,' I said. 'They've never seen a male agent with long hair.'

'Sure, it was the hair.'

The uniforms went off, leaving us at Dallas's doorstep in the morning light with her curious neighbors coming out in dribs and drabs to see what was happening at an hour past dawn on the quiet street.

'Would you like to come inside? I already started coffee.'

'Sure.'

Bernardo looked at me, but followed me in.

The kitchen was small, square, and neat like one that wasn't used much. But it was cheerful in a blaze of morning sunlight. 'What's really going on, Anita?'

I sat down at her table and opened the envelope with my name on it. It was written in block letters.

ANITA,

I KNEW THAT MOMENT IN THE CAVE THAT YOU WOULD THINK AS I DID. I FELT THAT YOU WOULD KNOW WHERE I WOULD GO TO HUNT. NOW HERE YOU ARE. I AM NEARBY.

That made me look up. 'He says he's nearby.'

Bernardo drew his gun. He stood and began to watch the windows. I went back to the note.

I HAVE WATCHED YOU COME TO THE GOOD PROFESSOR'S RESCUE. I WATCHED YOU TAKE THE ENVELOPE, AND I KNOW YOU ARE READING IT NOW. I BELITTLED EDWARD WHEN HE SPOKE OF SOUL MATES. I OWE HIM AN APOLOGY. WHEN I SAW YOU TAKE THE HEART, SO PRACTICED, I KNEW THAT YOU WERE AS I AM. HOW MANY HAVE YOU KILLED? HOW MANY HEARTS HAVE YOU RIPPED OUT? HOW MANY HEADS HAVE YOU TAKEN? YOU'LL ARGUE WITH YOURSELF THAT YOU ARE NOT AS I AM. MAYBE YOU

DON'T TAKE TROPHIES, BUT YOU STILL LIVE FOR THE
KILL, ANITA. YOU WOULD WITHER AND DIE WITHOUT
THE VIOLENCE. WHAT TRICK OF FATE HAS MADE YOU
PHYSICALLY THE WOMAN I KILL OVER AND OVER
AGAIN, AND YET PUT INSIDE THAT TINY BODY THE
OTHER HALF OF MY SOUL? ARE MOST OF THE
VAMPIRES YOU KILL MEN? DO YOU HAVE YOUR VICTIM
PREFERENCE, ANITA?

I WOULD LOVE TO HUNT WITH YOU AT MY SIDE. I
WOULD HUNT YOUR VICTIMS BECAUSE I KNOW YOU
WILL NOT HUNT MINE. BUT WE WOULD STILL KILL
TOGETHER AND CUT THE BODIES UP, AND THAT
WOULD BE MORE THAN I EVER DREAMED OF SHARING
WITH A WOMAN.

The note wasn't signed. Big surprise there, since I might have given
it to the police.

'You look pale,' Dallas said.

'What does the note say?' Bernardo asked.

I handed it to him. 'I don't think he's out there to kill us or even
her.'

'Who are you talking about?' she asked.

I told her, and she laughed at me. 'You know I'm a vampire
executioner.'

'Yes.'

'I killed another vamp last night. One I think that Itzpapalotl
wanted me to kill. She helped me do it. That's the heart that I took.'

Bernardo read faster than I would have thought. 'Jesus, Anita,
Olaf has a crush on you.'

'A crush,' I said, 'a crush. God, there's got to be another word
for it.'

Dallas asked, 'Can I read it?'

'I think you should because he didn't wait just to catch a glimpse of me. He waited because if I hadn't shown up, he'd have come in here and butchered you.'

She tried to laugh it off, but there must have been something in my face that choked the laughter and made her reach a shaking hand out for the letter. She read it and said, 'Who is this?'

'Olaf,' I said.

'But he was so nice.'

Bernardo made a harsh sound.

'Trust me on this, Dallas. Olaf is not nice.'

She looked from one to the other of us. 'You're not kidding, are you?'

'He's a serial killer. I just don't think he's ever killed in this country.'

'You should turn him in to the police,' she said.

'I don't have any proof of what he's done.'

'Besides,' Bernardo said, 'what if he was one of the vamps?'

'What do you mean?' Dallas asked.

'He means, wouldn't you protect one of the vamps from the police because you'd know that the vamps would take care of it,' I said.

'Well, yes, I guess.'

'And we'll take care of this,' Bernardo said.

She looked from one to the other of us, and for the first time she looked afraid.

'Will he be back?'

'For you, I don't think so,' Bernardo said. He looked at me. 'But I bet he'll find a reason to come to St Louis.'

I'd have liked to say he was wrong, but the cold tight feeling in my stomach agreed with Bernardo. I'd be seeing Olaf again. I just had to decide what I'd do when I met him. He hadn't done anything wrong on this trip. Not only couldn't I prove he was a serial killer, he hadn't done anything worse than I'd done this time round. Who was I to throw stones? Yet, yet, I hoped he stayed away from me.

For more reasons than I wanted to admit, maybe. Maybe for the same reasons that I'd kill him if he came. Because maybe there was some truth to what he wrote. I had over fifty kills. What really separated me from people like Olaf? Motive, method? If those were the only differences, then Olaf was right, and I couldn't let him be right. I just could not accept that. Growing up to be Edward was a problem. Growing up to be Olaf was a nightmare.

EPILOGUE

Marks tried to press assault charges, but Bernardo and I said we didn't know what he was talking about. Doctor Evans said that his injuries were inconsistent with being hit by a person. It wouldn't have worked except that Marks was in the doghouse about how he'd handled the case. He was in on the press conference where the public was assured that the danger was over, but Ramirez was standing up there beside him, along with Agent Bradford. And me. They put Ted and Bernardo up there, too. We didn't get to answer questions, but we got our picture in the papers. I'd have rather not, but I knew it would please Bert, my boss, and they did print it in several national papers that I was Anita Blake of Animators, Inc. Bert loved it.

Edward caught a secondary infection from something that had been smeared on the stake. He took a relapse, and I stayed. Donna and I took turns sitting by his bed. Sitting by Becca's bed. It got to the point where the little girl cried when I left.

Peter spent a lot of time playing games with her, trying to get her to smile. But his eyes had that hollow look you get when you're not sleeping well. He wouldn't talk to me or Donna. The only thing he'd admitted to her was the beating. He hadn't told her about the rape. I didn't betray his secret. First, I wasn't sure she could handle another shock. Second, it wasn't my secret to tell. Donna actually rose to the occasion. She was like this incredible pillar of strength for the kids, for Ted, even though he couldn't hear her talking to him. She never once turned to me in tears. It was like this new person had risen from the ashes of the person I'd first met. It saved me having to hurt her.

Ten days after the accident, Edward was awake and talking. Out of danger. I could finally go home. When I told them I was finally going home, Donna hugged me tight and cried and said, 'You have to tell the kids goodbye.'

I assured her I would, and she left us alone, to say our goodbyes.

I pulled the chair up to the bedside and studied his face. He was still pale, but he looked like Edward again. That cold bleakness was back in his eyes when no one but me was looking.

'What's wrong?' he asked.

'It couldn't just be because you nearly died,' I said.

'No,' he said.

I smiled, but he didn't smile back.

'Bernardo came to see me, but Olaf never did,' he said.

I realized then what he thought I'd waited around to tell him. 'You think I killed Olaf, and I've been waiting for you to get healthy enough to give you the same choice you gave me after Harley died.' I laughed. 'Sweet Jesus, Edward.'

'You didn't kill him.' I watched him relax against his pillows, visibly relieved.

'No, I didn't kill him.'

He managed a faint smile. 'It wouldn't have been the same choice. But if you'd killed Olaf, you wouldn't have wanted to owe me another favor.'

'You were afraid I'd press the point, make it the gunfight at the OK Corral?'

'Yes,' he said.

'I thought you wanted to see which of us was better.'

'I thought I was dying on the stairs. All I could think of was that Peter and Becca were going to die in there with me. Bernardo and Olaf were there, but you'd gone up the stairs and hadn't come back. When you came back around that corner, I knew you'd get the kids out. I knew you'd risk your life for theirs. Bernardo and Olaf would have tried, but the kids wouldn't have been their first priority. I knew they would be yours. When I passed out in the cave, I wasn't worried. I knew you'd see it right.'

'What are you saying, Edward?'

'I'm saying if you had killed Olaf, I'd have given you a pass on it because Peter and Becca mean more to me than that.'

I took Olaf's letter out of my back pocket and handed it to him. He read it while I watched his face. Nothing moved but his eyes. He had no reaction. 'He's a good man at your back, Anita.'

'You're not suggesting I date Olaf?'

He almost laughed. 'No, fuck no. Stay as far away from him as you can. If he comes to St Louis, kill him. Don't wait for him to deserve it. Just do it.'

'I thought he was your friend.'

'Not friend. Business associate. It's not the same thing.'

'I agree someone needs to kill Olaf, but why are you so adamant all of a sudden? You trusted him enough to bring him here to your town.'

'Olaf has never had a girlfriend. He's had whores and he's had victims. Maybe it's true love, but I think if he shows up and finds that you won't be his little serial killer pin-up girl, that he'll turn violent. You don't want to know what he's like when he's violent, Anita. You really, really don't.'

'You're scared he'll come after me.'

'If he shows in town, call me.'

I nodded. 'I will.' I had other questions. 'Riker's house sprang a mysterious gas leak and blew to Kingdom Come. No survivors, no bodies, no evidence that we did shit, or that Riker and his men did shit. Was it Van Cleef?'

'Not him personally,' Edward said.

'You know the next question,' I said.

'I know,' he said.

'You're not going to tell me, are you?'

'I can't tell you, Anita. One of the conditions to leaving was to never talk about it with anyone. If I break that, they'll come after me.'

'I wouldn't tell anyone.'

He shook his head. 'No, Anita, trust me on this one. Ignorance is bliss.'

'That is incredibly frustrating,' I said.

He smiled. 'I know, and I'm sorry.'

'No, you're not. You love keeping secrets.'

'Not this one,' he said. There was something close to sadness in his eyes, and for the first time I realized for sure that once there had been a kinder, gentler version of Edward. He hadn't been born this way. He'd been made like Frankenstein's monster.

'No answers, huh?'

'No,' he said.

We stared at each other, but neither of us seemed impatient.

'Okay,' I said.

'Okay, what?' he asked.

I shrugged. 'You won't answer questions about your background, fine. Answer another one. Are you going to marry Donna?'

'If I say yes, what will you do?'

I sighed. 'I was willing to kill you to keep you away from them when I got here. But what is love, Edward? You're willing to give up your life for the kids. You'd do the same for Donna. She's convinced you're her dream man. It's a good act. Becca told her what you did, what we did. Peter backed it. So in a way they all three know what you are, who you are. Donna's cool with it.' I stopped talking.

'Was there an answer to my question in there somewhere?'

'I won't do anything, Edward. You're willing to die for them. If that's not love, it's so close I can't tell the difference.'

He nodded. 'Nice that I have your blessing.'

'You don't,' I said. 'But I don't have room to throw stones at your personal life. So do whatever you want.'

'I will,' he said.

'Peter hasn't told Donna what happened to him. He needs therapy for it.'

'Why didn't you tell her?'

'It's not my secret to tell. Besides, you're his would-be stepfather, and you know. I trust you to do the right thing by him, Edward. If he doesn't want Donna to know, you'll find a way around it.'

'You're treating me like his father,' Edward said.

'How much did you see of what Peter did to Amanda?'

'Enough,' Edward said.

'He emptied the clip into her, Edward. He turned her face into spaghetti. The look in his face . . .' I shook my head. 'He's more your son than Donna's and has been since he blew away his father's killer when he was eight.'

'You think he's like me?'

'Like us,' I said, 'like us. I don't know if you can rebuild someone that got that broken that early. I'm not a psychiatrist. Healing people's not my job.'

'It's not mine either,' he said.

'I never thought you missed the pieces of yourself that you gave up to be who and what you are, but when I see you with Donna and Becca and Peter, I see regret in you. You wonder what life might have been like if you hadn't met Van Cleef, or whoever the hell was first.'

He looked at me, eyes cold. 'It took me a long time to understand what I saw in Donna. How did you know?'

I shrugged. 'Maybe, the same thing I thought I saw in Ramirez.'

'It's not too late for you, Anita.'

'It's too late for me to have the white picket fence, Edward. Maybe I can figure out something, but not that. It's too late for that.'

'You think I'll fail with Donna,' he said.

I shook my head. 'I don't know. I just know it wouldn't work for me. I'm not the actor you are. Whoever I'm with has to know who I am, warts and all, or it won't work.'

'You know which monster you're going to settle down with?'

'No, but I know I can't keep hiding from them. Hiding from them is like hiding from who I am. I'm not going to do that anymore.'

'You think I'm running from myself by going with Donna.'

'No, I think you always embraced the monster part of you. You're finding for the first time that not all of you is dead as you wanted it to be. Donna appeals to a part of you that you didn't know was left.'

'Yes,' he said. 'And what do Richard and Jean-Claude represent for you?'

'I don't know, but it's time I found out.'

He smiled, but it wasn't a happy smile. 'Good luck.'

'The same to you,' I said.

'We're going to need it,' he said.

I'd have liked to argue, but he was right.

I did call Itzpapalotl before I left for home. She was disappointed that I didn't come in person, but not angry. I think she knew why I didn't want to shake hands again. She'd killed every minion of every rival vamp that crossed her path for fifty years, but me she hadn't harmed a hair on my head. I thought she wanted the secret to the triumvirate, and that had interested her, but that hadn't been what saved me. She'd set me up to kill the Red Woman's Husband. She'd given me the power to both attract him and withstand his charms. I'd been her bait and her weapon. Now the other god was dead, and I was leaving her territory before she decided that I'd outlived my usefulness.

She extended an invitation to my master. 'We could have much to discuss, your master and I.'

I told her I'd pass along the invitation. I will, but they'll be ice skating in hell before I bring Jean-Claude down to meet Itzpapalotl. She'd gobble him up. Maybe Edward's right. Maybe Richard and

I would survive Jean-Claude's death. But surviving his death and surviving whatever Itzpapalotl would do to him are two very different things.

There are so many easier ways to kill Jean-Claude. Ways that would be less risky to Richard and me. I know that's what Edward wants me to do. Several of my friends are voting that way. But I get presidential veto, and I don't want him dead. I'm not sure what I do want, but I know I want him walking around so I can decide.

I'm going home, and I'm going to start by seeing all the friends I've neglected for the past few months. So Ronnie is dating Richard's best friend. So what? She and I can still be friends. Catherine's had two years of honeymooning. Time I stopped using that as an excuse not to see her. I think I'm just uncomfortable with how terribly happy she is with a man that I found ordinary and a little boring. But she glows around him. I haven't done much glowing lately around either of my two men.

I'm going to start seeing the werewolves in Richard's pack again, and Jean-Claude's vamps. First renew friendships, then if that works out okay, I'll see the boys. It's a cautious plan, nay cowardly, but it's the best I can do. Okay, it's the best I'm willing to do. Because the truth is that I am no closer to a solution to my love life than I was when I broke off with them over a year ago. The few times I fell off the celibacy wagon don't count because I was still trying to avoid them. I don't want to avoid them. I just want to know what exactly it is that I do want. Once I figure out what I want, who I want, the next question is can I have who I want or will the loser pull our little house down around us in bloody ruins. I would say it's the sixty-four thousand dollar question, but Richard and Jean-Claude are worth so much more than that to me. Maybe Ramirez is right. Maybe if I truly loved one of them, the choice would be easy. Or maybe Ramirez doesn't know what the hell he's talking about.

Edward loves Donna and Peter and Becca. They're all seeing a therapist together, but I think Peter is still lying about what really happened. You can't get good therapy if you lie to your therapist. But I think Peter is counting on Edward to be his therapist. Scary thought, isn't it?

Edward loves Donna. Do I love Richard? Yes. Do I love Jean-Claude? Maybe. If it's really yes for Richard, and maybe for Jean-Claude, then why don't I have my answer? Because maybe, just maybe, there is no one right answer. I'm beginning to worry that whatever I decide, I will be left mourning the one that got away. Once, I'd been afraid if I chose Richard that Jean-Claude would kill him rather than share me, but strangely the vampire seems willing to share, and Richard isn't. Maybe Jean-Claude loves the power of the triumvirate more than he loves me, or maybe Richard is just jealous. I certainly wouldn't share either of them with another woman. Fair is fair. Which brings me back to the original question: who is the love of my life? Maybe I don't have one. Maybe it's not love at all. But if it's not love, then what is it? I wish I knew.

It's time to satisfy your bloodlust . . .

Turn the page for a preview of the next sensational novel featuring Anita Blake.

LAURELL K. HAMILTON

NARCISSUS IN CHAINS

An Anita Blake,
Vampire Hunter, Novel

headline

I

June had come in like its usual hot, sweaty self, but a freak cold front had moved in during the night and the car radio had been full of the record low temperatures. It was only in the low sixties, not that cold, but after weeks of eighty- and ninety-plus, it felt downright frigid. My best friend, Ronnie Sims, and I were sitting in my Jeep with the windows down, letting the unseasonably cool air drift in on us. Ronnie had turned thirty tonight. We were talking about how she felt about the big 3-0 and other girl talk. Considering that she's a private detective and I raise the dead for a living it was pretty ordinary talk. Sex, guys, turning thirty, vampires, werewolves. You know, the usual.

We could have gone inside the house, but there is something about the intimacy of a car after dark that makes you want to linger. Or maybe it was the sweet smell of springlike air coming through the windows like the caress of some half-remembered lover.

'Okay, so he's a werewolf. No one's perfect,' Ronnie said. 'Date him, sleep with him, marry him. My vote's for Richard.'

'I know you don't like Jean-Claude.'

'Don't like him!' Her hands gripped the passenger-side door handle, squeezing it until I could see the tension in her shoulders. I think she was counting to ten.

'If I killed as easily as you do, I'd have killed that son of a bitch two years ago and your life would be a lot less complicated now.'

That last was an understatement. But . . . 'I don't want him dead, Ronnie.'

'He's a vampire, Anita. He *is* dead.' She turned and looked at me in the dark. Her soft gray eyes and yellow hair had turned to silver and near white in the cold light of the stars. The shadows and bright reflected light left her face in bold relief, like some modern painting. But the look on her face was almost frightening. There was a fearful determination there.

If it had been me with that look on my face, I'd have warned me not to do anything stupid, like kill Jean-Claude. But Ronnie wasn't a shooter. She'd killed twice, both times to save my life. I owed her. But she wasn't a person who could hunt someone down in cold blood and kill him. Not even a vampire. I knew this about her, so I didn't have to caution her. 'I used to think I knew what dead was or wasn't, Ronnie.' I shook my head. 'The line isn't so clear-cut.'

'He seduced you,' she said.

I looked away from her angry face and stared at the foil-wrapped swan in my lap. Deirdorfs and Hart, where we'd had dinner, got creative with their doggy bags: foil-wrapped animals. I couldn't argue with Ronnie, and I was getting tired of trying.

Finally, I said, 'Every lover seduces you, Ronnie, that's the way it works.'

She slammed her hands so hard onto the dashboard it startled me and must have hurt her. 'Damn it, Anita, it's not the same.'

I was starting to get angry, and I didn't want to be angry, not with Ronnie. I had taken her out to dinner to make her feel better, not to fight. Louis Fane, her steady boyfriend, was out of town at a conference, and she was bummed about that, and about turning thirty. So I'd tried to make her feel better, and she seemed determined to make me feel worse.

'Look, I haven't seen either Jean-Claude or Richard for six months. I'm not dating either of them, so we can skip the lecture on vampire ethics.'

'Now that's an oxymoron,' she said.

'What is?' I asked.

'Vampire ethics,' she said.

I frowned at her. 'That's not fair, Ronnie.'

'You are a vampire executioner, Anita. You are the one who taught me that they aren't just people with fangs. They are monsters.'

I'd had enough. I opened the car door and slid to the edge of the seat. Ronnie grabbed my shoulder. 'Anita, I'm sorry. I'm sorry. Please don't be mad.'

I didn't turn around. I sat there with my feet hanging out the door, the cool air creeping into the closer warmth of the car.

'Then drop it, Ronnie. I mean drop it.'

She leaned over and gave me a quick hug from behind. 'I'm sorry. It's none of my business who you sleep with.'

I leaned into the hug for a moment. 'That's right, it's not.' Then I pulled away and got out of the car. My high heels crunched on the gravel of my driveway. Ronnie had wanted us to dress up, so we had. It was her birthday. It wasn't until after dinner that I'd realized her diabolical scheme. She'd had me wear heels and a nice little black skirt outfit. The top was actually, gasp, a well-fitted halter top. Or would that be backless evening wear? However pricey it was, it was still a very short skirt and a halter top. Ronnie had helped me pick the outfit out about a week ago. I should have known her innocent 'oh, let's just both dress up' was a ruse. There had been other dresses that covered more skin and had longer hemlines, but none that camouflaged the belly-band holster that cut across my lower waist. I'd actually taken the holster along with us on the shopping trip, just to be sure. Ronnie thought I was being paranoid, but I don't go anywhere after dark unarmed. Period.

The skirt was just roomy enough and black enough to hide the fact that I wore the belly band and a Firestar 9mm. The top was heavy enough material, what there was of it, that you really ?couldn't see the handle of the gun under the cloth. All I had to do was lift the bottom of the top and the gun was right there, ready to be drawn. It was the most user-friendly dressy outfit I'd ever owned.

Made me wish they made it in a different color so I could have two of them.

Ronnie's plan had been to go to a club on her birthday. A dance club. Eek. I never went to clubs. I did not dance. But I went in with her. Yes, she got me out on the floor, mainly because her dancing alone was attracting too much unwanted male attention. At least with both of us dancing together the would-be Casanovas stayed at a distance. Though saying I danced was inaccurate. I stood there and sort of swayed. Ronnie danced. She danced like it was her last night on Earth and she had to put every muscle to good use. It was spectacular, and a little frightening. There was something almost desperate to it, as if Ronnie felt the cold hand of time creeping up faster and faster. Or maybe that was just me projecting my own insecurities. I'd turned twenty-six early in the year, and, frankly, at the rate I was going, I probably wouldn't have to worry about hitting thirty. Death cures all ills. Well, most of them.

There had been one man who had attached himself to me instead of Ronnie. I didn't understand why. She was a tall leggy blonde, dancing like she was having sex with the music. But he offered me drinks. I don't drink. He tried to slow dance. I refused. I finally had to be rude. Ronnie told me to dance with him, at least he was human. I told her that birthday guilt only went so far, and she'd used hers up.

The last thing on God's green earth that I needed was another man in my life. I didn't have a clue what to do with the two I had already. The fact that they were, respectively, a Master Vampire and an Ulfric, werewolf king, was only part of the problem. That fact alone should let you know just how deep a hole I was digging. Or would that be, already have dug? Yeah, already dug. I was about halfway to China and still throwing dirt up in the air.

I'd been celibate for six months. So, as far as I knew, had they.

Everyone was waiting for me to make up my mind. Waiting for me to choose, or decide, something, anything.

I'd been a rock for half a year, because I'd stayed away from them. I hadn't seen them, in the flesh anyway. I had returned no phone calls. I had run for the hills at the first hint of cologne. Why such drastic measures? Frankly, because almost every time I saw them, I fell off the chastity wagon. They both had my libido, but I was trying to decide who had my heart. I still didn't know. The only thing I had decided was that it was time to stop hiding. I had to see them and figure out what we were all going to do. I'd decided two weeks ago that I needed to see them. It was the day that I refilled my birth-control pill prescription, and started taking it again. The very last thing I needed was a surprise pregnancy. That the first thing I thought of when I thought of Richard and Jean-Claude was to go back on birth control tells you something about the effect they had on me.

You needed to be on the pill for at least a month to be safe, or as safe as you ever got. Four more weeks, five to be sure, then I'd call. Maybe.

I heard Ronnie's heels running on the gravel. 'Anita, Anita, wait, don't be angry.'

The thing was, I wasn't angry with her. I was angry with me. Angry that after all these months I still couldn't decide between the two men. I stopped walking and waited for her, huddled in my little black skirt outfit, the little foil swan in my hands. The night had turned cool enough to make me wish I'd worn a jacket. When Ronnie caught up with me I started walking again.

'I'm not mad, Ronnie, just tired. Tired of you, my family, Dolph, Zerbrowski, everyone being so damned judgmental.' My heels hit the sidewalk with sharp *clacks*. Jean-Claude had once said he could tell if I was angry just by the sound of my heels on the floor. 'Watch your step. You're wearing higher heels than I am.' Ronnie was five feet eight, which meant with heels she was nearly six feet.

I was wearing two-inch heels, which put me at five five. I get a much better workout when Ronnie and I jog together than she does.

The phone was ringing as I juggled the key and the foil-wrapped leftovers. Ronnie took the leftovers, and I shoved the door open with my shoulder. I was running across the floor in my high heels before I remembered that I was on vacation. Which meant whatever emergency was calling at 2:05 in the morning was not my problem, not for another two weeks at least. But old habits die hard, and I was at the phone before I remembered. I actually let the machine pick up while I stood there, heart pounding. I was planning on ignoring it, but . . . but I still stood ready to grab the receiver just in case.

Loud, booming music, and a man's voice. I didn't recognize the music, but I recognized the voice. 'Anita, it's Gregory. Nathaniel's in trouble.'

Gregory was one of the wereleopards I'd inherited when I killed their alpha, their leader. As a human, I wasn't really up to the job, but until I found a replacement, even I was better than nothing. Wereanimals without a dominant to protect them were anyone's meat, and if someone moved in and slaughtered them, it would sort of be my fault. So I acted as their protector, but the job was more complicated than I'd ever dreamed. Nathaniel was the problem. All the others were rebuilding their lives since their old leader had been killed, but not Nathaniel. He'd had a hard life: abused, raped, pimped out, and topped. Topped meant he'd been someone's slave – as in sex and pain. He was one of the few true submissives I'd ever met, though, admittedly, my pool of acquaintance was limited.

I cursed softly and picked up the phone. 'I'm here, Gregory, what's happened now?' Even to me, my voice sounded tired and half-angry.

'If I had anyone else to call, Anita, I'd call them, but you're it.' He sounded tired and angry, too. Great.

'Where's Elizabeth? She was supposed to be riding herd on

Nathaniel tonight.' I'd finally agreed that Nathaniel could start going out to the dominance and submission clubs if he was accompanied by Elizabeth and at least one other wereleopard. Tonight it had been Gregory riding shotgun, but without Elizabeth, Gregory wasn't dominant enough to keep Nathaniel safe. A normal submissive would have been safe in one of the clubs with someone there to simply say, 'No thanks, we'll pass.' But Nathaniel was one of those rare subs who are almost incapable of saying no, and there had been hints made that his idea of pain and sex could be very extreme. Which meant that he might say yes to things that were very, very bad for him. Wereanimals can take a lot of injury and not be permanently damaged, but there is a limit. A healthy bottom will say *stop* when he's had too much or he feels something bad happening, but Nathaniel wasn't that healthy. So he had keepers with him to make sure no one really bad got a hold of him. But it was more than that. A good dominant trusts his sub to say *when* before the damage is too great. The dom trusts the sub to know his own body and have enough self-preservation to call out before he is in past what his body can take. Nathaniel did not come with that safety feature, which meant a dominant with the best of intentions could end up hurting him badly before realizing Nathaniel wouldn't help himself.

I actually had accompanied Nathaniel a few times. As his Nimir-Ra it was sort of my job to interview prospective . . . keepers. I'd gone prepared for the clubs to be one of the lower circles of hell and had been pleasantly shocked. I'd had more trouble with sexual propositions in a normal bar on a Saturday night. In the clubs everyone was very careful not to impose on you or to be seen as pushy. It was a small community, and if you got a reputation for being obnoxious, you could find yourself blacklisted, with no one to play with. I'd found the people in the scene were polite, and once you made it clear you were not there to play, no one bothered you, except tourists. Tourists were posers, people not really into the scene, who liked to dress up and frequent the clubs. They didn't know the rules, and hadn't bothered to ask. They probably thought a woman who would come to a place like this would do anything. I'd persuaded them differently. But I'd had to stop going with Nathaniel. The other wereleopards said I gave off so much dominant vibe that no dominant would ever approach Nathaniel while I was with him. Though we'd had offers for ménage à trois of every description. I felt like I needed a button that said, 'No, I don't want to have a bondage three-way with you, thanks for asking, though.'

Elizabeth had supposedly been dominant, but not too much to take Nathaniel out and try to pick him up a . . . date.

'Elizabeth left,' Gregory said.

'Without Nathaniel?' I made it a question.

'Yes.'

'Well, that just fries my bacon,' I said.

'What?' he asked.

'I'm angry with Elizabeth.'

'It gets better,' he said.

'How much better can it be, Gregory? You all assured me that these clubs were safe. A little bondage, a little light slap and tickle. You all convinced me that I couldn't keep Nathaniel away from it indefinitely. You said that they had ways to monitor the area so no one could possibly get hurt. That's what you and Zane and Cherry told me. Hell, I've seen it myself. There are safety monitors everywhere, it's safer than some dates I've had, so what could have possibly gone wrong?'

'We couldn't have anticipated this,' he said.

'Just get to the end of the story, Gregory, the foreplay is getting tedious.'

There was silence for longer than there should have been, just the overly loud music. 'Gregory, are you still there?'

'Gregory is indisposed,' a man's voice said.

'Who is this?'

'I am Marco, if that helps you, though I doubt that it does.' His voice was cultured – American, but upper crusty.

'New in town are you?' I asked.

'Something like that,' he said.

'Welcome to town. Make sure you go up in the Arch while you're here, it's a nice view. But what has your recent arrival in St Louis got to do with me and mine?'

'We didn't realize it was your pet we had at first. He wasn't the one we were hunting for, but now that we have him, we're keeping him.'

'You can't "keep" him,' I said.

'Come down and take him away from us, if you can.' That strangely smooth voice made the threat all the more effective. There was no anger, nothing personal. It sounded like business, and I had no clue what it was about.

'Put Gregory back on,' I said.

'I don't think so. He's enjoying some personal time with my friends right now.'

'How do I know he's still alive?' My voice was as unemotional as his. I wasn't feeling anything yet; it was too sudden, too unexpected, like coming in on the middle of a movie.

'No one's dead, yet,' the man said.

'How do I know that?'

He was quiet for a second, then, 'What sort of people are you used to dealing with, that you would ask if we've killed him first thing?'

'It's been a rough year. Now put Gregory on the phone, because until I know he's alive, and he tells me the others are, this negotiation is stalled.'

'How do you know we are negotiating?' Marco asked.

'Call it a hunch.'

'My, you are direct.'

'You have no idea how direct I can be, Marco. Put Gregory on the phone.'

There was the music-filled silence, and more music, but no voices. 'Gregory, Gregory, are you there? Is anyone there?' Shit, I thought.

'I'm afraid that your kitty-cat won't squawl for us. A point of pride, I think.'

'Put the receiver to his ear and let me talk to him.'

'As you wish.'

More of the loud music. I spoke as if I was sure that Gregory was listening. 'Gregory, I need to know you're alive. I need to know that Nathaniel and everyone else is alive. Talk to me, Gregory.'

His voice came squeezed tight, as if he were gritting his teeth. 'Yesss.'

'Yes, what, they're all alive?'

'Yess.'

'What are they doing to you?'

He screamed into the phone, and the sound raised the hairs on my neck and danced down my arms in goosebumps. The sound stopped abruptly. 'Gregory, Gregory!' I was yelling against the techno-beat of the music, but no one was answering.

Marco came back on the line. 'They are all alive, if not quite well. The one they call Nathaniel is a lovely young man, all that long auburn hair and the most extraordinary violet eyes. So pretty, it would be a shame to spoil all that beauty. Of course, this one is lovely too, blond, blue-eyed. Someone told me that they both work as strippers? Is that true?'

I wasn't numb anymore, I was scared, and angry, and I still had not a clue to why this was happening. My voice came out almost even, almost calm. 'Yeah, it's true. You're new in town, Marco, so you don't know me. But trust me, you don't want to do this.'

'Perhaps not, but my alpha does.'

Ah, shapeshifter politics. I hated shapeshifter politics. 'Why? The wereleopards are no threat to anyone.'

'Ours is not to reason why, ours is but to do and die.'

A literate kidnapper, refreshing. 'What do you want, Marco?'

'My alpha wants you to come down and rescue your cats, if you can.'

'What club are you at?'

'Narcissus in Chains.' And he hung up.

Skin Trade

An Anita Blake, Vampire Hunter, Novel

Laurell K. Hamilton

'I'd worked my share of serial killer cases, but none of the killers had ever mailed me a human head. That was new.'

My name is Anita Blake and my reputation has taken some hits. Not on the work front, where I have the highest kill count of all the legal vampire executioners in the country, but on the personal front. No one seems to trust a woman who sleeps with the monsters. Still, when a vampire serial killer sends me a head from Las Vegas, I know I have to warn Sin City's local authorities what they're dealing with.

Only it's worse than I thought: several officers and an executioner have been slain paranormal style. When I get to Las Vegas, I'm joined by three other federal marshals. Which is a good thing because I need all the back up I can get when hunting a killer this powerful and dangerous.

978 0 7553 5255 5

headline

Now you can buy any of these bestselling
books by **Laurell K. Hamilton** from your bookshop
or *direct from her publisher*.

FREE P&P AND UK DELIVERY
(Overseas and Ireland £3.50 per book)

Guilty Pleasures	£7.99
The Laughing Corpse	£7.99
Circus of the Damned	£7.99
The Lunatic Cafe	£7.99
Bloody Bones	£7.99
The Killing Dance	£7.99
Burnt Offerings	£7.99
Blue Moon	£7.99
Obsidian Butterfly	£7.99
Skin Trade	£7.99

TO ORDER SIMPLY CALL THIS NUMBER

01235 400 414

or visit our website: www.headline.co.uk
Prices and availability subject to change without notice.